THE FAMILY MASHBER

a novel by
DER NISTER
("The Hidden One")

Translated from the Yiddish by
Leonard Wolf

SUMMIT BOOKS
NEW YORK

English language translation copyright © 1987 by Leonard Wolf
All rights reserved
including the right of reproduction
in whole or in part in any form
Published by SUMMIT BOOKS
A Division of Simon & Schuster, Inc.
Simon & Schuster Building
1230 Avenue of the Americas
New York, New York 10020
Book One originally published in the Soviet Union in 1939.
Book Two published in New York in 1948.
SUMMIT BOOKS and colophon are trademarks of
Simon & Schuster, Inc.
Designed by Levavi & Levavi
Manufactured in the United States of America
1   3   5   7   9   10   8   6   4   2
Library of Congress Cataloging-in-Publication Data
Der Nister, 1884–1950.
The family Mashber.

Translation of: Di mishpokhe Mashber.
I. Title.
PJ5129.K27M513   1987   839'.0933   87-6470
ISBN: 0-671-52768-1

Acknowledgments

In the course of translating *The Family Mashber*, I have been helped by a number of people whose patience, I am sure, I have often tried. Let me thank particularly Irving Howe of City University of New York, Ilana Howe, David Roskies of The Jewish Theological Seminary, Mordkhe Schaechter of Columbia University, Khone Shmeruk of The Hebrew University in Jerusalem, Yosef Haim Yerushalmi of Columbia University, and Sheva Zucker.

I want to thank, too, my colleagues at YIVO beginning with Dina Abramowiecz, that jewel in the crown of research librarians, then Fruma Mohrer, David Goldberg, David Rogow, Marek Web and Bina Weinreich.

It should be noted that my editor at Summit Books, Arthur Samuelson, saw the need for this translation and put the wheels into motion to get it done.

Mistakes, oversights and errors of judgment are entirely my own doing.

Introduction

BY LEONARD WOLF

"I burned and illuminated the circus for a long time."
—Der Nister, "Under a Fence"

Cyril Connolly, writing in *Enemies of Promise*, says, "The more books we read, the clearer it becomes that the function of the writer is to produce a masterpiece and that no other task is of any consequence." For us, who are readers, a corollary task is to see to it that lost masterpieces are restored to their place in the world's literary pantheon.

The Family Mashber, a lost masterpiece written in Yiddish by Der Nister, a Soviet writer who died in a Russian prison hospital in 1950, has begun slowly to emerge from the obscurity into which it was cast when its author, along with scores of other Yiddish-writing contemporaries in the Soviet Union, fell victim to Stalin's paranoia. This unfinished novel, of which volumes 1 and 2 were published in 1939 and in 1948, has refused to disappear. In the Soviet Union, where Der Nister has been rehabilitated, a truncated Yiddish version of the book is available. In 1962 a Hebrew translation appeared in Israel. A French translation was published in 1984 and an Italian edition is in the offing. Now here is *The Family Mashber* in English.

It is phenomenal how this book, written by an author whose name is hardly a household word even to the dwindling number of those who can read Yiddish . . . how this book, armed with its own excellence, has so tenaciously asserted its presence. The reader holding it now in his or her hand, will soon discover why.

Who is Der Nister?

Der Nister is a pseudonym that means "the hidden one" and it was the name Pinhas Kahanovitch used when he published his first slim volume. *Gedanken un Motiven: Lider in Prosa* (*Thoughts and Motifs: Poems in Prose*), in Vilna in 1907.

Der Nister, was born in Berdichev, Russia, on November 1, 1885, the third in a family of four children: Aaron, Hannah, Pinhas (Der Nister) and Motl. Der Nister's father, Menakhem Mendl Kahanovitch, who made a living as a smoked fish merchant, was an Orthodox Jew with ties to the Korshev sect of Hasidim. His wife Leah was evidently the one who encouraged their children to get a secular as well as a religious education. Of their four children, three would have secular careers: Hanna became a physician, Motl, who later settled in France, became a sculptor and Der Nister became our writer. Aaron, the oldest son, was drawn early to mystical experience and as an adult joined the sect that followed the teachings of Rabbi Nakhman of Bratslav (1772–1810). Aaron and the Bratslaver sect were to have a profound influence on Der Nister's imagination, especially on *The Family Mashber*.

Der Nister left Berdichev in 1904 hoping to evade service in the czar's army. Indeed it was the need for secrecy related to that evasion that seems to have been his first reason for acquiring his pseudonym. He moved then as a young man to Zhitomir, not far from Kiev, where he earned his living as a teacher of Hebrew.

Kiev, in those years, was hardly a literary center, but it did have a small cadre of young men who, as "the Kiev group," were to make a major impression on Soviet Yiddish literature. The Kiev group included the novelist Dovid Bergelson, Der Nister and the poet Peretz Markish, as well as the poets Layb Kvitko and Dovid Hofshteyn. They were a lively vibrant crowd, cultivated and literate, keenly aware of the winds of literary change blowing from the west and anxious to strike out in new directions of their own.

Nakhman Meisel, an early friend of Der Nister's who was instrumental in getting the young poet published, describes Der Nister's entry into the tiny literary world of Kiev in 1908:

Here, in gentile Kiev, far from the literary marketplaces, lived Dovid Bergelson ... and myself, Nakhman Meisel ... Asher Shvartsman ... S. S. Saymovtses ... The Kiev group which, for the time being, had not been fortunate enough to attract the attention of Warsaw and Vilna. . . .

And it was then that the charming Nister from Zhitomir or Berdichev slipped in among us ("slipped in," not "came in," boldly, directly). We knew, though not from him, that in Vilna he had published a strange little book with a strange title and strange contents called *Gedanken un Motiven: Lider in Prosa* [*Thoughts and Motifs: Poems in Prose*] . . . But neither we, nor Der Nister himself, took that first work very seriously.

. . . He was then twenty-four years old. He had delicate, refined manners and a modest way of walking and talking. He looked smaller than he was. His handsome head with its fine shock of hair was tucked between his shoulders as if he was ashamed to hold it up high. He seemed to be walking on tiptoe and as if on side paths rather than on the King's Highway. He had, too, another characteristic: he walked softly and was very silent—a ruble a word—and what he did say was cryptic, ambiguous and, moreover, spoken without stress or resonance. . . .[1]

He was silent and indeed secretive about his personal life and work. On the other hand, he was by no means a recluse nor was his silence a negative comment on the beahavior of others. He enjoyed being in company where he was always an attentive and friendly listener.

Gedanken un Motiven (*Thoughts and Motifs*) was followed by *Hekher Fun Der Erd* (*Higher Than the Earth*) (1910). While these books rather quickly established him as a presence among his peers, his work revealed a mystical cast of thought, a fascination with folklore and fantasy, with riddling speech and symbols that identified him as a difficult writer. In 1913, Sh. Niger, who years later would write a warm appreciation of *The Family Mashber*, was not happy with the early work. He complained that it was "not only without form, but without content." And Sh. Rosenfeld, writing in the New York Yiddish journal *Tsukunft* in June 1914, was harsher still. He wrote:

It is no coincidence that there should appear in our time such a clumsy, obtuse, absolutely opaque writer as Der Nister . . . It is a mistake to think, as some critics do, that Der Nister intends to be unclear, and so does not find the words that would clarify his meaning. He intends to be as clear as it is generally possible to be given the confused conceptions and mystical ideas and images that swim before his eyes.[2]

Despite his "uniqueness," which was the one characteristic on which the critics agreed and which should have marked him as rebellious to tradition, Der Nister's relationship to the classical writers of Yiddish literature, Mendele Mokher Sforim, Sholem Aleichem and Y. L. Peretz, was profoundly respectful. For Peretz he had a respect that bordered on the reverential. He writes:

> When I compared him with his contemporaries, with those who laid the foundations of Yiddish literature, he seemed to me always to be the sun over them: Mendele was the black, plowed earth, Sholom Aleichem, the grown ears of grain, and he [Peretz] was the sun that warmed, illuminated, blessed and made things grow.[3]

Peretz was living in Warsaw in the years when Der Nister was taking his first tentative steps toward fame in Kiev and there is a delicious story (told by Der Nister) about a visit he once paid him.

Peretz received Der Nister graciously and after seating him, he offered him a cigar. And here the fledgling writer experienced a cruel dilemma. He could not hurt Peretz's feelings by *not* smoking the cigar, and yet he desperately wanted to have the cigar as a memento of his visit.

> And so I pretended that I was smoking the cigar. But secretly I did what I could to extinguish it, my aim being to keep it so I could hide it somewhere. When I thought it was altogether out, and that Peretz wasn't looking, I slipped it into my vest pocket. Suddenly there was the smell of smoke and I saw my mistake: the cigar was still burning as was my vest pocket. Peretz, seeing this, understood at once what had happened, wanted to laugh, but unwilling to embarrass me, he turned his head away; and then, to give me a chance to extricate myself from my doleful situation, he pretended he needed something from the next room . . . Had the earth opened under me and swallowed me whole just then I would have been grateful.[4]

Evidently Der Nister saved both his vest and the cigar which became for him a cherished souvenir. More than that, since he already felt like a thief, he took advantage of Peretz's absence later that evening to steal a bit of notepaper on which there were some scrappy notes in Peretz's handwriting.

One should add that it was Peretz who observed about Der Nister that "That fellow ought to be treated the way one treats a rubber ball. The higher you want it to bounce, the harder you have to throw it to the ground." Der Nister, reports Nakhman Meisel, who tells the story, "sensed approval and encouragement in the remark and took it as a good sign."[5]

In 1912, Der Nister married Rokhel Zilberberg, a young Zhitomer teacher. Their daughter, Hodel, was born in July 1913, shortly after the publication of his third book, *Gesang un Gebet* (*Song and Prayer*).

At the outbreak of the Great War in 1914, Der Nister found work in the timber industry in the Kiev region. It was work which gave him a semimilitary status so that he was exempted from service in the army. He continued to write throughout the war years and produced the first of his books for children, *Meyselekh in Fersen* (*Tales in Verse*) (1918). It was about this time, too, that he translated various of Andersen's fairy tales.

In the meanwhile, Russia had become the Soviet Union and it is clear that in the early years of the revolution Der Nister's relationship to it was ambivalent. He continued writing in Kiev and he participated in educational and community work there. Then in 1920 he left Kiev and moved with his family to Moscow where, along with Marc Chagall and other artists and writers, he lived for a while in a Jewish orphanage in Malakhovke, on the outskirts of Moscow.

From there he moved his household first to Kovno in Poland and then to Berlin where his son Joseph was born and where, in 1922 and 1923 respectively, each of the two volumes of *Gedakht* (*Thought*) were published. Here, too, the stories were in the symbolist manner. A glance at "Ofn Grenetz" ("At the Border") is instructive.

As the story begins, we are told that there is a woman at the border between a desert settlement and the sea who spends all of her days straining for the sight of something. When she is asked what it is she is waiting to see, her reply is, "The two-humped desert camel . . . bearing two candles on its humps." Asked to explain her reply she tells the story that is the substance of "At the Border."

What we learn is that somewhere in the desert there is a giant, the last of his line who has conceived the idea that he must restore his race to their former power. He sets out to find a suitable mate. He is helped in his search by the arrival of a bird that brings him a letter from which he learns that there is such a woman waiting to be found. The letter tells him that the bird will lead the giant to her. And so he sets off. On the way he has various adventures and visions which encourage or discourage him. At one point he meets a leper who tells him that he, the leper, was once a giant who sought and found the same woman but her scorn of him was so intense that it diminished his stature, transformed him into a leper. His advice to the giant is to give up the search.

The bird, however, reasserts the truth of his message and provides the giant with a camel who also vouches for it, and the giant goes on. At one point, he has a vision of worshipers in a temple whose high priest, to encourage the giant's search, offers him two large candles. The high priest says:

> "Let him approach and let our benefactor, our temple rebuilder, take them [the candles] for his wedding and for his wedding night, and when he and his destined bride are united, then the wicks of these two candles will ignite each other and become a single fire that will be passed down to mankind which, seeing the light, will know that the ancient line has been reestablished, that old gods have been restored to life and that giants and the race of giants have resumed their powers."[6]

With this paragraph it becomes clear that we are reading another of Der Nister's cabalistic allegories. This time the armature on which the tale is wound takes its form from the

> sacred marriage, an idea that plays a central role in the *Zohar* and among all subsequent Kabbalists. What took place in this *hieros gamos* (*zivvuga kdisha*, as the *Zohar*, calls it), was primarily the union of the two *sefiroth*, [emanations of God] *tif'ereth* and *malkuth*, the male and female aspects of God, the king and his consort, who is nothing other than the *Shekhinah* and the mystical Ecclesia of Israel.[7]

And for cabalists, that unifying embrace is seen as the prerequisite for the coming of the Messiah.

As "At the Border" comes to its end, the giant finds the woman for whom he has been searching. And they pass the longed-for night together (while the camel moistens its feet in the water that laps the shore). With the coming of the dawn, the candles borne by the camel lean toward and ignite each other and the camel bearing the united flame moves toward the settlement to bring the news.

"And," the giantess tells us as the story ends, "it is that camel I await, for that camel that I scan the border and it is a long while that it has been in the desert, and it's a long while coming."[8]

In Der Nister's hands, largely because of the incantatory nature of his prose, the tale is occasionally moving. But finally it is a story impelled more by an idea than by an interior need, and one can see why, in 1924, the appreciative Soviet critic, Nakhum Oyslander, commenting on Der Nister's early work, could write that Der Nister would have found his place in Yiddish literature sooner "if at its center there had not stood the cosmic fable which, apparently, was outside of time and space."[9] More than a decade would pass before Der Nister would find a way to bring his fantastic imagination to bear on what most people call the real world.

In Berlin, Der Nister edited, "with Dovid Bergelson, the belles lettres section of the magazine *Milgroym* [*Pomegranate*]. Like other Yiddish émigré writers, he maintained his ties with the Moscow literary group around the influential magazine *Shtrom* which had Aaron Kushnirov, Yehezkel Dobrushin and Dovid Hofshteyn among its founders."[10]

In 1924, Der Nister left Berlin and took his family to Hamburg where they lived for two years. Irving Howe and Eliezer Greenberg write that this was a time when in the Soviet Union

> The growth of Yiddish culture was helped by the renaissance of Russian literature in the early 1920's, a modernist phase brimming with playfulness, impudence and raw energy. The powerful chants of Mayakovsky, the dazzling stories of Babel, the brilliant work of Zamyatin, Olyesha, Pasternak and Pilnyak— these mark a period of Russian literature second only to that of the mid-nineteenth century.[11]

Whether it was that he yearned to be part of that ferment or whether it was because he was uncomfortable with his life in Germany, Der Nister, in 1926, made a fateful decision. Like his fellow exiles, Dovid Bergelson, Layb Kvitko and Peretz Markish, he moved back to Russia where he settled in Kharkov. There, in 1928, he published a collection of still determinedly symbolist stories, *Fun Mayne Gitter* (*From My Estates*). Sh. Niger writes of that period that:

> In the first years of Soviet literature, the problem of Der Nister was not so severe. Soviet writers were themselves caught up in a

sort of romanticism, a new sort of flamboyance: the romance and glow of the elevated speech of embattled revolutionary heroes: and so room could be found for Der Nister.[12]

But by the end of the twenties, Communist doctrine vis-à-vis the arts hardened. The earlier postrevolutionary climate in which all sorts of artistic expression had been tolerated gave way to the severities of the party line. For writers, socialist realism became the approved way to serve the proletariat and Der Nister, who had been steadfastly pursuing his symbolist bent, came under attack:

> He was thought of as a mystic and a symbolist and was thus deemed rotten to the core by the Soviet critics of those years. Until 1929, they were reconciled to his existence, as they had been reconciled with other *poputsikim*, fellow travelers of his type. But in 1929, to impose the collective rule of the proletariat on Yiddish literature in the Soviet Union, they mounted a bitter attack on Der Nister and his works.[13]

There followed nearly a decade of hard scrabbling while Der Nister supported himself and his family with whatever "neutral" technical writing he could find or by writing journalistic accounts of his travels to Kharkov, Leningrad and Moscow. These essays, when collected in a book, were published as *Hoyptshtedt* (*Major Cities*) in 1934. And all the while he was doing his bread-and-butter journalism, it is clear that he was searching to find some way that would let him attend to his artistic vision and to feed himself and his family.

We know that he found the opening he was looking for sometime before 1935 because in that year, in a letter begging his brother Motl in Paris to help him with money, he writes:

> If you should ask why I have taken on technical work instead of writing original things of my own? I would reply that everything I have written until now is much denigrated here. It is a devalued article. Symbolism has no place in the Soviet Union and, as you know, I have always been a symbolist. It is not possible for someone like myself who has struggled to perfect my method and style of writing to turn from symbolism to realism. It is very hard indeed. It is not a matter of technique. What it requires is to be born anew to turn one's soul completely inside out.
>
> I made a number of attempts. At first, nothing worked. But now I seem to have found the right way. I have begun to write a book

which is, in my opinion and that of close friends, important. I want to devote all my energies to this book whose subject matter is my entire generation—all that I have seen, heard, lived and fantasized. It's been hard for me to get this book written until now because I've had to devote all my time to earning a living. I've not been able to recover so much as a kopeck from any of my past writings. And now, with the transfer of publishing houses from Kharkov to Kiev, I don't even get technical work to do.

And I must write my book. If I don't, it will be the end of me. If I don't I will be erased from literature and from the life of the living. I don't need to tell you what it means to be a writer who doesn't write? It means that he does not exist, that he has no substance in the world.[14]

In the event, the money from his brother was *not* forthcoming, and yet one way or another he found the means to devote himself to *Di Mishpokhe Mashber* (*The Family Mashber*). Its first chapter appeared in the pages of *Sovetish Haymland* (vol. 3 [1935]). Subsequent chapters of the book appeared from time to time in other Soviet journals. In 1939, the first volume of *Di Mishpokhe Mashber* appeared as a book published by the Emes publishing house in Moscow. Chapters from volume 2 continued to be published at intervals in Soviet journals. It was published in its entirety in the United States by YCUF in 1948.

In and out of the Soviet Union, Yiddish critics praised the novel. Communist critics saw it as demonstrating that Der Nister had been able finally to abandon his sinful symbolist habits to turn wholeheartedly to Soviet socialist realism while the others welcomed the book as an indication that Der Nister had returned to the broad road of Yiddish classical writing.

Sh. Niger, in an illuminating essay, tells us that he picked the novel up with some trepidation because having for years worried about how Der Nister would survive in the Soviet state, he now had to wonder whether Der Nister had not at last thrown in the intellectual and spiritual towel. What Niger finally concluded was that

though Der Nister had learned much from a quarter of a century of Bolshevism, he had forgotten very little and that the "socialist realism" of his present prose had not entirely vitiated his former folk and Hasidic romanticism. The odor of the tales of Reb Nakhman of Bratslav still rose from his characters and descriptions the way an empty esrog box still smells of the citron it contained. The difference between Der Nister's former tales and *The Family Mashber* is precisely this: that the tales were an extension of Reb Nakhman's fantasies, while in the novel we often hear the transmigrated soul of Reb Nakhman as it speaks the Mashber family chronicles to us.[15]

We will shortly have more to say about Reb Nakhman.

The Family Mashber is a family novel in the tradition of Dostoevky's *The Brothers Karamazov*, Thomas Mann's *Buddenbrooks*, I. J. Singer's *The Brothers Ashkrenazi* and I. B. Singer's *The Manor*. In *The Family Mashber* what we are given is an entire ethically intricate, psychologically seething, scrupulously re-created world in a real time and place shortly before that world disappeared for all time.

The place is the city of Berdichev (called N. in the novel). Berdichev is where Der Nister was born and raised. As we read *The Family Mashber*, it is well to keep in mind that Berdichev, in the western Ukraine, had been a Polish city from 1569 to 1793 when eastern Poland came under Russian control as its share in the third (this time Russo-Prussian) partition of Poland in the eighteenth century. In 1794, there was a rebellious outburst against the occupying powers. The Russians, led by General Aleksandr Suvorov, put down this Polish revolt at the Battle of Maciejowice.

After the Congress of Vienna in 1815, the so-called Congress Kingdom of Poland became a part of the Russian Empire and Czar Alexander I became also the king of three quarters of historical Poland. His harsh rule set in motion dozens of rebellious secret societies, often led by Polish noblemen, societies and movements which Alexander's secret police fiercely repressed. In 1830, under the rule of Nicholas I, there was another Polish uprising which was put down by the Russians who punished not only the rebels in Congress Poland but those in the eastern provinces as well. Estates were confiscated, deportations were ordered and key rebellious figures were impressed into the Russian army.

There was still another insurrection in 1846, and closer to the time of *The Family Mashber*, there came The Rising of 1863 that began in January 22, 1863, and lasted until April 10–11, 1864, when it was finally crushed. Again there were bloody reprisals and confiscations.

As for Berdichev itself, it was for centuries a major "fair" town which served the gentry and the peasantry as a distribution and banking center. In 1765 the Jewish population of Berdichev numbered no more than 1,220 people. In 1850 their number had increased to 25,000. Fifteen years later, that population had doubled and the Jews were at the heart of the city's commercial, banking and light manufacturing activity.

Mid-nineteenth century Berdichev was a turbulent place both in fact and in Der Nister's fiction. If, with Der Nister, we look closely into the mass, we see housewives, merchants, beggars, tradesmen, prostitutes, financiers, porters, tailors, clerics, physicians, maidservants, thugs, tavern keepers, weavers, dyers, teachers, gravediggers, rabbinical judges, mental defectives and thieves, as well as people so outcast that they cannot be assigned a place even at the bottom of a social ladder.

If Der Nister had only re-created that vanished world, we would have a tour de force of realism on our hands. In fact, however, we have something more and more distinctive. Because Der Nister, by manipulating detail with the tenacity of a Zola, has created a realistic novel and compelled it to serve his symbolist imagination. All of those seekers, those pilgrims, those fantastic creatures that haunted his earlier work, have returned to take their place in this most down-to-earth of fictions.

The trick is beyond easy analysis but it has three elements to which one may point: first, a scrupulosity of detail that turns what is real into the surreal; then a plot that is endlessly, ingeniously inventive; and third, by allowing his novel to be suffused by the light of the mystical teachings of Reb Nakhman of Bratslav, Der Nister manages to create extraordinary opportunities for transcendent writing.

Reb Nakhman of Bratslav, whom Gershom Scholem has called "perhaps the last Jewish mystic," was the great-grandson of the Baal Shem, the founder of that personalist, enthusiastic and mystical Jewish religious movement known as Hasidism. Nakhman, in his turn, was the founder of the Hasidic sect that bears his name.

Let me review briefly those of Reb Nakhman's teachings or practices that are reflected in *The Family Mashber*. First, there is the idea, derived from Lurianic cabalism, that the created world

came about as an act of divine contraction (*tsimtsum*) whereby God contracts himself, thereby creating space for a created world. This act is described in detail as catastrophic, the violent tempestuous clash of forces within God himself, a rending apart called *shevirat hakelim* ("the breaking of the vessels") that can be mended by the process of *tikkun* (remedying or repairing) in which man can take part.[16]

The sole duty of humankind, then, in *this* life is to gather up the shards of the shattered vessels of primordial light that have fallen into the world and restore them to their place in the primordial order. This can best be done by leading a life of piety and purity. If everyone could lead such lives, the broken vessels would be mended, at which time the Messiah would come. For the Hasid, the *tzaddik*, because of the purity of his life and the illuminated state of his soul, is the person most suited to effect the repair. For the Bratslaver, of course, the appropriate *tzaddik* was Reb Nakhman.

In Nakhman's lifetime, he and his followers earned the enmity not only of the *mitnaggedim*, the enemies of Hasidism, but of other Hasidic sects as well because of the exclusivity of the claims that Nakhman made or allowed to be made in his name: first, that he was the *tzaddik hador*, the holy man of his generation, and then that he himself might be the Messiah, or at least that the Messiah when he came would be born of his seed. That enmity against the Bratslaver sect continued on well past the time of Nakhman's death and was accepted by his followers as a sign of their distinction. In *The Family Mashber*, as we will see, that enmity becomes an important aspect of the plot.

The appeal of Reb Nakhman's teachings was primarily to the illiterate, to the suffering, to the dispossessed. His was a populist mysticism that assured his adherents that a passionately desiring heart would stand them in better stead than a learned head in the unequal dialogue between God and man. And that misfortune, disaster, personal anguish and poverty could ready them for redemption. Arthur Green writes that Nakhman's "was a doctrine for a very particular sort of spiritual elite: an elite of sufferers and strugglers who *knew* with Nahman [sic] as well as *through* him that 'There is nothing so whole as a broken heart.' "[17]

During Nakhman's lifetime, his Hasidim made pilgrimages to him three times in the course of the year: at Rosh Hashanah, the beginning of the year, on the Sabbath of Hanukkah and on Shavuoth. After Nakhman's death, it became a tradition for his disciples to visit his grave in Uman.

Because Nakhman demanded of himself that "he ever be the homeless wandering holy man, reviled by society as he rejected many of its conventional norms,"[18] the Bratslaver Hasidim accepted the spiritual efficacy of *oprikhtn goles*, penitential wandering. Another custom instituted by Nakhman as a way of binding his disciples to him was the practice among his Hasidim of hearing confession and a custom known as *hitbodedut*, aloneness with God. Here, the idea was for the Hasid to find a place, outdoors if he could manage it, where he could carry on a conversation with God, speaking to him in the Yiddish of daily life.

Other ways employed by the Bratslaver to achieve intimacy with God included singing, preferably songs without words, dancing, handclapping and reciting the Psalms and The Song of Songs, the latter because it was considered the holiest of all holy songs.

Der Nister's earlier tales, which owe a particular debt to *The Tales* of Reb Nakhman, serve primarily an allegorical function. They are garbed in meanings derived from the cabalistic tradition and their intent is to assert, or to reassert, mystical truth. Here, in *The Family Mashber*, positioning the Bratslaver sect at the center of a fiction in which, instead of giants or pilgrims or demons, all of the characters have names and addresses and bills to pay, provides Der Nister with several opportunities to make his plot and his characters more complex. In addition to the dramatic tension they provide because they are a persecuted sect, what they believe and how they are treated allows Der Nister to confront, within the pages of an implacably realistic novel, the question of redemption. Then, too, the Bratslaver Hasidim, because of their eagerness to leap across the abyss that separates humanity from God, provide Der Nister with an opening to the fantastic which in the form of dreams and visions gives an otherworldly and symbolic counterpoint to the novel's realism. Finally, the sect's appeal to the "insulted and the injured," to the declassed members of the community, provides Der Nister with occasions to introduce such Dickensian characters as Shmulikl Fist, Ten Groschen Pushke and Wednesday.

In Hebrew, the word *mashber* means "crisis" and crises are the stuff of which this fiction is made: the quarrel between Moshe, the businessman, and his brother Luzi, the *tzaddik*; Alter's fluctuation between lucidity and idiocy; Gitl's attempt to storm heaven to compel God's pity for her daughter; and the conflict between the Bratslaver sect and the established religious community led by Reb Dudi. Of course, the financial crisis that overwhelms Moshe Mashber's family is the one on which our attention is primarilly focused. Moshe, as the director of the family business, becomes the novel's protagonist, but his two brothers, Luzi, the Bratslaver mystic, and Alter, the idiot savant, both play equally important roles in the developing tragedy.

Moshe, when we first meet him, is very much a man for this world. He is a prosperous businessman and banker who is highly regarded, upright, decent and devout. He is also a loving husband and father. And yet, graced though he is with the attributes of decency and good fortune, the very first thing we learn about him when we meet him is that he has bought himself graveclothes and that he is on his way to buy a plot of ground for his grave. From this point on, what happens to Moshe Mashber, the pragmatist, the rationalist, the man immersed in this world, is the slow trying-out of his spirit. When, as the book ends, we take our leave of him, we are inclined to see him as more sinned against than sinning and we may be tempted to salute him as a hero of the way things are.

Luzi, the oldest of the three brothers, would seem to be at the opposite pole from his brother Moshe. Where Moshe is worldly, Luzi is aloof from the family business and attaches himself to the despised Bratslaver sect of Hasidim. On the face of it, he would seem to be the model figure of the spiritual seeker. He is the compassionate magnet for the despised and the downtrodden inhabitants of The Curse section of town. And yet, as his brother Moshe's tragedy develops, Luzi's role becomes ambiguous enough to keep us from being absolutely certain that we have the portrait of a saint before our eyes. Though Luzi apparently has the capacity of soul and the moral integrity required by the role, Der Nister distorts Luzi just sufficiently to create, if not doubt, at least ambiguity about what we see.

As for Alter, the youngest of the brothers, he has a very clear kinship with Prince Myshkin in Dostoevsky's *The Idiot*. He is one of those incompetents whose madness (if it is madness and not some form of epilepsy) seems to have purified him of all human dross. And yet Alter's story, more than any of the tales that are braided together in the novel, links the erotic with the spiritual life. There is no sensuality quite as powerful as that which is fully repressed, and Alter's sexual longings, linked as they are to the passionate purity of his gaze toward heaven, can make a reader giddy with confusion and shame. Alter, dazed and innocent, is the one who broods over the bedside of the sleeping kitchen maid, Gnessye, savoring her body's smell; and it is Alter who writes letters to God which, we imagine, God must weep to read.

The women in *The Family Mashber* seem at first glance simply to be playing the roles expected of them. Certainly Nekhamke and Yehudis, the two Mashber daughters, are, respectively, models of suffering and devotion. But there are other women who are vividly present in the fiction: sometimes they are authentic heroines like Gitl, Moshe's wife, whose gentleness shames a mob and whose resoluteness in confronting that archuserer, Yakov-Yossi Eilbirten, provides us with one of the subtlest scenes in the fiction. Then there is the portrait of Esther-Rokhl, the "Leather Saint," whose face, as a consequence of decades of ill nourishment, has turned leather hard and who, without the language to explain herself, has spent her poverty-stricken life patiently doing for others that next decent thing that needs to be done. The portrait of Esther-Rokhl is nearly as moving (and as ironic) as Y. L. Peretz's "Silent Bontshe" or as Flaubert's Catherine-Nicaise-Elizabeth Leroux of Sassetot-la Guerierre, who in *Madame Bovary* is awarded a silver medal for having served fifty-four years on the same farm.

Finally there is Gnessye, the young kitchen serving maid to whom the sickly Alter is betrothed. Gnessye, as ripe and full of life as she is poor and powerless, becomes a heroine beyond the clichés of the erotic which in the hands of a lesser writer might have hemmed her in. The series of scenes in which Der Nister depicts first her bewilderment as she suddenly faces the prospect of being related to her wealthy employers, and then later the strength of her resolution (and her action) when she confronts her dilemma, forms one of the great set pieces in *The Family Mashber*.

After Luzi, the foremost of the novel's spiritual seekers is Mikhl Bukyer, the primary-school teacher who preceded Luzi as head of the Bratslaver Hasidim in N. There is a telling difference between what happens to the poverty-stricken Mikhl as a consequence of his interior pilgrimage and what happens to Luzi. The well-educated, wealthy Luzi, though he is ostracized by the community, seems well (and not too uncomfortably) on his way to illumination, while the poverty-stricken Mikhl's uncouth but authentic spiritual adventures, linked as they are to his unstable psyche and to the Orthodox religious establishment's fear of his individuality, result in his destruction.

Almost as a counter to Mikhl's perfervid spirituality, Der Nister gives us the calm and competent figure of Yossele "Plague." Yossele is the secular seeker, the *Maskil*, the "enlightener" who generates projects for social change and to whom Mikhl comes, bringing his newly won unbelief as a gift. Yossele, hardly a radical figure, is however the nearest embodiment in *The Family Mashber* of the hidden revolutionary fervor which, Der Nister tells us in his preface, was brewing "even then in that stagnant environment."

Finally, in this partial list of complexly realized characters, we come to Sruli Gol, probably the most astonishing and most memorable character in *The Family Mashber*. He is a vital, mysterious figure. A voyeur of illumination, who, recognizing in Luzi a man who is tending an eternal flame, understands at the same time that Luzi himself needs tending. Sruli, out of concern for that flame, and no doubt because of less clearly understood psychological hungers of his own, takes that burden of care upon himself. He is a mystical pragmatist, a heavy-drinking monologuist who plays a shepherd's flute at the weddings of the poor and whose avocation it is to shame the rich. He is also, with the single exception of Alter, the most personally troubled character in the novel.

Two things more need some comment. First, the fact that *The Family Mashber* as we have it is unfinished, and second, that Der Nister, both in his preface and at intervals in the course of the novel, pauses to point the finger of doom at the world he has created.

As we have seen, volume one of *The Family Mashber* was published in 1939 and volume two appeared in 1948. In that year, Gittl Meisel, writing in the Israeli journal *Di Goldene Kayt,* referred confidently to *The Family Mashber* as a *trilogy.* She went on to say that "An enlarged, improved edition of all three parts together is being prepared for pub-lication by the author himself . . ."[19] And Khone Shmeruk, the most informed student of Der Nister's work, concluded his introduction to *Hanazir V'Hadgadyó* by saying,

> According to various reports, Der Nister was able to complete
> the third volume of his work, and perhaps even more than that.
> If, however, his writings were lost during the time of his impris-
> onment, our literature will have sustained the greatest and most
> painful casualties ever inflicted on them by the perversities of the
> Soviet regime.[20]

For the time being, it would seem that Yiddish literature has indeed sustained that heavy loss. Volume three has not yet come to light. Just the same it should be stressed that volume two of *The Family Mashber* is not a document torn from its author's hands in the very midst of com-position. It was clearly conceived as a coherent segment of a much longer epic fiction and it comes to a quite satisfactory stopping point. We may suppose that Der Nister thought so too from the fact that in 1948 he allowed the Yiddish version to be published in its present form in the United States.

As it happens, two fragments of Der Nister's work after *The Family Mashber* have been found. The Soviet writer L. Podriatshik describes how while working with various of Der Nister's manuscript fragments, he came upon the pages of "Nakhvort un Forvort" ("Afterword and Foreword"), which are part of a transitional chapter leading to volume three of *The Family Mashber*. Then he tells us that in 1962 he received a request from the critic Nakhum Oyslander, who in his capacity as an editor of *Sovetish Haymland* asked Podriatshik to decipher and untangle a 160-page manuscript of a novel of Der Nister's entitled *The Fifth Year*, which dealt with the Revolution of 1905. The manuscript had been sent to the magazine by Der Nister's widow.

In "Afterword and Foreword" Der Nister picks up Luzi and Sruli as they wander the highways and byways exactly as we see them at the end of volume 2.[21] After a few transitional pages in which Der Nister gives us some further details of what happened to the Mashber family, he then describes the economic and social changes that have taken place in N., and we are then introduced to the new characters who are to play their roles twenty years later in the projected fiction. "Afterword and Foreword" makes poignant reading. The fragment is shot through with occasional flashes of gentle humor, and it has on the whole the élan and the richly detailed descriptions of characters and events that we find in *The Family Mashber*.

The manuscript of part 1 of the novel, *The Fifth Year*, which Podriatshik untangled from the worked and reworked pages he was given, is altogether another matter. As published in 1964 in *Sovetish Haymland*, (no. 1), it is a surprising document to have come from Der Nister's pen because it is such a pat tale of revolutionary love and martyrdom. Its young protagonists, Laybl and Milye, are underground activists working in 1905 for the revolution. Laybl's middle-class mother, frustrated because she cannot wean Laybl away from his radical activities, betrays the revolutionaries, including Laybl, to the police. At the point where *The Fifth Year* ends, Laybl, whose remorseful mother has committed suicide, stands hand in hand with Milye beside the graves of martyred revolutionaries (including Milye's mother). Together they plight their love to each other and to the revolution.

If we remember that *The Fifth Year* was written at the same time as *The Family Mashber*, and that the manuscript never achieved even the status of fair copy, it is clear that what we have is the tentative draft of a fiction meant one day to placate a censor and perhaps put bread on the table.

Speaking of the censor brings us now to the matter of Der Nister's retractations in *The Family Mashber*. These come both as comments in the preface to the book and as occasional interpolations into the text where, usually, they take the form of an interruption of the narrative in which Der Nister, turning to his reader, points his finger at his characters and tells us that they and their world are doomed. These criticisms are often ascribed to a supposititious stranger, like this:

> Should a stranger come to the market and should he stay for a while, he would very soon get a whiff of dissolution, the first hint that very soon the full stink of death would rise from the whole shebang, the buying and selling, the hullaballoo of wheeling and dealing, the entire giddiness of all those whirling there.[22]

These disclaimers have the rote quality of a loyalty oath and they are clearly the price Der Nister paid so that he could get on with the work at hand. Interestingly enough, they decline in frequency as we move further and further into the narrative, as if, caught up in the making of his fiction, Der Nister had forgotten to attend to them.

As we have seen, volume 1 of *The Family Masber* was published in 1939. With the coming of World War II, Der Nister left Kharkov and moved to Tashkent. It was three years later that his daughter Hodel died in the siege of Leningrad.

During the war years, whether in Tashkent or later in Moscow, to which he and his second wife, Lina Singolobska, returned, Der Nister continued to write. He contributed short stories about Polish Jews under the Nazi occupation to the journal *Korbunes* (*Sacrifices*) at the same time as he worked on volume 2 of *The Family Mashber*.

After the war, Der Nister shared the general fate of Yiddish writers in the Soviet Union who came under increasing attack for individualism, for symbolism, for exclusivism, for bourgeois decadence. We get a glimpse of what life was like for him at that time from a letter he wrote to Itzik Kipnis in Kiev on December 7, 1947. Der Nister, commiserating with Kipnis's recent misadventure with the literary commissars, describes his own troubles:

> I share your literary fate. There are certain eager folk who would be glad to see me not only not writing, but not breathing altogether. Things have come to such a pass that lately I told our editor Kushnirov that I don't want to cross the threshold of the journal *Haymland*. I can't go on. No matter what I give them, they want to take its guts out. Well then, so I won't dance with the bear. So, I sit on the sidelines— Let Ivan blow [hot milk up his ass]. Let the Teifs [Moshe], the Zilbermans [Khaim], the Natovitshes [Moshe] write prose, criticism and so on. As for me, what

kind of a writer am I? Let what's said in this letter be strictly between the two of us; tell no one about it . . .

The letter ends with a reiteration of the earlier warning: "P.S. Again—the contents of this letter are between us."[23]

One by one, Der Nister's friends, Kvitko, Bergelson, Markish, were arrested. Finally it was Der Nister's turn. His wife reports that when the police came he was relieved that the long wait was finally over.

He received the N.K.V.D. with a broadly mocking smile which greatly irritated them. The officer who conducted the search began to laugh stupidly . . . To this Der Nister said in Yiddish: "Why are you angry? I am happy that you've come."

And he was indeed happy that he was to share the same fate as the other Yiddish writers . . . He couldn't understand why he was still free while the rest of the authors were already in prison.[24]

Professor Khone Shmeruk cites another account of how Der Nister dealt with the secret police. Evidently pushed by them to reveal where he had hidden his manuscripts, he said, "Forgive me gentlemen, that matter is none of your concern. It was not for you that I wrote them, and my manuscripts remain in a safe place."[25]

One can only hope that he was right. That it really is possible that one day someone searching through an attic or a cellar, or turning over old files of the Soviet secret police, will come upon the full text of volume 3 of *The Family Mashber*, or some other splendid surprise. Until then, here is *The Family Mashber*.

A Note on the Translation

This translation is based entirely and only on the two editions of *Di Mishpokhe Mashber* published by YCUF in New York. Volume 1 was published in 1943 and volume 2 in 1948.

NOTES ON THE INTRODUCTION

1. Nakhman Meisel, ed., *Der Nister: Dertseylungen un Esseyen* (New York: YCUF, 1957), 11.
2. Sh. Rosenfeld, *Tsukunft*, June 1914, 662.
3. Der Nister, "Peretz Hot Geredt un Ikh Hob Gehert," in *Der Nister: Dertseylungen un Esseyen*, ed. Nakhman Meisel (New York: YCUF, 1957), 289.
4. Ibid., 21.
5. Ibid., 282–83.
6. Der Nister, Gedakht (Berlin: Literarisher Farlag, 1922, 1923), 238.
7. Gershom Scholem, *On the Kabbalah and Its Symbolism* (New York: Schocken, 1969), 237–38.
8. Der Nister, *Gedakht*, 246.
9. Nakhum Oyslander, *Veg Ayn, Veg Oys* (*The Way In, The Way Out*) (Kiev: Cooperativer Farlag, 1939), 39.
10. Khone Shmeruk, ed., *A Shpigl Oyf of Shteyn* (Tel Aviv: Farlog Y. L. Peretz, 1964), 738.
11. Irving Howe and Eliezer Greengerg, *Ashes Out of Hope* (New York: Schocken, 1977), 5–6.
12. Sh. Niger, in *Yiddishe Shrayber in Sovet Russland*, New York: Cycco, 1958, 65–66.
13. Khone Shmeruk, Introduction to *Der Nister: Hanazir V'Hadgadyo* (Jerusalem: Mosad Bialik, 1963), 5.
14. Ibid., 12.
15. Niger, *Yiddishe Shrayber*, 71.
16. Arnold J. Band, *Nahman of Bratslav* (New York: Paulist Press; Toronto: Ramsey, 1978), 32.
17. Arthur Green, *Tormented Master* (New York: Schocken, 1981), 148.
18. Ibid., 153.
19. Gittl Meisel, "Der Nister," *Di Goldene Kayt*, no. 2 (1949): 169.
20. Shmeruk, *Hanazir V'Hadgadyó*, 42.
21. "Nokhvort un Forvort," *Sovetish Haymland*, 1967, no. 2.
22. Page 32, this edition.
23. Khone Shmeruk, ed., "Arba Agruth Shel Der Nister," *B'khinut* 8–9 (1977–78): 244, 245
24. Shmeruk, *Hanazir V'Hadgadyó*, 17.
25. Ibid., 17.

THE
FAMILY
MASHBER

My child, my daughter, Hodele, tragically dead. Born July 1913 in Zhitomir, died spring 1942, Leningrad.

May your father's broken heart be the monument on your lost grave. Let this book be dedicated as an eternal and holy memorial to you.

Your father, the author
[DER NISTER]

Preface

The world depicted in this book—the economic base on which it rested, its social and ideological conflicts and interests—disappeared long ago. It has not been easy for me to evoke that world, to animate it and to put its people into motion.

I have done it, however, for the sake of historical clarity, to give young people a sense of the great distance that separates our reality from that earlier one and to show them how far we have come in so short a period of time.

In depicting those people, who are physically and spiritually extinct, I have taken pains not to contend with them, not to cry out that they are doomed. Rather, I have let them proceed quietly on their historically necessitated way toward the abyss.

I have rendered them with all their sorry possessions, minimizing none of their characteristics so that I may show how pathetic the struggle was—even of the best of them—to make their way out of the dark toward some dimly discerned light.

Writing this book, I have held fast to the principle of artistic realism. That is to say I followed Goethe's famous injunction: "Painter, paint—and hush," fully confident that whatever was necessary and desirable would come in any case of itself, as a consequence of that painterly fidelity, and from the inner logic that controlled the fate of these people.

But the essential goal of my labors was not only to be done with an older generation that was up to its neck in the mire of medieval relationships—the essential goal of the book is to reveal the hidden strength of those who lay, profoundly humiliated, in the "third ring" and who perished so tragically under the weight of the yoke of their lives.

By that I mean the weak dazzle of the lightning that occasionally flares up on the distant horizon, those rebellious but as yet unfledged forerunners which, nevertheless, burst into light from time to time to reveal glimpses of the storm that is gathering in the distance and which will erupt—if not today, then tomorrow or the day after that.

Because, in a cellar or an attic, there *was* something brewing here and there, minute by minute, even then in that stagnant environment. And a bit of light showed that, depending on who chanced to see it, was either frightening or prophetic.

As we know, that vital seed from which would emerge first enlightenment and then the revolutionary movement was already ripening. The time was at hand that would mark the coming of those who would seize the rudder and steer society's ship in quite different directions. Those children were already growing who later would turn away from the ancestral traditions and would destroy by fire the mold accumulated in previous centuries.

It is, then, toward that fire secretly present among the young that I turn my gaze. It is essentially to that generation that I want to turn, to depict it creatively, and to return to it the honor, admiration and respect which, over a lifetime of walking hand in hand with it, I have acquired.

1939 DER NISTER

BOOK ONE

I

The Town N.

The city of N. is built in three rings. First ring: the marketplace at the very center. Second: surrounding the market, the great city proper with its many houses, streets, byways, back streets where most of the populace lives. Third: suburbs.

Should a stranger find himself in N. for the first time, he would at once be drawn, willy-nilly, to the city's center. That's where the hubbub is, the seething, the essential essence, the heart and pulse of the city.

His nose would be assailed immediately by smells: the smell of half-raw, rough or fine leather of all kinds; the acrid sweetness of baked goods; of groceries; of the salt smell of various dried fish; smells of kerosene, pitch, machine oil; of cooking and lubricating oils; of the smell of new paper. Of scruffy, shabby, dusty humid things: down-at-heels shoes; old clothes; worn-out brass; rusted iron—and anything else that refuses to be useless; that is, determined, via this petty buying and selling to serve someone, somehow.

There in the marketplace are shop after shop, squeezed narrowly together like boxes on a shelf. If one doesn't have a shop in the upper district, then he owns a warehouse in the lower. If he doesn't own a warehouse, then he has at least a covered booth outside a shop. If no booth, then he spreads his goods out on the ground, or depending on what he sells, holds his wares in his hands.

There, in the marketplace, it's a permanent fair. Wagons from nearby (or from distant) settlements arrive to pick up goods, and wagons from the railway depot endlessly discharge their loads—everything fresh, everything new.

Packing and unpacking!

Jewish tenant farmers, village merchants, come in from Andrushivkeh, Paradek, Yampole. They come from Zvill and Korets and even from the more distant Polesia. In summer, they wear their light coats and hoods. In winter, cloaks or fur coats with well-worn collars. They come to buy goods for cash or on credit. Some are decent and honorable—others are something else: their scheme is to buy on credit, then sell at a profit, then buy on credit again—then declare themselves bankrupt.

Wagons arrive empty and leave fully packed, covered with sacks, tarpaulins, rags—all of them tied down with cords. The wagons drive off at evening; others arrive at dawn.

"Sholom aleichem." A storekeeper hurries down the steps of his shop to greet a newly arrived old customer, to lead him from the wagon directly into his shop lest some other merchant get at him. *"Sholom aleichem,* and how are things in Andrushivkeh?" he says with a show of familiarity, then he gets right to business. "Ah, it's good you're here. I have just what you're looking for. A marvelous this . . . a splendid that . . ."

Rival storekeepers endeavor to strike up conversations with one's customer, to entice him away from his usual shop. They inveigle him in by offering lower prices or better credit terms. Often enough this can lead to real battles. Shopkeepers against shopkeepers, clerks against clerks. Only the porters and errand boys, who occasionally earn something from one or another of the shops, keep aloof, refusing to mix in, to choose sides.

Sometimes it's the market women who quarrel. Then women's cries are heard. Blows are exchanged.

But that happens rarely. For the most part, everyone is much too busy. Morning and night, there's work to be done to meet the needs of hordes of customers—and there's enough profit for all.

Clerks do the heavy work: weighing, measuring, carrying things out, setting them in place and so on. The shopkeepers do the bargaining: the persuading, cajoling, displaying of goods, arriving at prices.

It is, as has been said, a permanent fair. Wholesale and retail. In the more successful shops, the owners carry home bundles of hundred-and fifty-ruble notes. The less successful tradesmen take home coins in their linen pouches and not much paper money. But they make a greater racket than their richer competitors. Endless contentions, quarrels, shouts, cries. They fight over a groschen or a pound of soap, over the sale of a little starch, the price of a dried fish. And curse each other unsparingly with the same vehemence over small matters as over large:

"Break a bone!"

"Go to hell . . ."

"Drop dead."

"See you at your funeral."

But they make up quickly, too. The stallkeepers drink tea frequently with each other; they dart into each other's booths to arrange a free loan, to borrow a weight for a scale. They club together the money needed to take advantage of an opportune bargain offered by a Gentile. Or they play tricks on each other, or shout to each other across five stalls, across ten. Everyone shouting at once.

That's how it is normally on market days. On special days, the crowding is more intense. There's a greater press of wagons, of unharnessed horses munching hay. Those still harnessed have their noses deep in their feed bags. Colts nuzzle between the legs of mares. A stallion whinnies, making a horsey racket that resounds throughout the market. And along with the horses and people—dirt, filth. In winter, snow that is not snow. In winter and summer, cow flops, horse piss, puddles of kerosene, hay, straw, barrel hoops, barrels, boxes—rarely cleared away.

During important market days, like those during Lent, there's hardly room to move. A mob of varicolored peasant pelts; brown coats; yellow furs; men's coarse-haired beaver jackets; headscarfs, neckcloths, hats, fur caps, felt boots, knitted leggings for landowners and peasants, for men and women.

Well-to-do folk coming to town shop seriously. The poor search for some trifle or other—something that might easily enough be bought at home. But the yearning to come to town is great. The hunger to wander about the shops, to haggle over baubles. To haggle! To spend as much time as possible over a purchase. For the sheer pleasure of buying.

Those with money move about prudently. They know what they want and where to look for it. The shopkeepers make them welcome, greet them courteously, respectfully. Throughout the bargaining sessions, they take great pains to be accommodating, to keep them from leaving the shop. Naturally, given the press of the crowds, the poorer customers are not very welcome. They are instantly recognizable as they wander confusedly about, their eyes searching every shelf and corner of the shop. It's clear that they have more enthusiasm than cash and are therefore greeted with suspicion or driven away. Their diffident, poverty-stricken questions are not answered, and if a shopkeeper notices that one of his clerks is spending too long with such a customer he passes his clerk a note: "Don't waste time on this one. Can't you see what he wants, the damn thief?"

And, during the Great Market days, thefts are not infrequent. Occasionally it is a peasant who steals something from a shopkeeper, but more usually it is the other way around. There are certain specialists, well known in the market, who weigh with ten-pound weights instead of half a *pood* (twenty pounds). It's done quickly, skillfully. On the scale and off! And the peasant has no inkling of what's happened. Until later, when he comes back complaining bitterly. But then, those specialists, those *half-pooders* as they are called, don't recognize their customer. Often slaps are exchanged, blows. Until the red-faced, drunken policeman, the *buddoshnik*, meddles in the matter, blows his whistle and parts the combatants, and hauls off to jail precisely the one who ought not to be hauled off.

Or it may happen that a peasant slips some trifle into his breast pocket. If he's caught, he's tried unceremoniously on the spot. The shop clerk strikes the blows. If the clerks in the nearby shops get wind of the matter (and if they have the time), they too get into the action. Bringing with them whatever implements are available, they lend a hand at the beating. Male peasants are struck around the head and neck, a woman, whether old or young, is hardly beaten at all. But she is disgraced. Her shawl and babushka are torn off and she is made to stand, disheveled and ashamed, exposed to the scorn of the entire marketplace.

However, such things happen rarely. Now and then. For the most part, customers buy and are satisfied with their purchases, and sellers are pleased with their gains. Everyone's busy, everyone glows.

Whatever the weather—wind, frost, snow, blizzard—no one pays the slightest attention. The market goes on. Profit warms the merchants.

In the course of those busy days, people eat very little. Whatever was eaten in the morning at home before leaving for the market suffices until evening, until dark, until, red-faced, swollen, exhausted, one gets home.

One ignores everything. Trembling hands, freezing faces, noses, ears. Blows are overlooked, and splinters. Never mind. In the evening at home where it's warm, the splinters can be removed.

All of this takes place in the "Rough Market," but similar things happen in the "Noble Market" on a parallel street. There, too, there's no way to get through the press of wagons, though there are no peasants here and generally no retail buyers. Only wholesale.

There, the important cloth merchants and the major ready-made shoe and clothing dealers are. Dealers in all sorts of goods from Lodz, Warsaw, and Bialystok. From distant Polish towns and from others as far away as White Russia.

There, the customers are landowners, rich nobility, prosperous small-town Jews. There, the clerks are more neatly dressed. There, too, customers are received and treated differently. There, flattery and chicanery are of a higher order. There the shopkeepers move about before their shops in skunk coats, forming little clusters in which they carry on serious business conversations, while inside the shops, the sly-tongued, persuasive chief clerks bustle about displaying their goods so skillfully that it is a rare customer who can escape them.

Outside, the shopkeepers talk endlessly about the money market, exchange rates, bankruptcies, trips to Lodz or Kharkov, of rising or falling prices. Inside the windowless shops, where the only light filters in from the street door, there is a perpetual half-light, even by day. The customers stand at counters behind which the clerks display yard goods: linens, woolens, silks, cottons with English, German, Russian labels. Lying labels, false seals. And in the course of displaying and measuring the goods and persuading the buyers, one does—what one does. As the clerks put it, "You steal the suckers blind."

In the Noble Market there is the same busyness during the Great Market days described above. Here, too, wagons are packed, boxes torn open, goods are moved. Porters carrying loads in bump into clerks carrying bundles out of the shops. Shelves are emptied, cash registers filled. These are good days for the shopkeepers, who beam at the flow of money. Good days for the clerks to whom the customers "give a little something." And of course they get a commission on their sales. These are good days for the brokers, for the middlemen who, for a fee, introduce new customers, or who, for a fee, serve as consultants to regular customers in making their deals.

During those Great Market days, the shopkeepers, their wives and even their children are all in the shops. No matter how many employees one has, they are not enough. So one brings in family members. Those who can do real tasks, do them. Others who can only look on serve as lookouts. But no one thinks of leaving the shop, of going home until evening, until night, until very late when the shops are locked and chained, when the shutters, with an iron shriek, are lowered. Then, the contented shopkeepers, their cashboxes full, are accompanied home by their clerks and the members of their family.

And that's how it is in the market before the winter holidays. A little less noisy, but the market always is and remains the market, with its deals, its money hunger, its devotion to profit. And once in it, one is entirely swallowed up by it and becomes unable to understand or to welcome anyone who is not part of it. There's no time for such intruders. And in the eternally established organization of the market, no place for them.

So true is this that if, rarely, some nonmarket person—a clergyman or a child—should appear there (one does not count people who are merely passing through), their presence would be felt as a violation. Children are immediately shooed away by their parents: "What are you doing here? Get on home." A synagogue caretaker, or a cantor, may show up, but only to go from shop to shop to remind someone of a mourning anniversary, or to call shopkeepers to a circumcision or a wedding. But such an intruder must not linger. He must perform his errand quickly and leave. Because he is superfluous.

Even habitually insolent beggars, perpetual tramps, rarely receive alms in the market, but are turned away everywhere with the same sullen phrase: "Go. Go in good health. We don't give in the market. At home." Even the town's mad folk avoid the market, as if they knew that there was no place and no one to care for them there.

Market people are an earnest folk, worrying constantly. Those who don't have much money worry about where to get it. How to borrow a little. Those who have money worry about where to get it, how to borrow more. The prosperous merchants do their business with brokers and rack their brains for the means to pay them, and struggling shopkeepers worry about the weekly ruble they need to pay the interest to the loan sharks. But everyone is busy, heads whirring over profit when there *is* profit, or when there is none, over ways and means to meet expenses.

The clerks are less serious. More carefree. Since their time is not their own, they can be frivolous. The young ones who even at the busiest times are given to practical jokes turn especially silly when there is little to do. This is particularly true in the summer before the harvest, when the market quiets down and hardly anyone from the nearby villages (never mind those from the outlying districts) comes to town. Then, whole days go by with nothing to do.

Except hang around outdoors taking the sun, or cooling off inside the shops or cellars. And when things get particularly dreary, one thanks God for the occasional groschen in the till with which one can slip off to a nearby soda water shop for a drink and a snack. And when things get truly boring, one is grateful to the crazy noblewoman, the Panyi Akoto, notorious throughout the town, if suddenly she shows up in her old-fashined cloak (from the time of King Sobieski) with its tassels and fringes, her hat with its many ribbons, beads and dangling baubles.

The clerks rush to greet her, as if they meant to welcome her into their shops. One of the clerks outdistances the others and speaking to her in the most respectful, sidelong manner, as one does to the rich— says, "What does *kometz tsaddik* spell?"

"*Tso?*"

The clerks crack up because the Hebrew letters *kometz tsaddik* actually spell *Tso*, "What" in Russian. And so they have trapped her in their joke, and they laugh, pinch each other, go berserk until their game ends with a crowd gathering, outrage, shouting, swearing, and the cursing of Jews and Gentiles until even the older clerks, even the shopkeepers are involved.

Or another time the clerks may entice the feeble-minded Monish in from a nearby street. Monish, whose blond Jesus-beard frames the deep pallor of his face, is a sickly, gentle, usually silent boy who stutters.

The clerks press him into a corner where he is promised anything he wants if he will only answer, for the thousandth time, the question which, a thousand times before, they have put to him.

"Monish, why do you want to get married?"

"Three reasons," he says, smiling.

"What are they?"

"To c . . . c . . . cuddle. To k . . . k . . . kiss. And to t . . . t . . . tickle."

"And nothing more?"

"Wh . . . wh . . . what else is there?"

Thus the market in its off-season. The shops are opened just for the sake of appearances. There is a weary wait each day for the sun to move across the sky. Then lock-up time and home, only to return the next day for another round of wasted time. To stand in the doorway expecting no customers—because there are none.

And so pass the several weeks of the dead season before harvesttime.

Those who belong, those who are part of the market—shopkeepers, brokers, merchants who derive their livelihood from it, as their parents and grandparents derived theirs—have neither the time nor the inclination to wonder about its composition, or to doubt its permanence.

On the contrary, they take it for granted that the mezuzahs nailed to the doorjambs of the shops and the rusty horseshoes nailed to the thresholds of the meaner little stores are the guardians of their bit of luck. As the bat, killed with a gold coin and buried under the thresholds of the more prosperous shops, is the guardian of their prosperity. That's how it's supposed to be, how it has always been, from the beginning of eternity, and how it will be to the end of time, so ordered by God's law from generation to generation, a heritage decreed by fathers for their children.

Should a stranger come to the market, and should he stay for a while, he would very soon get a whiff of dissolution, the first hint that very soon the full stink of death would rise from the whole shebang: the buying and selling, the hullaballoo of wheeling and dealing, the entire giddiness of all those whirling there.

And especially if he came at night when the market, together with its main and side streets, was asleep, its shops barred, its booths and stalls closed down, its rows of dark warehouses behind heavy iron gates—locked and chained. And if he were to see the bored, yawning night watchmen sitting or standing about in clusters, or singly on various street corners, looking like dark, fur-clad manifestations of the wandering god Mercury, who, long delayed, has finally arrived here out of ancient times. If a stranger did show up, we say, and if he saw all this, if he was not already a prophet, he would not in truth become one. And yet, if he were a man with somewhat refined sensibilities, he would feel grief at his heart; he would sense that the thresholds on which the night watchmen sat were already mourning thresholds, that the sealed doors, chains and locks would never be replaced, and that to enlarge the picture, to frame it truly, one would need to hang a death lamp to burn quietly here in the middle of the market to be a memorial to the place itself.

That then is the market section of the city of N. The first ring. The second section: the city itself.

If on that same night a stranger leaving the market had turned toward the nearest houses, what would first catch his eye would be a series of one-, two- or many-storyed structures built in an old-fashioned way, and in a crazy style. Or better, in no style at all. He would know at once that these were not residences, but were destined for some other purpose. And if at first glance he was not able to tell that purpose, a second look would make everything clear. They were built by the religious community of the city of N. for their God and according to His requirements. He is a wandering and an exiled God, and does not ask much of them: no columns or airy spaces, no superfluous cleanliness. No exterior decor. Only that the guttering light of an economical kerosene lamp should reveal itself through a filthy window at night, that there be silence, and that a wounded spirit may rest on the threshold of the place, in its windows and on its roof. And that an old, somewhat slovenly bachelor sexton—a not particularly diligent servant of God—sleep in one of the buildings; and in others, let whole groups of homeless beggars lie sleeping on benches, on mountains of rags. Looking themselves like mountains of rags as they snore away there. And in other buildings, on the other hand, let all twelve of the windows that tradition requires in that God's structures be ablaze at midnight with the light of candles and burning lamps; and let there frequently be heard the warm singing of boyish voices which, as they study His laws and His commandments, serve Him, and are so accounted, as sacrifices such as in the days of His glory He received— and to which for a long time now He has been unaccustomed.

Here you have such a building.

Its front faces on a small, empty square. On the lower level, it is surrounded by shops and a few homes, meat and cereal stores and others producing income for the synagogue. On the second story, the synagogue itself, looking out at the square through the many windows of its entry corridor. The other three sides, each with three windows, look out on various little streets.

It is called the Open Synagogue.

Why?

In its builder's will more than a hundred years ago, it was specified in writing that the synagogue door must never close. Neither by day nor night, not in summer or in winter. Never. So long as the building remains standing—till the coming of the Messiah, it is hoped.

And so its door is always open to the town's inhabitants who come to say their prayers and to study there. Open also to those who in summer come in to cool off, and to those who in winter come to warm themselves. Open also to dealers, shopkeepers, porters and others who slip away from the empty tumult of the market so that they may breathe a bit of consoling air. It is a refuge for those poor wanderers for whom it is a pausing point in their arrivals or departures. Wanderers who sometimes stay for weeks, or even months. And nobody, according to the terms of the will, may prevent them.

In that synagogue, prayers are said from early morning to well past midday. Sometimes there are full quorums of ten men, at other times people pray alone. At night there is Torah study to which middle-aged and elderly men come in the evening, and who go home after their studies. Late at night there are sleepless young people.

It is rare then that one finds the Open Synagogue empty. The door swings in and out. Is never closed.

It is a gathering place for various interests. Here, there is a cluster of people talking about their workaday concerns. There, a young man, or an older one, is engrossed in a complex study problem that has no relationship to anything going on around him.

Those studying are of various sorts. Some of them are local young bachelors, wealthy or semiwealthy, whose parents support them. But for the most part, the scholars are from out of town, looked after by people who think it a benevolent act to provide them with their most urgent necessities. Among these young people are those who come from nearby villages as well as from more distant communities: from Volhynia and the Podolia borders—even from as far away as Poland: each with his accent, mannerisms, songs and gestures.

Now for the congregation. Very poor, tattered, carelessly or badly dressed—and therefore devoted to the impulse that brought them here; a congregation so inspired, so committed, so engulfed by the desire to reach the goal in which they believe that the days are not long enough and they stay up much of the night.

Then the synagogue is brightly lighted. A lamp from the ceiling or from one of the wall brackets hangs above each of the young scholars' heads. Those sitting in the farther corners hold candles above the books they are studying. The accumulated light illuminates not only the synagogue, but it also spills out-of-doors. And a pious passerby, or an inhabitant looking out of one of the nearby low houses, seeing the synagogue so brightly lighted on all sides might get the feeling that he was looking at a lighthouse set in the midst of the city's darkness. The sense that the lighted synagogue is the sleepy town's brilliant representative before heaven, and heaven's directors.

Especially if a pious passerby hears the young voices shouting or humming the famished, ascetic, yearning melodies brought here from the mullah and dervish schools of the godforsaken distant East. These young people, who have voluntarily immured themselves here, utter ecstatic yells, and express by means of those melodies their discontent with corporeality. Creating, we say again, the feeling in a pious passerby that he is watching young victims sacrificing themselves for somebody else's sins.

There you have one synagogue.

And here is another one nearby. The "hotheaded" synagogue, so called because hotheads, half-mad, fanatically pious Hasidic sects like the Kotzkers, the Carliners pray there, wildly climbing the walls, running about cooling their interior religious fervor with the sounds of their own voices.

Facing the "hotheaded" synagogue, the "cold" one.

A building in which, even if you enter it in summer, a cold breeze chills your bones. This, too, is a two-story building. Again, with shops on the first level. On the second story, the synagogue itself.

Highly polished railings, which over the years have been rubbed by many hands holding to them on the way up, lead to a vestibule like a cold-storage vault, then there are several steps up to the synagogue's entryway.

A high, broken ceiling divided into five parts. Beneath the fifth, the middle section, the Torah-reading podium on tall pillars. Chandeliers suspended from ropes make one think that neither the candles in their sockets nor the gas in the lamps could illuminate or warm anything.

Those praying are cold, those studying are dry—Lithuanians. A sense of withered life, an emptiness, emanates from their songs, their prayers. They are called the Ibn-Ezraniks, after the early medieval Spanish poet and philosopher whose rational spirit has found a place like a chilly, abandoned nest among this thicket of synagogues.

If it were not for the synagogue furnishings—the Torah-reading pulpit, the Ark of the Covenant, the podiums, bookcases and books— both the interior and the exterior of this building would be easily taken for some sort of burial structure, or tomb.

Now for the "old one."

The oldest synagogue of all.

As you approach it, you notice how dilapidated the entryway is, worn away by dark and unhappy generations over centuries. If you go in, you sense at once that all those centuries have left behind their despised and desolate breath.

The path to the door, and all along the facade of the building, is paved with flat, well-trodden river stones that have worn thin.

An iron door, broad as a gate and studded with huge round-headed nails, can be opened with a long, old-fashioned, very heavy key—an ancient masterwork with short, chiseled teeth whose like it would be hard to find anywhere. It is a key that needs to be turned several times in its keyhole, and no one except the synagogue's regular sexton knows how to put the key into its proper position.

Inside the gate you come to the synagogue vestibule. Dark, poorly illuminated by an exterior light, and even less by the light that filters through the varicolored panes of glass high up in the second door that leads to the synagogue.

If you open that door and cross the threshold, you will, willy-nilly, raise your head. It would seem that the architects designed the place for that express purpose so that the pious visitor must lift his eyes the moment he crosses the lintel. To make him think that someone higher than himself exists. Above him, and beyond his fate. Inducing in him the first religious tremor.

The ceiling is high and spacious, and if one looks closely at its center—amazing! A ceiling above a ceiling. An intensification not visible at first.

The synagogue: the east wall, and especially the broad pillar that reaches to the highest heights, are covered with gold-painted animals, birds, angels, fruits, flowers, musical instruments and woven branches.

The walls and ceiling are painted in oil. Folk painters, primitive masters, have lavished all of their devout skill, their naïveté and childish simplicity here. They have painted stories of myths, the lives of the Patriarchs. Abraham, for example, bringing Isaac to the sacrifice. Moses on Mount Sinai with the Ten Commandments; Isaac lying bound on the woodpile, and Abraham ready with his knife. And the angel appearing to keep him from killing his only son. Moses with the stone tablets, and around him the smoking mountain and bolts of streaking fire. Then the golden calf, and the shrine of the covenant and so on. And the same for the other walls, and the ceilings, too, decorated with such pictures.

The Torah-reading podium, with its many steps up, is screened on all four sides by artificial trees. Trees from which children cannot tear away their gaze, and even the hearts of devout adults beat faster at the sight of that tree-screened podium. From its height, the Great Ban used to be read against those who had merited it. At specified times, the appropriate sound of the ram's horn was blown from that podium: whether to announce heaven's decree or the news of a calamitous law of the state. From it, the deaths of great leaders of the people were mourned. From it, new ordinances and laws, whether of the community or the czar, were promulgated.

The synagogue is not very large, in fact, but on a holiday or a festivity, it has been known to absorb the entire population of N., with, naturally, some few left outside. First, the middle section was filled up, then the two side aisles, left and right. The people squeezed together so astutely; they filled every space so closely that it was hard to find space for so much as a pin. The press of bodies and the heated breathing of the multitude were so intense the walls perspired, and streams ran down the smooth oil-painted surfaces. That breathing could be sensed in the synagogue even when it was empty. The breathing of masses of people experiencing their lives on remarkable occasions.

The synagogue is especially for men. But there is a large, screened gallery running along three walls built so that men and women can be kept strictly apart.

But there have been times when the women were permitted to come down to the main floor. But even when they were not permitted, they sometimes seized permission for themselves. They came down an inflamed, angry, hysterical mob and opened the Holy of Holies and flung themselves on it with the sort of passionate outcries men are incapable of—on the occasion of a recruiting decree and the threat of draftee "catchers." Or when there was some other disaster in the town: a plague, an epidemic—cholera, for example.

This synagogue was not used only for the usual prayers. A quorum of men for morning or evening prayers rarely assembled there. There was no Torah study either. Sleeping overnight—strictly forbidden. And yet, essentially, this was the synagogue of synagogues, the only one of God's houses to which the townspeople attributed legendary holiness because it was the site of the martyrdom of a holy man who had suffered for his faith and shown great heroism there. This is why the place is held in such high esteem, why it is enfolded in legend and why the people have kept it closed at all times, opening its great doors only on the most exceptional occasions. And this is why, to repeat, it is closed during the day, and why at night, according to popular belief, it is a gathering place for the souls of the dead; and this is why those who need to pass that synagogue at night keep their distance from it, and this is why even the sexton knocks at the door first before he opens the synagogue in the morning. To alert the gathered souls to his coming.

This synagogue is the tallest building in N. According to decree, no other structure may be built higher. Only the church is taller, but it is not considered a building for comparison since it belongs to a foreign people, a foreign regime. And one has to yield to foreign power, especially when it has superior strength.

Then there are the workingmen's and tradesmen's synagogues according to their kind, those of the pious and charitable societies and institutes: shoemakers', tailors', smiths', wheelwrights', butchers' synagogues. Synagogues of grain brokers, fruit vendors. Of Don men, who travel on the Don River; of Muscovites, Danzigers, hospital workers; of Hasidic sects and other societies—and so on. And all clustered together in one place, cheek by jowl, above, beside, beneath each other.

And now, at night, in one of the synagogues a candle is lighted, in another, no light at all, in a third there are many candles burning. In the first, no Torah students, in the second, there are one or two, in the third, a number of scholars are studying. And overshadowing them all, standing guard over them all is the Old Synagogue, tall and somnolent, with its concrete walk and its mute doors.

A stranger—we say—a stranger who should chance to find his way from the market to this place at night would grasp at once the structure and the style of community life in N. Would perceive that the market is the town's living center, and that its God guards its pocketbook. That the people themselves live shunted into the nearby side streets and that they, the streets and their sleeping inhabitants, are not themselves of the essence—rather they are an excrescence on the essence, which is the market. The market which nourished them yesterday and which tomorrow will feed them again. And to keep from losing the restlessness of yesterday's market, to keep it from dissipating entirely, and as a way of recalling it in tomorrow's tumult, they have, during these quiet hours, set watchmen out, along with their God as well, who is permitted neither to doze nor to sleep; and to that end they have left their youngest children awake in the synagogues, with instructions to rouse Him to His old age and to His duties.

And we will add further that if that stranger, whether in summer or winter, should spend the night in one of those synagogues and should choose to wait there for dawn, he would observe that when it was time for day to open its eye above those places, he would see that when the eye did indeed open, it closed again almost at once, not only because it was not especially clean there, nor even because the houses are clustered as haphazard as in a Gypsy camp. No. The essential reason had to do with the sense of doom, of foreseen disaster, hanging over the place . . . over everything: over the market, and especially over those synagogue structures which, though they would appear to be the guardians, would appear to be the lookouts, the caretakers of the community—were, if the truth be told, already a sight to occasion pity. And later, who could tell? Perhaps they would be hung about with the rusted locks of memory; perhaps they would be sold at auction. Or (in the event that nobody bought them) . . . they would collapse from sheer age; or to imagine the best case possible, they would, with the changing times, be renewed and put to other, quite other, uses.

Everything's possible. The day, however, as it opens its eye, sees:

A large city divided in two by a river. Along its banks, the river is screened by rotting old tree trunks, by the dense tops of willow trees. The trees, with their feet in the water, turn it dark green, and in that darkened water live fish, frogs, snakes and all sorts of plants and swarming other things.

Early in the morning a few old fishermen in small boats wait beside nets or beside the fishing rods whose lines they have cast out, hoping to be rewarded for their early morning patience with small river fish.

Flocks of ducks and geese, each flock led by its respective drake or gander paddling in advance of the flock, quietly swim the breadth of the river from one bank to the other.

Occasional washerwomen, early in the morning, are already doing their laundry at the river's edge, and the sound of rinsing and beating is so insignificant it does not even disturb the fish swimming nearby.

There's a presunrise light on the river, with trees bending over it, and the shadows of night still on the water.

Not far above the level of the river there are meadows which, here and there, are still moist with water left by the spring floods: green meadows, tinged with mildew, covered with the myriad heads of yellow dandelions.

At this time of day there is seldom anybody stirring in those fields, except for an occasional suspicious-looking cluster of people who have come there to conduct their secretive discussions or to divide up the loot of an already achieved theft.

Higher than those meadows, on both sides of the river, the town whose two sides are united first, downstream at the point where the river narrows, by an old-fashioned footbridge that can accommodate three or four people walking abreast; and farther upstream where the river is wide, by a modern bridge made of wood and set on numerous timbers, but broad and handsome with room for two sets of wagons coming and going as well as sidewalks (with handrails) for pedestrians.

At the moment, both bridges are still asleep. No one to be seen. And not only the bridges, the whole town is still asleep.

The first people that the town sees stirring are:

1. The oldest rabbi of the town. An intelligent, politically astute, scholarly featured graybeard. He stands on the porch of his small two-story house that is on the square facing the Open Synagogue. He is not dressed, as one might expect of a man of his age and station, he is not dressed in a loose white cloak. No. He already wears his black caftan, which, despite his years, is very neat and clean. He stands there, his hand at his forehead, shading his eyes from the sun.

He is the first to rise. Whether (as one has to consider) it is because of his age, or as the town says, it is because his mind is so keen and his thoughts so pressing that they will not let him rest and continually drive him from his bed early in the morning.

That is Reb Dudi, who is known to the whole town, who is respected by the entire region, who has a reputation for scholarship, for grammar, and for mathematical knowledge.

He inhales the early morning air, when there is no one abroad as yet, when the sun has not yet mounted to the sky, when everyone else is still asleep. When even the Open Synagogue, from which all night long various voices could be heard—when even it, because its scholars have grown weary, has finally gone to sleep. And only rarely at this time of day does anyone go in or out through its door.

2. The second, Yanovski, the Polish doctor.

Also an old man. With a grandmotherly gait, and a countenance that already has the look of clay, and shaved, except for pure white side-whiskers, in the Franz Josef style.

He is a leader in the Polish-Carmelite church on the other side of the marketplace. That church on whose entrance gate facade there is a semicircular panel on which has been painted a view of Mount Carmel at whose foot sits Elijah the Prophet enfolded in a Roman toga while birds fly overhead bringing him food in their beaks.

He, Yanovski, the earliest of the believers, comes to say his prayers before dawn in that chapel which is in the old fortress, itself a remnant and an ancient reminder of the Cossack revolt of the time of Chmielnicki and Gonta. The fortress is old and supported by recently built sloping buttresses. Willows grow along both the old and the new walls. The cannon and the entrenchments serve as nesting places for birds. And the only thing left alive is the courtyard in which are to be found the red-roofed Gothic chapel and the fire lookout tower that sets up new alarms in case of fire, and which with its swaying bell serves as a clock, announcing to the town its quarter, half and fully rounded hours.

Yanovski is always, summer or winter, the first one in the street. But as he approaches the perpetually open gate that leads from the church to the street, he finds a couple of beggars sitting at the doorjambs as if they had congealed their yesterday or the day before, a couple of ancient Polish old women who, with their dresses drawn up above their knees, look like statues in church niches. They sit begging wordlessly, in the well-known attitude of Catholic humility, their eyes lowered.

Sometimes, Yanovski gives the beggars something, or else he does not, but in either case he is always the one around whom they have built their day's first beggars' expectations.

And thus it is that Yanovski, with his grandmotherly gait and his clay countenance, comes first to wake the Polish god for the small Polish community in the same way that Reb Dudi wakes his God for the Jews (nearly one hundred percent of the population).

And soon thereafter—after those two have waked and risen—the town itself wakes up. With blundering about in the streets, confused movements in lanes and back alleys, among houses which—never mind how often they have been leveled by fires (no one can remember how many)—have been rebuilt by the same inhabitants, the same householders, and seem prepared one fine day or night to go up in flames again.

The town wakes. That section—the second ring, where the bulk of the population lives and where the roofs are shingled, rarely covered with tin—not only in the mostly unpaved but also in the paved streets; where the houses are so low, so dwarflike that a man of normal height can touch their roofs with his outstretched hand; where every court-yard is barren, its earth dry; where a tree is a guest and a bit of garden a rarity; where over low fences and palings the inhabitant of one court-yard looks right into his neighbor's court; and where the people living in those enclosures are perpetually at war with each other; where sometimes the entire street—so closely packed are the houses—the entire street takes part in the quarrel.

That section of the town stirs which, were one to look at it on a map, would reveal neither hands nor feet, neither beginning nor end. Nothing but a mixture of whorls and lines, a strange braiding of insane arabesques. Except that in the very midst of the density, as in all towns of this sort, one would find small squares of shopping markets, for fish or meat and so on, toward which, from every side, the newly wakened housewife population makes its way—to the meat market, for instance, where the butchers, readying themselves for the day's business, are already hacking at the meat on their blocks while the dogs lurk nearby hoping to have bits of meat or bones thrown to them.

The day comes into being in a tumultuous time-honored manner with samovars put on to boil, with the warming of ovens, with the smoke emitted from one courtyard gracing the inhabitants of the other.

The day comes into being with the thrusting open of shutters, doors, rooms and stables. Often, beginning very early, with the sounds of quarreling women's voices. Then with the news of what transpired last night: a disaster perhaps, someone in a nearby house who has been ill for a long time has died suddenly. Or, on the other hand, a festivity in someone's home. A woman has given birth to a child, or a cow to a calf. The women are always in a hurry, yet they gather in clusters and though they have not yet fully washed themselves that morning, hastily trade news of the events of the night.

The day comes into being with the noise of the shopping markets, of the meat-fish-flour-groats-merchants who call out their wares; and the noise of the customers jostling to buy, turning over the various goods and bargaining at the tops of their voices; with the cries of little children whose mothers often bring them to the shopping markets and who frightened by the racket in the place burst into tears; with the sound of dogs who prowl between the legs of the merchants and their customers—and who frequently receive violent blows—their legs stepped on or something heavy thrown at their backs—so that they yelp for pain; with the cries of crippled beggars who also have been in the market from a very early hour, and each of them cries out his particular disability, his blindness, his lameness or whatever other fault, hoping at the top of his voice to waken the market's pity; with the cries of thieves who not infrequently set off a deliberate racket to create a crowding, a jostling, so that in the throng they may more easily take possession of the purses and wallets of strangers; of mad folk who support themselves and regularly spend their nights in the market—at night, they sleep in the merchant's stalls, and in the morning, with the first market noises, they are assailed by their first seizures of madness, and thereby attract to themselves the first of the compassionate souls who drive off the small mobs that have gathered around to torment them; or they attract those who, on the other hand, have come to torment them even more, and who will continue to tease them for the rest of the day.

A stranger, we say once again, who chose to come in the morning to this, the second ring of the town of N., would see the sorts of things that were in those days to be seen in such sections of such cities: house and market confusion, street and courtyard filth, rarely a lane in which the eye rested on a bit of greenery, on a tree, on grass, on cleanliness, or a place where the ear might experience the delight of silence.

And he would also observe that all of the architecture of N. was a mockery. The most that one could say about the very best of the buildings in the town was that they were second-rate. As for the rest, the best that could be said was much worse.

Old folk might have pointed out certain streets or lanes which had miraculously survived very ancient fires. And the stranger might notice that the new streets, those built after the fires, are hardly any different from the old ones. The same planlessness, the same narrowness. Tiny courtyards. And again, house pressed against house, roof against roof, as if to be ready, when the time came, for the next fires . . . as if to be ready to snatch the flames up and pass them quickly along.

He would have noted, too, leaving the question of fires to one side, that the town must have had a sudden spurt of growth within a particular span of years.

Townsfolk would point out to him the old cemetery which now was in the center of the town, though formerly, in obedience to the injunction to set aside a "field" for such a purpose, it was undoubtedly outside the town. And seeing it would serve him as the first indication of the way in which the town had grown, and if then he actually went out to visit the cemetery, he would in that place, seeing the small square enclosure fenced in on every side, get a clear sense of how the town some hundred years ago had been really small, since this minuscule plot had sufficiently served the infrequent burial needs of the community. Not like the modern enormous cemetery.

Certainly the town had grown. Had he wished to compare the inscriptions on the headstones, the greater part of which had survived and were easy to read, with the inscriptions on the modern stones, he would be struck by how little the new inscriptions differed from the old ones: the same style, the same headstone language and honorifics, as if there was an identicality in the people themselves who were buried in both places.

He would in either cemetery have read with only slight modifications of names and dates, "Here lies a young cabalist of three and twenty years."

"Here lies," he would further have read—in either cemetery—"a famous rabbi who wore the rabbinical crown for thirty years" . . . and so on.

In passing, he would have noticed groups of evergreens whose spiny leaves intermingled with each other like thorns growing above the graves of the most respected members of the community just as similar groups of trees grew above the graves of the most respected members of the community in the new graveyard. And in the new cemetery there would be the same tall, overhanging linden trees with nests of crows in their branches growing above important graves just as they did in the old graveyard.

And just as the old cemetery and the new resemble each other (except in matters of degree), the stranger would observe that so, too, the living town differs only in small details from its earlier self.

The third ring. That is the circle that forms a circumference enclosing the town. Here are to be found the outlying villages like Popivke,

Peigerivke, Katshenivke and so on. With hills and valleys, with clay and swampy places.

Various of these places are sprinkled with inhabitants as if with poppy seed—a hut beside a hut, one ruin beside another. No sign of a street, no hint of a sidewalk, permanently filthy, muddy. And there no grass ever grows.

In other areas the houses are set at considerable distances from each other. Already there's a whiff of the country. Of the stillness of tiny hamlets.

In this third ring, the most extreme poverty imaginable. Most of the houses are held together only by a miracle. Inside, the walls are warped, moist, perpetually mildewed; outside, unpainted; the roofs, badly mended if at all. Most of the children are naked to the waist, the older ones wear torn, ragged or patched shirts. Dirt and poverty are acquired there by inheritance, and no one anymore even dreams of freeing oneself from that legacy.

There, the poorest of the poor, as well as the town's human detritus. The lowest of the underclass. Incompetent workers—the sorts of patch makers to whom even second-rate work is not given. Who are capable of patching only the shoes and the clothing of the town's and the outlying district's very poorest folk.

For the most part, such are the inhabitants of that district.

There, too, ragpickers, beggars and professional paupers, organ grinders and poor porters, agents for servants and wet nurses, card readers and whores.

There, removed from the community of the town, sundered and estranged, their customs are the same, but their laws are not those of the town.

The God of N. had here, as it were, loosened His reins. This community was badly harnessed to the wagon of His ways, and a great many of them seemed not to be in harness at all.

Here, on a bright summer day, on some sandy spot, one might encounter a group of young folk sitting or lying about, playing cards, or having a picnic under the open sky.

There, one day, a town dweller might have seen the sort of sight that in town he would never have seen in his life. In some barren spot, some fellow not dressed like a Jew. He had a short jacket, a shirt, and his trousers embroidered with peasant designs were tucked into his long polished boots. He had a cattle prod in his hand and he stood talking to a woman whose young pretty face was framed in a shawl. Or, if one saw her from behind, one noticed her largish, rounded shoulders.

At first they stand quietly. They have evidently something of importance to discuss. It is clear that the man has called the woman out here from her house because the matter between them is serious.

She casts her eyes down guiltily. He taps his boot with the prod and looks at her, then following the estranged silence that encloses them both for a while, a shriek is heard. It is the man who suddenly and with all his might has slapped the prod full across her face.

After the shriek, silence once more. The woman makes a great effort to control herself. The pain has made her cry out, but becoming immediately aware of her helplessness, she has restrained herself and is now prepared to receive in silence whatever further blows are to come.

Because that is the custom there. When a man beats a woman who is subjugated to him, and she cries out, no one will respond. No one will help her. On the contrary—the less anyone takes her part or comes to her aid, the less any bystander or stranger has to do with the quarrel, the better it is for her.

Thugs live there. "Emperors," toughs who beat up people for a fee. "Dry" beatings, or "wet," a few broken bones, or downright hospitalization.

There, too, among the agents for servants and wet nurses one finds a couple like Perele and Iliovekhe—both of them partners in the same business which is conducted as follows: when a maidservant in a prosperous and proper family makes a slip and is already in the later months—no way to hide it anymore—and when the respectable wife of the rich family wishes to hide her husband's or her son's guilt from people and to avoid improper talk that can lead to scandal—then Perele comes onto the secret scene.

A large, fifty-year-old woman, with a porter's beefy shoulders covered always with a skimpy shawl, with a certain masculine hoarseness in her voice brought on by drinking, with features that have turned red for the same reason, and with a mouth well known for its strong language.

She begins by threatening the maidservant and gets her thoroughly frightened. She warns her never to dare mention a certain unmentionable name. She threatens her with the police, with all sorts of dire consequences: rotting in jail for a frame-up and for false accusation until at last she, the maidservant, cowed by her misfortune and her fear, agrees to everything, accepts her kind words . . . her motherly advice: to live with Iliovekhe who will be paid with the money that Perele will get from the respectable housewife by devious means. Money for room and board and general care until the time for "having" comes.

Then Iliovekhe puts the "suckling," as she and Perele call such a child, on the sort of diet that ensures that it is "carried off"; or in case the infant is too strong, or too stubborn, then they do "what's right"— they throttle it. After which Perele places its mother as a wet nurse in a respectable household for a good fee, not a groschen of which the wet nurse ever sees.

There's pure gold in the partnership between Perele and Iliovekhe: Perele drinks, frequents the company of other servant finders in the town and visits wealthy homes. There for a fee she receives "the fallen ones," and replaces them with fresh, healthy women—again for a fee. And Iliovekhe does the housework: feeding and throttling. Until—one may say in passing—until one fine day the town will see the partners linked to the same pair of handcuffs led off by the police, only to be freed to go back to their work again.

Thieves and gang leaders live there.

There's a place there where a nobleman's stolen horses can be sold, or depending on someone's need, where they can be safely kept until the time of a major fair. There's a place there where stolen dry goods can be redyed, or where they can be cut up and packed in "thieves' boxes," and where they can be bought later. And there is where rich people's paired candlesticks find a home, and there is where one goes to find a soothsayer or a card reader who promptly sends for a gang leader who takes his cut and arranges for a burglary in the home to follow not long after.

Jewish rope braiders live there, and non-Jewish pig dealers. That's where full-bosomed young women grow up; and "dove boys," future picklocks, gold chain snatchers and pickpockets.

The dog killer goes there to get his dogs flayed, and the wagoner brings his fallen jade—the horsemeat for his dogs, the hide to be sold.

There, every Saturday, summer or winter, were fought the well-known battles of the "royal" gangs led by their emperors: their leaders who lived at the expense of rich youths who stole (or enticed) money from their parents to pay the weekly or monthly protection charges the gangs levied to refrain from beating them or to protect them from other gangs. The gangs gathered there from every part of town. At first they fought with their bare fists, then as they grew heated, or entered into a "passion," they used sticks, stones, knives. Such encounters always ended with broken heads, with several victims taken off to the town hospital—half dead or crippled.

Though these outlying districts had certain affinities with N.—the same god, identical customs, the same days of mourning, the same festivals and holy days—still, as has been said, God was not quite as stern and required less of His servants here, because He knew that it was useless to expect much from them.

There, the festivals were celebrated for the sake of the delicacies associated with them. And on the days of mourning, nobody mourned.

There, in the outlying districts life was more relaxed. One despised the town and its religious bureaucracy, calling them simpleminded and stupid. There one called them in only at need: at a circumcision or a wedding or at such other times as custom and law required. Then they were essential. One gave them their due and got from them what, alas, they had to give, but one did not prolong their visits. They, for their part, felt equally constrained by the people in that part of town. And once they had done what they had come for and had received what they were given, they turned their collars up and left without delay.

Those in the outlying districts lived their lives among each other and, except for matters necessary for their livelihood, did everything they could to avoid being dependent on the town.

They had their own synagogues in which even on Sabbaths and holidays, prayers were over sooner than in the town. Here, the congregation was worn with fatigue, had very little understanding of Hebrew, and though it was generally faithful to the daily prayer book, said its prayers hurriedly, anxious to finish as quickly as possible so that it could leave the proximity—and incomprehensibility—of God and get on home to its own, to what it understood.

There, tradition—as has been said—was still tradition. But religious laws were not held in very high esteem. The fine points of the law, they said, were not for poor people. And they said that too much study or psalm singing would give one lice.

In summer, for example, they said their prayers quickly so that entire households, entire streets full of wives and children carrying cushions and bedcovers, could get to the green spots outside the town, to the wagon routes and the walks along the railway lines leading out of the city. There, they sprawled out, Gypsy fashion. Some lay down to rest, but for the most part they merely passed the time: men and women, boys and girls, scattered about, like Gypsies, gesticulating freely and speaking freely, too. So freely that any one from the second ring of the town (no matter who he might be) who chanced to pass and saw and overheard them would hurry off like one scalded, hiding his face for shame and stopping his ears against obscenities.

Yes, in the third ring, as has been said, the outcasts of the town. Houses as well as people. But in the final analysis, the outcasts are but a minority of the inhabitants of this ring. Its absolute essence is the mass of the poor exhausted by hard labor who lived there. And anyone with a keen eye might even then have been able to see the seeds of the future floating in the air.

It is true that in the days of which we speak, the community of workers who lived on the outskirts were not highly regarded by the town and that they lived isolated from it. But there will be times later, much later than those of which we speak, when the town will press an attentive ear to just these places. It will be from there, from those very swamps of poverty, that it will feel the current of an overthrowing, an extremely refreshing, wind. And it will be there, to those huts and ruins, to those poorest of workers, to those patch tailors and laborers—it will be to them that the finest youth of the town will come with trembling hearts to hear unusual news and to participate in historically pleasing events. Better educated and wiser heads than those of the inhabitants will bow before them at the low doorways and thresholds of their hovels because in the course of bringing knowledge to them, in the course of teaching them, they will themselves carry away a new knowledge.

It will be there that the first small circles will form for whom, in the course of time, the sense of the narrowness of the walls that enclose them will grow, and they will begin to gather out-of-doors—though still only in small groups. Then as they feel their strength and spirit ripening, they will (and the town will remember it as the beginning of an era) gather into a great mass—not quite bold yet, because not used to taking such steps—but still, in disciplined ranks, heading toward the town.

The evening will conceal them in darkness, and out of the concealment a humming, like the sound of distant floodwaters, will rise.

The calm, bourgeois householders accustomed to a lassitude sanctified by generations, will, when they hear the sound, step out to see: a strange human wave, with a flag at its head that has never been seen before, singing a song no one has ever heard before. Then, greatly frightened, the bourgeois householders will not know whether it is a plague advancing, or some other visitation with its roots in earth or in hell.

Averting their eyes from the sight, they will, like brood hens clucking for their young in time of danger, hurry their children indoors under the safe wings of their own roofs, under the generations-old eaves, and will lock the doors behind them, and will put the chains firmly on the latches.

That will happen much later. And later we will devote time to an extensive account of those events. But this is not the moment for it. Now we must turn again to the second section of the town and to a house where our narrative will be detained for a considerable while.

II

Family Chronicle

Introduction

In truth, the earliest memories and the great prestige of the Mashber family are intimately linked with Uncle Luzi. Uncle Luzi was Moshe Mashber's older brother. The two of them were sons of a rabbinical judge, a scholar of Jewish law, well known in his time in a large Volhynian town on the border of imperial Poland.

The brothers saw each other rarely. They lived apart: Moshe in N., the large Jewish commercial town where he was well known for his wealth and his generous conduct, and Uncle Luzi, who was not rich, and was unknown, and made no effort to be noticed, lived in an isolated little town somewhere near the border. And yet Moshe deferred to his brother and took great pride in his prestige. Luzi's occasional visit to Moshe's house was always eventful, not only for Moshe, but for everyone in his household: for his daughters, his sons-in-law and even for the children.

Here's what one child remembers.

Usually, it happened in summer. In the evening. The child, coming back from somewhere, slips into the house for a bite to eat or to change some article of clothing before going back outside to join the other children in their summer evening games. Then suddenly he notices a change—something has happened in the house. The floors are swept, the members of the household are dressed in their Sabbath clothes. Voices are hushed and everybody is curiously restrained—like in-laws.

Must be a guest, the child thinks.

"Who?" he asks the maid, because it is instantly clear that the members of the household are too busy and won't put up with a child's questions.

"Hush, now. It's Uncle Luzi. Uncle Luzi's come," the maid replies in a hurried whisper.

The child knows at once that Uncle Luzi is not in any of the common rooms of the house, but rather that he is closeted with his grandfather, Moshe.

Because that was the custom. When Uncle Luzi came, he first shut himself in for a while with Moshe Mashber, and showed himself to the family only later on.

And that's how it is now. Even as the family, strangely tense, waits, the door of Grandfather's alcove opens and Uncle Luzi appears on the threshold. Behind him, Grandfather. And Grandfather is in his Sabbath clothes, and his cheeks are tinged with red, and Uncle Luzi is taller than Grandfather because Grandfather is of less than average height, and Uncle Luzi is taller than average, and his beard is rounded, dense, white, and his eyes are grayish and strange.

The men say, "Shalom," and the women blush as they greet Uncle Luzi, tucking their hair under their headscarves or wigs and ask how he is—Uncle Luzi. Uncle Luzi, smiling, replies to the questions, but looks away; he does not look at the women.

Later, the child sees Uncle Luzi sitting in a chair in the living room and Grandfather stands beside it as if supporting himself on the armrest. The men stay in the living room and carry on conversations, and the women leave to go into the dining room and to the kitchen where they start to prepare something for Uncle Luzi.

Then strange talk is heard in the kitchen. Uncle Luzi will not eat "flesh from the living." Neither fish nor meat. And the women consult and consider for a long while, pooling their skills and experience until finally they settle on something to cook.

At night, when all the children have come in from outdoors, they are led one by one to Uncle Luzi. Shyly, they say "Shalom" to him. And the child on whom Uncle Luzi's gaze rests or whose hand he holds a bit longer than the others is thoroughly petrified. The children back away one by one, each child seeking its father and mother, embarrassed.

Much later in the evening, when they have washed up and taken their places, the men near the head of the table, the women at its lower end, the children notice that their grandfather is sitting not quite in his usual place. He is not at the head of the table. Uncle Luzi is. And their grandfather's prestige seems in some way to be diminished today. His weight less. And this troubles the children for their grandfather's sake, at the same time as they appreciate the magnitude of Uncle Luzi's esteem.

After that first day, the first night, there is the following morning. And in the morning the children get to observe Uncle Luzi's character and demeanor. He says little. One never hears him utter a superfluous word. And yet any room in which he is to be found seems to be filled with a presence. And those who are near him seem to have been put there expressly to obey his every command.

This is the experience of the children, but the adults feel it, too. Not even Grandfather Mashber and Grandmother Gitl are excepted.

So long as Uncle Luzi is a guest in the house, Grandmother Gitl never leaves it. She doesn't go to town to do her shopping. Instead, she is constantly in the kitchen. Her headscarf tied loosely behind her ears, she perspires, gives orders, supervises the servants, examines their hands, their pots and pans, making sure that the ritual rules governing food are more strictly enforced than ever.

And Uncle Luzi, it is noticed, goes nowhere and he conducts himself as follows: he prays late, eats late and alone. He is served by Grandmother Gitl who will let no servant wait on him.

That's how it is on weekdays. When sometimes Uncle Luzi is in the house over the Sabbath, the children notice that he prays at home on Friday night and on Saturday morning, and that Grandfather Moshe stays home on his account too. And the listening children notice that Uncle Luzi's manner of prayer is different too. He prays in the Sephardi fashion. And when Uncle Luzi is not in the house, the curious children steal into his room to look at his prayer book and they see that it's true. It *is* different, not like other prayer books. The prayers are in a different order and not set out in the usual way, and some of them are entirely unknown.

And the children learn that Uncle Luzi received this very prayer book from his father, and that that father had it from a grandfather and so on and so on; and that the prayer book has been rescued many times from conflagrations; and that it is a talisman which, when it is put under the head of a pregnant woman, helps her through a difficult labor.

And that during the Sabbath meals, Uncle Luzi is silent. Will not, it is said, utter a secular word. Everyone knows this and avoids troubling him on any matter; if he is spoken to, his replies are brief, and in Hebrew.

That then is the manner of his coming and his going. And with each departure, the children learn more about the family's prestige, about their grandfather and their great-grandfather. And based on various conversations and remarks let fall by the adults, they acquire more and more information.

And here is what they learned.

They come from an ancient stock that reaches as far back as the Spanish exile: rabbis, holy men. And finally that their great-grandfather, Reb Luzi's and Moshe Mashber's father, died young—from too much fasting. And that he became a hermit in the years before his death. His wife, at that time still terribly young, made a complaint about her husband, Reb Yoel, to a well-known holy man, but the holy man was unable to help her at all and Reb Yoel remained a hermit for the rest of his life.

He spent entire days in prayer, and studied Torah at night. And the children heard how adults, boasting, recounted how on a summer's night a great preacher passing grandfather Yoel's open window overheard him studying Torah. Tearing his shirt, the rabbi said, "Lo, how a Jew studies Torah for its own sake. But what a waste," he added, "that what he gains by Torah he loses by fasting."

The fasts, it was said further (and now a bit covertly, as if it were a secret), the fasts were undertaken because of the sins of Reb Yoel's father, who, the story went, was a member of the sect of Shabbatai Zevi. He was misled by them for a long time. And when there was a notorious assembly of Shabbatarian rabbis who locked themselves in a room in some market town where they danced all night around their priestess, a naked woman, Grandfather Yoel's father was one of the dancers.

Later, he repented, and when the Shabbatai Zevi sect was put under a ban, he spent his days weeping, beating his breast night and day. He would not change his clothes and would take only bread and water and, even on the Sabbath, slept on the ground. Then he disappeared and no one knew what had become of him. Some said that he rejoined the Shabbatarians and went off with them to Istanbul. Others said that he became a wandering pilgrim.

And it was his sins that Reb Yoel undertook to expiate. Not only Reb Yoel, but also Uncle Luzi of whom it was said that when as a small child he heard the story of his grandfather's fate, he took it very much to heart and wanted to follow in his father's, Reb Yoel's footsteps. And things took an ugly turn with him. Much fasting made him very sick, but since he was still young, his friends and relatives prevailed on him to go to Velednik. And when Uncle Luzi appeared before the rebbe of Velednik, the rebbe shouted, "Ha! What do you think you're up to, young fellow? You're going to make your grandfather's lot easier with your fasting? He was a soul killer; his son was a soul killer. And now his grandson is a soul killer. Just what do you think you're up to, young fellow?"

And Uncle Luzi allowed himself to be persuaded. He wept for a long while in the presence of the Velednik rebbe, and realized finally that he could not help his grandfather by the way he had chosen. From then on he attached himself to the Velednik rebbe and allowed himself to be guided by that firm hand.

But recently, it was said further, with the death of the Velednik rebbe, Uncle Luzi had felt himself to be out of sorts. He traveled from rabbinical "court" to "court," searching. Always melancholy, and always unable to choose a new rebbe. He had little to do with people. The only human intercourse he had were the occasional brief visits to his brother Moshe Mashber. And if Uncle Luzi delayed a visit for any length of time, Moshe Mashber went to see him.

And because of these visits of Uncle Luzi's, his image was permanently impressed on their minds, and what they remembered is this:

A man of more than average height with grayish eyes that do not look at one directly, but seem to look over one's head. Dressed always in a long, durable shiny coat during the week, and on Saturdays, a coat of silk. He stood erect, and when he walked, people seemed naturally to move out of his way. He spoke little. Generally, he was seen seated, wearing his tallis, and when not in his tallis he had his hands stuck in his back pockets as he paced meditatively about the room, pausing frequently, still immersed in thought. He had a way while thus engrossed of putting his index finger over his right eye and moving it back and forth as he brushed the hair of an eyebrow.

1.

Immediately after rising, on an early, already very hot morning in the month of Ab, Moshe Mashber, as soon as he had washed and dressed, went into the narrow, metal-paneled corridor where clothes were hung. He put on his summer topcoat, took his umbrella from its corner and without saying a word to any member of his still sleeping family—not even to his wife, Gitl—and without saying his morning prayers, or taking his cup of tea, he left his house and started off to the cemetery that lay some distance away—nearly at the other end of town.

No sooner had he left his own courtyard than he crossed his still-slumbering street in the vicinity of the non-Jewish ones—those streets where there were hidden gardens surrounded by high fences—after which he walked onto the bridge that united the higher and the lower sides of the town.

In the middle of the long bridge over the river, there was a wide lane for horses and wagons, while on either side, along the handrails, there were narrow paths for pedestrians. The now nearly empty bridge echoed the sounds of horseshoes striking timber.

As Moshe ascended the bridge, he could see how one bank of the river lay still dark and sleepy, like a silent herd, while the other side was already sunny, with the morning's residual coolness touching the surface of the water where it formed a roiling haze.

Leaving the bridge, he arrived, via an upwardly sloping street, at the higher part of the town where most of the shops—the expensive ones—were to be found. At this hour, they were still closed, their doors and shutters secured by locks or intertwined chains. Though on the sunny side of the street, there were, here and there, clusters of early-rising, half-sleepy laborers, men in work-grimed clothing sitting or standing before or on the steps of a shop, their tools in their hands, waiting for someone to come who might hire them for the day.

From here, from the city's center, Moshe made his way down the longest of the town's streets where, so far as any eye could tell, all of the shutters in the single- or two-story houses on both sides of the street were still closed, all of the inhabitants still asleep. Only rarely did an early-rising housewife, carrying her basket, cross the street to turn down a side lane on her hurried way to the market, or an occasional shopkeeper returning from the synagogue, with his morning prayers already said, his tallis and tefillin under his arm, hurried, for the sake of his business, toward home.

On the whole, the street was still empty. Sometimes, far, far away—almost at the lower part of the town—one caught a glimpse of an exhausted driver in danger of losing his bobbing head as he dozed on the front seat of an empty, sleepy-looking carriage.

But the farther that Moshe went on his way, the more the street began slowly and little by little to wake up. Sleepy women, men, maidservants and children just out of their beds came out to open the shutters, and one could hear a stirring in the houses and smell the fumes of charcoal under samovars put on to boil, and the odors of singed foods rising from courtyards and wicket gates.

Then the street ended for Moshe, and now what presented itself before him was an open field with a paved footpath down the middle. No houses, no settlements, anywhere alongside it. From that point on, one could see the distant railroad line that divided the town from its suburbs. On both sides of the line, leaning diagonally, one to the right the other to the left, there were two black-and-white-striped barriers. And it was toward these that Moshe now turned his gaze, toward them that he directed his steps.

Once he reached and crossed the tracks, his path forked: one way— paved with white stones—led to the suburban settlements, then to the horizon and to far distances; the second, descending, unpaved, led to a redbricked, unpainted fence with a low gate. Moshe took the second path.

And when he had gone some way along the length of that fence and had walked beside it for several long minutes, he arrived at the precise middle of the fence, at the cemetery gate, then through it, passing through a high-walled and dark mortuary enclosure until he came to the "field" of the cemetery.

It was, as has been said, very early in the morning. The cemetery, with its many and closely set graves which for the most part were shaded over by walnut trees the size of a grown person . . . as well as, here and there, by tall, scattered linden trees in whose branches many crows' nests clustered—the cemetery, then, at its lower level lay in the half-dark, in the cool grassy shade, while at its upper level, early though it was, it was awake and unfolding itself to the summer day.

Moshe went through the dark cool mortuary enclosure, through the two doorless openings (first the entrance, then the exit facing it) where, on the mezuzah doorjamb, he saw hanging a signboard containing "a justification of the law" written in large prayer-book letters.

Leaving the enclosure, he came upon an open, not yet occupied space—and there, from the tall sun-filled trees, there erupted a babble of sounds, the racket of crows in the presence of the warming, early morning sun.

As Moshe crossed the open space and ascended by a footpath, he felt his heart constrict at the sudden sight, on his right, of the tomb of a famous holy man.

The holy man's vault, with its mute windowless walls and its red tin roof, stuck out from among the mass of tombstones that surrounded it like a mushroom surrounded by grass. And it took Moshe several minutes of walking down a side path before he reached the vault's old warped door.

The door hanging crookedly on its hinges before the warped opening of the vault gave Moshe a pang of loneliness. He did not stand there long but leaned his umbrella along the wall, then put his hand to the doorlatch and went in.

Despite the darkness of the vault and though his eyes were still filled by the dazzle of the outdoor sunlight, Moshe could see that there were wires stretched from wall to wall on which lamps had been hung, lamps so darkened, sooty and begrimed that one could hardly see the glass in which often the flame had gone out or had not yet been lighted, so that only occasionally did one see lamps that were burning, their short wicks snapping and sputtering in oil as they weakly lighted up the surrounding dark.

No sooner had Moshe entered, than a vague figure detached itself from beside a wall and hurried toward him.

This was Liber-Meyer, the vault's caretaker, who, summer and winter, was always at the cemetery, and who, from morning till night, could be found in the vault. In the mornings, a book always in his hand, he was to be seen hurrying to it and at night hurrying away. He was a short, stocky dark brown man who had the smooth face of a castrato—except for the three or four gray hairs on his chin which, when he had time, he chewed. He was nearsighted, and had his spectacles always at the tip of his nose, and his gray eyes, like those of an owl, peered perpetually through them into the dark. His coat, shiny with the spattered oil that had dried on it, was because of his various duties frequently gathered up and bound by his waistband whose two fringes hung down over his hips.

As soon as Moshe appeared, Liber-Meyer rose from his bench beside a wall and put aside his book, that book which he perpetually studied when he was not busy, when there were no visitors to the cemetery, when there was no reciting the annual memorial prayers for the dead, when it was not the time of year for visits to the graves of parents, when no one required him to write petitions or to light memorial lamps.

Now, no sooner did he see Moshe and recognize him (since he knew everyone in town), than he went over to the wires at once without even asking whether Moshe desired it of him, and busied himself quickly with one of the lamps, pouring oil from a bottle, but being nearsighted and in a hurry, he spilled the oil. With his clumsily seeking hands he fussed at the lamp, and in his awkward sexton's fashion adjusted the wick, after which he lighted it.

In the meantime, while Liber-Meyer was busy with the lamp, Moshe was looking at the ground and at the holy man's tomb, noting how it, too, glistened with oil that had spattered and dried, and how its boards had warped, and how the petitions, stuffed over many years into the cracks, stuck out of them.

Taking a book of psalms from his pocket, he stepped back a respectful distance and took up a position facing the tomb, but it was only when Liber-Meyer had finished lighting the lamp and gone back to resume his reading at his place beside the wall that Moshe began to say his prayers. He recited the psalms warmly and at length, and the more he recited, the more fervid he became. Words streamed from his mouth—the sorts of words that remind people of their weaknesses and of their sins, of their own insignificance and of the inevitability of death.

For my sins are over my head,
They press upon me like a heavy weight,
And You have given me but a small measure of days
And my world is as nought beside You.
And vanity is all that man is. So it has always been.

At once, he forgot his surroundings, and as he felt himself fused with the streams of his words, his grief and faith (more grief than faith) grew stronger within him—till, his masculine strength overcome, he wept aloud, he sobbed.

Liber-Meyer did as he always did in the presence of anyone reciting prayers. He kept his face averted the whole time Moshe was saying his. He stood to one side and looked occupied, his eyes fixed on his book. But as Moshe's voice subsided, and he came to the end of his prayers, Liber-Meyer put his book aside once more on the bench, and slowly, respectfully, approached Moshe, who was now much calmed by his burst of weeping, and asked what was the occasion that had brought Moshe to the "field" today.

"Just so . . . yes . . . just to buy a bit of earth?" Liber-Meyer said, repeating Moshe's reply humbly as he usually did when he was in the presence of a prosperous man, as if he admired every word of the answer.

"Yes," Moshe agreed, his voice still dry, his throat hoarse with weeping. He stayed awhile longer in the crypt, talking with Liber-Meyer of cemetery matters. And since he saw Liber-Meyer rarely, he asked how things were with him, and what his earnings were like.

Then in the easy fashion of a prosperous man, he paid Liber-Meyer for having lighted the lamp, being careful not to humiliate him; and Liber-Meyer sensing the high value of the coins between his fingers—much higher than he was used to getting from other poorer visitors—was visibly very pleased. Raising his gray, nearsighted eyes, he peered up over the rims of his glasses at Moshe, and in a shy, hesitant, sextonlike manner, murmured his thanks.

After that, Moshe and Meyer had nothing further to do with each other. Moshe, before he left, looked around again at the walls of the crypt and the tomb. Then he faced the tomb, and backing carefully, respectfully, toward the door, he opened it and went out.

But Moshe did not walk away from the crypt, nor did he go toward the exit leading to town. No. When he came to the empty square before the crypt, he turned aside to the right where stood, built right into the fence, the caretaker's little house with its tiny windows and the door of its tack room opening toward the "field."

That house, like all such cemetery caretakers' structures, reminded one, because of its poverty-stricken look, of a tavern set down on a road near a settlement. A couple of timid children who had risen early were playing before the door. Their downcast villager's eyes avoided meeting the gaze of the newly arrived stranger. Cropping the cemetery grass not far away stood a single nanny goat, tied with a rope to a new and as yet unplaced and unlettered wooden sign. As always in such houses, dishes, pots and pans were drying and bedding had been set out to air in the passageway leading into the house.

Moshe went through the passageway, which smelled of empty jugs, moldy barrels and water, and when he opened the door of the house itself, he found more than half of a prayer quorum of Jews already there, gathered, evidently, by prearrangement and expecting him.

They were: first, Hirshl Liever, the caretaker himself. A stocky fifty-year-old of average height with yellow tobacco stains on his beard, though most of the rest of his hair was quite white. The buttons and the buttonholes of his coat were greasy, but not from frequent buttoning and unbuttoning or because he handled his coat too frequently. Rather it was as if they were coated with belly grease from his protruding belly. He was a very calm man, with a sly, derisive, amber gaze. He was an influential town personage. And his profession was—to tear money from the living and the dead, from the rich and the poor, and thereby to procure income for the cemetery and for himself (for himself, money to live on, and for the cemetery, money for whatever needed to be bought or repaired).

He lived in the cemetery and was called "the cemetery man." But he was rarely seen among the graves with anyone except the well-connected and the rich. He kept the cemetery's record book and knew the location of the tiniest plot in the "field." No grave, no matter how small, was hidden from him. That was why, when it was time to visit parental graves, if a poor man came to him to ask, "Reb. Hirshl, I can't find my father. Please tell me where he lies," his answer was likely to be, "Beside a twenty kopek coin." It was a reply that was understood at once. And indeed Reb Hirshl helped to find the father—and was himself helped thereby.

That was Reb Hirshl.

Also waiting there was Itzikl Tchitchbabeh, an honorary Burial Society officer. A deformed-looking little fellow. It was not his body that was misshapen, but rather his tiny hairless face, like a withered fig, and his eyes like narrow slits and his thin little voice like that of a newborn kitten.

He is very pious, Itzikl! And because of his piety, he frequently nourishes himself by drinking air like soup. On his own he is silent, never saying a word. But if someone else speaks, he stands to one side and echoes his phrases.

He wore a hat with a very broad crown and a short Sabbath coat and for the sake of his income and to emphasize the honorable nature of his work, he wore his cincture from early morning on.

There were also several pallbearers wearing very long coats that reached to the floor and ankle-length unpolished boots. Silent, numb-looking folk, half stupefied from seeing and working with so many dead. There were, too, a couple of gravediggers of the sort whose heads one sees sticking out of unfinished graves. Men at the brink of old age. One of them wore a sleeveless vest, the other a padded cotton jacket thrown over his shoulders. They were clumsy and broad-shouldered men who had grown old digging graves.

These, then, were the ones who, as has been said, appeared to have arranged to meet Moshe. And now as he came into the house, they were already standing around, expecting him; Hirshl with the cemetery book in his hand, the others—as Hirshl had done the moment he caught sight of Moshe—turned toward the door. Then after the group had, out of respect for Moshe, continued their interrupted small talk for a little while, Hirshl said, "Come Jews," and they all went through the door and with Moshe made their way to the "field."

Then it was that the cemetery and the tall sparse linden trees (those whose branches held many crows' nests) might have seen a densely packed cluster of Jews making its way, with Hirshl Liever and Moshe in the lead followed closely by the others.

Hirshl, clutching the book, looked like a merchant who has gone out with a customer to his warehouse and is showing him what he owns and what he is willing to sell. He knew who was buried where, which sorts of locations were prestigious, and just where various important people would like to lie. "And this one," he said, pointing, as he led Moshe from one spot to another, "this one, as you can see, is already taken, and there, that one is sold. I have only a few selected spots left, near the graves of some very great people, and those places are reserved and won't be sold to just anyone. Not even great sums of money can buy one of those. But let Moshe look around for himself—because what was the point of talking—and let him, Moshe, choose wherever and whatever pleases him: a place in accord with his honor."

"Certainly, certainly, in accord with his honor. . . ." It was Itzikl Tchitchbabeh springing up to one side with his wide crowned hat, his tiny face and his kitten's voice. Itzikl agreeing with Hirshl, even as he seemed to be helping Moshe to decide.

"Yes, yes," the stupefied sextons also said, and were echoed, in their own coarse way, by the pair of gravediggers.

A little bit later one might have seen that the cluster of Jews stopped at a particular place, that it lingered there for a considerable while. Hirshl was seen to write something into his book, then he ordered the gravediggers to clean up that spot and to put up a TAKEN sign. And in fact the gravediggers promptly went to work and in a little while put together a temporary sign made of thin boards.

Moshe, while the gravediggers were making the sign, stood immersed in thought, his eyes lowered. The others, as if sensing the importance of the moment for Moshe, drew apart from him to keep from disturbing him.

Just at that moment a young crow in one of the tall trees cawed into the sun-filled, expansive morning, and Moshe, startled out of his musing, turned around.

His eye sought the tree and was unable to find it, and instead of seeing it, he suddenly noticed a locomotive on the distant railway line emitting pitchy smoke and white steam as it hauled a heavily laden freight train with a long row of uniformly red cars, its black wheels hurrying along, all turning at the same speed even while they seemed to be standing still.

The train accorded with his own thoughts about arrival and departure, then as if immediately to confirm them, the locomotive signaled to the station, emitting a piercing, attenuated whistle. The unexpected sound shook Moshe. He turned toward the gravediggers whom he had left at their work behind him and saw: the sign was finished, the gravediggers' work was done.

Then the cluster of Jews, with the same people in the lead as before, started back through the cemetery toward the mausoleum, and toward Hirshl's house, and on the way back each one of them had a reason to feel cheerful and satisfied. Moshe for buying, Hirshl for selling, Itzikl, because Moshe and the others were satisfied, and the sextons and gravediggers were cheerful because they looked forward to the drinks they would get at the "moistening of the cemetery plot."

And indeed, they did "moisten the plot." When they had all come into Hirshl's house, Hirshl went at once to an old-fashioned low glass cupboard from which he took goblets, a bottle of spirits and various snacks which he always had on hand for just such occasions (and not only for them). He poured the spirits out for everyone except Moshe who had decided to make this day a fast day. The gravediggers, delighted by the drink and affected by the high-grade spirits, coughed and shook themselves like dogs coming out of the water. The sextons, after they had drunk, snatched up snacks, all the while keeping their heads or their eyes averted. Itzikl hiccoughed and his tiny face turned pale. Hirshl, who was used to him, shifted attention from him by making a toast and drinking to Moshe. And the others, too, joined him in wishing Moshe well.

When the drinking was done, they stayed where they were for a while longer talking expansively of cemetery and of town matters and exchanging bits of news. Finally, before Moshe's departure and as he was taking his leave of them, Moshe turned and invited those who had been at the purchase of the plot, and those who had been there drinking—he invited all of them without exception to his home for a celebration that night.

"Come, Jews. All of you come," he said, turning also to the sextons and to the gravediggers.

2.

For a long while now, Moshe had not had a letter, a greeting or any kind of news from his brother Luzi.

In truth there was nothing new in Luzi's long silence, or in the absence of any word from him. Moshe was used to it. He is either, Moshe thought at such times, he is either in that distant little town of his somewhere on the border, or else he is on one of his pilgrimages, traveling from one rebbe's court to another, sometimes here, sometimes there, devoting himself to study as he stays longer in one place, less in another.

Thinking about Luzi, Moshe habitually saw him in his mind's eye: With a pleasing fraternal possessiveness, he would imagine Luzi in one or another of those "courts," but most of the time in the court of his own rebbe whom Moshe used sometimes to visit.

This, then, is what Moshe saw:

A small town, like every other such small town, poor and dusty, streets that were hardly streets, low, half-warped houses crouched close to the earth. Within the town, unswept, filthy. And yet as if in compensation, the town stood between two mountains covered by pine forests. Because of the forests, the town, seen from a distance, looked as if it were dozing. The road leading in and out of the town also appeared to be sleepy. And empty for the most part; not a soul stirring, though sometimes a peasant, also dozing, rode by on his wagon. Sometimes, more rarely, one might see a Jewish wagon driver, his deafening bell ringing, his wagon packed with a crowd of noisy, dusty Jews, and one could hear their Yiddish gabble as it went hurrying by. Very rarely, one might also see a nobleman's phaeton driving along that road, as if it were a wanderer who had lost his way.

The town, as Moshe was seeing it (he was imagining it at midweek), was empty. A long time had passed since the last market fair and it would be a long wait until the next one. In the half-dead streets, the little shops had no one to whom to show or to sell their wares.

The more prosperous merchants kept their goods displayed in baskets set out before their doors; the less successful displayed samples of their wares by hanging them over the doors or on the shutters: a string of salt fish, a cluster of bagels, a wreath of shrunken Turkish peppers.

There was no one now to be seen in the streets. The Jews were in their shops, boys since early morning in their religious schools, and girls were at home with their mothers, cooking, cleaning and being generally helpful around the house.

The rebbe's court was in the center of town in the middle of a rather large square and was distinguished from the other houses in no way except that it was taller by a story, and because there was a house of study within its walls.

The courtyard itself was spacious and the earth showed the effects of much trampling, of coming and going.

In that courtyard there was always, but especially on the eve of the Sabbath or on holidays, a great deal of activity and noise. Sextons were

constantly carrying tables and chairs from the house into the courtyard. There was always someone cooking fish in a frying pan held over
a fire built in a trench, and always a crowd of courtyard dwellers and
street urchins gathered around to watch the fish cooking.

That courtyard, because it is neither a holiday nor the time of the
New Moon, is now empty. There are no synagogue officers nor sextons
to be seen. At this hour they are for the most part in their own inns—
inns run by their wives to provide lodging for travelers. Such places
are called by the names of the women who run them: Sarah-Hannah's,
Gittl-Leah's and so on. And since the sextons have little to do for the
rebbe now, they make themselves useful at home.

Frequently now, one such officer or sexton can be seen at home in his
inn running out of an empty guest room, all disheveled, ill-buttoned,
the way he usually is when he is serving at the rebbe's table or waiting
on the rebbe himself. He runs out through the tack room that divides
the house in two and in whose depths, under a high, badly thatched
roof inhabited by bats and swallows, there is room enough for a horse
and wagon. He runs about, trying to catch a glimpse of his wife who is
supposed to be in the kitchen on this side of the house, but he does not
see her, though he finds a strange dog that has stolen in and is standing
there; and he calls, "Sarah-Hannah, chase the dog away. He'll steal the
meat," or "Sarah-Hannah, there's a pig in the tub—drive it away—the
pig."

It is late morning in the rebbe's courtyard, and, as has been said, the
place is silent. There's nobody there. Except that from time to time one
catches a glimpse of a couple of the rebbe's daughters who with nothing to do have been bored since early morning and who now, like prisoners in a jail, stand looking out of an upstairs window.

The house of study, too, now that the early morning quorum has
finished its prayers, the house of study, too, is silent. There will be no
other quorums that day because there are not enough men available
either from the neighborhood or from out of town.

And this is where—as Moshe imagines the scene—he sees Luzi sitting alone in a corner of the house of study. Earlier in the day, he wore
his tallis and tefillin. Now, later, he wears only his tallis. He is looking
into a book. Studying.

A purblind, feeble old sexton is wandering about on the west side of
the house of study. Sometimes he wipes a soot-grimed lamp with a rag
wrapped round a stick, or else he hangs the morning's wet towel out to
dry for the day.

Then this is what happens:

A stranger, a recent arrival who had urgent business with the rebbe and whose business was concluded sooner than expected, has come into the house of study to say his prayers. The stranger sees Luzi engrossed in his book, and he senses that this is no local man, and that he is neither one of the rebbe's disciples nor his guest. Luzi appears to have too much leisure to be one of the local people, and clearly he has too foreign a look to be one of the rebbe's disciples.

And the newcomer develops an interest in Luzi—and wants to know who he is—because Luzi's stately look marks him as an exceptional man. Turning to the caretaker (or whoever else may be there just then), the stranger, indicating Luzi with his eyes, says, "Be good enough to tell me, who is that man?"

And the caretaker (or whoever else it is who is being asked) is astonished at the question and replies with another question: "You don't know? Really? Why, it's Luzi. Luzi Mashber."

"Ah, really." The stranger is surprised and ashamed of his own ignorance. And his eyes fasten on Luzi and he studies him for a while from a distance. Because, hearing the word "Luzi," the stranger, who a moment before had been uninformed, now knows that this is a man who is welcomed with honor and hospitality into the courts of all of the rebbes everywhere. This is Luzi, for whom a privileged place has been set aside at the tables of the greatest of the rebbes. And whom every court would feel honored should it be fortunate enough to acquire him for its permanent leader.

Those were the stranger's thoughts, and they were also the secretly prideful thoughts Moshe had about his brother as he conjured him up. And especially since, as has been said, he had not lately had either a greeting or a letter from Luzi.

Then one day, a wagon driver brought him a letter from Luzi. A strangely surprising letter which considerably excited Moshe and which disturbed his previous images of his brother. Luzi had written:

> The Name of the Lord be praised . . . the name of the Torah portion of the week . . . the year . . . the date . . . the town Uman.
>
> To my honorable brother, flesh of my flesh, may his light shine . . .
>
> After inquiries about your health, I make known unto you the important events that have befallen me since I parted from you a year and some months ago.
>
> You know, dear brother, of my grief since the death of our holy rebbe of Velednik—may his memory be blessed—whose death was a crown falling, a sanctuary of sanctuaries lost. To whom, even in my youth, I was united and bound with an un-

breakable bond of love. Into his hand I yielded up my soul, into the hand of that holy man, the foundation of the earth, and felt myself secure in him and safe in my yielding. I was always firmly in his grasp and he led me in his ways, in the way of the living God. Thus it was while he lived.

But after his death, when he had left this lower world, he left me in perplexity, like one lost in the desert. I lost him—and lost all. I wandered from town to town, from the home of one holy man to another. Yet not one of them has raised my soul to that degree to which I had attained by means of my own powers or the powers of my great rebbe while he lived, and I have descended ten degrees since his death.

And it is well known to you, my friend and brother, flesh of my flesh, that one needs a holy man to help and intercede for him with God, and that this is especially and most often true when one begins to age, when his sun starts to decline in the west and he sees (may heaven preserve us) his shadow lengthening. . . .

I had almost concluded that I would not be able to find what I was seeking, and I spent long days in prayer until a compassionate heaven pitied me and hearkened to my prayers.

And now my heart and my mouth are filled with praise and gratitude to a merciful God who extends His hand to those who are drowning, and who has kept me from sinking into the depths of the mire—that is to say, into the degradations of spiritual poverty.

And certain it is that the merit of our parents—and especially the merit of our sanctified father—stood me in good stead. For now the Almighty has rewarded me, has led me and brought me here to this place where I have formed a new and a powerful bond with those imbued with the spirit of that great and godly man, the holy rebbe, Reb Nakhman, the grandson of the Bal Shem-Tov—may his memory be blessed—he who is called the Bratslaver—the man from Bratslav. And my soul has been uplifted.

And now for some while I have been here in the town of Uman, the town in which the above-mentioned holy man is buried. Each day I visit his grave, and I say my prayers in his house of study. I have gotten to know and have become intimate with those who love his name. I have studied the books he once studied, I have plumbed his profundities and have brought up many pearls.

And dearest brother, I know that I have chosen an untrodden path and that there are many obstacles and impediments in the way of those who walk in it; and I know the essential fact that the name, the system and the teachings of the above-mentioned Reb Nakhman have roused many enemies and ill-wishers, yet with the help of the Almighty who gives strength to the weary, I will oppose myself against all who hate him, and those who speak malice against him, and I will render their arguments and their arrows (though they be dipped in venom) as naught.

As you will soon see when, with God's help, I shall come to you and we will discuss all aspects of this matter.

Therefore, I will be brief because God's work is long and time is short. I come to you with wishes for your happiness and with greetings to your lady wife, Gitl, may she live long, and to all of your household, children and adults alike, all of whom are dear to me and whom I clasp to my heart.

These are the words of your brother Luzi, the son of our lord, our father Yoel, may Eden be his resting place, and may he stand at our right hand at the End of Days when the Messiah shall come. Amen.

On the night of the day on which Moshe received this letter, he dreamed:

He was standing before a mirror—at the long wall mirror in his living room. There was no one there. He looked at his image and said, "See, it seems one is no longer young. Already a grandfather, and yet not so much as a wrinkle in that face. And in general not the least sign of age. Hair and beard still blond, face fresh, genial. And the tiny wrinkles in the corners of the eyes are what come of his habit of squinting at the light, as well as from much inner pleasure. The body is stout, firm. His clothes fit snugly."

He was, to a certain permissible degree, pleased with himself, but his immediate impulse—because he was afraid of being boastful, of being too involved with things of the flesh—his immediate impulse was to turn away from the mirror. But suddenly—"What's that, what's this I see?" There was something on his forehead, something red as a wound, like a stamped seared letter of the alphabet. He examined himself closely. It was a letter *tav* on his forehead. Fearfully, he asked himself, "What can it mean?" Then he remembered what the letter *tav* could signify. *Tkhiya:* You will live. Or else, *Tmus:* You will die. As he brushed his hand across his forehead, he was afraid of his hand. Just then he woke up—and he was afraid. But the fear was of brief duration and he was able to fall back asleep. And dreamed again:

There was a celebration in his home. Many people in the house. All the relatives and friends toward whom he felt warm and close. The rooms were full, and though Moshe was in the candle- and lamplit dining room, yet it seemed to him that he could see everything happening in all the other rooms, as if there were no walls dividing them.

He was wearing his black silk coat and his waistband. The left side of his coat was a bit askew because of the handkerchief there which he frequently returned to his pocket after wiping the sweat from his forehead. Moshe's bosom was so swollen with joy that it actually made him feel the pressure of the handkerchief. He was feeling expansive surrounded as he was by children, grandchildren, relatives and friends. As always at such moments, he could hardly keep his eyes open, but squinted out at everyone through half-closed eyelids.

All was well. Yet Moshe felt a small cloud over his festive sky. He had the feeling that there was some stranger in his house and—as if it were someone not Jewish. And whichever way Moshe looked he saw the stranger there. And see, it was the nobleman—the one from whom years ago, when he, the nobleman, had lost all his money and was on the verge of bankruptcy just when Moshe was having a good year and had been able to buy from the nobleman his courtyard, the house, its surroundings and its furniture. In fact, Moshe had then had an astonishingly good year and all of his ventures had been exceptionally prosperous.

And Moshe was amazed. But yes, it was the nobleman. But how did he happen to be here? Who needed him? And who had invited him?

Just at that moment, Moshe was surrounded by another group of people who toasted him. He accepted their toast and drank to their luck in return, and for a while he forgot about the stranger—forgot what it was not pleasing to remember.

And all at once, Moshe was aware that the light in the room, and especially the light behind him, was going out. When he turned around he sensed a sudden silence. As if the festivities had been abruptly interrupted. Everyone, either in small circles or in clusters, turned away from him. Withdrew.

Everyone turned pale and, in the waning light, looked like shadows.

Then, as if someone had called him, he turned his head toward the door and saw someone standing on the step, someone whom at first he did not recognize. But as he looked more closely at him, he realized that it was his father. He was wearing a somewhat dusty travel cloak, and when he, Moshe, meant to come near to greet him and to lead him into the house, Moshe saw that the cloak was unbuttoned and that his father was wearing a prayer shawl under it.

And now, Moshe felt a chill at his back. As if without warning someone had opened a window. And when he turned to discover from where the cold breeze was blowing and who had opened the window, the light behind him suddenly went out and there was nobody there, or else in the dark they were all invisible.

When he turned once more to his father, he saw that there was light only on his father where he was standing on the doorsill, and Moshe saw that his father was pale, and that he must have come from a great distance. And he could swear (Moshe, that is) that he saw something resembling frozen tears on his father's face.

"What's the matter, Father?" Moshe asked.

"Come with me," his father replied.

"Where?"

"Into the courtyard."

"Why?"

"A spark has been kindled. Part of your house is on fire."

"Where? It's dark. There's no way to see anything."

"Come, and you'll see."

And his father turned and led the way and Moshe followed.

As they descended the porch steps, his father pointed to a section of the house below the roof, high up near the gutters. And it was true. Moshe saw a small fire. A small fire that flickered unsteadily, and Moshe wondered why it was that he was not afraid. Why he did not call for help.

Then it seemed to him that he was being watched by someone behind him. He turned and saw what seemed to be the nobleman in the very middle of the courtyard. And Moshe was perplexed once more, but as he looked more closely he saw: No. It was not he, but rather it was his brother Luzi.

Then all at once, a candle seemed to grow beside Luzi. A tall wax candle about the size of a man and it reached to Luzi's chest. And the little fire descended from the roof, from the gutters and moved across the floor to Luzi's candle, climbed up its side to the top and there it ignited the wick.

And then a second person appeared beside Luzi. A man like a sexton wearing a waistband. He had a frying pan nearby in which wax was boiling. And the sexton continually poured wax from the pan, and cooled it, kneaded it and put a wick into it. And each time, Luzi lighted the candle thus made.

And the sexton's work proceeded quickly and Luzi, his head raised to the heavens, stood between the two rows of light, his head pointed up, his throat exposed, his gleaming eyes half open, half closed.

Then Moshe heard his father weeping, his father, who had all this while been standing nearby and who had, like Moshe, seen all that had transpired . . . but who now had turned his eyes away from the sight of Luzi's magic making under the moon. And his entire body shook with fear and trembling.

And Moshe asksed, "Why are you weeping, Father?"

And his father, speaking through his tears: "Can't you see what shame and disgrace Luzi is causing us? Let's get away from here."

"Where?" asked Moshe.

"With me," his father replied. And his father started off and Moshe followed. Then after taking a few steps Moshe woke up.

Is it possible? Luzi, he thought immediately after he woke.

No. He drove the thought away.

But is it possible? He returned again to his former thought. Can it be that he is following such a crooked path that Father had to come down on his account? And why he turned his head away from Luzi, and wept for sorrow and shame.

No, he said, resisting again the turn his thought was taking.

He spat three times when he remembered the nobleman and Luzi. How Luzi had stood with the candles in the courtyard facing the moon. He tried to drive his thought of it away as if it were something unworthy, some dream bleakness that he had dreamed.

And if his heart was oppressed by the turmoil of his dream, he accounted it as his own fault. His father, he said to himself, had, after all, appeared to *him* and called, "Come with me." And though Moshe hitherto had only rarely thought about death—and had had no cause to think about it, since he was physically healthy, there was no lack or failure of his strength, and he was the master of all his faculties—nevertheless, now, following the two dreams, the idea of death entered his mind so that what a few days earlier would have seemed wild and improbable now seemed a reasonable and very present thought. And who could be sure? (he thought). Perhaps the time had come . . . in any case how was one to know? One ought to be ready.

And so this is what he did: As soon as he woke from the dream that morning, he washed, dressed and went at once to the synagogue where he prayed. Then he addressed himself to interpreting the dream.

Nor was that all. He went that day, secretly, so no one in his household would remark his going, he went to a shop where he bought grave clothes and took the package home—again, so no one would notice—and put it in a bureau drawer in his room. Then he locked the drawer and pocketed the key.

Nor was that all. On that very same day, he sent a special, and secret, messenger to Hirshl Liever, the director of the cemetery, fixing a particular day and hour when Liever was to expect him, Moshe, to visit him in order to look about for a grave site. And not merely to look about, but, in fact, to buy one as well.

3.

It was not yet noon when Moshe appeared again back home from the cemetery. Outdoors, the late morning sun was blazing. Moshe's street smelled of hot dust and paving stones. The nearby non-Jewish streets with their set-back gardens and mute fences were silent under the heat-wilted, fainting trees.

Moshe's tidy courtyard, whose center was paved with large round stones, and whose walks along the walls were made of small flat stones set in cement, had been swept that morning. And in the midst of the whiteness of cobbles and cement, there grew individual stalks, and in some places entire clusters, of grass.

The well, looking like a covered chest, dozed before the door to the dining room, not far from the rear entrance to the house. The windows of every room in the house were flung wide open.

In the kitchen, as was usual for this time of day, everything was quiet. No sound of quarreling servants' voices . . . all of which signified that a quarrel had just ended or was about to begin. There were no children to be seen and all the adults, too, were dispersed. Gitl, Moshe's wife, wandered from room to room, disoriented from having nothing to do. Finding herself in the dining room, she moved vaguely about from place to place, turning continually from one unnecessary task to another.

And Moshe, just then, made his appearance on the threshold. He had just finished taking off his coat and was hanging it and his umbrella in the hall closet. Gitl could see that he was still perspiring heavily and had not yet cooled off from his journey. His forehead, pale and wet at the top, was otherwise flushed. And since Moshe was not usually home at this time but was, rather, in town in his office, Gitl, seeing him here now, was frightened and understood that something important had happened to him today.

Turning to him, she asked, "How come so early?"

"Nothing. I just had to come home."

"And where did you go that made you leave the house so early in the morning? Before your prayers. Before breakfast."

"I went to the cemetery."

"Why just now?"

Gitl could see that whatever was on Moshe's mind, it was something that he would just as soon have kept from her, and about which he would have preferred to say nothing. But he did not hide it. Smiling, he said, "I bought myself a 'place' out there, and since you want to know, you may as well know everything. I also bought 'clothes' for that 'journey.' "

"What sorts of clothes, and which journey?" Though Gitl was beginning to get the idea, she refused to grasp it fully and herself interrupted her train of thought. "What are you saying, Moshe? I can't for the life of me begin to understand you."

"Come with me and I'll show you."

He left the dining room at once and Gitl, feeling apprehensive, and bracing herself against surprise, followed him from room to room until they reached their bedroom. Moshe walked with his back to her and never looked around. Nor did he look back when, followed by an anxious Gitl, he entered their bedroom. He went at once to the bureau, opened a drawer with a key, then stood bent over the drawer as he searched for something. Finally he found it and only then did he turn around.

And Gitl, even before she saw his face, caught a glimpse of the unwrapped package of linen cerecloth he held in his hands.

"Don't be frightened, Gitl. These are my 'clothes' for the time when, if the good Lord permits, I'm a hundred and twenty years old. Don't be scared."

At this, Gitl was assailed by a weakness in her knees. Like someone about to faint, she untied the knot of her headscarf. "Oh," she cried, and before Moshe had time to say a reassuring word she sank weakly down on her bed like one stricken. With a feeble movement of her hand she waved Moshe and his package away and then, as if she could not bear to look at either of them, said, "Don't let me see it. Take it away, I beg you." She sat apathetically on the bed as Moshe set the package down somewhere then turned to reason with her, to reassure her.

"It's just foolishness, Gitl. It's nothing at all. I had a dream . . . all the world is no more than a dream."

And Gitl allowed herself to be consoled. But all the while he talked as he stood over her, she looked up at him with a devoted look in which reproach was mingled. Reproach that he should have put into her mind a matter about which she had never thought, and about which she had never had any wish to think. She put the corner of her headscarf frequently to her eyes to wipe away the tears.

Finally, after a considerable interval during which Moshe reassured and consoled her, he saw her face relax and a calmer look came into her eyes. And he, too, felt himself heartened and put an encouraging hand on her shoulder and asked her to get up from the bed. And when she had obeyed him and stood up, he urged her to leave their bedroom, "There now, Gitl. Go on. Get yourself ready. I've invited people to dinner tonight. You invite whom you want. And let us rejoice among Jews."

An hour later, in the sunlit dining room the Mashbers used by day, one could see Gitl seated at the head of the large table. Beside her sat Menakhem the sexton who also did odd jobs. Menakhem, a short, continually worried-looking man who spoke so rapidly he was hard to understand, was always busy, seeming always to be hurrying somewhere. He had pens stuck in his hat and in his hair (because of his confusion and haste, one would suppose).

Menakhem sat now immobilized, and as if asphyxiated by the indoor and the outdoor heat, before a long sheet of paper, a pencil in his hand. Gitl called out the names to him of the people who needed to be invited to the dinner that evening and Menakhem wrote them down. There were only the two of them in the dining room, except that every so often the kitchen maid came into the room to ask Gitl a question, and, as soon as she had her answer, went back to the kitchen.

It was, as has been said, hot in the dining room. Gitl sat back in her chair more relaxed than usual, her headscarf tied behind her ears—a sure sign that she was busy and in a great hurry. From time to time she moistened her dry fingers on her lower lip as she pulled another nearly forgotten name from her heat-stricken mind. "Just see, we've forgotten Moyshe Feigenson, too," she said, amazed. "Write him down, Menakhem."

From time to time Gitl got up from the table and left Menakhem alone while she went off to the kitchen, when suddenly remembering

· 83 ·

something, she added new instructions to those she had given earlier for the preparation of the dinner.

In the courtyard where the stables and storerooms were, one could see Mikhalko the old watchman bent double under a load of wood as he went back and forth from a storeroom. Mikhalko was always sleepy. He had an old man's moist eyes, the color of brandy. Now he muttered and cursed irritably, because lazy as he was he was being expected to do a little more work than usual—as if today were a holiday.

His short-legged yellow dog, Watch Chain, might also be seen coming out of a stable. Watch Chain suffered a disability very painful for a dog. He had no voice, he could not bark. He was never far from Mikhalko and followed him about quietly with downcast head and sagging belly as Mikhalko, loaded down with wood, went from the kitchen to the storeroom.

All at once there was movement and noise in the kitchen. The quick blunt tapping of the cleaver on the chopping block could be heard throughout the house and as far as the courtyard, the coppery ring of a pestle undertaking to outshout the sound of the cleaver. And the voices of servants interrupting each other's loud and quarrelsome cries heightened and hurried the sound of the cleaver and the ringing of the pestle as they kept time with them.

The stove in the kitchen was already being heated to prepare for the dinner that evening. Every so often one or another of the servants opened it and looked in, shoved in a fresh log of wood, or shouted for Mikhalko: "What? Are you deaf or something? There's not a drop of water in the house. Get some at once."

And by then Gitl and Menakhem had finished the list of invitations. A weary Gitl fanned her face with one corner of her headscarf and from time to time wiped the sweat from her upper lip with the other. Menakhem, also tired, held the tip of his pencil near his mouth, using it only rarely. For there was nothing left to write down. All the names were accounted for. And finally when Menakhem rose from the table with his completed list and started toward the door, Gitl, too, got up and went with him. Standing at the threshold, she asked uncertainly, "Ah . . . what do you think, Menakhem? Have we forgotten anyone? Has everyone been written down?"

"Everyone. Everyone."

"So hurry, Menakhem. Don't waste any time. And don't leave anyone out. Yes. And don't forget to buy candles for the candlesticks and the lamp fixtures."

"I'll buy . . . I'll buy . . . Good, Gitl. Good."

4.

That evening, to the degree that one could judge by looking through open doors, the dining room and the nearby other rooms were brightly lighted and gave off a festive air. In the dining room there was a long white-clad table that reached from one wall to the other. That table was for the honored, important guests; and there were tables also in the other rooms, but those were for the less important folk.

A three-branched candelabrum hung down from the dining room ceiling with candles in all of the brackets, and there were candle brackets set along the walls at intervals between the windows.

Serving the tables, there were:

First, Menakhem, with his soiled, brass-colored beard and his child's distracted and unseeing eyes. He was sloppily dressed, his coat unbuttoned and his hat shoved higher up on his forehead than it should have been. Every few minutes, he came hurriedly, and fully laden, from the kitchen to which he quickly returned empty-handed, only to come once again loaded down, trying each time to carry more plates than before. Then, sweating, hurrying, running, he was once more off to the kitchen.

Then, Gitl dressed in her best holiday garb: her black silk dress and her jewels. Her dress widened at her feet where it was gathered in flounces. Her jacket was puffed out over her breast, and it was edged with embroidery and drawn tight at the waist where the edge of the jacket draped over the bustle as if over a saddle. She was wearing her oblong, two-tiered diamond earrings, gold rings on her fingers as well as a golden "heart." And yet she did not look the way she did during the happy holiday season, but rather as if it were Rosh Hashanah or Yom Kippur time—because she was not wearing her wig. Instead, her hair was covered with a white silk headscarf.

She stood receiving the plates as Menakhem brought them to her and passed them over people's heads and across the table. Each time that her hands were free for a moment, she reached up behind her ears and under her chin and adjusted her headscarf.

And now Menakhem came again and again, and Gitl leaned across the table serving what needed to be served. Removing what was no longer necessary. Taking care that everyone was served, that no one was overlooked. That everyone was content.

Both of Gitl's daughters helped her to wait on the guests. Yehudis, the older one, an extremely sociable woman, resembled her mother physically, but she had the movements and manners of her father. She felt comfortable and unrestrained around the guests. And like her father, she screwed up her eyes with pleasure in the celebration. Then there was Nekhamke, the younger daughter, who was somewhat shy and withdrawn and who, though she had her father's stature, was nevertheless more like her mother. She was stiff and self-conscious and blushed before strangers, and each time one of the guests addressed the slightest word to her, she got confused and did not know what to do with her hands.

Moshe himself, dressed in his Sabbath clothing and wearing his waistband, presided over the chief table. He got continually up from his place to fill one glass after another, as far as his arms could reach, for those at his end of the table.

In the other rooms where the guests of lower rank sat, the waiting on table was done by people of lower rank: maidservants, poor relations and Moshe's grandchildren. At those tables, placed for the most part along the sides of the rooms, there sat the indigent and the poor. They kept their eyes focused on the tabletops and only on what was on the table. They ate quickly, making swift movements toward the plates set before them, at the same time as they reached toward the heaped mounds of bread and rolls that were piled on platters or scattered about on the tabletop. As soon as they had eaten one dish, they waited irritably for another, saying little, either to each other or to those serving them. And the servingmen and maids looked on with contempt at the hurried way in which "those folk" ate. At how "there's no way to fill their bottomless guts." And they set food brusquely before them and turned away quickly, unwilling to watch the grasping of the poor folk or the eagerness of the paupers.

But at the table in the dining room, there were townspeople of consequence: merchants, well-known municipal functionaries who kept their handkerchiefs in the back pockets of their coats. When they needed them, they reached for them with their hands low, with sedate movements—slowly, calmly.

There were also Hasidim at that table. Hasidim from the same rabbinical court to which Moshe was allied. Hasidim who traveled with Moshe when he went to visit their rebbe. And these folks were more boisterous, less calm, and they had *their* handkerchiefs above their waistbands; and when they had need of them, they were ready to hand in their breast pockets; and they pulled them out and tucked them back hurriedly with mechanical, aimless motions.

It was noisy and bright in the dining room and in the nearby chambers, Menakhem, supervising, hurried from the hall to the kitchen, from the kitchen to the hall. Servants and servingmaids hurried back and forth, ran into each other, stepped on each other's toes, bumped foreheads or platters together. The guests were well past having taken the edges off their appetites, and were beyond their first glasses of wine.

A little while later, a general hubbub (and an occasional shout) could be heard. Bottles were passed from hand to hand. Some folks left their places, poured out wine and passed it to those more distantly seated. Hands holding glasses reached toward those pouring from bottles, and those who stood and poured made sure to satisfy all those who reached toward them. They poured, they filled to overflowing.

Entire tables were engrossed in tumultuous talk. People talked loudly, simultaneously. Those who were at one end of a table shouted to those at the other; at intervals some half-drunken person stood up, made a gesture . . . an unsuccessful effort to call out something, then sat down, unheard by anyone.

Someone else, his feet already tapping, rose from one end of the table and, stepping out, pulled a second dancer with him, the second in turn drew a third along, and so on until, one by one, more and more men clasped hands and fully half of the people at the table were on their feet and all of them dancing in the middle of the room. And these were followed by those who remained until within moments all the chairs at the table were emptied and the formerly empty center of the room was now crowded with dancers.

The first of the dancers were the more agile people at the table—young and intoxicated. These were followed by the older, calmer, more or less sober folk. At the very last there came the very old men who entered the dance slowly, silently, separating two who were already dancing, joining them to make a quiet third.

The Hasidim danced with each other, hand in hand, or head to shoulder or clinging to their neighbor's waistband with their hands. Merchants danced apart: prosperous, polite and quiet folk. It was easy to see that the paces of the dance did not come easily to them.

By now, the circle was large. Servants and family members moved the tables to the wall in order to make room for more dancers. Everyone was dancing. The members of the household were outside the circle at whose center Moshe was dancing alone: Gitl, her daughters, granddaughters and various relatives. The servants and maids looked on with pleasure from a distance. They jostled each other and made conspiratorial gestures about the paupers and beggars who had by now also entered the dance, but who danced embarrassed, unwillingly, feeling themselves unwanted.

Back at the tables after the first dance, with the initial drinking over, the new drinking began, this time with greater enthusiasm, with more warmth, more license. New bottles appeared at the table; long untouched old bottles were brought up from the cellar. Moshe poured for those who sat near him while those farther off poured for themselves. Mouths everywhere open, arms outstretched or entangled. Shouts heard at the tables—often directed at Moshe.

"*L'khaim*, Moshe," Hasidim turned toward him—his companions, those who traveled with him when he went to visit his rebbe—called to him as intimates, as brother to brother, as to an equal without any title.

And some who felt themselves still more intimate with the family, seeing Gitl standing nearby, were attentive to her, poured wine in her glass, urged her to drink, calling out to her also, "*L'khaim*, Gitl. Remember what we've wished you: may you and your Moshe, together with all Israel, live to see the Messiah. Remember, it's what we wished for you."

Others cried, "*L'khaim*, Gitl. Remember our wish: that Moshe may never have need of his 'place' in the cemetery." "And that the cerecloths—" Someone else interposed: "the 'clothing' we mean, may rot here in the house."

They beat upon the table, emphasizing the word "here," beating the table again and again as if they had not been understood, as if the earlier "here" had not fully completed their thought.

Gitl drank, pleased to have so many people wishing her well, pleased that there were so many hands, mouths, shouts and tumult surrounding her. She swallowed an inadvertently large swallow and turned pale, embarrassed. She looked guiltily at Moshe, but along with her sense of guilt, she felt a certain warm sweet trembling of her knees that made her think that if they were to dance right now, she would get to express that warmth by dancing.

When a little later the guests began to dance again, and the table was once more emptied, and the middle of the room was crowded, nobody noticed Gitl's sudden departure. She was gone for a little while—during which she went to the bedroom which she and Moshe shared. And there she took a package from the bureau drawer.

And once again nobody noticed just when she reappeared in the midst of the dancing circle with a package in her right hand, as with her left she raised the train of her dress a little above her shoes.

She danced as if in a daze, as if some strange power were leading her. She did not notice that several people, suddenly aware of what it was she held in her hand, stopped in middance. Or that her children, also aware of what she was holding, restrained themselves from crying out, "Mother," or that Moshe, too, kept himself from calling "Gitl." Nor that several extremely pious old men, arbiters of religious law and custom, already had the words "Desecration" and "It isn't right" on their tongues. She noticed none of this.

She held the hand with the package more and more rigidly outstretched. And with her fingers held the train of her dress up—as before—in a light, womanly fashion. And dancing that way from the center of the ring, she calmed her children's fears—and her husband's anxieties too—and even the extremely pious old men, the arbiters of law and custom, were robbed of their most irritable murmured complaints.

The daze in which she danced did not last long. Her expression became more and more domestic, intimate, and then in the midst of the large crowd, her eyes met those of her husband, and her smile seemed to promise: "Never mind . . . never mind. With the power of happiness, with the joy of faith, we will overcome all dangers, and all evil decrees will be null and void."

Then Gitl resumed dancing. She was by now a bit tired, so she transferred the package from her right to her left hand and held her dress with her right hand as before she had held it with her left. Held it just above her shoes to make her dancing easier.

And when she was really quite tired, her eyes roved about as if looking for help and support from somewhere within the circle. Then, seeing her children, she called, "Children—my daughters!"

Her children understood, and at once her two daughters, Yehudis and Nekhamke, came dancing before her and took their places on either side of their mother: mother and daughters, three in a row. Yehudis, the older one, sought her father's eyes as she danced and Nekhamke looked down at her mother's feet.

And because the guests were caught up watching them, no one heard, no one heard the wagon drawing up before the entrance to the house.

The sounds of the bells subsided as the wagon stopped. A man who had been sitting on the seat climbed down. Then the driver, carrying several bundles, climbed down from the wagon and joined him and both of them started toward the gate of the house.

Watch Chain came out of his kennel intending to attack, started to bark, but was left with the intention only. And so, a dog that had not barked, he turned himself around several times and returned to his kennel.

Then both the passenger and the driver entered the courtyard, the passenger surprised to see that in midweek, on an ordinary working day, there was light blazing in the living room windows. And in addition to the strangeness of the lights, he had the feeling that he had glimpsed a number of people in the room.

Still in the courtyard, he walked along beside the living room windows until he climbed the stairs to the back entrance. He opened the door and crossed the long corridor in which the wardrobes stood until he stood on the doorsill of the dining room. Because he had come in from the out-of-doors dark, he was for a moment blinded by the bright light.

He was a tall, dignified-looking man in a cowled summer traveling coat. His beard and eyebrows were slightly dusty from traveling. He looked on at the festivities and his eyes seemed to smile quizzically—as if the smile were saying, "They don't notice me. Never mind—very soon they will notice me."

And as it happened, just then, as Gitl with her daughters, one on either side of her, was dancing, and just as she was turning toward the door she raised her eyes and saw something . . .

At first she could not believe her eyes—thought certainly because it was so unexpected that she was seeing a vision. Just an instant before, she had noticed nothing at all. But now the longer she stared, the more believable the vision became. Abruptly, she tore herself away, and leaving her place between her two daughters, she left the circle and went toward the door where she cried out, "Luzi."

She looked like a child who has caught a glimpse of a beloved guest—or of her own father—and started forward meaning to fling herself upon his breast. Then she remembered her age, and his age as well, and restrained herself. But she continued to look like a child who, in a moment of utmost danger, unexpectedly sees a rescuer who has in his hand the key to all help. And she was happy that of all the wishes she had ever hitherto wished for herself, the one she had most longed for was about to be fulfilled.

She held out the package in her hand to Luzi and called, "Luzi."

"What is it, Gitl? What's the matter? What's going on?"

"A celebration. And I won't let you into the house, I won't let you stir one step, until you make a wish for Moshe."

"What kind of a wish?"

"Wish him length of days—and see—" And here she showed him her package once again. "See, these are the 'clothes' Moshe has prepared for that journey."

"What are you saying, child? Length of days? Certainly, length of days. Certainly I wish him length of days."

As Luzi and Gitl were having this encounter, all of the members of the household, with Moshe at their head, gathered around them. The brothers embraced, and the children helped their uncle remove his travel cloak, and they took the bundles from the wagon driver who all this while had been standing behind Luzi. And Moshe immediately led Luzi off to a room that was always kept set aside for him. There, water was brought to him so he could wash up, and there, too, he changed from his travel coat to one more suitable for a banquet. A little while later, to the delight of the company and to the members of the family who had been waiting for him to return, he came back to the dining room.

He was given a place next to Moshe at the head of the table. Servants hurried, servingmaids waited on him, and Gitl and her children stood beside and behind him ready to get him whatever might be necessary.

Luzi ate what was given him. As he ate, he spoke but sparingly to the people at the table who were Moshe's intimates. And though it was clear that he was relaxed and happy to be in an ambience of celebration, yet he spoke as sparingly with his brother and to the other members of the family.

Later, when the festivities flamed into life once more and the company had forgotten the guest who earlier had interrupted them and when everyone had resumed what they had been doing—conversation, boisterousness, drinking or all of these—then the dancing, too, began again.

And this time, Uncle Luzi also danced. He appeared like one who had arrived fresh and new; all eyes were on him, seeming to demand something of him, and he, though he danced together with them, seemed nevertheless to be going his own way, setting his own pace as he moved—profoundly inward, like someone chosen, exceptional, his movements exuberant and spare at the same time, his eyes half closed as if he was in a state of ecstatic joy.

And later, when the company was entirely intoxicated—some exhausted, dozing and silent where they sat, with their heads on the table, while others, excited by drink, sat red-faced and ready for further revels. There were some who flung themselves about, trying to pick quarrels, ready to do battle with everyone. Others spoke rudely to the host and hostess, while still others argued over dredged-up ancient sins.

It was then, in the hubbub and clatter, that the two brothers, Moshe and Uncle Luzi slipped away unnoticed by the guests and made their way to a distant quiet drawing room where the noise of the festivities did not reach, a room in which guests were only rarely entertained.

A lamp suspended from the ceiling burned there. Rectangular rugs were laid out on all sides of the room. In all four corners there were clay pots of fig trees, or oleanders with thick, oval leaves. A repose of growing things emanated from them, a repose of night when growing things are still, a repose, too, of rugs laid out in rectangles, of soft overstuffed furniture under cloth covers: footstools and a deep couch, also covered with cloth.

And it was here that the brothers met, without prearrangement and as if reluctantly and unintentionally. No one noticed their absence from the dining room. They were of no further concern to anyone there, except for Gitl and her grandchildren who, ever since Uncle Luzi's arrival, had not let him out of their sight. Now, seeing him suddenly gone (him and Moshe), they went looking for them, room by room, until they came to the drawing room.

They paused at the threshold and watched the brothers walking and talking quietly together. Restrained by respect and reverence from going into the room, Gitl and her grandchildren stood at the threshold, as if from a distance, they were appreciatively watching two moving lights.

The discussion between the brothers was brief but revealing.

Among other questions, Moshe also asked Luzi, "So, then . . . you've come from . . . the place from which you wrote?"

"Yes," Luzi answered.

"And you've really," Moshe inquired further, "you've really decided to join them?"

"Yes," Luzi said again.

"I must tell you, Luzi, I never would have believed it. The thought never entered my mind."

"Is it such a strange direction, then?"

"No, I don't say that. I only say that the world does not go that way. It was not a direction our father took. You've really surprised me."

"Is it such a crooked way, then?"

"I don't know. I never thought about it. But it is bizarre—and disagreeable."

"Think so if you will, dear brother. Now, let's drop it for a while. Traveling's worn me out. Another time." And with that the conversation ended and the brothers started to leave the drawing room. The family—Gitl, Moshe's wife, and the grandchildren who had been quietly waiting on the threshold—noted the small cloud that now hovered over Moshe's face. There was a look of sadness in his eyes, eyes that were now wide open and not as they were used to seeing them in the course of a festivity, half closed with pleasure.

5.

One evening a few days after the events described above, Mikhalko, who had the key to the garden always with him, made his dragging, age-crippled way to the garden gate.

As always when he had work to do, he muttered and grumbled to himself in dotard fashion. He puttered around the lock for some while unable to find the keyhole. Finally, he unlocked the gate and opened it as if he was making way for someone. This was a clear indication that one of his employers—Gitl or Moshe—with one or more guests was coming to the garden where in the expansive way of the rich, they would spend an evening in the fresh air.

And indeed:

From the elevated main entranceway to the house that traversed the courtyard and led to the street, and passing through a glass-enclosed corridor, Moshe, and then his brother Luzi, now came. They descended the steps, crossed the courtyard, passed the dining room and the rear entrance to the house and arrived at the garden.

When Moshe left the main gate, he was perspiring and looked flushed and a bit confused, while Luzi, his head held high, looked pleased and cheerful. Moshe appeared like a man who has just emerged from a battle and who is about to go into another one that he will lose. Luzi, his gaze calm, a bit playful, looked victorious.

The brothers had just finished the discussion that began on the night of the banquet. They had just broached the subject then, when one of them—Luzi—pleaded fatigue from his journey and the other one—Moshe—wishing to spare him, had agreed to put off the conversation until another time.

And it had been put off. Meanwhile, a perspicacious observer might have noted that Moshe was now frequently irritable and impatient and overly distracted. Children (and other members of the family) noticed that in the intervening days Moshe untypically involved himself more and more deeply in the affairs of the household. Often the children saw him go to the table, pull a chair out as if he meant to sit on it, then change his mind and thrust it back under the table, only to change his mind and pull it out once more.

This much the children observed. Gitl, however, who was closest to him of anyone, noticed how frequently now his lower lip trembled. And how, to keep people from noticing the trembling, he pressed his lips together or clamped his mouth shut.

"What is it?" she tried asking him one day.

"Nothing. Nothing," he replied unwillingly as he pushed her aside. But Gitl knew at once that the source of her husband's distraction during the days that followed Luzi's arrival was nothing else but Luzi himself. Because shortly after Luzi's coming, she noticed (nor was she the only one) a change in Luzi: He was not as he had always been, immersed in thought, silent, self-enclosed. Now it was as if he had opened up. As if he had grown a new skin. Not as before when he had seemed to be looking past things toward the sky where he appeared to be searching for something. It was as if he had found it, and made happy by what he had found, he looked everyone in the eye, allowed them to approach him, carried on conversations with people in the household—with men and women, with children or adults. He spoke and allowed himself to be spoken to.

It was while she was serving Luzi a meal that she thought the time was ripe for her to say, "Luzi?"

"What is it, Gitl?"

"Pardon me—and don't take it amiss. I don't mix in men's business because I don't understand it. Moshe says . . ."

"What does he say?"

"That you've made a turn in some new direction."

Luzi regarded her with a smile and said, "Well, if it's new, that's good. Something new . . ."

"Yes, but Moshe . . ."

"Then leave it to me, and to Moshe," he interrupted good-naturedly.

And Moshe himself waited several days, still distracted, still too deeply involved in household details. Then one night when he and Luzi were alone in Luzi's room, Moshe decided the time was right to talk as brother to brother to Luzi. And this time there was no delay. Looking—and sounding—distressed he went right to the point.

"I don't understand—and I can't begin to understand—who 'they' are. What have you to do with 'them'? Or they with you. You—and they: workingmen. Criminals. That's what's said about them in N. and everywhere else as well. And how, if it comes to that, is it that they own the truth and everyone else is wrong? 'They,' only they, have the straight of it?"

Luzi, aware of his brother's distress, wished not to reply in the same way. He appeared—and felt himself to be—like a fully loaded ship in deep waters that is entitled to a safe and calm passage. He merely said, "Well, what if they are workingmen? What of it? And if they are ignorant, are they any the less Jews for that? Is it only their way of life that troubles you? Then talk about that and not about them."

And at this point, Moshe saw his opponent clearly before him and he sensed at once that the game from its beginning—and from here on—was lost. Suddenly he found it hard to breathe. The four walls narrowed and throttled him. It seemed to him then that if he went out-of-doors his thoughts would come more readily, and that he would be better able to resist his opponent. He ordered Mikhalko to open the garden gate so that the discussion could be continued in the fresh air.

As they came into the garden, an observer might have noticed how Uncle Luzi, as he entered the first path, had to bend beneath the low-hanging branches while Moshe, shorter than Luzi, continued to walk erect. Later, they might have been seen strolling together on a more distant path. The one tall and slender, the other, shorter, walking beside him. Both in black caftans as if in the middle of the week they were dressed for the Sabbath. And both of them now, in the last light of evening, had the look of a couple of old sages in an ancient garden, dealing with great matters which only they might be expected to understand.

But if one looked more closely, it was observable that one of them, Luzi, had his hands all the while calmly in the back pockets of his caftan while the other, Moshe, walking a bit ahead of him, kept turning his head toward his brother and making restless movements with his hands as if he meant to attain to his brother's height.

The taller man's paces were measured, while the other one continually interposed himself in his brother's way. But the taller one was not affected by the other's disorderly movements. On the contrary, Moshe, the shorter one, was constantly having to adapt his speedier steps to his brother's more measured rhythm and had often to return to his side.

The discussion had caused Moshe's ears and face to flush. Nor did the evening coolness quiet his temper at all. On the contrary, it inflamed it. Luzi, on the other hand, had, in order to think more clearly in the open air, pushed his hat higher and higher up on his forehead.

Luzi spoke then of various paths, directions, doctrines, and of various holy men. And he likened the majority of them to a fixed candle that illuminates only its immediate surroundings. If the candle is small, it sheds little light, if large, it sheds more. While others he compared to a moving light which, no matter where it goes, gives illumination and serves as a beacon. Some sages he compared with a river flowing in summer that gives of its abundance only to the lands along its banks, while others he compared to a springtime river in flood that waters and makes fruitful the most distant places.

Luzi spoke also of various kinds of joy. Of the joy that reaches only to the ceiling, and of others that elevate and purify, doing wonders: making the old young, turning the crudest thing into something capable of aspiring to ultimate heights.

He said, and demonstrated, that these things were not to be found in all the leaders of any generation, but only in some exceptional ones. And certainly not among those of the present age. Rather, they were to be found only among those of a former time, among "the forefathers."

And Moshe struggled, resisted and tried to disprove what was said.

Luzi, with remarkable calm, spoke of various kinds of measure. Of tall and short, of the measure of good and evil. And he showed that the standards of measure were different at various times. That in particular epochs even the measure of good and evil was different. And that that was why "what everyone accepts" is not an objective or an imperative for everyone. Especially not for unique or exceptional persons, for those capable of changing the measure of things, those capable of blazing new trails. And it was on that account that all of Moshe's proofs and objections in defense of the beaten path were not valid because an exceptional person had a right to his uniqueness, a right to create his own path which would at first be for his own use but which later would serve many, and finally would be of service to all.

And Moshe continued to object.

Had a stranger been a witness to this discussion, he would have seen—he would have imagined—that he saw before him a tall ladder and two people mounting it from different sides. One climbed calmly, easily, step after step, and achieved his ascent without the least difficulty. On the contrary, his very climbing seemed to lend dexterity to his feet, enabling him to climb farther, higher; while the second man, on the other side, who wished to follow the first, was afraid of heights. As he mounted, he kept his eyes fixed on the other climber's feet. He studied them, imitated them. And yet he could not profit by their instruction because the other one's climbing pace was not his pace. And besides he was afraid of heights. They made him dizzy.

The end of it all was that when Moshe had used up all of his accumulated knowledge and laid it all out on the table, he grew weary seeing that despite his struggles there was no sign that he had made any sort of structure at all; while his antagonist seemed to be standing on a high fortress that had been slowly and surely constructed, and from whose height he looked down at his adversary as if he were looking at a child armed with worthless, childish means, who was getting himself ready to do battle with an adult.

And the conclusion of it all was that when Moshe had used up all his reasons and answers, he searched long and distractedly, the way one searches in a pocket, until he found a final bit of coin which he laid out—a final reason: "All right, then. But why is it that every one else does his seeking and finding among the living while you've gone off to do your seeking among the dead?"

To which Luzi, as if pitying Moshe's weakness, and like a victor who puts his hand out to help his defeated foe to stand, Luzi, with a sympathetic smile, replied, "What difference does it make if they are dead? Our teacher Moses is also dead. And Yokhanan ben Zakkai. And the Rambam and the holy Bal Shem are dead. Well then—God forbid—is their holy Torah dead?"

And with that the brothers ended their discussion. It was already late in the evening. Time for late evening prayers. A chill emanated from the trees, from the garden itself. Not a trace of the sun left, but on the opposite side where the sun had just gone down there had risen an early, golden month-of-Ab moon, huge and pale, which promised to fill the evening and the night itself with a calm golden radiance that would illuminate the garden, the house, the courtyard and its surroundings.

The brothers left the garden, crossed the courtyard and entered the house where candles and lamps were already lighted. They paused at the door, blinking as their eyes grew accustomed to the light. Then they addressed themselves to their prayers.

The members of the family could see that Moshe, as he came in from the garden, had a defeated look on his face. And he kept his distance from them, and especially from Luzi. Luzi, on the other hand, was relaxed and cheerful, as if nothing unusual had happened.

The family, seeing their father's discomfort, curtailed their usual dinnertime sociability, both at the beginning and at the end of the meal. They did not form into clusters. Instead, just as soon as they had eaten, they dispersed. Moshe and Gitl went to their bedroom and the children to theirs.

This time Uncle Luzi did not sleep in his room; instead, at his request, a bed was prepared for him in the glassed-over corridor leading from the main entrance. The corridor was used at the Feast of Tabernacles as a succah. Its ceiling was divided into six squares and each square was diagonally set with bars made of colored panes of glass: red, green, yellow, brown and so on.

In this corridor, then, Luzi's bed was set up. And Mayerl, Moshe's daughter Yehudis's oldest son, was given the task of "guarding" him. Mayerl, whose thoughtful, silent bearing—remarkable in a child—distinguished him from the other children in the house . . . Mayerl, of whom Uncle Luzi always took special note when he came to visit.

The word "guard" frightened Mayerl. He understood that some sort of important responsibility had been laid on him but he was not sure just what being a "guard" entailed. Just the same, as well as being frightened he was tremendously pleased by the responsibility.

And now, when everyone in the house had gone to sleep and the house was silent, when there was nothing to be seen in the rooms except the golden light from the ascendant moon, there were now in Moshe's silent, silent house only two people who were not asleep.

They were:

Moshe himself who, after the conversation with his brother, was restless for a long while. Restless during the late evening prayers, and later also during the meal, and restless now, here, in his bedroom as he readied himself for sleep.

As he removed his caftan, he stood musing for a while with one sleeve on and the other off. And after the caftan, the same thing happened with his shoes: one off and the other on. And a long, silent musing.

The second person awake was Mayerl who, as he was settling down to sleep, saw Uncle Luzi open the corridor door. Saw him go outside and stay outside for a much longer time than seemed necessary. Mayerl was frightened. First for his Uncle Luzi whom he, Mayerl, was supposed to be guarding, and second for himself because he was left alone late at night in the corridor.

Which is why he stood up on his bed and pressed his face against a pane of glass (a red pane, as chance would have it); and looking through it, he suddenly saw Uncle Luzi in the middle of the courtyard with his head thrown back and staring vaguely at the moon.

The sight frightened Mayerl who had never seen anyone facing the moon at midnight in that way—with his head thrown back, his eyes staring at the empty air.

Trembling, Mayerl fell back onto his bed, wrapped himself in the quilt and went to sleep. But all night long he tossed about in his bed, shuddering with fear. And indeed the vision of what he had seen stayed with him for the rest of his life.

And Moshe, too, before settling to sleep, found himself drawn to the window by something—what it was he could not say. He leaned forward and suddenly saw what Mayerl had seen: Luzi in the middle of the courtyard, head and beard thrown back, looking up at the moon.

An "oh" nearly escaped him, but he restrained himself, not wanting to wake Gitl who was asleep in the other bed before him. For a long while he did not look—could not look—at Luzi. It was clear to him that Luzi, having accepted the way of "his" people, had also accepted their discipline of "being alone." And that before going to sleep, he, Luzi, like all of "them" was celebrating the "hour of being alone."

Then Moshe remembered the dream he had dreamed: Luzi in the middle of the courtyard and the magic candle, and their father weeping as he gazed at Luzi, and how Moshe had turned his head away to keep from looking.

He was stupefied because of the way his dream was now confirmed. Then he remembered his father's words: "Can't you see," his father had said, "can't you see what shame and disgrace Luzi is causing us?"

III

Luzi Among His Own

At that time, among the numerous rich and noisy Hasidic sects in the town of N., there was also a small and not much respected group of Bratslavers.

They numbered not much more than one and a half or two prayer quorums—fifteen or twenty men. They were, for the most part, poor workingmen, but they were all of a type whose like had never been seen before. Given their small numbers and their poverty, they did not have—and did not dream of having—a synagogue of their own. They were, moreover, a severely persecuted sect. Sometimes they rented a place, but more usually they pleaded for and were given permission to say their early morning prayers in the synagogues of others.

Sometimes a young artisan who spoke with a musical lilt came to the sect from a distant part of Poland. He brought with him a skimpy pack of things from home as well as a sack of tools. He wanted to linger with them for a while so that he could study their teachings, their habits and their mode of life.

He was warmly welcomed and befriended. At first when he was still unable to support himself, he was helped out of the community funds—because, as they put it, money "is neither mine nor yours, but

God's." Later, when he could look after himself, he shared his earnings with the others and contributed to the support of those poorer than himself.

On the other hand there were times when some rich man joined the sect. It was clear from his clothing and his demeanor that he was a prosperous man, one who was used to important business affairs, to an expensive home. He was, in short, a man who could take his ease. He stayed with them for a certain while and treated the members of the sect as if they were his own relatives. Any money he had left over after he had met his immediate expenses, he shared with them. Nor was it ever observed that the one who gave was prideful in his giving, or that the taker ever felt humiliated. Such was their custom, always. Among them money passed from hand to hand, from wallet to wallet. But it was rare, very rare, that money from a rich man fell into their hands. For the most part the general purse was empty, and it was that emptiness which members of the sect usually shared.

Many of the Bratslavers, grown fanatically religious, had abandoned their trades. Their wives, influenced by their pious husbands, did not ask them for money. And their emaciated, dejected children, condemned to anemia, made no demands either, knowing full well that there was nothing to be got from their parents.

For the most part, the members of the sect lived on prayers and fasting. They did not, as other people did, occupy their time with daily tasks. Their days were spent in prayer, and their nights lying on the graves of the town's holy men. As for doing something for the world or for themselves or for their families—they ignored all that to a criminal degree.

Some of them stand before us now:

First, Avreml, known as the Three Yard Tailor. Still young. In his late twenties. Smooth cheeks, sparse, colorless hair on his chin. A complexion so pale that it actually looked green—like pus under an abscess.

He is tall, withered, thin. He has given up his craft and occupies himself with books that are beyond his understanding. But chiefly he devotes himself to pious prayers and with spending his nights in the cemetery. A chill emanates from his mouth, and his breath is bad—the result of his fasts, of hunger.

"Ah! Ah!" He is often ecstatic at prayer, and, in the midst of a discussion, is sometimes overwhelmed by religious fervor.

"Avreml." Thus his wife sometimes wakes him out of his trance in the synagogue where he spends his evenings. "Avreml, the children have had nothing to eat all day. Have you got something?"

And Avreml has. A long, folded wallet with many compartments, segment after segment; and as he unfolds it, unwinds it, there is in the very last segment a six-kopeck piece. Though sometimes that last segment is empty.

His wife stands somberly by. She wants to leave but cannot. Wants to stay, but sees no point in it. And her husband is tall, withered, with a green complexion, the Three Yard Tailor with a sparse beard. And she sees that waiting is useless, that he is preoccupied. She sees, in the declining light of day or by the light of a candle that has been lighted before evening prayers, that he is already far from her world, absorbed in his book.

Second:

Moyshe-Menakhem, the dyer. Middle-aged, of middle stature, with a very black beard, and black brows and eyes. His right side warped above his left so that standing, walking or running, he moves a bit crookedly. He has a sewn harelip, but the edges of the wound have not healed so that his upper jaw shows through. And this is why he always sucks air as he speaks, and if he says something once, it seems to him that he has not finished and he sucks air and repeats his words again. He is an energetic fellow, inwardly mercurial, always in restless, feverish motion, never able to stand still.

Menakhem, when he was not stupefied by piety, found time to practice his craft—dyeing.

Winter or summer he might be seen alone beside the river rinsing or beating a bundle of dyed clothing. He was never dressed appropriately for his work, but wore, instead, his usual gabardine even as he did his work. But one could tell that his mind was elsewhere. Even in winter in the coldest weather, when as often happened he interrupted his washing and went away for a while, it was not, as it would have been with anyone else, to warm his frozen and stiffened hands—but rather because he had gone to think through some important consideration, some exalted, pious thought that had occurred to him.

And therefore he was frequently robbed. In summer in the fenced meadows beside the river where he did his washing, on those occasions when he went off with his bundle and turned his attention to his beloved book, *The Duties of the Heart*, and particularly to that chapter of the work that he specially loved, "The Gate of Hope," thieves, then, knowing that he was preoccupied, stole up behind him and filched some customer's shirt or dress at the very moment that Moyshe-

Menakhem, immersed in hope, was furthest from any worldly concerns.

And it goes without saying that Moyshe-Menakhem had, then, to pay for the loss. Since such thefts had lately been very frequent, he would very soon reach the point at which he would be without customers—and therefore without an income. And then his wife, too, would come to beg him for something, the way Avreml's wife did. Like her, Moyshe-Menakhem's wife would leave with empty hands.

Third:

Sholem, the porter. A huge man with a chest and shoulders of legendary proportions, with a milk-pale complexion and an ash-gray beard. His porter's garb—a coarse canvas apron with a hole cut in it for his head—had dangling corners bound with rope in front and in back. Because he was so tall, his apron was twice the size of any apron worn by the other market porters.

His arms and legs were in proportion to his size. Before he became a member of the sect, there were fabulous tales in the marketplace concerning his great strength: it was said that he had lifted a nobleman's enormous horse by its forelegs, that he could climb or descend a staircase carrying, entirely unaided, a hogshead of sugar weighing a thousand pounds, and that he could devour all the contents of Zekhariah's food shop, swallowing up the good things meant to last all the porters in the market for an entire day—all the shop's dumplings, chopped liver, gizzards, crackling and goose legs. And that he could drink up the Jordan River.

Whenever there was heavy work, he was the first to be called. Everyone bragged about him, clustered around him and was eager to work in his company.

Then without warning he was stricken with piety. No one quite knew how it was that he came to choose the Bratslaver sect. Perhaps because among them everyone was warmly welcomed and treated as an equal. Or perhaps because the sect had no living rabbi at its head. A relationship with a living rabbi would have troubled him. The formal routine of visiting a rabbi was alien to Sholem: the careful coming in, the greeting, would all have seemed strange to the porter. Among the Bratslaver, he was spared all of that.

Whatever his reasons for choosing them, he was completely altered when he became a member of the sect. He did not know what to do with his enormous bulk and was ashamed of it. He kept his hands folded in his apron, his eyes lowered. He tried to stand shorter than he was, to contract his shoulders. And little by little he succeeded. His eyes lost their natural luster and he acquired a melancholy look. His shoulders seemed yearning to be covered with a gabardine. And when he dressed for the Sabbath, he seemed to have shrunk to only half his usual size. And if the other market porters chanced to see him, they laughed. At other times of the week, they poked fun at him as they went by: "Sholem, what's going on in the Bratslaver's world beyond?"

And it was reaching the point at which very soon there would be no more legends told about Sholem, and as they disappeared, so, too, would his income.

Now, here is "The Couple" (their names are not important): They are both short, slight, nearsighted. One of them, a blond—a sort of goat with a broad, sparse beard—the other, a defeated-looking fellow with a dense black beard. Both of them smoke and take snuff passionately since they have nothing to do and spend entire days in idleness.

They can no longer remember what they once were nor how, once upon a time, they supported themselves. But now they make their livings by being in motion from morning to night in the synagogue. One walks from east to west while the other meets him moving west to east and back again. Back and forth, both of them deep in thought, occasionally bumping nearsightedly into each other, at which time one of them takes a pinch of snuff or the unsmoked stub of a cigarette from the other.

These two do not have wives coming to ask them for anything. Evidently it would be a waste of time. Because, as has been said, they live from being in motion, from thoughts. Sometimes they are given the task of sitting up at night with a corpse and earn a couple of five-ruble notes that way.

And here is one more of their number.

Yankl the shoemaker, who formerly had led a charmed life. To whom the whole town used to throng with orders for shoes. Mountains of completed shoes for adults and boots for children were piled high on his workbench. And then there were the shoes and boots in progress. He employed more than a dozen workingmen, sturdy young fellows from distant Lithuania, who, working for him, never had a slack moment—not even in the interval days of a holiday. All year long, every day, including the days before festivals, they worked late into the night and sometimes all night long.

Other shoemakers envied Yankl. As for himself, he was a quiet, modest, simple man who had no idea why he was so lucky, nor how to appreciate or safeguard it.

And indeed he did not properly appreciate it. He did not think highly of himself, was in no way boastful. Because his shoemaker's success, his workingman's achievement in *this* world, gave him no special pleasure. He did not pursue wealth, was rarely grateful to his customers and frequently confused their shoe sizes, offering large shoes to customers with small feet, or narrow shoes to people with wide feet. He got finally so confused that the book in which he wrote his orders became absolutely useless.

And the reason for all this was that Yankl was afflicted with a grief so great that neither his prosperity nor the abundance of his money gave him any relief. Yankl had no children and he passionately wanted them. At least one boy who would be able to say Kaddish, mourning for him after his death.

It was for this reason that he had made gifts to various wonder rabbis, that he bought talismans from various female conjurors and finally consulted a doctor. But nothing did any good.

But what did help—when, once, his good fortune exceeded all his expectations—was the year of the eclipse of the sun, a time when, as everyone knows, barren women can conceive. And Yankl's wife conceived—and gave birth.

The whole town was delighted by his good fortune—as it was for all those who were similarly blessed—although among the shoemakers, no doubt because of jealousy, a certain slander was current. It was said that in addition to the good he had received from the eclipse, he had also had some help from a young journeyman shoemaker from Pinsk, a handsome giant of a man with disheveled hair, who worked for him.

Whatever the truth of the matter might be, Yankl was made so giddy with happiness that that year it seemed that he worked entirely without using a measure. Long, short, wide, narrow—he got the piles of shoes on his bench so confused that even the most faithful of his customers went away displeased or angry because he did not get their shoes done on time or because they were ill made. In that year his customers had a revulsion of feeling, and many of them (along with his luck) left him to go to other shoemakers.

And with each succeeding year, things got worse and worse. The disheveled Lithuanian youths who worked for him left him one by one to work for more respected shoemakers. His customers were gone, his workbench empty. Even during his prosperity, Yankl had forgotten the secrets of his craft. Little by little he lost his skill until at last he could do nothing.

And thus we find him, still bearing the name Yankl Eclipse, now one of "them." A member of the sect described above. And poor like all of them. Modest and very pious. And even more naive than before, with eyes gleaming because of the miracle that had happened to him, that had so fulfilled his utmost hope that he had no need of anything else. Anything more would be superfluous happiness.

And here, now, is the chief of the sect: the one who has lived through more trials than any of them, who is truly worthy to be their leader, because of the various transmigrations of spirit he has experienced, or because of the struggles he lived through in his frequent waverings between belief and unbelief.

And the marks of that struggle could be seen in his physique. His upper body seemed always to be quarreling with the lower. He walked quickly, distractedly, pushing his head and upper body before him, as if he meant to part them from the rest of him.

And there were signs of struggle in his face too. Though he was middle-aged, with a complexion solid and browned as leather, it was already deeply plowed with wrinkles. The hair of his beard, the color of dull brass, was prickly and hacked sharply off at the edges, like thatch. He gave off a powerful smell of cheap tobacco which he smoked, rolled in coarse cigarette paper—inhaling deeply, passionately, sucking the smoke so deeply into his belly that the tears came to his eyes.

Always distracted, he rarely looked anyone in the eyes. He kept his head lowered, but when he raised it one saw eyes as dark as smoked amber that frequently had a troubled look. When his eyes cleared, they took on a look of intelligence that was at once ironic and even teasing. The wrinkles at his temples and around his eyes were signs of much suffering, but in his head and forehead one saw signs of stubborn vigor, a readiness—if it should be necessary—to endure suffering once more.

His name is Mikhl Bukyer.

Now he is a primary-school teacher. There was a time when he was the author of various essays which now he disavows, rejecting them utterly to the point that he does not even want to recall them . . . they are so distant from anything that now concerns him.

In the days when he wrote those essays he had been so far gone that once on a Sabbath in the synagogue where he had gone to pray, he had had the audacity to say openly to a group of Jews sitting around him that when the Bible says that Moses went up to God in heaven, it does not literally mean that he walked there in his boots, but that he went there in spirit. And for saying so, he was immediately slapped in the face twice by an old graybeard Jew—not a particularly learned man, but a fanatically pious one. "One slap," the old man said, "is for Moses' first boot, the next one is for the second boot."

In those days he was so far gone that he had looked into the kinds of books which true believers avoid as they would the fire; though in fact such books have their place among other holy works, and have in fact been written by certain very great Jews The *Sefer ha-Kuzari* (Rabbi Judah ha-Levi), *The Guide of the Perplexed* (Rabbi Moses ben Maimon) and so on.

He was so far gone that his mind was constantly filled with such thoughts as, The universe may be anarchic. It has neither creator nor master. It has always existed. And if it has been created, it is not necessarily the work of one being. And from there he came to the point of denying the very foundations of the ancestral faith of his people, foundations that had been established for all eternity.

He had by then separated himself from the community, and the community from him. And things had come to such a pass that he had the choice of starving to death or of changing his faith.

But finally he mastered himself. And so it seemed to him, heaven, too, helped him to free himself from those thoughts and to redeem his soul.

He had, as has been said, a very changeable nature, and he changed from one extreme to another: from the profoundest belief to the outer reaches of unbelief. And the struggle had begun when he was still very young. He was some sixteen years old, still living in Buki, his village, when on a Thursday night he crept up to his mother's chest of drawers where the linen was kept. He took a shirt from a drawer, and with that . . . with a single shirt and the sack containing his tefillin, he started off toward Sadigure on foot. And the following morning, Friday, when he got to the nearby town, he went, as everyone does on the day before the Sabbath, he went to the bathhouse and there discovered that in the haste of his leaving, he had mistakenly taken one of his mother's shirts.

Then later he was arrested and beaten by gendarmes for trying to cross the Austrian border without a passport. He dragged himself home, sick and coughing. He was cared for for a long while, and given goats' milk to drink. Thanks to his natural vigor, his wounded lungs healed, and his parents, because of their son's miraculous recovery, borrowed or pawned everything they could to furnish him with a passport and expense money so that he might be sent to the Sadigure rebbe toward whom in his youthful thirst he had been drawn.

Later on his convictions changed again and he returned to his origi-

nal faith, but fearful lest he be overtaken by the great disaster of unbelief, he refused to look into those dangerous books and would not
permit so much as a phrase from one of them anywhere near him. For
a considerable time he moved about among the holy men of his generation, trying to find one to whom he might be able to bind himself
until having searched among the living holy men, he came at last to
"them." To the Bratslavers.

But even now he lived an uncertain and troubled life, and though he
kept a firm hold on his faith, yet he continually trembled with fear. Always, he had at his lips the prayer created by his rebbe: "Creator of the
World," said the prayer, "help us. Make us happy in the strength of
our faith in Thee and in Thy true saints, and in Thy true faith. And
keep us from entering into any inquiry. Keep us from looking into
those books that explore the meaning of things, even if they have been
written by the great masters of Israel."

This, then, was the prayer he had continually on his lips, at his rising
up and at his lying down, at his walking on his way. Sometimes even
when he was in the presence of others, he would move away and one
could hear him whispering it.

He devoted himself to his new beliefs with a special ardor, stronger
and more diligent than that of people who had believed for a much
longer time and who had had no doubts. He took on himself exceptional duties. For instance, in winter in the extremest cold, he went at
dawn to bathe in holes cut in the ice. On Fridays when he trimmed his
fingernails, he kept his eyes averted from his fingers so that his scissors
drew blood. And he took on himself other penances of body and of
soul such as people in those days assumed.

He was indifferent, also, to his own great poverty. The reasons for
his poverty were first, that he had a large family. And second, that the
wealthy, the established people of the town, knowing of his former
eccentric ways, had no confidence in him and would not entrust their
children to him to be educated. So he was forced to content himself
with the children of the very poor and with the small sums of money
they brought him. But none of that mattered to him. And if from time
to time his wife and children got something in the way of money from
him, he himself was contented with a cheap cigarette whose smoke he
sucked deeply into his stomach. And in that way he got through the
day. As for the children who were sent to him, he did what was necessary, whatever it was that a teacher was required to do. The rest of his
time he spent among his fellow sect members, guiding them, sharing
with them whatever superior portion of spiritual nourishment he had.

And the sect was composed of such as these who have been described and of others like them. Avoided by the community, they were a persecuted group that acquired converts only rarely, though, as has been said, sometimes a poor young artisan from outer Poland, carrying his sack of tools, came to them, or, also rarely, a rich man who after some interior crisis turned away from his wealth and left his family, his prosperity and his business and chose to come to *them*, the poorest and the most rejected of all.

And it was to them, to this sect, that Luzi had come.

It was in the Living Synagogue ("Living," because no one wanted to refer to a synagogue as "Dead"), which was built at the entrance to the old cemetery in the center of town, and whose windows looked out over the field in which the tombstones lay, half buried in the grass . . . it was in the Living Synagogue that the sect had paid for (or begged) permission for their prayer quorum to gather.

And it was there that they were already gathered very early on a Saturday morning, when the sun had just risen and the town was still pleasantly sleeping. All of them had been to the ritual bath, and their heads and beards were still damp and uncombed; they were pale from a whole week of poor nourishment (nor was what they had on the Sabbath any better or more pleasing). They all wore their one vaguely black Sabbath caftan, faded from its original hue and frayed from long years of use.

Luzi was among them. He had taken a place at an open window that looked out on the cemetery. He, richer than the others, had his silk gabardine, and his summer coat of marengo stuff with its narrow velvet collar was draped over a bookstand. Awhile later, the sect saw him wearing his silver-edged prayer shawl. And that made a deep impression on them all because, though the congregation was just then deeply self-absorbed as usual before prayers, being eager, though no one drove them to it, to bend themselves to the yoke of their dear servitude, yet they could not, just the same, keep their eyes from Luzi. All of them, not even conscious that they were doing so, turned toward him who was their pride because he had recently come to *them;* he who, as they well knew, would have been a source of pride to any other sect to which he might have adhered.

Then there began the usual tumult of prayer. Some stood fixed where they were, others ran about from place to place as if they meant to climb the air, as if they wanted to separate themselves from their bodies. Some seemed to see ladders before them up which, with trembling hands and feet, they meant to climb. Still others plunged forward toward great expanses which only the synagogue walls prevented them from reaching. The consequence of so much plunging and climbing was that the synagogue was soon filled with cries of yearning. Cries like those of Avreml, the tall, withered tailor, from whose mouth a cold breath constantly emanated and who at his prayers, though he was weak and helpless, managed to summon up a last bit of warmth to cry "Ah! Ah!" as if he were screwing up his courage even as he was giving himself up to delight. Menakhem the dyer ran about like a caged beast, sucking back with his split lips the words he uttered because it seemed to him he had not put sufficient life into them the first time. Some of the congregants clapped their hands, others stamped their feet. Still others tossed their heads and screamed as if they were being slaughtered, and those who had neither voice nor strength stood facing a wall and vibrated in silent ecstasy. Some shook only half of their bodies, others their whole selves. All of them were impassioned as they uttered one or another exalted passage of praise:

Sing, with God, oh, saints, the praises due to the righteous.
Favor us, O Lord, for our hopes are in Thee.

And so on.

All twelve of the windows facing on the cemetery were open. The newly ascending sun, now low in the sky, sent its first stripe of sunlight from the edge of the eastern horizon. The town was still sleeping the last sleep of the night and here, in the Living Synagogue, the little community was already raising its exalted, wildly rapturous sectarian Sabbath song. They were ecstatic with themselves and with the knowledge that they were, as always, the first to sound God's praises on this Sabbath dawn. And they were especially exalted today, when among them they had such a notable new adherent, one from whom, in the midst of their prayers, they had not taken their eyes because he had inspired them with courage and a desire to praise.

So they had watched him standing there, when his face was turned toward the open window that looked out on the cemetery and later when he turned to face the praying congregation making its mad movements.

And Luzi, too, was in a good mood—because he had left his comfortable bed at his rich brother's house and had come here to join this ill-dressed congregation whose members must have found it very easy to rise from their mean beds and who, so early in the morning, were capable of so much exaltation.

It had been long since he had had the taste of such prayers in his mouth, and the overflow of sheer delight he experienced made him catch his breath. He turned to face the open window and sent his heartfelt words outdoors. And then so he could unite himself again with this congregation, so that he could experience that joy again, he turned to face them in the interior of the synagogue, and stood that way throughout the course of their prayers, which lasted a considerable while.

Then the prayers came to an end and all of the congregants, some still wearing their prayer shawls, others without them, wished each other "A good Sabbath." And then excitedly they gathered around Luzi.

"A good Sabbath. A good Sabbath," he returned their greetings.

And then, as was their custom, they danced. For a long while and on empty stomachs, and until they forgot themselves in the residue of the pure joy they still felt from their prayers. Forming a circle around the reading desk, the whole congregation danced heatedly, passionately, hand in hand, head to shoulder, unable to tear themselves away from each other—engrossed as if there were no real world. For a long while—until the sexton representing the synagogue's real owners appeared in the doorway and seeing the circle of the dancers (whom he neither respected nor was fond of), he formed the ugly word he habitually used for them, "Demons." But this time he did not say it: because he saw that among the others whom he knew only too well, there was now one whom he had never seen before: Luzi, tall, proud, stately who stood there in his silk caftan giving off an aura of wealth. So the sexton restrained himself and waited. Then still standing on the threshold, he saw, when the dance had come to a stop, how everyone formed a circle around Luzi, and he heard someone ask, "Well, and who will take Luzi home as his guest for the Sabbath?"

"I will," Mikhl Bukyer called first, before any of the others.

And on that Sabbath, Luzi was Mikhl Bukyer's guest for the entire day: for the meal in the morning, for the brief nap following the meal, for the short Sabbath conversation after the nap, and so on until it was time for early evening prayers when Mikhl brought Luzi back to the same synagogue where Mikhl served as a preacher to the small sect.

Mikhl Bukyer, as did all the poor, and especially those who were like himself, lived far away at the very edge of town—almost in the Sands, where his street, or, better, where the twisted maze of streets, gave on to the district of the flayers that was not far from the slaughterhouses.

His small squat house was set deep within its compound. On one side it looked out over an empty garden in which grew various badly sown vegetables and a tree that might be a willow or some other kind of tree. There was no way to know since it had practically no leaves. The tree was warped and its trunk had a hollow in the middle from which decaying wood dust oozed. Wood mites moved up and down the trunk, doing their wood mite business.

Luzi had to bend as he went through the low vestibule that led into the house. Inside, there were two small rooms. In one of them there was an oven and a table around which Mikhl and his pupils sat on two benches when he was instructing them. It served now, as it always did, as a kitchen and a dining room. Next door there was a smaller room. The bedroom.

There was also a wife and five children. The wife, a tall woman whose mouth was continually open. The oldest of the children was a girl with a freckled, yellowish complexion. The two after her, well-grown boys of fourteen or sixteen, were already employed, one of them at a bookbinder's, the other turned a knife-and-scissors grinder's wheel. The last two, a boy and a girl, were still quite small.

And now the entire family was sitting at the table. At the same table at which, before Mikhl Bukyer joined the sect, he used to sit every night writing by the light of a cheap lamp those commentaries which now he rejected. The same table at which he could be found teaching the Bible to his pupils—especially his beloved book, Job. Job, whose wounds and sorrows he felt as if they were his own. His pupils often saw him weeping during a lesson. His eyelids turned red and a tear coursed down his cheek—a tear for the griefs he shared with Job with whom he, too, uttered the curse: "May the day of my birth be obliterated."

And now the whole family was at the table with Mikhl Bukyer himself, and Luzi, his guest, in the place of honor. Pale loaves of bread badly baked in an inferior oven graced the poverty of the table which had been covered with a coarse linen tablecloth.

The foods that were then brought to the table had been cooked on a "cold angel," and, what's more, sparing amounts of inferior wood had been put on the fire.

Nevertheless, Luzi felt very good. He knew that in his rich brother's handsomely decorated, capacious and comfortable dining room, with its windows opened to the courtyard, a place was waiting for him at the head of the table, beside his brother; and yet, precisely because of that, the poverty-stricken primary-school teacher's little room with its stale air, and its ceiling pressing down on his head, and its low windows that were rarely opened to let fresh air in, was dear to him, as well as the frugal foods and the coarse linen tablecloth, and the coarse salt and the inexpensive chipped or warped dishes and silverware.

He felt good, so good that he could not remember when his usually closed-off self had ever been so relaxed. So good that he felt like embracing, like absorbing, the entire impoverished family as well as the poor room with everything in it.

And in fact Luzi had provoked something like a look of joy in his host's ... in Mikhl Bukyer's face and in his eyes where there was rarely the least sign of anything that might suggest pleasure; and yet now it was there in his face and perhaps something even more was expressed there because Luzi, in the brief time he had been in the house and at the table, had responded with such freedom, with such a lack of constraint to the children—to the whole family—he had made himself so much at home that it seemed to them all that the house had grown taller and more spacious and that Luzi had become its sole occupant. And that the heavy weight of daily life that hung like a rod perpetually over the place and oppressed them even on the Sabbath had now vanished—disappeared.

Luzi and Mikhl and the oldest boy chanted while Mikhl's wife, the daughter and the smaller children listened, entranced. After the final blessing, the children ran outside and the adults, Luzi included, went to take their Sabbath afternoon naps.

After they had slept, Mikhl's wife brought fermented pear juice and various fruits into the garden. She also put a bench under the hollow tree with the leafless branches from which decaying wood dust poured and on whose trunk wood mites moved busily up and down.

Luzi looked about at the sad remains of the poorly sown garden. He knew that people were strolling in the courtyard of his brother's house. People from all over town—young and old—strolling, drinking at his brother's well. The town was cramped, and in summer people took walks into the more distant streets, like the one where his brother's house was, for example. The gate there was left open and people came and went—all of them strangers. Mikhalko complained that they muddied the place around the well, but he was ordered to keep still and was forbidden to scold anyone.

The members of his brother's family were also in a garden, but on quite other benches, under quite other trees, than the one here under which he sat with Mikhl Bukyer.

And yet he felt good where he was, he breathed more freely, and the conversation between himself and Mikhl Bukyer became intimate and warm. Their talk was relaxed, comfortable. At first, they spoke of their work, then, little by little, of personal matters, then about the sect, of its growth and its present situation and then of each of the individual members. And both Luzi and Mikhl sat contentedly on the bench until they noticed that it was getting late. More than half of the tree was in shadow. Only the leafless crown still had the evening sun in its branches. The men stood and said, "Time for the first evening prayers."

And now here they were, after the long walk back, once more in the same synagogue.

Again there were the same congregants, but refreshed now after their Sabbath rest. And ready to pray again, just as they had prayed at dawn. And as before to do it in their wild fashion.

In the dusk that preceded the early evening prayers, a rumbling could be heard in the synagogue, a rumbling as of beasts who might utter their cries at any moment, and without warning—though for the time being they repressed them, keeping them in their bellies where they gurgled and droned.

Again they prayed while in motion, their bodies shaking wildly, uttering cries and moans of pleasure. Among them it was not as with anyone else for whom the early Saturday evening prayers were a signal of the day's decline and therefore an occasion to invite grief into the melodies they sang because they would soon be separated from the Sabbath, would face once again the ordinariness of the coming week. No. These people did not take leave of the Sabbath. They clung to it and treated the whole week as if it were the Sabbath.

"Thou art one and Thy name is one and unique and who else but your people, Israel, is one and unique in the world?" they sang now with the same enthusiasm that they had had at dawn.

When the prayers were finished and it was already dark, they pushed a couple of tables together at the west wall of the synagogue and, as was their custom, gathered around for the "third meal" of the day. There was very little to the meal but portions of a Sabbath loaf and salt preceded by the ceremony of handwashing and when the meal was over, further prayers. While they ate, it was their custom to honor someone with the opportunity to "speak" to the company. This time, naturally, that honor fell to Luzi. He started to speak at once, very moved to have before him, seated at both sides of the long tables, a company of such devout listeners.

On one side he had beside him the huge-bodied Sholem, the porter unaccustomed to wearing his Sabbath capote. On his other side there was the long and lean Avreml the tailor, a man with almost no body at all, with only the slightest trace of the corporeal about him. As for the rest of them along both sides of the long table, they were very much like these two, sharing the same destiny—people of great poverty, fated to have but minimum pleasures in this world and contenting themselves with that minimum.

And it was about just that, about contenting oneself with little, that Luzi spoke to his faith-hungry audience, and also about the joys of being contented with little. Luzi, unaccustomed to addressing a group, had difficulty speaking and perhaps for that reason his words had a special sincerity. There were times when they seemed to have been drawn from exceptional depths. The eyes and heads of everyone sitting at the tables were turned toward him, and from time to time one could hear a sigh of pleasure coming from someone in the audience.

Even the sexton, coming in just then for evening prayers, the sexton who, as has been said, had no excess of love and even less respect for the members of the sect, even he, who rarely bothered to listen to any of the sect's speakers, listened to this stranger's speech, to the words of this strange Jew whom the sexton had already taken notice of that morning; he listened and stood still and entirely lost track of his sexton's duties, and of the lateness of the hour, and forgot entirely that it was time for evening prayers.

And Luzi set himself the task of raising this community that had gathered together in the dark of a Saturday from the darkness of its reality. To light its way toward even greater faith, and to strengthen its hopes. And the sexton who stood at one side heard Luzi talk of real and of vain wealth—real wealth that need not to be searched for afar, since it is within the self, and which when it is found, can be possessed both in this world and in the world to come; and he heard him also speak of vain wealth—vain because one pursued it as one pursues a shadow, and it is not lasting but disappears in an instant like a shadow. And then to lend force to his words and to end his discourse, Luzi told a parable taken from an old book.

"Once upon a time, as the old book says," Luzi began, "there was a recluse. About the time that he became a hermit, he made a voyage to a distant land in order to earn his livelihood. He arrived in a town in that country and there he met an idolater. The hermit said to him, 'How foolish, how confused you all are that you worship idols.'

"The idolater replied, 'And you, whom do you worship?'

" 'We,' said the hermit, 'we serve Him who feeds all, who nurtures the whole creation. And beside Him there is no comparable god.'

" 'In that case," said the idolater, 'your words do not sort well with your deeds. There is a contradiction.'

" 'What do you mean?' said the hermit.

· 115 ·

" 'I mean that if what you say is true, then you would not have needed to travel such a great distance in order to get your livelihood. You would have found what you needed in your own country, in your own town.'

"To that, the hermit was unable to make any reply. He returned home and never left his country again and remained a hermit there for the rest of his life."

That, then, was the story. And the moral was so clear that Luzi did not bother to explain it.

The month of Elul came. And in that month it was the practice of the members of the sect to go off by twos to some place of isolation and recount to each other all that had happened to them in the course of the year, and each one confessed the other.

And here, then, one evening, well after the evening prayers, when everyone had left the Living Synagogue, two people still remained: Mikhl Bukyer and Luzi.

Luzi, at the east wall, sat on a bench before a podium while Mikhl stood before him in the attitude one takes standing before a teacher, or a spiritual guide, or a director of one's conscience. As if he was prepared, with great meekness, to open every drawer within himself which all year long he had kept closed, so that Luzi might have the opportunity to search among them, turning everything over, digging deeply so that he might reveal what needed to be revealed and judged.

The entire synagogue was dark except for the hanging lamp that feebly illuminated the place where the two of whom we are speaking stood at the east wall. Nevertheless, had anyone standing at a distance, even from as far away as the west wall, looked toward Mikhl, he would have seen the redness of his eyelids, reddened as they always were when he studied the Book of Job and was exalted by Job's grief and suffering. And now Mikhl was moved even more: he wept, and one could see tears running down his hard cheeks and into his dull-yellow beard.

And Luzi stern before him. He had, in the role of inquirer and judge, looked deeply into the exposed soul of the guilty one. He had stood silently by and listened, seeming to require of Mikhl ever greater revelations.

And Mikhl, standing there before Luzi, continued his confession:

He had a flaw. He had been touched by a heavy hand. Despite all his efforts, all of his struggles, since then and now, he had not yet recovered all of his former faith. It was a curse. He had been stricken somewhere in the innermost depths of his being. He felt as if strange winds were blowing in the structure of his self, as if very soon and violently, they would open its doors and shutters, creating such havoc as would leave him helpless to control whatever had been his own. Then he would be flung into the depths from those heights that had cost him so much pain and struggle to reach. And he would become like a dog on a chain dragged here and there according to the needs or the will of some unknown power.

It was an unhappy struggle. Lord, what had he not tried in the way of mortification of the flesh and of the spirit. And all to no avail.

He confessed that he had not been able to master a single human passion. On the contrary, they had mastered, defeated, imprisoned him. For example, bodily passion in him was intensified as he grew older. When he walked in the streets, he had to keep his eyes on the ground in order to avoid meeting—to avoid seeing—temptation, and just the same forbidden sights seemed to leap out at him as if from underground, and as a result, he saw—and sinned. It had reached the point that he found himself seeing only nakedness before him so that he trembled and was confused in the midst of his prayers and studies.

And the same was true of the other passions—for example, money, honor, envy, hatred and so on.

But worst of all was his tendency for denial—a tendency that in him was a passion and which had various consequences for him. Sometimes he found himself emptied, as if every bit of spirit had fled from him and he looked at his surroundings with indifference, and as if all the threads that bound him to the world and that ordered the world had suddenly snapped and he found himself walking in the void. Or, on the other hand, he felt sometimes as if a wild madman possessed him and made him frightful, excitable, and pushed him to want to spoil or to destroy everything, to break all bonds.

All of this, without mentioning the "trivia." For example, on the Sabbath when he stood before a lighted candle, his impulse was to blow it out. Or worse: when he was alone in the synagogue, he was seized with an impulse to run up to the Holy of Holies and tear down its curtain and (God forbid) to dash the Torahs to the ground. And worse, much worse. He could hardly bring himself to let his mouth form the words—but it had actually happened that he had held a knife to his own throat desiring to cut himself off both from this world and the next. Evidently out of a fear of denial, but the truth was that this was the greatest of all forms of denial.

And all of this because of his conscience, that interior destroyer and corrupter who sometimes took the guise of a beggar at his threshold and sometimes of a beast howling on the other side of his door.

And what was he to do? And what sort of counsel could he give himself?

Here, Mikhl was silent for a moment. And Luzi averted his gaze in order not to embarrass him. Then Mikhl resumed his narrative:

And this is how it was. When sometimes he felt himself oppressed and things were bad, he went, as was the custom among the members of the cult, to the cemetery to spend the night at the grave of the town's famous holy man in order to purify his thoughts by wakefulness and study. And, as Luzi knew, such visits helped everyone—but they did nothing for him.

And here he found it necessary to tell of something that had happened to him this past summer when he was lying on the holy man's grave. The memory of what happened still filled him with revulsion, but since he was making a confession he was required to tell everything—nothing must remain hidden.

As was his custom he arrived at the tomb late in the evening when there was no one else left in the cemetery. And as always there was a weak lamp left burning for the night by the tomb's sexton. He, Mikhl, stood under the lamp, studying his book for a period of some hours until, deeply exhausted, he evidently fell asleep standing there. And he had a dream.

Raising his eyes he saw: the town, the entire town was upside down. The marketplace and the shops, the streets and their houses, synagogues and study houses. Everything hung upside down and only the church stood in its place. Everything that was topsy-turvy was for the moment whole and stable, but then things began to move: goods fell out of stores, furnishings out of houses, sacred objects and Torah scrolls began to fall from the synagogues, forming a pile, a great mound. Everything was obscured by dust, and there was nothing to be seen. But then—oh, Lord—he saw that the dead, too, were falling from their graves, falling onto that heaped-up mound. And only the church was steady in the place where it had always stood.

Then all at once there were flames in the mound as everything on it began to burn, and he found himself standing beside it, a stick in his hand, and wherever he saw any object that lay at some distance from the fire, whether it was pure or impure, he pushed it within range of the flames so that they might be fed, so that nothing should be left out of reach of the fire, so that everything might burn.

And the fire grew stronger. Household furnishings, scrolls of the

Torah and bones smoked, fumed and crackled in the flames, while he, Mikhl, at the edge of the mound, shoved more and more things into the fire.

He looked about, wondering what he was doing there. How was it that he could stay in such a place, let alone to take upon himself the acts he was performing with his own hands. But he did not go away. He stayed and did not put his stick aside, but, like a paid employee, continued to push objects into the flames, committing the most atrocious blasphemies.

And the fire increased in intensity. And now living voices could be heard coming from the mound, and he could swear that the name those voices called was his own and that they cursed him, bone and marrow forever and ever. Until they were silent, those voices. And the fire was quenched and there was only ash left.

And then—oh, Lord! Out of the wide-open door of the unaltered church, He came . . . theirs . . . the Nazarene looking as he usually does in their paintings: bareheaded and barefooted, and wearing a long cloak, he looked like a shepherd. And indeed he was driving a large flock before him. And at the beginning, it appeared to be a flock of sheep, but then there was a crowd of people. A crowd, and only he, Mikhl, was distant from them, and he was assailed by a feeling of separation and he longed to join the multitude, and then from some unidentified source, he received a signal to join them and he moved toward the flock.

Then he saw a dog running before the flock—a shepherd's dog—and it appeared to be wearing a sort of crown on its head—and it ran before the flock crying, "Way, make way for the holy shepherd and his faithful flock."

And in the course of recounting all this, thick tears rolled down Mikhl's cheeks and into his beard, and Luzi, too, lost the calm that he had maintained throughout the course of Mikhl's recital. He stood up, leaving Mikhl at the lectern while he, greatly agitated, greatly moved, paced some distance back and forth along the east wall. Then he sat down again in the place he had occupied before in the role of a counselor authorized to look closely at Mikhl's spiritual ailments, but now there was a look of wonder on his face and he expressed that wonder with a mute shrug of his shoulders and some half formed words: "So . . . so . . . Dreams, then . . . well . . ."

And Mikhl, with Luzi once more sitting before him, resumed what he was saying.

Then when he saw himself running and crying out like a dog before the flock, he was suddenly frightened. The book that he had been holding in his hand when he fell asleep now fell to the ground and he woke up with a start and saw where he was.

And now the door to the burial vault opened and the sexton, the lamplighter who usually worked in the vault from early in the morning until evening, came in and, seeing Mikhl there, spoke harshly to him and drove him from the vault, as he usually did any member of the sect whom he found there at dawn after a night spent in the tomb. And he, Mikhl, left the vault without being able to think about the dream or how to assume its burden of shame and anguish.

It was not until he was outside and standing on the threshold in the broad light of day that he was so oppressed by the weight of all that he had seen that night that he set his face against a blind wall, feeling that he would stay there, paralyzed, forever. And for a while it was like that. He continued to stand. People went by—and he did not notice them. Hours went by, and he was unaware of their passing.

Finally his wife, seeing his pupils arriving for their lessons in the morning and knowing where he might be, came to the cemetery and found him. When she took him home with her he was like one made drunk by the night, defeated and confused.

And to the present day—Mikhl continued—he could not shake the effects of that vision. It irritated him and caused him pain. It troubled his sleep so that he spent whole nights without closing his eyes, and during those nights he saw such repulsive things that he could hardly survive the days that followed: demons on the walls or in the air or descending from the ceiling or starting up from the floor, sometimes in great numbers, sometimes silently as if stealing by, sometimes noisily, as if on their way to a wedding. Sober demons and drunken ones, playing music and dancing. And he felt a kinship with that ugly mob, and felt that they had a right to come into his house, and that one night they would require him to go with them to take part in their celebrations, to dance in their dances, in short, to become one of them.

Spitting three times did not help, neither did reciting spells against them. He spat, he recited, and they went on with what they were doing: they came and went, came and went. He felt that they wanted one particular thing from him: blasphemy—if not in action, at least in speech, and if not in speech, at least that he look on while others blasphemed.

And in truth they came once bearing Torah scrolls which they unwound before him and made him watch as they did atrocious things to them, things so appalling that woe unto the eyes that beheld them, things impossible for human speech to describe and that can only be compared to the deeds of the tyrant Titus in his time and to those of other tyrants like him.

Mikhl, seeing such things, was in mortal terror and broke out in a cold sweat. He was left enervated for days afterward and was unable to recover his strength or get any rest. He went about not knowing what he did or what was said to him, with the result that he often scanted his duties as a teacher. Sometimes he did not meet with his pupils, or he could not abide the sight of a holy book. And he was drawn once again to those other learned books whose study would truly lead him to lose his faith, but which at the same time would free him from all the ugliness and hatefulness that clings to . . . that lurks around or accompanies faith.

And here Mikhl stopped talking entirely and stood before Luzi as if he were waiting to be sentenced. But Luzi continued to avert his eyes, thinking that Mikhl still had things to say . . . that he needed—that he must—say more. But when he sensed that there was no more, he looked up at Mikhl suddenly and measured all of his length with his eyes as if he wanted to confirm now what he had thought while Mikhl was speaking. And that was that Mikhl was not merely touched by a flaw, by some minor imperfection, but that there was some rupture, some unhealable break that could not be mended, and that such people generally finished badly, and that that would be Mikhl's fate, and that one could not repose confidence in such people, because not having the strength to support themselves, they could not muster the strength to support anyone else.

Luzi thought all of this, but of course he did not say it. On the contrary, he said what one says—what one must say—in such circumstances, simply to console, to lighten the burden of the heart. And for that task, for such remedies, Luzi had skill and spiritual experience enough. Anyone watching Mikhl as he listened to Luzi, though unable himself to hear what Luzi said, would have been able to tell from the changes in Mikhl's face how little by little he was freeing himself from the depression which, in the course of his own recital, had so visibly marked it. Mikhl's dark amber eyes cleared; his skin had a new fresh look to it because Luzi had understood and participated in his feelings and had extended a hand to him in the abyss into which he had sunk, because the guidance and the remedies Luzi offered were precisely designed for his situation and his capabilities so that by their means he might lift himself up and climb once more toward the blessed light of day.

At that point, Luzi finished speaking.

There was, as has been said, no one else but these two, Luzi and

Mikhl, in the synagogue. The one lighted lamp hanging from the ceiling near the east wall which earlier had revealed a deeply depressed man standing before one who was sitting, now showed an exalted man standing while the seated one was deeply depressed, as if the two of them had changed roles.

It was Luzi who, having said what needed to be said to console Mikhl, now sat there worn and exhausted. He had the look of a man who has just survived an extremely difficult experience, but who is about to confront an even more difficult event, because he sensed with absolute certainty that Mikhl's just completed confession would be followed by some other event which he, Luzi, had already thought about and about which he had taken a position.

But it was getting late, and it was time for Luzi to go home. He stood, put on his coat and then as was his usual custom before he left the synagogue, he went up to the Holy of Holies, raised its curtain to his eyes and then kissed it. But this time he lingered before the curtain for some time, looked longer at it when he held it before his eyes, as if he was taking counsel with it, as if he was asking it for advice. Then with Mikhl beside him, he left the synagogue.

The air, after a very hot day, was stuffy at that hour. One sensed that somewhere away on the invisible horizon the warm weather was getting ready—either that night or the following morning—to turn stormy, but for the time being the air was calm with no hint of any coming change. It was dark, but the distant stars of the month of Elul shone brightly, and the streets were lighted by lamps set here and there at longish intervals.

And those two, Luzi and Mikhl, now left the center of town in which the synagogue was where they had spent the day, and moved toward the outskirts where Luzi's brother, Moshe Mashber lived. Their way took them through streets and lanes that seemed emptied by death of all passersby. And it was here that Mikhl, now that he was alone with Luzi—as he had been before in the synagogue—finally said why it was that he had chosen Luzi before whom to make his confession and to nobody else. Because, as Luzi had suspected back in the synagogue, Mikhl after his confession had planned to say still more. And Luzi now was prepared to hear whatever that was.

Mikhl said that it must be clear to Luzi now what state he, Mikhl, was in: he was a defeated man who had more than he could do to plumb the depths of his own self; how could he be expected to be a guide to others, how take up their burden, or how could he be a help to others when he needed healing himself? Though "our" sect was not numerous, still they were a certain number and the need for guidance was great and he, being so very, very needful of guidance, was not fit for the task—someone else was needed, older than himself, more experienced and stauncher in his faith than Mikhl, someone beside whom he could stand, upon whom he could lean and from whom he could get counsel when he needed it.

And it was certainly true, as Mikhl well knew, that the other members of the sect would be happy to have someone like Luzi, for example, at their head, because leaving to one side the fact that the group was small, still, as Luzi knew, the town was large and there were many classes of people who might be drawn to and be taken into the group, thereby greatly enlarging its numbers. But for that, one needed someone whose capabilities were greater than any of those possessed by any member of the sect—Luzi, naturally, excepted. Luzi was famous, he possessed the spiritual weapons the situation required, and he would unquestionably inspire the sort of respect that it was impossible that anyone else but himself could elicit.

Well then! Perhaps Luzi would think the matter over and would decide to stay in N. and become the leader of the community?

"To stay," said Luzi, as if he had known all along what the proposal would be and was by no means surprised by it. Then he was silent.

"Yes," Mikhl continued, "because a two-front war is developing here: first against all the classes of the town which have concerted to oppress us, to swallow us up, and on the other hand, against the general foe (ours and theirs)—the ever more powerful and growing number of heretics who believe in violence and who intend to devour us as well as those who persecute us."

And here, Mikhl recurred again to matters of the sect itself and spoke of the hardships he had to endure, the confusion that overcame him in the course of which he had no idea what to do or whom to turn to for advice.

For example, lately a young man from some town very far away had come to them and no sooner had he arrived than he commenced to weep, and he continued to weep to the present moment, and there was nothing anyone could say that would quiet him. And what was he crying about? Well, from his infancy, he had been raised with a half sister, and when the two were older, something apparently happened between them. What it was he did not specify, but that was the reason he left his home and his town. For some while he wandered about until he came here, and he had no sooner joined the sect when he began to weep: night and day. Whenever anyone so much as looked at him, he burst into tears. And if anyone tried to console him by saying, "Enough weeping. Penitence and contrition will help," it only made him weep the harder and he said, "That's not it. That's not why I weep. I'm crying about a new sin—because my head is stuffed with sins."

And here, for example, was another case, one of many recently. The wife of Avreml the tailor came to complain that it was now a very long time since Avreml had behaved like a husband to her. He did not come to her or take her as custom and the way of the world required. Well, so much for Avreml's wife. She came quietly, wept silently and went silently away. But then here came the wife of Sholem the porter with the same complaint. She was quite another sort of woman, openly shrieking and shouting her grief: "What have you turned my Sholem into?" she cries. "What sort of magic have you used to change him? He doesn't earn a living; he doesn't treat me like a wife. Well, what does he want . . . a goat in his bed, perhaps?" And she sets up a clamor demanding that we give her back her former Sholem or else she threatens to pluck beards and go crying her wrongs through the streets.

And here, Mikhl smiled as he told the story, and so, too, did Luzi.

By now after their slow walk through the streets, they had come to the wooden bridge that linked the upper with the lower part of the town and which led to the street Luzi needed to take to get to his brother's house.

Because of the lateness of the hour, there was no one, neither rider nor pedestrian, to be met on the bridge. But there were two lanterns, one at one end of the bridge and the second at the other, which cast a weak light on the middle of the bridge. That light was refracted in the water on both banks of the river.

The river, after the heat of the day, flowed quietly, calmly. There was no breeze to ripple the surface of the water or to make the slightest sound in the reeds along the river. The stars overhead were reflected without distortion in the water. And anyone passing along the bridge just then would have shared in a certain portion of the star-studded sky and the calmness of the water.

We have our two passersby in mind: one of whom, Mikhl, now that he had made his confession, felt freed and refreshed, like someone who has left a place of great heat to come into the fresh air; and his surroundings—the bridge, the river with its calm banks and the water at dusk—strengthened his hopes for a fresh renewal. And Luzi, too, was cheered because he had encouraged someone else, despite the fact that it had left him preoccupied with particular questions: namely, whether to go or stay, and what reply to give to Mikhl when sooner or later he would want to know what conclusion Luzi had come to.

And thus it was that they crossed the bridge and entered the street on the other side which led to the house of Luzi's brother. And it was here that both of them sensed a slight coldness touching the skirts of their coats. Somewhere far away to the southwest there was a break in the horizon; the air stirred and there were flashes of lightning and clouds began to gather—though it was not yet clear whether a storm was or was not building up. Our two walkers tightened their waistbands, and when they reached Moshe Mashber's courtyard, they paused before the gate to chat awhile as a way of ending their conversation before they took leave of each other. And it was when their talk was finished that Mikhl turned to Luzi and speaking hurriedly put a final question to him. "Well . . . Luzi—about the matter I've put before you. What do you think?"

"We'll see. We'll think about it," Luzi replied.

And now, after their good nights, they parted. Mikhl, the skirt of his coat lifted by the wind, hurried off on the long way to his home, while Luzi opened the courtyard gate and went into his brother's house.

When Luzi came into the house, none of Moshe's family were still in the dining room. It was already late, and this time even Gitl had grown weary of waiting for her brother-in-law. Only Moshe was there, waiting for his brother.

As was usual after an ordinary, somewhat prolonged working day, there was a particular sort of air hovering in the room: the residue of a variety of people—of the employees who worked in Moshe's business who came to make their daily report and to receive their instructions for the next day.

Cashiers came, confidential employees, portly, neatly dressed, with refined hands and suave speech and manners, and simpler employees, too, who did the rough work in the shops who had come for the evening without having made much change in the clothing they wore by day. Men who felt themselves under constraint because their hands were but poorly washed.

There were others, too. Merchants of the same class as Moshe who came to conduct ongoing old business, and brokers who had new business to propose, and borrowers who came to get or to repay money and so on.

At that hour of the night, Moshe Mashber always looked a bit fatigued and pale. Usually when he had finished his many conversations and interviews, the table was freshly reset and a light supper was laid out for him. But light as the meal was, he usually sat down to it wearily and without much enthusiasm.

And so it was now.

When Luzi came into the dining room he found a tired Moshe, who was more than ready for bed, waiting for Luzi to show up for his dinner. Luzi, then, did not delay but washed his hands quickly and took his place at the table.

The brothers, as they had been lately doing, carried on a cool, somewhat dutiful conversation that seemed designed to help them avoid uncomfortable silences and above all to avoid serious matters.

Moshe asked no questions about what Luzi was doing or what direction he might be taking because he knew without inquiring; and even if Moshe had asked any questions, Luzi, for his part, would have turned them aside simply to avoid getting into arguments from which Moshe, Luzi was convinced, would only emerge feeling once more besieged and ashamed. And Luzi did not want that.

The one thing Moshe did feel he could ask in his detached fashion, was where, he, Luzi, meant to stay now that the High Holidays were approaching. Whether here in N. or did he mean to go, as members of his sect usually did, to Uman to pray during those days over their rabbi's grave?

Luzi replied that he would be going to the rabbi's grave.

"Yes, and after that?" Moshe asked.

"I'll come back here," Luzi replied.

"Back?"

"Yes, to be here, to stay here . . . always."

Moshe, astonished, raised his eyes and gazed at his brother, as if studying him so that he could understand better what he had just said, but just then a voice from the threshold of the dining room intruded itself into the quiet late-night fraternal conversation. The unexpected voice said, "To stay here always. Ah, that's good."

It was then that the two frightened brothers turned to look toward the doorway and saw:

A short, poorly dressed person was standing directly in the doorway. He was a young man still, in his thirties, though from his very blond, unkempt beard, his neglected and shabby clothing and the particular intensity of his pupils which contrasted sharply with the whites surrounding them, it was hard to guess his age. Perhaps he was really young and it was his clothing that made him seem older; perhaps he was older but his eyes made him seem young.

This was Alter, the third of the Mashber brothers. And one could

· 126 ·

tell at a glance that he was—more a misfortune than he was a brother. He was abnormal. Despite the sweetness of his speech and his simpleton's smile, his head, his forehead and his eyes seemed to have survived some great storm. His forehead looked rough and hard, as if, though for the time being it was still unshattered, he had frequently struck it against a wall. His eyes, though at first glance they seemed gentle, nevertheless gave one the impression that they could make adults as well as children tremble with fear and run to be miles away.

And here we must interrupt our narrative in order to say a few words about Alter and his biography.

It may be that this is not the place for him, and it may be that generally speaking there ought not to be a place here for someone like him who does not—who cannot—take an active part in the narrative, and we might simply have passed him over or mentioned him only occasionally here and there. But we have not done that, and after much consideration we have introduced him here and we mean to occupy ourselves with him for a little while longer because, though he does not play an active role, still, it is a role, if only because he existed and because he existed in the household about which we have been speaking, and since blood is thicker than water, and because we have in mind the researcher who two or three generations from now may find in later members of the family a tiny kernel of that sickly inheritance which in the generation being discussed here was unhappily Alter's portion.

Well then, let us turn to Alter.

He was the last little one, the youngest child of Moshe and Luzi's parents. As a small child, he grew normally, naturally, and until he was old enough to go to religious primary school, he was no different from other children. But it soon became evident that he paid no attention to what he was being shown; his eyes wandered away from the prayer book whose use he was being taught and if he was told, "Say *aleph*," he repeated the words, "Say *aleph*." And the same thing for the letter *bet*—he repeated "Say *bet*."

At first it was thought that he was a somewhat distracted child and that later he would become more attentive and things would get better, and for a year—and more than a year—such explanations comforted both his teachers and his parents. And then they had to confront the truth. The child was not improving and he was taken to one doctor after another, and such remedies as were available in those times were applied: charms, magic formulas and so on.

Nothing helped. The parents grew desperate, but there was nothing to be done. The child grew, a simpleton, a spiritual cripple. And he had been entirely given over as lost when one fine day when he was about seven years old, his eyes suddenly cleared and a look of intelligence appeared in them and the child, with a more than childlike avidity, became attentive to everything he saw and heard around him as if he wanted to make up for the years he had lost.

The change was instantly observed and measures were at once taken to help him. The finest teachers were hired, and the child seemed to swallow rather than to study his lessons. What took others a year, he learned in a month; what they acquired in a month, he grasped in one day. His mind was swift, penetrating, all encompassing. So much so that his parents and teachers, to avoid giving him the Evil Eye, spoke to each other about him in secret. And though his parents, without knowing quite why, found themselves trembling now with even greater anxiety over his acuteness than when he was retarded, they nevertheless rejoiced in his amazing progress and foresaw that he would accomplish great things.

In the course of the years, this younger brother far surpassed the two older ones in learning, in diligence and in what was regarded as wisdom in those days. Nor was it only his brothers he surpassed. He was superior to all other students like him and his fame spread throughout the town and beyond.

But then when he was seventeen years old, there was another sudden change: as if someone had burned a thread in his brain, the light of intelligence in his eyes went out. This time the grief of the mother (the father was no longer living) and that of the family was overwhelming. Now they were not satisfied to consult their own local doctors. The young man was taken to a distant Russian regional capital to visit a doctor or professor of some kind who was at that time very famous. As the family later told the story, the doctor spent a long while inquiring into the facts of Alter's childhood, about his early diseases and his other illnesses. The doctor was especially interested in the mother's account of something that had happened when Alter was still quite a small child. He had collapsed one day and had then been assailed by a high fever. The local doctors attending him had prescribed leeches under the ear. And the leeches had been set there. And then (as his mother recalled) they had left the boy in the charge of a maidservant who neglected to remove the leeches at the proper time. . . .

The famous professor then asked questions about the boy's parents.

He wanted to know who Alter's father was and what he had died of, and in spite of the halting and confused account given by a woman speaking a language unfamiliar to her, the professor finally understood what she had to say and shook his head sympathetically. "Ah. I see. I see. A rabbi. A recluse."

Alter's mother, unconsoled, having received not the slightest promise that the boy would improve at any time in the future, left the professor as if from a last place of hope. And then it was that the illness fully manifested itself. There were violent headaches whose onset blinded the boy. It was clear that he was in torment, that it required all his strength to keep from crying out against the pain or from dashing his head against a wall to end it.

Later, he did cry out—cries so appalling that no one (relative or stranger) could bear to be near him. A leopard's cries, so ghastly that it seemed that at any moment his intestines would spew from his throat. So awful that people who knew him were perpetually amazed that such inhuman sounds could emanate from him.

It was like that until the seizure was over. Then for several days he was fearfully pale and exhausted as if he had survived some atrocious interior storm.

It was about that time that the pattern set in that was to repeat itself throughout the course of his unhappy life: from time to time the headaches and outcries described above, then exhaustion, then a period of quiet during which his cast of mind, though it was calm, grew ever darker.

During those quiet periods, he seemed to be especially drawn to music. Sometimes he would disappear from the house only to be found later by members of his family who early learned to look for him in some outlying home where a wedding was being celebrated and whose music had drawn him, though no one else at that great distance had heard it being played.

And when he was not at such festivities, he stayed at home in his room where, with nothing to do, he either paced back and forth or, as he sometimes did, he tore his clothes into minuscule shreds, or else he gathered rags and tatters and made careful heaps of them. Sometimes he would gather perfectly useful household implements which he carried out and threw into the outhouse. Or with a wild and mad tenacity, he might set himself the task of gathering up bits of dust which he persuaded himself were bits of unswept garbage.

His mother, still a young woman, was so oppressed by the misfortune that had overtaken her son that she took sick and died. His brothers then looked about for a home in which he could be placed and where he could be cared for. A poor widow was found, a fee was paid and Alter was brought to her home. But a few weeks after he had been consigned to her care, when Moshe, who went alone, came to see how Alter was, his brother threw himself into Moshe's arms and begged to be taken home. Alter's eyes cleared for a moment, and like someone being punished, he clung to his brother and promised faithfully to behave himself. Moshe's eyes filled with tears and he took Alter back home with him.

And from that time on, Alter lived in Moshe's home. At first, in the days before Moshe became so very rich, he lived with Moshe's family in somewhat narrow circumstances. But ever since Moshe acquired wealth and a nobleman's house, Alter had been given a small upper room which, when the house had still belonged to the nobleman, had been a servant's quarters. This room could be reached through a door leading from the kitchen up a flight of stairs. There was a single small window in the room that looked out on the garden at the bottom of the courtyard. Alter stood before this window, deep in thought, sometimes for hours at a time.

Everything he needed was sent up to him in that room: food, clothing. And it was there, night and day, that he spent his time. Only rarely did he go downstairs to visit any of the members of the household. And it was equally rare for any of them to visit him.

And everything went on with him as it had before. Sometimes his cries were heard. But an attentive watcher would have noticed that the onset of his headaches was linked to changes in the weather. In summer, just before a storm, in winter, when the weather changed.

The adults in the family were used to his cries. Children, in the midst of their play, stopped, stupefied, and looked toward the kitchen ceiling from which the great cries seemed to come.

But most of the children, like the adults, got used to the cries and, after the first startling moment, resumed their play. Only one of them was more affected than the others and that was Mayerl, who has already been mentioned—only he, on the days when Alter's cries were heard abovestairs and Mayerl was down below, turned pale and weak.

He was drawn at such times to go up to Alter's room to see him, and not only then. He often found his way up the stairs and, to the degree that it was possible in Alter's situation, spent some time chatting with him.

And Alter, therefore, singled Mayerl out from all the other children. And though he had difficulty remembering who they were, yet Mayerl's name, along with those of his brothers, was engraved on his mind.

"Mayerl, Mayerl," he greeted him joyfully when he chanced to meet him, but especially when Mayerl appeared at his door to pay him a visit. And Mayerl, much later, would tell how he found Alter in his little room in the upper reaches of the house, sitting at his table with paper, pen and an inkwell before him, deeply absorbed, but with something of an air of intelligence in his eyes.

At such times Alter used to be much preoccupied with writing, and if a curious family member should happen to come upon his bits and pieces of paper, he would find that Alter had been writing letters. Always to important personages; to the great biblical figures, or to people whose names can be found in cabalistic writings. Names evidently which Alter still remembered and which floated in his now darkened memory. And some of the letters were addressed to no one—except God Himself. Letters that were part prayer, part complaint, though sometimes they were businesslike letters, reproachful or confiding and written as between equals.

Among a number of other papers, a small collection of such letters survived, thanks to Mayerl himself, to much later times, but we do not think it necessary to cite even one of them, but by way of characterizing them, we will list some of the addressees.

All of the letters were written in Hebrew, and they were addressed to:

Akhi of Shilo . . .
Nebuchadnezzar, king of Babylon . . .
Rabbi Bakhia Hasfardi . . .
The angel Gabriel . . .
The angel Raziel . . .

And a letter of a different sort. A "Letter to God Who Responds When One Is in Great Need."

And it was the above-mentioned Mayerl who was among those who first noticed (and who remembered later) that the onset of Alter's headaches was related to changes in the seasons and in the weather. And this made such an impression on him (Mayerl, that is) that he became exceptionally sensitive in such matters, and such sensitivity was his gift and it served him for the rest of his life so that he, too, intuited not only the changes in seasons and weather, but even as a child he was able to anticipate minor family events, and when he was older coming changes in society itself.

But more of that later, when Mayerl will be our theme. But here we want to note a trait of Mayerl's that was now characteristic of Alter. Whenever some event was about to take place in the family, he would come down, day or night, and appear in the doorway where he stood, his gaze pure and radiant, after which, with a few thoughtful, sensible words or astute phrases, he intruded into whatever conversation was going on.

And so it was this time, too. As the brothers sat at the table at this late hour in the evening carrying on their quiet talk, they heard Alter entering into their dialogue as he crossed the threshold into the room.

Startled, both of the brothers rose from their seats and moved toward the doorway where Alter was. And a moment later one seemed to see an amazing sight: triplets in the doorway.

Having come together, they stood there for a while, the two brothers looking at Alter, Alter returning their gaze. Each of the brothers had a hand on Alter's shoulder. Alter bowed his head and rested it on Luzi's breast, and Moshe said pleadingly, as he usually did when Alter showed up without being asked, "Go on now, Alter. Go on to your room."

And Luzi looked sorrowfully on, one hand on Alter's shoulder as with his other hand he caressed his head while he whispered, "Ah, our unhappy, sinful soul."

Suddenly, there was a knocking at the shutters.

It was as if a wind that had been in hiding during the course of the hot day and the stifling evening had broken loose from its place on the banks of the river or from a corner of the sky.

Clearly that wind had already been stirring up the dust in the street, in the courtyard and in the garden, and had been whirling about in the treetops, but the two brothers had noticed nothing. Alter, on the other hand, standing by the window in his upper chamber—or maybe he was not at his window—Alter had noticed it and that was what had brought him down here; and his being here now was the signal that tomorrow—or perhaps even tonight—a miserable time awaited him: his atrocious headaches and his cries.

For the time being, however, he was calm. Indeed, very calm, and stood, simply one of three brothers, his head still resting on Luzi's breast. Then he raised his eyes and made a brief, sensible remark: "So, Luzi, you're going to be with us for always. Ah, how good that will be. For always."

IV

Sruli Gol

For the sake of clarifying what is yet to come, we have now to introduce still another person. But in the interest of brevity, we will for the time being provide a sketch only and will develop more about him later. We are talking about Sruli Gol.

Sruli Gol is a man who wears an earth-colored caftan. On weekdays, he also wears a peaked cap with a lacquered visor—the only lacquered visor in town. On the Sabbath and on holy days, he wears an exceptionally long caftan of shabby cloth that is not belted at the waist the way caftans usually are. Rather it is buttoned in front with a great many buttons so that it looks like the soutane of a Polish priest. On the Sabbath and on holy days his cap, too, is made of shabby cloth, but it is curiously shaped, like a high tower, and it has false earflaps that are fastened in the middle of the crown with a button.

Who concocted it for him? Who made his clothes? No one. He himself. He has nobody, he owns nothing. He has no family, no roof over his head. He eats in other people's homes—usually in the homes of the rich.

He is always a guest in their homes, though "guest" is a figure of speech and it implies that the inhabitants of a house more or less welcome their visitor. But here this is not the case. No one welcomes Sruli. For the most part, people fear him. And what they fear is his mouth. If anyone irritates him or fails to respect him in any way, he swears and curses so that people cover their ears. He calls down flames and plagues and does not even hesitate to wish the death of children.

He can be seen often looking at a house as he stands in some rich man's courtyard, or in the street before a rich man's gate, his head tilted back as he looks up at a gutter on the roof, or at a window corner into which swallows have daubed their nest of straw and feathers. He stands, his head thrown back as he grumbles curses at them. "Swallows! Some swallows. Just look at them. They brought the firebrand that burned the Temple, but they can't find one to burn a rich man's house."

No one knows just why he is so angry. Nor how long it has been since he has led his vagabond's life. No one dares ask him what town he comes from, what his origins are, or what is his family name. All that is known is that he is not a local man, that he is someone to be reckoned with, and that rich people especially must endure—and support him.

See him now coming into a house where he will . . . when he will: early for tea, or later in the morning, or in the middle of the day, or late in the evening at suppertime. He never says, "Good morning," or "Good evening," as he comes in, and he never says "Good day," or "Good night," when he leaves. He sits right down at the table and eats and drinks until he has had his fill. If he chooses to, he may go away after he has eaten. If he does not choose to, he stays on.

He almost never participates in the table talk but he is keenly alert to what is said. And yet everyone knows that he is familiar with everything that happens in a home, and what's more, with what is going to happen.

His presence puts a constraint on all the members of a family, and when he leaves, everyone breathes more freely. No one can abide his earth-colored caftan or his lacquered cap pulled down over his eye on the left side of his face. When he is in the house, people feel as if an undertaker's silent assistant is there, waiting for misfortune to strike so he can carry a body away.

One rarely sees him working. Though sometimes when somebody dies—and generally when it is a rich man—he will suddenly appear out of nowhere and stand by while the body is being washed. He does not offer to help, but he stands by watching as the corpse is given its due, and from the look on his face, it is evident to everyone that he is pleased by what is going on.

When he has special rancor against some rich man's corpse, he can behave violently. He drags sheets from the beds and tears them to strips on the pretext that they are necessary for washing the dead. He demands extra candles so that he can set them around the corpse, but he does not light them; instead he passes them out among the crowds of poor folk jostling each other in the rich man's house.

At other times he will deliberately turn off the spouts of the urns in which water for washing the dead is being heated, and when the sextons waiting for the water to get hot ask why he has done it, he replies furiously, "Never mind. It's none of your business. No need to hurry. He'll get there in good time. Let him stink here a little longer."

Thus in the presence of the dead, and he behaves in the same way at the weddings of the rich. He will interfere with their contented and happy lives just the same way that he interferes with their noisy and tumultuous funerals.

At weddings, he never sits where he could—at the head of the table, or indeed anywhere he might please, because who is there who would deny him his choice of a seat? No. He always sits at the tables prepared for the vagabonds and beggars.

He takes command of those folk and issues orders. "Eat, eat, you rascals. Fill your filthy guts."

Or, more gently, somewhat later, "Eat. Eat your fill, and take some with you. Keep in mind that this food belongs to no one but you and God."

When the banquet is over and the beggars have stuffed themselves, when their pockets and sacks are full, Sruli continues to shout at the servants, demanding that they bring more food and still more. And when a table is completely reset with food, just as the beggars are leaving, Sruli, as if it were happening by accident, entangles a button in the fringe of a tablecloth, then starts to move away dragging the tablecloth with him so that all the food, wet or dry, tumbles to the floor in a heap along with the broken crockery.

This, then, is his behavior at a festival.

It was said that he had lost his faith because of anger, that he feared no one but God, that he had no respect for holy men or miracle rebbes or for any other representatives of God on earth. He laughed at them all. Especially at the famous ones whom the rich visited and in whom they believed.

And yet he never picked on any of the faithful poor. If they believed, he let them. But he would tell off the rich as sharply as he could and at every opportunity. So that Sruli, who was habitually silent and about whom no one could boast that he had ever heard anything from him but insults . . . Sruli, when he had an opportunity to get his hooks into some rich man, went at it with all his might, no matter how rich and powerful his victim was, whether it was in the very middle of the synagogue or in the center of a circle of people; and his attack was so sharp, so biting, that there were those who feared merely to stand in his vicinity and turned away to avoid him as if they were afraid of being infected by him. There were others, on the other hand, who stayed where they were, gaping and unable to tear themselves away.

On such occasions, when Sruli got fully started, he had a great deal to say, and those who chose to stay got quite an earful.

One gathered from what Sruli said that he was widely traveled. Whatever he had not personally seen, he had heard about. And things about which he had not heard, he seemed to have discovered for himself. He gave one the impression that he could hear through walls and that his vision encompassed great distances.

It is true in any case that when the seizure of speech was on him, he might be seen in the very midst of a crowd of the faithful telling a tale of events that had taken place in some well known rebbe's court. A tale about the rebbe's daughter-in-law who hated her husband and who would not live with him. And bitter because she had wasted her youth in a marriage that had been forced upon her, she now refused to accept a bill of divorcement from her husband. And Sruli told how she was made to accept it by force, though at first persuasion was tried. But when that didn't work, angry threats were made. Still, she would not budge. Finally, she was offered money, but she was obdurate.

All this while, they were secretly gathering the signatures of a hundred rabbis (the number, according to religious law, needed to impose a bill of divorcement). And Sruli described how the daughter-in-law, who had spent years in seclusion to avoid being pursued, how she went out of her house one day and was set upon by people hired by the rebbe, who laid her down on the ground, and . . . here Sruli, ending his tale, smiled a coarse and cynical smile . . . forced her to receive the divorce.

Another time, before the same company, he told another story also set in a rebbe's court. It was a tale about an unmarried son of the rebbe who got a chambermaid in trouble, and of how she was quickly married off to a dull-witted workingman and of how they were sent off to live in some distant town, and of how they were supported for some years with money sent from the rebbe's court. Payments made to hide the rebbe's shame.

It is true—as people in town said and believed—that Sruli had on one occasion been taught a lesson for his behavior—or at the very least he had received a warning. It happened, so the story went, on a summer's day in a house not far from the river in the home of people he knew, or perhaps did not know, when all at once a cloud appeared. There was a storm, there was dust and darkness, and as Sruli sat at the table in the half dark a terrific crash was heard. Sruli thought the roof had caved in upon him or that a fissure had opened in the earth. At that very moment a streak of white fire came in through the open door, it whirled above his head like a flaming bagel, then it twisted and turned, and turned as if seeking an exit, then it made its way outdoors through an open window opposite the door and vanished.

Sruli was not easily frightened, nevertheless because of the sharp detonation and the flame, he felt now a certain emptiness, a hollow feeling in his head. He took his hat off and passed his hand over his head. His hair, suddenly gray, came away at his touch and began to fall on his clothes and to the ground.

He got up, went to the window and looked out toward the river where he saw the hundred-year-old bent willow tree broken in half, with the top half in the water and the bottom standing on the shore burning like a candle in the storm.

There had been thunder and lightning.

Later, there were people who reproved him. Believers said, "You see, Reb Sruli, it's because of such and such; it's because of your words and blasphemies that you've been given a warning. First the hair and then the head." Sruli laughed and said irritably, "Hair? Who needs hair? In fact, things are better for me now without it. More relaxed and ideas come more easily. No need for anyone to worry about my head. Anyone who does is an idiot, much good may it do him."

From that time on, his cap was pulled even lower down on his face and its visor turned even more to the left, and from that time on, his silences were even sterner than before. He continued to hate what he had formerly hated, to frequent the homes of the rich where as always he continued to be received with bad grace.

For years that had been his mode of life; he had assumed the right to do as he liked and that right, whether they liked it or not, was acknowledged by the rich as well as the important people of the town. Hostile though he was, he came and went into their homes like an habitué. More than that, he had the right to sit at the wealthiest of tables without asking permission of anyone, or to pass the night if he liked.

And not only one night, but on those occasions when he felt like it, he could spend a week, a month—months sometimes—and there would be no one to deny him with a word.

That's how it had been for a long time, practically always. He always showed his hostility to anyone who angered him. But he never revealed any attachment, any affection—or very rarely. And when he did, it was usually on some holiday. One or two times a year, he might dance with some poor guest at the feast of a rich man. He would lead him away from the table or pull him away from a circle of dancers—some poor man, some defeated fellow who kept himself always apart—and dance so intensely with him that no one, no matter how many were there at the festivity, no one could keep his eyes from the two of them dancing. And he exhausted his partner; placing his hand on the poor man's shoulder, he compelled him to dance and dance until both he and his partner were streaming with sweat.

Only then did he let him go, and turning to him said loudly enough for everyone to hear, "Listen, and I will prophesy. All that you see here is for you, and for all the other poor folk like yourself . . ." And here he would point a menacing finger at the rich householders and at their rich guests and then, usually, he was silent, though he might add, "Hard labor convicts, in chains."

And he could be remarkably congenial at the weddings of the poor.

Occasionally, dressed in his earth-colored gabardine, he might appear—without invitation—in the very midst of the festivities in some poor home where a wedding was taking place. No one knew him or knew anything about him. If anyone asked him what he wanted, he would reply, "To bring joy to the bride and groom."

"By all means," was the reply.

Then taking a flute from one of his pockets, a simple wooden pipe with holes in it—a flute bought no doubt from some shepherd—he would start to play.

He made then a strange and somewhat lovely sight as he stood and played. He was certainly not a professional musician, nor even a trained player, but his fingers were agile and closed or opened the holes in his flute at just the right time. The tones he produced were pure and always in a low or middle register.

His stance was curious. His body seemed not to be taking part in the music—nor did his face. He stood entirely rigid without the least change in his expression, nor the slightest movement, so that those who had seen him arrive and had heard him express a desire to take part in the festivities were inclined to smile a little the way one smiles at the efforts of a not very skillful wedding jester or at a hoarse beggar comedian; but once Sruli put the pipe to his lips and started playing they looked on with wonder (and not a little fear). He, however, paid no attention to anyone, as if he were not playing before an assembly but rather as if he were playing in the open air.

And he played a sad melody. So sad that softhearted women, relatives of the betrothed pair as well as the others, wept.

He played softly, and with his simple and ancient pastoral instrument, he brought into the wedding household things such as its walls had never seen or heard, redolent of green fields and woods, of sunny as well as cloud-shaded ease. And the relatives of the couple as well as the guests felt that they had been transported into another world and they forgot the celebration taking place in the house and everything that had preceded it.

But Sruli, though he was capable of making them forget, did not abuse his skill and would not let them forget for long.

Always, the same thing happened: Sruli interrupted his playing the moment he saw that the audience was in his power. And then in a fashion unremarked by his listeners, he managed by a sort of sleight of hand to give them the impression that he was still standing before them with the flute in his mouth when, in fact, the flute was already resting in his pocket.

The audience then, awed by the sleight of hand with the flute, stood abashed, but before anyone had a chance to look around, there was Sruli beside the bride with his hand out as if he were demanding payment for the entertainment he had just provided. But it was not money he wanted, not payment. Rather, he liked to say, "Pay me with a dance, bride." And if the bride hesitated for a while, uncertain whether to pay or to refuse, then Sruli would hold his other arm out to the audience as if asking whether he was entitled to make his request or not.

"Certainly, of course," the guests called, reassuring Sruli.

So the bride danced with Sruli. And Sruli did with the bride precisely what he was wont to do with a poor man at the weddings of the rich. He danced with her until she was completely exhausted. The result, however, was that she remembered this man with his earth-colored caftan for the rest of her life. And she cherished the dance throughout the grave and difficult years that were to come as one of the best of her memories of youth and marriage.

Then he was welcomed and given a seat of honor at the table, and he was served with all of the things that had been prepared for the wedding. And before Sruli left—always well before the banquet was over—he would take one of the parents of the bridal couple aside and put into his hands a silver ruble as a wedding present, or a small silver cup or some other silver object.

We do not know whether the money or the small silver objects that he gave were his. But if, as was sometimes rumored, there was coincidentally an empty place on the shelf of some rich man's collection of silver, it was not important and neither we nor the rich man, nor anyone else—and certainly not Sruli himself—will shed tears over the matter.

A remarkable man, this Sruli. A somewhat mad, contradictory person, spiky as a thornbush, neither to be grasped nor understood.

There were some who, speaking of Sruli's antagonism to the rich, offered it as their view that it derived from the fact that Sruli himself was or had been related to a wealthy family.

This view was based on his conduct, his arrogance and certain of his habits, his grandiose manner and his irritability. He was perfectly capable of indulging himself in gestures like sitting down in the middle of the market square to remove his shoes, which then he presented to a stranger either because the stranger had no shoes or so that the man might sell them to get out of some trouble he was in (a charge of theft, for instance—or some other distress).

Or it could happen on another occasion that he became so deeply involved in rescuing the shabby bedding from a poor man's blazing hut that his eyebrows and beard began to smolder.

Or, further, he would suddenly take on a quarrel with the greatest and most famous of the town's rabbis over a matter of ritual purity put to the rabbi by some poor woman. The matter at issue was some dish the poor woman had cooked for a sick person in the family, and when the rabbi prevailed and declared that the food was ritually unclean and could not be eaten, then Sruli would ask the woman who was already leaving . . . where she lived. And very soon after he would show up at her door bringing another and more costly repast. And he would say that the rabbi had sent the food to replace what had been declared unclean, but the truth was that he had himself taken the food from the kitchen of the rabbi's wife, taking it out of her hands by force, shouting grossly at her that the law was shit, and that it would do the rabbi no harm to miss a meal, let him, too, be deprived of something once in a while for the sake of the law. There, then, one of his eccentricities. And now, the other. On the very same day he found money somewhere or other and brought the price of the meal he had taken from her to the rabbi's wife and gave it to her with a gracious "Thank you."

"And stop being a rabbi's wife," he called scornfully back at her as he was leaving.

When this last tale reached the ears of the town, there were those who admired his cheekiness, there were others who laughed delightedly, but everyone without exception was amazed by him: Just think! Who would have supposed that he, Sruli, whom nobody has ever seen with a book in his hands, who does not even know *how* to hold a book . . . that he would undertake to quarrel with a rabbi. And to pit himself against so learned a rabbi at that.

There you have the sorts of capricious, strange tricks he was continually pulling off to astonish the world. But he did not spend much time at causing astonishment. Whenever he became aware that he had become the object of people's curiosity, and that the curiosity was growing, he would lower his head between his shoulders and assuming a surly look would not let anyone get near him, as if he were trying to erase any memory of whatever had been unwonted or bizarre in his behavior, so that by the next day or the day after there should be no trace of it in anyone's mind.

And it was not only the emergence of the hidden thorns in his nature which, having emerged against his will, that he tried to repress, treading them out as it were with his feet. Sometimes it was Sruli himself. Every year he would disappear from the town's ken. Sometimes for a long while—even for months at a time.

No one knew why. Whether it was because he was suddenly sick of the place, or whether he had a revulsion of feeling against his ongoing anger against the people into whose homes he went daily, or whether there was indeed something in his nature which he had to conceal. Whatever it was, whenever he sensed that he had been in the public eye too long, he arranged to duck out, to disappear.

Whatever the reason might be, he disappeared each year. Usually it was in the winter after the last snows had melted, when the last mud of the season was already drying; though sometimes it could be as late as the beginning of spring, when the air was light and the chestnut and lilac trees were in blossom, when every vista turned limpid and bright and every windblown and neglected road and field gate was flung open; and from the sky's upper reaches one heard the hushed and secret noises of flocks of geese, swans and herons returning from distant lands to make their nests here.

It was then that one noticed Sruli's irritability, his bemusement. He looked about erratically and listened with double his usual intensity, as if he were listening to something that came from a very great distance, bringing news.

Then on one fine morning, without taking leave of anyone or giving anyone any hint of his intentions, he took from its usual hiding place, where he had put it in preparation for just such an occasion, a sack into which he put the few things from his poor wardrobe that a man like himself might need on a journey.

He threw the sack over his shoulders and without so much as a good morning or a good day, he left the courtyard of the house in which he had spent last night. Sometimes as he left a courtyard, he might turn and make an obscene fig at the house with his hand. The movement shoved his cap lower down on his face and tilted its visor more to the left. Then, with his caftan unbuttoned and the sack over his shoulders, he started off, meeting no one, exchanging no greeting with anyone he chanced to meet, and in this fashion he traversed the town until he came to its outskirts.

It was something to see—Sruli striding along always in the very middle of the highway that he preferred to take when he left the town because it was arrow straight and paved with white stone; he liked it, too, because it was somewhat lower than the other roads so that when he had gone a certain distance he could, if he turned, look back and see the whole town to which he could then make the same obscene fig he had made when he left the courtyard.

Always, he kept to the middle of the road. He never turned aside for any of the simple peasant wagons that came his way, nor did he turn aside for any other vehicle. No matter whose it was, not for a merchant's horse and wagon nor a nobleman's coach, not even one harnessed at tandem. And on more than one occasion some nobleman's coachman lashed at him on the direct orders of the nobleman himself, who stuck his head out of the window to urge the coachman to hit him again . . . and again.

Walking on the highway with the wind in his face, he looked disheveled, his earlocks flying, the skirts of his caftan blowing backward, like a devil torn loose from his chain. Whether there was a wind blowing or not, he would not step aside for anyone who caught up to him from behind. Instead, people, coming upon his frightening, unresponsive shoulder, his rigid and stubborn walk, avoided him.

That's what happened when he met someone. For the most part, at that season of the year—in the spring—there was no one on the road because people were occupied with work in the fields. And Sruli could walk the entire day without meeting anyone, entirely rapt in the pleasure of the silence of the road that filled his ear, as well as from the humming of the telegraph wires of the single telegraph line that passed through the district. On such days, Sruli had no need either to eat or drink. Nor even to rest, because everything about him was pure, specially created for him, a holiday that freed him from the town.

It was only at the day's end that he would turn off from the highway and enter a village—Dvoretz it was called—situated on the road he was taking toward the towns in the distant forests of Duneshi and Shumsk where there lived various farmers and tavern keepers of his acquaintance with whom it was his custom to spend the long summer months.

It was late in the evening when he turned aside into a Shumsk or some other such village and showed up in some farmer's house where he had spent the summer before and was still remembered.

He put his sack down and was immediately invited by the rudely pious farmers to eat with them their standard food of fresh rye bread with sour cream or curdled milk.

He felt himself refreshed by the country calm which penetrated deeply into his marrow, by the silence or the polite speech of the farmers and by the deference they showed him as a man from the city. By the rare silence of the fields surrounding the village, by the head-scraping low ceiling of the rooms in which one had the smell of simple tavern brandy in one's nostrils, and by the water that came from a stagnant well, by the fowl that moved familiarly through the house—the hens and the geese which at that time of year when the winter was over were done setting and went about leading their young. They were kept in the hearth, and the faint cheep-cheep of the newly hatched chicks could be heard there, even at evening.

Sruli felt good there, from the first evening of his arrival, and especially good the next morning when he heard the first cry of the shepherd outside the window calling and assembling his flock; the newly risen sun made him happy, and the dew, and the hushed waking of the village to its labor, and the women going to draw water from the well, and by the quiet shyness of the village children wearing their fathers' hats who from the very beginning of the day knew exactly how they would use their childhood hours.

All of it pleased him. And from the very first day it made him forget the city and the irritations the city roused in him and one might have sworn that Sruli himself had been transformed into someone else. His anger dissipated; his cap was not pushed down so far over his face; the distrust and the skepticism, and his habit of separating himself from others, all of which had manifested themselves sharply in the ways he walked and talked and looked at people, were now all softened. The change was most clearly seen in the manner of his prayers, which when he was in the town, he often abbreviated. But here, wearing his prayer shawl, he stood before a window and took time with his prayers, even smiling occasionally as he prayed. And the change could be seen, too, in the manner of his dealings with the farmers with whom he stayed. It was not that he was particularly congenial with them or in any way intimate, but at least he did not grumble angrily at them or cast suspicious looks about him, nor, when someone addressed him, he did not immediately reply with some biting gibe.

And so a day . . . two days . . . a week . . . and more went by. In one place, in one village. Then he went off to another village. Again to someone he had known the year before, and again to some quiet place, even farther off in a forested region where the sun had difficulty crawling its way out of the branches of the trees in the morning and where it was swallowed up much earlier in the evening than in other such flat steppe lands.

The villages became smaller and smaller the farther he went into such distant regions, and the roads less deeply incised into the soil by foot or vehicle traffic, and a living city dweller was for the peasants in those forgotten regions an even rarer sight and they looked upon him as if he had come from a foreign land. And the Jewish farmers, who rarely saw anyone from the city and went there less frequently, felt themselves even more estranged and removed from him.

A great ignorance reigned in those places. The Jewish farmers lived in darkness and superstition. Sruli had encountered a farmer who refused to sell brandy to the person identified by everyone as the village witch. His explanation was that on one occasion, when he had sold brandy to her, long green pins had appeared in every barrel of his brandy, in every glass that was being drunk. Several peasants had been seized by the colic, and some had actually died.

In those places, every Jewish farmer conjured away the diseases of the peasants in his own language, Yiddish, while the peasants conjured away Jewish illnesses in their Polish tongue.

In those regions, will-o'-the-wisps gleamed in the wells at night. Mares wearing crowns circled the wells, and on the near or distant roads, ghosts on horses rode bareback and without bridles; and men and animals were misled by will-o'-the-wisps into bogs from which they never escaped—where they died or became emperors among frogs.

Sruli encountered such things, and others like them, and despite his love for the village, they made him feel constrained—as if he lacked air, as if he were choking.

Usually that happened in one of the mot distant of the villages, the one from which, after a long summer's visit, he would return to the city. In one of those sparsely settled villages in whose midst there might be a single thatch-roofed Jewish hut, such as the one in which, for instance, Menashe Tryeder lived. Menashe was an old dotard who was looked after by his children. He spent the entire summer in front of the house lying on an old cloth spread out on the ground. He was so deaf that he heard very little and understood even less. And the single reasonable gesture he was still capable of was that he thrust out his hand to greet whatever visitor might chance to come by, forgetting entirely that he had already greeted him not long before. And he continued to make this greeting all day long till everyone was wearied by it.

And it was beside this Menashe that a bored Sruli could be found, shouting into the old man's ear after Menashe had, with his last strength and according to the old village custom, uttered the few sensible words still left to him by asking, "And what's the news from town, Reb Guest."

Sruli shouted into his ear, "There's news, Reb Menashe. Great news. The Messiah has come."

And out of sheer boredom, he would joke with the old man or recite nonsense to him as if he were speaking to a child. For instance:

"Yes, Reb Menashe. The Messiah has come and the whole city is packing up; they've rented wagons to go out to meet him; rabbis in prayer shawls are riding on donkeys; rabbis' wives are wearing fringed four-cornered undergarments, piled on top of each other. The ritual bath has been hot all week and neither men nor women want to leave it. Cows and oxen go of their own accord to the slaughterhouses; the tax collector has disappeared and butchers are selling meat for free. Dogs drag whole heads away, trailing guts behind them; thieves have cut everyone's purses and bellies; poor people are wearing gold, and the rich are in rags."

"Really, really," the deaf old man said, amazed.

In this and in similar drolleries, Sruli passed his time, and it was clearly because he had nothing else to do. He no longer found the place interesting, and he felt that he was stuck in cement, and that it was time for him to leave.

And that always took place on a fine day at the end of the summer. The fields had been harvested, the barns were full; the woods engrossed in their after-summer meditation slept earlier and rose later each day, attentive all the while to the sound of the squirrels gathering their nuts as they prepared for the winter's dearth.

Then it was that Sruli, taking leave of no one, took up his sack once more. The roads back to the highway led him back through the villages he had passed before. And all the while that he was making his way back to the city, one could see emerging in his face a look of quiet contempt for the dotards among whom he had just been, for the foolish Menashes and for those who were not yet dotards and who were now a matter of indifference to him. He came to the highway with pleasure and breathed deeply, as if he were freeing himself from the dense air of the summer, and keeping his eyes straight before him, he made for the town from which he had been so long absent and for which he now yearned.

V

The Quarrel
Between the Brothers

1.

Early on the morning after the evening we described above, when the three brothers all met in Moshe's dining room, Alter, as everyone foresaw, had a seizure of screaming. But this time it was so unusual—even for him—that it was something to wonder at.

The morning was still dark when he was first heard by the housemaids who slept in the kitchen just below Alter's chamber. It was the older maid who woke first who, frightened out of her sleep, woke the other young woman. "Do you hear? It's so early in the morning and he's already begun."

They lay in their beds, wide-eyed, and though they were separated from him by the ceiling, they heard his cries as if he were lying in the same room with them. It seemed to them that such cries were produced not by one woman in the final moments of her labor, but by ten all at once, as if ten bodies were being ripped apart and the shrieks of ten times ten were struggling to be uttered by human mouths too narrow to allow them passage.

Later, members of the family sleeping in rooms farther away also heard him. Gitl, Moshe's wife, was the first and she was assailed at once, while still in her bed, by the headache that always came to her on the day that Alter's screams began. A headache that confined her to her bed all day, or compelled her to tie something around her head as she dragged herself about the house. Later, Moshe heard him too, and after him all of the adult members of the family, then finally it was the turn of the older of the children to hear him, and Mayerl was among that number.

There was a wind blowing outdoors, a wind that promised fall. A wind that had been gathering in the gardens all night and which, despite the coming of day, had not yet left them. It continually moved the treetops back and forth. It bent the branches toward the ground and sometimes broke them.

The dust-impregnated sky looked as if it might rain or as if it had rained. It hovered low over the streets and houses, and had anyone chanced to look out of a window that morning, gloomy thoughts would have occurred to him, as happens always whenever the weather changes for the worse.

A little while later, everyone in Moshe's household was up. The servants were busy getting tea ready for the adults and breakfast for the children. Dishes were washed and dried and the samovar was carried to the table in the dining room.

And one could already discern signs of a particular sort of anxiety in the faces of the adults in Moshe's household, one not caused by the bad weather which normally depresses people who have not yet eaten, nor was it because of Alter's cries which generally oppressed everyone in the house and turned them mute without exception. No, the essential reason was that there was news quietly being bruited about the house, and which derived from Gitl, that Uncle Luzi had decided to stay in N. and that Uncle Moshe was not especially pleased with his decision.

As the word spread, everyone felt that the quarrel between the brothers which had begun imperceptibly and which had been carried on with great restraint was now about to burst its bounds. It was felt that this decision of Uncle Luzi's, which, at any other time would have been received with great joy, was at this point like wood freshly added to a fire—stuff to make the flames leap up.

The adults drank their tea in silence and as if they were keeping up appearances. They stole glances at Moshe, the father and head of the family, and saw the general anxiety expressed on his face. At the same time their glances turned to the door of the dining room through which Uncle Luzi was likely to come for his morning tea. And this time they did not look forward to his coming. Given the tension which affected them all, what they were afraid of was that the quarrel might flare up over some trivial thing. What they hoped was that if they could avoid a conflict today, it might be possible to cool emotions that were at fever heat and that the spark that might set off a battle would be extinguished.

But Luzi was delayed by something—or was intentionally late. No one came through the doors through which he was expected. Instead, an unexpected guest came through the other door, the one that led from the kitchen to the dining room. It was Sruli. Sruli Gol.

Now as always he came in quietly, moving sideways. With his sack over his shoulder, he had the look of someone just returned from his travels. But in fact that was not so, as one could tell from the look of repose on his face that showed he had already spent the night since his return in some home or other. It was also evident that he was aware of what was transpiring in the room, the gloom over what had already happened as well as the anxiety about what was yet to come. One way or another, news of it had already reached his alert ear. And it was clear, too, from the look of malign pleasure in his eyes that it was all giving him delight, as if he was taking pride in a piece of good fortune that was about to befall him.

As was his wont, he did not greet anyone as he came in. He merely set his sack down in a corner—an indication that he meant to spend a little more time here than usual. Then, unasked and uninvited by anyone, and as if he were one of the members of Moshe's household, he found a place for himself at the table where they were all taking their tea and sat down.

It was clear, too, that Sruli had no interest in drinking tea. Perhaps because he had already had his breakfast or for some other reason—it made no difference. His eyes, all the while, moved from one member of the family to another, as if he were searching among the faces he had known so well and for so long a time for one that would be new to him; and when he did not find what he was looking for, he turned his gaze toward the doors of the dining room through one of which, he sensed, the unknown person whom he sought would be sure to come.

It was then that Moshe rose from the table and went off to his room. A little while later Luzi came in through a different door, as if the brothers had made an agreement not to encounter each other.

Sruli, who, as has been said, was waiting for him, marked his arrival at once: Luzi, who had carefully attended to his morning ablutions, was an imposing figure—the sort of man who gives off a holiday air and focuses attention on himself the instant he appears.

Sruli gave him a sidelong glance meaning, in his usual fashion, to turn it away at once and then give his face that look of irritability which he customarily turned on people. This time, however, that look—entirely against his will—failed to materialize. Instead something quite different took place. He found himself drawn to Luzi and to such a degree that when Luzi came through the door and made his way into the middle of the room and to the table, Sruli, who almost never did such a thing, now, as if unaware that he was doing it, offered Luzi his hand and said, "Shalom."

It's true that he was almost immediately angry with himself for what he deemed a show of weakness, but what was done was done, and there was no way to retrieve the gesture.

Putting his hand out, in any event, established several things at once. First that he, Sruli, was not always in control of himself, that there were times when he went beyond his self-imposed limits and that in certain circumstances he was incapable of sustaining the role he usually played. And second, it demonstrated that Sruli must already have heard about Luzi, that he might even have seen him here in the house on some occasion—or if he had not precisely seen him, he had at least formed an idea of him as an exceptional person of a sort that roused in him, Sruli, feelings such as he never had toward anyone else. And third, it demonstrated that Sruli had come this early in the morning to Moshe's house for no other reason than to see Luzi—whether it was done out of curiosity or for other reasons, we will not know until later. For the time being, at least, it was unclear, and nothing could be read from Sruli's behavior.

As for Luzi, he showed no apparent interest in Sruli, as if he were someone he had known from before or in any case as if his being there was not a matter of importance. On the contrary. Luzi was bewildered to notice that his own arrival at table had put the family under the same constraint as Sruli's presence and that they were all hastening to finish their tea so that they could leave the room. They, for their part, seemed not to be aware of his feelings. One by one they rose from their seats and went off to various parts of the house.

Only Gitl remained. She sat, a compress bound round her head to combat the migraine from which since early morning she had been suffering. She remained first of all because she wanted, as she usually did, to pour Luzi his tea and pass him his cup, and, too, she remained behind when the others had gone because she wanted to be the one to ask him (though it was a question for form's sake only) whether he had heard Alter's cries at dawn. And when he had replied that he had, then she asked about the matter that most interested her, and about which her husband Moshe had informed her early that morning while they were still in their bedroom, and which she had then passed on to the members of the household: the news of Luzi's decision to stay in N.

"Luzi, is what Moshe told me really true?"

"True," he replied. And this time, as was usual with him when he did not feel like enlarging on some subject, he created the impression that he would not welcome further questions and would be displeased to have to say anything more.

Gitl, aware of how he felt, could not, nevertheless, restrain herself from putting one more question to him. "And what will you do with your house and property?"

"Sell them."

"And then?"

"Rent something."

"Rent something? You'll live among strangers and not with us?"

"Yes," was his laconic response.

His answer deeply discouraged her, and she felt her headache increase in intensity. Too exhausted to stay longer at the table, she took her leave of Luzi and went back to her bedroom.

There began, then, a difficult day for the members of Moshe's household. Difficult for him, for Moshe, and for all of his dependents, as well as for such visitors who chanced to arrive, and difficult, too, for almost anyone who had dealings of whatever sort just then with the family.

When Gitl had left the room, Luzi, as was his custom before his prayers, began to pace back and forth, his hands in the back pockets of his caftan. He was today considerably upset because Alter's cries which had subsided sometime during the morning were now beginning again. Coming as they did through the kitchen ceiling they seemed to him to be very close, and one could see in his face the fraternal anguish they elicited in him. When finally Alter's cries became stronger than ever, Luzi interrupted his pacing. He stood quietly for a while, then he made his way to the kitchen and mounted the steps leading to Alter's room.

When he got there, he saw:

Alter's bachelor quarters with its bed, table and chair had an untended look, not at all as if he had relatives living right below him, but rather as if he were in a hut lost in a wood or on an island.

It seemed to Luzi that the room, the walls, seemed to be mourning Alter's lost youthful years. He had the impression that the dreary view onto which the window facing the garden looked out was permanently there and was not merely the result of today's bad weather: a view of trees whose branches the wind broke, and a permanently overcast or cloudy sky.

Alter stood in the middle of the room and was far indeed from manifesting any human reason. He kept wringing his hands with such speed and ferocity that it seemed as if he meant to tear them off at the joints so he could throw them away. Meanwhile, his gaze kept wandering and from time to time he beat his head with the knuckles of his fists and panted like someone who had been laboring hard.

But when he saw Luzi, the look in his eyes grew clearer; he stopped wringing his hands or beating his head and for a moment—for a single minute—he had sufficient presence of mind to say, "Ah, it's bad. Ah, brother, it's bad." But then he became disordered once more; he had the look of a man who was continually attentive to someone calling him, and who, when he heard the cry for which he listened, responded with one of his own that as it left his mouth seemed about to tear both at his jaw muscles and at his bowels.

When one seizure was over and done with, he tried to fix his eyes on some object in the room: a wall, a window—anything at all that would help him escape the domination of that cry and would keep him from responding to it with his own; but he remained in its power and once again his eyes began their wandering and he uttered a new and wild reply once more.

Luzi went up to him and tried to calm him. He caressed his head and wiped the sweat from his forehead. For a while, Alter permitted the attentions, then he began to shriek again. . . . And Luzi saw that here was an instance in which no one, not even a compassionate and sympathetic intimate, could be helpful; he turned his head so as not to have to see Alter's implacable anguish, to avoid seeing him in the grip of his destiny. And it was then that he saw a boy in the doorway . . . Mayerl. He had not noticed him before, but now he saw him leaning against a wall with his head turned away because he was scared to watch Alter, though at the same time he seemed rooted to the spot as each of Alter's cries sent a shudder through his body so that he burst into fresh tears and sobs each time.

Without a word, Luzi led Mayerl out of the room by the hand. Together they descended the steps, and without letting the boy's hand slip out of his, Luzi led him through the kitchen and into the dining room.

When Sruli, who had been sitting alone all the while Luzi was out of the room, saw him crossing the threshold leading the boy by the hand, he found himself, against his will, standing up respectfully. But he mastered himself a moment later, and as if justifying his gesture, he advanced toward Luzi and looking directly at him said offhandedly what a moment before it had not even occurred to him to say, that if Luzi had the time he, Sruli, would be very pleased for a chance to talk with him about a matter of some importance to Luzi.

"To me?" said Luzi, looking at him with surprise, as if he were seeing him for the first time. "Not now," he said, and then, as if that were the reason for his refusal, he nodded toward the boy whom he still held by the hand, though in fact he was thinking less of Mayerl than of himself, of the distress he had experienced in Alter's room. "Not now," he said. "I'm not able to do it now."

"When?" Sruli inquired.

"After my prayers, morning or evening. Just as you like."

Sruli, offended, was already considering the sort of crudely insulting and unforgiving response he usually permitted himself to certain sorts of people whose slights he paid back with interest. This time, however, the harsh words did not pass his lips, though their sense might be gathered from the look in his eyes. If he did not speak them then, it was not so much because, as has been said, he behaved differently with Luzi than with everyone else; rather, and perhaps this was the real reason, it was because Luzi, after refusing to speak to Sruli, left the dining room at once and made his way to his own chamber in a distant part of the house.

A little while later, Sruli, left alone in the dining room, busied himself with his knapsack from which he took his prayer shawl and phylacteries. He put them on and in his usual fashion mumbled through his prayers. Then he removed prayer shawl and phylacteries and returned them to his sack. Only then did he leave the dining room to make his way to the kitchen where, as he often did, he meant to spend some time with the servingmaids.

This time things did not work out as he planned. The feeling of oppression that reigned in the house had affected the servants and they, who usually were fond of gossiping with almost anyone at any time, greeted Sruli now with no show of eagerness, and one of them—the cook—when she saw him in the doorway, said irritably, "Well, look who's here. Reb Sruli."

But the words were no sooner out of her mouth when she took fright. Regretting her tone, she tried to smooth it over with more considerate speech. Sruli, however, pretended not to have heard her and did his best to give both the women the impression that he had not come to the kitchen on purpose but that he was simply passing through it. And indeed he left it at once and made his way out into the courtyard.

A little while later he could be seen standing before the closed garden gate. The wind from the garden blew gusts into his face; it whipped his beard about and made the skirts of his gabardine flap around his legs.

He stood for a while, disturbed and thoughtful, with nothing to do.

Later he could be seen at the well in the same attitude—immersed in thought. He looked like a man who, having had nothing to do since early morning, was bored and was trying to find a way to pass the time.

And it was this very boredom, this pressure of time on his hands, that sent him at last into Mikhalko the watchman's tiny and narrow hut. The hut, furnished only with a wooden cot, a chair and a table, was permeated with the smells of sweat, rye bread, dried herbs and coarse, cheap tobacco. The hut was dark even during the daytime because whatever light there was had to come through a tiny window cut into the wall beside the door. A cheap lamp hung by wires from the ceiling illuminated a smoke-smudged icon in a corner of the room. On a shelf just under the light there were a couple of dried-out palm fronds left over from last year's Palm Sunday and a bottle of filthy gray water from a Twelfth Night celebration. There were a couple of crude village-made pottery bowls and plates and a paint-faded wooden spoon. And not one other utensil or piece of furniture anywhere. And the sole inhabitant of this sparsely furnished place was the old, bent Mikhalko, purblind and nearly voiceless.

And on that morning it was into this little hut that Sruli came, after much purposeless wandering in the courtyard. Because Mikhalko was old, it almost never occurred to him to take up his day's work unless someone required it of him. And if it chanced that he had a visitor— never mind whether the visitor came too early or at some other wrong time, and even if it was someone in no way like him, or whose visit could not possibly please him—still, the need to honor his visitor served as an excuse for him to stay in his hut and to avoid getting to his work.

And strangely enough, Mikhalko had the impression that Sruli was really pleased with his company and that he wanted to encourage Mikhalko's laziness. "Never mind," Sruli told him, "there's no need for you to hurry. The work won't run away. You've done plenty of hard work in your time, so where's the harm in taking a rest once in a while?"

There was an ironic look on Sruli's face as he spoke. He seemed to be speaking inattentively, as if he was not thinking of Mikhalko at all. And yet without thinking of him he nevertheless guided Mikhalko's pathetic cluster of aged thoughts into a particular direction. Toward those matters concerning the relationship between a servant and his master, the sorts of things that prompt even the most devoted servant to tell tales of the way his master mistreats him, and how there is no point in devoting himself body and soul to his master's service because it is not appreciated. Because everyone knows what sorts of tricks his bosses play. Some tricks.

And Sruli meanwhile sympathized with Mikhalko's complaints. He said that Mikhalko was certainly right that the house servants ordered him about much too much, that they made him do work that was properly their responsibility, and moreover it was certainly true that whenever Mikhalko and the servants quarreled, his employers always came down on the side of the servants. And if the truth were told, what sorts of servants were they? Here today and gone tomorrow, while he, Mikhalko, who had served them for so many years, had no more importance in their eyes than a dog.

"You're right," Mikhalko. You're right."

The hut was dark, primarily because it was a hazy day, but also because very little light came into the hut through the tiny window that looked out on the courtyard. Now, too, there was the smell of rye bread in the hut and the odor of dried herbs, and the stink of the thick tobacco fumes rising to the ceiling from Mikhalko's ancient, thoroughly caked pipe.

And Sruli, an ironic smile on his lips, continued to sympathize with Mikhalko. "You're right," he said. "When you get old you get treated like a dog, especially if you work for others as a watchman. It may be that you should be thinking of the world to come."

"You're right," said Mikhalko who took his visitor's words to be solid gold. "I've been thinking just that—and I've been getting ready." Then as proof of his words Mikhalko reached for something under his pillow and showed Sruli the present that his village daughter had given him not long ago: an embroidered white shirt and a pair of linen trousers—the clothes he would be buried in.

Then as a way of thanking Sruli for the pleasing idea of death he had introduced into their conversation, Mikhalko went on to confide to Sruli that his daughter was looking after a bit of money he, Mikhalko, had saved, and that she was raising a small pig for him. All of this so that there would be something with which to buy liquor, and food to serve the good people who would gather to remember him at his burial feast.

Having said this much, Mikhalko cited other signs that he had lately observed which demonstrated clearly that his, Mikhalko's, time on earth was nearly up, and that he ought to prepare himself for his final journey.

Here's one sign, for example. Whenever he ate his evening meal and washed up his dish and his spoon, he always left them with their bowls up. But lately when he woke in the morning, he found them with their bowls down.

Sign number two: When in the morning he started out of his hut, he tripped on the doorsill, as if one of his shoe soles were torn and were hooked on the sill, when in fact there was nothing wrong with the sole at all. More than that, each time he left the hut he found himself being pushed back inside, as if someone were trying to tell him that there was nothing left out there for him to do.

And there were other signs as well. But the most important of them all were the cries that he had heard Alter, his employer's brother, make today. Alter (God have pity on him) had never cried that way before, and that was a sure indication that something was about to happen, that the *domovoi*, the spirit of the house, was hungry—and demanded a victim.

And he, Mikhalko, had sensed this from the very first moment that he, the Other One, had come to the house. And here, Mikhalko looked about as if he were confiding a secret, but he did not say who the Other One was or refer to him by name.

"Who is he?" Sruli asked.

"Him . . . the boss's second brother." The guest who (Mikhalko was sure of it) was neither a rabbi nor a Hasidic rebbe. He was, rather, a warlock related to the *domovoi*, the spirit of the house. Again this was said as if he were telling a secret and in a stage whisper as if he were repeating a magic formula.

Making his voice even more mysterious, he then confided to Sruli that he, Mikhalko, remembered the way the Other used to come to visit, but that he had never seen him behave as strangely as now. Mikhalko went on to say that ever since his coming to the house, he, Mikhalko, had seen the Other moving about behind the windows and doors of the house at night, and not only in the house but he had also seen him hovering outside his, Mikhalko's, door. And, said Mikhalko, he was afraid to run into him, even by daylight. It was as if he had brought with him something that was not good. "Don't laugh," Mikhalko said. "It's not a laughing matter. I know about such things."

And here, Sruli turned serious for a while, but then he was seized with a fit of laughter again, and all the curiosity that had brought him into Mikhalko's hut and had kept him listening all this while suddenly evaporated. He looked irritably at him and stopped listening to the old man's prattle.

But Mikhalko did not notice the change and would have gone end-lessly on and on with his tale now that he had a listener, but just then a voice from the kitchen was heard calling him. Mikhalko himself, being occupied with Sruli, did not actually hear the voice, but Sruli, eager to rid himself of the watchman, called it to his attention. Pointing to the door leading to the kitchen, he said, "Better go, Mikhalko. They're calling you."

Mikhalko left the hut reluctantly and out of sorts. He was gone for a considerable while and as it turned out was occupied with a number of errands.

Sruli, meanwhile, with nothing to do and with no desire to go back into the house, found himself, without being fully aware he was doing it, stretched out on Mikhalko's cot. He lay there in a stranger's bed, a visitor in a watchman's hut. Above his head gleamed the lamp over the icon; the hut was suffused with the odor of willow and dried herbs, of old sweat and Mikhalko's trapped breath. Imperceptibly, Sruli grew sleepy.

One should add that the weather outside was dreary and wintry so that everyone was driven to find something pleasing or familiar to do as a way of cutting the gloom. The darkness and the stifling smells fi-nally put Sruli to sleep. It was not long before his snoring could be heard in the hut.

Much later, when Mikhalko, done with his work in the kitchen and the courtyard, returned, he found Sruli snoring away; out of respect for the sleeper, he refrained from waking him. For a little while he stood quietly watching him, then even more quietly, he left the hut and went off to the stable where he performed various labors, freely and without constraint of any kind.

2.

When Moshe Mashber left the house that morning to go to his of-fice as he usually did at that hour, various things were pressing on his mind: first, there was Sruli, the sight of whose earth-colored caftan in-duced a pang in him, as if it were a sign that everything he would un-dertake that day would turn out badly. If he encountered Sruli by day, it presaged a bad evening; if he met him in the evening, Moshe could be sure that he would dream bad dreams that night; and if he met Sruli in the morning, it was a sign that the rest of the day would be spoiled.

And that's how it had been this time. He kept having the feeling that there was someone ahead of him continually scratching on glass with a diamond. Sruli, with his sidling walk, his crooked glance and his way of coming silently into a room without exchanging a greeting with anyone, was constantly before his eyes. And he remembered, too, the silence of his family the minute that Sruli had come into the room that morning.

Then, second, there was Luzi. A heavy weight on Moshe's conscience. He sensed that the quarrels and the discontent did not come about simply because Luzi had left the common way and chosen one that differed from what the world accepted. No, well-intentioned people could tolerate each other's mistakes; they could file away the sharp points of their differences; and one way or another they could make peace with each other's errors and still get on together.

No, that was not the principal cause, not *the* reason. The heart of the matter was, and Moshe felt this keenly, that his brother had taken a stand against an essential principle that animated and was accepted by all the world: that one had a right to struggle for acquisitions, to work for wealth, and to become wealthy without feeling ashamed. Luzi, who had heretofore been indifferent to all questions of wealth, who had never thought much about whether anyone was rich or poor, seemed now on such matters to have had a change of heart. It seemed to Moshe that Luzi now looked down at wealth, that he despised it, as if it was sinful merely to look at it—how much more sinful to take pleasure from it.

Moshe had become aware of this throughout Luzi's recent visit. It could be read in his glance, in the way he held himself, in his evident indifference to everything that was of importance to Moshe. Things which at other times Luzi had been sufficiently interested in to ask questions about, to wonder how things were going, and so on. This time, however, Luzi behaved like a stranger who was not merely indifferent but who, if one started to tell him anything, turned his head away as if there was no place in his ear for such information.

True enough, Moshe did not particularly care whether his brother paid attention to him because he, Moshe himself, had come a long way from those times when earlier in his career he used to stop at intervals to ask his brother, as one might ask of one's conscience, whether his success was honorably attained or no.

And those years, too, were gone when he used to pause deliberately between pieces of business as if he were restraining himself, as if he were saying, "Enough for a while." After which he would devote a certain time to higher matters. A visit to his rebbe or to his brother. The point was to spend a little time with spiritual matters, to remove himself from his daily business affairs.

Those days were over. Now there were no intervals between one business matter and another. He was so absorbed in them that it was not so much that he was occupied with business, but that it occupied itself with him. He thought continually about his work. He could not stop even had he wished to, and as it seemed to him, he did not really want to stop.

And his brother came as if to remind him of a sin, especially recently, and particularly with his decision to remain here in the town— a decision that he must have known would produce friction; he felt, moreover, that a certain contempt had taken root in his brother's heart—for him and for all the concerns that occupied him night and day. And he could not abide that contempt. The result, he knew, would be petty quarrels at first and later serious battles.

More than that, he had in recent times become aware that in addition to the expansion of his business ventures and the degree of respect his name elicited in town, and abroad, from merchants and financiers—important people of their sort; and in addition to the good fortune that had come streaming in on all sides . . . he had lately, and against his will, begun to feel a growing pride. A sense of ambition he had never known before. The sort of ambition he had never known before, that was new to him as it had always been, so far as he could remember, for any of his father's descendants. But now this ambition was intensified day by day and had become a sharer in his good fortune and would not abide opposition. And this ambition, he noticed, manifested itself in his business relationships so that no matter what the issue might be, no matter what it might cost him, he meant to prevail. And now his relationship with his brother seemed to be turning into a matter of honor. It seemed to him that his brother's decision to stay in N. was somehow directed against him, Moshe, and was calculated to irritate him. And yet he had these thoughts about his brother with whom he had lived in peace, and whom over the course of many many years he had profoundly respected, having indeed regarded him as a sort of rabbi—a spiritual guide. Despite all of this, his brother's decision to stay in N. he found nearly as oppressive (though it was not a comparison he liked to make) as his meeting today with Sruli had been.

These then were Moshe's thoughts this morning as he left his house.

He went very quickly through his quiet, unfrequented street and crossed the bridge over the river—the bridge that led to the upper part of the town. This time he did not respond as he usually did to the friendly greetings of the passersby. No, this time he noticed no one, neither those who were coming toward him nor those who came up behind him and went on.

He did not even notice the mean gusts of wind that kicked up dust at the riverside, darkening and bending the thickset reeds that grew right down to the water's edge. Nor did he take notice of the somewhat senile fisherman of whom at other times he was always aware and for whom he had some sympathy, the fisherman with the swollen legs and watery eyes who, every morning throughout the summer and well into autumn, sat in his leaky little boat in the midst of a thick growth of reeds, that very same fisherman whose income and whose life achievements he, Moshe, had added up as if the old man, too weak-minded to do the sums himself, had authorized him to do them.

Nor did he notice how he reached the street where his office was, and he did not remark the britzka drawn up beside the sidewalk near the courtyard of his building, a britzka whose presence ought to have told him that he had a visitor—someone who, on an errand from the distant estate of a nobleman, had left his coachman outside and was now waiting for Moshe in his office.

The visitor might also be some wealthy small-town Jew, some prosperous merchant who, having urgent business with Moshe, had started out véry early in the morning so that he would arrive just as the office opened.

On the other hand it might not be a stranger at all, but rather one of Moshe's own representatives, most likely his young son-in-law Nakhum Lentsher who, because he spoke fluent Polish, was often sent by Moshe to do business with the nobility: to collect the interest on old loans or to arrange new loans for them.

This time, as it turned out, the britzka belonged to Moshe himself and it had just then returned bringing his son-in-law back from a journey to the provinces. But unlike his usual practice, he had not driven it home but here to the office, all of which would seem to indicate that Nakhum's journey, too, had had an unusual result.

Evidently, Nakhum had brought back either desirable or very undesirable news which had compelled him to come to the office at once so that (if the news was good) he might brag about it to his father-in-law the way he usually did: at the top of his voice so that everyone might hear and take part in his triumph. Or if, on the other hand, the news was bad, he could whisper his justification, doing what he could to put himself in a light that would make it clear that if he had not handled the matter, things might have turned out much worse.

And that is precisely what happened.

The moment that Moshe came into his office, and even before he had taken in the presence of the usual hangers-on who spent whole days there talking to the employees or with each other—people like Sholem Shmaryon, Tsali Derbaremdiker and others—his tall, portly son-in-law threw himself at Moshe.

A word about the young man. He was ambitious and he took no little pride in the fact that his family over many generations had only done business with Poles. There was a certain prideful affectation, too, in the way he spoke Yiddish. Since he came from Kamenets he said *Ekh* instead of *Ikh;* and like everyone else from his semi-Bessarabian district he had his own way of saying the words for "long" and "went."

His clothes were a mixture of the Hasidic and the Polish styles. He was always impeccably dressed, and the way he wore even his weekday clothing distinguished him from Moshe's other son-in-law whose income equaled his. His short, restless nose was set in a face whose pallor was emphasized by his black little beard.

This time his face was paler than usual. When one speaks of a white face as growing paler, one assumes that it is because of strenuous journeys or the sleeplessness that follows the fatigue of travel. But that was not the case with Nakhum. His pallor was the result of something more than fatigue; clearly, something had befallen him.

One could tell this not only by the frequent nervous sniffing of his short nose (that was a habit he had even when he was not especially tense) but also by the physical impatience expressed by his whole body. An impatience which, now, prompted him to pace about the office unwilling to answer any questions put to him—or answering them abruptly, unwillingly, as he seemed to be looking over the heads of the employees and the hangers-on or swung his gaze repeatedly to the door through which at any moment he expected his father-in-law Moshe to come.

He, Nakhum, had in fact arrived just as the office was opened. Seeing Nakhum's anxious mien, Shmaryon, an early riser who was always among the first to arrive, sidled up to Nakhum and in his most sly-fox, flattering manner tried to sniff out what the matter was. He wondered where Nakhum had come from, which of the local noblemen he had visited, and how things had gone. But a quick look into Nakhum's eyes showed him that he would get no answers to his questions.

Nakhum would not let himself be led. He replied to Shmaryon's questions with vague, short answers and would not let himself be drawn into lengthy discussions. He interrupted the conversation abruptly, as if he had to ask one of the other employees something, when all he wanted was to turn away to be left to himself so he could wait impatiently for what was most important to him—the arrival of his father-in-law.

Then there Moshe was. At once there was the usual rush toward him of the office hangers-on. Some had important matters to put before him, others had no serious business but were regularly there because they enjoyed greeting an important businessman in the morning. But when Moshe saw his son-in-law's pallor, occasioned evidently by something that had happened on his journey, he hastened to extricate himself from the circle of clients and petty brokers.

As he approached Nakhum, the very first words that issued from his son-in-law's mouth and the strained look on his face told Moshe that the news Nakhum brought back from his journey was bad.

"Come in here, father-in-law. I have something to tell you." Nakhum indicated an adjoining room—the so-called Council Chamber where Moshe usually sat when he was in the office. It was there that he received his most important clients where, seated at a round table, merchants, noblemen or their representatives quietly conducted their business with him.

As they came into the room—Moshe first and then Nakhum—Nakhum closed the door. This was meant to be a signal to the others in the office that they, father- and son-in-law, were busy and did not want to be disturbed. Moshe turned immediately to Nakhum and asked, "What happened?"

But then even before he heard whatever it was that Nakhum would say, he recalled where Nakhum had been sent and from whom he had now returned. Nakhum had been sent on business a few days earlier to the nobleman Rudnitski, who some time before had sent a messenger to ask Moshe to send him various promissory notes that were about to become due so that he could pay them off.

Moshe recalled Rudnitski. A profligate, an exhausted wastrel who, it was well-known, had squandered the better part of his fortune. He remembered, too, that on an occasion when Rudnitski was pressed for payment of some loan or other, Moshe had, for the sake of the high interest the nobleman was willing to pay, and, too, because he was egged on to it by Shmaryon, or by someone else in the office, Moshe had lent Rudnitski a large sum of money, an impermissibly large sum and one that no one with sound judgment would have made. But the high interest rates had been irresistible and Moshe had risked the principal against his better judgment and despite the warnings of people who knew Rudnitski well.

He remembered all this in the instant before he heard and before he

understood anything of what Nakhum had to say. He knew that Nakhum's business had turned out badly and that Moshe, to the tune of
some thousands of rubles, had marched into a quagmire. But without
knowing any of the whys and wherefores, and with no clear sense of
any of the details (and because he was unwilling to believe his bad
luck as one is always unwilling to believe in one's own misfortune), he
said again to Nakhum, "What happened?"

"The Rudnitski matter—it's not good," replied a pale Nakhum,
turning to his father-in-law.

"What happened?" Moshe said again. "He's run off? He's bankrupt?
He won't pay?"

"No, it's worse."

"What could be worse?"

"Even if he pays, we won't get anything."

"What do you mean?" an enraged and baffled Moshe shouted.

"I mean that we've lost our promissory notes."

"Lost! How lost, how lost? Speak *words*, damn you. Where? When?
And how?"

"No, not lost, but we don't have them anymore."

"I don't understand you and I don't begin to understand you."

And it was here, then, that Nakhum gave his father-in-law a circumstantial account of the whole dreadful adventure, a series of bizarre events (bizarre even for one dealing with the nobility, even with a
nobleman like Rudnitski).

Nakhum said that when he arrived at the nobleman's courtyard he
had announced himself to the nobleman's estate manager and told him
that he, Nakhum, had brought the promissory notes that he had been
asked to bring and that he wanted a meeting with the nobleman. But
the estate manager had put him off. It was impossible just then. His
master had been up late last night with other noblemen and had not
gone to bed until early morning. He would sleep late today and Nakhum would have to wait.

When, finally, the nobleman was up and had breakfasted and had
sent for Nakhum, Nakhum could tell at once that he had arrived at a
bad time. The nobleman was strangely disturbed: he seemed not to
hear what was said to him or was unable to understand what he did
hear. Undoubtedly he had lost a great deal at the gaming table the
night before or else he was troubled by some other distress incidental
to the nobility.

But when finally he grasped why it was that Nakhum had come, he
became very excited. He treated Nakhum with great warmth as if he
were greeting an old friend whom he had not seen in a long time, call-

ing him frequently by name and using the honorific, "Pan Nakhum, Pan Nakhum." Then he put his hand on his shoulder, or taking him by the arm, he walked about with him from one room to another of the many rooms in the manor, turning Nakhum giddy with a stream of unconnected stories that had nothing to do with Nakhum's mission—the payment of the notes. He described in the most minute detail encounters with various people: how much time he had spent with them, what sorts of business he had transacted, what he had bought or sold or traded: a dog for a dog, a servant for a servant, a forest for a meadow, a meadow for a wood. Deals he had made with peasants or Jews or with neighbors of his estate, with innkeepers, farmers and with strangers. And how the deals had come out.

In the course of his narration, his manner was very expansive. He bragged that recently things had been going very well with him, that luck seemed to be with him no matter what he did. He said that the people who used to conduct his business, his estate manager and his steward, had continually stolen from him to line their own pockets. But he had exposed them and driven them away. And he had replaced them with new responsible men. Things would be different from now on. His financial stability was secure. More than that his fortune would grow and he would no longer suffer from the bad reputation he had had as a result of the wicked dealings of his former employees. From now on there would be a complete overhaul. He, Pan Nakhum, could be sure of that.

Rudnitski had been expansive and confiding. He had told Nakhum privately that, ". . . she, no doubt you know who I mean, who had gone back to her people in Warsaw, is going to return to me very soon . . . it's true that I have promised her an expensive present. In fact, the present has already been bought, and in order to pay for it, I have had to mortgage to some Jew, and at disadvantageous rates, a considerable portion of my oak forests—but what does that matter . . . that's a trifle. What is important is that things are going well. The critical thing is that they are getting better—as Pan Nakhum himself can see."

After that he dragged Nakhum with him on a long tour of the stables and from there to the kennels, showing them off and bragging that there was nothing like them anywhere, not even among the nobility who were richer than he was. He, Rudnitski, loved the horses and the dogs and was an expert in such matters. The others did not have his understanding; they had no feel for it and no taste and they never would have any.

And thus it had gone on till evening, from the courtyard to the stables and to other sights worth seeing. Finally he had brought him back into the house. It was already beginning to be dark. Rudnitski, fatigued by his wanderings and bragging, took Nakhum into his trophy room, on whose walls from top to bottom an array of weapons was hung. A small table with a mirror on it stood in the middle of the room. Rudnitski went up to the mirror and stared at his reflection in it.

Then suddenly he was transformed. His feverish braggadocio vanished and he stood, a figure of grief. He took a chair beside the table and ordered a servant to bring in wine for himself and for Nakhum, and when Nakhum refused the wine, Rudnitski drank it himself. He was silent now, cold, and deeply depressed. Nor did the frequent glasses of wine he downed warm him in any way, nor lift him out of the depression into which he had so suddenly fallen.

Then, abruptly he stood up, and with the help of the weak light provided by the single candle in the room, he sought for something among the weapons on the wall. Finally he found a pistol which he took down and then went back to the mirror. There he pointed the pistol first at his heart, then toward his open mouth, then to his temple, as if he were testing which of these places, if he shot himself, would give him the easiest and quickest death.

Nakhum, seeing what Rudnitski had in mind, stood there in a blue funk. Rudnitski burst out laughing. Nakhum, hearing the laughter, went up to him, and with the sort of respect one shows to a nobleman, especially a nobleman in his cups (as Nakhum believed him to be), and who was in addition very unhappy . . . Nakhum, then, tried to restrain him, saying, "Please, my lord, no more joking, it's dangerous. I beg you, you've been drinking, you could have a very serious accident. Please put the pistol away." This provoked another laugh from Rudnitski, but then his mood abruptly darkened. He stood up and holding the pistol the way he had before, he said, "Bankrupt, I'm bankrupt. There is no other solution for a nobleman."

Then he went quietly to the door through which earlier the servant had brought the wine. Rudnitski locked it. Then turning to Nakhum he said, "We are alone and there is nothing to stop me. I am at the end of my tether, my fate is in your hands, Pan Nakhum. You, Nakhum, you're a businessman and you know that these are critical times, and for me, Rudnitski, this is a time of crisis. I have no money. I have recently gambled and lost a great deal, and other of my affairs have gone badly. But I am not yet utterly lost. I have hopes of getting out of this situation. But there is no way I can pay these notes or any sum comparable to what I owe you and your father-in-law. But that's not what matters. I am a nobleman and my parents taught me that a nobleman may not survive bankruptcy. You'll have to give me back the notes.

Otherwise, I'll end it all here. You know, Nakhum, that I will never speak of the matter to anyone. The sum is a large one, and if it became known in the world of finance that you returned unpaid notes, it could harm you in business as well as in other ways. Which is why you may be sure that for the time it may take before my situation improves and I am once again in a position to pay my debt honorably and honestly (as, Pan Nakhum, you may be sure I intend) . . . for that time, then, the matter will rest entirely between the two of us and your father-in-law. But if, Nakhum, you do not give your consent, why then I have no other choice—"

And here he added a few words that were fraught with meaning. "But you ought to be aware that if I have now to shoot myself, it may very well produce very bad consequences for you. We are alone, just the two of us in the room: on one side, there is you, Nakhum the creditor, on the other, myself, your nobleman debtor."

"And you gave him the notes?" Moshe cried, beside himself with rage as he listened to this story the circumstances of which were unbelievable even in the world of the nobility, even among the most sanguine of them who were capable of anything.

"Yes, Father-in-law. And what would you have done in my place?" Nakhum asked.

"What do you mean? What kind of question is that?"

"Well, in your view what else could I have done?"

"Done! What done? You could have dissuaded him, distracted him. You could have waited him out. Or told him that there was no need to pay the notes just yet. That no one was pressing him, that no one would need to know about the delay."

"What if having done all that, what if, after I had given him my word of honor that I meant all that I had said, what if, after all, that his reply still was, 'Hand over the notes or I'm a dead man'?"

"There was a door, a window. Something through which you could have called for help. For a servant. For witnesses. You could have done *something*. You don't just hand over the notes."

And here, Nakhum, on whose shoulders there lay a heavy weight of guilt for having, with his own hands, turned loose a considerable sum of money . . . it was here that the scene with the nobleman rose up in his mind. He remembered the look on Rudnitski's face and the sound of his voice, like a dying man's, as he made his desperate threats. And how, as he spoke, Rudnitski had held the pistol up to Nakhum's eyes; and how he had stared at him as if he, Nakhum, were the Angel of Death. And he remembered how much more than money had been at stake; and that he, Nakhum himself, had been in terrible danger: first of being mixed up in a blood libel, or second (who knows?), he might have been shot where he stood. And so it was that, remembering all this (and setting the anguish of the lost money to one side), Nakhum felt considerable relief, the way a man might feel who had been rescued from mortal danger. And this was why he was able to muster the courage to reply to Moshe's further accusations. To his, "How, why, how could you?" Nakhum replied as follows.

"Listen, I know what kind of folk the nobility are. I know them better than you do and I tell you that you should thank the good Lord that it's only money you've lost. I can imagine you grieving over something much worse."

"Worse? What could possibly be worse?" shouted Moshe.

"I could have been killed and then you would have had to grieve over me. I'm a father of children and I tell you I know the nobility better than you do."

And here, Moshe, looking at his son-in-law, seemed to realize that Nakhum had perhaps a little right on his side. Still the matter continued to gnaw at him. His son-in-law stood there safe and sound, but Moshe would never see the money—the notes—again. And though Nakhum continued to reason that one could never know—the nobility were still the nobility—it was just possible that Rudnitski was not really interested in cheating him, that he might, after all, treat it as a matter of honor, that he would keep his word to pay the notes at the earliest opportunity—despite all that, Moshe felt himself seething.

He paced back and forth from one wall of the room to the other. Nakhum, standing in the middle of the room, heard him muttering, "Swindler, profligate. I'll see you in jail. It mustn't be left this way."

And then after being absorbed in this fashion for a while, and pacing the room like a caged beast, he returned again and again to the same theme. "But it's unheard of. Not once in a thousand years." And his son-in-law time and again defended himself or offered Moshe such consolation as he could. "You'll see, this isn't the end of the matter. The whole thing could turn completely around. It's much too soon for despair."

It was then as Moshe was turning over various remedies in his mind that a single sensible practical thought occurred to him. That was, that he would go to his lawyer, to his confidential agent to whom he always went when he was in a tight spot or when matters were especially delicate. That was the first thing that had to be done. After that, he would see.

And that was the reason that he made no move to take off the coat he had put on when he left the house that morning. He told Nakhum to leave the office, to drive home. Naturally, he warned him not to speak with anyone about the Rudnitski affair. And Moshe himself went through the door that led into the room where his employees and the office hangers-on were. He talked with none of them, nor allowed any of them to delay him. Instead, he went off to make the visit which earlier he had decided needed to be made.

For Moshe, the blow was a serious one. Another one like it, added to various other adversities, and even a man as rich as Moshe could find himself ruined. If not actually downright ruined, still, he could be seriously injured. It could be the first trembling of the earth under him. His reputation could be touched by it, and business people such as those that surrounded him—people like Sholem Shmaryon who hovered around him, endlessly sniffing and flattering him in their canine fashion, people like Shmaryon would turn away the minute they caught the scent of death and go off to hunt someone else whom they could sniff and flatter.

Moshe knew well how to guard himself against such folk. And whenever he had had problems of any sort, he had made very sure that such people were never given any inkling of them.

Which is why, now, he kept his face averted so that he would not by any chance have to exchange glances with any of the visitors in the outer office as he made his way through it to the exit door. He was determined to give them no opportunity to suspect anything, to keep them from putting to him their usual sly-dog questions, to prevent them from poking about and pawing over every nuance until they had plucked some kind of knowledge out of thin air.

He left the building and was out in the open when he remembered that he had been upset when he left home that morning, that he had had something pressing on his mind and that he had had various premonitions that today would turn out badly.

Luzi came into his mind, and then Sruli who irritated him even more. Sruli and his earth-colored caftan. And Moshe was assailed by a somewhat anxious thought . . . a wish . . . a sort of prayer: "It's still early, and the day has already gone badly. Please, God, let nothing more happen today."

This time, however, Moshe's wish was not destined to be fulfilled. Something did happen that day. True, it was not something that actually happened to Moshe himself or to any member of his family, but its results seriously and closely affected him.

It all took place in the second of his business places, the one situated in the middle of the marketplace. There he had a kerosene depot that consisted of a store and several warehouses.

That business was run by Moshe's second son-in-law, Yankele Grodshteyn (who will be spoken of more fully later, in another place). He was assisted by a man named Liberson who was at once a book-keeper and confidential clerk. The heavy work was done by two senior employees, Elyokum and Zisye, who were helped in turn by a boy named Katerukhe.

These three, then, were the ones who served the wholesale customers (there was no retail business done there). While some of them were local people, most of the customers drove their wagons in from the surrounding countryside to have their barrels filled with kerosene.

The three employees served the customers and they were helped sometimes by market porters when things got too busy for them. They hauled the barrels up from the warehouses, loaded them onto the wagons, arranged them, packed them in and finally tied them down with rope.

Elyokum, whose short, stubby fingers seemed to have only two joints in them instead of the normal three, was the strongest of the workmen. He worked quickly, with quiet confidence in his hands and in his guardsman's build. Always silent, always with the hint of a smile on his face, his physical strength was discernible in his eyes and in the high color of his complexion. He had, among the porters in the marketplace, a hero's reputation. They avoided a blow from his fist as they would avoid the plague because, they said, anyone struck by that fist might as well make his deathbed confession.

The second employee, Zisye. Still young, in his thirties, but already worn out, exhausted from being badly paid: a ruble and twenty-five kopecks a week. He was, moreover, a father of many children. And yet poor as he was he kept himself looking decent. On the Sabbath or on holidays, he was dressed so resplendently one would hardly recognize him. His trousers were neatly pressed, his boots were shined and in winter he wore the fur-lined coat that dated from the time of his wedding.

That, then, was the way he lived and that was how he raised his children. He was the son of a certain Kosman who had died long ago and whose children, even when their father had been alive, had been forced to leave home and take up service elsewhere—rough labor. And Zisye had gone to work for Moshe, to whom he was distantly related.

Zisye's cheeks above his neatly trimmed beard showed an unhealthy pallor. Though he was strongly built, and was still possessed of considerable power in his hands, he had been tremendously weakened by ill nourishment and by the heavy work that exhausted his energies, as well as by his frantic efforts to satisfy the demands of the *vokhernikes,* the loan sharks.

His wife and his mother, the widow Malke-Rive, often groaned inwardly seeing him come home late in the evening worn and weary. Because they knew that he came from a family with a history of illness, and that his own health was frail, and that he really ought to be doing some other kind of work, but they knew, too, that he had no alternative . . . no way to improve his situation. And that, finally, *vokhernikes* were *vokhernikes* and had to be paid; and that Zisye's employer, though a relative, was an employer just the same. And that one's bread was earned with hard labor.

That, then, was the second of the workingmen. There was a third. The youngest of them, Katerukhe, still a boy. A spirited, lively fellow. A perpetual wag, a prankster, a *hotzmakh,* as the porters and everyone in the marketplace called him. Everyone who met him felt compelled to pull his cap down over his eyes or snap a finger at his nose or pull off some similar stunt. And none of it ever bothered him. He was on good terms with them all. He had a snappy reply always ready and was quick to play tricks of his own.

He was a biddable boy, always at everyone's service, but he was most especially devoted to the two older workmen: to Zisye and Elyokum for whose sake he would have gone through fire.

On the day of which we are speaking, Zisye did not feel quite well the moment he arrived at his work. He was frequently chilly, and the chill was followed by fever. He had no appetite, not even for his sparse breakfast. Elyokum and Zisye did what they could to spare him all but the most essential labor. But sometime later in the day, when a customer drove up who announced that he was in a terrible hurry, and then stood over them insisting that his wagon be immediately loaded because he had to get home that evening . . . then all the workmen had to pitch in.

In the excitement, Zisye, who most of the morning had been sitting down, forgot himself. Out of habit—and because he could see that the others could not really do without him—he joined them at their work. They, for their part, taking this as a sign that he was feeling better, let him help. Why not?

They all descended into a basement warehouse from which they began to drag a hundred-and-forty-pound barrel. Using ropes, they started to haul it up a flight of stairs that had been splattered with kerosene. Elyokum and Katerukhe pushed up from below, Zisye and the customer's wagon driver pulled from above. When finally the bar-

rel reached the top, and Elyokum and Katerukhe came out of the basement dark and into the light, they found Zisye standing quietly there,
the loose rope in his hands, looking very pale.

There was something very wrong with him. He seemed to have lost
his powers of speech. His hands shook, his eyes darkened and he
looked as if he might fall at any moment.

Katerukhe ran up to him, and Zisye leaned lightly against him. As
Katerukhe led him toward the stairs that went from the warehouse to
the store, Zisye grew visibly paler and paler. His eyes were beginning
to close and it was clear that he had hardly the strength left to reach the
stairs.

And indeed when he did reach them, he simply collapsed and fell
and lay with his head to one side as in a faint, then he gave what
sounded like a hiccough. He opened his mouth as if he meant to vomit,
but instead there was a sudden gush of blood from his throat.

An alarmed Katerukhe cried out. Elyokum raised Zisye's head and
shoved some sort of ragged clothing under it to serve for a pillow. The
confidential clerk came out of the store even as porters and shopkeepers' assistants and passersby gathered around from the marketplace.

At first they stood, uncertain what to do. There were some who said,
"A doctor . . . send for a doctor." Others suggested that he be taken
home. There were some bystanders who splashed water in his face;
others said, "That's not a good idea." Fridl, an old market porter, came
up to Zisye and made as if to wake him: "Zisye, don't give in to it. Pull
yourself together."

But it was soon clear that he was beyond that, and the large crowd
that had gathered around him broke up now into smaller clusters and
drew away from him a little. Those who stayed near—the employees
who knew him best—seemed helpless to do anything for him. Seeing
the condition he was in, and remembering their own situation, they
stood considering him sympathetically, like animals gathered around
one of their number who has fallen sick.

Others having watched him pityingly for a while could not bear to
look on any longer and moved off to talk quietly to each other, to share
their feelings and add their remarks to the general expressions of
compassion.

"He wore himself out," some said.

"Our kind of luck."

"Yes," said a woman passerby who seemed herself to be very poor,
and who seemed to be reminded by the sight of Zisye's bloody face of
secret troubles of her own. "Yes, of course. The rich pour gold down
their throats while blood flows from the throats of the poor."

"Woe to his mother, Malke-Rive. He was her last and only support," said a pitying marketwoman with a knitting needle above her ear who had just come from knitting a stocking.

"Why are you all standing about? Why do you just let him lie? Is that the right place for him? He could die there," cried several newcomers.

"Someone get a wagon. Quickly. Don't just stand around."

It was then that Liberson, the pious confidential clerk with the well-groomed beard, who, cold and impassive, had been standing there as if he expected the unconscious Zisye to forget the blood he had spilled and get up from the ground simply to keep from being talked about . . . to keep from being pitied by strangers—it was then that Liberson, hearing the cries demanding that something be done, that help be sought quickly for the sick man, but above all hearing the name of his patron being mentioned in a not very pleasing context, Liberson, like the faithful employee he had always been, a man turned watchful and attentive by the very word "employer," a word that was dearer to him than the hairs of his well-trimmed beard, he, now, Liberson, pulled himself together and ran into the store where he went up to the cashbox from which he took several coins. Locking the box quickly he went back to the group around Zisye. There he spoke to Katerukhe who stood there downcast like everyone else. "Go get a cart, Katerukhe. Here's money . . . but be sure to bargain."

Moments later, Katerukhe was back with a cart. He and Elyokum grasped Zisye under the arms and, moving slowly, put him into the cart. Elyokum stayed behind in the store because there was still work left for him to do while Katerukhe was given permission to take the sick man home.

The crowd gathered silently around the cart until Zisye was settled into it, and even after the cart started off people did not disperse but stayed together talking over what had happened. But Liberson, the faithful bookkeeper with the well-trimmed beard, detached himself from the crowd and went into the store. There, standing up, as was habitual with him, he held the long account book close to his left eye (because he was a bit nearsighted) and made an entry in it: "A cart for the employee, Zisye . . . kopeck."

And it was just then that Moshe Mashber, having crossed the marketplace on his way in from town, showed up at the store. It was a place he came to rarely because he regarded the business as a secondary investment. Now as he came up he was astonished by the clusters of people before the store.

The animated crowd was suddenly still. Silently, people made way for him and watched his progress as he made his way up the stairs. The moment he got into the store he turned to ask the squirming Liberson who was hurrying respectfully toward him, "What's the crowd doing out there?"

A meek Liberson tried to reassure him: "Nothing. It's nothing. It's Zisye . . . he's not feeling very well . . . he threw up blood . . . and he was driven home just a moment ago."

3.

Certainly it would have been better if there had not been people gathered in Moshe's home on the evening of the day just described. Given his low spirits, he would have preferred being left to himself. But as it turned out there was a considerable crowd in his dining room that night. First, there was Liberson, the bookkeeper, who, sensing that Zisye's accident during the day would have further consequences, judged it wise for him to show up so that he could play his usual role as a yes-man.

Liberson moved about the dining room on the alert to be polite to any of Moshe's household, ready to agree to anything any of them might say, no matter how absurd. Meanwhile, as was his habit, stroking his beard upward with his left hand, so he could glance down at it as if it were a favorite toy he was caressing.

Nakhum Lentsher, Moshe's son-in-law, who had his share in the harassments of Moshe's day, was also there. Though he rarely left his rooms, generally preferring to spend his evenings with his family or busied with business matters, he, too, was in the dining room now.

From the look of him, he had not yet rested from his journey, nor had he recovered from the distressing conversation he had had with his father-in-law that morning. He, too, seemed to expect that there would be consequences of the events of the morning. It might well turn out that Moshe would have things to tell him about his conversation with his lawyer, or that Moshe might want to consult with him about what further steps to take in the Rudnitski matter.

The third of the people there, Yankele Grodshteyn, the second of Moshe's sons-in-law, was called the quiet one by the members of the family and other people as well. The servants called him, "the one in stockings" because his tread was so light. Even he, the very retiring Yankele Grodshteyn, who was withdrawn even from the members of the household, was present in the dining room. There he took a seat beside the silent Liberson and asked him for news of the store from which he, Yankele, had been absent for a considerable while that day.

It was a not unusual absence, since Yankele frequently shirked his business responsibilities to disappear from his work.

Sholem Shmaryon, too, showed up. This, contrary to his usual habit of avoiding evening social events. He preferred to pay visits in the daylight hours only. Then he could be seen and heard. And then all of his canine senses were heightened and he could sniff out the news he was seeking. Which was why he was to be seen nowhere at night. That was the time he was holed up in his doggy lair gnawing at the bones of the news he had gathered by the light of day. But this time daylight had not been sufficient for his needs and he had come to sniff about, to spy out the land, on the alert for every word or gesture, for anything that might be a clue to what had taken place between Moshe and his son-in-law in the office that morning.

These, then, were among those gathered in the house. In the kitchen on this occasion there were also Elyokum and Katerukhe who rarely came to the house except on a Sabbath evening, on a holiday or on some family festivity, or sometimes in the middle of the week when Katerukhe brought some market bargain Liberson sent which he thought might prove useful in his employer's kitchen.

Katerukhe was normally a cheerful soul who enlivened the kitchen the moment he came into it. He always had something funny to say to the cook, as well as to Gnessye, the kitchen maid, on whose vivid high bosom under her jacket he liked to gaze. Invariably, he made the same joke. With a sly look in his eye and his forefinger all but touching her jacket, he would say, "See, Gnessye, there's a button missing." And Gnessye would gasp and slap his hand away. Then she and the cook flung good-humored invective at him. "Plague take him. That bastard Katerukhe. He's turning into a lout, a good-for-nothing, a scoundrel."

But today neither Katerukhe nor Elyokum had come bringing a market bargain. And Katerukhe did not make any of his usual jokes. His face still bore the marks of seriousness imposed on it by what had happened that morning to Zisye and what had followed later when he had driven him home in the wagon, and still later when he had helped Zisye into his house past his mother, Malke-Rive, and past his wife and children.

Though the conversation in the kitchen (conducted, naturally in whispers) was about Zisye, everyone there was eager to know what was being said about him in the dining room.

There, however, Zisye was not being discussed. For one thing, the people there had other things on their minds. For another, Zisye's accident was known only to one or two of the people in the dining room. This may be because when Liberson came into the house and saw that

Gitl was pale and apparently still suffering from one of her daytime headaches, he decided, out of sympathy for her, to put off telling her what had happened to Zisye. Or else he did not say anything because he himself had forgotten about it.

It would be easy enough for him to forget, since, when he was in his employer's home, he moved about as if he were animated by springs. He was constantly jumping up to be respectfully attentive to some member of the family, or constantly ready to murmur something soothing to anyone who might be even remotely connected with them.

The people in the dining room were taking tea. Gitl had noticed that Moshe's dark mood when he had left the house that morning had turned darker in the course of the day. That something else had happened to disturb him in addition to whatever it was that had been troubling him then. At any other time, in a similar situation, she would simply have urged him to get to bed. But today and without herself quite knowing why, she did quite the opposite. She not only did not make any effort to get him out of the room and away from the noise and the tension of the presence of strangers—from everything that could exacerbate his situation—instead there came into her mind the idea, on which she acted, to send someone to ask Luzi to join the company at tea.

The messenger went off toward the more distant rooms of the house and a little while later not only did Luzi appear, but he showed up accompanied by Sruli. They came from Luzi's room where they had had the interview which Luzi had promised Sruli earlier in the day but which he had put off until early in the evening. The meeting had evidently taken place, though we will not give any details about it at this time because doing so would delay us for an unnecessarily long time. But we will return to them later on.

The two men seemed to be pleased with each other, though Sruli treated Luzi with greater respect than he received from him, as was clear when they came into the room and Sruli paused at the threshold and stepped aside to let Luzi walk in first.

The surprise, the astonishment, in the dining room was general. The members of the family wondered how it was that these two had met and what the two of them, Sruli and Luzi, could possibly have in common. They stood together on the threshold, their arms linked in brotherly fashion, making everyone wonder how it was that they had formed such a congenial bond.

No one that evening had remarked Sruli going to Luzi's room. No one had had the slightest suspicion that they were meeting. And now when Gitl saw them standing on the threshold, she had to restrain an amazed cry. Moshe rose uncertainly from his seat, and so did the other members of his family.

The two newcomers, Luzi and Sruli, took their places at the table. Each of them accepted the tea served to them. Because they were seated beside each other, it happened that when Sruli turned to face Luzi he had to turn his back on those who sat on the other side of him. Moshe, seeing this, was tempted to leave the table as he had done earlier that morning. The temptation was especially strong now that Luzi and Sruli were in an alliance that irritated him.

Gitl, seeing Moshe so upset, was afraid of that which she had good reason to fear—that at any moment now there would be a confrontation between the brothers, a confrontation intensified because it would take place in the presence of strangers. The situation was indeed so tense that Gitl could feel the returning pain of the headache which had receded earlier in the day.

She was just putting her hands to her temples to test the degree of her pain when a tallish woman wearing a shawl over her broad shoulders came through the doorway. This was Malke-Rive, Zisye's mother.

Despite the great misfortune that had overtaken her today—the sudden illness of her last surviving son, an illness whose seriousness (God grant him a speedy recovery) her previous experiences had already taught her to recognize—Malke-Rive had, as she started off to visit her son's employer and her dead husband's distant, and rich, relative, chosen to wear her Sabbath wig, the one with the part in the middle and the hair descending in smooth waves down both sides of her head. She wore, too, a pair of dangling brass earrings, the last remnant of her former prosperity. Earrings which no one was ever willing to buy and which in hard times could not even be pawned anywhere.

Yes, in the face of everything, Malke-Rive had worn her wig and her earrings. Because that's how Malke-Rive was. A remarkable woman with a tenacious character that had, especially in times of trouble, a certain masculine quality. No! She was stronger, more tenacious than a man.

Everyone knew her, everyone respected her—and for good reason. Because there was a diminutive Job in her character. Like Job, she had been assailed, but unlike him she had not been broken.

She had had to put up with much in her life. Survived much. But the set of her shoulders was steady and her step and her voice were firm.

She began having babies soon after her marriage, and with each delivery she shed a great deal of blood. Buckets of blood. They had thought her end was near, but once the child was born, her health was restored and she became pregnant again. And bled just as heavily

· 176 ·

again. The doctors regarded her as a phenomenon and gave up prescribing medicines for her. And midwives, too, gave up being astonished by her. She was Malke-Rive, after all.

She poured out seven sons that way into the world. When times were good, she fed them well. In bad times, she sent them off to work for strangers. But what sons they were! Tall, well built, graceful, with high-colored cheeks.

And that was where the trouble began. It waited until they were grown and then one fine day one of them, an eighteen-year-old, took to his bed. For a couple of months he was assailed by seizures of dry coughing, his cheeks glowed. Then he was gone. A second son had his two months of coughing and came to the same end. And thus it was, one after the other. The curse established itself in the house like an unbudging guest.

Each time a fresh corpse was carried from her house, especially with the last of her sons . . . the fifth . . . the sixth, even the most closely related, the healthiest of their kinsmen, avoided coming to the funeral. Because who could bear to see so much grief? But those who did come encountered Malke-Rive there, her shawl over her shoulders, her eyes dry. She neither wept nor wailed, but each time the moment came for the ablutions for the dead, she would accost a relative . . . by preference one of the older, pious men. Giving him a dry look she would say in a low businesslike voice, "They say there's a god in heaven. Well, what do you think?"

"Hush, Malke-Rive. What are you saying?" the man would reply, overwhelmed by sympathy for her but terrified nevertheless that she might speak blasphemy.

"Well, where is He, eh?"

And today, when they brought her last son, Zisye, pale and stricken, the hair on his face all bristly . . . when they brought him home to her she put him to bed at once and behaved as she always did. She made no outcry, but she shunted Zisye's wife and children aside and went up to the bed. She studied him for a moment and said, "My son." And that was all. For the rest of the day, she allowed Zisye's wife to attend to him and she permitted his children to stand around his bed. Then in the evening she retired to some corner of the house where she put on the wig and drew her shawl over her shoulders and started off from the distant part of the city where she and Zisye lived (almost in the third ring) and made her way to the other side of town to Moshe's house.

As she went through the kitchen she passed Elyokum and Katerukhe and then the kitchen servants. They said nothing to her and she did not speak to them. But everyone in the kitchen gazed after her as she went by and started up from their places, hardly aware that it was Malke-Rive's shawl over her stately shoulders that was starting them into motion.

The first person to see her as she came into the dining room was Moshe, who sat at his place at the head of the table. And he saw, too, how his shop people and kitchen folk, in single file, quietly followed her into the dining room as if they had come to see, as if it were a scene, in a play, how Malke-Rive's arrival would be received.

After Moshe, it was Gitl who saw her next. She, too, observed the train of people who followed her in and as usual when she was embarrassed or perplexed, she turned to Moshe for an explanation.

Liberson, too, marked Malke-Rive's arrival and was instantly poised to leap up to ask "How are you?" Not because he was himself interested, but because it was clear that her presence there was certain to be a matter of concern for his employer.

It was then that Sruli who, as has been said, was facing Luzi and therefore had his back turned away from the head of the table . . . Sruli, then, since he was looking toward the kitchen, also saw her. Sruli, with his alert intelligence, understood at once that something had happened that day about which he was ignorant. What it might be he could not guess, though he could read something in Malke-Rive's face; but he could read even more in the curiosity and the fear he saw reflected in the faces of the employees and the servants who followed her in. And this it was that made him get to his feet, that turned him completely around so that he stood entirely on the qui vive like a warhorse that has heard the trumpets sounding to battle.

After Sruli, the members of the household and the guests saw Malke-Rive.

Malke-Rive, who had had a long walk from her home, an enormous distance . . . practically across the whole of the town which by and large was badly lighted, except here and there by the glow of candles and lamps shining in the lower windows of the houses she passed . . . Malke-Rive, then, who had been walking in the dark, found herself suddenly in the brightly lighted, expensively furnished dining room where guests sat around the table drinking tea. The sight was in sharp contrast with the poverty-stricken, shabby and bare, though neat and clean room (for Zisye demanded neatness and cleanliness from his wife) from which she had come. It intensified . . . it doubled, tripled her sense of the poverty of that room which was shabby and bare when everyone was in good health, and was now by that much shabbier, barer now that Zisye was ill. Feeling all this and having the bright light from the chandelier in her eyes, she paused at the threshold for a while, as if unable to stir a foot to enter the room.

But then she started forward and made her way to the head of the table so that she might stand beside Moshe whom, it was clear, she had come to see and with whom she had business to conduct.

Everyone at the table lapsed into silence. Sruli turned completely around in the direction which earlier he had avoided facing . . . that is, toward the head of the table where Moshe sat. And Luzi, too, without a word to anyone, turned in the same direction.

Malke-Rive said, "Moshe, maybe you know (she did not use the honorific "you" because he was a relative, because he was the same age as she and it may be because she generally made no use of the honorific "you") . . . maybe you know why I've come. You know what happened to my Zisye today."

"Yes, I know."

"And you know, too, what kind of poverty-stricken home I come from. Especially now when doctors and medicines and the like are needed."

"Yes. Well, what else can I do for him except to keep on paying his wages as if he were still working?"

Clearly, Moshe was irritated that Malke-Rive, without allowing any interval to pass, had come to his house on the very day of the accident, had come in the role of a beggar asking for alms. Worse, since she had come she ought to have put her request to him quietly in private and not in this public fashion. Properly she ought to have spoken first with Gitl, and Gitl would have discussed the matter with him. And one way or another he would have done whatever it was possible to do.

With his very first words, then, he wished to cut the interview short. He had, after all, committed no crime. He knew what was the right thing to do in such matters.

But Malke-Rive just then was incapable of seeing his situation from his rich man's point of view. She had other things pressing on her mind. She knew perfectly well that her Zisye was gravely ill. She knew, too, that the loan sharks were unmoved by illness and that they would be demanding their share of Zisye's one and a quarter rubles per week. And that even if Moshe did not weary of paying the wages, there would hardly be money enough to shut the gaping maw of the least of their most pressing needs.

And Malke-Rive said all of this to him, straight out and in the full presence of everyone there at the table as well as in the hearing of the employees and the kitchen help standing in the doorway.

"Well then. What *do* you want?" Moshe said, getting up from his chair. "What else can I do? For my part, it's more than strict justice requires. No one is immune from illness. And if it turns out to be hard to look after Zisye at home, he can always be sent to the hospital."

"The hospital. Do you know what you're saying, Moshe? The hospital? You're a trustee of the hospital. You know who gets hospitalized and how patients are treated there."

"They are treated," Moshe interrupted, unwilling to hear any more, "they are treated as well as can be, according to the sums of money the community sets aside for their treatment. What more—or better—can be done?"

Malke-Rive made a movement that made her brass earrings tremble and her shawl slip down her shoulders. "Moshe, may the Lord never put you to the test. I have been tested, and I tell you that I haven't come here to ask you for alms, but to demand justice. Zisye took sick working for you. He wore out the last bit of his strength working for your prosperity, and according to all the laws of the Torah, you are responsible for him. And if there are no such laws, there ought to be."

"Responsible?"

"Yes, Moshe."

"Well then, what do you want me to do?"

"Do?" interrupted the voice of the bizarre Sruli who had not been asked for his opinion and from whom, naturally, no one expected a word. He spoke so clearly, so loudly, that his words rang in everyone's ears. "Do? Do what is necessary. What you would do for yourself. And if the trustees think so highly of the hospital, let them lie there for a while and see how it is for people in good health, much less for someone who is spitting blood."

This time Sruli's impudence was so unexpected, so dreadful, that everyone gazed at him as they might have done at something that had suddenly fallen from the ceiling.

Gitl stood up as if to defend her husband. Liberson, unable to believe his ears, also rose. Everyone in the room was tense. Luzi threw a glance at Sruli, a glance that made it impossible to guess whether he approved or disapproved of him.

For Moshe, then, who had had a particularly hard day—in the morning there had been his son-in-law's news, then later at his lawyer's from whom apparently he had come away with very little that might console him, and now this matter of the sick man and Malke-Rive and the employees clustering in the doorway listening to what was none of their business—as well as other people. And now to top it all off, this uninvited madman who always had an ugly effect on him, especially today, this Sruli, after such an insult, to stand at his brother's right hand—we say that for Moshe then there was naturally nothing left to do but to leap to his feet, to strike the table with his fist and in the sharp voice of a man who was rarely angry, to cry, "Out of here. Leave my house."

Then Luzi, who until then had not participated in the discussion and who apparently had not even thought of participating in it, Luzi, now, hearing Moshe's cry, was stunned like everyone else, first because no one could have expected such anger from Moshe—enough to drive someone from his home! and then because he could not imagine how Sruli would reply. Luzi, too, got up and, taking his place beside Sruli, said in a voice loud enough to be heard by everyone, "Moshe, apologize to him at once. You've humiliated a man in public."

"I! Apologize to *him*."

"Yes. You. Him."

"Is that it? I've humiliated a man. But that isn't a man. It's a disaster that delights in the misfortunes of others and it's long past time that he be driven from every home."

"How can you talk of 'driving away'? And from 'my house'? Since when is the house yours? 'This house is mine,' saith the Lord."

"Then you're taking his side? In that case," Moshe shouted, beside himself, "do you want me to apologize to you along with him?"

"Moshe," cried Gitl, understanding Moshe's meaning and the enormity of the insult to Luzi implicit in what he said. "Moshe."

"Father," his daughters called out, aware of it, too, as they moved toward him, toward Moshe, as if to prevent his rage from putting more such dreadful words into his mouth.

"Father-in-law," cried their husbands edging fearfully toward him.

And Moshe, realizing what it was that he had said in anger, grew even more heated, and turning once more to the apparent, to the primary, cause of his extraordinary violence, to Sruli, he raised an arm as if he had snatched it from the circle of his surrounding family, and pointing toward the door he again shouted, "Out of here. Don't dare to cross my threshold ever again. And," and here he turned to Luzi, "if that thing is a man, then you, Luzi . . . are no brother of mine."

"Moshe . . . Father . . . Father-in-law . . ." came the trembling voices of those around Moshe.

And amazing to behold, Sruli made no insulting rejoinder; he made no resistance whatever and said not a word—as was his usual manner in situations less serious than this one, when the insult he received was by comparison with what had just happened a trivial one. Instead, he simply turned away from the table, and his head bent he moved away from it and toward a corner of the room in which that morning he had left his bundle.

No one could understand why Sruli this time did not behave in his habitual fashion, why he did not show what he was capable of. Perhaps it was because what had happened was a surprise to him, and he had had a glimpse that other people, too, were capable of behaving as he did, of being unrestrained and insulting to the last degree.

No. That was not it. What is more likely is that he had noticed that in the very instant that he, Sruli, was moving away from the table, that Luzi, too, who had been standing there all the while, also moved away from the table and that while Sruli was busying himself with his bundle, Luzi, followed by all eyes, quietly left the room.

Everyone confidently thought that Luzi, because he was Luzi, seeing that his brother's rage was not to be restrained and knowing that any show of opposition to it would only make things worse . . . that Luzi, because he was the older one, had for the sake of his dignity chosen to leave the room and swallow in silence the insult he had received. At that moment, then, though everyone in the room stood as if transfixed, still a glimmer of hope showed in their eyes that soon, very soon, the storm they had witnessed would be over and its turbulence would subside.

But just as Sruli, who in the interval had busied himself tying up his bundle . . . just as he started toward the threshold, everyone's attention was drawn to the kitchen door through which a moment before Luzi had passed and through which he was now returning. With his summer topcoat on and fully buttoned, he was ready to go.

And when Sruli saw him, he did something that was very rare . . . something that no one could boast that he had ever seen. His mouth opened to form some sort of smile. And here, everyone was able to observe that every other tooth was missing in his upper jaw. And it was with those teeth, present and absent, that he formed the grimace of silent and vengeful pleasure that he turned on those who watched him; and when Luzi moved toward the threshold on his way out of the house, Sruli's grimace widened even more. He stepped aside to let Luzi pass, then he, Sruli, followed him as if he were his servant or the squire who carried his weapons.

His pleasure was even greater when he saw Gitl tear herself away from her husband and run toward the doorway after Luzi. And at that moment, Moshe's daughters, too—understanding the seriousness of what was happening, that Luzi was really leaving—started after him, as did others who were there.

Gitl was the first to reach the door. "Luzi, you can't go," she cried. "You can't put us to such shame."

"Uncle," the daughters called, their arms out as if they were fending off misfortune.

"Uncle, Luzi," everyone cried—Gitl, her daughters, the sons-in-law.

But Luzi, quietly and determinedly, without saying a word, moved Gitl aside with a gesture of his hand. She was first, then in the same quiet manner he motioned aside the others who tried to stand in his way. And thus it was that they left, Luzi first, looking straight before him, followed by Sruli whose grimacing face was turned toward the family. They left and disappeared from their sight.

One would think that that would have been enough for one evening. And that members of the family who had lived through these events might have been allowed a few moments of silence in which to deal with their amazement, their shame, unable to speak with one another, after which they might have parted in whatever manner and to whatever place.

But that was not what happened. What followed then was that at the very moment that Sruli and Luzi left the house, everyone—those at the door and those who were still standing at the table—everyone suddenly remarked the appearance of a fearfully pale figure, the glow of whose pallor seemed to reach from the darkness of the doorway to those standing around the dining room table. Someone half dressed, without a hat, someone who seemed to have come out of a grave, and before the people in the room had had a chance to recover from the shock of what had just taken place, a second shock followed. It was Alter.

It would appear that he had been in the room for some little while. In any case he had been there during the last interchange on the threshold at the time of Luzi's departure. He came in now, pale, exhausted, looking like a wandering sleepwalker, and as he came in he could be heard repeatedly whispering the same words, "He's going away, he's gone." When he was in, he passed through the cluster of people in the room and beyond them, and as he went he raised an arm as if he meant to catch a fly. In the same instant he uttered a sharp cry such as a tiny creeping creature might make as it was being crushed, then he stumbled and collapsed with a crash to the floor.

At that moment no one had a thought for Sruli and Luzi who had left only minutes ago, and certainly no one was thinking about the still-present Malke-Rive, nor about any of the events that had so recently taken place in the house.

Now there was a man lying on the floor surrounded by a circle of family and visitors who, in the first moment after he fell, stood about stupefied and helpless without any notion of what to do or where to turn.

Liberson, a visitor whom we have already met, was the first to pull himself together. Leaving his place at the table, he approached the cluster of people standing around Alter, and before any member of the family could move or say anything, he turned to Katerukhe and, speaking for everyone there, gave him an order: "Katerukhe, run and bring the doctor. Dr. Yanovski. Tell him to come here, at once, this minute. Hurry."

For Alter, falling was something new. In all the years of his illness he had never fallen like this. One might suppose that the strange events of the day and the intensity of his cries—worse than any he had ever experienced before—had so exhausted him that he had fainted. But no. Anyone with half an eye could see that it was not exhaustion brought on by the intensity of his cries that had made him faint. Alter was frothing at the mouth, foam flowed from it as from a fountain. And this was a symptom of an illness which until now had not afflicted him. A symptom of an illness which, when old Dr. Yanovski came, he identified, though only after much beating about the bush. It was a symptom of epilepsy.

"By the way," said the reasonable old doctor, "it is quite possible that this illness, which at first glance may seem to be a worsening of Alter's condition, will indeed serve as a sort of crisis, a sharp turn in the course of his earlier disease which retarded his mind. It may be that this illness will serve to clear his brain. Yes," he said, "medicine has taken note of such cases."

That night Alter was not taken back up to his attic room. He was left in the dining room because after he came to from his fall, it was clear to everyone who saw him that he did not have the strength to get up, that his eyes wandered confusedly so that he was not able to see or comprehend things even to the degree that given his mental illness was usual with him.

A cot was set up for him in the dining room. Dr. Yanovski stayed for a considerable while, and members of the family sat with him. When he was gone, they stayed on quietly, like mourners, until late in the evening.

This time, as always when remarkable things happened in the family, Mayerl, too, was present. He had been asleep in his room when he heard the sound of Alter falling and the strange silence that lasted for several minutes after it. It was that silence that had prompted him to leave his bed, to come half dressed to the dining room where his parents found him standing in one of the doorways.

And that night in another house at the far edge of town, practically in the third ring, on the Sands, in one of the rooms in Mikhl Bukyer's poverty-stricken hut, three men sat talking under the light of a cheap oil lamp. These were Luzi, Sruli and their host, Mikhl Bukyer.

We are not certain how this came about, but when Luzi and Sruli found themselves in the street outside of Moshe's house, they walked across the bridge that led from the lower part of the town to the upper. There, Sruli, after a brief consultation with Luzi (we do not know what they said to each other), called a coachman and gave him the name of a street to which he and Luzi wanted to be taken. They took their places in the cab and after much riding about from one dark and pothole-ridden street and alley after another, they came finally to their desired destination.

Mikhl Bukyer's family was already in bed. Sruli knocked at the door and Mikhl opened it. For the sake of his guests, Mikhl waked his wife and she put on the samovar—the tin samovar with the brass faucet. When his wife had done her part, Mikhl sent her back to bed; later, when the water in the samovar boiled away, he added charcoal and more water several times. And it was there, later, after a long, quietly friendly conversation and frequent cups of a poor man's tea and such food as a poor man could offer, that Luzi and Sruli spent the night.

VI

Sruli, Again

In the morning Malke-Rive's door opened and there on the threshold stood someone whom she would never have expected to see under her roof.

That was Mazheve, the butcher's apprentice who was well known in the Sands and in the town itself. He had, too, a somewhat ugly nickname. He was known as Mazheve the whore. He had a considerable reputation among his peers—the pimps and troublemakers of the district.

In summer, especially on Saturdays, he passed most of his time after work on the riverside meadows bathing or playing unsavory tricks, accounts of which were later, and for a long while, the talk of the town.

After work he went about decked out in the style much admired by butchers' apprentices: a short jacket, brightly polished boots, an embroidered shirt, and carried—it was a symbol of authority in his rough crowd—a leather riding crop.

He was handsome to look at and had made many a young woman of the town very unhappy, not only those who lived in the vicinity of the meadows, but others as well who lived outside the town. And those who had not been made miserable by him gazed after him as if they were anticipating pains yet to come. Nor was it only servant girls or simple workingwomen. No. Women from prosperous homes, young middle-class housewives, would cast swift glances at him as they were buying their meat from his employer, the butcher Meyer Blass, whose apprentice Mazheve was.

He had a certain calm energy. His roseate features glowed with self-confidence, as if he expected to be continually triumphant. Though he was clean-shaven, tiny hairs sprouted in his face. Generally he stood beside his chopping block, but his real use to his employer, the well-known and prosperous Meyer Blass, was not the meat cutting for which ostensibly he had been hired, bur rather Mazheve served as a sort of attractive sweet to entice the young servant girls who had been sent from the rich homes to do the marketing. While the other butchers stood beside their chopping blocks and meat counters with comparatively little to do, the crowd around Mazheve was always dense.

Mazheve served as a kind of advertising sign for Meyer Blass. A sign that seemed to promise much, it attracted the women to him, seeming to promise warmth for every heart as well as the fulfillment of every desire. Which is why Meyer Blass overlooked the thousands of scapegrace tricks Mazheve played and why he was not particularly concerned about the bad reputation that might come to his shop because Mazheve worked in it. What mattered to Blass was that there should be customers clustering around Mazheve's chopping block. Assuring thereby Meyer Blass's prosperity.

It was then this Mazheve who this morning had been pulled away from his work at the chopping block (though there was already a fairly dense cluster of customers around it), and who was shown which portions of meat he was to take with him, and who was then sent like an ordinary errand boy to deliver it to the particular address that he was given.

Home deliveries were simply not made! They were rare even to rich people's homes. Not even on great occasions when quantities of meat were bought. And, of course, such small amounts of meat as he now carried were not delivered. Especially not to the poverty-stricken houses built on the Sands.

Something was going on. But whatever it was, it was beyond a butcher's comprehension. Certainly Mazheve's mind could not fathom what it was. He was even more flabbergasted when he entered Malke-Rive's house and saw how poverty-stricken it was, and saw, moreover, a sick man in bed, surrounded by his children, and his wife doing what she could to look busy, though she had nothing to busy herself with. And the sick man's mother, looking very out of place and also doing nothing.

But his wonder was no greater than that expressed in the faces of the householders when they beheld Mazheve standing on the threshold. Then after a moment's hesitation he moved farther into the room where he handed over his package of meat to Zisye's wife, the person nearest to him. "It's from my boss, Meyer Blass," he said. "This is for today. He asked me to tell you that tomorrow all you have to do is send someone to the shop for more. It's already paid," he added, seeing the looks of astonishment that Malke-Rive and her daughter-in-law exchanged.

"For us?" said Zisye's wife, looking down at the package of meat in her hands.

"Yes, for you. From my boss, Meyer Blass, who sent it today, and he says that tomorrow you can send to the shop for more. You don't have to send money. It's already paid," he repeated because he could find no other words and because indeed he had nothing else to say.

When Mazheve was gone, the people in the house stared at each other: the sick man, and the children, too, who had never seen anyone delivering food to their home before. The children had no idea who had sent it, but the adults thought they had an inkling who it might be. Certainly it had to be someone who felt twinges of guilt, someone who, feeling compassion and humanity stirring in him, wanted to ease his conscience.

They accepted the gift in silence and avoided meeting each other's eyes. But finally the sick man's wife, in her role as the wife of a sick man, partly embarrassed, but partly also pleased, started off with the package of meat toward the little kitchen nearby where she meant to exercise her housewifely function in preparing something for the sick man to eat.

But she had hardly taken a step when the door opened just after Mazheve's departure and a second unexpected visitor appeared.

It was a prosperous grocer named Laybush who had his shop in the neighborhood where Malke-Rive lived. It was a shop in which goods were displayed in sacks and in barrels, and not in the way that the paltry goods (if they could properly be called that) were set out in half-empty paper bags and conical sacks in the hole-and-corner shops of that district. No, in Laybush's shop, things were different.

He even had an all-around clerk to help him—something rare for that neighborhood. It was a sign of his prosperity, showing as it did that his shop had so many customers that to serve them it required more than the help he could get from his wife and children. In a word, his was nearly a wholesale business compared with the others in that district.

And it was this Laybush who now came into Malke-Rive's house—and not only Laybush. He came bearing a basket filled with sacks. And once inside the house, he asked whether this was where Malke-Rive lived.

"Yes," everyone in the house replied in unison, but, as it were, more with their eyes than with their mouths.

This was the second surprising event of the day. It was apparent that once again they had been sent something, again some sort of gift. In their amazement they stood silently, waiting for the man who brought it to do something.

Laybush turned to Malke-Rive and said, "Good morning," as to the oldest person there, and also as to the one who was clearly in charge, more nearly the householder than the householder herself.

"Good morning." He pointed to the basket and to the filled sacks. "It's for you. From me—from my store . . . though you're not one of my customers, I think you know who I am; everyone knows who I am. 'Laybush,' thank the Lord, is a well-known name."

He was known as Laybush the Splutterer, because preoccupied as he was and always in a hurry, he spoke rapidly and not always clearly. And when he talked he continually turned his head to one side to avoid looking into anyone's eyes. He did not generally like to talk much, but now, because "Laybush" was, thank the Lord, a name well known to everyone on that street and in that district, even to those who were not his customers, now, because he, Laybush, had early that morning taken the trouble (though he had become something of a wholesaler who kept a general assistant because his wife and children alone were not able to keep up with the work in the store), since he himself, then, had taken the trouble that morning to fill a basket with groceries and had himself made a home delivery, like an ordinary errand boy, he wanted, therefore, to explain, and in his spluttering fashion to make all of that clear to the astonished family.

"Yes, it's all from my store, my goods, my basket. Will you be good enough to empty the basket? No . . . no. I'm not asking you for money. I don't want any money. But I do want a receipt showing that you received it all. And for anything else you need, you have only to come for it yourself. Or send a child for anything else. I don't want any of your money. Just send a note. A note will do."

In Laybush's basket, there was indeed everything that a household might need. Groceries of all sorts: tea, sugar, rice and other things as well. So it took a little while to empty the basket. It took awhile because, as has been said, there was *something* to empty, and second, because it would seem that when Zisye's wife bent over the basket and started to take out all of the packages and sacks, her hands trembled. No. Not "it would seem." Rather, it was certain that her hands trembled. Because even on the sick Zisye's face—Zisye, who had all the while lain quietly in his bed taking in what was happening in his house—first Mazheve's visit and now Laybush's—even on Zisye's face which had since yesterday turned yellow and which had dark, sharp hairs sprouting from it, one would have sworn that even on Zisye's face a tinge of color appeared; and on the faces of the children who had formed a circle around the stranger and the things he had brought, there was a look of joy and wonder . . . more wonder than joy, because they were unaccustomed to anything like this, so that they stared at their parents all the while as if inquiring if they might stare; and even Malke-Rive, who was, as should be clear by now, a strong woman—even she had, from the time that Laybush came into the house and had begun to turn over to them what he had brought—even Malke-Rive stood the whole while watching silently. Was she wondering who it was that had sent such an abundance, or did she perhaps know? Whichever it was, what is certain is that her heart was warmed by the event, not so much by the things that were sent, but—and here is the essence of it—it was because neither she nor her family had been forgotten. She stood there and cast a look toward the bed at her sick son with whom she exchanged a silent glance, and then compelled by the pressure of her emotions to manifest them in some way, she told the children to move away from the unknown visitor whom they had surrounded.

"Remember, then. Just a note," Laybush said when the basket was empty. "You can come yourself or send one of the children. I don't want any money. It's all paid for."

What happened after Laybush was gone is the sort of thing that sometimes happens in a tale.

Before Zisye's wife had even begun to put into their appropriate place the things that Laybush had brought, and even before the family had had a chance to consider whether they ought or ought not to discuss what had happened ("ought not" was the most likely answer, because that would have been Malke-Rive's established manner, and Zisye, after all, had inherited a good deal from Malke-Rive, including a considerable portion of her character), even before anyone in the room had had a chance to move from where they were standing when Laybush left the house, they heard—the children first, and then the grown-ups—they heard a fiacre pulling into their street and pulling up to their door.

The vehicle was instantly recognizable, first from the sound of its well-oiled wheels, then from the solidity and pace of its arrival before the house, much different from the sound an ordinary peasant's wagon would make. Above all, it was recognizable because a fiacre seldom came to that district and the sound of fiacre wheels on those poor streets was rare enough to seem festive.

It was a doctor who arrived. Dr. Boymholts, who had his own fiacre and who in addition to his regular fee for a visit charged the families of his patients a fiacre fee, just as if he had come in a rented carriage.

The doctor was a great scrounger and moneygrubber whom the town knew well and was not particularly fond of, but whom they called in more frequently than anyone else—because he was old and experienced.

He was the first to start his rounds early in the morning and he was among the last to return at night. And even when he had no place to go, he drove out in his fiacre so that people seeing him drive about would suppose that he was so necessary to the town that it could not do without him.

Poor people, because they could not pay his high fees, had no access to his services. As for his visiting the home of a poor person, that was unheard of. He was portly and tall and would have had to double over completely to get through a poor man's door. He had, moreover, a limp—he dragged one leg strangely after him, as if it didn't belong to him. Which may be why he was always in a bad mood. He was particularly irritable with the poor to whom he was usually rude and to whom he never repeated anything.

"I've already told you once," he would say gruffly if anyone forgot any part of his instructions.

The children and the adults in the house, hearing the sound of wheels, went to the window from which they saw Boymholts getting down from his fiacre right before their house and saw how without inquiring of anyone, he moved toward their door with the instinct of a doctor who knows where his patient lives.

This time, as always when he made one of his rare visits to a poor home, he bent low as he crossed over the threshold. Nor when he was inside did it take him long to find the patient. Boymholts went at once to his bedside.

There was, naturally, a rush to hand the doctor a clean chair. He dropped heavily into it from his whole height, then, shoving his lame leg into place one way or another, he started in with his questions.

What had happened, when, how long had Zisye been sick, bedridden since when, how did he feel now, was he in pain, and what was his chief complaint?

It was amazing! This time Boymholts, contrary to his practice when dealing with the poor—this time, Boymholts, as if he were dealing with well-to-do folk, took the time to make a lengthy inquiry of the family about various details regarding the patient. It was immediately clear that Boymholts was not behaving in his usual fashion—which was to look quickly at the patient, make his recommendation, write a prescription, then say something rude, after which, having been paid his honorarium, he left hurriedly without so much as a good-bye. No, this time his pace was actually leisurely.

More than that. When he had made full inquiries of the family and the time had come for him to approach the bed to look closely at the patient, he did not, as was his custom in such a case, he did not require that the patient sit up ... or if he was unable to do that, that some member of the family prop him up or hold him, so that he, Boymholts, could examine him while sitting down since it was hard for him, because of his lame leg, to bend over the bed. No. This time he made no such demand. Instead, tall and portly as he was and difficult as it was for him to make the move, this time he bent over his patient, though it required him to stick his lame leg out the way a rooster does with a leg and wing when it yawns.

His difficult posture bent over his patient made him breathe hard, nevertheless he listened carefully to Zisye's heart and lungs. He tapped his ribs and looked his body over, and it was clear from the look on the doctor's face that he already understood the nature of Zisye's illness, what it was he lacked and precisely what course of treatment he would prescribe to effect his cure.

He looked at Zisye a final time, and one would have sworn that it was not with just a doctor's smoothly impersonal look.

Then in that melodic, slightly hoarse voice of his that resembled a wisewoman healer's or a fortune-teller's, he started in as he always did, in the third person, "The doctor says ..." Then looking into the faces of the family, he spoke to them like one who was deeply interested in them, teaching them how to care for the patient, how to feed him, how to give him his medicines and so on. This time he was not sparing of his advice, nor did he wait for anyone to ask him to repeat any of it. He repeated it himself and then again without any show of irritation or fatigue.

Malke-Rive, seeing the doctor in the house and knowing that there was no money with which to pay him, gave her daughter-in-law a wink that was a signal for her to go out, while the doctor was examining his patient, to borrow what money she could from their neighbors. And now the daughter-in-law was back with the painfully borrowed money which she slipped into Malke-Rive's hand so that she, Malke-Rive, might pay the doctor for his visit as she accompanied him to the door.

But that, too, like the doctor's unexpected visit, turned out not quite the way they had expected. When Malke-Rive tried to put the borrowed money into the doctor's hand as she walked with him to the door, Boymholts pushed it aside. "It's not necessary," he said. "It's been paid. And should the doctor need to come again, you won't have to send for him. He'll know when he's needed."

A stunned Malke-Rive stood clutching the money in her hand. Her daughter-in-law, who had had such difficulty borrowing it, was also stunned and stood there, the words "Thank God," hovering on her lips. The patient, Zisye, too, who had not yet fully absorbed the preceding events, was especially overwhelmed by this final one—this visit of the doctor whom no one had called, and who had refused to take any money. Zisye was overwhelmed, too, by his untypically friendly behavior toward them, and by his promise to come again of his own accord, without being sent for. Zisye, who could not bring himself to say anything, turned his head away, unable to look even at Malke-Rive.

When the doctor had gone, the atmosphere in the house was appreciably improved. Despite Zisye's illness, despite the fact that so many troubles had overwhelmed the family since yesterday, there was, nevertheless—and this was a consequence of the various helps that the hidden hand had extended to them—an easing of tension. The first to feel the change was the daughter-in-law, who, when the doctor was gone, turned busy at once tidying up the common room, then pleased to have something to work with, she started to cook a variety of things.

The children, too, sensed the new mood. While they did not understand what was happening in their home, still, seeing the arrival of strangers, none of whom came empty-handed, they were grateful for their father's illness which, as they saw it, had produced the various visits and all the gifts.

As for Zisye, he said nothing, but in his eyes, too, there was reflected the same sense of relief that someone had offered a shoulder to help carry the heavy load that was oppressing his family. And Malke-Rive, watching her son . . . Malke-Rive, who was not much involved in any of the household tasks, Malke-Rive took up her prayer book and, seating herself beside a window, looked down through her spectacles the way a man does and began to read her prayers.

But before she would let herself pray for her son, as would have been natural in the circumstances, she wanted to express her thanks for the generous help that had been extended to her. Though she was a strong woman she felt herself flooded now with humble gratitude to those people who, distant as their lives and their circumstances might be (a distance that might have made it easy for them to forget her circumstances), had, just the same, remembered them. Just see how they had remembered! On the very first day and in such a fine and delicate manner: remembering everything that a household needed—food, support, medical help . . . everything. Without doubt the first words of thanks she read from her prayer book ought to be addressed to them—God, of course, should come first. But certainly the first words after that should be uttered for them, for those who, far distant though they were from her life, and who, though it was unlikely that they could have any understanding of it, had, just the same, understood it and taken it to heart.

Who?

They—Moshe Mashber's family. He, Moshe Mashber himself, Zisye's employer who had always behaved like the kinsman he was to Zisye and to his children—and especially now in their time of trouble. Certainly the first prayers of thanksgiving should be addressed to them. Of course.

But as we will very soon see, she had made a small mistake—Malke-Rive.

What does that mean?

Listen . . .

Had anyone seen Sruli on the street on the morning after he and Luzi had passed the night at Mikhl Bukyer's would have known that no one had ever seen him looking quite so mixed up, no one had ever seen him in such haste or running about so feverishly as on that morning. He had the look of a man whose business was under attack and who had frantically to liquidate a great deal in a very short space of time. As if he had undertaken something that required extreme speed, something that had drawn him out of his habitually slow and meditative manner and had made him rise early on that fine morning.

He was evidently in such haste that he had left the Bukyer house without even having time to wash.

Awhile later he was seen among the butchers' stalls, wandering about until he came upon Meyer Blass with whom he conducted a strange conversation. At first the butcher seemed not to understand what it was Sruli wanted, because Meyer Blass had never in his life conducted business of this sort. "Did you ever hear the like? Imagine, delivering meat to someone's home. And for whom? Not a rabbi, not a Hasidic rebbe, nor a rich man's celebration. Instead it's for some widow or other who lives on the Sands. Just who and what is she? Is she too young to come and get it herself. Why does it have to be delivered? And where will I get someone to do the delivering? I've only got the one apprentice, Mazheve, and how can I drag him away from his butcher's block at this time of the day when there are already customers waiting to be served?"

That, then, is the way that Meyer Blass expressed his puzzlement in the first few moments of the conversation as he stared at Sruli as if he were a man who was out of his senses, but when Sruli took several bank notes out of his pocket and paid in advance for a supply of meat for that widow for a whole series of days—equal portions for each day—and when Sruli specified that delivery was to be made to the home one time only and that after that someone would come to the shop to get the order . . . when the butcher had seen the bank notes and had held them in his hands and raised them to the light and saw that it was real money he held, money that could be counted, then he became considerably more understanding and gentler and what had seemed bizarre before became slowly, slowly, something that could at least be considered, though at first glance not quite comprehensible. Nevertheless, as he received the bank notes for Sruli, he looked him over from top to bottom as if he was dealing with a man who might be half mad.

The same story was repeated later with Laybush, whom we have already met, and to whom Sruli went just as quickly as he could after he had done his business with the butcher. Laybush, who was generally a bit addled, understood what was happening even less than the butcher. Explaining the matter to Laybush cost Sruli considerable effort and time during which Laybush regarded him as he would a madman. Finally Sruli abandoned words and explanations and turned to more efficient means. He took his wallet from his pocket and extracted from it several bills of large denomination and paid for several weeks in advance for whatever that household might need that could be bought from Laybush. And finally Laybush understood. Then jostled, harried and confused, he undertook to deliver the purchases himself.

Sruli had still a third struggle with the doctor into whose home no one would admit him or receive him at that early hour. Not even when he said he was there to call the doctor to a patient. Nor, even, when he said that he himself was the patient and wanted the doctor to visit him at his home. The doctor's maidservant, made suspicious and distrustful by Sruli's dress and features, would not let him cross the threshold nor would she open the door more than a crack, ready at any moment to slam it shut in his face.

It cost Sruli considerable effort and time before he managed to be admitted into the house and finally to see the doctor himself. But once that was achieved, once he was in the doctor's presence, everything went quickly and smoothly. Because the doctor was a singularly understanding man—especially when he was paid in advance for several visits and especially since what he was paid covered not only his visits, but a fee for the use of his fiacre as well.

On the evening of the day described above Sruli could be found in Sholem-Aron's tavern.

This particular tavern was in a distant, half-dark back lane not far from the Noble Market; it was in an old brick house built long, long ago—at the same time as the old fortress to which, evidently, the house had had some particular relationship. It seemed to have served as a town hall or to have performed some other equally important government function for which in its time the ancient city had had a need. But now that the old dilapidated fortress was unused, the house, too, was run down.

For the most part, the house was now inhabited by small and middle-level local merchants, because as has been said, the lane in which it stood had declined over the years, and because as has been said, it was distant and dark, not at all attractive as a place to live for people with greater means.

The old building smelled of decay, of primordial darkness, smells that came from its old-fashioned apartments, from its three worn and half-buckling stories. The corner bricks were worn away—gnawed away as if some sort of worm that ate stone and brick had sharpened its teeth on them. The bricks had lost their natural color, having passed from reddish yellow to dark brown. There was a door almost at ground level near one of these corners of worn brick, a door which led one by means of a steep flight of steps to Sholem-Aron's tavern.

It was a very old tavern. It smelled of antiquity. It had the sharp smell of soured old wine, of building and cellar damps and of air that had been enclosed for years. Because the only bit of fresh air that could reach the place had to come through the aforementioned door and down the steep flight of stairs as well as through a window set in a sloping niche that from outside the building was not visible at all, while from inside the tavern, not only could one not detect any light through that window, but it was rare that one could even make out the feet of passersby out on the street.

And it was there that Sholem-Aron kept his tavern. He and his only assistant, Naftali, a Bessarabian youth inclined to bacherlorhood whose beard was ash gray and who wore a long sacklike caftan that had no slit in the back and that was never buttoned in front. Night and day, Naftali was always busy in the depths of the wine cellar pouring wines from one barrel to another. He worked by the light of a single candle, and for the most part he worked alone, so that he spoke rarely whenever he came up into the light.

When there were visitors in the tavern, and at such times as Sholem-Aron was unable to handle all the customers himself, Naftali helped him out. When there were no customers and no work to be done in the wine cellar, Naftali usually sat rigidly in a chair, never saying a word. He was not interested in anything: neither the tavern nor what was going on outdoors. He sat so still that occasionally a fly would settle on his nose. He did not drive it away and seemed not to be bothered by it at all. On the contrary, he would stare intently at it as if it were the one thing in the world he was interested in.

Sholem-Aron, with his refined features, his milk-pale complexion and his well-combed, respectable-looking, longish dark beard, had the look of a well-bred lamb. He greeted his customers with selected polite stock phrases that bore the marks of frequent repetition. He served them and they paid him. There was never the hint of a quarrel, never the slightest wrangling even when some of his customers were drunk. That happened rarely, and mostly on a Friday evening when shoemakers who had delivered work to their customers and had been paid by them came in. Then as was usual with them when they were drinking, they turned rowdy and then quarrelsome until some of them were ready to do battle. Even then Sholem-Aron stayed to one side of the fray, refusing to take sides with anyone. It was only when things took a turn for the worse that Naftali interfered. He knew well what was required of him. He seized the most quarrelsome of the combatants and quietly hustled him up the stairs and out of the shop.

All that Sholem-Aron knew was the five kinds of wine he had in his wine cellar. His only concern was to keep those five kinds of wine from running out. He had no interest in any other wines at all. What were the five? Hungarian wine for the petty nobility and Christian government officials who sometimes came into his shop; Soudak wine for the knowledgeable Jewish merchants and brokers; Vymorozek for workingmen—and especially for shoemakers; Tsmukim, raisin wine that everyone in town bought for the Friday night Kiddush, the blessing over wine; and finally, there was "borsht," as he and Naftali called it, for those customers who were not themselves clear as to which category they belonged.

There was no one in the tavern when Sruli made his appearance. It was the middle of the week, so there were no workingmen there; it was also the middle of the harvest season, so there were not even any merchants present because business was slow. It was also the time preceding the great annual Prechistaya Fair, celebrating the birth of the Virgin Mary—a time during which the tavern was being readied to receive the grand and the petty Polish nobility who would be at the fair. Everything was now ready—what had needed to be mixed had been mixed, what had required adulterating had been adulterated—sugar poured, or water (boiling or cold) added, and Naftali and Sholem-Aron had nothing more to do. Expecting no one, Sholem-Aron, with a lazy look on his face, stood resting behind the counter while Naftali, on a chair near the entrance, sat staring at the flies that had settled on his nose.

At Sruli's entrance, Sholem-Aron did not even look around. The man was clearly a stranger and not, moreover, of the kind who might have engaged his interest. Naftali appraised him according to his clothes and his exterior and brought him a glass of borsht. Sruli made a grimace, but he drank it down. Then he ordered another drink, and Naftali handed him another glass of the same. But it was not until Sruli had ordered a third glass of wine that Naftali took a long and wondering look at this Jew whom, as far as he knew, he had never seen before.

The man puzzled him: first, because though it would seem that he was neither a businessman nor a merchant, yet he was able to indulge himself in a third glass of wine; second—and this was the heart of the matter—there was his manner of drinking. Sruli sat with his back to the counter, facing the window in the niche on the opposite wall. That window through which, as has been said, light hardly ever passed and through which one only rarely caught a glimpse of the feet of passersby. Sruli, as he drank his first drinks, looked out of that window; later, he turned his eyes away from it and stared at the glass from which he was drinking. At first he simply looked at the wine-filled glass; later, when his face had acquired a rosy tint—as usually happens by the third glass—he began (so Naftali thought) to talk to the glass itself.

"Na. You think it bothers me? You think I give the slightest damn?

D'you think for a moment I'm grumbling like this . . . d'you think I'm complaining because of the way that fellow insulted me yesterday in his house and before his family, and before strangers? None of that's worth taking seriously, because . . . d'you understand . . . I don't hold that one can be shamed by the insults of inferior people. And that's why I, Sruli . . . that's why I kept still so that no one might suppose that his words had any effect. Because if truth be told, who was it who was insulting me? A man who could not bring himself to confront a great injustice that had befallen his poor sick employee, and who, because of his petty merchant's pride, could not bring himself to apologize. Because if he had, it would follow that he would have to do something about the injustice—and that's something his rich man's heart won't allow.

"Oh, no, that's not why I'm complaining. It's not the so-called insult. But . . . I don't know what it is, but since yesterday I don't feel quite right. It's as if someone had turned my soul inside out. And it's all happened since I opened myself up to Luzi, revealing myself to him, from top to toe. Something that's never happened before."

He had exposed everything he had kept hidden for years, as well as the grief that gnawed at him for having concealed it. That deep inner grief which would not let him rest, that kept him from any sort of pleasure beyond the occasional relief he got from cursing. He had also spoken to Luzi about his money which until then he had kept hidden away as if he were forbidden to use it. And then having talked about it, he had had to reveal it, to drag it out into the light of day, and at the very first opportunity that presented itself, he had had to spend it, and he had indeed spent it. As he had today, for example, used it for the poor sick employee who worked for Luzi's brother and whose misery had touched his, Sruli's, heart after he had seen how Zisye's mother, Malke-Rive, had come to complain to his employer about their distress. And after that first occasion, once the sack had been as it were untied, one expenditure had followed another, of its own accord, and now here he was pulling money out once again, to pay for his drinking—something he had not done in a very long time.

It must be that there was something wrong with him. It might well be some physical illness. No, whatever was wrong with him came from the fact that he had let go of the discipline he usually practiced and he was experiencing a sort of spiritual relaxation, a lightness, as if a pocket had been turned upside down and emptied. He felt the need to refill it with something—with whatever might come to hand. Even with wine . . . even with such a bad wine as that which stood before him, whose foul taste he had registered on his tongue and palate when he drank his first glass. A wine that was making his knees bend and his head spin.

"Damn the stuff," cried Sruli. Raising his eyes, he saw Naftali, the waiter, with his long caftan and his graying beard sitting there with nothing to do, looking as if he were listening to all that Sruli had said and smiling, or so it seemed to Sruli, smiling at what he had heard.

"Waiter," Sruli cried angrily, turning to Naftali as if he intended to abort even the insolent possibility that Naftali might be willing to think, or was actually thinking, of smiling at him. "Waiter, take this borsht away. I ordered wine."

"Wine," said Naftali, getting sleepily up from his chair and moving toward Sruli with his hand outstretched as if intending to correct some small mistake he had inadvertently made.

"Something else?" he asked foolishly.

"Yes, something else," said Sruli casting a look at him from where he sat, a look that implied that another such mistake was impermissible.

By then, Sruli was already considerably affected by the wine fumes. One could assume that even if he were not given a different sort of wine, he would keep on with his drunken discourse, affected as he was by what he had already drunk. "What you drink / Shapes what you think." He would maunder on until, as some drunks do, he would become noisy and would have to be carried out, or else he would, as other drinkers do, turn into a drunken lamb and lapse into silence, his head bent over, dozing where he sat. But Sruli's case was not like either of these yet. Sruli, in fact, was still right in the middle of his drunkenness, so that Naftali, the waiter, could see that it was much too soon to try to cheat him—as he often cheated others by giving them the same cheap wine when well into their cups, they asked for something better. Sholem-Aron, too, who all this while sat thinking his lazy tavern keeper's thoughts behind his counter . . . he, too, did not think the time was right to exchange with Naftali an appraising glance about this drinker. Nor was he as yet concerned about whether his customer would pay his bill, nor whether he was likely to cause some other disagreeable trouble.

For the time being, Sruli continued to sit where he had been from the beginning, his face turned toward the window cut in the niche in the wall. Sholem-Aron stayed where he was and paid no attention to the drinker. And when Naftali returned with a better wine, he found Sruli muttering where he had left him.

Naftali resumed his seat as if he meant to watch a fly—or the drinker. It did not matter to him which. And now he heard Sruli talking, but not as before as if his words were intended for his glass, but rather as if he were talking to some living person, someone who was his equal and who sat before him on the other side of the table.

"I know," he said, "I'm a little bit drunk. But you've no cause to laugh at me . . . the way the waiter did. I'm not yet someone to be laughed at. I can put you all . . . you, and the waiter and the landlord and the tavern, all into the same sack and sell you—or buy you. Because I've got money—and not only for one tavern, but I can buy up half the world's taverns. I can prove it to you if you like. I've got the money here, in the wallet in my breast pocket. It'd scare you to death if you saw it . . . you and the waiter, and the landlord and the whole neighborhood—and the whole damn town. . . . If you could see . . . this . . . this packet that I've got here in my breast pocket, what a bunch of scared faces you would be, every last one of you, every one of you wondering the same thing, 'Where did he get it? How did Sruli come by it? He must have robbed a church, or maybe he deals in counterfeit bills.' Crowds would gather and some would say, 'Tie him up and turn him over to the authorities.' Others wouldn't believe that and would stand up for me saying, 'Maybe it's his, after all. Maybe he inherited it. Maybe heaven's been good to him. Who knows, he may have found a treasure. Or pulled off an advantageous business deal. Or a nobleman lost the money and he found it.' In a word, the town would have something to do, something to talk about. And the waiter would have work to do: to hustle me out of the place as a drunk. And the landlord would have something to worry about; he'd be so worried he'd even forget to collect for the wine I drank. Anything to end the matter. Never mind if I pay . . . just get rid of me. Never wants to see me darken his door again. Ha . . . oh, yes. Oh, I see the waiter eavesdropping. And he's worrying about being paid."

And it was true: Naftali, hearing the sorts of words the stranger uttered: "robbed a church," "tie him up," "turn him over," even Naftali, who was used to what drunkards said and who never paid the slightest attention to their words—even he, Naftali, suddenly sat up straight and turned an amazed look at the Jew who was, he could see, fully under the influence of his liquor; and he could see, too, that the latest glass of wine he had brought Sruli had weighed his eyelids down so that he had the look of a droopy-eyed chicken—Naftali, then, was suddenly frightened, and because he was frightened he uttered a sort of cough that was meant to be a signal to his employer, Sholem-Aron, who sat behind his counter utterly unmindful of any harm, and entirely unsuspicious. But that cough—the moment Sholem-Aron heard it—caused him to turn uneasily toward Naftali whom he interrogated with a look, after which he understood at once that there was something wrong with the Jew, the sole drinker in the place. Something very wrong.

He left his place behind the counter and approached Sruli, first passing behind his back so he did not see his face, as he had not seen it when Sruli had come in. Now when he stood near him he greeted him the way one usually did in such cases, "Reb . . . what, may I ask, is your name?"

"My name?" The moment Sruli heard the question, he turned toward Sholem-Aron, and before the landlord had a chance to look into his own face, he replied, "My name is the name I was given."

"Ah, well now," Sholem-Aron said when he caught a glimpse of Sruli's face. There was a caressing note in Sholem-Aron's voice, as if he were greeting someone he knew well; at the same time there was a certain edge of surprise in it, because he recognized Sruli, and, like nearly every landlord in town, knew his reputation well. He was, then, truly amazed because Sruli had never been in his tavern before, neither as a visitor nor as a drinker; and knowing about Sruli's strange public behavior in town and regarding Sruli's present visit, too, as strange, Sholem-Aron concluded that nothing very good would come of it. One thing, anyway, was certain: at the very least he risked not being paid.

"Well now. What do you know?" he said. "If I'm not mistaken it's you, Reb Sruli?"

"Whom did you expect?" Sruli asked angrily in the tone of a man who has been interrupted right in the middle of some important matter.

"Whom did I expect," Sholem-Aron replied, more than a little offended in his turn. "I only meant to say . . . that is, if someone means to buy something . . . well, he has to have money. In a tavern, too. That's what I mean. Do you have any money, Reb Sruli?"

"Money?" Sruli said at once cranky and half drunk, as he looked Sholem-Aron over, taking the full measure of his pettiness, his foolishness, the absurdity and the impropriety of his questions. "Money? Rich people have money."

"And that's why they're the only ones who drink. And those who have no money stay home. They don't come into other people's places and ask to be served. Money, Reb Sruli. One has to have money."

"Money," cried Sruli, getting to his feet as he put his hand into his breast pocket from which he drew a package of bank notes the like of which, for thickness, was rarely to be seen even in the hands of people who looked much richer than Sruli.

"Take it, carrion. There's money for you." Sruli waved the packet of notes under Sholem-Aron's nose. The landlord, seeing the money, was speechless. To see *that* in the hands of a man like *that*—he was unable to believe his eyes.

"Take it, carrion," Sruli shouted even louder. "There's rich people for you, there's money for you. Take what's coming to you, and may it choke you!"

It was already evening when Sruli left Sholem-Aron's tavern after he had paid him and had been followed by Sholem-Aron's wondering looks as he was escorted by Naftali, the waiter, up the entire flight of steps all the way to the door and out into the lane where Sruli paused for a while. He was considering something—or perhaps not considering. Perhaps, like anyone drunk who has just left a tavern, he was standing there to rid himself of the tavern's air so that he might be steadier on his feet as well as clearer in his mind. And when finally his face felt cooler and his vision, after so long a time in the obscurity of the cellar, had readjusted to the light, he started off toward the main thoroughfare where Moshe Mashber had his business on the second floor of one of the buildings in the Noble Market.

As we have said, it was harvesttime, when business was slow, when the town saw almost no customers. Merchants and their assistants, who had spent a long harassing day broiling in the sun, were gathered now in cool clusters prior to shutting their shops and going home. They were waiting for night to fall, so that there might not be the slightest possibility that a customer might show up. They waited, absolutely certain that it would not happen, yet they were driven to waiting by their mercantile consciences that would not let them ignore the least "maybe" or "might."

It was then that Sruli neared a shop that was directly across the street from Moshe Mashber's business. And in the way that was habitual to him when he sometimes stopped to look at a nest built into the corner of a window so that he could scold the birds the way he scolded rich people, he now stopped and, facing Moshe's building, assumed a rigid stance, evidently deep in thought and unmindful of anyone. He just stood there, his eyes fixed on the entrance to Moshe's office as if he was waiting for someone who was certain to come out now that the day was done and all the stores and shops were closed, as Moshe's soon would be.

He was waiting for Sholem Shmaryon or for Tsali Derbaremdiker. For one of these two whom he needed to see because he meant to involve him in some important business. The two of them were constant habitués of Moshe's office; they worked with him and helped him and were practically never out of his sight. They were the first in the office in the morning and the last to leave it at night. They were involved in every financial transaction, and no office business was conducted without them.

Both in the office and on the street, the two were always seen together, though they kept a certain distance apart. If one of them was on one sidewalk, the other was across the street. As if they were following each other's footsteps, as if they were afraid of losing sight of each other. Though they were both concerned with the same thing—with money, with interest rates on money—and though they both hovered around Moshe's office, finding him clients to whom he lent money, or from time to time finding him someone who lent him money when he needed it; and though they both drew their income from the same source, they were bitter rivals, like two hyenas who though tearing at the same body have their heads turned in different directions.

The difference between them was that one of them, Sholem Shmaryon, was a short, quiet, sly sort of person who kept his head turned continually to one side and who when he walked kept close to walls and fences as if hoping not to be noticed, or as if he was looking about for a courtyard or a doorway through which to escape from possible danger.

He, Shmaryon, with his pious features, was almost as deeply instructed in the religious texts as a rabbi. In addition he had a most remarkable memory for detail; he knew all the terms and times of every transaction: who had borrowed or lent money to whom and at what percent, who had repaid, who had not. And he knew all this not only about the local merchants, clients and moneylenders, but also about those in the surrounding region who came to town on money matters, whether to Moshe's office or to some other lender. Beyond all that, he knew by heart the current rates of currency exchange, as well as stock and bond prices—and not only the rates in the local money market, the local banks, but those abroad as well. He knew them all.

On the other hand, Tsali was his complete opposite both in his appearance and in his skills. He was as tall, smooth and straight as a planed board. When he walked it was in the middle of the sidewalk or more than likely in the middle of the street. He walked with his head high, as if the whole town was expected to get out of his way because it owed him something. And indeed it did. Because except for high-rate investments, he derived his income chiefly from usury, lending money to whomever: laborers, petty merchants and even to people without any significant place in society: middlemen, servants, market peddlers and so on.

He was crude in every sense of the word: crudely educated and with crude manners. Crude at home, in his relationship to his wife and children. And he was extraordinarily cruel in his treatment of those to whom he lent money.

The town buzzed with stories about his methods of collecting occasional bad debts. He balked at nothing. He would seize the last bits of clothing from some poor family, the last goods from some poor widow's shop. Nor was that all. The story was told of how he came to the home of a man who owed him money and climbed into bed with the man's wife and announced he would not leave it until he had been paid down to the last groschen. That's how despicably clever he could be—Tsali.

There was nothing of the scholar in him. Though his only son was a scholar, an enlightened young man who among his associates made fun of his father and was more than a little ashamed of Tsali's profession. And Tsali, for his part, did not hesitate to fling the most terrible curses at his only son. Because as he saw it the boy was a ne'er-do-well, an enlightened scholar who lived off the usury money his father earned lending money to the poor.

And now Sruli waited for one of these two. This time the first to come out was Tsali. And Sruli, seeing him, went toward him.

We don't know what might have happened had Sruli encountered Sholem Shmaryon instead. How would Shmaryon have greeted him after having seen him insulted and driven out of Moshe Mashber's house last night?

But Tsali was indifferent to insults and we are certain that even if he had been at the Mashber house last night, it would not have kept him from making any business arrangements with Sruli. And all the more readily since he had *not* been there, and more especially still since the first word he heard Sruli utter as he approached him was "money"; and we know already that the word "money" was capable of waking Tsali from the profoundest sleep, because when it came to money, Tsali let nothing stand in his way. It made no difference whose the money was, so long as it was obtainable. "Because," said Tsali, "money has no smell." And now when Tsali heard Sruli speak that word, he became instantly alert, sensing the possibility of business and though it was late—almost night, in fact—and though the place of their encounter was the very middle of the sidewalk, and though the man who stood before him looked strange and was by no means, so far as he could tell, a businessman, still, Tsali was more than willing to listen to whatever deal or proposal he had to make.

"I have money to put out at interest," said Sruli. "I want to put it in safe hands—in Moshe Mashber's, for instance. I'm not going to dicker over the rate. What matters to me is the safety of the investment."

Tsali, hearing this, gave Sruli a curious look. He was much taller than Sruli, and looking down at him, Tsali seemed to be peering into his skull to decide whether the man had lost his mind.

This time, even Tsali was amazed and could not believe his eyes. What he thought was that a man like Sruli would come to him to borrow some small sum at a high interest rate—a transaction appropriate to a man of his rank and station. If Sruli had proposed something like that then he, Tsali, would have paused to consider the matter carefully; he would have asked a number of questions and only then would he have asked for a pledge or for collateral. But instead—look what he had here! Sruli was offering to put money out at interest, and apparently no small sum either, and he said he was not concerned about the rate, so long as the capital was safe.

And this is why Tsali stared, unable to conceal his surprise.

"You . . . Sruli . . . You want to lend money," he said, half joking, half amazed.

"Yes. So what?" Sruli demanded.

"Where did you get it?"

"That's none of your business. I'm making a deal. You can say yes or no. If you don't want to do business, I can go somewhere else."

Tsali was perplexed, uncertain whether he should believe Sruli or not. He wondered, too, whether he might not be wasting his time dealing with what might be a madman.

Someone other than Tsali, we think, would have concluded that Sruli *was* mad. He would have spat three times, turned and gone away. Tsali, however, was, as has been said, neurotic on the question of money, and where money was involved was capable of believing the unbelievable and the mad, sane. Still, he hesitated for an instant and wondered whether to take the matter seriously.

Then to test Sruli he asked, "When can you bring the money?"

"When? Whenever you like? Whenever it's needed. Today, if necessary. Now," Sruli replied and reached his hand toward his breast pocket as if preparing to take the money out to show it.

"No, that won't be needed. There's no hurry. We have time," Tsali said, now fully convinced, as he put his hand out to keep Sruli from reaching for his wallet. "Not now," he said. "Later, after I've asked around, I'll get in touch with you."

"Get to it at once. Remember, I want it done as quickly as possible," said Sruli as he turned and walked away, leaving Tsali as perplexed as he had been at the beginning of their conversation.

We are aware that what we have just narrated will raise questions and create some misunderstanding.

How did Sruli come to have money? What sort of a borrower was he? What sort of a lender? What means were at his disposal, what secret hoard did he have?

Well then, in order to answer and to clarify, we must now return to that conversation Sruli had had with Luzi the day before—the conversation he had asked for that morning but which had only taken place in the evening, a conversation whose details for various reasons we refrained from giving at that time.

But we will now return to that discussion.

When Sruli kept his appointment with Luzi, he, Sruli, had the look of a man who had not slept at all—or who because his heart was heavy within him had slept too much. He began the conversation angrily, his head turned aside as if he were seeking some petty reason to wound the person with whom he was speaking. The moment he came in, he said, "I've come to you because I don't know anyone else in town. They're all a bunch of cattle, or as much like cattle as they can be."

That, then, for a considerable while that day was the irritable manner of his discourse, until finally his tone softened and he relaxed enough so that he was able to say, at last, just why it was that he had come.

Here is the story he told:

To tell his story, he told Luzi, he would have to go back a considerable distance in time. He had been raised by an old and very capricious grandfather in a village in Galicia very near to the banks of the San River. The grandfather had once had great holdings, and after that he had run a tavern much frequented by the landed nobility. Later when his grandfather was overtaken by the misfortune, about which Sruli would shortly have more to say, he turned all of his properties into cash and cut himself off from the world.

He, Sruli, had lost his mother when he was very young. Not that she

had died. It was rather, as he learned very soon, that she had "run off."
For his grandfather that had been a triple disaster. First, because the
old man was left alone, without wife or child, without son or daughter;
second, the running off was a dreadful scandal itself. And third, as
Sruli learned, his mother had not run off with a Jew. "Worse," was the
word quietly added as people looked toward the boy, toward Sruli.
What "worse" meant, the boy did not know. What he did know was
that soon after his mother "ran off," he lost his father, too.

His father disappeared from the house one day and Sruli was left
completely orphaned, in his grandfather's care and under his tutelage.

His grandfather's behavior, which had always been capricious, became worse after the flight of Sruli's mother. He withdrew, as has been
said, from the world. He went nowhere and received nobody in his
home. He had a little synagogue built for himself that people called
"the little synagogue for friends." There he and a carefully selected
prayer quorum of poor Jews whom he paid were the only worshipers.
He had a bathhouse built as well: "the bathhouse for friends" into
which only he and a few intimates were permitted to enter.

His grandfather used to spend days studying, but he spent even
more time just sitting in his chair with his head thrown back. Since the
chair was backless, his head rubbed a hollow in the wall which, because it was left unwhitewashed, grew dirty over time.

He, Sruli, lived in a room some distance away from his grandfather.
A room that had its own outside entrance and which was not connected with his grandfather's rooms in any way. Sruli was taught and
looked after by harsh teachers and unfriendly servants and chambermaids. He never saw his grandfather. He was never sent for by him.
More than that, the old man had evidently ruled that the boy must not
be allowed to come to him even if he wished it. And Sruli was aware of
this so he only rarely—and then only when his loneliness was too
much for the child to bear—violated the rule and made his way to his
grandfather's door.

On such occasion he would find the old man sitting with his head
thrown back against the wall, deep in thought, his eyes closed, his
beard upthrust. Invariably the old man sat muttering the same words:
"Ah, woe unto me and to my household. Ah, woe unto me and to my
household."

When sometimes his grandfather saw the boy standing there, he
would react with a start. His eyes widened as if he did not know who
Sruli was or how the boy had found his way to him. Then as he remembered, he would beckon the boy to him, and with a trembling
hand would make a hasty attempt to touch him, to caress him. But

then, another memory would come to him, and he would thrust the boy fiercely away, whispering so softly that only he and the boy and nobody else—not even the walls—might hear: "Bastard! Bastard son of a whore."

He, the boy, though he did not understand the words, was nevertheless frightened by them and went away until a later time when once again oppressed by his loneliness, he reappeared at his grandfather's door and was thrust away once more. Such scenes were repeated often enough so that they became etched ever deeper in Sruli's mind.

And that was how Sruli was raised—until his grandfather grew old and felt death approaching. It was then that he called the most respected, the most important, leaders of the community together. The very people whom he had avoided over the years because of his shame, the very people who, for their part, had pitied him for his misfortune and who had avoided seeing him so as not to intensify his sorrow. The old man called them now together to get their help in writing his will.

Beyond a few bequests such as are required by custom to charitable institutions, there was no one for whom the grandfather had to make proviso in his will so that everything else would normally have been left to the boy, his one and only heir.

But then, on the very edge of the grave, the grandfather demonstrated that he had not forgotten the shame that she, his daughter, the boy's mother, had brought down on him in *this* world and which he was sure he would be reproached with in the *next* as well. And so, remembering all this, he paid no attention to the opposition of the respected members of the community who argued long and hard with him that, after all, the child was innocent of all wrongdoing . . . a child is a child . . . and so on. . . . No, he continued to believe himself right and decided once and for all to disinherit the boy.

He kept repeating firmly and bitterly the same citation: "The offspring of a serpent can be no more than a serpent." Beyond that he would listen to nothing at all. Just the same, after the notables of the town had brought to his attention various citations from famous books which tended to contradict his reasoning and proved him wrong, he finally yielded some ground and agreed to accept the following formula: So long as the boy was a minor, he would, at his grandfather's expense, continue to be given the care he had had until now. On this matter the notables did not have to struggle with the old man overlong because he himself saw that as his obligation. But where he did not see an obligation, the notables had a much harder time of it, and finally wrested from him (or bargained out of him) these concessions regarding the boy: A specified large sum of money was to be put away for him into secure hands. But this money was to be his only—and this was a condition to which the old man held adamantly—if this was denied him, he would refuse everything. The boy would get the money only if it could be shown that he had chosen the right path—the path that the grandfather and the community would wish him to have taken. What this meant was that he would have to fulfill the duties and obligations of a Jew. If all that happened, then when the boy reached a specified age, the sum of money would be given him. "Why this condition? Because," said the old man, his mouth trembling but his words still harsh, "while it's true that I've let myself be persuaded by people who, having a better understanding, may know more about these things than I do, and I have yielded, still, I believe what I believe. I carry my misfortune in my heart—and, woe is me, I will no doubt take it with me to the grave. But there is no way to hide either from God or from men that the boy has impure blood in his veins, and who knows what consequences may yet follow from that. It's not my responsibility to help such a creature. But since I can't be there myself, why then let God and men, when they have seen what he becomes, be the judges."

And here Sruli wished to add in that regard that when he heard about all this—because it stands to reason that the matter was being talked about in the town and it was of course the constant subject of conversation of the rabbis and servants who came and went in his grandfather's house—when Sruli began to hear the various words that were continually being repeated all around him, words like "disinherit," "inherit," "money" and so on, it seemed to him that he was sick at that time; it may have been that hearing all that talk brought his illness on. However it was, he remembered that one day, hearing the word "money," he was suddenly assailed by a headache and a profound pain deep in his bowels, and from that time on the word always produced nearly the same effect on him—a ghastly sense of revulsion, not only against the word "money" itself but even against those who owned it.

It was then that he tasted the full flavor of loneliness, of rejection by the one person who to some degree could have mitigated it—his grandfather. And that sense of isolation was intensified in the last days before his grandfather died when the house was opened to all sorts of townspeople who came to pay their respects to the dying man, many of them people who had never been there before because of the isolated life his grandfather had, for reasons already described, chosen to live. And now that there was a continual coming and going and all the doors of the house stood open, he, the boy, also ventured one day to go to his grandfather's room. The old man was already far gone, but when he saw the boy standing there, the dying man feebly waved him off. Weeping, and at his last gasp, he begged, "Get him out of my sight. Don't let him cast a pall over my final moments. . . ."

Then his grandfather died.

He would not dwell on what he had then to endure because of the nickname that clung to him, first from his guardians and teachers of his own town, those appointed to look after his education, and then from their children, and then from the children of the town. Nor would he dwell on what he endured later from other of his teachers in other towns to which his first guardians sent him when they perceived that he would never be permitted to lead a quiet life at home—because of that nickname; that nothing good could come from his staying there, either while he was still young or later when he became an adult.

That accursed nickname followed him everywhere. It made no difference that he had a good head for study and that he worked hard. His nickname robbed him of his rest by day and of his sleep at night. Indeed, even his various talents, his excellence as a scholar, produced reactions from those around him quite the opposite of those elicited by other people with similar talents. In his case his brilliance and his skills were contemptuously linked to his shameful family background, as if his very quickness, his scholarly aptitude, were not achievements of his own but were derived from something outside of himself: his bastard's head.

His entire youth, then, was oppressed in this fashion as he wandered from one place to another without finding repose. His one dream was to grow up as quickly as he could so that he might be freed from dependence on those people to whom his circumstances—and his grandfather's will—had subjected him. To escape their spiritual and financial domination, to become older so that he could receive his inheritance, then he would make his way to distant places where his name was not known and where it could never reach. He would find rest there and finally do what he liked, think quietly about his life and what direction it ought to take.

When that longed-for time finally arrived and his dream became a reality, his joy was so great that all of his repressed energies exploded at once—and he got sick.

It was then that he was possessed by his fixed idea: that he must find his mother. Sooner or later he would be sure to see her. She would come toward him unexpectedly and would reveal herself. He wandered about half mad believing that every unknown woman he met might be his mother. When he was young, he believed she would be a young woman; when he got older, he imagined she would be older too. And the mania became so strong that he actually made several voyages to the region of his hometown and there he sought news of her from every possible source. He spent money on the search, but to no avail; and when each such journey was over, he returned home dejected and weary, as if he had been thrown from a very high place into an abyss and had been left to lie for a long time like a sack of broken bones. Until finally that mood passed and he gathered his strength once more, only to be seized again by the same dream, which once again he believed he could turn into reality.

And this process was repeated several times until overwhelmed by despair—he forgot her.

And it was then that he was seized by his second fixation. It was the same one that he had as a boy when he was nauseated by the talk of wills and money while he was yet living in his grandfather's house. He found that the very least reference to money induced the same nausea, but this time with greater force.

And so he had made a vow. He swore that he would renounce the use of the money he owned and any money he might own, and that he would take no personal pleasure from having it, and that he would not please himself by using it to help others.

It was then, too, in middle life that he changed direction. By then, given his education and attainments, he might have chosen to follow the beaten path taken by people like himself: he might have become a scholar and linked his life with that of other scholars—with rabbis, for instance. Particularly since he had a fairly tidy fortune of his own, which, as everyone knows, is useful to anyone who wants a career in scholarship.

But he had chosen not to do that. In fact, he chose to descend—steeply. He felt himself being pulled downward. And then—it was pure accident—he had a friend who pointed the way for him. He, Sruli, was not quite sure how it all came about—he hardly noticed it at the time—and it was as if it had happened while he was asleep, while he was dreaming, however it was, there he was. . . .

Where? Why, there where someone of his rank and circumstance was seldom to be found, in the sort of place that a man of his birth and education (first at his grandfather's house and later in the care of his teachers) might only be expected to imagine . . . in *shefel hamadrege*—at a low level. No, lower than the low.

How did he come to be there and why did he stay there so long? Perhaps because there nobody tormented him with reference to his birth, as had happened so often among his peers. No one paid the slightest attention to his past or to his rank. They had no interest in such matters, and if occasionally someone among them did know about his birth, it was regarded as a small blemish. Because they were all like that. Besides, they had all seen worse. Perhaps that was it—in any case, he felt at ease among them, relaxed and not hemmed in by those constrictions which the rest of the world (with the exception of the people among whom he now was) found it necessary to impose on their relationships with each other—and with God.

He felt so comfortable among them that he had had no difficulty accepting work as a waiter in a tavern where simple peasants and Christian townspeople drank and were made drunk, and where they were taken advantage of by the tavern keeper as well as by the waiters who played dirty tricks on them without compunction—robbery included.

Nor had he, Sruli, after his work in the tavern, hesitated to join a group that wandered about from courtyard to courtyard. One of them played a fiddle and Sruli played a flute, which he had been taught to play and to play well by some hole-and-corner band. His companions were both Jews and non-Jews: Hungarians, Moldavians, as well as others. At the beginning he wandered with them through his homeland; later he sneaked across borders to continue his wanderings in foreign lands.

He was then in the first flush of his youth. And it was clear to him that he could not obey the usual advice: Turn eighteen, become a groom. That was for people who lived normal, rooted and approved lives. By then his mode of life was far from normal. He lived among people for whom laws were neither impediment nor restraint. He had violated every rule and had committed the most unspeakable of sins. Indeed, he had reached such a pass that he was no longer able to recognize sins for what they were and committed them in all innocence, without thinking about them, without being aware that others behaved differently, without remembering that he had only recently abandoned teachings in which he had been deeply instructed, and that while he was under their sway it had never even occurred to him that it was within the range of human nature for anyone to do the things he was now doing.

In a word, he had gone a long way downward. So far indeed that when he became aware of what he had become, one day, after a particularly ugly episode, he found himself cursing his mother and the day of his birth; and there sprang to his lips those words with which his grandfather used to greet him when as a boy he came to the old man's room: "Bastard. Bastard son of a whore."

Yes, he had to confess that throughout that whole period of his life, he had felt regarding himself the same sort of feelings that had kept his grandfather from acknowledging him when he saw him—that is to say, it was those feelings that had caused him to make such a sharp, unregretful and violent break with the past, and with the man that his heritage, education and training had made him. It was those feelings that had plunged him into a wild, unbridled manner of life. What he meant to say was that he blamed it all on the circumstances of his birth and on the blood he had inherited.

He felt, too, that he had to justify this sudden change in his life, and the best way he knew to justify it was to sink deeper and deeper into his situation, to sink into it over his head until he forgot completely that he had ever known anything else.

And that, then, is what he did. Until one day he stopped. And just as he could not explain the circumstances that had started him on his downward track, so he could not explain what caused his return to his former condition.

He only knew that there came a day on which he parted from his low companions and became again what he had been. And that he returned to that station in life which some while ago he had abandoned—and that the whole interval of his absence was simply wiped from his memory.

The experience had left him completely unmarked. He brought nothing back from the lower regions: there was no spot, no sign, no gesture. It was as if he had never been there. No one noticed any change in him: neither intimates nor strangers. No one, not even himself. When he spoke to those he had known before he left, his speech was as it had always been. So that no one expressed any suspicion about what he had done during the time he had been away. Had anyone had the least inkling of it, he would certainly not have been received in any home nor would anyone have had the slightest dealings with him.

They did not notice because having left his companions, he did not return to the place from which he had come. No, he made his way to a different town, to a place where he was completely unknown, where no one had or could have the slightest knowledge of his recent—or his distant—past. And there he was received as an equal among equals, as a good scholar who was, in addition, a quite presentable man whose thought and behavior were in no way suspicious. So that there was no reason why he should not be treated any differently from anyone else.

Later, however, he slipped once more. He had observed himself growing quarrelsome in a way that made his gorge rise, that made him gag, that drove him to leave those who thought of him as one of themselves and to reject, with words or deeds, things which had been believed and venerated for generations.

Naturally enough, persecution followed. And so he left and began a wandering life, but wherever he went he attracted persecution—and for the same reasons. In some places things became so bad that he was regarded as a sort of cancerous growth, or as a corrupter of the community, a man at war with it, and who not content with that was willing to betray the people of his own faith to strangers. So that finally he was excommunicated and declared a target of attack—even of assassination.

And it was true that driven by rage he had gone almost as far as denunciation. On one occasion, he became closely acquainted with a priest, and things had progressed so far between them that the fears his grandfather had had about him and which had caused him to want to disinherit him—those fears were nearly realized.

But at the last moment he realized what he was doing and terrified went off on a quite opposite course of behavior. He visited the courts of renowned rabbis who at that time lived in his region. He stayed among them for some while and did everything he could that might make it possible for him to join those who warmed themselves at those fires of faith; he tried his best to believe with them, to avoid thinking too deeply and to avoid noticing those things which none of the faithful ever noticed.

But he could not do it. From some of those courts he was driven away with anger, from others, with worse. And in one of the courts he visited last, he was treated like a madman. That came about because he had seen a terrible sin committed. A number of respected and well-known rabbis who were anxious to seem serviceable to the rabbi who presided over the court gave a false interpretation of a particular ritual rule, twisting and turning its meaning in a way that was absolutely unauthorized. When he, Sruli, interposed and revealed the falsification, demonstrating with a thousand citations that the rule had a completely opposite meaning, the rabbi's intimates saw no other way to deal with the situation than to declare him, Sruli, mad. And that's what they did. He was tied and thrust into a dark room where he stayed for a long while.

Finally he left that place too. By then he was somewhat older. And yet he did not have a house of his own; he was not married and had no children. Well, yes. He had been married and then divorced. He had tried many professions and given them up, learned many trades and abandoned them. And strange to say, never in all that time did it occur to him to break his vow regarding his money. In fact, the thought never occurred to him because he behaved as if he did not have it. He carried his fortune with him from town to town and wherever he came, he saw to it that it was put somewhere in a safe place—and that was that. He thought no more about it, and it was as if it had never existed.

And everywhere he went, he tried to find someone in whom he could confide, to whom he could pour out his heart, but no matter whom he chose as a confidant, he was always left disappointed and defeated. Because if it happened that he, Sruli, made the slightest reference to his own origins, the man would look at him as if he were a leper, as if it was dangerous to be near him, as if it was necessary to put space between them if he was to save his life and soul.

And so Sruli concluded to have nothing more to do with anyone. And the only thing that from time to time still gave him any pleasure was—sometimes silently, sometimes aloud—to indulge himself in curses.

It was then that his third illness came upon him. What he meant by that was the personage—a sort of dybbuk, a reincarnated spirit, who was seated opposite him one day at a banquet table. A ragged, barefoot fellow who reminded him of the sorts of people with whom he had lived during his wastrel and poverty-stricken days.

The man appeared unexpectedly and Sruli, seeing him, rubbed his eyes, unsure whether he was really seeing him. And when it was clear that he was, he became thoroughly frightened. He spat as one does when one sees a ghost or after waking from a nightmare. But the spitting did not make the man disappear. He continued to sit calmly as he had from the beginning, and looked quietly at Sruli. Later he talked with Sruli and then little by little insinuated himself into his friendship.

From that time on he became an inseparable companion, sharing Sruli's life whether for good or ill, until finally Sruli became so accustomed to his presence that on those occasions when the creature was absent for a while, Sruli missed him and found himself yearning for his friendship.

That creature put a number of inchoate ideas into Sruli's head and prompted him to various undertakings, some of them good, others evil. One of his most recent suggestions had been for him, Sruli, to come before Luzi, to confide in him.

Certainly he, Sruli, knew that the creature was a manifestation of an illness and that one could not base anything on such an apparition, and yet he was grateful to the creature because he had not abandoned him to loneliness, and had roused him from lethargy, spurred him on. And it was because of him that he, Sruli, had been prompted to approach

Luzi and to confide in him those matters that pressed on his heart—including the following matter:

He, Sruli, needed to find some sustaining strength, someone to lean on. It was painful to live with both wallet and soul tightly bound. Lately he had had frequent thoughts of breaking his vow about money and to make use of it—either for himself or for others . . . which of the two he was himself not quite sure. And so he was seeking a relationship with someone stronger than himself, someone who would counsel and direct him, and—here Luzi must pardon him—Sruli thought that Luzi had the sort of strength he sought. He wanted to turn himself and all that he had over to Luzi—to do whatever Luzi might want, to go in whatever direction Luzi might indicate. If that meant toward faith, then faith it would be. If toward impiety, then so be it. It depended on Luzi, and if Luzi did not guide him he feared that he would move again toward some disaster: drunkenness, perhaps—and here he had to confess that in this regard (drunkenness) he had indulged himself considerably lately and had already broken his vows about money for the sake of drink.

We will not pause here to describe how Luzi regarded Sruli after he had heard his confession, nor will we repeat what he said. Whether indeed he said anything, whether he consoled him, or whether he guided him in some new direction—as sometimes happens in such cases—is not our concern nor is it essentially related to what has been described above.

It will, however, be necessary to remind the reader that it was shortly after that conversation had taken place that someone was sent from Moshe Mashber's dining room to Luzi's chamber to invite Luzi to join the family at tea, and that he had come accompanied unexpectedly by Sruli with whom he seemed now to be intimate, as if they shared some understanding. And that Luzi's brother Moshe, we will recall, observing that intimacy was irritated by it, and that irritation was no doubt an additional provocation to the quarrel that then erupted between the brothers, So that, keeping all this in mind, we may conclude that Luzi had *not* rejected Sruli as Sruli had been rejected by so many others, and that indeed he had evoked Luzi's compassion. But we will learn later, in the narration of events to which we now turn, whether that sympathy was of long or short duration, whether it was lasting or ephemeral.

VII

The Prechistaya Fair

At any other time, the town would have been abuzz with the news. Just think of it, the famous Luzi Mashber, who could have been the pride and the adornment of any Hasidic community of his choice—including the finest and the best known—had unexpectedly turned from his path, had lowered himself to join those who had neither reputation nor numbers, yes ... people of no importance, of whom no one spoke or who if they were spoken of, it was in tones of scorn and contempt such as one might expect would be used toward a people that kept itself at such a distance from the community that it was all but forbidden for anyone in the Hasidic world to intermarry with them.

Just think of it. Luzi among the Bratslaver. A fact that had already occasioned a quarrel between himself and his brother Moshe. And what a quarrel! That brothers should part over what was not even a family matter. The town had never seen anything like it. That a younger brother, Moshe, should so shame his older brother, Luzi, that he in reaction had abruptly and insultingly left his brother's house and that before the eyes of the entire family as well as strangers (and before the eyes of the town which soon learned of it ... as was only to be expected). Left it by night, as one might leave a ruin that was on the verge of collapse.

It was unheard of. And as if that were not all, he had left the house with that strange fellow, that Sruli, in whose company nobody, nobody at all, was ever to be seen and with whom nobody at all had the slightest thing in common. A man who shared no common path with anyone, and who was nobody's friend, nobody's comrade. And now just think of it, he who was *nobody's* friend was suddenly *Luzi's*. And such intimacy between them, such closeness that Luzi had felt obliged to defend Sruli's honor and had made of the insult he had received from Moshe a sufficient reason to break with him and bind himself to Sruli.

Certainly the town would have buzzed with the news at any other time. And it would have fantasized freely over the money that Sruli seemed suddenly to possess.

It is true that those who first heard the story refused to believe it. But when Sholem-Aron, wearing prayer shawl and phylacteries, stood before a crowd of worshipers in the synagogue, people who knew him for what he was—who knew that whatever else he was, he was neither a liar nor the sort to make up stories—and when Sholem-Aron, wearing prayer shawl and phylacteries, stood before a crowd of worshipers and said, "As I hope for the coming of the Messiah, I swear that I saw a pack of bank notes in his hand. And what a pack! You don't get to see anything like it often, not even in the hands of the richest men. A thick packet—enough, I tell you, to provide for the dowries of half the poor young women in town." And when Sholem-Aron added the details of how Sruli had come to his tavern, and how many glasses of wine he had drunk, and how Sruli had talked to himself in a way that had seemed suspicious even to Naftali, Sholem-Aron's assistant, then his story was believed beyond all doubt. At first the crowd was stupefied—and silent. Then there was a rush of speculation—each more preposterous, more ridiculous, than the others. Speculations such as would have been beyond the reach of the most practiced of fantasists.

"Can you believe it? A fellow like that Sruli, with money. And with so much money. Where did he get it? And how come none of us had the slightest suspicion that he had it?"

There were those who tried to show that there was some link between the two stories: the story of Luzi and the story of Sruli's money. What teased at their minds especially was that both events had taken place on the same day—as indeed they had.

As we have said, at any other time the town would have been startled by the news. There would have been a great deal of talk, and the stories would have been bruited about for a considerable while. Everyone would have added a little something, and the wonder of it would perceptibly have grown. At first, the tale would have traveled from house to house and would have been an amazement for the town, but later it would have expanded out into the surrounding region until finally it would have rung in the ears of half the world.

Yes. At any other time.

Now, however, the spreading of the news came to an abrupt halt because it was the season of the Prechistaya Fair, the great annual fair celebrating the birth of the Immaculate Virgin. It was the fair for which the town prepared throughout an entire year. And in the days immediately preceding it, even those synagogues and Hasidic courts that were normally crowded with worshipers were but sparsely attended. At such a time people, for the most part, did their praying at home. So it was that in those hotbeds of news and gossip—the synagogues and Hasidic courts—the news was only scantily heard by those who had hardly time to repeat it. As a consequence, the story did not elicit the usual wonder nor attract the sorts of additions and expansions that would have set it circulating still farther.

There wasn't time enough. Because the Prechistaya Fair was coming.

Here may we be permitted to pause for a while to describe the fair in some detail, not only because of the weight and the importance the fair had, as we will see, for the citizens of the town of N., but also because of the importance it will have for us.

During the fair, the town gave the impression of a city under siege. Thousands upon thousands of peasants, petty nobility, merchants and noblemen, contractors, Gypsies, beggars and thieves converged upon N. from regions near and far. They came in wagons and in carts, in coaches, calèches, on horseback and on foot. The streets of the town were too narrow to accommodate them all. Many people, therefore, found places to stay in the environs. But there was a great number of lucky persons who found their way into the town and occupied whatever space was available: a square, if one could be found, and if there was no square, then a street, a back street, a lane, an alley—anyplace at all where wagons might be lined up behind each other so densely that there was no room for people to go by.

The day before the fair, the roads and highways into N. were jammed with wagons bringing in the harvest from the fields, the produce from truck gardens and orchards, as well as cattle that had been fed at home and in the fields. Some of the wagons had cows tied to them, some had calves, some had colts trotting beside the horses, others had one or several squealing young pigs bound inside sacks.

There were thousands of voices to be heard when that crowd of vehicles arrived in the town: the mooing of cows that had been dragged away from their familiar meadows and barns, the neighing of young horses and colts who were not accustomed to the narrowness of the streets and to so much noise, and the squealing of the pigs whose throats seemed ready to burst as if they were already being slaughtered.

An extraordinary racket because of everything that had been brought into the town and that would be displayed and sold in it. And to buy city goods at once with the money that would be realized. There was bargaining over haberdasher's goods, belts, harness leather, clothing, shoes, headscarves, scarves for men and children, but especially for peasant girls and women whose taste in textures, colors and designs the merchants of the town had studied well.

The crowd was especially dense in the region of the "wrangling" part of the market where cattle and horses were bought and sold. There, where the dealers had brought entire herds of horses: good ones for the nobility, mediocre ones for the petty nobles—and where they showed off for their customers their horses' gaits and speed. It was a place where the sound of whips could be heard all day long, where the horses, on long lead ropes, were made to run, sometimes in a circle, sometimes not. And always surrounding the action, there were crowds of buyers or of the simply curious, of busy folk or of hangers-on.

There, too, were swift-tongued Gypsies with horses for the peasants, doing what they could to cheat their customers—who, because they knew the Gypsies well and had no faith in what they said, refused to be cheated. The peasants spent hours at their haggling. They stood around in clusters, exchanging advice, examining closely and frequently testing what they were bargaining for. Then they resumed their haggling until finally they managed to get themselves cheated—more or less.

At the grain market, the merchants were mostly Jews—sweating and cheating. Each of the merchants wanted to do business with those peasants with whom he had a long acquaintance. Naturally this was more advantageous for the buyer than for the seller, but in any case—and within certain limits—it was advantageous for them both, since each of them had over the years become familiar with the other. It follows, of course, that the merchant, dealing with chance customers whom he did not know, was more inclined to shady manipulations; in short, he was willing to cheat those customers more.

There, too, one could see dense crowds of peasants gathered around the grain wagons where grain was being weighed and put into huge sacks—grain that had been brought from peasant homes or from the estates of the landed gentry. The peasants and the estate stewards accompanying the grain had precise numbers in their minds regarding the amounts and the weight of what they had brought. And there right before their eyes they watched as their property or the property of the nobleman they represented shrank in value on the scale. And that because the grain broker falsified the weight of the grain by putting his foot under the scale. And this was at the risk of his life, because if he had been caught in the act he would not have emerged from the cluster of peasants with so much as a single unbroken bone in his body. The buyer, then, and the seller were both bathed in sweat—the buyer frightened to death and the seller stunned, overwhelmed, unable to understand how he could have made such gross miscalculations back home where he weighed the grain, stunned now to see his profits slip out of his hands, and yet he was helpless to do anything about it because a scale, after all, is a scale.

This was true for the petty merchants, poor middlemen for the most part, but it was also true of the Gypsies and contractors as well as of landed proprietors who stood to one side some distance away looking as if they were not taking part in the sale of whatever it was they had brought to the fair: horses, flax, samples of grain in knotted kerchiefs (grain which later would be sold in grand lots on the grain exchange). But their representatives—stewards or managers—were all the more ardent on their account and did all that in such situations at such great fairs in which cheating and furious haggling were in the air.

And there were thieves, too—simple pickpockets thronging the scene who practiced their metier as targets of opportunity presented themselves to them. In addition to the local contingent, there was an influx of others who came from near and far, people who had skilled hands, who prowled among the wagons wherever there were crowds in narrow spaces, who thrust themselves profitably in among the throng, using all their skill to get out of the crowd as quickly as possible; and even when their timing was off and they were caught they cleverly saw to it that those who beat them, beat them only on those parts of the body where there was likely to be less pain, and so contrived it that if they had to be hurt, the wounds they suffered might not incapacitate them for any length of time.

There they were, then, the cheats and thieves. Some stole more, some stole less. But how much made no difference. Thievery is thievery and the fair is always the fair. And from one fair to another, the thieving was forgotten because life went on and the need for intercourse between country and town was in no way diminished by the thieving. And if this is a truth governing fairs in general, it was truer still about this fair.

But the fair was something more than a fair. It served as a sort of holiday for everyone. For the peasants who went to the taverns when their business was finished. Those who could not squeeze into the taverns drank alone or in company with friends from their home—or from nearby—villages. They drank outdoors under the sky, in the streets, in courtyards, in squares, in their wagons, or seated on the ground, or stretched out underneath their wagons.

It was a holiday, too, for the peasant women who always found something new to buy at the fair. A brightly colored babushka, an apron, a dress, boots and so on. As for the children who were sometimes brought along—one saw them sometimes wearing a cap of a size clearly intended for the father—a cap with a high crown and a lacquered visor—pulled down over the child's head so that it could hardly see; and yet the child wore it, to the evident delight of its parents.

Despite the thievery, the peasants at the fair found ways to indulge themselves. They put away for a while their parsimonious rural habits, and in addition to those foods they brought with them from home— bread and pork—they eagerly sampled a variety of town goodies: loaves of partly white bread, for example; sometimes—for women and children—a cluster of bagels hardened from being sun-warmed in the summer and by exposure to cold in the winter in those bakeries where they hung until they finally found their way to the fair. Sometimes someone bought a bit of candy, or a herring, or a glass of kvass or other town goodies. And they bought, too, the sorts of fruits that were not usually seen in their villages: especially watermelon, for example, whose sweet juices men, women and children sucked so avidly that their faces were damp and sticky up to the eyebrows.

That, then, was the way it was for ordinary folk. Those who were more prosperous indulged themselves in more complexly prepared tavern meals. With fish and meats accompanied by various alcoholic drinks and very loud song.

The town's taverns were packed. Prosperous peasants and their wives, their faces already flushed with drink, occupied every chair. The men's jackets were unbuttoned, the women's headscarves loosened. And conversation was carried on at shouting level and all in unison, with no one able to hear anyone else. And always, at intervals, between speech and song, there were kisses and embraces. The dense air of the place—and the racket—could be sensed from afar.

Peasants, then, in the inexpensive taverns. In those of a slightly higher grade, like Sholem-Aron's, for example, the petty nobility were the customers. They knew something about wine and brandy and expected more refined cooking and somewhat more elevated company and better service.

Then there were the superior inns, reserved for the landed gentry with ranks as high as counts or princes. Here, the finest meals were ordered to be brought in from the town's best restaurant. From The Paradise Shop as it was called. None of the local people, not even the richest, could afford the sorts of delicacies that came from there. Foods prepared only for the nobility by a management that had been counting on their custom for the better part of the preceding year.

In these "better" taverns, various entertainments were organized to take place at the close of the business day. Entertainments so memorable that the noblemen who participated in them returned to the same inns the following year to participate in more and similar such celebrations.

The tables groaned under the weight of the food. The proprietors of The Paradise Shop exerted themselves to have the finest brands of local or imported wine for their customers. The best fruits were brought from the most distant places in the land and others were imported from abroad—from places as far away as Turkey. Fresh fruits, as well as dried. Fine smoked meats and fish. The walls of those inns witnessed absolutely unheard of forms of extravagant expenditure and princely self-indulgence.

So much, then, for the older noblemen. As for the younger, they liked to meet in small groups out of range of prying eyes and out of the presence of those who could report their behavior to their parents or guardians. In those youthful groups, debaucheries were accomplished of the sort that were only to be seen in those places in Europe to which young noblemen were sent, ostensibly for their educations, though it was to spend their madcap youthful days in wasting their patrimonies.

And it was on their account that during the time of the fair a whole mob of servitors from their own regions—people sent after them by their parents to look after them on their travels—as well as certain other people who descended on them in N., sinister folk, the sort of people who skulk alongside walls, brokers (whether of money or vice), by whose means were provided whatever feverish pleasures the younger noblemen might imagine during the course of the fair. Those debauches began with uninhibited drinking parties and ended in the company of the sorts of women (local women as well as those imported) who were to be found in the town's brothels. They were driven—whole flocks of them—into the bathhouses of the town by the brothel keepers so that they might look clean and freshly scrubbed. Then they were made up and dressed to the nines so that they would be pleasing to their distinguished clients.

That was for the nobility.

But local people, merchants, brokers, middlemen from the countryside who came to town to buy and sell, to initiate deals and to connive, were all busy hustling about each in his own fashion—that is, depending on the amount of money he had available to him to invest or on the amount he could realize from what he had to sell.

In the course of those days, everyone ate in haste, prayed in haste. There was little or no Torah study. Even the rabbis were busy judging disputes between partners. Even the greatest, the most renowned of the rabbis such as Reb Dudi, the most famous of them all, were caught up in the turmoil. Especially Reb Dudi, to whom merchants came with ancient and tangled lawsuits. For him, then, as for the merchants, this was "the time of the fair," a period looked forward to all year as a time when there was income to be derived from judgments and arbitration, income that was reflected positively in rabbinical budgets.

In a word, everyone . . . everyone . . . bustled about, hurried, sweated—first because of the fair itself, then because of the broiling sun which shone continually down on the fair during the month of Elul.

The air was laden with odors: the smell of coarse peasant clothing, of sheepskin pelts, the sweat of people and horses, the scent of dried hay, straw, grain, flax, honey and fruit. It sounded with the cries of those shouting their wares in the various markets, booths, stands or stalls erected on every street, and the cries of those, too, whose goods were merely displayed on the ground: potters, barrel makers, wheelwrights and harness makers. There was the sound of whips cracking in the air, the shouts of those putting their horses through their paces. Cries and lamentation when someone discovered he had been robbed, and cries of the thief when he was caught in the act, and even when he was not. Tumultuous voices: the voices of drunks leaving taverns, quarreling voices, sounds of brawls and the pleased voices of successful thieves.

The mélange of sounds hovering in the air made a noise like the sound of many dikes that have suddenly burst and been carried away by a flooding stream. One heard the voices of cattle, fowl and people mingling with the songs of the blind folksingers . . . the bandura players who gathered at the fair wherever the crowds were dense, bandura players who squatted at street corners, sometimes alone, but for the most part in groups. Blind singers who were served or led about by one or several sighted people.

The singers sat cross-legged on the ground, holding their banduras close to their chests with their left hands as they turned the tuning knobs with the right. They sat, their mouths wide as they sang, their blind or empty eyes turned up toward the sun. They played mournful old Cossack songs and wagoner's melodies which touched the hearts of the bystanders—especially those of the women who wept openly as they listened. Sometimes someone tossed the singers a dry bagel or some other bit of food and sometimes someone might put a small coin into a blind man's cap.

Yes, for them, too, for the bandura players and the folksingers, the time of the fair was a time to make money, a time of large and attentive audiences.

Thus it was at every Prechistaya Fair.

But this year—the year of which we speak—the fair took a grim turn. As early as midsummer, the town had begun to hear disturbing rumors coming from the villages of the surrounding region that this year, because there had been no rain since spring, a calamity was in the making: drought.

And in truth the sky that summer was, as it were, sealed. The peasants stared long and longingly at the sky. They made pious processions following priests around their fields. They crossed themselves and prayed—with no results. The grasses in the meadows, the grain in the fields, parched.

And yet the fair took place.

No matter how bleak the prospects of the summer were, no matter how shaky a foundation the fair might have, and in spite of the abuses nature had heaped on them, still the peasants came to the fair. From near and far, along every highway and byway. Some bringing more, others less—still others with even less. But in every case, they brought something. With the result that when the sum total of this and that was added together, the fair was as tumultuous as ever and no one who saw it for the first time would have imagined that it ever had a different look.

But that would have been the view of a stranger.

Those in the know, those who had a stake in these matters, sensed the difference at once between this year's fair and those of past years.

This was especially true of the petty brokers who, looking into a peasant's wagon, found it to be half or three quarters empty; and the peasant presiding anxiously over that half or three-quarter emptiness was demanding a price as if his wagon were entirely full. And, moreover, that expansive geniality which was the peasant's usual manner was certainly missing now. On the contrary, he seemed irritable, harassed; and his eyes, shaded by the lowered visor of his cap, had an angry, a malevolent, look in them.

One had to haggle long and hard to persuade him to sell what he had at the price the town had established for his product. He hesitated, unwilling to part with what he had; he tried to snatch back what he had sold. Or he was cranky and decided not to do business with the customer who first approached him, chose to wait out the unpropitious day, to wait until tomorrow, when if he could only hold firmly to his original price, he might make a better deal.

But that isn't what happened. The customers who came later did not make any better offers and he was finally forced to accept the original offer.

Because the buyers, who would not normally have arrived at such a thing, this time presented a united front. That is, at a signal given by a first bidder who was haggling with a peasant, each of the subsequent bidders who, at other times, would have snatched business out of each other's hands, offered him the same price. A stubborn peasant might wait out an entire day without ever getting a bid one cent better than the first he had been offered. It was as if he stood before an iron wall of collusion, and seeing that his stubbornness availed him nothing, he was constrained to retreat, yield, and to accept half of the amount he had mentally fixed as his price.

That's how it was for the poorer peasants, embittered because of the little they had to bring. As for those who were slightly more prosperous and who had more to sell, they were deceived by other means. On the scales, or by measure, or in the record books (which they had difficulty understanding). In other years the buyers could afford to be a bit more honest, more generous and rarely cheated so meanly or so heavy-handedly as now.

So it was that even the more prosperous peasants had little occasion to be pleased at the fair. And what could one say of the rich—horse dealers, for instance, who came to the fair with entire herds of horses that had been driven long distances, who had had to hire drovers to look after them, to feed them, to keep their hides in the high gloss that was necessary for horses that were being taken to market; and the high-quality horse dealers who sold exceptionally fine horses to the small landholders and to the nobility ... and their slightly less fine horses to simpler sorts of folk were left now with the horses on their hands, as if they had come all that distance merely to display their animals. There were very few buyers because who could afford such prices? The result was that though people stood around and watched, nobody came too close or made the slightest gesture, no matter how wildly attracted they might be to any particular horse.

The horse dealers fumed. There was no sound now of galloping horses or of cracking whips or noisy deals being concluded in the horse markets. No clapping of hands between sellers and buyers—with the result that many of them, out of sheer bitterness, gathered in clusters in the smaller taverns where simply to do something, any kind of business—never mind with whom—they found themselves dickering even with Gypsies.

Nor were things any better with the nobility: counts and the sons of princes who, as has been said, came annually to the fair accompanied by stewards and managers of estates whose task it was to sell the produce of the estates while the young men, though they made a show of being present at the transactions, had other things to do. Carousing, for instance, and spending such moneys as were made at the fair. They, too, had a grimmer time of it this year.

There were no samples of grain brought to the fair this time; there had been no harvest to speak of. And the rural brokers, hearing what had happened in this district, stayed away for the most part. And those that did come were in no great hurry to buy the little there was for sale. They thought things over very carefully, afraid, first of all, to risk the high prices, and second, worried that their competitors in other districts, hearing about the scarcity in this district, would harm them by bringing grain from districts where there was no scarcity to sell here at lower prices.

As for the nobility, they had little money just then—almost none. And all those who depended on them ... that is, those who did business with them throughout the entire year, who lent them money and counted on being repaid during the time of the fair, felt themselves suddenly cheated. Those who had lent money by means of middlemen sent them now to collect what was owing only to have them return looking very pale because they had been driven away by infuriated noblemen who would not allow them so much as to cross their thresholds. As for those moneylenders who went themselves, they fared no better, and were sent away with not so much as a kind word or even the hint of a promise that they would be paid later.

Clearly, the moneylenders had no choice but to absorb the temporarily defaulted loans of the nobility. What else could they do? The moneylenders knew that they could not call in the promissory notes at this time. It was simply not done because to do so would be to create a rupture between themselves and the noblemen which would make it impossible for them ever to do business again.

These things happened this year to everyone and naturally it happened to Moshe Mashber also—because, after all, how was he any different from the rest? But things were even worse, because the nobility not only did not pay their debts but, as one might have expected, feeling themselves pressed for money, they were exigent about making new loans, and they signed notes that imposed both harsh conditions and high interest rates. They put important parcels of land up as security for their notes just so that they might realize some cash and avoid for a while any diminution in the style of life they felt was suitable to the nobility.

The nobility, then—the minor as well as the greater nobility—were experiencing hard times, and those people who were their usual recourse in such circumstances, the town's money brokers and moneylenders, were, with the best will in the world, unable to help even those of their clients with whom they usually did business.

In addition to the money problems the nobles were suffering that year, there must be added the details of an event that took place during the fair—an event in which most—and the most highly respected and the richest—of the nobles were involved. It was an event that posed all sorts of dangers for them since it involved disloyalty to the government and carried the implicit threat of Siberia, of imprisonment and exile, of confiscation of property and perhaps worse. . . .

We are talking here of events that took place in the seventies of the last century, the years immediately following the Polish revolution of 1863, in the period when most of the nobility, even the district of which we speak and which, though it was a little bit removed from the sphere of great events, and though very few of the local nobility actually participated in the revolt because the battlegrounds were elsewhere, still, they manifested considerable sympathy for the anti-government movement and aided it with money and various other forms of help—espionage, or hiding those who, after the outbreak of the rebellion, one was forbidden to hide.

Some of the nobles, those who were more foresighted—and less rich—managed after the rebellion to make some accommodation to the regime. They swallowed what had to be swallowed (as one might swallow a repulsive and greasy medicine); they wore such masks as suited the occasion and, overtly at least, seemed to yield. But silently, when they were among themselves behind closed doors in their castles and on their estates, they raged and dreamed of better times to come and waited for help to come from various quarters.

There were others, richer ones, who, incapable of tolerating the new regime, lost patience and sold their estates, turned everything they had into cash and left the country to live abroad. There were still others, also wealthy, who were so conscious of their family honor and of the estates they had inherited from grandfathers and fathers that they could not bring themselves to part with them. They stayed on their lands and though they were not openly rebellious still, those who needed to know knew what their true sympathies were, that they secretly tended the flame, that they fumed with poisonous hatred against those who had done them so much anguish and harm, and had taken from them their age-old rights to govern their people as they saw fit and to dispose of their lives and property.

The authorities, therefore, kept them unceasingly under surveillance in order to be as closely informed as possible about their secret thoughts and deeds. Hired spies from their own class, loyal to the authorities and traitors to the nobility, were placed among them.

This, then, is what happened: we do not know whether it was because the landed gentry had had misfortunate financial dealings at the fair, or whether it was because of the shame they felt because they could find no way of paying last year's debts, or if it was that they were depressed because of the difficulty they were having floating new loans this year and so were seeking some distraction. Or they may have had some other reason altogether. In any case, they decided that they had to have one great spree, and a night for it was chosen.

Those who participated:

Primarily, young men-about-town and older bachelors—men who would never marry, whether because of certain illnesses they had suffered when they were young and whose consequences they were now feeling, or whether they stayed bachelors because of some caprice or hypochondria of the nobility.

Other participants were those who on their home estates had families and who conducted themselves according to the usual proprieties, but whenever they came to the fair they allowed themselves indulgences which at home for particular reasons, they would never have considered.

But those who set the tone for the evening were the young people. They took it upon themselves (with the help of the servants who accompanied them from their paternal estates) to see to it that everything such an occasion required should be provided. So it was that there were a considerable number of backstairs arrangements made (because one did not do business with such people in the house) with male and female purveyors of various disreputable sorts. And money was found for everything: for food from The Paradise Shop whose shelves would shortly be thinned out because the gentry were great consumers, particularly when they let themselves go, and most especially when they were on a spree.

Tables would have to groan under all that was required to please such high-ranking pleasure-seekers. And deals had been made, too, with those shady representatives of houses of ill fame, pimps and bawds who ran about feverishly and, in their zeal to accommodate everyone, enlisted the services of our old acquaintance, Perele, so that if the whorehouses should prove insufficient, Perele would be able to make additional "goods" available from among her pregnant or post-abortion servant maids to the nobility when the party was over and they retired to their rooms.

The party was to take place in Nosn-Note's inn, a relatively distinguished place, one of the town's best, a place in which very rich merchants stayed as well as government and administrative officials: judges, for instance, who were sent from distant regional capitals to preside over a local trial, liquor tax collectors, inspectors and the like.

The rooms, therefore, were better furnished than in other inns. The chairs and couches had coverings over them, the floors were carpeted and on the walls of every room there were portraits of generals. And one of the large rooms was designated as a dining room in which there was a large table to be used when a numerous crowd would be eating together. There, there hung a portrait of the czar wearing his coronation crown—a cheap picture on stiff glazed paper like all such portraits sold cheaply and in great numbers in every marketplace, portraits meant to appeal to patriotic and lower-class tastes.

Now all the doors of the rooms were open because all of the guests knew each other very well. Their gathering point was the table in the dining room which was lighted not only by candles on the table, but also by a sort of spotlight that hung from the middle of the ceiling.

Nosn-Note, the owner of the inn, who was accustomed to greeting and serving guests of the highest respectability and who, therefore, in his role as a hotelier wore a silk skullcap and kept his beard clean and well combed . . . he, Nosn-Note, had been busy from the evening preceding the celebration, setting the table, putting out the chairs, cleaning the lamps, wiping plates, spoons and glasses, but most important of all, during those moments when Nosn-Note was unobserved by any of the nobility . . . when he was almost entirely alone setting things out on the table, it was then that he kept back some of what was supposed to be on it, putting aside a little of everything so that later he might re-sell it to the owner of The Paradise Shop or to someone else. He was in constant motion, to the table or away from it, his brain furiously working all the while as he considered whether he had or had not taken too much from the table or left too much on it. He ran continually to the cases of wine which had been set aside in another room (not counting those bottles he had already put on the table); he examined them wondering how many he would be able to keep for himself or for resale once he had gotten his noble guests thoroughly drunk.

In addition to those thoughts buzzing about in his head, he had certain moral qualms regarding the troop of scrubbed and bathed women occupying an entire room in some distant part of the inn where they waited out the time until they should be needed. Nosn-Note tried not to think about them because he did not deal with such matters—that was left to some low-ranking servant . . . and it happened, in any event, only rarely. Nevertheless, aware of their presence, he spat, and he was irritated when he saw the door of their room open and caught a glimpse of a woman's head and a portion of her body. He acted as if he had seen nothing and hurried by, but inwardly he sighed: What choice do I have? Ah, what one has to do to earn a living! Particularly when one has to deal with people like this whom it is out of the question to resist and dangerous to deny.

And in truth, Nosn-Note was dealing this time with the flower of the nobility, as coddled as they were depraved.

Above all—for example—there was the only son of Count Kazeroge, a nobleman famous throughout the region. And it was enough to know the old man to guess at the sort of man the son was.

The old count was no more. But there were legends, each one stranger than the other, still extant about him. As for instance the one about his passion for collecting all sorts of porcelain. He had whole rooms in which he maintained a crammed display of teacups, large and small platters, trays, portraits of various sizes on porcelain which he had ordered from various countries.

Nor was that all. He had another passion: for tobacco pipes. And he had whole rooms full of pipes as well—the walls from ceiling to floor were hung with them: pipes of clay, of wood, of amber, sent to him from everywhere. Local pipes as well as pipes from Persia and Turkey; there were pipes even from Venice and the devil only knows what other places.

And then he had coins. Especially, it was said, coins that came from before the time of the ancient Christ. Disinterred, defaced, with illegible letters, they had no value for most people but he, the old Kazeroge, was mad about them and was ready to give away half his estate for an antique coin that would be a source of amazement in any of the world's great museums as something exceptional—indeed unobtainable.

But these fixations and caprices were still more or less tolerable. A nobleman's foibles, but still they were human. But in his old age, the count became more and more fantastic. First, he began to collect coats from around the world. Then he turned to collecting living creatures: cripples of various sorts, male then female dwarfs. Stunted people, midgets, idiots with aged, wrinkled yellow faces. But collecting them was only the beginning. He got it into his head that he wanted to pair them up—to marry them to each other. "And *pfoo . . . pfoo . . .*" people spat as they told the story, "he caroused at their weddings and conceived the idea that he and his guests should be bystanders at what follows after a wedding. To stand right there, insanely drunk, and watch, laughing until his sides ached."

He came to an ugly end. He did not himself take part in the rebellion because he was old and lived far from the battlefields. But he did not keep his opinions to himself, and the authorities, who watched people like him closely, kept him under surveillance and knew very well what he was thinking. Because of a curious habit he developed: whenever one or another of the authorities was about to visit him in his castle, he pretended to be sick and then ordered that the official be brought to him in his bedroom. And the official invariably found the count apparently asleep, his face turned to the wall and always with a naked— how shall one put it—with the least respectable part of his anatomy uncovered. Each time, he started up as if wakened by the sound of the official's step, and apologized, but everyone knew that he had not been startled awake at all, that what he had done had been done on purpose as a way of expressing his contempt for the authorities.

At first this was a trick he played on minor Russian officials, then later to increasingly more important ones until the matter became known in very high places. Finally he tried it on a high-ranking military man who was passing through our district and who came to the count's estate leading a troop of soldiers. The military man was highly offended and, acting on his own responsibility and without inquiring further of anyone (or perhaps it was not on his own responsibility—it may well be that he had been given an approving wink from higher up—but the end of the matter was that he, the old, highly privileged, highborn Polish Count Kazeroge was whipped across that same naked portion of his body on which he had himself wielded the whip when he made his defenseless peasants drop their trousers. The difference was that they received their strokes across their backs while he, because of his age, was whipped on the buttocks.

The old man could not bear the shame of it, and after the beating, he took to his bed and would not let anyone except for his servant come near him. Nor could he bring himself to have any eye contact with him—with the servant. He lay with his head continually turned to the wall and his back to the room because he was so ashamed, and it was in that position, turned away from the room, that he gave up his aristocratic ghost.

The young count, his only son and heir, had lived abroad from his earliest years where ostensibly he studied sometimes in Liege in Belgium, sometimes in Lausanne in Switzerland. But one had only to cast a glance at him to understand his real situation and to know what sort of man he would very soon become.

He was hardly thirty years old but his features were pale, emaciated, bloodless. He gave the impression of being asleep with his eyes open. And in fact he used to fall asleep in the mornings under the hands of his barber when he came to shave him and get him ready for the day. His head would drop forward and often enough he would sustain a cut from the razor.

He was half empty spiritually and physically. True enough, he had, from a spiritual point of view, very little to lose, since from his earliest childhood he had not acquired much spirituality and certainly he had not inherited any. Physically, he was a man whose feet were always dragging. It did not take much medical skill to know that very soon he would lose the use of his legs, and his speech, which was already thick, would fail him, and the little confused memory he still had would be extinguished and he would become one of those bedridden people with glazed eyes and spittle continually drooling from their lips, or at best he would be moved about in a silent, rubber-tired wheelchair—and this is what did happen not many years hence.

Meanwhile, he was still moving about, and for the time being, a bit of flame still sputtered in him. He was, moreover, the only heir of his father, the count, and owned hundreds of villages, estates, breweries, distilleries, mines and other wealth which he had no idea what to do with any more than he knew what to do with himself or with his more than half-wasted life or with anything else in a world that filled him with revulsion.

For the moment he was still himself, surrounded by aristocratic finery and the richest of all the rich men in the region, still likely to commit the maddest of pranks—despite his dragging feet and his nasal voice. He had a lorgnette always in his hand . . . a lorgnette he could not do without even when he went to the toilet, though in fact it made very little difference whether he had it or not—he could not see in any case, just as he could not understand anything since his mind no longer functioned.

Still, he was the principal personage of the planned festivities of which we have spoken above, since their costs were coming mostly out of his pocket and since their chief design was to entertain him, to keep him from boredom during the time of the fair—as well as, of course, his guests, people of his own stripe or very like it.

We will not list here all the participants in the festivities that night, because they are not that important to us and because they were not particularly distinguishable one from the other.

And in truth what is the difference between Count Gedroyts, the grandson of that famous Polish voivode of the time of Chmielnicki, of whom it was told that he traded a cellarful of old wines for an Arab racing mare with fine legs and a fiery temperament and with such form and gait and power that the count lost his head completely over her. So that when the mare was taken ill, he rounded up every horse doctor in the region and when the horse doctors could find no remedy, he turned to the local sorcerers; and when they proved ineffectual he went on bended knees to the priests and begged them to pray for his horse with the same fervor as for himself.

We ask what is the difference between Count Gedroyts and a certain young Prince Denike, of half-German, half-Polish descent, who devoted himself to raising a particular species of pig—white-haired and with rosy snouts the size of a three-groschen piece. He employed people to give the pigs special feeding until they became so fat they were unable to move because their bones had become too brittle to support the mountains of flesh they turned into. Forced to eat lying down they lay there night and day, their eyes closed, mortally sick, stinking quietly. As for the prince, nothing delighted him more than to stare at those pigs for hours at a time, enchanted, when they were healthy, but how fat they were; but inevitably they took sick and then the prince, along with his veterinary and his swineherd, would, by the light of a darkened lantern, stay with them all night long, standing guard over their souls. The prince's goal was for his pigs to reach a certain maximum weight and fat distribution, but the animals could not tolerate the forced feeding and died off—alas—before the goal was achieved.

What, then, is the difference between them? The company of celebrants were all of a kind and well chosen: all of them noble parasites. One of them, however, was exceptional: Lisitsin-Sventislavski, a man with a double ancestry: one part Russian, one part Polish, neither a nobleman nor a landholder. He did not own a local estate, but was in government service in the town. Once he had been a petty official collecting taxes on alcoholic beverages, then for various reasons he had been promoted and given a post in the municipal council of some Russian town, and then—no one knew just why—he was sent back to our district, to N., and again given a post in the local government.

It may be that the authorities sent him back to our district where there were a great many Polish nobles so that they could keep their eyes on him. Particularly in the period just after the uprising of the Polish nobility, when surveillance over them was increased. It may be that he had been given certain secret orders because he was so deeply involved with the nobility—it may be.

He was part liar, part buffoon—at once foolish . . . and sly. One of those people who is easily accepted and trusted by everyone, and particularly the sort of fellow the nobility liked: a devoted drinking companion who could be found wherever there was a carousing crowd. Fraternizing with Russians, one of the boys with Poles. And the butt of his jokes today were always the people with whom he had been drinking yesterday. He had the latest news and told the most recent anecdotes; he knew every money, family or love scandal current among the local nobility and was a boon companion and on intimate terms with them all. The ambiguity of his name and the double nationality of his family served him so that he could move in every society. Both government administrators and highly respected Poles treated him as one of them. He crept like wild grass from one group to another. Everyone had something to whisper to him about everyone else. He had the appropriate flattering word ready for use with everyone. And so it was that all doors were open to him, all purses were put at his disposal, and he was prepared to hear the latest secrets from them and to whisper them into ears for which they were *not* intended.

He could easily have been a sponger, a permanent guest in the home of any of several Maecenases who were his friends, and to move about, passing the time in one court or another. But it was clear that he enjoyed living in the town, he felt at ease there; as for his employment, that seemed to have been given him more as a matter of form than anything else. Unlike a regular employee, not much in the way of work was required of him and he rarely put in an appearance at his office. Essentially, his work was to mingle socially, to insinuate himself, to sniff about, to lend an ear to what was being said, to keep an eye on what was happening among the nobles—or among others. And where he himself belonged, what his true world was, no one could say. If you liked, he was a Polonized Russian; if you liked, he was a Russified Pole ready, for the price of a drink or a little more, to sell the one to the other.

He would sometimes disappear from town and go off into the provinces for a few days, staying now with one now with another of his old friends, drinking companions or gambling partners. He liked especially to go where there was a celebration of some kind: a party for a guest from one of the provinces, or when a large group gathered—as now at the fair where such a large group had come together. Certainly, Sventislavski's presence was required on an occasion like that. And there he was, Lisitsin-Sventislavski, at the banquet.

Almost from the beginning of the festivities, when all of the guests had not yet even gathered, Count Kazeroge, who managed to look drunk even when he was not—though in fact he may have had an earlier drink or two—even early on, then, the young count repeatedly called the innkeeper Nosn-Note to him whenever he made his appearance on the threshold of the dining room—whether to bring something in for the noblemen or to take something away, as his duties required—each time the count waved drunkenly at him, signaling to him to come over because he needed something; and each time that Nosn-Note came up, the count, speaking with a drunkard's candor, said contemptuously, as if he were speaking to a domestic animal he was trying to tame, "Hey, there, No-San. Sing me that song—what's it called?" . . . And always he was unable to remember the name of the song he meant. The song was one that the Polish nobles frequently required their subject Jews to sing when they, the nobles, were feeling expansive—and the Jews, out of fear and dependency, were afraid to refuse. It was the famous Sabbath song, "Mayofes."

Each time, Nosn-Note turned away with one excuse or another, at first pretending not to know what the count meant, then promising to do it "Later, later." A third time, he managed skillfully to elude the count's hand when the nobleman reached to grab at his coat, at his beard and earlocks, endeavoring by that means to keep him there.

From the beginning, the police official, Garletski—no one could be sure whether it was the higher-ups among the authorities who, having heard about the gathering, had sent him (as they usually did on such occasions) to keep some sort of an official eye on things, or whether he had come on his own initiative and responsibility. It may be he came of his own accord, imagining the free drinks the innkeeper Nosn-Note would bring him on the sly (because he had neither the authority nor the courage to go into the dining room itself) while Garletski stood eavesdropping on the other side of the door. He might sometimes open the door and poke his head in and it could happen that a nobleman might see him and send him something to drink. Or it may be that Lisitsin-Sventislavski, having some kind of plan in mind, had invited him. Or perhaps he had no such plan at all.

That notion—that is, the idea that Sventislavski had invited Garletski—seems reasonable and has a certain basis in fact. Because this time it was very noticeable that Sventislavski kept sending Garletski glass after glass of spirits.

Yes. Things had reached the stage at which Garletski, the police official with the three folds of flesh at the nape of his neck and a belly protruding like a drum, Garletski who sweated continually—and especially when he was performing some official duty (a parade, for example, or standing guard for one of the authorities)—it had reached the stage at which Garletski, who was continually wiping the sweat away with a handkerchief, and who, as has been said, had been standing behind the door because he had no authority (and was afraid) to go in—it was now to be observed that Garletski, as the festivities moved forward and he heard what was taking place inside, now ventured to open the door wider and wider, occasionally even poking his head inside, thinking, evidently, that no one in the dining room would take notice of him.

The truth is he was mistaken. Inside the dining room, things had not reached such a point that he could pass absolutely unobserved. And in fact every time he looked, someone saw him, and his appearance was regarded as a comic event—as if a cat had silently and unexpectedly opened a door. Someone would say, "Psssst!" and Garletski, averting his eyes, would pull his head back and quickly shut the door.

That began to happen early, when the full complement of guests had not yet arrived. Later in the evening, the nobles who had been invited to participate began to show up one by one. Some were young, others already middle-aged, some were sober, others—who had just left their rooms in the same inn (or who arrived from other inns of the same caliber)—already half drunk.

Among them, Rudnitski, whom we have described in a previous chapter. He had a poor reputation, not just among businessmen, but among the nobility as well. Even among his peers, he was greeted with a certain mistrust. Neither his word nor his promises were taken seriously. It was as if they kept their eyes on his hands because they thought him capable of stealing if he was unobserved and could avoid any risk of scandal.

On this evening, the first to greet Rudnitski was the host of the banquet, Kazeroge who from the beginning of the festivities had been drunkenly heated. Kazeroge, his withered face recently powdered, held the handle of his lorgnette carelessly in one trembling hand and moved at his usual half-paralyzed pace, dragging his feet. At first he cast an indifferent look at the newcomer; this was followed by a look of profound disdain—as if it would be treating the new arrival with altogether too much honor to take him seriously (even if contemptuously). As if the only way to greet someone of that sort was lightly, humorously. As if Rudnitski was one of those creatures who made not the slightest difference to the outcome of any human calculation.

Kazeroge, moving at his trembling gait, approached him then and, as if he were meeting Rudnitski by accident, tapped him contemptuously on the forehead with the palm of his hand.

"Ah. So it's Rudnitski," he said. "It's you."

"Gentlemen," he cried. "See. It's he, Rudnitski, who, they say, plays at cards and doesn't pay his gambling debts, who has a mistress but has no money with which to keep her, who borrows money from the Jews and compels them at pistol point to give back his promissory notes. Here he is, gentlemen, the very same man who . . ."

But here, his half-paralyzed tongue caused him to trail off. Unable to find his last word, his concluding idea, he was forced to end his speech with a tasteless and meaningless giggle and a lazy wave of his hand.

"Hee, hee, hee." He waved his hand and was rendered helpless by a fit of senile coughing.

Someone else in Rudnitski's place—someone with more dignity, with a greater sense of pride—would certainly have responded differently to such an insult, even though (as in this case) it was put in the form of a joke. Rudnitski, on the other hand, who had fully earned every word of the reproach made to him, was forced to bear it without response, without any sign indeed that he had even heard it. He sought then to go off to one side, to join some other group in which the count was *not* present, and to ignore him; but the count, when he was done with his senile giggling cough, followed him into the new group where he sought him out and repeated everything he had said when he first met him. This time he added, "Do you see, gentlemen? Rudnitski feels insulted, and if that's true, then all is not lost. I, for one, am quite ready to give him satisfaction. I'll be glad to meet him on the dueling ground—with pistols. And let Rudnitski, here and now, choose his seconds."

With that, the count drew a pistol from one of his pockets and showed it around to the circle of noblemen—holding it for a somewhat longer interval before Rudnitski who had to swallow this insult as well, though he offered the transparent excuse that the count, as everyone could see, was drunk, and one did not demand satisfaction from a drunken man who after all was not responsible for what he was doing.

If the truth be told, it was not only the sickly, weak-minded young count who was not responsible for what he was doing; everyone else who was there had had a considerable amount to drink, as was evidenced by the disordered state of the table as well as by the inflamed faces of those sitting around it or standing in convivial groups of two or three people.

At intervals one or another of those who were drunk was seized by some new impulse. One of them climbed up on a chair meaning, though he did not know why, to extinguish the lights in the chandelier so that they might be in the dark. When he was unable to reach the chandelier, he turned to blowing out the candles on the table.

Someone else decided that there was insufficient light, and he demanded that more candles be brought in. "Candles, lamps—and if you haven't got any then—why not—let's light the place up. Let's let the whole house burn to light up the street, light up the whole town and the fair as well.

"I'll pay for it," he cried. "I'll pay all the damages. The losses of everyone here as well as of those who are not. All the losses—of anybody at the fair. Because what the hell, I've got the capital, I've got my estates. I'll pay."

Someone else, hearing "I'll pay," confided to the man beside him that he had indeed been burned, that he was a victim, that he had lost everything in the flames of the fair, that he had been left completely stripped, that he deserved the compassion of the others because he was penniless and unable to pay his way home, that the nobles ought to do something to defend his name and his honor because if they did not then all the nobles would be held up to scorn and their reputations stained.

There was a terrific racket in the room. The air, made dense by tobacco smoke, wine fumes and the presence of the packed crowd in the narrow room, weakened the light from the lantern. There were those who, feeling choked by their collars, unbuttoned them; others sought the door, meaning to escape outside for a bit of fresh air with which to fight the nausea that was oppressing them; while others sought out corners of the room in which to let the nausea have its way. Still others, on the other hand (and these were generally the latecomers), felt as if they had not yet had enough to drink and demanded more and still more from the waiters, and Nosn-Note, the proprietor, whose visits to the dining room were increasingly more widely spaced because he did not want to be noticed by the nobles who by now had grown extremely wild—instead, Nosn-Note, whenever he could, sent the servants and servingmaids in to deal with them in his stead.

All sorts of wines in flasks and in bottles, local and imported, were served, and there were connoisseurs of drink in the crowd who, with skills they frequently practiced at home, now put their minds to work to fashion various mixed drinks. They told the waiters which sorts of wine to put together to make hot drinks. And the more they drank, the more wine was spilled on the table. There was not much pleasure to be derived from it all, but the racket seemed loud enough to pierce the ceiling on its way to the roof.

Garletski, the police official, who was continually being handed different sorts of drinks by the proprietor of the place as well as (and this is of greater importance) by Lisitsin-Sventislavski, who had evidently been keeping an eye on him all evening so that he would know where to find him if he needed him . . . Garletski, the police official who on the other side of the door had already drunk as much as half a dozen of the guests, was showing the effects of all he had had; this was particularly shown by the state of the handkerchief with which he continually wiped the sweat away from the nape of his neck. He sweated first because he always sweated when he was on duty, and then because of the effects of the wine.

Garletski, seeing how tumultuous the dining room had become, and that no one was any longer taking any notice of him, risked leaving the door ajar for longer periods and poked his head in at will.

But it was true—no one paid him the slightest attention, with the single exception (as has been said) of Sventislavski, who all this while had been moving from one group to another, putting in a word here and there to show that he was participating in the tumultuous conversations, but in fact he hardly knew what he was saying, since even as he said something to the first group he was already eavesdropping on the second as he went from one conversation to the other.

The result was that his eyes, like those of a mouse, were in continual motion as if searching for something to focus on and no sooner did he overhear a snatch of conversation that seemed important, than his eyes swiveled toward it.

And though he did drink, it was always in such measure as would enable him soberly to see and hear everything that was taking place in the uproar: who was saying (or shouting) what to whom. And always he was on the alert to note, to remember, everything.

To do that required an exceptional talent: to be able to drink and keep sober. To hear everything, and to pretend not to hear and at the same time to avoid being noticed. But that, precisely, was Sventis-lavski's genius. He seemed to have a natural talent for it, to have been called to the work—and no doubt it served his interests as well. It was generally a difficult task, but it was to a considerable degree easier now, in the chaotic conditions prevailing in the room—in the half-dark and drunken disorder.

Various of the noblemen were by now so drunk, so addled and confused that they groped their way along the walls, imagining that they were at home and were trying to find their way up the stairs leading to their bedrooms where they meant to rest awhile in their beds.

Others, stouter drinkers who were still on their feet but whose heads were whirling, carried on thick-tongued and fragmentary conversations, babbling and jabbering to each other without understanding what anyone said.

Some bragged about their wealth or their happiness to acquaintances or to strangers, maintaining all the while, despite their drunkenness, a certain aristocratic mien. Others on the other hand, inspired by wine, opened their hearts and confided secrets that had they been sober they would never have revealed: tales of imminent . . . or nearly imminent . . . bankruptcy. And as proof of what they were saying, they turned their pockets inside out and showed them to their confidants, as if to say, "What's to be done? Might as well turn beggar."

One could see—or, more nearly, one could feel—that the nobles were heavyhearted. Had they been sober, of course, none of that would have been revealed, but now there were many signs that they were troubled.

As an example, let us take Prince Denike, the famous pig raiser who himself looked a bit porcine—fat and with close-cut hair. After downing his many glasses of wine, he leaned his head to one side on the table and lay there, groaning like a pig perishing in its own fat. No matter how much they pushed trying to move him, trying to make him get up, he continued to resist, and like an ailing pig that is being poked, he emitted a grunt from his belly to show that he had heard what was said but that he had neither the strength nor the desire to move.

As for Count Gedroyts, he sees scenes in a nightmare: it seems to him that he is playing cards and has lost everything. But he can still wager one last thing on which his whole destiny depends—his beloved mare. He sees himself leading the mare out to show her to the nobles with whom he is gambling. Whoa, there. Whoa. He holds the bridle and stands before them and they can see his eyes starting from his head. The hand holding the bridle trembles. Whoa, there. Even as he calls for cards, he stands and waits for the noblemen to admire his mare. "Cards, here," he cries.

Yes. He wagers it. His horse, his final treasure . . .

So, too, the ailing Kazeroge. The one who might most properly be called the host of the banquet. At the beginning he had been quite haughty—that is to say, to the degree that his dragging feet, feeble intelligence, babbling tongue and purblind eyes permitted. At the beginning, in his role as a host, he had moved about greeting the newly arrived guests, and trading inanities with them. He invited them to the tables, offered them drinks and then forgot them as he turned to greet still other newcomers. He, too, Count Kazeroge, looked weary and worn now; he could hardly drag himself about, or make his mouth shape any clear words. He lay sprawled, with his feet outstretched in the single overstuffed chair in the room.

He looked ill and pale and seemed indifferent to everything going on around him. But in addition to that, his spirit seemed dark and heavy—if, that is, a man like that can be said to have any human spirit. The dark mood might have been the result of the depressed business atmosphere that affected everyone at this year's fair. It may even be that the entire festivity had been designed to combat the general depression. Or perhaps there had been some other reason. With Kazeroge there was no way to tell. Or perhaps the depression was the result of his illness which lately pressed ever more on his heart. And to the degree that he still possessed a mind, he found himself, in the very midst of the celebration, with his strength and his courage failing him, and he lay sprawled, faint and exhausted, with his feet stretched out before him.

Whatever the reason, he, too, the host of the banquet, was out of sorts. At any other time, the festivities would naturally have subsided slowly. One by one, the guests, whether they needed to find a place to vomit or under some other pretext . . . the guests would have found their way quietly to the door and would have gone out, not to return. And as with most such celebrations, that would have been the end of that.

This time, however, it happened that just as the guests were getting ready to disperse, they noticed, drunk though they were, that one of their number, dead drunk and with his eyes closed, stood trembling before the wall on which was hung the portrait of which we have already spoken, the cheap glazed paper color picture of Czar Alexander the Second. The nobleman raised his head sharply and seemed to take note of whose portrait it was that hung above him on the wall, then he took several steps backward and took up a stance facing the picture. Then, after standing and staring thus for a while, he burst into a full-throated laugh that involved all of his features, including his eyes which were now open and apparently sober. He laughed as if he were being tickled by several hands in secret places, laughed so that everyone who saw him took the infection and shook with laughter as they pointed to him or to the portrait; and the finger pointing redoubled or tripled the mirth and they laughed till their sides ached. Had a stranger come into the house just then and into the room, he would have thought he had walked in among madmen and, taking fright, would have made his escape—or else he might have stayed and joined in the laughter.

"See," cried the nobleman who had initiated the laughter, "there he is, King Ahasuerus himself, who rules from India to Ethiopia; from ocean to ocean; from the White Sea to the Black Sea; over the khans of Kazan, Astrakhan and Crimea; over the Cossacks of Zaporozhye; over Poland, Lithuania and over our Zemaitija—one hand, one iron fist, one boot, one Siberia for all, one gallows, one rope and one noose for all."

The speaker paused. Having lost his drink-inspired train of thought, words failed him. With neither words nor ideas at his command, he ended by spitting.

"*Ptui, ptui.*" The sound of spitting was heard from all sides, as the whole crowd, whether they intended it or not, repeated his action. "*Ptui.*"

The spitting and the sudden seriousness of what was happening had a sobering effect on everyone including even Denike, who all this while had been sleeping with his head on the table, breathing hard like a sick pig.

He woke with a start, opened his eyes and saw that all those who not long before had been creeping along the walls or moving toward the door so they could leave . . . as well as those who, as he remembered it, were like himself still drinking alone or in groups, now suddenly they were all standing, awake, sober and alert as if they had been splashed with cold water.

The seriousness of what had happened before the portrait, and the mass spitting, left the noblemen speechless. More than that, as if they had suddenly come to their senses, they looked about to see whether there was anyone among them who in the present situation ought not to be there.

It was then that everyone remembered Garletski, the police official who, they vaguely remembered, had been standing behind the door. During the festivities they had scornfully noted his presence, as they might have noticed a dog. But now they remembered him—perhaps, indeed, the door more than him. Who could say who might chance to look in or who might come into the room unexpectedly?

Naturally, no one suspected any of those who had just participated in the scene in the dining room, not even Sventislavski, though if anyone had scrutinized him closely just then they might have seen that there was reason enough to be suspicious of him; but since no one in the room regarded him as in any way different from any of the others—all of them people who could be trusted absolutely—it did not even occur to them that he might be capable of evil; and since their blood had been stirred by their confrontation with the portrait, they found themselves remembering all the wrongs they had endured: they remembered the rights and privileges that had been taken from them (though, despite all, they still had large fortunes left); but above all they remembered those who not only had had their fortunes confiscated by the state, but who had also been driven away or exiled to Siberia; and they remembered still others who had been hanged or shot or beaten to death; remembering all this, the noblemen could not repress the hatred they felt for the man who looked down at them with royal self-confidence from the portrait that hung before them on the wall, and who, as they thought, was mocking them because there was no one among them who would dare lift a hand not only against himself, the living czar, but even against the cheap picture of him hanging on the shabby wall of a shabby inn—and *that* was more than they could endure; so, however sober they were, still, now, as if they had planned it, they raised their fists toward the portrait as one of them threatened (with words) to punch its face, while still another reminded the picture that judgment between the czar and themselves had not yet been handed down, that the partition and the despoiling of Poland would not last forever, that there would be payment demanded for blood already spilled, and someone else, shaking his fist at the portrait, began to sing "Poland Is Not Yet Lost," and it was beginning to seem that at any moment they would all take up the song, and had that happened, it is possible the matter might have ended there, that the noblemen who were becoming increasingly sober would have left the room after the absurd battle of words before the portrait, and fearful and conscious of their weakness would have crept back to their chambers.

Except that just as the singer was bringing the song to an end, suddenly—no one could tell from where—a shot was heard. Stunned, frightened, everyone looked around wondering where the shot came from. It was then that they saw the pale and sickly young Count Kazeroge who stood beside the easy chair holding one of its arms with one hand and a pistol in the other. It was clear that he had pulled off one shot and now, his finger trembling, he was trying to press the trigger a second time; but, whether because of his fear or his trembling, he could not manage it, and instead of a shot from his pistol, another shot was heard, but where it came from nobody could tell.

One may say in passing that no one seeing the count and noting his ruined condition could believe that a hand like his could have fired that first shot; and there was reason to suspect that someone else had done the shooting, that he had seen the count holding the pistol in his outstretched hand and had taken advantage of it to use it as a cover.

However it was, as everyone turned in the direction toward which the shot had been fired, they saw two holes clearly visible, one in the crown and one in the chest of the portrait. The pistol holes were still smoking; the portrait had been dishonored and there was a dumb anguish in the faces of those who looked on.

"Gentlemen, who did that?" It was a voice that did not belong to any of those in the room but of someone who had just opened the door.

It was Garletski who, no matter how drunk he was from the frequent drinks he had been given by Nosn-Note, the proprietor of the inn, and the even more frequent secret drinks brought to him by Sventislavski—drunk though Garletski might be, when he heard a shot in the room, the policeman, the guardian of the law in him, came wide awake, and half-frightened, half-bold, he opened the door and put his head in.

Sventislavski, however, anticipating that move, was right there. He calmed Garletski down and told him to shut the door, with the result that the words "Gentlemen, who did that?" were not even attributed to him but to someone else.

The noblemen in the room understood at once what were the implications of the situation. Every face there reflected guilt, because, in fact, they were all guilty. The first shot was certainly the count's, but since nobody could be sure who had fired the second, it could be imputed to any of them.

Just at that moment, someone—nobody knew who it was for sure—jumped up onto a chair and put out the spotlight that hung overhead. Then everyone moved it would seem by some vague fear, reached for the nearest candle and extinguished its flame. One might have thought it was done for the sake of concealment, so that they would not have to look at each other, to give them an opportunity for reflection, and perhaps, also, to provide them all, whether more or less guilty, with a chance to slip away.

At that same time, the picture on the wall disappeared, and though the noblemen searched high and low for it, it was as if it had sunk into the earth without a trace.

And at the same time, it seemed to each of the noblemen that he heard a voice in his ear whispering hurriedly, "Gentlemen, the matter is serious, though it may be one can do something about it. But it will take money. A great deal of money." With that, the voice named a sum so great that they trembled even worse than they had before at an event that had smacked of high treason, of lèse-majesté, and which, given the times and their rank as noblemen, could have the most dreadful consequences for them: from whippings, to exile, to execution itself.

But the sum that had been named was not only beyond the limited resources of the noblemen who were suffering financially from this year's half-dead fair, but it would have been beyond them even in prosperous times; it was a sum that was not only beyond the reach of anyone of them, it was more than any group, putting its resources together, would have been able to raise.

"It's a grave matter," continued the voice. "Consider, gentlemen. The event took place in a Jewish inn, and, moreover, in the presence of a government official. The whole thing may well be reported by tomorrow morning. The news could spread, throwing the whole town into an uproar. And the critical evidence—the portrait—has disappeared, and who knows who has it now? It has to be found and destroyed. Still, all is not lost. But it will take some heavy bribing. If you don't do it, gentlemen, you will have much to regret."

Late that night in the very same inn, there was a meeting of noblemen. Sventislavski (because the others were immobilized by fear) presided over the meeting and was the most forthcoming with suggestions. The decision of the group was to collect the money and to turn it over to Sventislavski to use in any way he saw fit.

Everyone by then was sure that the money would stay in Sventislavski's pocket, as they were convinced that he had the portrait in his possession. By then they all knew him for what he was but there was nothing they could do about it unless they chose to throttle him at once right there in the inn, but evidently there were no volunteers for that task. All that was left was to accept what they knew to be a charade and to treat as genuine his offers of help. One thing they did do, however, and that was to dicker with him to lower the price, and this they accomplished. But even the lowered price was so high that there was not one among all those noblemen who could even in his wildest fantasies imagine how, in the present financial climate, the sum could be collected.

"Where, gentlemen, will we find the money?"

"The Jews have money. We'll have to ask them for it. The Jews won't abandon the nobility. They'll help us. They'll find the money."

Sventislavski undertook this task, too. It was he who would be able to present the matter in such a way that the personal fears of the nobility (because of the danger that threatened them) would be seen as related to the general welfare and security of the whole town.

How it was that Sventislavski made contact with our rabbi, Reb Dudi (who was famous not only in our town but in the entire region) ... whether Sventislavski approached him on his own, or whether it was through the intercession of some Jew of his acquaintance ... we do not know.

We know only that a meeting was called early the very next morning, in the very midst of the fair, at a time when people were at their busiest and time was most pressing. Of course it involved important leaders of the community, but naturally this time it did not involve rabbis or those who were simply honorable men. Essentially, it was a meeting of moneyed men to whom Reb Dudi turned—the sorts of men from whom something might be expected on this occasion.

Reb Dudi presented the case as one that had implications not only for the noblemen, but also for the entire Jewish community. "Just think of it," Reb Dudi said, "this thing smacks of rebellion—and there will be payment required. Those who are guilty will certainly be punished—what that means is clear to everyone. And the noblemen, swimming in debt, cannot buy their way out of this on their own—especially this year when money is so scarce because of the drought. One has to remember," Reb Dudi went on, "that if the noblemen suffer, it won't be only the village Jews—innkeepers, tenant farmers and leaseholders—who will suffer along with them, but the town Jews, too, with whom the nobility have financial ties—including those of you who are here at this meeting. Think, too, that if the noblemen are carried off, you may as well say good-bye to the sums they owe you. If on the other hand we drag them out of this mire, the nobles will remember it with considerable benefit to Jews.

"It is true that there is danger in that course as well. If it became known that Jews were involved in this matter, it may be that the community will be charged with false accusations. On the other hand, there is a defense against that. The only witness of the events who might give damaging testimony is only interested in extracting money—a particular sum of money—out of the situation. People we can trust assure us that he wants nothing more than money. And there's a real suspicion that he is himself the culprit—that it was he and not any of the noblemen who fired the shots, and that he has been a long time planning to make himself rich by taking advantage of a situation like this. And luck has at last been with him . . . the outcast, the informer! There's no way to prove any of this, but the fellow, it is clear, doesn't feel entirely safe since he's in a great hurry to get the money so he can get clear of this business as quickly as possible. He has the portrait, but he won't get any money until it has been delivered to the noblemen so that they can destroy it. There is no need to worry that the fellow will start the whole blackmail process over again after he has been paid because, first of all, who will believe him when the evidence is gone? And second, should the noblemen prove innocent, he will be in danger for having contrived the whole plot. But the noblemen, fearing him because the portrait is in his possession, have agreed to yield to him. But none of them has any money; and meanwhile, the fellow is exigent: he wants his money now, at once, immediately, or else the matter will be allowed to follow its course, after which no remedy will be possible. It is incumbent on us to think of something. The money has to be found today—or tomorrow.

"I know," Reb Dudi said, "that times are bad for everyone and that money is in short supply. But the welfare of the nobility—and our own welfare—requires that we do everything in our power. And the good Lord will help us."

One of those present at this hastily convened meeting was Moshe Mashber who was selected to find a portion of the amount required. This because of the prestige his name carried in the town and because he had large sums out at interest to the nobility.

Naturally, Moshe, like the others, when he first heard the story, wanted—and intended—to have nothing to do with it. Let the profligates get out of this the best way they can. But the more they considered the matter, looking it over from every angle, and when they had thought through what consequences might come of it, not only for those who were at the meeting, but for a large number of Jews who were not there, they concluded finally that they really had no choice; that there was no one, except those who were there, who were in a position to do anything—and that indeed something would have to be done. So, though they groaned and scratched their heads and their beards, they had finally to agree and each of them promised to bring on the following day the amount apportioned to him.

Following that meeting at Reb Dudi's, Moshe Mashber went to his office at once and there he asked his son-in-law Nakhum Lentsher (who is already known to us) to join him in his counsel chamber. Lentsher, as his confidential consultant, knew every detail of Moshe's business. Moshe told him the whole of the story involving the noblemen; he discussed the matter with him and then asked, "What does our balance sheet look like today?"

"Well, we have a balance, but there's no cash available. You know our situation. You don't need to hear it from me."

Nakhum was right. Moshe knew. He knew that the annual fair was not a fair at all but a conflagration—for everyone, but especially for those who like himself were moneylenders and agents whose notes had not been paid on time. This was a year in which creditors had not even ventured to stand in their doorways, as they normally would have done at this season, to greet their smiling debtors coming to clear up their debts or to discuss ways of contracting new ones. It was different now. If anyone did show up, one could tell at once from his sad and guilty look that he had come to plead for an extension of time on his loan and perhaps for an additional sum to be added to the previous principal.

Moshe knew this all very well. And yet there was no way that he could avoid participating in the new loan for the nobility. His name and his position required it of him. His credit and his standing with the merchants of the town. Had he refused to participate it would have been a sign that he was facing difficulties. That he was in financial trouble. And that was something that no businessman—especially not anyone like Moshe—would allow to happen.

And there was a particular reason why Moshe had now to participate in the loan. No one is quite sure how it happened—whether the nobleman Rudnitski himself had while he was drunk confided the matter to someone, or whether Jewish brokers had sniffed it out for themselves—but it had become known that Rudnitski had defaulted on a large sum of money he owed Moshe, and the story itself was retailed and became a topic of discussion among merchants and brokers: how he had cheated Nakhum out of the notes. Moshe had done what he could to keep the whole thing quiet—but this, too, was given a sinister implication. "It just shows," it was said, "that things are not going well at Moshe Mashber's. Why else would he want to cover up the story?"

Things had reached such a pass that those agents who were permanently ensconced in Moshe's office and who when they spoke to him accompanied their every word with lickspittle flattery—men like Sholem Shmaryon and Tsali Derbaremdiker, and others—things had reached such a pass, then, that when such folk heard the story and, irritated because they had not been able until fair time to discover it for themselves, they now took to looking frequently and insultingly into Moshe's eyes, as if to brag that they knew the details of the story that he had tried without success to hide from them.

Yes, things had reached such a pass that Moshe, in order to keep up his reputation with the merchants and the financiers in the town with whom he had participated at the meeting at Reb Dudi's house, as well as with such agents as Shmaryon and Derbaremdiker who would regard him with even greater contempt should they become aware of the story of the noblemen—(which for the moment was still unknown to them); and it would certainly not have done his reputation any good had they learned that at the meeting where everyone was required to contribute only Moshe had not paid his share. In that case, the insolence of the whole tribe of agents and moneylenders would be justified.

And this was why, after he had discussed the matter with Nakhum, he called his various agents into his office and assuming his usual rich man's manner—haughty and indifferent—as if the request he was about to put to them was the most ordinary sort of business request, specifically, that he needed to have a certain sum of money at once and that they must find it for him, and in order to speed their work and to obviate their need to return to the office each time to get Moshe's promissory notes whenever they found a lender, he provided them with signed notes right there and then for small (and even very small) sums, because he knew that no matter how diligently they searched, it would be impossible for them to find large sums in the hands of individual lenders.

When the agents had left, Moshe stayed where he was. Occasionally he groaned, and his hands traveled frequently to his breast pockets, feeling about in them as rich men often do when they are feeling relaxed and self-confident; but this time he found them empty—an experience he had not had in years and which seemed to him strange, even unbelievable.

He felt a chill at his heart. Nothing went well all the rest of the day—especially in the evening when it was time to close the office. Nothing had happened to ease him all day. Then his agents and brokers gathered in his office and, though they brought him the money he required, he could see that they had been able to find it only after the most strenuous searching. When prompted by curiosity he inquired where they had found the money and to whom they had given his promissory notes—though he knew full well that this time, because of the scarcity of money, the notes were not in the hands of well-known or reputable people—Tsali Derbaremdiker told him where his share of the money came from.

"Do you know where I got it?" There was a spiteful, an insolent look on Tsali's face.

"Where?"

"From someone that nobody in the world would believe could have access to money."

"And who might that be?"

"That surly fellow who frequents rich people's homes, who wears an earth-colored caftan and a cap with a lacquered visor. Sruli Gol."

"From him? From Sruli? Who told you to go to him? How could you bring yourself to do it? Have you gone mad? Are you in your right mind?"

"What do you mean?" And here Tsali, because he was weary after his day of running about, and, it would seem, because the Rudnitski affair had eroded some of Tsali's respect for Moshe . . . Tsali replied sharply, "What do you mean? Money has no odor, Reb Moshe. Money doesn't smell. Money is money, wherever it's found. What counts is that it's there."

"But the thing is impossible. How does a fellow like that suddenly come to have money?" cried Moshe.

"That's none of our business. What counts is that he has it, and that it isn't counterfeit," Tsali replied.

An embittered Moshe returned home after this conversation with his head still buzzing. He was dumbfounded, utterly unable to understand what had happened. But we, who know the facts, are not surprised, and we ask our readers to keep in mind that it was during the fair on the day after what happened to the noblemen, and after the meeting at Reb Dudi's house, and on the same day that Moshe sent his agents out to search for money, on that same day Moshe, much to his chagrin, became Sruli Gol's debtor. He, Moshe, was the man in need, and he, Sruli, was the man who helped him. He, Moshe, the man who felt about in his breast pockets and found them empty, and Sruli, who, had it occurred to him to put his hand to his breast pockets, would have found there a packet of promissory notes signed by Moshe Mashber. Let us keep that in mind.

We will not recount here how and where it was that Sruli and Tsali did their business—the giving and the taking of the money. We will not recount it because it would be superfluous. It is enough to know that (as we learned in the previous chapter) Sruli had approached Tsali on money matters once before, and that Tsali had hesitated whether to take him seriously or not, and finally he had taken him seriously so that when he went searching for money on Moshe's behalf, he remembered Sruli and sought him out as Sruli, for his part, was seeking him. And when two people are looking for each other, they are sometimes helped to find each other by chance—as happened to Sruli and Tsali.

One way or another, the business was done. What Sruli felt at that moment, we do not know. Nor do we know what he intended by the transaction that made Moshe Mashber his debtor. It may be that when it happened he did not fully know what he intended. We know only that Moshe was profoundly troubled and felt that Providence had abused him. Had touched him with the finger of poverty as a signal to him that there was no stability in wealth, that it was wrong to take pride in it. The signal was clear: he had been forced today to have recourse to a man like Sruli, a man whom he had driven from his door not so long ago as a person of no account. So much for Providence. But beyond that, what bothered Moshe was that the news of the event could—and certainly would—spread. The story would be in everyone's mouth, and it would be told as a joke, and the fact that he owed Sruli money would be linked with the Rudnitski matter. It would not sound well, it was not a story to be proud of. It smacked of scandal and the sort of unpleasantness that one would prefer to wish on one's enemies.

That evening when Moshe came home, he recited his late evening prayers in a mood of embittered piety. He did not eat supper but went to bed at once. Sensing his irritation, no one in the household asked him any questions.

Moshe was restless even in his sleep. So restless and embittered that (as always happened when he went to sleep with something disturbing on his mind) his tension finally dissolved into images and he dreamed:

A table. It is a Sabbath or a holiday. Everything as always. His children and grandchildren at table. The house . . . as always. Everything in its usual order. But see, there where Moshe usually sits with Gitl, a guest now sits beside her.

He looks closely. It's Sruli, acting as if he were the man of the house. And Sruli noticing that there is a guest at the foot of the table orders that he be given food. And he encourages the guest to eat and to enjoy himself.

Moshe gazes at the guest—and recognizes himself, Moshe, a guest at his own table. Wearing, moreover, Sruli's clothes, and looking like Sruli, with Sruli's bowed head, his sullen downcast eyes looking at no one.

Moshe is in agony. He hears Sruli at the head of the table saying to Gitl, "Why is our guest angry? Why doesn't he eat?" And he, Moshe, wants to cry out, "You've got it wrong!" He ought to say it, because he is the man of the house. But Sruli laughs in his face. Then he turns to everyone at the table and puts his hand into his breast pocket from which he draws some kind of packet which he shows everyone as proof that he has a right to sit where he is. "Who," he asks, "owes whom? Who holds the promissory notes?"

Moshe is helpless. He bows his head and leaves the table and goes into a nearby room where he finds the knapsack that he has always supposed belonged to Sruli. He takes it up and then, before the eyes of all the household, before his wife and children who watch him pass, he goes to the door, ready to cross the threshold. There, he kisses the mezuzah, and, weeping, says farewell, leaving his home, leaving his family who sit silently at the table.

VIII

Two Outside the Fair

Ah, if I were to meet him now, thought Moshe Mashber on the morning after the night on which he dreamed the dream described above. "Him," of course, meant Sruli whose name he could not bring himself to pronounce—more than that, whose face he would not permit himself to imagine, the way one refuses to remember something hateful . . . a reptile or some other loathsome thing.

Ah, if I were to meet him now. He was not quite clear what it was that he would do but several vague and improbable things swirled about in his head . . . that he would do to the man who had disturbed his sleep, who had marred his relationship with his brother and who, above all, had robbed him of his fragile rich man's honor because, when the world heard about the promissory notes—when it learned that a man like Moshe was financially beholden to a fellow like Sruli—he, Moshe, would become a laughing stock.

Ah, if I could get my hands on him. He would do God alone knew what. Such things as in other and even worse situations had never even occurred to him. Now, however, he considered having the fellow seized and turned over to the proper authorities to have him searched, to have the source of his money investigated. Because how else if not by robbery could a fellow like that have come by money?

Ah! he sighed on that same morning as he thought of his brother, and linked the thought with the events of the last few days, that is, with the first indications he had had of financial difficulties. And when he let himself think of what had caused his problems, he was assailed by the pious fear that he had, perhaps, sinned in some way, and perhaps it was in regard to his brother that he had been most guilty.

Ah! And now it was of his brother he was thinking. If I had him here, I'd stand before him with a grieving heart and say, What's happening to us? Have I violated any part of the law or any of the customs established by our eternal lawmakers? It's what he should have done except that Luzi's heart had turned away from him some time ago so that finally the two of them had come to that bitter rupture.

Had he sinned? Moshe wondered, when for the sake of wife and children and to maintain his condition in life, he had conducted his business the way everyone did? That is, one was no sooner on one step of the ladder of commerce then one sought to climb to the next one up. But how was that sinful? That was the question he would have put to Luzi. After which, instead of dealing with his brother with hostility and anger, as he had before, he would change his approach; he would be gentle, forgiving and soft-spoken as he sought to find a mode of accommodation that would unite them in their former accord.

Because, speaking between ourselves, Moshe had a real need for such an accord just now. All that had happened following the Rudnitski affair, especially the events of yesterday involving the empty cashbox, the borrowings, the need to give over signed promissory notes to a fellow like Sruli . . . all of that weighed on Moshe like a ponderous stone, and he had a frightening premonitory chill in his bones. Perhaps, who could tell . . . perhaps the signs he was receiving were indications that his luck was leaving him? That he had achieved the highest rung on fortune's ladder. And from now on, all that waited for him was a descent. Things like that happened often enough.

Ah, if I only had him here . . .

But both of them—Sruli and Luzi—were just then far away; it was impossible even to know just where they were. On top of everything, there was still the fair which would go on . . . tomorrow and the next day . . . for nearly the whole of the week. A time in which for the sake of business one had to keep a clear head so that he, Moshe Mashber, could not afford to be preoccupied even with such grave and important thoughts as these. And indeed, pressed by the demands of the fair,

Moshe managed to shake himself free of them, and soon after rising he turned once again to business.

But on his way to the office, first Luzi, then Sruli, obtruded into his mind where he carried on a silent conversation with them while his lips, though he was not aware of it, murmured. As for the two who preoccupied him, they were both far away, unaware of him or of his sorrows.

Sruli, after he had been subjected to humiliation in Moshe Mashber's house, and after the confession he had made to Luzi, and especially after he had succeeded in putting what had been his secret horde of money into safe and carefully selected hands—that is, in Moshe's hands—Sruli from that time on was no longer seen in any rich man's home. One might have thought he had taken a vacation.

Once the fair began, he could be seen wandering about in the marketplace, moving, evidently deliberately, into the most crowded places, though he seemed to have nothing to do and no interest in buying anything. But there he was, a stranger in every crowd that gathered. Sometimes he was regarded with suspicion, as if he might be some sort of thief, or as a madman who without point or purpose had attached himself to a circle of people doing business.

And there he is, early on this morning of which we will now speak.

He stands there against one of the town's old fortress walls that faces the dike and the river. Now, because of the fair, a number of booths, tents and enclosures have been built at the foot of the wall, and there the press of the crowd, the hubbub and the noise of sellers hawking their wares and of buyers milling about is intense. People in motion, people standing in groups, in clusters, making a murmur like the humming of bees.

Sruli is standing beside a booth that has two canvas walls; the third wall abuts on the fortress. The fourth is no more than an open door. It is a booth where nothing is either bought or sold. It is a place of "healing." Of "slicing." There swellings, boils and abscesses are opened; it is a place for haircuts and shaves; leeches (dry and wet, but mostly wet) are applied; teeth are pulled; eyes are healed; and the chief doctor is old Layb, the barber-surgeon, peering through his two pairs of spectacles through which his eyes gleam, strange and huge, like those of a fish. There is also his helper, Menashe, the doctor's apprentice, who wears shiny boots and is constantly ready with a biting remark or a gross quip.

The patients—peasants who have saved up their illnesses at home for the barber-surgeon, Layb: they come to have him look at hernias that have opened; they report long-neglected sharp pains and other things for which the local village doctors (sorcerers, old women, female healers, conjurors) can find no remedy, and which, therefore, they have put off dealing with until they came to the fair.

There are two benches, one along each of the canvas walls on which the peasants sit as they wait their turn to be dealt with by pincers of the sort one uses to pull nails out of a wall and that here are used to pull teeth, benches on which, after the patients teeth are pulled, they can rest the way one rests when one has come into a cool place from the heat. Others, their hands at their jaws, spit blood and leave the booth in greater pain than when they entered it. They are Menashe's concern . . . Menashe, who holds the pincers, while Layb, the barber-surgeon, works with more refined implements to open abscesses and swellings after which he applies various colored salves and plasters.

Sruli stands there looking at basins filled with rags soiled with blood and pus. He watches the peasant patients: those who are healed and those who are not, those who leave the booth feeling better and those who feel worse; he watches them pay, healed or not, for their treatment. Some pay with cash, others in kind—half a dozen eggs, a fowl, a quantity of boar's bristles, garden produce . . . everything piled in a mountainous heap.

Sruli leaves this booth and we see him at the edge of a crowd on a street corner. There, too, the press is great. The bandura players have gathered there because it is an intersection of many streets and lanes through which all sorts of people have to pass.

A group of blind beggars have seated themselves on a pile of straw over which they have thrown their coarse coats. Their eyes are widely various: some of them stare sightlessly; others have their eyes closed, sunken, showing no sign of any pupil; some seem to have white peas floating in their eye sockets while under the closed eyes of still others, one senses the movement of pulsating pupils. But all of them have one thing in common—they are all blind. And no matter whether they have their heads raised to the sun or bowed low over their chests, whether they have deep voices or speak in a soft whisper, they all press their instruments close with their left hands while they turn the cranks with their right.

There is a large crowd gathered around them. The day is hot. One feels that later it will turn hellish. People press close around the bandura players and the crowd grows. Mostly, they are peasant women who have come to hear a pleasant word accompanied by music, a song whose simple melody is close to everyone's heart and over which one can shed a few sweet tears about fate. As, for instance, in the tale of a certain Kishko Samoylo, who was a prisoner of the Turks in ancient

times. And the tale tells what torments he and his whole band of Cossacks endured, first at the hands of the Turkish Janissaries, and later
from one of their own, a certain Liakh Buturlak who, because he had
betrayed his Christian homeland, had been made an overseer over his
breathren, the Cossack prisoners. And the tale goes on to tell what else
happened, and how finally they were rescued.

They hear, too, that other tale of a prisoner that begins with the
words *Nye yasni sokil kvilit prokvilyaye* and that goes on to tell how the
prisoner begs a falcon to fly to his home and there to plead with his
parents to sell their land and all that they have so that they may come
to ransom him. The song, like all such songs, ends with the words:

Free us, O Lord,
Poor miserable prisoner
From the dire captivity
of the Moslem faith
Take us back to
the holy bank of the sacred
Russian river
To the clean dawn
To the calm water
To our joyful land
To a Christian world.

Peasants, young and old, weep. Sometimes a bandura plays a solo.
Sometimes they play in chorus. There, in the midst of the racket of the
town and the fair, in the tumult of buying and selling, and the shouting
of thieves, a small island of people has been formed around the musicians, an island of people who have taken time to feel compassion for
ancient captivities—national or individual.

And Sruli is in the midst of this crowd. And he is just a hairbreadth
away from reaching into his pocket for the reed flute with which he
delights newly united poor couples at their wedding feasts; he is just a
hairbreadth away from joining the bandura players at their song.

But he does not take his reed flute out; instead, he finds a large coin
... Yes. And the peasants in the crowd are amazed at this strange fellow, this curiously dressed Jew: where does he come from: why, like
themselves, does he have tears in his eyes; why is he taking this tale of
Christian suffering so much to heart; what is it that makes him give the
bandura players such a large tip?

A short while later, Sruli might have been seen leaving the environs

of the fair and heading for a part of town that was a considerable distance from the region of the commercial marketplaces and the fair: to
the third ring, in the Sands area. There he found his way to a small
house, to the home of Malke-Rive whom we have already met. He
hovered about the entrance for a while. When nobody was looking, he
knelt at the doorstep and seemed to be picking something up from the
ground. Evidently amazed, he looked at whatever it was, then he rose
to his feet and knocked at the door.

To Malke-Rive's daughter-in-law, who opened the door for him, he
said angrily, "Look here, woman. Are you so rich that you leave
money lying about on your doorstep? Look what I've just found
there."

"Money? What money? Where?" she asked, astonished.

"Here. Right here on your doorstep."

The children of the house, hearing a conversation being carried on
in loud voices on their doorstep, came to see who it was who was so
angry with their mother. And Malke-Rive, who, with her spectacles
perched low on her nose, was reading the prayers in her prayer book,
as she did every morning . . . Malke-Rive interrupted her reading and
came to the door where she beheld Sruli, whom she knew to be a poor
man who was a frequent visitor in the homes of the rich, and whom
she especially remembered seeing last in Moshe Mashber's home on
that evening when right before her eyes Moshe had quarreled with his
brother on Sruli's account. And now here he was standing in her
doorway pressing a large denomination bank note into her daughter-
in-law's hand, and when the young woman refused to take it, shouting
at her, "Are you so rich that you leave money lying about on your
doorstep?"

"Money? What money?" Malke-Rive asked in her turn.

"Here. This," replied Sruli. "I was just passing by and caught a
glimpse of this money on your doorstep. I picked it up and brought it
in because it has to be yours. It was lying on your doorstep."

Malke-Rive stood perplexed. Like her daughter-in-law, she tried at
first to reject the money, saying that it had nothing to do with them,
that they had no money they could have lost, but at this, Sruli turned
furiously on both of the women. "Well, so what? So it isn't yours. But
it's certainly not mine. Do what you want with it. Throw it back on the
doorstep. Or give it away to the poor."

As he spoke, he glanced at the sick man in the house and saw at
once that his condition was getting worse. There was an unusual dry
and feverish glitter in his eye, his cheeks were sunken and the wrinkles
on his forehead had deepened, as if to indicate that inside his skull

there was a nest of thoughts that were not like those of a man who is long for this world.

As Sruli turned to go, he noticed a look on the faces of everyone in the household, the sick man included. It was like the one on their faces when all in one morning so many good things happened to them on an occasion described in a previous chapter. They had tried then but had been unable to guess who was the source of so much kindness. And now again they felt a hidden hand extending help in a way that could only be interpreted as miraculous.

Awhile later, one might have seen Sruli going back to town, but this time his pockets were crammed with bottles. Now he was on his way to the Living Synagogue which, like all the other synagogues during fair time, was deserted at midday—no one at prayers, no scholars studying Talmud. But there was one person there: Luzi—who lately had been spending his mornings and evenings in the company of his fellow Bratslaver, and the rest of the day in the synagogue alone because everyone else was busy.

But Sruli did not go into the synagogue. Instead, he went through a gate that led into the old cemetery. It was a quiet cemetery, one that did not even have paths because it had been so long since anyone had been buried there.

Had anyone been looking through a synagogue window or through a gap in the ancient fence, they would have seen Sruli moving in a crouch through the tall grasses. The ground sloped downward and the undergrowth, grown tall and dense over the years, smelled of moss and of grass that grew thicker each year. The place was silent except for the sound of grasshoppers. Graves and gravestones dozed, overgrown and so neglected that one could suppose that even the grandchildren of those who were buried there must be among the dead by now, and that this was why the paths of the place had been reclaimed by the grass. The place had a double silence. First, the silence that one generally finds in a cemetery, and then the additional stillness of a cemetery in which no one is buried anymore.

Sruli made his way to the one tall old tree that overhung the tomb of a famous holy man, Rabbi Liber, whose grave was closely hemmed in by the graves of others as holy as himself. His grave was deeply sunken and surrounded by imposing headstones that had been artistically carved. And it was here that Sruli lay down, hidden from sight by the tall grasses. Moving slowly, he took the bottles out of his pockets. Then after a brief rest he settled down to drink.

It is necessary to see the scene clearly.

It is a fearfully hot day. In town, young and old are preoccupied with the great fair. There is an appalling racket in every market square. And here, in the center of town, in the neglected cemetery, under a shady old tree, is the grave of a profoundly reverenced man. There is a legend about him that says that the Old Synagogue was built on the spot where, once, the great Rabbi Liber stood reciting the Eighteen Benedictions under a tree when the place was still a forest. He was so engrossed in his prayers that he did not notice the approach of a nobleman's coach. The nobleman's horses, startled at the sight of the Jew in prayer shawl and phylacteries under a tree, ran off and the nobleman was nearly flung from the coach. The nobleman instructed his coachman to give the Jew a sound drubbing. The coachman wielded his whip with all his might—as a coachman can—but the great Reb Liber did not interrupt his prayers until he had finished the last of the Eighteen Benedictions. And it was there, beside that holy man's grave and near the graves of others like him, that Sruli lay sprawled, tippling from his bottles.

Had anyone passing by seen him thus occupied, he would certainly have been torn to bits. But that thought did not occur to Sruli. He did what he had in mind to do. He had just endured the heat of the day as well as the racket in town and now, drinking in the cool space between the graves, his mood was at once elevated and dark. Dark because he lived set apart from the world, and elevated because he loved solitude.

And there he commenced to unburden himself, complaining first to his dybbuk, that creation of his morbid imagination, and then to the letters carved on Rabbi Liber's tombstone. He addressed himself to them as if they were living persons. He even (one is ashamed to say) invited the great Rabbi Liber to drink with him as with a boon companion. And when, as he supposed, the rabbi refused, he forced him to drink, pouring the rabbi's share of the liquor over his gravestone.

"Never mind. Drink, Reb Liber. You're a truly holy man, and I'm an excommunicant who may not be admitted into the community of Jews. But money, after all, is a purifier of bastards. And I have money. If not cash, then promissory notes—which are as good as cash."

And here, Sruli took the promissory notes out of his breast pocket and showed them to the gravestone. "See. Look at them, Reb Liber. And don't put on any airs and don't shrink away from old Sruli. Notes are money, just as long as the fellow who's signed them doesn't go bankrupt. And it's not just his notes that I have. Not just Moshe Mashber's. I have them from others greater than he is. From the richest of the rich. I tell you I have them from Him who can say, 'The silver is mine, and mine is the gold.' I have them from the Creator of the World Himself, and I beg you, dear Rabbi Liber, to tell Him up there that he, so and so, son of so and so, Sruli Gol has claims and complaints against Him. One day I'll come and stand before His throne and make them myself, but meanwhile, Reb Liber, be good enough to make them for me.

"Never mind," Sruli went on, speaking to the headstone and to the great Rabbi Liber, "it's a perfectly honorable errand for you to run. Well, we know that you're a venerated saint who was horsewhipped by a nobleman. But that happened to you only once. But it's happened to me, Sruli, ah . . . many, many times. And if they built the Old Synagogue on account of your one beating, then I, who have been frequently beaten, am entitled to have them build me—never mind an Old Synagogue—but at least one new one. Yes, I'm entitled to be honored by one synagogue."

The sun's heat beat down on his head. Sruli sat in a partly cooled space among tall grasses sharing his liquor with the rabbi whose name was inscribed on the headstone. A sip for him, a sip for the rabbi poured over the stone. Until finally the bottles were empty and his head—full. It felt heavy, things around him began to whirl: the cemetery, the gravestones. The tree above him seemed to rise up, roots and all; heaven and earth changed places; and everything he had seen that day at the fair—Layb the barber-surgeon and Menashe his apprentice, cutting into abscesses on the breasts or under the armpits of peasant women, the teeth extracted with pincers, veins opened or blood drawn by leeches, and what he had seen of the blind beggars, their eyelids open or closed; and what he had seen later in Malke-Rive's home—the sick Zisye, with the sunken and yellow cheeks of a man who was more than half dead, and who bore the sign of death on his forehead; all of that, and the liquor he had drunk or poured out on the ground, mingled in his head making the world turn. He felt a spasm of nausea. Leaning his head against the gravestone he rested there awhile, then the nausea overwhelmed him and he threw up, covering the headstone from top to bottom with his vomit.

He felt better, and was instantly ashamed when he perceived what he had done. His head cleared a bit, and he glanced back in the direction of the Living Synagogue whose eastern wall looked out on the cemetery and it seemed to him that he saw Luzi's head at one of its windows. It is possible that it actually was Luzi, but also that Sruli had imagined seeing him; in any case, he felt ashamed when he thought that Luzi might have seen him profaning the gravestone.

He tried to get up but couldn't. Half drunk and trembling, he spoke, but this time only to himself. "Didn't I say that I needed help? That left to myself, who knows what might happen to me. This isn't the first time I've done something like this and been left feeling so ashamed I can hardly face myself. How, then, will I be able to look into Luzi's eyes?"

He got to his feet as best as he could and moved off to one side, away from the gravestone where he had done his unseemly business. There he leaned against another stone, and there, his head bowed, all thought left him and he dozed off. He does not remember how long he slept, but it was long enough so that he was wakened by the sun whose rays, no longer shaded from him by the overhanging branches of the tree, were shining directly on his head. He got to his feet and made his way to the synagogue. He stood at the entrance, and there he found himself facing Luzi who sat behind a lectern at the eastern wall.

It was still midday. All of the synagogue windows that looked out on the cemetery were open. There were bushes, saplings and grasses mirrored in every window, something rarely to be seen in the windows of other synagogues. The silence and solitude were also unusual, because the synagogue was some distance from the hubbub of the town.

Evidently Luzi had been sitting at the eastern wall for some time after his prayers because he was no longer wearing his pylacteries—only his prayer shawl, studying for hours after his devotions. And this was especially true during the month of Elul. But now he was not studying. He was reading penitential prayers and he was so engrossed in them that he did not, as he usually did, read them quietly and with his eyes only. No. He read them aloud and wept loudly as he read.

He did not notice that Sruli had come in. Sruli had in the course of his life seen many manifestations of piety; added to that, he was now at least half-drunk so that one might have expected Luzi's praying to have little effect on him. And yet seeing Luzi rooted Sruli to the spot, as if he could muster neither the strength nor the will to move.

Here, it is necessary to interrupt our narrative to make the following remarks:

Those of our readers who are little acquainted with Luzi's biography may find it incredible and inexplicable that a man like Luzi could bind himself to a fellow like Sruli. What was it he discerned in him? What was it that attracted him? And what did Sruli get out of the relationship? These are questions one might well ask, especially now when one sees Sruli, half-drunk and newly wakened from sleep, keeping Luzi under the intensest scrutiny.

It is very true. Everything would have been clearer and all doubts would have been allayed had we been able to see Luzi in action. But that will not happen until we have passed over from part one of our narrative in which we have undertaken to describe only people, to part two where we intend to describe events. Meanwhile, we feel that we have not done justice even to the description of people. Luzi's biography, for example, has been neglected in this part of our tale, and so we will use this space to sketch in (however hastily and out of sequence) a few of the most salient details.

We believe that even the insufficient details we mean to add will be enough to explain to some degree that Sruli who felt himself to be an outcast was drawn to Luzi who seemed in one sense to be an outcast as well. Sruli may have imagined that the two of them would smolder together, giving off smoke until, who could say when, they might burst into flame.

Well then, back to Luzi's beginnings.

But one needs first to recall that we are dealing here with an epoch in which people of Luzi's caliber were constrained to live through various superstitious phases intended to corrupt and deceive everyone, and which for the most part had corrupting and deceitful effects on them as well. The result was that what they built with their imaginations or their dreams served that world by covering up or enhancing what, if it were not concealed, would result in great harm to its material and spiritual structure.

We turn now to a period in Luzi's life when he was doing penance for his grandfather's adherence to the teachings of Shabbatai Zevi. Luzi slept on the ground, he put stones in his shoes. He would spend hours, especially when he was at his prayers, with his hands rigidly at his sides, refusing to let them make the slightest movement until the hands swelled to the size of pitchers.

When he allowed himself to lie down, it was only during days of celebration: on holidays or on the Sabbath. But even then he lay on a bare bench that was only a board or two wide and on which there were no bedclothes. In addition to that he placed his head in the middle of the bench so that his feet would be forced to dangle over the edge.

He still had a youthful appearance but physically he looked fearfully worn. It gave one the chill to see him. That period, which we have described at the beginning of our narrative, lasted some little while and his condition deteriorated so much that it was likely he would have to take to his bed. But then, as has been said, he was brought to the rebbe to whom he became so attached. And it was the rebbe who berated him roundly, and forbade him to live like an ascetic, and Luzi obeyed him.

What happened then without anyone taking notice of it was that Luzi, who was still young and in the very bloom of his youth, filled out physically: his shoulders broadened, his bones strengthened, and his clothes, which had hung on him loosely, now burst at their seams.

It was as if he had acquired a whole new skin. Luzi turned into the complete opposite of the person he had been. He became the rebbe's most cheerful—and favorite—disciple. The older men saw him as the most youthful of the young, and the young men (even the very youngest) envied him his overflowing high spirits.

At every rabbinical festivity or holiday or wedding, when great crowds gathered together and when ordinary (or even extraordinary) men might pass unnoticed, Luzi stood out. He was noticed and admired as a shining light whose brilliance illuminated them all. The rabbinical court that nurtured Luzi in its bosom was the envy of all the others.

The cheerfullest man, the best prayer leader, the finest dancer, the man best loved by everyone and the one who was closest to the rebbe. He ate and drank joyfully, but beyond that there was joy in the very set of his shoulders, and he was manifestly delighted to be alive.

He studied, he prayed, he lived with such intent pleasure that anyone standing near him had his view of the world changed. It became delightful, gleaming, presenting itself in such a way that one could not help loving it. Luzi had the rare gift to imbue those around him with the warm light that streamed from him.

And this was especially evident at festivities where many people were gathered and hearts were expansive. Where joy was great—and would grow, as soon as it found a midpoint, a focus from which it would radiate outward to shine on those in its circle and on those around it. It was then that Luzi was seen—as if he had wings. He drank, his voice could be heard above everyone's. It was he who uttered the first brilliant and joyful words that bound all hearts together in an intimate unity.

One had to have seen him at one of those truly thronged festivities, such as a wedding in a rabbinical household when there were many Hasidim with their fur hats and black silk or white satin coats seated around the main table. One ought to have heard how he was praised by them all, and seen how faces lighted up when he appeared in the midst of a huge crowd that had absolute confidence that he would not embarrass them, and taken note of the way that all of the assembly—onlookers, guests, relatives and relatives-in-law who had come from other rabbinical courts—envied this one.

At such times, Luzi was generally already a bit drunk, but there was no indication of it in his graceful carriage or on his energetic, youthful and still lightly bearded face.

Luzi looked out at the crowd, his eyes avid and feverish the way a child who is learning to walk keeps his eyes on his mother, confident that she will not let him fall or hurt himself, that if he should need it she will help him restore his balance.

Luzi danced.

The event always took place in a huge shed specially built for weddings, one of those buildings in which Jewish artisans outdid themselves to transform a one-story structure into two, doubling thereby the number of seats so that those who were not lucky enough to find places below might look down on the festivities from a sort of gallery.

The place was terribly crowded. People were standing cheek by jowl. The sextons, however, who knew what was coming, made way for Luzi and cleared a circle for him despite the crowd.

Luzi stepped forward. At first, as always, he kept his eyes on the toes of his boots, as if something had embarrassed him, as if he were uncertain and wanted for a while to study his feet, to determine whether he could count on them when he made his appearance before such a large crowd. He looked them over the way a fine workman studies his tools before he begins a task.

He was soon reassured. Then Luzi moved, keeping at first close to the wall of people who formed the circle, so close that he almost touched them. Then he took off like a delicate bird that circles its mate, creating space and air around him first so that it may have room to move when he advances to possess her.

Luzi circled the ring once, and then again, and the audience—those sitting below, as well as those seated above in the gallery—was already in his power. As if nothing in the world existed for it (the audience) but the ring at whose center there stood Luzi who looked as if he had been given some great riddle to solve, or who had been told that there was a treasure buried in the circle—and now he was required, silently and with the power of a hidden instinct, to guess the riddle and for the good of mankind to find the treasure.

And now Luzi was on its track. He moved with the care of a hunter in a wood hiding among bushes and so engrossed in the hunt that he does not breathe. The tension in his slim young body was visible to all. Sometimes he leaped from one place to another only to hide once again. The hunt continued, as if the hunter had to pass through dark then half-dark cover. Then he had it . . . or was about to have it.

And here, Luzi was delighted. He looked down at his feet as if grateful to them for their help, and because they had proved dependable whenever he had counted on them. He took to pacing now, and every step seemed to be an act of gratitude, a praise of the earth on which

Luzi flourished and which had rewarded him. He lifted the skirts of his coat as if he were walking in gold up to his knees and turned and gave the people who encircled him a look of smiling approbation and gratitude for their support and for maintaining the circle while he had danced.

Luzi's delight intensified. And here, the audience, watching him, learned what *one* man could do in an instant to a massed crowd. Everyone's eyes were so intently focused on him, their very breathing depended on him; his least movement was so precisely in tune with their desire to make the same movement that they found it difficult to tell whether it was *he* and not *they* who were moving with such precision.

A wild whirlwind in the shape of an agile young man was moving before their eyes. Sometimes, Cossack-fashion, with his hand at the nape of his neck, he went round and round, a wheel within a wheel, seeming to circle himself and his superabundant energies; and sometimes, on the contrary, he moved as if he were a weak old man, but one who had therefore been purified and moved now with a rare self-possession, as if he had acquired the best of experience in its calmest form.

Sometimes as Luzi danced he seemed to be strolling at sunset in a garden over which an evening stillness reigned. Everything that lived, every winged creature, everything that whistled or hummed by day was being led to its rest; and one man was there summing up and interpreting their deeds for each of the creatures. And sometimes Luzi himself was seen as a winged creature waking at sunrise who, in sheer joy at being awake in sunlight and not knowing what else to do, flung himself off into space, but finding space to be too constricting swooped back down, then up again, all the while feeling a constriction in his throat because it was too narrow to permit him to utter his praise of light.

It was then that Luzi was seen to turn his head toward those in the audience who surrounded him and on whom it would seem he had focused all his life energies, turned and greeted them with a cry that proceeded from an an overflowing heart: "People! I haven't the words to express what I feel. I have only these. . . ." And here he indicated his feet. Then, like a young stag whose horns have newly grown, he made a lyric leap back into the center of the circle, so deeply engrossed in the display of his own abundant energies that the bystanders were afraid to watch him, feeling themselves in the presence of a man whose wild and excessive happiness might drive him—God forbid—beyond the limits of sanity.

"People! Say unto Him whom I have not the words to name—say unto Him that even if *'kol etsmosi tamarna*, my bones sang,' it would be no more than if one of its droplets were to praise the sea."

It was in such dazzled tones that Luzi was spoken of in those years by those who shared his views, who lived in the same world as he and who were nourished by the same ideas. His character and acts were seen as worth emulating, as helping to unite the community.

Still dazzled, they would go on to say that when the young Luzi was a participant at a festivity or a holiday celebration at which older folk regarded him as their heir apparent and young people saw him as a model to be imitated—Luzi, under the influence of the drink he took before he danced (afterward he could drink the Jordan up) became exalted in a way that everyone understood meant that he would appear before them soon and, screwing up his courage, would address them:

"Gentlemen, I want to demonstrate *gevuras-haboyre*, the power of the Creator." With that he would strike the edge of the table. . . . If it was an old, weak table, he would beat at it till it fell apart, and if, as was usually the case, it was not old, he would beat it until his hand bled. It became the custom of synagogue sextons to stand by holding wet towels with which to stanch the blood whenever Luzi was about to make one of his demonstrations.

That's how it was with him when he was young and turbulent, and he often confided problems to his rebbe who gave him various kinds of advice that sometimes comforted him and—sometimes did not. Because Luzi felt like a young animal in a cage that flings itself against the bars—which is what he called the passions that assailed him.

Naturally, as he grew older, he calmed down. On the other hand, his love for the religious faith to which he had attached himself increased, so much indeed that his soul seemed to be inextricably bound to it. For years he lived under the shadow of his rebbe as under the shade of a many-branched tree. And there, he found spiritual peace. He was the greatest and best beloved of the rebbe's disciples. Whenever there was any event in his rebbe's court, he, Luzi, was called in for advice even before any of the rebbe's confidants; and, face-to-face with him in his private chamber, the rebbe confided the most intimate matters to him. On the other hand, when Luzi had need of the rebbe, he was certain of access to him night or day. Even when the rebbe was busy with other people, it was Luzi who was given priority.

And that was how things were until the rebbe grew old and feeble and sensed that his end was near. It was then, as he was dying, that he had a conversation with Luzi during which no one was permitted into the room but the two of them. The rebbe said that he was very unhappy to be leaving the world without discerning a successor who could preside over his court. He said that he thought that the world was in a decline—and that faith was diminishing. Luzi, hearing him, wept. He foresaw what would be for him a setting of a sun but the old man consoled him and told him where to go after he, the rebbe, was dead. And Luzi wept even more.

There, sitting beside the dying man's bedside, he had felt as if his head were already covered with ashes, and knew that his life would be a lonely one. He felt a chill stirring in his garments because lately he had sensed that the old paths had become overgrown, and that there was something new in the air, something about which previous generations had not needed to be concerned and which now it was already too late to do anything about. There was a sort of illness abroad in the land, an illness that chilled faith. There was something profoundly wrong; counsel was needed and now the man with whom one could take counsel was dying.

And when the rebbe died, Luzi was, as we have already recounted, overwhelmed by solitude. He undertook a new pilgrimage, and visited many rabbinical courts but could not attach himself to any until at last he found and joined the Bratslavers, his group.

And now we see him sitting alone in that synagogue, all of whose twelve open windows reflecting trees and shrubs looked out upon the old cemetery from which there came an odor of greenery, decay and silent growth. Outdoors the day was hot, one of those latter days that, gathering its force, becomes the hottest day of the summer.

A day, then. And a town in tumultuous disorder, and here, in the synagogue removed and distant, sat Luzi like the blind singers with the banduras in the marketplace whose songs called up ancient folk yearnings, servitudes and captivities, Luzi who was also a sort of singer, and who was in his own way equally blind as he looked into his book and the tears obscured his sight. He read aloud, weeping, and mourned another sort of captivity, the captivity of a people in the grip of an ancient and blind destiny, mourned it because, as it seemed to him, it was a people that had grown weary and whose capacity for faith had declined. At the same time he felt that his own energies had passed their peak and were subsiding as he moved toward old age; and Luzi mourned for the summer, too, which, though its reflections were still green in the synagogue windows, yet a sensitive heart could not help feeling that the intense heat of the day was but a symptom of the summer's end, a presage of those inevitable cooler, overcast days that would bring with them a calm like that which now reigned over the cemetery.

Luzi wept for his wasted life, for the waste of a people which was destined from on high to be the grief bearer for all nations. A destiny whose metaphor he saw in the Messiah. Luzi saw him as the legend describes him, seated before the gates of Rome, wounded, leprous—bandaging, unbandaging and rebandaging his sores.

And here is what Luzi, the blind singer, sees as he recites his prayers:

The first scene: It is dawn. His gaze turns first toward a mist. Then the mist clears away and he sees a town in the distance: houses—each one taller than the next, each one above the other; he sees whole sections of the town—some built on the heights, others in valleys.

It is still early morning. The town is asleep. But there is a grandeur rising from that sleep. Soon now the town will wake from its satiated and sinful sleep and will see a new day, and a new night ready for new sins.

And now it is fully daylight. There is movement *from* the town and movement *to* it of people from all parts of the country bringing supplies. Peasants from distant villages, merchants, secondhand-clothing dealers, soldiers, cripples, tax collectors, slaves, tumblers, beggars, and every variety of whore, some more, others less, highly painted, who have been sent from the most distant parts of the country in anticipation of night pleasures still to come; and everyone, those leaving the town and those coming toward it, becomes aware that there is a man sitting at the city's gate. His features are radiant, but his clothing is ragged and his body is covered with sores. He has not been permitted to enter the town and tonight, as on every other night, he will sit here before the gate. And everyone, as if by prior agreement ... everyone stops and, as if it were a debt he was paying, spits at him and on his wounds.

Some spit on his head, some at his face, some on his ragged garments. Sometimes the man wipes the spittle away, but most of the time he sits mute and immobile as if it were not at him they were spitting but at someone else.

And here, when the blind singer sees the man with the radiant face being spat on by coarse and bestial soldiers, by merchants and old-clothes dealers, by cripples and by whores, he utters a wail and all of his limbs tremble as he remembers passages and fragments of passages from ancient poems of prayer and from the angry poems of ancient folk singers. And, in unison with one of those songs, he cries out like a wounded man:

פצעי לא רככה וחבורתי רצח
ועיני הוכהתה צופה לדודי צח.

My abscess has hardened, my tumors are fearful . . .
And mine eyes have gone blind with long watching for my
     Savior.

He seeks consolation and cannot find it, but there is one thing that does help: he imagines himself taking the other man's place, himself ulcerated, spat upon, condemned and yet silent, knowing, like him, that this is a destiny sent from on high, and that what is destined must happen, that destiny is a gift of sorts handed down by a blessed arm.

And here is the second scene:

Night. Darkness. And one can sense that in the dark, people are searching without being able to find each other, but they feel a certain consolation because, though they are scattered, yet they can sense each other's presence and they know that the place is swarming with people searching for each other.

One is aware, too, of the presence of a profoundly faithful, and lost, mass of people. And one feels that if a single ray of light should suddenly shine there, then the whole of the fasting, thirsty and exhausted mass . . . would, as if it were half mad, rush to follow the ray of light into whatever passage might open before them—a sea . . . an abyss . . . or both. They would follow that light toward disaster with song and with praise as if they were flying to salvation.

And there at the edge of the sky, there is a blaze and the whole mass is suddenly illuminated: sleeping children, their heads on their parents' shoulders; the parents weary with senseless wandering; old people, more than three quarters bent to the ground—all moving toward that fire in the sky.

One sees:

Some are being dragged to the fire by strangers. They do not want to go, they resist. But when they are finally cast into the flames, the others who are next in line now go of their own accord. Still others hurry toward the fire. They fling their children in first, their wives and old people next, then they, too, leap into the flames, serving thereby as examples to the massed crowds who, seeing what these have done voluntarily, pause for a moment like a great herd dazed in the presence of some catastrophe, and then their herd instinct comes to their aid—that instinct that allows them to blind themselves to danger and enables them to move with enthusiasm toward death and destruction. The greater the herd, the greater the enthusiasm, and as the sense of danger lessens, the pressure of movement increases until, like sheep before an unavoidable precipice, they hurry to push and jostle each other into the arms—into the lap—of death.

קדש את שמך בעולמך על עם מקדישי שמך.

Sanctify Thy name in Thy world through Thy people that sanctifies Thy name.

Here, the blind singer hears the cries that come from the pyres of ancient times and he mourns along with them; he feels as if he, too, has been thrust into the flames and that his clothes too are smoldering and that soon the flames will reach his body and touch his soul. He sees himself as one of a group of those who in ancient times rushed into such fires as this, and now, after all those years, he smells the scorched odor of their clothes as well as of his own.

And now, a final scene:

Again, before dawn: Off in the distant dark, at the night's edge, in a place where there is neither sunrise nor light, a shape is seen to emerge that has the form of a gate with a pillar on each side. Above it, a semicircular arch. And as the gate becomes increasingly visible, it becomes clear that through it, and only through it, will the light of the sun appear.

And soon thereafter it does indeed appear: the father and the son: the famous Reb Shimon and his son Eliezer. These two who hid for years in caves and who, when they left, brought with them cool predawn remedies for those who leaped into the fires, and brought ladders, too, to help them mount upward toward their goal, and lamps to illuminate their way.

All this is a way of saying that they brought with them their two books, the *Zohar* and the *T'kuni Zohar* over which the singer sat bowed. Books which he thought—as did many others like him—relieved the people's weariness and were like moist bandages on fevered wounds.

Then the gate disappeared and in its place there appeared a great spacious square in which all those things that are mentioned in the books were to be seen. Bears that speak in human voices, birds that carry messages from one part of the world to another, brooks and wells beside whose calm waters certain secret shepherds rest, herbs that heal or kill, children who look old, aged folk that look like children, prophets, seers, wanderers, pilgrims with ashes on their heads and dust in their eyes. In a word, everything that is touched on in those marvelously begun and incompleted tales and half tales, forming a fantastic arabesque of God's Name braided with flowers and with the dead, and those as yet unborn, the dead from whose bodies emanates a persistent odor that covers the world; and with the shades of those tormented souls who wander about unable to find a resting place; and with still other forms: shape shifters, ghosts, wandering spirits, plagues, demons, good and evil angels and various people who have been cursed—all inhabitants of those wildly imagined writings whose authors, with evil intent or because they are themselves misled, have written to blind or to deceive the world.

Sruli waited. He had observed that Luzi, all through the recitation of his prayers, had been trembling like a man who has chills or fever. That at the most touching moments in the prayers, he had passed a hand across his forehead, or over the top of his head and sometimes, even, over the back of his neck. At intervals, he had left his place, as if unable to keep seated. It was not his usual way to pray. His eyes had been often darkened by tears, and sometimes he had uttered a curious sort of cough.

Sruli waited. And when he saw that Luzi was done, that he had calmed down and that his features were clearing (though there were still marks of moisture in the corners of his eyes), then Sruli left the spot where he had been waiting throughout Luzi's prayers.

He took one step forward, then another. Step by step he approached Luzi's lectern, and as he walked, his hand moved slowly to his breast pocket from which he removed a packet of paper which he handed to Luzi. "I've been to the fair and I . . ." he began to stammer and repeated the same words he had used in Malke-Rive's house. "I happened to be passing by and I looked down at the doorsill and saw these—so I picked them up and brought them in. And I'm returning them to their owner."

"Fair? What fair? Owner? Which owner? And what are you giving me?" Luzi said, more with his eyes than with his words. And it was now that he observed a pale Sruli standing before him. Sruli, with the sort of wan look drinkers get after prolonged drinking and before they have completely sobered up. And since Luzi had himself just returned as it were from a distant, distant place where things of *this* world had been of little interest to him, he did not at first grasp the meaning of such words as "fair" and others like it. He had completely forgotten that there was a fair and that people might have all sorts of reasons for being interested in it.

"What fair? And what are you giving me?" He stared without comprehension at Sruli and at his outstretched arm.

"This is the money I told you about. I've put it out at interest—actually, I've lent it to your brother Moshe. And I'm afraid to carry the promissory notes about with me—worse, I'm afraid I might get drunk and lose them. So I want to give them to you. You can do what you like with them. Use them at your discretion . . . help needy people . . . anyone at all . . . whatever you think proper."

"Oh . . . ah . . ." Luzi pushed Sruli's hand away. "Oh . . . ah . . . I don't meddle with such things . . . I have nothing to do with them. They don't concern me." Then more clearly he added, "No. I'm not the man for that. Give them to someone else or keep them yourself. I have to say no."

Again, Sruli waited as Luzi put the prayer shawl and tefillin away, and then as he put on his coat. Then one might have seen them leaving the synagogue together, Luzi first and Sruli behind him until at the middle of the staircase they drew even with each other. But even there, Luzi was a trifle in advance and Sruli just behind as if maintaining a respectful distance. In the conversation they had as they walked, it was Luzi who did most of the talking, while Sruli listened. And anyone seeing them would have noticed how Sruli strained to hear what his companion said because his head was still unclear, his step still unsteady and the ground on which he walked still wobbled.

IX

A Little Bit of the Ordinary

It was in the final days of the month of Elul. At the Rough Market, where at various vending stalls various small but important things for shoemakers were sold at retail all year long: nails in packets, loose nails, thread and shoemaker's pitch. Now in those stalls there appeared rounds of wax shaped like large, medium or small plates. This was wax that the town's most pious women would be needing soon to make memorial candles for use during the most awesome of the imminent holidays: the New Year and Yom Kippur, the Day of Judgment.

In the days between the New Year and Yom Kippur, those women would gather in family enclaves, each family meeting in the home of its most pious member. They would cluster in rooms from which men and children would be excluded. There, various magic things would be done to each of the wicks, and they would be wept and sobbed over, as the women invoked the names of the dead to which each thread in the wicks was to be dedicated.

As has been said, long thin candles would be made in those rooms for their fearful God and His fearful Judgment Day, on which He is especially stern, requiring of those who pray for His help that they use special candles of an exceptional holiness and made of the purest natural materials available: beeswax—a product of bees and flowers.

In town, people readied themselves for the holidays in various ways. For the whole of the preceding month long lines of women might have been seen on every Monday and Thursday going out to the cemeteries in the morning and returning later in the day tearstained and hoarse because of the loud laments they had uttered earlier over the graves from which they returned now eased and relaxed as if they had left intense heat to come into a place that was cool.

The numbers of these women had multiplied on the most recent Mondays and Thursdays by an influx of poverty-stricken women who, in torn shoes and shabby shawls, brought with them the collected griefs of the entire year which now they poured out to their dearest dead: their parents, their relatives, their children.

Liber-Meyer, the guardian of the tomb at the "field" was kept very busy in those weeks and earned considerable money for lighting lamps and for extinguishing them. He ran about from one client to another. And to make things easier for him, he now had an assistant to help him with the writing of petitions, but the assistant, too, had a hard time getting quit of the many women and maidens who crowded around him wanting him to write to the holy man, or to his sons or sons-in-law who were buried there in the men's section of the tomb; or to his wife and his daughters and daughters-in-law who were buried on the other side of the wall in the women's section.

The place was acrawl, too, with vagabonds, beggars, cripples and various sorts of clergy whom nobody needed but who had need of everyone. People who had nothing except their various disabilities, or the curses—or blessings—in their mouths. These vagabonds, beggars, cripples and clergymen besieged the entrance and the exit to the tomb—they were everywhere. They found their way to the most distant graves—and whoever gave them something, received their blessing, and those who did not, went unblessed. But who at such a place and at a time like that wanted to remain unblessed. So it was that poverty-stricken women untied the knots in their kerchiefs or opened their purses and took out their last groschen to buy the goodwill—and the blessing—of these good-for-nothings who had waited all year long for this occasion.

So much for the women during those days. But men, too, made ready for the holidays. The members of the various Hasidic sects of the town gathered in their places of prayer—in synagogues and in their rebbes' courts—and in the evenings of the last days of the month, they talked among themselves, deciding who was to "make the journey" and when; they formed groups, collected money so that they might share in the costs of wagon drivers, and the members of those sects whose rebbe lived at a great distance arranged to go a few days earlier so that they would arrive on the evening before the holiday. The result was considerable hubbub at various wagon depots as the drivers made promises to do the driving, then broke their word when someone else offered them more money.

Thus it was with those members of Hasidic sects who were traveling overland. The first priority was for oneself to go, to appear before the rebbe on the holiday, but there was also the need to prepare a list of names of those who could not make the journey so that on the last day of the year it could be handed to the rebbe so that those names too might be mentioned in the rebbe's prayers.

But there was one sect that was in no hurry. Because the road to their rebbe, though distant enough, was not to be traversed with the help of any wagon driver. One had to go by train. This was the Bratslaver sect whose tradition it was to start on their journey the very morning of the day before the holiday. They did not hurry, even on the day of their departure, even at the train station. Because one of their members, a rich landowner of the district, provided a special car for all the members of the sect who were going. A special car because years of experience had taught them that when they traveled in the company of strangers there was no way to avoid insults, taunts, laughter and even, God forbid, blows. The landowner, a few days before the journey, took it as his pious duty to lease a railroad car and, wherever it was necessary, to bribe the requisite officials. After that those who could pay their share of the costs did so. Those who could not, traveled without paying a cent.

And now, here it was, the morning of the day before the holiday. The town's railroad station, though one would not call it large by any means, was a very busy place—particularly at arrival and departure times. Because travelers from the entire district gathered there, and there was a great pushing and hurrying about, an extraordinary stream of people pressed against each other like sheep, standing or moving together. All of them, a bit frightened of a place to which they rarely came, waited for their trains.

And now, here it was. That stream of people, led by the landowner of whom we have spoken and who leased a car for them, now moved across the platform to get on board.

The two gendarmes who were always on duty maintaining the peace during the arrivals and departures of the trains were on the platform now decked out in their gendarmish best, wearing their Caucasian lambskin hats with the white brush in the front, their chests covered with gleaming silver medals and decorations—awarded to them by the highest authorities for their exceptional and exemplary service as gendarmes.

Zshouk, who stood a man and a half high and ramrod straight, chest and shoulders rigid, looking altogether like the embodiment of a powerful golem . . . Zshouk, with the shaven cheeks and the long black mustache, never smiled, first because it was not in his nature to smile and then because he thought that being a gendarme was not compatible with laughter.

Matvei, the second gendarme, was much shorter than Zshouk, but he was broader, especially in the chest where his spreading Russian beard covered all of his medals.

These two, seeing that stream of people, paused to watch it, leaving the rest of the station to look after itself. They were so taken by what was going on at the specially leased car that they had no attention to spare for anything else. It made no difference that both of them were local people and that the crowd they were watching was made up of town dwellers (and out of towners) whose customs, manners and clothing they knew well, or that their long service had accustomed them to unusual sights, still they could not keep their eyes from that crowd.

Those people looked, as they clambered aboard the car, like so many creatures being taken somewhere to be displayed. Among them, there was the tall Avreml, the Three-yard Tailor, his head bent with fear. Sholem, the porter, half the size of an elephant, who was continually hunched in his effort to seem smaller than he was. Menakhem, the dyer, frightened at being looked at by strangers, and afraid of the unfamiliar train station air which seemed to threaten him from every side. He kept his head close to the man who preceded him and whispered a prayer to be kept safe from the dangers of the journey as well as from those that—God forbid—might overtake him here in the station.

And then there was "The Couple" who here, as well as in the synagogue, kept close to each other like a pair of nearsighted little creatures who were still suffering from the light of day. They wore shabby caftans over their skinny shoulders, and as they waited in line for their turn to board the train, each of them had a cigarette stub in his mouth from which he hastily tried to suck whatever he could.

These were local people, who one way or another still looked human. But then there were those newly arrived from the provinces who lived all year long in distant godforsaken settlements. They were truly wild. They wore the sort of clothing that provoked laughter even in people who were quite used to them, never mind the effect they had on those to whom they were an unaccustomed sight—strangers . . . or gendarmes at a train station. So that when the gendarme Zshouk saw these frightened people crowding each other in their haste to get into their wagon, he made a sign to Matvei, who stood beside him, to take a good look at them. But as the two laughing gendarmes stood before the car, they observed the arrival of three new people at the end of the line. These were Mikhl Bukyer, Sruli and Luzi. Luzi, tall and stately in his summer coat. The instant the gendarmes saw Luzi, the smiles disappeared from their faces. They recognized him as a chief of sorts, a leader. A man of some wealth and dignity. And these two deferred to wealth and dignity, whether they encountered it in the merchant class or the clergy without regard to nationality or religion.

The gendarmes, still standing before the leased car, saw Mikhl Bukyer and Luzi go into it. Then there was only one person left standing on the platform: Sruli, a strange fellow.

Sruli had taken his leave of Luzi on the steps of the car. They had seemed to exchange farewells. Then, when Luzi got into the car, Sruli stood on the platform until the train began to move out of the station. It was then that Sruli seemed to come awake, seemed to remember something he had forgotten in the car. He started off after the train and, at the very last moment, caught hold of the railing with his right hand and pulled himself up on the step where he stood for a while, like a conductor, with his two hands on the two railings, the skirts of his coat blowing in the wind. He looked back at the receding station and at the gendarmes standing there who at any other time would certainly not have permitted such a thing to happen. But now—it was too late. Sruli—and the train—were already far away.

And now it was the eve before the New Year. That morning, Moshe Mashber had done what everyone like him did on that day. First he went to the cemetery where Liber-Meyer, despite the pressure of the crowd at the tomb, immediately noticed him. At once Liber-Meyer passed him through before everyone else and put himself at his service—for which, naturally enough, he was well paid.

According to custom, Moshe conducted no business when he returned. He whiled away the time at the synagogue with others at prayer or at home with his family.

That day he divested himself so completely of his usual concerns that in the middle of the afternoon just after the midday meal, when the house smelled of the holiday clothing the family had put on, and of the foods being readied for the table on which the candelabra would soon be set in preparation for the holiday candle-blessing that preceded the last meal of the year—then Moshe did something rare for him: he had the gate of the garden unlocked and walked about alone among its well-trodden sandy paths.

He looked around at the trees, whose yellowing leaves touched him with sadness, partly as an expression of the time of year—nature's fall—and of the imminent holiday that signaled the human fall. He walked about taking note of the trees that had lost their foliage (some earlier in the year, others later) and noticed that fruit still clung here and there to a branch.

He walked about until the sun declined toward evening. Then as he turned onto a path that bordered the fence, he looked toward the courtyard and saw lighted candles on the table reflected in the panes of an opened dining room window (opened because the day had been calm and warm—almost a summer's day). He remembered then that it was time for the benediction over candles which Gitl, on holidays like this one, tended to make a bit early. He left the garden and went into the house.

And indeed there at one edge of the freshly set tablecloth, stood a row of candelabra: large, silver, newly polished and gleaming, and in their midst there was one that was an heirloom, used only on the High Holidays. It was a demi-menorah with three branches with a fourth rising out of the middle branch and curving forward.

There were white candles in all the candelabras and wax candles in the menorah. And, because the candelabras formed a large cluster—the menorah, especially, was quite tall—and because Gitl was of middling height (perhaps a bit shorter) and would have difficulty encircling the candelabras with her arms as she recited the benediction, her usual footstool had been set beside the table to help compensate for her lack of stature and to make it easier for her to stretch out her arms.

And indeed Gitl was just about to step onto the footstool. But even before she touched it, there were tears rolling down her cheeks as she looked around the table at her husband and children for whom she would be praying as she made the benediction over the candles. Praying for all of them together, and for each one separately, but first and foremost for her husband.

Moshe, too, looked around: at her, at his children, at the members of his household, and then he noticed that someone was missing. Alter. He decided then, before the blessing of the candles and before he had to leave for the synagogue, to go up to Alter's room and find out how he was, and whether anything had happened to him since that night when he had appeared before them. Was he better? Worse? If better, then he would wish him a Happy New Year. If not, he would at least have looked in on him and would later remember him in his prayers. And so Moshe left the dining room and made his way toward Alter's attic room. On his way there, he noticed that because of the mild summer weather, Alter's window looking out on the garden was also open, and the light of the setting sun, softened by its passage through the branches of the trees, had reached into his room. Alter, his face toward the light-struck window, lay on the bed whose linen had been changed for the holiday. He lay with his hands folded over the quilt, looking pale and exhausted by the severity of his illness, but his eyes were clear and intelligent, like those of an animal that has just given birth and in whose look one can still see traces of the pain it has endured but the creature has no words with which to share the contentment it feels for what it has overcome.

When Alter first heard and then saw his brother on his doorstep, he turned and looked at him for a moment, then with a look at once wan and delighted, he invited him in.

Moshe bent over the bed, "How are you, Alter?"

"I think I'm getting well, Moshe." Moshe heard the words coming weakly out of Alter's chest.

And indeed Moshe perceived in Alter's tone, in his look and in his demeanor that some new change had taken place in him. He recalled Dr. Yanovski's words on that night when Luzi had left the house and Alter had had his fall. Alter, despite his pallor and weakness, seemed to Moshe like one newly born. Moshe was amazed by the change, but then, feeling that he had to go back to the dining room, he bent over Alter and shouted into his ear, "Happy New Year. It's the day before New Year. Do you know that?"

"The day before New Year? No. I didn't remember."

Moshe went back to the dining room. Gitl was standing on the footstool. Her white silk headscarf was drawn down over her ears, and she held her hands over her closed eyes from which the tears flowed over her fingers. Gitl's daughters waited for her to finish. Moshe and his sons-in-law, ready to go to the synagogue, were already wearing topcoats.

Then everyone left the house. Only the servants—and Alter in his attic room—remained. The setting sun illuminated his lonely bachelor's chamber and shone, too, on him where he lay weeping quietly for the years that had passed without his having been aware of them, and for the uncertainty of the years still to come. Slowly he pushed the quilt aside and left the bed. Then, half naked, he dragged himself weakly to the window. There, with eyes half closed by fatigue, he followed the failing sunlight through the trees.

X

Storm Clouds

It is not known how it was that the distant authorities came to know the story of the banquet and of the portrait at which the noblemen shot. It had become clear on the night in question that Sventislavski had been responsible for the shooting . . . and it may be that Sventislavski, fearing that the matter would one way or another come to the attention of the authorities (in which case his actions would appear in a bad light), had, after collecting his ransom money, reported it to them himself.

There is reason to think that that is what happened. In any case, Sventislavski dropped from sight for some little while and it was rumored that he had been arrested. Who knows? That, too, might have been a trick of some kind. Or it may be that the arrest was intended by the higher authorities to avert the suspicions of the noblemen from him. To create the impression that *he*, too, was under suspicion, that *he*, too, might be in danger. And by this means to preserve his credibility in the eyes of the noblemen—at least so far as this case went. So that the noblemen would be convinced despite all the evidence that it was not he who had betrayed them. People in high places—so it was rumored—meant in this way to keep Sventislavski as one of their own. A deceitful practice that was not uncommon with secret government agencies that made use of informers.

In any case, an entire commission of inquiry showed up in town one fine day. And nearly everyone who had been present at the banquet during the Prechistaya Fair was summoned to appear before it. It is true that at the beginning the requests to appear were not especially threatening. The noblemen received ambiguously worded requests to present themselves for interrogation in the regional capital at N. The subject of the inquiry was not specified, but the noblemen, trembling in their boots, immediately understood that it was a consequence of the pistol shots and the portrait.

Such people as, for example, young Count Kazeroge were already being counseled by their friends and relations to make plans to steal across the border as soon as possible. Because who could say how the matter would begin—or end? "Everyone knows that right or wrong is not the issue here. Essentially, they want to get rid of you. They're looking for some guilt or other as an excuse to harass you. To drive you from your estates, so that the government can confiscate your lands and goods."

And Kazeroge, at least, was prepared for flight. It was said later that on the evening of the day on which according to his summons he was supposed to present at N., the district capital . . . on that evening, his harnessed carriage, laden with the baggage that his loyal servants working by torchlight had carried down, stood waiting for him in his courtyard. Everything was ready. Kazeroge too. But then at the very last moment, as he made his trembling way out of the house and down the stairs, he made a strange turning movement, as if he had bumped into something. He would have fallen if a nearby servant had not caught him. The servant thought his master had slipped. But no, it was far otherwise. The count was unable to budge. He lay like a log, completely paralyzed and speechless, lay like a corpse with his full weight in the servant's arms. He was immediately carried into the house where it was observed that his mouth, dripping saliva, had twisted to one side. One of his eyes had a bizarre, glazed look, and half of his body had turned blue as a spleen. The result was that Kazeroge, anyhow, was dropped from the list of those called. And for the time being he was left in peace.

Everyone else, of course, showed up at the inquiry. Each of them was interrogated and at first, as if by prior agreement, everyone denied everything. They even denied knowing that any shooting had taken place. But it availed them nothing. As the interrogators completed more and more interviews, the clearer it became that what needed to be established was not whether shots had been fired, but rather who was the first, who initiated the shooting and who among the others was sympathetic to him. Because, as the interrogators established, all of the noblemen had sung the forbidden Polish hymn. So that in general the situation at the banquet became clear enough, and various of the summoned noblemen did not return to their homes but stayed in N. under arrest. And while the interrogators were at it they found a thread that led them to the rich Jews of the town who had put up the ransom money that had helped the noblemen hush up the affair.

The result was that various rich Jews were also summoned to the inquiry, occasioning such distress and fear in various homes that the secret, which had at first been known only to a very few participants, that is, only to the men who had been at the meeting held at Rabbi Dudi's house—that secret, then, was no longer a secret. It was known first to the wives of those who had been there, then to their children, then to relatives and friends. The excitement and confusion were comparable in intensity to that induced by a fire or a flood—when one is helpless to know what to do. Various of the wives, friends and relatives hurried off to wonder rabbis for advice; others went to the cemetery where they "measured" the graves. And so on.

For the time being, the rabbi, Reb Dudi, was still left in peace. He was not called before the commission. Perhaps it was out of respect for the clergy, or it may have been because of the consideration that if the others who were implicated should fail to confess, it might become necessary to put them under oath, in which case the rabbi might be urged to persuade them not to take that step, since oath taking was such an offense to the community that even the government required it only when all other measures had failed. So for the time being Reb Dudi remained unscathed. But that did not prevent the mood of Tisha Bov mourning from pervading his home. There, too, there was panic. The rabbi's wife was so dismayed that one thing after another fell from her hands and broke. It all seemed to her to be an augury of what was to come. Reb Dudi himself, however, remained silent. But his daughter-in-law, whose sole distinction came from the fact that for many years she had not borne the rabbi's son any children, and because, therefore, her belly was constantly being scrutinized as people waited for her to achieve her feminine capabilities, she, the daughter-in-law who usually went about all day veiled and in silks, changed her clothing habits and went about now half-dressed, complaining to her husband, a defeated, misfortunate man who sent her to his father, Reb Dudi; and Reb Dudi, who made everyone in town and in the entire region tremble obediently before him, now had to put up with his daughter-in-law's accusations.

"Just why had it been necessary? What reason did you have to meddle? Lives are at stake here."

"Oh, woe is me," she wailed. "What will become of us? Where will we go?"

There was panic also, as has been said, in the homes of other rich Jews. There, too, heads were in motion. And before the men went to the interrogation, and after they returned, their wives shed plentiful tears over them: "That's what comes of going off on one's own without so much as asking the advice of anyone in the family, not even one's own wife . . ." And after having made such remarks, the women went with their men to the place where they were to be questioned as if they were accompanying them to the scaffold.

And all the while the men were being interrogated, households were completely disordered. There was neither life nor rest. People ran about as if they had been poisoned, seeking advice wherever they could hope to find any, and sometimes even where there was no such hope.

The same, of course, was true in the home of the family that we know: Moshe Mashber's home. For him, too, the commission of inquiry was like the approach of a dark cloud. Until now, no one in the household had known the ins and outs of the matter because, except for Moshe's younger son-in-law, Nakhum Lentsher, the story of the noblemen and the meeting at Reb Dudi's house had been kept secret from everyone, Gitl included. But there was no way to suppress the story any longer—and the family was overwhelmed by it.

He was regarded by them as a condemned man and they cast mournful farewell glances at him as if he had been taken dangerously sick. Gitl was beside herself. Wringing her hands, she wandered from room to room, from corner to corner, trying to think of some way for her husband to find his way out of his dilemma. The thing confused her, and this time, the matter was so grave that she could not ease her heart by the shedding of a few easy tears. So she went about silent and depressed, confiding in no one.

The same was true of Moshe's daughters. Only Nakhum, the son-in-law, because he was a man and because he was better informed, having been entrusted with the secret from the first, said a few words to Moshe about the matter—in the sort of reproachful tone one has when watching *someone else* being foolish. In his quiet way he went about now to demonstrate his own superior intelligence as he reminded his father-in-law of errors that it was too late to do anything

· 287 ·

about and succeeded thereby merely in rubbing salt into Moshe's wounds.

"How was it that you didn't think the matter through before letting yourself become a part of it? Even if someone like Reb Dudi encouraged it, even if all the others agreed to do it."

In a word, there was sorrow in every one of the households in which the fathers or the husbands were in any way involved in the affair of the noblemen. Sorrow before they were interrogated, but even more after the interrogation when they returned to their homes silently and with their heads bowed, like mourners following the corpse of a loved one.

Because they got themselves all tangled up. Whether it was because they had not discussed what their answers should be in advance, or because they had different notions about what they should say, the fact is that each of them, on his own responsibility, chose at first to deny flat out that there had been any meeting or any agreement to lend money to the noblemen. But when it was clear that the investigators knew all that had happened, down to the smallest detail, down to the number of those who had been present and the amounts of money that had been subscribed, then they saw that nothing would be achieved by any further denial or pretense of ignorance. And that one way or another they would have to yield up all of the facts pertaining to the meeting. Speech was required of them and by then they were ready to speak.

The truth is that the demeanor of the investigators toward the Jews was by no means as stern as it was toward the noblemen. Evidently the investigators knew from the start (or it may be that this is what they were told by their superiors) that the part played by the Jews in this matter was in no way comparable to that played by the noblemen. The Jews were by no means to be suspected of subversive sympathies, of opposition to the state. Their guilt essentially lay in their habitual willingness to help the noblemen when they were in financial trouble. From the point of view of the Jews, the affair simply was a business matter involving interest rates and profits.

It is also true, however, that one could put quite a different interpretation on the matter. It is a crime to help a criminal. In this instance, the Jews and the nobility are united: the noblemen acted and the Jews concealed the act. The Jews not only kept the secret themselves, they also paid bribes to keep it from being revealed.

Yes, it could be interpreted either way. Still, if those who were questioned had not been utterly panicked, they would have noticed that they were being handled quite gently. One indication, for instance, was that not one of those interrogated was detained after being questioned. And even during the questioning, it was clear that the investigators were searching only for the facts related to the money that was lent, but that they themselves were of no interest to anyone. But those being questioned were in no condition to notice any of this, and the result was that when they returned home from the interrogation they looked dazed, like men who had been fasting for a long while, or confused and fearful, as if they had been struck by lightning. All of them—nor was Moshe Mashber any exception.

These events took place after the holidays, around the beginning of the month of Heshvan. A stormy fall: rains by day, unending rain, for weeks. It was the month which even in normal times pressed upon the town like a weight of mud upon the heart. A long fall that would be followed by a difficult winter. Difficult for everyone: for workingmen who, after the holidays and the closing of the fair at the end of summer, saw their incomes shrink; difficult, too, for the middle-class businessmen who do not do too well until the midwinter holidays by which time the roads are fit for sledges. Difficult, too, for more prosperous folk—the weather itself, all-day and all-night fogs, and rain coming down as through a sieve, hovering over the town, over the entire region, creating an oppressive darkness in which it was hard to breathe. Most important of all, even the prosperous classes had a hard time finding goods by this year. Because as one might have predicted at summer's end, the bad harvest was sure to have negative consequences for every sort of business without exception. Even Moshe Mashber's business was not excepted. Or, to put it another way, the consequences for Moshe Mashber's business were particularly bad.

Because the truth is that anyone who knows anything about the way such financial businesses were conducted in the old days will know just how a banking house like Moshe Mashber's was founded and run. A venture like Moshe's was a sort of "Credit and Discount House," as years later they would be called. And the financial transactions conducted there were indeed of the sort that would take place in credit and discount establishments. But the true foundation of the business, its credit (over and above the owner's basic capital), was of a quite different order than that on which the later credit and discount houses were based.

In those distant days of which we speak, such businesses were somewhat primitively organized. What was most important to them was not the amount of credit available to them from large banks; no, what mattered in those days, in such provincial cities as N., was the esteem in which those establishments were held by the inhabitants who sought a safe place to put their savings. So fearful were they for their nest eggs that they often paid no attention to the rates of interest offered them, settling for less just so long as they felt that they had put their money into reputable hands.

Those who kept their money in such establishments might be from the middle class or even working-class people who had put by a little money for a daughter's dowry, or to build a house; or they might be old folks who had saved some cash for their declining years, with a little extra for burial expenses and so on. Such financial houses served as fireproof safes for the sorts of people who were afraid of keeping their bit of fortune at home and who were wary of entrusting it to undependable strangers. Their faith in these financial establishments was on a par with their faith in God.

To sum up, it was this sort of confidence on which such financial houses were based and people like that from whom they obtained most of their funds. And so it was that the slightest rumor—well founded or not—that there was something wrong could destroy the confidence of such investors, and just as they had devotedly relied on that banking house before the rumor, so now, without making the slightest effort to trace the rumor to its source, they invaded the premises with cries, with imprecations and curses and stones thrown through the windows as they demanded the return of their money.

It's true, thank God, that in Moshe Mashber's case, things had not yet reached such a pass. And, as has been said, the tale of the noblemen, to the degree that it was possible, had been hushed up and kept from the general populace. And indeed, even when the story did manage to reach someone's ear, it was not regarded with much interest: "What noblemen? What gunshot? And if they did shoot, so what? On their heads be it. Profligate louts. What's it to do with respectable folk like Moshe Mashber? No. It's not to be believed. It simply makes no sense." That, then, was the general response, at first. And those who were most incredulous were the people from that stratum of which we have just spoken, the small creditors: those nearly overwhelmed folk who never went beyond the small circle of their lives, who lived in poverty and in that poverty managed to put aside a poor groschen which then they guarded like the apple of one's eye, tied it and knotted it in its handkerchief until little by little there grew a hard-won sum, large enough so that it could be respectably put into respectable hands for safekeeping—and for that they invariably wore their holiday coats, and when they arrived at the home or the office of the important rich man to whom they were bringing the money, they stood with the humility of poor folk before his door as if hoping he would do them a kindness.

It was such folk, then, we say, who, even if the tale of the noblemen reached their ears, could not understand its significance for those who were involved in it, and understood even less how any of it had anything to do with their own lives. "Who cares? What's it to do with us?" For all the effect the tale had on them, one might think they heard it through ears that had been stuffed with cotton.

Still, with frequent repetition, the tale, even if only half-understood among those poor folk, still it began to stir a certain uneasiness about the safety of their tiny nest eggs.

And therefore one might observe such persons putting aside their ill-paid work one morning to go home. There, they could be seen standing before an old-fashioned clothes press or if there was no clothes press in the room, kneeling beside a folding bed under which they rummaged among clothes that smelled of fungus or decay until they had found and pulled out their holiday coat which they put on. Then in the broad light of day, making their way to Moshe Mashber's office.

They arrived there at the wrong time and uninvited. Embarrassed, mute, their tongues cleaving to the roofs of their mouths as always happened when they found themselves in the offices of rich and important folk. We can imagine such a person—a man, for instance, who had saved money for his daughter's dowry, or one who had put together a sum with which he intended to buy a small shop—we can imagine such a person beginning to stammer, "I . . . uh . . . I . . . I have heard . . . there are . . . rumors of some kind in town . . . Maybe . . . would it be possible that . . . now . . . actually, yes, now . . . today, that is . . . could I have my money now?"

"What happened?" the office employees asked him. "Is the term of your note up?"

"No. The term isn't over," he replied. "No one said anything about the term. For my part, I'd let the money stay where it is for several terms. But there's talk in the town. And there are rumors."

"What sort of rumors?" he was asked, angrily.

"They say that some noblemen . . . did some sort of shooting."

"Well, what of that?" came the teasing question. "Did you get hit? Now, go in good health," he was told. "When the term of your note is up and you want your money, it will be given you with all due respect. But there's no money paid before the term of the note is up. Good-bye. Go in good health."

And that was how the office employees, to whom the task had been given, dealt with those folk. And these poor people went away with nothing to show for their pains, and yet somehow consoled because, having put on their Sabbath coats to make their visit to the office, they felt themselves in some small degree to be partners in the business.

There were others, however, more energetic and less easily intimidated (because more anxious about their investments), who, from the moment they arrived in the office refused to deal with the lower-level employees. And when they were asked whom they wanted to speak with, they replied Moshe Mashber or the son-in-law who speaks for him.

"Perhaps *we* can help you?" the employees asked. "The bosses are busy."

"Never mind, we can wait."

And they did, indeed, wait out the time and were finally admitted into Moshe's office where they set themselves to checking whether the rumors were true by studying Moshe's comportment and the way that he spoke to his creditors.

Certain of those visits affected Moshe badly. More than once he was tempted to shout at his visitors, to drive them from his office. But, because his situation was indeed serious and because reports of his behavior to creditors of this kind would certainly be broadcast and wrongly interpreted, he restrained himself. But he restrained himself at great cost. When one such miserable interview was over and the creditor was gone, Moshe heaved a huge sigh and sat for a long while sunken in his chair, breathing occasionally with difficulty. Finally, he reached for his coat and got ready to leave.

But there was worse, still. There were those for whom coming to the office was not enough. They went to Moshe's home. These were people who one way or another felt themselves to be related to Moshe, or who traveled with him on his visits to his rebbe, or who prayed in the same synagogue with him and so on. They calculated the time when Moshe would not be at home and made their appearance before Gitl or before Moshe's daughters. And the moment they began to speak, their tone implied that they were speaking of an imminent bankruptcy and that they had come to make their complaints knowing what tender consciences Gitl and her daughters had.

"To do something like this to one's relations. Who would have expected such a thing from a Moshe Mashber?"

"What do you mean, 'expected such a thing'? What does that mean, 'from a Moshe Mashber'?" Gitl and her daughters asked such people, utterly ignorant of what they meant.

"The idea was to put the money 'into safe hands,' and whose hands could have been considered safer than Moshe Mashber's?" they replied.

"Then what is it you want?" the relatives asked.

"We want our money back," they said.

"But why did you come here for that? That's what the office is for. We didn't take the money from you here. We know nothing about it. Business isn't conducted here."

That was how they were answered. And yet, when such people were gone—the very moment they left the room in which Gitl had received them—Gitl went to her own room where she wiped away a tear—and often, more than one.

Indeed, it was by no means a pleasant situation. And here we want to reveal a secret. Things had reached such a pass just then that Nakhum Lentsher, Moshe Mashber's younger son-in-law, was thinking of leaving the business.

Up until now he had worked with Moshe as a partner. That is, he had been entitled to take from the general income whatever he needed, first for household and family expenses, and then a certain variable percentage of the profits. An amount that depended on the condition of the balance sheet at the end of the year. If it had been a good year and the business had grown, then his percentage was higher; in a poor year (something which in recent times had rarely happened because the business had continually expanded), his percentage of the profits was smaller.

But now Nakhum said to himself, "No. It's time to leave." It may be that in addition to the trouble the business was in, Nakhum's character played a certain part in this decision. And this because from his first moment as a member of the household, he had brought with him a heritage of long-ingrained family pride. A pride which had to do with the fact that his family had always done business with Poles and had adapted itself to their ways.

It was a pride that in his grandmother Krayntse variously manifested in the way she came to his wedding dressed in a style different from that of any of the other women her age, as well as in her deportment and the way that she refined her speech by slipping Polish words into it. It manifested itself even in the baked sweet goods she brought with her from Kamenets: tarts of some sort, half white and half black, and holiday loaves with candied fruits in them and the like. And that pride was evident again at Nakhum's wedding where she had stepped in front of the wedding canopy so that she could rearrange some jewel the bride was wearing in a Polish rather than in a Jewish fashion.

After the wedding, the nickname she was given, "Grandmother Pardon Me" lingered in Moshe Mashber's home. There was some hostility toward the old woman who the moment she stepped from the carriage had managed to give her in-laws the impression that they ought to be grateful to her for setting foot on that soil. Nor was it only Grandmother Krayntse. Her daughter Shayntse, too, and her grandson Nakhum who, because he had no father had come to the wedding bringing two women with him, also behaved in the same haughty fashion.

From the first moment of his arrival, Nakhum had behaved as if he was different from the other members of the household. He was different in his food habits (he ate little because of the gastritis he brought with him from home), in the clothes that he wore. Even the cigarettes he smoked were different from everyone else's—women's cigarettes of some kind, which Nekhamke, his wife, was required to roll for him, cigarettes which he smoked only halfway after which he put them out by spitting on them. Then he tossed them into the spittoon.

He kept himself apart from the family. And it would seem there was no way anyone could please him, and least of all his wife, whom he frequently reduced to tears. And it was clear that because of him and his capricious treatment of her (treatment of which she never complained, and which she concealed even from her parents) . . . that her cheeks frequently turned pale. "God grant that things work out for her. May the Lord keep her from getting sick," people whispered. Because it was frequently to be observed that even in summer she suffered from a chill and sat with a shawl over her shoulders.

He spoke little, but he grumbled often. And generally it was to express some dissatisfaction to his wife. Sometimes it was food he complained about, sometimes it was something else. Or in a roundabout way, he would express his dissatisfaction with the way that her father, Moshe Mashber, his father-in-law, treated him. There were times when, as it seemed to him, Moshe did not value him at his true worth. At other times he complained that he was being treated unjustly, that he was being paid too small a percentage of the profits, because a man like himself, if he were working for anyone else, would be rolling in gold.

From the moment he joined the household, he thought continually that he would be doing better if he was in business for himself. Ah, then . . . then he would be able to sprout wings. But until now he had had no reason for leaving since the business had been prospering at such a high level that it would have been sheer madness to abandon a sure thing in order to involve himself with a new project which, as is always the case with anything new, would involve a considerable risk. And so until now he had not revealed his ambitious thought to anyone except occasionally to his wife, and even then only in a roundabout way.

Now, however, when there was a spoke in the wheel, Nakhum resumed his complaints. It seemed wrong for him to have to participate in his father-in-law's destiny and not his own. Moshe Mashber was older, and it was possible that his heyday was done. He, Nakhum, on the other hand, was still young, and there was no reason why he should be forced to suffer because Moshe was on the skids. Now was the time, he thought, to avoid imminent danger. While he still could and before his own foot was caught in the trap.

Naturally, he did not even now reveal to his father-in-law nor to anyone else what he was thinking, because, after all, he was not so crude as to talk about the matter at such a delicate moment. He would have been regarded as an outcast. And so he spoke to no one except to his wife. Nekhamke who lately had been worrying about her parents—and especially this past autumn when she saw that her father's luck had somehow turned. It was to her, then, that Nakhum one night revealed his hidden thoughts and complaints as she sat in their bedroom which recently she often did; she sat wrapped in a warm shawl and shivering. He knew that she would reveal nothing of what he said—not even to her mother. At the most she might quietly shed a tear into her shawl, but that was a matter of indifference to him.

He argued as follows:

Everyone has his own goals. Father and mother are well and good ... but they, Nekhamke and himself, were also the parents of children for whom they needed to provide. Her father's business was in bad shape. For the time being nobody was telling Moshe because they wanted to spare him, but nobody took that kind of pity on him, Nakhum. And she ought to see the sorts of looks a fellow like Tsali Derbaremdiker gave Moshe when he came to or went from his office.

And it would be well for her to understand that fellows like Sholem Shmaryon and Tsali Derbaremdiker often knew the balance sheets of the businesses they were involved with better even than their owners. It was a fixed rule: if you want to know how any merchant is doing, you look at the Shmaryons and the Derbaremdikers to see how they treat him face-to-face or behind his back. That was the best and the truest measure. And now those two were practically ready to leave Moshe's service. And just as they had served Moshe faithfully, so now they were looking after their own interests: first, they were seeing to it that they would not be personally damaged—that is, if they had invested any of their own money, they would get it out at the first opportunity. And they would do the same with "intermediary" money. That is for such moneys as had been lent to Moshe because of their intercession. They would do what they could to see that the investors whom they served would be safe. They would keep those investors informed and would advise them to withdraw their money the very first moment that some note became due and payable.

In a word, those fellows had the good standing of the business in their hands. For now, it was safe; perhaps tomorrow it would still be, but if the situation did not improve soon, they would be the first to malign its reputation. Then one fine morning the office would be besieged by a swarm of creditors, like bees. Money would be snatched from hand to hand, people would curse and shout and come to blows—as often happens in such cases.

That's the situation. And what's clear is that one fine day we'll have the roof tumbling down on our heads; what's clear is that things may get so twisted about that one won't be able to tell what belongs to whom and whoever's caught in the middle is likely to get hurt.

Now, what was it he wanted and why did he tell her all this? He told her because it was he who was in the middle. Because, though it would be neither his fault nor hers, nor anyone else's, yet just the same he, Nakhum, could be drawn into the disaster so that every bit of his previous hard work would come to nothing.

As Nakhum explained all of this to his wife in their bedroom, he paced back and forth from one wall to another, smoking his cigarettes all the while. The ailing Nekhamke, her cheeks turning even paler, sat silent, wrapped in her shawl, and looked up at him as he paced. She waited expectantly, but her heart told her what direction her husband's thoughts were taking. And even before she heard the words she could tell from his lips that he was getting ready to say them: "We have to leave."

To leave. It was a thought that could never have occurred either to her or to her older sister, or to her mother and father or to anyone in the household until now. First, because until now there had been no need for anyone to go. And second, even if, as now, there might even be such a need, how could anyone imagine that in a household where everything was held in common, everything was shared—money, air, breath—in a household in which, until now, there had been no way to distinguish anyone's interests from anyone else's—whether in larger or in smaller matters—in a household in which even the children of the various parents shared family traits in common, and in which the words "mine" and "yours" were almost never heard, then how, in such a household—and especially at a time like this, when her father was in such straits—how could one even have the idea of leaving on one's mind?

Nakhum writhed. Though he was not actually a son in the household, but only a son-in-law, still, it would be hard to say those words. Not only to his in-laws, but to his wife as well. Nevertheless, he spoke them: "We have to leave."

Nekhamke could not endure this conversation for very long. She got to her feet and Nakhum could see that she was crying. In order to spare her, he said nothing more about the matter on that evening. But with each passing day the evidence was clearer that the business was in trouble, and yet he did not have the courage to discuss the situation with his father-in-law.

On the other hand he did send a letter home discussing it. He had always been a frequent letter writer who kept in close touch with his family. And even now, just as he had when he was a boy, he regarded his grandmother Krayntse and his mother Shayntse as wisewomen to whom it was perfectly permissible to turn for advice in a difficult time—just as he had when he was a boy.

In his letter he let fall a phrase or two which he knew would immediately alert them: "Certainly, they would understand that though he, Nakhum, was a grown man and entirely independent, they could, just the same, be helpful to him, especially since it was he who was turning to them for help.

"To my dear grandmother, and mother," he wrote. "We are, thank God, in good health, Blessed be the Name of the Lord. Only Nekhamke, may her health improve, feels a bit poorly from time to time. She wraps herself in shawls because she is for some reason continually cold. Actually she does not look too well. My father-in-law's business affairs lately have not prospered. He seems confused. In addition to that, there is some sort of involvement with noblemen that smacks a little of a false accusation. My father-in-law is not actually involved in it, but who knows how such a matter can turn out? As regards my own personal business affairs, they depend, after all, on my father-in-law. And because we are, after all, partners, what happens to one of us may happen to the other. Who knows whether I may not be destined to suffer because of what happens to him? I don't want to be misunderstood, here. The matter of the false accusation in no way touches me, but I am involved in what happens to my father-in-law's business. Yes. *Ma yoled yom*, who knows what the morning will bring? I really need advice, but there's no one here who can give me any. Nekhamke is not the right person for it; as for my father-in-law, he is too deeply involved. I'm inclined to do something on my own, without my father-in-law, to make a move out of this risky business. But how is that to be done? It might be useful to have someone else here—a hint to the wise is sufficient."

With this formulary phrase, used usually only when writing to men and only in situations in which one means to provoke action, Nakhum ended his letter.

The hints in the letter did indeed inform his grandmother Krayntse and his mother Shayntse off there in faraway Kamenets that something was happening in N. in which it might be proper to meddle.

A short while later, Grandmother Krayntse herself showed up in N. Her journey began with a wagon ride, then she took a train and she arrived at the Mashber house in a local vehicle with ringing bells. The woman who arrived after all this travel was very old, but she had a fine head on her shoulders and eyes that were still quick to discern what anyone might be trying to conceal.

She looked about, and then after a brief interview with her Nakhum, understood what she needed to know, and then with her quick, practical intelligence, she saw at once what needed to be done.

First off, and on that very evening, she had a critical conversation with Nekhamke. She wanted to prepare her, to get her on her side. She approached the matter with great care, understanding that any child is likely to be made unhappy when a father is in trouble—especially when that trouble is brought on by strangers. And especially in this case, how could she stand by and watch her father's fortunes decline and then by leaving him become a part of his misfortune? How could Nakhum and Nekhamke even think of such a thing?

All that was certainly true. On the other hand, Grandmother Krayntse reasoned, perhaps Nekhamke did not quite understand what was at stake. In fact, the issue was her father's welfare. He was not the first, nor would he be the last, with financial problems. And each time one had to be alert. It might turn out that they simply had to wait out a particularly bad time. And if that was the case, would it not be better—in the event that, as could happen in such a case, creditors showed up and demanded to be paid and there was insufficient cash— would it not be better to do what was sometimes done—that one of the partners left the business, taking with him whatever assets it was possible to sign over to him? Then later when the bad times passed and the creditors were paid off—or even if they were not paid off, and one had simply got rid of them by paying them a small percentage of the debts outstanding—then the partners could turn to the one who had the moneys entrusted to him and the business could be re-created once again.

With a stranger, an arrangement like that might be very difficult to arrive at because one had to be specially careful, but in the case of one's own child, as in *this* situation with Nakhum and Nekhamke, what could be more ideal?

As she saw it, Grandmother Krayntse said, if Nekhamke was truly her father's devoted daughter, she herself must want this. Because, she said, just let us suppose the worst case: even if your father, God forbid, was unable to set himself on his feet again, then what conceivable good would it do him to have his children go to smash along with him? And particularly since the situation was not really that grave. It's only that this is a bad year that one has somehow or other to get through—and that business with the noblemen, too, will take care of itself.

There's no need to weep. Quite the reverse. She herself, Nekhamke, ought to be helpful to Nakhum in any way that she could. And if the matter came to a discussion, Nekhamke ought to ease her father's burden by making him understand that things were not at a desperate pass. That such things had happened often before. And that, finally, businessmen were businessmen—and wriggled out of such troubles.

This, then, was the way that Grandmother Krayntse reasoned with her granddaughter-in-law. And Nekhamke, inexperienced as she was, especially in business matters, and understanding little of what was said to her, allowed herself to be persuaded. Though her heart was heavy, she could find nothing with which to oppose Grandmother Krayntse's arguments.

Grandmother Krayntse said nothing more on the subject. Nor did she say anything to Gitl, nor to Gitl's older daughter, Yehudis, though earlier it might have occurred to her to do so. Instead, she addressed herself directly to Nakhum's father-in-law, Moshe Mashber.

"Kinsman," she said one evening after her arrival as she drew him into a corner, "kinsman. I have something to discuss with you privately, just the two of us."

The conversation took place in the large room in which important visitors were entertained. And here, Moshe and Grandmother Krayntse faced each other, seated in large easy chairs.

Grandmother Krayntse armed herself for this conversation with greater care than for the one she had had with Nekhamke, because in this instance she had before her the proprietor of the business itself, the man most deeply involved and the one in greatest danger. And she was on that account better prepared and devoted a longer time to preliminary side issues before she turned to the dangerous matter.

Finally she addressed herself to it. "Kinsman," she said, "I know that you don't ask for my advice, and I know that you don't need it. You have, praise God, a head upon your shoulders. Just the same, as a member of the family I want to say something to you, and in fact that's my reason for coming here. The trip here was not an easy one—I'm no longer in the years when . . . From something in one of Nakhum's letters we . . . myself and my daughter (your daughter-in-law) got the impression that there was something he was not telling us. So we decided that I would come and see for myself. And of course we wanted to see Nekhamke and the grandchildren too. And here it has been brought to my attention that . . . It is difficult for me to reproach you . . . but I believe that you, kinsman, a man with so much intelligence, a man from whom, they say, the world could take instruction . . . it seems to me that you ought to think seriously . . . first, for your own sake, and then for the sake of the children.

"Clearly, kinsman, nobody can have too many friends. Particularly rich businessmen like yourself, God keep you. There are envious folk in the world who would like to swallow you up. Certainly your present difficulties are not so grave as they could be if certain evil-intentioned people had their way. Among people like ourselves, merchants, the heart of the matter is our reputation. Without reputation, we are nothing: nobody, no credit—nothing at all. And who can say when we may be overwhelmed by the sort of disaster you know only too well: there is a rush of creditors, our own loans are lost? One feels oneself throttled and there is no way out of the noose. One needs then to be well prepared. You have, praise God, loyal children and with their help there is much that you can do. What that is, I don't have to tell you. Clearly, those assets that your creditors might grasp at should be put into safe hands, out of their reach. Everything that can be transferred should be transferred to the ownership of trustworthy children. As if you were dissolving your partnership. As if they were in business for themselves and that you had gone your own way. For instance, your fuel-oil business could be turned over to your older son-in-law, Yankele Grodshteyn. The business license can be taken out in his name. The financial brokerage can be signed over to Nakhum and your house can be put in your wife's name. Jewels and cash, too, can be put into safe hands for a certain time.

"Certainly, these are measures to take only in a crisis—when one has to take a final stand.

"It's hard, I'm sure, for you to have to hear all this. Of course there is nothing more precious to a man—and especially, kinsman, to a man like yourself—than his good name. And God keep us from hearing even the slightest ill word about oneself. But I can tell you from my own experience (as we know, one may take counsel from a woman in matters of experience) . . . I can tell you from my own experience that one has seen such things done before, both in my husband's business and elsewhere. But there was never any intent to rob anyone, God forbid, but simply to stay afloat in a troubled sea. And so, what happened, happened. And the hard times passed and the world did not fall apart, and we remained what we had always been. And certainly the good Lord forgives such things.

"I can see, kinsman, that you are wondering how I could have brought myself to say all this, and you are wondering, too, what makes me think I have the right to say anything about matters in which you would not permit even your own wife to meddle. I can see that you want to ask who sent for me. And who gave me permission to give advice—especially the sort of advice which, as you see it, even your worst enemy would not have given you.

"None of this is pleasant to hear, I know, nor is it pleasant to say. Especially for a member of the family. But it's precisely because I'm a member of the family, and loyal, that it has to be done, just the way that one sometimes gives bitter medicine to a patient. And never forget, kinsman, that you and I are after all in the same family. What we are talking about is what will be good for our children. There is nothing you can suspect me of beyond the knowledge that in a situation like this the person with most at stake does not always have the best judgment. He is blind. All he can think of is how to rescue his honor, his name. And it is then that his family has the duty of showing him the right path; that honor may be set aside for a while, that pride may be bent, that one has to think of what is essential, and if that is preserved, then all else follows from it: honor, reputation, pride. All of it is rebuilt, and nobody remembers yesterday's dishonor any more than they remember the day itself. And so, kinsman, hear me and take the advice of one who is older than you. I mean no harm, God forbid. My concern is our welfare and the future of our children."

Moshe Mashber was silent as he heard Grandmother Krayntse's long speech. Sometimes he seemed to be watching her, sometimes he looked away. There was no way to guess how he would reply to her because he was deeply affected by what she said and there were various responses he could make to it: a restrained anger, for instance, in which he might coldly ask, "As a matter of fact, who did send for you?

And who asked you for your advice?" Or, worse, he might have exploded at her, as he had vis-à-vis Sruli when Sruli had so offended him that Moshe had forgotten where he was or what he was saying. Now, too, as then, he could cry, "Out of my house." Anything was possible. A man is no more than a man—and especially when one finds one's destiny being discussed without so much as a by-your-leave—as if he had become so critically ill that even his illness was a matter of indifference to him.

Any answer, then, was possible, but Moshe made no reply. But he had the look of a man who had received a heavy blow to the head and whose fear and astonishment were so great that not even the loudest scream would suffice to express them. He sat quietly as if he was not aware of Grandmother Krayntse's presence and therefore had no duty to give her any sort of reply whatever. And if he did say something to her, it was as if he were saying it to himself, as if his ears did not hear what his lips whispered: "Ah . . . well. So then, it's time for advice. And there was nobody closer by to talk with, so that one had to write away for help the way a country patient sends for a city doctor. And, it would seem, before the matter was thought of elsewhere, the idea had occurred to my own children. Well!" Moshe said, his voice muted as he got up from his chair. Then disregarding Grandmother Krayntse as if there was no need to make the slightest respectful gesture or to utter so much as a single word to her, not even to wish her good night, he rose and, having said the words recorded above, he left. Finished.

Of course, this was no way to behave. This was certainly not the kind of behavior one expected from Moshe Mashber. And yet, if one were to put oneself in his shoes, would one have behaved differently?

In a word, that was the way, more or less, that Moshe left the room. Perhaps it was not quite this way. But we have said "more or less" so that even if his manner of leaving was slightly different, it hardly matters. The point is that Grandmother Krayntse felt humiliated and that her mission had accomplished nothing.

It was not long after this conversation that she left N. and hurried back home. But before she left, she took Nakhum aside and said, "My boy, I've done what I could—what a parent can do in a situation like this. I came. I spoke. And I did not succeed. He said nothing to me, but it doesn't matter. He's heard the knocking at the door, and when the time comes, he'll respond. He's overwhelmed just now so there's nothing more to be done. As for later on, I'll leave that up to you. When the time is right, you'll do what's needed."

The interview with Grandmother Krayntse profoundly unsettled Moshe Mashber. He went about confused; often he did not hear what was said to him and it was necessary to repeat questions before he understood what was wanted. But silent and perplexed though he was, he was clear about one thing: he avoided Nakhum and rarely spoke to him. Sometimes he watched him warily as if he was looking at someone who had done him a particular harm . . . who had tried to strangle him in the middle of the night.

That, then, was the Grandmother Krayntse episode. But things got even worse. And here we will reveal another secret: One evening, after his conversation with Grandmother Krayntse, Moshe Mashber sent secretly (so secretly that none of his employees—nor any family member either knew about it) for his confidential adviser, the so-called lawyer, Itsikl Zilburg.

At other times, and under other circumstances, Moshe used to go to Itsikl's home. Because no one was eager to invite Itsikl to his own home. But this time Moshe departed from his usual practice and sent for him. No one, as has been said, was particularly fond of Itsikl because he was one of those people whose friendship is not sought and who is generally avoided except when his services are needed.

This Itsikl would make an interesting chapter in himself, but to describe him in detail would carry us too far out of our story. Still, to link him with the present business, we will say a few words about him. He was a man with a good head on his shoulders who was possessed of various useful skills. Though he had no higher education and had never been in universities or law schools, he was, nevertheless, so deeply learned in both civil and criminal law that even profoundly competent professionals could benefit from his instruction.

All this was well known and the marketplace merchants consulted him frequently. Particularly since his fees were not excessive. They were not based either on the difficulty or on the importance of the case that was brought to him, but rather on the client's status and on his capacity to pay.

A strange fellow. Undoubtedly, anyone else in his place would have become rich. Not he. He had his idiosyncrasies. Sometimes he demanded a fantastic fee from a wealthy client. "If you don't want to pay it, never mind," he said. "Go to someone else." But people had faith in him and brought him the most difficult cases, the most tangled lawsuits that might arise from badly written contracts, and Itsikl set himself the task of unsnarling them—and that, often enough, when the cases were already deemed lost. The result, much to everyone's surprise, was that such hopeless cases, thanks to his skill, were won.

All of that, then, would have been well and good except that Itsikl suffered from an illness: he was a compulsive gambler. He was a passionate cardplayer who lost his own considerable earnings and who had gambled away a considerable portion of his father's wealth. The father, a quiet Jew, had been reduced almost to beggary by Itsikl, his only son. Itsikl had also gambled away whatever money he had been able to get his hands on from his rich father-in-law. First he borrowed money, then he took it, then he begged what he could from his wife to whom over and over again he promised that he would not gamble again, that he needed the money to pay the debts he had acquired the last time he had played. In a word, Itsikl gambled away whole fortunes. Nor was that all. He dragged down and corrupted young people who came from fine, wealthy families. They, too, were finally ruined. They and their entire families.

He was destined to have an ugly finish: hanging from the end of a rope. And in a particularly ugly place—a latrine. But now, the market merchants made much use of him and he was regarded with respect and authority because, in addition to the skills of which we have already spoken, he had other virtues that are particularly rare among cardplayers: he was honest, a man of his word and—most important of all—he was an absolute master at keeping secrets. One could rely on him as on a fortress. He was as silent as the tomb. He never spoke a word that might harm a client. He was not like others of his profession who, if each of the parties to a case confided their side to him, made use of what he learned from the weaker confidant to choose the side that promised the easier victory. That was not his practice. Whoever came to him first and confided his problem to him became his client. If the other party also came and asked Itsikl to represent him, Itsikl stopped him at once by telling him he was already engaged by his opponent.

And it was this Itsikl Zilburg whom Moshe Mashber had invited home so that Moshe could consult with him in his own room behind closed doors.

Moshe told him that he had been lately much troubled. That he felt confused. That though his situation was not yet dangerous—the balance sheet was normal—still, the cash flow was weak. He had huge notes outstanding, but the times were such that those who owed him large sums of money would certainly not be able to meet their notes on time. On the contrary, he, Moshe, owed moneys that he would have to pay because otherwise, as he, Itsikl, understood, if a man like himself, Moshe, did not pay it was like putting a razor to his own throat.

Someone like himself must pay. Wasn't that right? Or else there was bankruptcy, his credit ruined, never to be restored. And he would not be able to pay. He could see that already—for various reasons and because of circumstances some of which Itsikl knew and others of which he was ignorant. It was true, for the time being, that one was not, God forbid, at such a pass. But it could happen, it could happen any day now, any hour, and then not only would those creditors whose notes were due come demanding their money, but the others as well. It's what happens.

In a situation like this, a businessman looks for a way out. Moshe, too. He, Moshe was well known. Everyone knew that he, Moshe, was not about to enrich himself over a business disaster, God forbid. He simply wanted to get past this bad time—the way one waits for a flood to subside. And when it was all over, he would be able to face the world again and resume his respectable and settled ways. Of course, it was possible nothing of all this would happen and then there would be no need to take such precautionary steps, in which case he relied on Itsikl to keep the knowledge of this conversation confidential. In any event, however unlikely the danger, he had sent for Itsikl to discuss it with him.

What did he think? Was it a good idea, and was it feasible and proper, for him to dissolve his partnership with his children and to put the business in their names? Would it be possible to distance himself from them in a way that would make him appear to be the sole person responsible for the firm's debts so that in the event that he defaulted, the default would be his only, leaving his children and the firm uninvolved.

As Moshe spoke, his lips writhed, as if he could not quite control them, as if he could not get them to frame the words he meant to speak. Sometimes he had literally to put his fingers to his lips to keep them from disobeying him, to keep them from trembling.

Moshe's first words and the quaver in his voice alerted Itsikl Zilburg to the nature of the crisis toward which Moshe was heading. To avoid looking at him, Itsikl kept his eyes lowered. Then he set his quick intelligence to work to find some way to calm Moshe and to ease his heart. The result was that even while Moshe was still speaking, Itsikl, like a skilled doctor who grasps the nature of his patient's illness from the first account of his symptoms and has no need to hear more, was ready with his response.

"Certainly it's proper. Of course it can be done. For the moment, as you say, it's still too soon, but when the time is right, we'll see.

"How is it done? In a variety of ways. The very first thing to do is to see to it that the license to operate the heating oil business is taken out in your son-in-law Yankele Grodshteyn's name. And then, Reb Moshe, you should see to it that the house and whatever other immovable goods you have are transferred to someone else's name. As for the movables—jewelry, cash and so on, they should be taken out of the house and put into safe hands. As for the firm itself . . . we'll see. It may be necessary to write promissory notes for large sums of money apparently borrowed from your son-in-law, Nakhum, if you want to make it seem that he has a controlling equity in the business. There are other techniques we don't have to think about just now. In any event, you should keep me informed at intervals. When the time is right, we can apply the proper remedies. You can rely on me, Reb Moshe."

It was clear that Itsikl Zilburg, who had a wide experience of such business crises, had nevertheless a more than professional sympathy for Moshe and was eager to relieve his client's anxieties.

And to some extent, he succeeded. Moshe allowed himself to be reassured. He thanked Itsikl, but he was so overcome with emotion that he reiterated his good-byes. Of course he still had plenty to worry about. Who, for instance, could have imagined that a man like Moshe would be compelled to invite Itsikl Zilburg to his home to consult with him behind closed doors on matters such as these?

Well, what was done was done. And in a lifetime one could be overtaken by all sorts of things. Moshe was already calming down, but even before he could accompany Itsikl to the door, a messenger came from Reb Dudi with the request that Moshe come to him at once. The rabbi was waiting for him; the matter was urgent.

This transpired just after Reb Dudi had taken to his bed pretending to be sick. Pretending? Yes, though in fact he did not feel too well. Still, he was not so sick that he needed to take to his bed, but take to it he did . . . so that he might have an excuse to send for Dr. Yanovski with whom he had the discussion we will now describe.

The two old men, Reb Dudi and Yanovski, were both municipal leaders. Reb Dudi represented the majority population—the Jewish community. The other was a leader of the Polish minority and served as an economic administrator and as church treasurer. These two, Reb Dudi and Dr. Yanovski, frequently had common interests touching their two communities. They always treated each other with respect and worked well together on the solution of their problems. So that they had achieved a sort of official friendship and consulted each other on all sorts of matters not necessarily related to their roles in the community. Whenever they met, they greeted each other politely. As for Yanovski, on those occasions when he paid Reb Dudi a professional visit, he sat with him much longer than he usually did with any of his patients. They talked of all sorts of things, and when the doctor left, he refused to accept his usual honorarium.

This time, when Yanovski arrived at the rabbi's house, Reb Dudi said at once, "I'm suffering from anxiety more than from any physical illness. No doubt the doctor knows about the incident of the noblemen, the portrait and the pistol shot. And about the charlatan Sventislavski who has manipulated the situation for his financial advantage. And the difficult choice the noblemen faced: on the one hand, chains, exile or, conceivably, even worse. Or, they could pay Sventislavski and the matter would be dropped."

And of course the doctor knew that because of the ill success of this year's fair, the noblemen did not have the money with which to pay off Sventislavski. And that Reb Dudi, feeling sorry for the noblemen with whom the Jews have been involved over the years in all sorts of business matters—he, Reb Dudi, had regarded it as his duty to do what he could to help them. And so he had called together the appropriate people, the money had been collected and the payment had been made.

Obviously, he, the rabbi, did not believe that the noblemen had, God forbid, intended any disrespect to the government. Indeed, quite the reverse. It was precisely because he believed the noblemen were absolutely innocent and were the victims of a false accusation that he had done what was humanly possible and what Jewish law commanded: to give help to those in need.

But the matter became known—no one knows how or who it was who revealed it. It may be that the charlatan Sventislavski, afraid of the consequences of his plot, revealed it himself. Or it may have been someone else. In any case, as Dr. Yanovski no doubt was aware, the noblemen have all been tarred by the same brush. Some have already been detained, and those Jews who helped to gather the money have also been interrogated. And he, Reb Dudi, is terribly distressed. He feels guilty for having entangled innocent people in the matter. Because if things go on as they have been, then, according to what one hears, it may very well end, God forbid, very badly for everyone.

And that was the reason he had sent for the doctor and not becasue of any illness. But rather for a chance to discuss the matter. Perhaps he, the doctor, had some idea of what to do, what measures one might take.

Throughout this discourse, Reb Dudi lay propped up in his bed and Yanovski sat on a chair beside it. Reb Dudi, an old man with a sparse white Jewish beard; opposite him, Yanovski, also an old man, but he had white-woolen Emperor Franz Josef sideburns. Reb Dudi with a certain fire in his keen eyes. Intelligent, politically skillful; Yanovski opposite him, his eyes lusterless, because of old age or because nature had made them that way.

For his part, Yanovski listened, understood, but made no suggestions, whether it was because he did not want to become too deeply involved, or because he saw that there was not much that could be done. Still, he let it be known that, in his view, since this was not an ordinary matter but one that had high-level governmental implications, everything depended on the commission of inquiry and on how it would present the matter to the higher authorities. His point was that if anything could be done it would have to involve the members of the commission. Access to them had to be found—through high-level contacts or other means. If that could be achieved, one could learn first of all how the inquiry itself was progressing, and second it might be possible to persuade them, to demonstrate to them the innocence of the accused. That, it seemed to Yanovski, was the only direction in which one might proceed.

On the whole, Reb Dudi was not particularly satisfied with the results of his conversation with Yanovski. But one thing did stay with him and that was the notion that it might be possible, with the help of minor government officials or through other contacts, to get at the commission members.

And that was why he had sent for Moshe Mashber who was one of the select group of those who had collected the money for the noblemen. Because what Reb Dudi now had to say could only be said to selected highly trustworthy men.

To begin with, Reb Dudi recounted to them his conversation with Yanovski and the effect it had had on him.

Then he added, "There are rumors, gentlemen, that the noblemen are in grave danger. There is something here that needs to be understood: In all instances when there is a commission of inquiry into antigovernment behavior, the members of the commission are inclined to find more guilt than actually exists. It's in the nature of the situation. The commissioners don't want to be charged with taking such evils lightly. Their tendency, then, is not only to establish who is in fact guilty, but also to include in that guilt those who, however slightly, can be said to have helped the accused or who failed to report their behavior to the authorities. The rule of such commissions is: the more you accuse, the more you are praised. As the commissioners see it, if they are sedulous to accuse, they will be seen as faithful servants of the crown and will be rewarded. You may be sure that the commissioners will make good use of this opportunity to distinguish themselves.

They will indict more than the noblemen; they will involve in their accusations even those who had only the faintest connection with the affair: ourselves, for instance—though they know well that the Jews have nothing to do with the substance of the indictment. But he who helps the criminal is considered guilty of his crime.

"What, then, can we do? First, an appeal to God and then to the members of the commission. One has to find the means to get to them. That's Yanovski's suggestion and I agree with it. The question is, how to reach them. If there are legitimate ways, then well and good. But if we cannot reach them through acquaintances, through friendly intercessors, then we must use other means. Small sums of money if they are necessary to bribe petty officials, larger sums for those more highly placed—if they 'take' money. And of course they all 'take.' There is no other recourse.

"It's true," Reb Dudi added, "there are, as in all such ventures, certain risks here. When one approaches such high officials and is about to pay them there is always the danger that the official will cry 'bribery.' Then our guilt is doubled, it grows mountain high. Because, after all, innocent people don't need to pay money for bribes. Yes, there is that danger. On the other hand, we have no other options, and we have, therefore, to be especially careful. To investigate *whom* to pay. To be very sure that they are willing to 'take.' How, and how much. And of course one has to be clever at giving as well."

Clearly the news Reb Dudi brought was not pleasant. In any case, the select group of those who were at the secret meeting left Reb Dudi's house without coming to any decision. Reb Dudi himself did not firmly urge his proposal, first out of fear, and second because even if they had accepted it, no one knew whom to entrust with the task, or who would be willing to risk doing it—or, most important of all, how much money would be needed and where it could be found. As a result, the meeting ended inconclusively—though there were headache and heartache enough for them all. What a disaster! What miserable luck!

Moshe Mashber left that meeting profoundly depressed. The hour was late—nearly midnight. None of his children were in the dining room when he got home; and, though Gitl was waiting up for him, he urged her to get to bed, saying he would make do with the supper that had been prepared for him. And he wanted to be alone after supper because he still had some things to do.

He was left alone. As for his supper, he might as well not have eaten it. He sat at the head of the large table where the light from the hanging lamp in the ceiling obscured the door to the kitchen. Which was why Moshe did not at first notice that someone had silently appeared in the doorway. It was Alter, dressed as always—shabbily, the way someone dresses who does not expect to be remarked, and for whom clothes, in any event, have no great importance. He stood there now, looking as he always did when he made one of his surprise appearances. But now anyone looking closely at him would have observed that a strange change had come over him.

We do not, on this account, want to delay our story. We do, however, want to say that the change that had taken place in Alter would have perplexed even a great doctor. And he would have had great difficulty explaining it. Not being a doctor, we will make no attempt at explanation but we will offer the following facts.

After Alter, on that memorable night of which we have spoken, had had his fall, no one in the family had much of any notion of how he passed his time up in his little room. He was not visited often there. He was given what he usually required, but beyond that not much attention was paid to him. It had been observed that he had recovered quickly from his fall. What no one noticed was that Alter, even when lying in his bed, had, with an infant's delight in such things, taken to playing with the sun's rays.

When he had recovered from his fall and was able to leave his bed, the first thing he asked for was a prayer book. There was some wonder about it in the household, but he was given the book and the matter was forgotten. Later, he asked for a particular book whose title he specified. Again, there was some surprise in the household, but again, the book was given him and the request promptly forgotten. When Mayerl, whom we have already met, the only child in the household to take a continuing interest in Alter, visited him, the conversations he had with Alter frightened him. Not because they were bizarre (Mayerl was used to that) but rather because they were so focused. Mayerl stared at him, hardly able to recognize him, and was more frightened than ever.

The first to notice the change in Alter were the maids in the kitchen. When Alter passed through the kitchen on his way into the courtyard or returning to his attic room, he paused there longer than usual. And standing there, he gazed at the kitchen maids, and particularly at the younger one, the high-bosomed chambermaid, Gnessye. When for the first time the older servant saw him at it—that is, staring at Gnessye— she was horrified and cried (when Alter had gone), "Ah, woe is me. Did you see that?"

"What?" asked the other.

"Woman! You mean you didn't notice?"

"Notice what?"

"It's beginning to look as if Alter's becoming normal."

"What makes you think that?"

"From the way he was looking at you."

On another occasion, she cried out, more convinced than before, "Why is he looking at you that way, woman? What does he see in you?"

On a third occasion, with still greater certainty: "I see which way the wind is blowing. He's got something on his mind."

And it was true. Alter was now staring in amazement at what had been of no concern to him before. Often he felt himself hemmed in in his room and felt the need to go out into the open air, into the street, but he was too ashamed. And with reason. In the eyes of others—in his own eyes—he would be an object of derision. And then, too, he was ashamed of his clothes. In a word, Alter was now conscious of his situation, and was aware of what had transpired until now. And he wanted his situation to change. He wanted to step over the threshold of his room, to enter into the life of the household, but he did not yet have sufficient courage. And so for the time being he concealed the fact that he was restored to health, that his mind was whole, and waited for an opportunity to be alone with his brother Moshe to whom he would reveal himself, counting on him, then, to reintroduce him to the family.

Meanwhile, he was putting on weight. It seemed to him that his food had a different taste and its effect on him was now different. His pallid features, it is true, remained pale, but his face was filled out, and from time to time one could even discern some color in it. If the family, overwhelmed with worries, had not just then been going through such a difficult time, any of them meeting Alter would have noticed the changes in him. But everything was disordered. Especially Moshe, about whom the older servant said one day to Gnessye. "Do you know what? Alter's changing places with the boss!"

"What does that mean, changing places?"

"It means that the boss is going crazy and Alter is turning sane."

Alter, meanwhile, had the time and the tranquillity he needed. In his attic room, he was like a chick still in the egg under the mother hen, warming his new growth and understanding until he should feel himself ready to crack his shell, to emerge, to stand alone on his own two feet.

During this period, if anyone had come into his room, they might have found him turning his gaze this way and that as he studied his clothes, his hands and his feet and even his face as it was sometimes reflected in the panes of the window when the changes in light and shade turned the glass into mirrors.

And so it went, until one day he was drawn to go down to the family. This happened on the night when Moshe, having returned from his meeting with Reb Dudi, was sitting at the table in the dining room. Alter, as he usually did, paused in the doorway. Moshe, as we have seen, did not at first notice him because of the light from the overhead lamp. When he did see him, he cried out, surprised, "Ah, Alter. Is it you?" Alter came in and approached Moshe who was at the head of the table. And in the brief space of time it took Alter to move from the doorway to the table, Moshe became aware that Alter's pace was somehow different and that his manner was not as he remembered it; and beyond all that, the look in Alter's eyes was of a sort one could not have expected to see there: a look of humanity, of intelligence. And precisely that is what now terrified Moshe: that look of human intelligence with which all men are gifted.

At first, in his fear, he did not know what to do. He did not, as he usually did when Alter made one of his surprise appearances . . . he did not send him back to his room with, "Go. Go on, Alter. Go to your room." No, this time Moshe got to his feet, as if he wanted to make room for Alter, as if he meant to invite him to sit down. But he did not do that because it was not something he had ever done. Instead, Moshe stood for a moment, then not knowing what to do, he asked confusedly, "What did you want, Alter?"

"I wanted to discuss something with you."

From the very first words that Alter uttered, it was clear to Moshe that he had an amazingly new man before him. He remembered how Alter had come to see him on the day before the New Year to report to Moshe that he thought he was getting better. Moshe remembered, too, Yanovski's words on the night we know of, when Alter had had his fall: that it was possible that the fall might produce a crisis in Alter's illness. . . . Moshe remembering those words now, with Alter standing before him, a new man, did not know what to say or what to do. But at this point, Alter himself came to Moshe's aid. Without waiting for Moshe's questions, Alter said, "Moshe, I've come to say that you must arrange a wedding for me."

This was said in a tone of such pure sincerity as only a madman might have used, or someone so unaccustomed to human society that he did not know how, when or where certain things might be said— and the way the words were spoken . . . it was enough to break one's heart.

There was nothing to blame Alter for. He was like a man who had come from some distant place. He was a man who had been cut off from people and from human ways. And so he spoke not as people in society usually speak, but he said directly what he meant, and what he meant was that he was like everyone else.

"What?" Moshe asked, as if he had not heard. As if he could not believe his ears. And greatly baffled he could think of nothing better to do than simply to repeat. "What? What is it you want? Alter, what is it you want?"

Alter replied that what he wanted to say was that he was now like everyone else. That his room had become too small, that the world was opening up, that it was time for him to live and that, therefore, something had to be done for him. And that he was turning to Moshe because, as he remembered, when their father had died, he had made Moshe his guardian, and Moshe was therefore responsible for him.

At first what Alter said was so amazing to Moshe, so incomprehensible, that for a while Moshe did not seem to know where he was. He saw neither the lamp, nor Alter, nor where he stood in relationship to his chair. He turned, then, and began to search for it, presumably to sit down again because he was unsteady on his feet. As he turned he murmured the phrase he habitually used when he was dealing with Alter: "Go. Go, Alter." But this time he added, "We'll see. We'll think about it."

Alter stood there awhile longer, then he went away. Moshe was so confused, so perplexed, that he hardly heard the sound of Alter's receding footsteps. It was only when finally he had found his chair and had seated hmself in it that he was able to understand what it was that he had heard a moment ago. Then he heaved a sigh of relief and said, "Dear God in heaven, what's happening here?"

XI

Before the Crash

Late one very drizzly evening in the month Heshvan, in the time of which we speak, a rain-drenched coach drawn by a couple of steaming horses who were exhausted by the hours of their long haul over badly maintained muddy autumn roads drove up before an inn in the town of N. A lone reflecting lamp was fixed to the right side of the coach. It, too, looked as if it had long ago grown weary of its insignificant and sooty light which nevertheless allowed one to see the two persons who now descended from the coach after their long journey from abroad.

They were Sruli and Luzi who were now returned not only from their most recent trip to Uman, but also from another journey which, it would appear, they had undertaken after Uman—a journey to Luzi's distant little border village so that Luzi might turn the little bit of immovable property he had there into cash, and to bring back with him what *could* be moved—the sorts of things everyone has need of (bedding and the like).

Yes. This was evidently so because Luzi this time came back more laden down with baggage than he had on his last journey. The coachman had all he could do to get the packages and bundles into the house, while Sruli, who in truth had nothing to do with the packages—obviously they did not belong to him—nevertheless hovered over them as if they were his. First he supervised how they were being carried, and then he counted those that were brought in. He gave instructions where to put them so that they would not get dirty or pushed about. It was Sruli who busied himself with all these matters before which Luzi was helpless because he had neither the experience nor the knack to deal with them. He seemed, moreover, exhausted by the journey.

And all the work that Sruli did with the packages and bundles and the settling in of Luzi that evening had to be done again, and more, when next morning he sought out a house which it would appear had been previously found and rented with the help of various brokers. And now Sruli had to install Luzi in it. First, there was the move from the inn to the house, after which there was a great deal to do: the walls had to be painted with whitewash, the floors washed, the furniture and housewares had to be set out, and whatever they needed and did not have had to be bought. Sruli took all these tasks upon himself, and accomplished them efficiently, as if to the manor born. As if he had had long practice in settling people into their houses.

Luzi had settled in not far from The Curse. This was a section of the town which, without question, some sickly, angry old prophet had cursed with misfortune and with a look of ruin so dreadful that a passerby who saw it could not repress a shudder and left it with the feeling that he had caught a whiff of the tomb.

This was the third part of the town—it had a certain number of streets. Actually, they were not exactly streets. Rather they were small, narrow lanes wide enough for one or two people. These ran crookedly between rows of houses, three quarters of them in ruin. Some had no roofs, though they still showed some sad and naked timbers. Others, though they seemed to have shingles on their roofs, had been so withered by heat, time and wind that they appeared rotted and full of holes. The walls of these houses were made of thin, cracked, unplastered boards. Those that had been plastered had the look of swollen bellies, their doors and hinges were crooked, their windows warped or without panes—the holes stuffed with rags or something of the sort. In those houses, water was a rare guest: the houses were unwashed and so were their inhabitants. And therefore dust over everything. Filth and dirt that had endured for generations on the walls, on the few remaining panes of glass that no longer served to let in light, because light, in any case, did not exist in those streets; it was an idea that only exaggerated the prevailing dark and the abandoned, uncared-for condition of the house.

There was a populace there. People of the lowest class: cripples who made their livings from their illnesses and handicaps. Because these people (those who still had feet) dragged themselves about the town and went from house to house as beggars. But for the most part, those who lived there were no longer even beggars, and how they made a living only they and God, and perhaps the prophet who had put the curse on them, could tell.

Just imagine how they lived. Pillows, filthy to the last degree, lay about in the streets for them to lie on in summer. Who knows where, or on what, they lay in winter? Because who, after all, had ever looked at them besides the Angel of Death? He was a very frequent guest in that quarter, even when there were no epidemics in the town. And when there were, he was there constantly, peering in through the filthy rag-stuffed windows. And, after each of his glances, more than one of the inhabitants was made ready for the journey—today or tomorrow—to the cemetery.

The Curse, too, provided candidates for the poorhouses and hospitals. Old people, and the young who were condemned from childhood on not to get old: defeated, half crippled, half mad. Children who were born there were destined, if they died while they were still small, to be carried in the skirts of Moshe-Mote, the stretcher bearer's coat, the way one carries a melon when one hasn't got a basket. If the children died when they were a little older they were picked up by the gravedigger's wagon—not singly, but several at a time—because corpses there were as common as bread.

Here and there, and from time to time, there lived in that quarter artisans of the very lowest grade whose only reason for living there was that there was no place else that they could live since they had neither work nor craft nor tools. And if they lived anywhere else, they would at the very least be required to pay rent. And here, a landlord who might demand payment was frequently absent—unless it might be the prophet who had put his curse on the place.

It was in that district, not far from those crooked streets, that Sruli had found a house for Luzi to live in. There, a solitary old woman undertook to clean, cook and wash up for Luzi. The little house with its entry hall, two rooms and small kitchen had, since Luzi moved into it, acquired a look of some respectability. It was not very clean on the outside because it, like all the other houses in that district, was on a muddy street. It goes without saying that at night the street was unlighted, but, given the kind of help Luzi had, conditions inside the house were quite pleasant.

One needs to add that no sooner had Luzi moved into the house than it became a sort of gathering place for the members of Luzi's sect. This happened because this district was quite far from the center of town and from their synagogue; and since the autumn weather was wet and muddy, and because most of the members of the sect, because they were poor, lived in the district anyhow, Luzi's house very soon became a place where they could slip in to say early evening and evening prayers after which they could spend some time sitting over a glass of tea and a rude sort of supper, talking about sectarian matters, or telling tales, or listening, or pouring their hearts out to each other.

Nor was it only members of the sect. With each passing day, Luzi's house became increasingly better known to other pious Jews. And from time to time, young people from other sects who, it would appear, felt a lack of piety in their own communities, slipped into the house, drawn to it by their sense that greater spiritual demands were made on them there. Drawn, too, to Luzi to whom, as they had heard, such a strange thing had happened—and this they found especially exciting. And so they came, stealthily, slipping away from parents and in-laws, from friends and comrades, in the evening, in the interval between light and dark, approaching the little house with secrecy and care, crossing its threshold the way one steals into a place of sweet sin.

And, little by little, the house began to draw people from the neighborhood, people who had no interest in the nuances of meaning that separated the sects. They were simply drawn to a house that was always open, and from which nobody was ever sent away. And why not go in, why not look around? Particularly since at night one heard strangely passionate songs coming from the place, and saw, if one looked through the small windows, packed clusters of people, sometimes sitting around the table, sometimes standing, but always engaged in heated conversation. Then why shouldn't one of the local inhabitants open the door and, without so much as a "Good evening"—a greeting never demanded of anyone—why shouldn't he, then, join that crowd and lend an ear to the proceedings?

Luzi's house was soon so well known that even the cripples who lived in The Curse began, in their dull and clumsy way, to frequent it. Naturally enough, they came without invitation. But it became a not unusual sight, in broad daylight or late at night, to see one of them who still possessed feet and some intelligence going toward the house.

As, for instance, Ten Groschen Pushke, a ragged and tattered fellow dressed in wadded old cotton clothing that he never took off, neither in winter nor in summer, so that his stink could be smelled a mile off. He wore, too, a great many rings made of tin or lead which, since they were never removed, were sunk into his flesh. The result was that his hands were brownish blue and swollen. He never spoke. With his bundle of clothes on his back, he looked like a tortoise when he moved. And, because of the weight of his burden, he sat or stood more frequently than he moved. And this Pushke, too, was one of those who went to Luzi's house. He did not go in; he simply wanted to be near. To stand rigidly in the glow of the lamp that shone from its windows. Or, sometimes, simply to press a somewhat deaf ear to the wall, to listen to the songs that were being sung within.

Or, still another: Wednesday. He was very like the first. He had been an abandoned child with neither father nor mother who had found his way here, to The Curse. And he was called Wednesday for the day in the week when he was found, and because no one had been able to think of a better name. One of his eyes was the size of an apple and was glazed and protruding. With his second, normal eye, he looked out at the world with an idiot's sweet gaze. And that's who Wednesday was: himself and his two eyes. Wednesday: whose smile moved from his good eye down his cheek like a brook moving downhill. He owned nothing except perhaps the shirt he wore, and the idiotic smile on his lips, and a very little bit of speech and reason. And always ready to reply if he was asked who he was, "I am Wednesday. My name is Wednesday, because I was found on a Wednesday." And this personage, too—only the Lord knows how or why—found his way to Luzi's house.

In a word, Luzi's house became a gathering point to which young people, whispering stealthily, came. Their elders muttered and tried to warn the young people off, and the aged grumbled angrily and used harsh language to describe the house. They called it "impure" and "church," and they discussed how they might rid themselves of its owner.

It had indeed reached the point at which the town was beginning to concern itself about the house. Though it was so distant and remote that one would have thought that no one could care what went on in it, still there were those who cared a great, great deal and who had it very much on their minds. So that certain pious folk met quietly and decided, since Luzi was a distinguished man and the brother of a distinguished man, that before undertaking any action against the owner of the house, against Luzi, to get Moshe Mashber's opinion on the matter. What they wanted to know was whether he would have any suggestions for what steps to take other than the severe ones that they had considered.

Just imagine, then, that a considerable group of well-known personages came together one evening in Moshe's house where they discussed the matter, examining it from every point of view in a manner that was at once animated and restrained. Everyone was excited, but Moshe only half heard what was being said. He had other things on his mind. Distracted and confused, he seemed to be living in another world.

Because just then things were going very badly for Moshe Mashber. His business affairs were declining, his troubles and misfortunes, mounting.

In addition to everything else, his younger daughter, Nekhamke, was taken seriously ill. It was not known whether the illness was a result of repressed anxiety regarding her father's situation or because of her husband Nakhum Lentsher's quiet harassment of her, or whether she had caught a chill of some sort, or whether there was an inherited illness at work in her. Whatever the case might be, her condition grew steadily worse. Her cheeks turned increasingly paler. She shivered frequently and she was now wrapped in her shawl from the time when she rose in the morning until she went to bed at night. And recently, because of the bad fall weather, she had taken entirely to her bed. Her feet were swollen. The doctors advised a summer climate, but where was that to be found just now? They suggested journeys to tropical countries—but in those days that was an idea that was not well understood. And even if it had been, the times through which the family was living were not of the sort in which one could even think of such a solution.

For Moshe, Nekhamke's illness was one more visitation. He felt that there was the weight of a heavy hand upon him, and who could say how far down it would thrust him. Often when he came home and went into this daughter's room to see how she was, he simply stood there without saying a word, and the two of them, father and daughter, had tears in their eyes which they repressed for each other's sake. Nekhamke, lying in her bed, wiped them away secretly, while he did the same in some corner of the room as he left her.

There was reason enough for tears. In the room where his wife lay, Nakhum Lentsher, Moshe's son-in-law, paced the room like a wolf, chain-smoking cigarettes whose unsmoked ends he spat out too frequently into a cuspidor in a corner of the room. He had reason enough for anger, but he was angrier still because now he had no one to whom he could confide his feelings nor whom he could torment. He understood enough to know that it would be criminal to talk with Nekhamke about his projects now, so he kept silent, but his father-in-law understood what he was doing, and so did Nekhamke, so that his silence made nobody's lot any easier. It would have been better, they thought, for him to speak out.

In addition to all this, something happened just then in the household that made a deep impression on everyone, including Nakhum, and which affected them the way a sudden sharp sound in the ear can make people leap to their feet, trembling.

One evening, Shmulikl the Fist showed up in Moshe's house. Everybody in town knew him. He was a man of medium height but built like a block with high, level shoulders. His face had a pale look to it because of the effect of the white film of a cataract over one eye. His dark yellow hair and beard were bristly. His single eye coupled with his bristly beard were enough to frighten anyone whom he meant to intimidate, and his lean, dry hands, the size of boards, could make a whole town tremble. Mostly, his clients were primary-school aides and teachers or artisans who hired him to teach some colleague a lesson that his bones would never forget. A blow from Shmulikl's fist could turn a man's face into a pulp seeded with loosened teeth, or it could make the whole face look like a swollen pancake.

There was a time when he, too, had been a school aid, but he could not make nearly as much money at that as he could from being a thug. It was a trade acknowledged by the town—in extreme cases, one had to employ extreme remedies. When Shmulikl was a youth, he had been a member of one of the town's gangs, ne'er-do-wells who lived by raising pigeons, or fighting, or who were supported by fallen women; or from protection money they collected from the middle class youth of the town, the sums varying according to their fathers' wealth. Now, when he was no longer young (he was certainly in his forties), he had nothing more to do with such youthful ventures. He had more serious projects. He was an "enforcer" and made rather a good living at it. Good enough so that he could always afford a bit of drink before he went out on a job, and a drink after he had done his enforcing. And sometimes a drink while he was doing his work.

This time his client was a usurer, a Jew nicknamed The Kitten. A small man whose face was hidden by his beard and who had worn, for as long as anyone remembered, the same frayed winter coat without buttons so that he habitually huddled against palings to avoid the cold winds of winter.

He was a dreadful miser, though he had a house with a large front garden in the district near the dikes. But the house was invariably leased to strangers while he, himself, because he had no need for anything more, lived in a tiny room he rented from his neighbors. He had neither wife nor children. Or if he had, he had parted from them so that he would not need to support them. As for his own keep, he sometimes made a trifling payment to a neighbor for an occasional Sabbath meal. Beyond that, he had no needs. As for such trifles as wood and fuel, he stole them when he could from his neighbors. He had amassed, people said, rubles by the thousands in addition to a considerable amount of silver and gold plate which had been pawned to him, and which, when their owners failed to redeem them, had become his property. All of it was hidden under laundry so filthy that one would be too revolted to reach under it to find out what was there. The Kitten's dirty laundry was *so* foul that its stink could be smelled from afar, and pregnant women getting a whiff of it had been known to miscarry.

He came to an ugly end. He was strangled by a gang of Gentiles to whom he used to rent his garden and from whom, in addition to the rent he collected, he used to get presents of rotting apples or wormy plums—from which during the summer months he used actually to nourish himself. It was said that his murderers had very little trouble strangling him because he was so small and malnourished. After a brief spasm, he yielded up the ghost, with interest. There was a squeak out of his mouth and another sound from somewhere else. And that was all the profit his murderers got, because they could not imagine that there could be anything of value in the midst of all that filth. And he never kept any cash, though, since that was how he hoarded his money, there were promissory notes enough, and for large sums.

Moshe Mashber was one of his debtors. When The Kitten first began to hear rumors in town about Moshe from other Kittens like himself, he would not at first believe them, because he had been a regular visitor in Moshe's office where (dressed in his threadbare coat) he went often for news, and he had seen no change in the office. It was all business as usual. But when, over time, the rumors failed to subside, he began to get queasy tremors in his ugly little belly—though the term of his loan was by no means up and he had no money coming to him just then. Whether it was the bellyache from eating rotten apples or the dreadful thought that he risked losing such a large, such a vast, lump of money—whichever it was, he woke frequently at night and had to go outside to relieve himself beside a paling, and, standing there, he raised his eyes to the heavens where there were unreachable coins chiming, coins that only rarely fell to the ground. . . . No, he could not sleep and racked his brain to figure out how, without creating complications, to get his money back from Moshe Mashber before it was due. But there was nothing he could think of except the one plan that he usually put into effect when he was dealing with smaller, less important debtors than Moshe Mashber and that was: send Shmulikl.

It was altogether curious to see how The Kitten, this little fellow with the hoarse, stringy voice—like the sound one makes playing music on a comb—this fellow who even in winter lacked buttons on his coat, who managed to keep it closed with bits of string the way a poor porter does, who sidled along palings to protect himself from the wind . . . it was altogether curious to see how this fellow got on with Shmulikl. How, indeed, he had sought him and found him. And how he and Shmulikl did their business together.

It's true that The Kitten invariably tried to cheat Shmulikl or to get him to give him a bargain price. He would promise to pay *after* Shmulikl had done his work. But Shmulikl did not budge. He was tough and knew what he was worth, and he always made the same reply: "A drink before, a drink after—and the price of the job is fixed." But when finally The Kitten and Shmulikl had come to an agreement, The Kitten pressed himself close, very close, and as if he were climbing a ladder and lifting himself toward Shmulikl's ear, he said, "Remember, Shmulikl, beat their guts out. My money. Those crooks. It's hard-earned money. Bitterly earned. Got without food or rest. Beat their guts out."

This time, however, when The Kitten discussed Moshe Mashber with Shmulikl, he said, "Now remember, Shmulikl . . . remember where you're going. And remember who you're dealing with. Don't touch him. Don't lay a hand on him—beyond banging on the table. Because the truth is, he doesn't owe me any money. The term of the loan isn't up. But he needs to be scared. So that he doesn't take the matter lightly. So that he can see who is on my side and what measures I'm willing to take when the time comes."

Shmulikl himself was not entirely comfortable with this assignment. He was, in fact, unhappy with it. He had never before been sent into such a respectable, such a wealthy, home. And, too, he was not much given to speech; all of his power resided in his fist and with it, when he was dealing with people like himself, he always prevailed. But now in this case with Moshe Mashber, how could he raise a hand? Especially since The Kitten had expressly forbidden it.

So that he was already a bit confused when he entered Moshe's house. And the house itself: its air, its candles and lamps sapped his energy so that he felt as if he had left three quarters of his enforcer's strength on the other side of the threshold.

It was already night, a time when, as he had calculated, he could expect to find Moshe home from his office. Moshe and his sons-in-law with him. If it had happened that Elyokum or Katerukhe had been in the kitchen, or that some office employee was in the house, as was often the case, then Shmulikl's appearance would not have had quite such a startling effect. But just then nobody from the household staff was there, so one may guess what sort of look there was on the faces of the people in the room when they found themselves confronting this fellow whom the whole town knew. One glance at Shmulikl and at his cataract-covered eye and they could tell at once that they were dealing with a man who would stop at nothing—not even at crime.

He was asked what he wanted and he was invited to sit. He accepted the invitation saying, "The Kitten sent me. I've been sent by The Kitten. Money."

"Money? What kind of money?" they said, without understanding him. "Does anyone owe you anything, God forbid?"

"No, not me. The Kitten."

"But what's that got to do with you? Why doesn't he speak for himself if anyone here owes him anything?"

"I," shouted Shmulikl, "am Shmulikl. My name is Shmulikl. The whole town knows me, and you should know who I am. I've come for him. It's for him I've come."

Shmulikl's presence itself, and the stagnant smells that came from the old clothes he wore—the same clothes he had worn when he was a school aide—and the very way he used his unwashed hands in whose folds there clung encrusted bits of blood as on the hands of a butcher, all of this was enough to turn the stomachs of those in the household who saw him, and to nauseate those with delicate natures. Is it any wonder, then, that having the fellow sitting so near to them at table, and fearing that at any moment he might do the sorts of things they knew he was capable of . . . all of this, we say, explains why those who were there turned pale and why secretly their hands and knees trembled and why no one was able to utter so much as a word. No one, that is, but Moshe Mashber who, as the head of the household, and as the person to whom Shmulikl had spoken, somehow found the means to reply, "Be good enough, then, to tell your Kitten that he is an ugly Jew, an ugly person with an ugly mind. And that there is no money due to him just yet, and that when it is due he will have to ask for it himself, and that there is no need to send messengers. Tell him . . ."

"Our money!" Shmulikl remembered The Kitten's standard instructions: "Beat their guts out." Then remembering that he had been forbidden to use his hands, he cried again, "Our money. Give us our money." With that he struck the table such a blow with his fist that everything in the room—glass, china, furniture—made such a clatter that people from other rooms in the house came running, even those servants in the kitchen who normally never appeared in the dining room, sensing now that some calamity was lowering over the house, showed up. And of course they were not wrong: what else could it mean? Whoever heard of a stranger pounding the table with his fist, and what a stranger . . . a fellow who at any other time would not have been allowed to cross the threshold; and surely he was not pounding the table for no reason; it must be that he was owed something.

"What's going on there?" It was sick Nekhamke's voice that reached them suddenly from her distant room.

Everyone was silent. Somebody went off at once to reassure Nekhamke but, after the banging on the table and after Shmulikl had left the house, people for the most part stayed where they were in the dining room staring at each other, helpless with shame and not daring to say a word because the sound of the fist banging on the table still rang in their ears.

Fortunately for them there was no stranger in the house just then who might have carried the tale of what had happened into the street. But there was trouble enough. Enough so that later on that same night a greatly distressed Gitl, wringing her hands, asked Moshe as they were getting ready for bed, "Moshe, what's happening to us? What's going to happen? Isn't there anything we can do? Or somewhere to turn to for help?"

And trouble enough so that Nakhum Lentsher, Moshe's younger son-in-law, unable to contain himself, ignored his wife's condition. Coming into their room, he exploded openly and angrily: "Ah, what did I tell you? Have you any idea who was here tonight? Who it was that banged on the table? And the situation we're in? Did anyone bother to take my advice? And now it's too late—a waste of words."

And even Yankele Grodshteyn, Moshe's older son-in-law who was gently quiet in all circumstances, good or bad, and who never raised his voice—even he said, "Sinking to a low level. The lowest, the absolute lowest."

And the events of the evening caused Yankele Grodshteyn to remember something that had happened to him earlier in the day when he was standing near a group of merchants in the marketplace. It happened that Sruli Gol was going by just then. At any other time, nobody would have noticed Sruli. Now, however, everyone turned to watch him as if he were a phenomenon, and at the same time they looked quickly and furtively at Yankele Grodshteyn as if Sruli's presence in the marketplace closely concerned him, Yankele. Yes. By now everyone knew that Yankele's father-in-law owed Sruli Gol money, and what Yankele noticed was that the people in the marketplace were not as surprised to discover that Sruli Gol had suddenly become rich as they were to learn that Moshe Mashber had had to borrow from someone like Sruli.

"Did you see?" someone in the crowd said. "He's walking about as if the market were already his. As if he had an investment of his own in it."

"He has an investment in it," someone else said. "Tsali Derbaremdiker can tell you the precise amount that he lent Moshe Mashber. He knows it because it was he who arranged the loan. He was the broker."

"Well," said a third bystander, "it happens sometimes that some poor fellow wins the lottery and a rich man buys a losing number."

Now that conversation had taken place in Yankele Grodshteyn's presence, and those taking part in it counted on Yankele's well-known shyness and his somewhat foolish honesty which would require him to turn away from, or to pretend not to hear, a discussion that had anything to do with him or his.

Now that was how the market talk dealt with Sruli. What would they say when the story of Shmulikl's visit to the Mashber house got out?

Now, even Yankele Grodshteyn said, "Sinking to a low level. The lowest, the absolute lowest."

Naturally enough, Shmulikl's visit had its most dreadful effect on Moshe. Almost as soon as Shmulikl left the house, the members of the household noticed how Moshe, stunned and ashamed, had suddenly a crowd of old sayings and citations in his mouth. He spoke them more or less unconsciously, as a man might all of whose inner constraints have been torn so that he no longer knows what's happening to him or how to impose any controls. "The song of David fleeing from Absalom, his son. 'Lord, mine enemies are many,' he said. 'My flesh trembles with fear. I am in dread of your judgment . . . I raise mine eyes to the mountains from whence cometh mine aid.' " One verse after another, without any order or sequence, mingled bits and pieces of text and citation. Then all at once he was aware of himself: "What's happening? What am I doing? What am I saying?" And he put the palm of his right hand over his mouth to prevent his lips from moving as, ashamed, he looked around at the members of his family who, perplexed and worried, encircled him. Abruptly, he stopped reciting, but the shame and the pain were by no means lessened, nor did the fact that Shmulikl had been there become any less of a fact. And what exacerbated his pain was the memory of his sick daughter's cry coming to him from her distant room, a cry that had made him tremble far worse than the blow of Shmulikl's fist on the table. He had been prepared for anything. Except to be unable to protect his sick daughter from a fellow like Shmulikl. For anything! But Moshe Mashber had not been prepared for that. Now that was sinking—to the lowest level of all. And then the thought passed through his mind that everything that had just happened was merely the trivial beginning of the doom that was yet to come. This was but the momentary first blow, and not even properly a real blow since it was possible to turn it aside, to eject from his house the fellow who struck it. But what would happen later when those who had rights in the matter, when his creditors came thronging to his house and no further discussion was possible, and not one word more could be said in the way of self-justification or excuse; and then there would be loud demands for repayment—and blows.

He cast a look at his son-in-law Nakhum and knew that he, Nakhum, was in a hurry to get back to his sick wife's room where he could lodge his complaints; and Moshe looked, too, at his second son-in-law and read the pitying words that hovered on his lips; then he looked at Gitl and had a clear understanding of what she would say to him tonight in their bedroom. And he could find no consolation, either for himself or for anyone else. His forehead turned pale as did the tip of his nose, and it was some little while before they resumed their natural color. And from that moment on Moshe Mashber acquired traits and patterns of behavior and experienced states of soul which before that time a man like himself could not have imagined would happen to him under any circumstances.

For instance:

When, on that same night, he and Gitl were in their bedroom and she began the serious conversation she wanted to have with him, he put her off: couldn't she see that he was in no mood for it, that his head ached, that he was in no condition for it just now. He asked her to put the discussion off until tomorrow and urged her to get a good night's sleep. And when she had gone to bed and was finally asleep, Moshe Mashber lay there for a considerable while longer, his eyes wide open. Then he got out of bed quietly, put his slippers on and began pacing, first in the bedroom and then through other rooms in the house, the dining room included, where no one was sleeping, then he came back to the bedroom and stood at his window looking out at the night.

An end-of-the-month moon shone through streaks of clouds making a network of autumn silence in the night sky. In that half-light, everything looked vague and formless especially to someone seeing it through a windowpane.

Then all at once, Moshe Mashber saw a man standing in the court-yard. He was not entirely sure that he had seen him, nor was he partic-ularly frightened as formerly he might have been. Certainly he would have wondered who the stranger was who was wandering about in his courtyard. What did he want? But now Moshe was calm and because he was calm he was able to recognize the man: Alter. Alter whom Moshe had put out of his mind since their last conversation, though each time in recent days that he and Alter chanced to meet, Alter re-minded Moshe of his promise to find someone for him. And it was clear, too, to Moshe that Alter was wandering about at night this way because in daylight and in the presence of others he felt ill at ease, hemmed in. At night, he troubled no one; walking about at night he could clear his mind and think about his situation.

Then all at once Moshe felt that there was nothing separating him from Alter, as if there was neither wall nor window between them, and it occurred to him that just as he stood there looking at Alter in the courtyard, so Alter could see him, Moshe, standing there only partly dressed. And that may even have been true, since Alter's face was turned toward Moshe's window.

At that moment Moshe in the house and Alter in the courtyard each felt a chill in their bones just as the moon chanced to show itself through a rent in the clouds; and at the same time, both Alter and Moshe heard a cry—was it human? No, not human . . . Was it a dog's? No, not a dog's. It was a sound that emanated from the vicinity of Mikhalko's hut, from the doghouse there. And it was the dog Watch Chain's voice. Watch Chain who was voiceless all year long except now in the fall and at night, when there was no one to hear him, and when the moon, desperate to shed a little light, was fortunate enough for a few rare moments to penetrate the clouds—then it would seem Watch Chain found his voice and uttered his anguished and muted cry, a cry that came from deep within his dog's bowels. Usually he did not feel the need to repeat his cry more than a couple of times. But now, seeing a man standing in the courtyard, a man wandering about at night—even though it was someone he knew, and, furthermore, sensing with his dog's instincts that there was a second man, his owner, looking out at the courtyard from the window—given all that, he sent forth from the hidden depth of his entrails a long series of agonized and muted howls.

Then both of the brothers moved. Alter left his place in the court-yard, and Moshe his at the window. We do not know what Alter did next. But Moshe went back to bed—whether to sleep or to lie there sleepless, we cannot say. In either case, Watch Chain's howls echoed for a long while in his ear—a reminder of a dreadful day and a prophecy of a tomorrow that would not be much better.

Yes. The next day was no better. And when that evening an exhausted Moshe Mashber came home from the office and went in to his daughter's room to see how she was, he could not bring himself to stand at her bedside for very long because he could see that she was very far from getting any better. He stood silently at her bedside unable to say more than, "I think you're looking a bit better." Then abruptly he left the room to avoid seeing her pain.

He went at once into the dining room where there were no guests, since in recent days business people, as if by agreement, avoided the house. It was clear to everyone that there was no new business to discuss, and that ongoing matters were not going well. There were no visits from financial brokers nor from his own office employees, with the exception of an occasional, and urgent, visit from Liberson, his cashier.

It was as if the doors to the house were resting, and the walls, too, had no occasion to see any new faces. And the members of the household could be sure these days that when they sat down among themselves at table there would be no newcomers to greet before the evening was over. Though sometimes there were exceptions—as last night there had been Shmulikl Fist. And tonight Malke-Rive.

She did not simply come in, but she carried some object covered in a white cloth. It was some sort of clothing and it was obvious from the protective way she carried it that it was very precious to her.

She came in via the kitchen door and as she passed through it, something in the kitchen displeased her. Usually, there was a gathering there of kitchen servants chatting, cracking jokes, quarreling. And always there were piles of washed or unwashed dishes and pots and pans. But this time there was none of that. It was as if the spirit of the kitchen had been drawn off—or as if it were after a holiday when everyone was weak, worn out. Indeed, the whole house did not feel as it usually did: she could not be sure whether it was that the lamps were somehow shedding a different glow, or that the walls were darker or whether people's expressions were different. And she could have sworn that she could smell the odor of camphor or some other medicament coming from a distant sickroom.

She stood uncertainly for a moment. She had come here on a matter which as she saw it could only be resolved in her favor here, in this house. She had come to pawn her Zisye's skunk fur coat. She had come here instead of to the usurers because in the first place, they only gave one a trifle for such things, and second, because if one pawned clothing—or anything else—with them and was late with a payment, then they sold it at once or for want of the ridiculously small sum they had lent on it, they kept it for themselves and then that was the end of it and good-bye forever.

As usual she was wearing her earrings and her veil. She was certain that here she would be treated better than by the usurers. She would get more money here, and the coat itself would be safer until, with the help of God, she could redeem it.

She had been confident that this would happen especially after all the good that had come to her since Zisye's illness. Was it not these rich relatives who had, after Zisye had been taken sick, sent them a free doctor whenever he had been needed? And who had paid the butcher so that they could get meat from him? And had paid the grocer for food? And had done all that without being asked? It followed naturally, then, that today, when she came to pawn an object like this one, practically new, hardly worn—because her Zisye took great care of things—and this coat was the last and the best of the things they had already pawned, and the most expensive and the one most treasured—certainly a thing like this would not be rejected and so she would not need to risk being insulted by the pawnbrokers and of course she would get more money on the coat here than she would from the pawnbrokers.

And she had worn her earrings and veil. Then why was it that she felt as if she had chosen the wrong time to come? What was it that made her feel that no one in the household, including the people in the kitchen, were particularly eager to welcome any visitors just now?

But, since she was already there, and had gotten herself all dressed up in her best clothes, and since she had brought her last precious possession with her, she plucked up her courage and sat herself down even closer than usual to Moshe Mashber and nodded more familiarly than ever to him.

"First of all, Moshe, I want to thank you for everything you've done for us until now. What I mean is the doctor, the butcher and the grocer whom, and for a considerable while, you paid in advance, thereby saving Zisye's life and the whole family's. . . ."

"What?" Moshe Mashber asked, perplexed. "What doctor, what butcher, what grocer? I haven't the faintest idea what you're talking about."

"What do you mean, you don't know what I'm talking about? There was a while when none of them would take any money from us. Not the doctor for his visits, nor the butcher for his meat, nor the grocer for the food that he sent. But maybe you didn't want anyone to know?" Her voice fell and she looked around as if she expected everyone there to avert their eyes from herself and Moshe because Moshe, out of modesty, did not want to be thanked openly for such things. "Maybe you meant to keep the whole thing hidden, like those who practice charity in secret."

"What kind of charity? And what kind of secret?" Moshe said, more perplexed than ever. "I haven't the faintest idea who your benefactor is. In any case, whoever he is, I'm not the one, nor, I think, is it anyone here?" he said, turning to the members of his family for confirmation. He looked first at Gitl who throughout the conversation had been sitting nearby.

"No," Gitl said, rejecting the idea with a shrug of her shoulders.

No. No one. Not even Yankele Grodshteyn, who occasionally and secretly and over fairly long periods of time did support people who had run into a streak of adversity. He, too, denied being the one and actually blushed at the idea that he was suspected of doing something in which he had had no part.

"Then who?" Malke-Rive said, her speech of gratitude hovering, as it were, in midair. "Well, in that case," she said, as if talking to herself, "then maybe it was from him. . . ."

"From whom?"

"You know the man, Moshe. Everyone knows who he is because he goes everywhere. You remember him, Moshe, he's the one you had the quarrel with when I was here the last time, after Zisye was taken ill. You shouted at him and drove him from the house. Maybe that money also came from him."

"What other money was there?"

And here, Malke-Rive recounted what he had done not long ago. How Sruli one morning during the time of the fair had shown up at her door with a bank note of a large denomination which he claimed to have found on her doorstep. She had at first refused it, because how in the world could anyone suppose she had a note of that sort to lose? But he had been stubborn, and had insisted that it was certainly not his. It had to be hers since he had seen it lying on her doorstep as he was passing by and all he was doing was giving it back to its owner. And when she, Malke-Rive, continued to refuse it he had shouted at her, "You don't want it? Then throw it into the street . . . or to the dogs. Or do anything else you want with it . . . give it away to the poor if you like." It was clear to her that he had not found the money, but, since the money was neither stolen nor the work of witchcraft, and because she was afraid of him, she finally accepted it and it had certainly proved helpful. "Then . . . what do you think? Can it be that everything else was also his doing? What do you think, Moshe? What do the rest of you think?"

"I think," Moshe said, as if confused . . . as if not conscious of what he was saying, "I think that, yes. Certainly it was he. Surely, because who else could it be?" Then he got abruptly to his feet and they all saw how his hands went irritably to the nape of his neck, as if a fly, or some other creature, had landed on it; indeed, he actually turned his head as if endeavoring to see what it was.

"And what did you want now, Malke-Rive?" he said, still confused, still standing there.

"Well, I came . . . I came to pawn a coat, because the charitable help we received is all used up, and I brought the coat because the pawnbrokers, as you know, will take the skin off your back; and here I'm sure to get more for the coat than I would from them."

"No doubt . . . more . . . Certainly more than from them," Moshe stammered after her, and the family watched as his hands moved, searching his pockets as if he was prepared to give Malke-Rive her money without bothering to look at the coat. He looked first in his vest pockets—in the lower vest pockets, then in the upper ones—then, not finding anything, he felt around in his trousers' pockets, then in his inside coat pockets, returning empty-handed each time to where he had begun. Finally, with a strange and frightened cry: "Nothing. Empty. I haven't got anything, Malke-Rive." Then, to everyone's amazement, he added in the same frightened voice, "I have a sick child, too, Malke-Rive. And it won't be long before I'll have to pawn something also."

"Father!" Yehudis, Moshe's older daughter, cried as if she were trying to prevent a disordered person from saying or doing something wrong.

"Father-in-law!" The two frightened sons-in-law were both suddenly on their feet.

"Moshe!" cried Gitl, trembling like everyone else.

We do not know whether Malke-Rive left the house *with* or *without* money. *With* or *without* the fur coat. All we know is that after Malke-Rive's departure, Moshe Mashber, like a man half mad, spent most of the rest of the night continually searching his pockets, and that later that night, when once again he was unable to sleep, he took to pacing from room to room in his bedroom slippers until, as he had before, he found himself leaning against the window in his bedroom, and, just as he had seen Alter yesterday, he believed he saw him now in the half-light of the moon, standing in the courtyard. But it was not Alter. He felt, rather, a heavy weight pressing on the nape of his neck. A man's weight, and Moshe kept turning his head to see who it was and each time it seemed to him to be the same man—that fellow, Sruli. And every time that Moshe caught a glimpse of him, he felt the gathering in his throat of a terrible scream which soon, soon, he would be within a hairbreadth, of uttering—like Alter.

At that time Moshe had the feeling that Sruli was astride his neck, but where was Sruli just then?

Sruli was living with Luzi.

Yes. For a while after they had returned from their journey, and Sruli had settled Luzi into the house we know of, Sruli was an occasional visitor there, but it was not long before he became a more frequent and familiar presence, sometimes even spending the night. At first he made space for himself in the second bedroom where he could nap at need. Later, he acquired a sort of convertible bed which he put in the room in front of the house so he could spend the night there when he felt like it—as began to happen more and more frequently . . . almost daily.

Eventually, he ended by supervising Luzi's household more or less entirely—he and the woman of all work. He participated, too, in the inner workings of the household, mixing in whether his opinion was asked for or not. For example, if any of the newcomers from other sects who came secretly to the house at night met with his disapproval, he stopped at nothing as he sought to reprove Luzi because he, Sruli, was convinced that he had an eye and an ear for such matters though, in fact, they did not directly concern him. Luzi listened attentively to him and took what he said into account, even when it was entirely capricious. And there were certain occasions when Sruli's was clearly the ruling hand.

For instance: It happened one day that Mikhl Bukyer, the former head of the sect, sent a child to Luzi with a letter that began with the words, "To our beloved brothers, I ask you to pray for me." Luzi read the letter and it made him at once thoughtful and depressed. Sruli asked to see the letter. He read it and then, his eyes on Luzi, said irritably, "So what? It's not as if you didn't know that Mikhl was on a slippery path, and that one fine day he would fall and break his bones. Didn't you expect this?"

And it was a noticeable fact that ever since Luzi had taken on the leadership of the sect, Mikhl Bukyer had as it were moved off to one side. He began to come less and less frequently, even to Sabbath services; and when he did come, it was obvious that neither the prayers nor the discussions about the Torah delighted him the way they did the other members of the sect, and it was also clear that something was fermenting—something that rendered him mute, that made him lower his eyes and kept him from looking directly at anyone.

Then at last it surfaced. Mikhl's faith was wobbly once again. But more, and more intensely, than it had when he had made his confession to Luzi. He had begun to doubt the order of the universe and to wonder whether he could justify everything that the faithful were expected to believe. All at once, it was as if a veil had once again been lifted from his eyes: he saw everything under a new light, so that everything had to be reseen and reexamined. And all of this was expressed in his letter to Luzi. Evidently he had been unable to find the courage to come and discuss the matter with him directly: Luzi, he believed, would certainly reject him. On the other hand, he could still feel faith touching his bones. He felt himself doubting faith—and lack of faith. In the circumstances, all he could think of was to ask the members of his sect to pray for him: "Pray for me, my people. And particularly, you, Luzi, the leader of the community. Pray for Mikhl, son of Sore-Feygel, who once more is sinking into the abyss. I've reached such a pass that I am in danger of succumbing to the man from Dessau [Moses Mendelsson]. And I've all but decided to go far away, to Lithuania to join those from whom it is said all negation and all denial derives."

All of this had been developed in detail in the letter in which he also described how he had come to have these unhappy thoughts. Among other things he described how one day recently his wife had given him his scanty meal—a bowl of soup, as usual—some sort of fish soup, thin, with nothing in it except a few noodles. Hungry as he was, he was swallowing it down when suddenly he stopped eating and burst into tears. "The world is so huge, so rich, and the master work of creation, mankind, is hungry. And he's entitled to no more than a bit of soup with noodles. As punishment for what sin? And who can survive such degradation, and how is it justified?"

Beyond that, he added a list of family problems that he could no longer endure.

"My daughter Esther," he wrote, "has reached a marriageable age and I cannot give her a dowry, nor any hope of finding one and she will, God forbid, be left an old maid. And she is, moreover, not gifted with beauty. She is not well endowed, either physically or with any household skills, and, because I cannot bear her unhappiness, I beat her frequently and drag her about by the hair like a brute of the lowest sort.

"My son, Berele," he wrote, "is a sickly half-blind idiot who turns the wheel for a knife grinder and works beyond his strength to earn practically nothing—may the Lord see his sorrow. My son Yankele works for nothing doing hard physical labor for a bookbinder. I'm afraid that my daughter Khanele is also an idiot.

"Beyond all that, I no longer have any pupils because householders won't send their sons to me given my earlier bad reputation.

"My people, pray for me."

It was reading this letter that had saddened Luzi, and Sruli laughed. "He wants to be prayed for? Why? He's not old enough himself? A man with feet praying for crutches? What? He wants to go to Dessau? Those people with cold heads, cold caps and cold justice? By all means, let him! What point does the luckless fellow think he's making with his soup and his noodles?"

In this case, as in others, Sruli intruded himself and had his say. He always spoke up and it made no difference to him whether or not his advice was taken.

He took on himself nearly the full responsibility for running the household, admitting people into it who he thought might prove useful to Luzi, and barring those who were not, or those who in his judgment would prove encumbrances.

And he discouraged the nearby residents of The Curse from coming to the house: those lame and mad and half-mad folk who were drawn to the house during the day and even more frequently at night when they were drawn by the light in the window and the sound of singing.

And, too, he kept himself informed of what was going on in the town, and he reported to Luzi whatever he thought he should know. It is true that lately Sruli had avoided the homes of the rich, appearing among them only rarely, even rejecting such invitations as he was given. Just the same, he knew what was going on in those houses.

It was through Sruli that Luzi heard the story of the noblemen, and from him, too, he learned that his brother Moshe's affairs were in a decline. And it was Sruli who had given him to understand that this had been a bad year for business and that one could expect numerous bankruptcies. It was Sruli, with interests of his own in the matter, who let him know that it was widely expected that Moshe, too, was in danger of bankruptcy.

Yes, Sruli was well informed of everything. He seemed to know what went on behind closed doors—nor was what had happened in

Moshe Mashber's house any exception. He knew even about those events which only the family had witnessed: like Shmulikl, the Fist's visit to Moshe. Did he have some secret source for his information or did he simply sniff it out of the air? Whichever it was, he was well informed. One may even conjecture that he knew about Itsikl Zilburg's visit to Moshe and what the two of them, closeted together, had discussed, and that Sruli knew that there was an imminent likelihood that title to the house and the business would be signed over to somebody else.

He knew it, and seemed to be waiting for it to happen. He knew, too, what no one else at that moment had any inkling of—not even Moshe Mashber. And that is that Moshe Mashber would finally feel so hemmed in by his misfortunes that it was not at all out of the question that he would come here, to Luzi, whom he had, along with Sruli, driven from his home—that Moshe would come here to take counsel with Luzi, to pour his heart out to him, and perhaps to shed a tear.

He sensed that this would happen and he looked forward to it. Strangely enough, he found himself at this time particularly caught up in household matters: cleaning more, tidying, rearranging things. Buying a larger lamp, a finer tablecloth for the table, as if readying the house for a reception or for a holiday. He had no idea what good would come of it for him, but he felt himself tingling with expectation, intrigued by the image he had of a humbled Moshe crossing Luzi's threshold.

He said nothing of this to Luzi. But his mind toyed with the image of what was to come. And as he toyed with it, he was busy with preparations: getting things tidy, buying what was needed for the encounter.

And now the moment for it arrived.

One evening Sruli, sensing Moshe Mashber's imminent arrival, found himself growing uneasy. He used all of his powers to get the visitors from town, young or old, not to delay their departure. To some he merely indicated with a look that they should abbreviate their visit; with others he did not hesitate to speak out boldly, telling them that today, for various reasons, their presence in the house was not wanted. Would they go now, please, and come back some other time?

That was how he dealt with strangers. It goes without saying that with acquaintances he was even less ceremonious. Immediately after the evening prayers, he sent them off, telling them that Luzi was not feeling well and that in all fairness they ought to let him rest.

So that finally there were only the two of them left in the house. They did not speak to each other.

Sruli had been readying the place since morning. He had given orders to wash the floor, polish the glass lampshades, put out a new tablecloth, arrange chairs and benches in their proper places. Luzi, for his part, was not particularly surprised, imagining that Sruli did this every day.

Sruli's intuition had not deceived him.

When Moshe Mashber came home from the office that day, the members of his family were struck by the ashen look on his face. He had that day learned that a note to one of his major creditors was due. It was a note that would have to be paid or else it would signal the beginning of the end. If it was not paid, everyone would know and his other creditors would come running. The money to pay it would have to be found.

Moshe Mashber had exerted all of his energies to find some way to put off the due date of the note. Delaying payment was the sort of thing that could happen even in prosperous times. One was short of cash and one asked for an extension of time. Yes, it could happen, even in good times. And when the creditor found that his debtor was short of cash, he thought nothing of it: later is later. Nor was the debtor particularly distressed. In the world of business it was a commonplace occurrence—just as long as the times were good and the debtor solvent, it was not unusual to delay payment.

But now in these hard times that was impossible because of the distrust with which the business world was being eyed just then—and especially those businessmen who had been involved in the case of the noblemen. And this was particularly true where Moshe Mashber was concerned, about whom rumors were now continually rife that he was on the verge of bankruptcy.

Moshe Mashber was thrashing about like a fish out of water. At his office he was continually sending for one or another of his intermediaries to whom he made all sorts of promises as he begged them, with tears in his voice, to go to the creditor and persuade him to give Moshe an extension of time. Just now, as they could see, times were bad for everyone. If he wanted an additional percentage point or two, very well then. Just as long as he removed the razor poised at his throat by delaying his demand for immediate payment. The intermediaries undertook this errand reluctantly. It may be that they did as they had been asked and urged such reasons as one could on the creditor. Or it may be that, having accepted the mission because they were afraid to refuse Moshe, they performed their task indifferently—perhaps because, having no confidence in the task, they were unwilling to address themselves to it with much energy.

In any case, whether the intermediaries went in good faith or indifferently, the fact is that, having interceded for Moshe Mashber, they all returned with the same reply: No. He won't grant an extension. He's not interested in a greater interest rate. All he wants is his money, his principal.

A greatly distressed Moshe Mashber went off then to see Itsikl Zilburg, knowing perfectly well that Itsikl could be of no immediate financial help to him. Advice was all he would get from him—not cash. And advice was not what he needed. His first priority was to get out of his present bind. Later would be time enough to discuss other remedies with Itsikl.

As it happened, Itsikl was not at home, and Moshe had to wait for him. It was an uncomfortable wait for Moshe who dreaded running into strangers there who would see how impatient he was for Itsikl's return.

And yet he felt that he had to wait. In Itsikl's foyer, he paced back and forth, back and forth, like an animal in its cage. Had anyone seen him pacing this way, it might have seemed that Moshe Mashber had been struck by a poisoned arrow whose agony he could not endure even as he could not bring himself to tear it from his flesh.

But when finally the long wait was over and Itsikl Zilburg returned home, Moshe Mashber had very little time left for any discussion. Hardly time to sit down, though indeed there was little need of that. Because, as has been said, Itsikl could not help him with cash—only with advice. And it was as Moshe was leaving that Itsikl murmured into his ear. Moshe, stunned by grief, only half heard him. "Yes, I understand. Well, given the situation, now is the time and as quickly as possible to resolve the matter. I mean, sign over to someone else the ownership of your property and business as soon as you can: movable and immovable property. Because, as I see it, the situation is grave and you haven't a moment to lose. Have you heard me, Reb Moshe?"

Moshe heard—and did not hear. Leaving Itsikl Zilburg's house, he felt as if the arrow in his flesh had been driven deeper. Then, with noplace else to go, he started to walk home. No. Not walk. He ran. Because now that he was outdoors he could still feel the pressure of the nervous energy that had made him pace as he waited for Itsikl Zilburg in his foyer, and that he had had to repress while he was listening to Itsikl's counsel. That pressure was with him still as he crossed the bridge that divided the river in two and linked the upper part of the town with the lower, and when he looked down into the water it seemed to him that he was thirsty—no, not thirsty. Rather, that he wanted to swim. No. Not to swim. To plunge into the water never to leave it—the good Lord keep us from such thoughts.

When he got home, his face, as we have said, was ashen. Then when the ambience of the house had somewhat calmed him and he felt the effects of the day's tumult subsiding, he called the members of his family together into a room where behind locked doors he and his wife Gitl, his sons-in-law and his older daughter Yehudis held a secret meeting.

They discussed the need to pawn, wherever they could, the family's jewels and plate and any other gold or silver items that might be in the house. It would be important to remember what had been pawned and with whom, so that when the time came, they would know where it might be redeemed. Because now the family's first priority was to meet the pressing note so that Moshe might have a breathing space. As for the other debts, they were not due to be paid for a while. Later, there would be time enough to think about them.

Gitl was taken ill several times during the course of the meeting and someone had to go quietly to the kitchen to bring her some water. Nakhum Lentsher's nose turned pale and he kept up a continual sniffling as he paced the room. Yehudis, the older daughter, cracking her knuckles all the while, kept her eyes fixed on her father. And her husband, Yankele Grodshteyn, was regarding the vest pocket in which his gold watch reposed as if he were already asking himself whether he ought to take it out *now* and offer it to be pawned or whether it could be put off till later.

All of them left the meeting feeling depressed and unwilling to meet each other's glances. The family scattered to different parts of the house, leaving Moshe and Gitl in the room. He continued the conversation, trying to console Gitl. He pleaded with her to wipe away her tears lest a stranger coming into the house should see them—or a servant coming to her from the kitchen with a request of some kind.

Later, when the family had had a short rest and was gathered once more in the dining room, Moshe abruptly stood up from his chair and went out into the corridor. There he took his coat from its hanger in the closet and made ready to leave the house.

"Where are you going so late?" he was asked.

"I have things to do."

"They can't wait until tomorrow?"

"No."

Seeing that he had not found it necessary to say a word of what he intended, no one asked any further questions. It was clear that nothing they might say would make him change his mind.

• • •

Moshe Mashber, as Sruli had known he would, now started off toward his brother Luzi's house in the third section of the town, in The Curse. Evidently he had made previous inquiries because he knew where the house was. When he came to the upper part of the town, it occurred to him to take a fiacre, but then he thought better of it.

It was a very dark autumn night. Even if he had taken a fiacre, it would have been easy to lose one's way. On foot, it was easier still, and now without a lantern to guide him it was a walk that threatened broken bones at every turn.

But that did not deter Moshe at all. Driven by some sort of inner force, he was able to find his way through the dark, and avoided the pitch-black, muddy sinkholes which even the residents of the neighborhood were not always lucky enough to escape.

Anyone seeing his face just then would have recoiled from him in fear. He resembled King Saul of whom it is narrated that when the Philistines encircled him and he felt himself in great danger he called on God for help, but God made no reply—then he addressed himself to the prophets, and then to his own dreams, but neither of them made any reply. Then, though he had himself commanded the destruction of all the witches and sorcerers in the land—yet now when his need was great, he asked his servants to find him a witch to whom one night, wearing a disguise, he went. And Moshe, now, was in a similar situation.

And now, having walked a long way in the course of which he had frequently to ask for directions from late-night passersby, he had come at last to Luzi's house.

There was no one either in the kitchen or in the vestibule when Moshe got there. Sruli, on one pretext or another, had just then left the house to visit a neighbor. Moshe, having crossed through one room was about to go into another when he saw a sight which, had he not seen it with his own eyes, he would not have believed—Shmulikl Fist sitting at Luzi's table. It's true, Shmulikl was drunk, as one could tell from the exceptional pallor of the film over the eye with the cataract, and from the fact that his good eye seemed to be floating in a fine oil.

Yes, Shmulikl was at that stage of drunkenness whose characteristic is a high good humor, the stage at which the drinker's whole body has been so bathed as it were in drink that it seems ready to fall asleep, or if not actually to sleep, at least he is so deeply under the influence of drink that he is very unlikely to make trouble of any sort even if he is normally a troublemaker. At the very worst, one might expect from him a very brief flare-up that would quickly die down.

A greater wonder still was that Luzi sat calmly at the head of his table as if, in truth, there was no Shmulikl there. Or as if Luzi, even if he *had* noticed Shmulikl's presence, was no more affected by it than if it had been a child or a well-known acquaintance who, because of fatigue or the lateness of the hour, had fallen asleep there.

As Moshe crossed the threshold, Shmulikl, drunk as he was, was the first person to see him. He tried to stagger to his feet to greet Moshe as if he meant to apologize to him for their last encounter a few days ago, or, who knows, drunk as he was perhaps he meant to repeat what he had said to him then.

His move frightened Moshe. It was all too unbearable that now, here, when he had come with a heart overflowing with grief, and perhaps, too, with regret for the wrong he had done to his brother; it was altogether unbearable that now when he had come to be advised by and to be reconciled with his brother, that the first person to meet him at the threshold should be this fellow. No. Moshe had been prepared for anything but this.

Moshe stood speechless and frightened but Shmulikl, given the thickness of his tongue, and the small degree of self-control that he still possessed, did what he could to modulate his voice, to moderate his drunken movements, as if he meant, as he rose from his seat and went forward to greet Moshe, to convey to him his peaceful intent, to make clear that the Shmulikl who was here was not the same Shmulikl Moshe had seen, that he had not come here on some wicked errand and that, in general, so long as he, Shmulikl, was in Luzi's house there was no need for anyone to fear him. "Here, I am not me. Here, I am not Shmulikl," he said, smiling.

He sat down again. Then, before Luzi was fully aware who it was to whom Shmulikl had been speaking, The Fist, whose limbs had grown heavy with drink, let his head fall to his chest and was fast asleep in an instant.

We do not know who was responsible for Shmulikl's visit to Luzi. Perhaps it was Sruli, with some scheme of his own in mind, who had deliberately sent everyone, including intimate friends, away. And who had contrived that someone like Shmulikl should be the only one left. Or perhaps not. It may be that Sruli had nothing to do with it. Perhaps it was pure chance that Sruli had been out of the house when Shmulikl arrived so that there had been no one to turn him away. Because, as we have said, no one was turned away from that house—and this was especially true when Sruli was not there.

Whatever the case may have been, it was evident that this was not Shmulikl's first visit to Luzi's house. His reasons for being there—what he wanted or what he received in that house—is not known. And yet his words, spoken with drunken candor, "Here, I am not Shmulikl," are evidence enough that when he came there his thoughts and his intentions were of a wholly different sort than anywhere else. Certainly he was not there in his role as an enforcer. Indeed, he may have come there because he wanted to cool the combative fevers in his blood. And there is reason to believe that he did feel changed there—to the degree, that is, that someone like Shmulikl could change in the ambience that surrounded Luzi. While he was there, he was to some degree improved: he was more humane, calmer, as if impressed by some great presence, and it may be that in Luzi's house he forgot, if only for a while, how he made his living.

And now, as Shmulikl's head nodded, Luzi raised his own and saw his brother Moshe standing in the doorway. He was tremendously surprised. Moshe's visit was entirely unexpected. Though he knew from Sruli's accounts the condition that Moshe's affairs were in still it had not occurred to him that his brother might be so depressed as to be impelled to leave his cozy rich man's home on a dark autumn night and walk such a great distance to this remote district of the town, to this little house in The Curse. Luzi could hardly believe it.

He did not, therefore, stand on ceremony. Instead, Luzi, because Moshe was his guest—and a brother experiencing troubles which no doubt were the occasion for this visit—Luzi rose and went forward to greet him and to invite him in. "Ah, Moshe. How are you? And what's happening to you? Welcome."

"Shalom," Moshe replied, putting out his hand but without moving from the threshold as if he was not quite ready to accept Luzi's invitation. Indicating the sleeping Shmulikl he asked, greatly perplexed, "What's going on here? What sort of people have you taken up with?" Of course he meant Shmulikl and from his tone it was clear that he regarded him as absolutely dangerous, the sort of man who would not be admitted into any respectable household.

"Who are you talking about?" Luzi said, perplexed in his turn, and looked around as if it could not possibly have occurred to him that Moshe's comment might in any way refer to Shmulikl who with his head on his bosom slept at his table like a child or a relative and whose sleep could in no way be regarded with suspicion nor as an occasion for reproach. "Who do you mean?"

"Him," said Moshe, indicating Shmulikl. "How does he come to be in *your* house? Have you any idea what this fellow's profession is? How he makes his living?"

· 341 ·

"Yes. I know. What, then? What do you think? Would it be better for him if I didn't let him into my house?"

"I don't know about better for him, but better for you, certainly." And what his words were meant to imply was that the fellow was a town bully, a ne'er-do-well, a brute who was employed on the most appalling missions, who was paid to beat people to a bloody pulp with his fists, who was one of those "who lives by the sword." And how could one invite such a man into one's home?

Just then Shmulikl started up out of his sleep, raised his head for a moment, and, opening his drink-bleared eyes that seemed to be swimming in oil, he looked around.

"Our money!" he cried. It was the war cry that was habitually on his lips—either when he was sober and at his work, or when he was drunk and it made no sense. And seeing Moshe Mashber before him, Shmulikl's mind cleared for a moment and he said good-humoredly, meaning again to reassure Moshe as he had earlier, "I'm not really talking to you, Reb Moshe. It's not you I mean." He smiled broadly and promptly went back to sleep.

"Well, there you have him," Moshe said, indicating the sleeper. "That's what he is. Now, what's he doing here? What sort of job is he on?"

"Here? Where else should he be?" Luzi asked irritably. Then in a tone of accusation he replied to Moshe's question: "Where else should he be? It goes without saying that you wouldn't let him into your house."

"No? What makes you say that?" Moshe said, also with a tinge of accusation—and a touch of mockery—in his voice. "I have recently had the honor of a visit from him in my house—just as you see him, except that he was not asleep, as he is in your house. No, he visited me in his professional capacity on a mission for The Kitten, a client of his for whom he demanded money, though it was not yet due him. He banged so hard on my table he frightened the entire household out of its wits."

And it was at this point that Moshe accepted his brother's invitation to come in and sit down. To tell him what was happening to him at the office and at home, and especially the details of the troubles that were assailing him and about which Luzi had, for his part, only heard from a distance. And now Luzi, listening to his brother, was anxious to get all the details. And Moshe recounted one event after the other and, in the course of the recital, he told Luzi, too, of the family meeting at which it had been decided to pawn the family's jewelry and plate (his own and his children's) in order to meet a pressing debt *at once*, or else bankruptcy stared him in the face. And then all those to whom he owed money would come in a mob to demand it.

He was hemmed in and had no breathing space. It would not be long before he had to sign over the titles to his house and to his business, and to everything else he owned to other people until he could find a way out of his present distress and things returned to normal. It was what he had been advised to do by his confidential legal counselor, Itsikl Zilburg, whom he, Moshe, and others as well consulted in such a situation. And now Moshe, too, thought that it was his best recourse. And this is why, Moshe added, he had come here now to Luzi. First to discuss his situation with him before he undertook such grave steps, and second to apologize to him and to reestablish their friendship as brothers. Because, after all, with whom else was he as close as with him, Luzi? And third he wanted, if possible, to transfer the ownership of his house to Luzi's name. Because everything else was to be put in the names of his sons-in-law; but it was not prudent to put it all in their names. The word would get out and there would be an outcry. Those to whom he owed money would be outraged. And it wasn't possible to sell the house now because to begin with buyers were not that easy to come by, and second, as things stood, if it was known that he was selling his house, it would be taken as confirmation that the rumors flying about him in the town were true. And Luzi could not possibly imagine what the consequences of that would be for a man like himself, Moshe. Nor could he mortgage the house, as he might have done at any other time, for the same reason—the news would get out with disastrous effects. And so he could think of only one recourse, and that was quietly to turn the ownership of the house over to someone he could trust—as he would be doing with his other property: the fuel-oil business and the financial establishment.

"Ah . . . well . . ." Luzi shook his head and made a grimace as if he meant to refuse, but Moshe interrupted.

"It's true," said Moshe, "I know that you're no businessman; you've never had anything to do with such things. But in this case there's nothing you need to do. You can stay put at home, and everything that needs to be done will be taken care of. All that's needed is your permission. You have simply to agree and everything else will be taken care of by my financial adviser, my lawyer, Itsikl Zilburg."

"No," said Luzi tersely. "I don't want to, and I beg you not to ask me."

"Why not?" Moshe asked.

"Because I've never done business with my name, and because I don't want to be involved in covering up anyone's wrongdoing."

"What wrongdoing?" asked Moshe. "It's just the way of the world. It's what everyone does when things get tight and one has to buy time. It's what any businessman would do."

"Businessmen, yes. But not me. I beg you, don't ask me to do it."

"You mean, then, that you're saying no. At a time like this, you refuse to help me."

"That's right," Luzi replied. "First, because, as you see, the times are not yet quite as bad as you think. There are people who have been in much worse shape than you are to whom it would never have occurred to make this sort of outcry, or to believe that because they have had a run of ill luck that their fates have been sealed forever."

"What are you getting at?" Moshe asked.

"Why so much noise?" Luzi replied. "Where did you get the idea that what has been given to you as a pledge, as something that belongs to someone else and that has been only left in your care for a while . . . where did you get the idea that it was yours forever? Who gave you that assurance? And why, when the owner to whom it all belongs comes and asks for it back, are you so frightened and confused? More important, more honorable things are also given for a brief time only."

"Well?" Moshe said. "Have I, God forbid, stolen what I have so that I have no right to keep what is mine? And who forbids me to protect my property and to try to keep it always."

"True. Yes," said Luzi, "you haven't stolen it. And yet, very close to theft. As is evident from the wrongs you are willing to commit to protect it."

"Wrongs! Again wrongs," Moshe cried.

"Yes. And you are even ready to involve me in dealings intended to deprive your creditors of the chance to get back the money that rightly belongs to them."

"But it's only for a little while. And the whole point is to avoid bankruptcy."

Luzi stood up. He seemed to be much taller than his brother as he said, "Moshe, I'm not going to preach to you, and I'm not sure you'd listen to me if I did. But I think it's time for you to consider who you are and from whom you derive. You were not raised among silks, nor, God forbid, are you destined to rags. You can get along perfectly well on whatever you have left after you have satisfied your creditors. There's no need for you to cling so vehemently to that high and slippery place to which you've climbed, though in fact it is not so high. And even if it were, it is by no means safe—it's a place to turn you dizzy. And the means you are willing to take to stay there are not for you . . . not for us . . . not for those with our heritage; not for those who have received the warnings we were given in our father's will. Just remember: 'Before all,' our father wrote in his will, 'beware of pursuing honor or false wealth which are both likened unto that passing shadow left by a cloud as it moves over the earth and which has neither permanence nor substance.' "

Moshe Mashber heard his brother say all this and, though he understood the words, he was not clear about their meaning. Because the two of them seemed to be speaking quite different languages. Moshe Mashber had come here following a cataclysm in his business; Luzi was altogether indifferent to such disturbances. Not only had he never experienced anything like it himself, but he was utterly incapable of imagining what it was like.

"So, then," Moshe said after a long silence, "it appears that I've come for nothing. No advice, no brotherly reconciliation. No help. Even though the help would cost you nothing at all. So I've come for nothing. And you won't agree to do what I want?"

"No. I won't."

"Who, then?" asked Moshe.

"Who?" Luzi, seeing his brother so unhappy, so humbled, tried without success to think of some way that he could ease his situation. "You want to know who?"

Just then as luck would have it, Luzi looked up and saw Sruli in the doorway. And almost without thinking he cried, "Him." Then the idea that had come to him almost as if it were a reflex, began on consideration to make real sense. There would be no chicanery involved because, as Luzi recalled, Sruli was one of Moshe's creditors and was therefore entitled, like any other creditor, to accept Moshe's house as security for his loan. Moreover, he felt certain that if Sruli had it, the house would be in good hands, that Sruli would not take unfair advantage of Moshe's desperate situation, and if the house was worth more than the sum of the loan, that Sruli would not take possession of it for the smaller sum.

"Him!" cried Luzi.

"Who?" said Moshe who had not yet seen Sruli in the doorway. Then when he turned in the direction indicated by Luzi's hand, he saw him.

If a tomb had opened before him, or if a perilous abyss had yawned at his feet, Moshe would have preferred them to the sight of the man he now saw standing in the doorway.

What's going on here? a distressed Moshe thought, and in his surprise nearly said the words aloud. What's going on? Where am I? Am I really at Luzi's. And why is this bearded Shmulikl sleeping here? And, then, what's he doing here? This other fellow in the doorway who looks as if he has been here for a long time, for years, standing coldly, rigidly, there in the doorway—watching?

"What . . . Why so surprised?" The words coming from Sruli in the doorway sounded as if a clay figure had spoken them. "Why are you so frightened? Has anyone cut the lapel of your coat? Or do you think someone's going to cut it? Is that why you're so startled? Or do you think you've fallen into a den of thieves?"

And now there occurred that which, if Moshe had been thinking clearly, would certainly never have happened. He was unable to reply to Sruli. For one thing, he had not expected to encounter him there, and he had certainly not counted on Sruli's overhearing his entire conversation with his brother or that he, Sruli, would be the mute witness to the way Luzi had rejected his request for help. Nor had he expected that his brother would then designate Sruli as his Good Samaritan. Sruli—Moshe would rather die than be beholden to that man in the slightest way.

And then suddenly something else happened. Whether it was shame that prompted him or great distress he did not know, but in any case he staggered to his feet and stumbled over against a wall where he stood, unable to meet either Sruli's or his brother's eye. He stood there with his face against the wall as if in prayer. It seemed to him that he said "Ah!" more to himself than to anyone else. He stood there, oblivious to everything for a moment or two—or perhaps for a while longer. When at last he turned back, he found that Luzi and Sruli were standing together in the doorway. It seemed that in the interval during which Moshe had stood there, dazed, Luzi and Sruli had had a discussion whose conclusion Moshe now heard as Sruli said, "As far as I'm concerned, it will be all right. I have no objections, though I myself won't guarantee my honesty. Who knows what temptations I may have once I'm the owner of the house, but if you're willing to vouch for me—why not?"

"I'll vouch for you," Luzi said, turning to Moshe as if he, Luzi, had taken no notice of the withdrawn moment in which Moshe had stood against the wall. Then as if nothing had happened in the interval, he resumed the interrupted conversation he had been having with his brother. "I'll vouch for him," he said.

And now a third thing happened which, given what follows, will seem unbelievable, though it is a fact: Moshe made no reply. It was as if, after his dazed interval leaning against the wall, nothing he might hear or see could surprise him or make a difference to him in any way. Not even anything as appalling as that Sruli, through Luzi's good offices, should acquire temporary ownership of Moshe's house because of the money Moshe owed him.

Moshe simply let it happen. He looked stunned, like a man who had been felled and whose passions and energies have been exhausted, as if he was beyond all shame, all humiliation.

"Are you willing to do it? Do you have any objections?" Luzi asked.

"No, none." Moshe could not be sure whether he had actually replied. But an answer was in any case superfluous. By then one could do what one liked with Moshe. He was prepared to agree to anything at all.

And yet no one took advantage of the situation to do him any harm. Luzi asked Moshe to resume his place at the table, and a moment later Sruli found occasion to leave them, and one could hear him moving about in the next room preparing something to eat—supper, perhaps. And indeed, shortly thereafter, Luzi invited his brother to eat with him.

And now there happened that which had happened to the biblical King Saul. Yes, as it is written:

And the woman came to Saul and when she saw that he was terrified, she said to him, "Now therefore hearken to the voice of your handmaiden; let me set a morsel of bread before you and eat so that you may have strength when you go on your way . . ."

Yes. Just as the Witch of Endor offered Saul a meal after she had obeyed his request and called up the dead Samuel, who revealed Saul's fate to him, just so did Luzi now invite Moshe to eat with him because Moshe, like Saul, had come a long way—the long distance to The Curse. And now Luzi did what he could to ease Moshe's mind.

It was Sruli who served the meal because the woman of all work was not there. He laid the cloth and set the table. Then he roused Shmulikl and tried to get him to keep his drowsy head up. "Go on, wash up. Dinner's going to be served." And Moshe, too, washed up before dinner.

At the meal, Luzi inquired about Moshe's household and asked, among others, about Alter. At this, Moshe livened up a bit and shaking off the effects of what had happened earlier in the evening, he replied in detail. He particularly emphasized the recent change in Alter. His sense that Alter's condition was improving, and that he needed to be treated like someone who had been in the dark for a long while and was only now coming into the light, but that he, Moshe, preoccupied as he was lately with his own affairs, had been unable to devote himself to Alter. Among other things, Moshe told Luzi also about Alter's recent request (and here, Moshe leaned forward to speak into Luzi's ear) about which nothing conclusive had yet been done for the same reason—that is, Moshe's presently unsettled situation.

"One must . . . one must . . . quickly, without delay . . ." Luzi spoke gravely and now in his turn he leaned forward to speak into Moshe's ear since the matter was so delicate that even men like themselves dealt with it in circumlocutions. "He lives without wife, without children," he whispered confidentially. His words clearly conveyed his belief that it was criminal for anyone to live that way, but it was particularly wrong for an unfortunate like Alter. "Yes. Soon. Without delay," he said again.

The quiet meal of the three table companions, Luzi, Moshe and Shmulikl (with the occasional participation of the fourth—Sruli—who in the intervals between serving courses managed to sit silently with them) was coming to its end.

Throughout the meal, Shmulikl kept nodding off, though, in deference to the others at table he did his best to behave properly, so that when he started up from his dozes, he instantly started in to chew something, but slowly and without much interest; and then, his mouth full, he fell back asleep. Neither Moshe nor Luzi—not even Sruli—paid much attention to him, though they had to take him into account since he would have to join them in their after-dinner prayers.

Moshe spoke as if he were in a daze. Sometimes he actually forgot that he and his brother were now together after a period of separation, and forgot, too, what had occasioned his long walk here. Indeed, what with his stupor and the effect his brother's little house had on him, he might even have yielded to an invitation to spend the night, just as he had earlier consented to wash his hands and then to seat himself at the table and to take part in this meal.

Well, that meal was now coming to its close. Just then there was a new and entirely unexpected presence in the doorway: a strange, indeed bizarre, fellow—especially strange to Moshe who had not in years seen or imagined such a sight in his own home.

It was Pushke, Ten Groschen Pushke. No one, not even Sruli, had heard him coming through the kitchen or the next room.

He stood, weighed down with a heavy burden of clothes and rags, filling the entire doorway with his silent mass. His face was dark, unwashed, and the eyes in that unwashed face looked even paler than the eyes of those who habitually work in the soil. He stood in the doorway, apparently fixed there, coming neither in nor out. But his stink assailed those in the room, and Moshe who all this while had been sitting there thinking that there was nothing in the world that could surprise him again ... Moshe, seeing Pushke and inhaling his terrible moldy stench, got to his feet and became once again the fastidious rich man that he was just as Sruli, surprised though he was by Pushke's entrance, greeted him in a voice that was at once genial, welcoming and pleased: "Ah, Pushke, Ten Groschen Pushke—" Just then Moshe, as if outraged, as if finally feeling all the insults and the abuses to which all evening he had patiently submitted ... Moshe then, without himself knowing why, erupted: "What is this? What kinds of people are these ... and who let this fellow in?"

"What?" Sruli interposed before Luzi had a chance to say anything. "There's no harm in it. Come on in, Pushke." And Pushke, moving like a vast tortoise, came in carrying his rags.

"Come in, Pushke. You're a welcome guest. You feed on your own stink. You're not a rich man who needs to borrow money from anyone else."

Now, surely, something might have happened. After all he had endured, Moshe certainly could not have put up with such words, and the evening, because of them, must have ended badly. But just then Luzi, as if he had not heard what Sruli said, passed Moshe the beaker with the water for after-dinner ablutions and said, "Moshe, conduct the blessings." It may be that he did it to keep his brother from replying to Sruli, or it may be that he actually had not heard what Sruli said. In either case, Moshe had no recourse but to conduct the prayers. He washed his hands, then Luzi and Shmulikl washed theirs. Then with great rapidity, as if hurrying so that he could leave the house soon, he opened the prayers: "Gentlemen, let us pray."

Finally, then, the evening ended well. When the prayers were done, Moshe got ready to leave. As Moshe was putting on his coat in the doorway, Luzi, standing beside him, spoke gently, consolingly to him, as if he were finishing the earlier conversation of the evening: "Never mind. Let it serve as a form of penitence. You've learned that it is wrong to drive someone from your home, and that he may own that home one day. It's all right, Moshe. These are matters that it will do you good to think about."

Sruli was no longer in the dining room when Luzi and Moshe were having their final conversation. He had gone into the next room and from there into the kitchen where he busied himself with something. When Moshe, accompanied by Luzi, came through the kitchen on his way to the vestibule leading to the street door, Sruli was holding

Moshe a lighted lantern, and as Moshe opened the street door, Sruli put the lantern in his hand. Then he said, "I have agreed. Come to me when you need me."

Moshe made no reply beyond a bare "Good night." But the light of the lantern Sruli had given him served him from the moment he left the house and all through the time he walked through the third section of the town; and he continued to use it even when he reached the wealthier neighborhoods where it was no longer necessary. And yet he did not extinguish the lantern, but carried it, lighted and shining, all the way home.

XII

Alter's Three Visitors

Inevitably, the first person to become the target of Alter's reviving masculinity was Gnessye—with the high, full breasts, and the soft, velvet bodice: Gnessye, the younger kitchen maid whom he encountered daily as he passed through the kitchen on his short journey between his little room and the courtyard. She entranced him so that when he saw her he stopped dead in his tracks and turned speechless. And if his heart beat at the sight of her by day, when he passed her bed in the kitchen at night and was assailed by the warmth that came from it, his bones seemed to melt, his head spun; he felt his knees weakening, and it was all he could do to keep from kneeling at her bedside, or indeed to keep from flinging himself into the bed.

He often contrived errands—real or imagined—that required him to go through the kitchen so that he could come once again into the presence of that female warmth, so that he could inhale it and even, if luck was with him, touch, in passing, a warm hand. A hand or a foot—or perhaps something even more delectable.

The older kitchen servant was not wrong when she said to Gnessye, "Girl, why is he looking at you like that? What does he see in you?"

After one of those night passages through the kitchen where Gnessye slept, Alter would return to his room panting, sweating, his heart constricted. And it would take him a long while before he could get comfortable in his bed, and it was much later than that before he finally went to sleep.

It was then that he dreamed again of the woman who used to come to him in dreams when he was still in his passionate, early youth. The woman with the black crown on her head who came to him fully clothed but who moments later was entirely naked. That woman who always comes to young people who have not yet tasted the sins of the flesh. And who gives herself to them.

Alter was terribly afraid of her. And yet he could not keep from looking after Gnessye, the live young woman with the high, full breasts. Nor was it possible for him after he had stared lustfully at Gnessye to refuse the consolations the woman with the black crown brought to his bed in his heavy, passionate dreams.

His only comfort—all that he had been able to do to raise his spirits given the whirlpool of feelings in which he found himself—had been to muster the courage he needed to approach his brother with the request that he, Moshe, arrange a betrothal for him. It had cost him considerable anguish, as we will remember, but, on that night when Moshe had returned from the meeting at Reb Dudi's house, Alter had blurted out his wild request.

It had undoubtedly been both strange and dangerous, but Alter had felt himself literally burning, clothes, flesh and all; and, as sometimes happens to people who are threatened with fire, he had found himself possessed of an unwonted strength.

Because things had taken a really serious turn with Alter. It happened one night when he was in the kitchen. He found himself in the dark standing much longer than usual beside one of the beds of the two sleeping kitchen maids. It may be that he had made a mistake and was standing beside the older servant's bed; or it may be that he was beside Gnessye's bed and that the older servant, tossing in her sleep, had become aware of his presence and that her female instinct warned her—whatever the case may be, the older woman was suddenly conscious that it was not sheer chance that had brought Alter there, that he had come with some particular male purpose, and that the situation might end with violence against Gnessye and with appalling scandal for Alter and her employers.

In the morning she asked the younger servant whether she hadn't either heard or sensed anything the night before. Gnessye was unable to say, but a night or two later as she was sleeping she became aware that a hand was moving toward her private parts. And in the morning she reported this to the older servant who said, "Yes. It's clear. You've just confirmed my suspicions. Oh, no. I didn't just think it all up. I saw with my own eyes the way he stood over you, brooding. As if he didn't have the same needs as all the others. Well? He's not a log with a wood-pulp soul."

As for Alter, the welter of his feelings stupefied, irritated and overwhelmed him. Crushed him to the ground. And that was no metaphor. He was literally, actually, crushed. There were times when, unseen by anyone and alone in his room, he leaned his back against a wall as if he were supporting some great weight and lowered himself slowly to the ground.

We have seen, then, the distressing first consequence of Alter's recovery from his illness.

The second was that everything he had ever learned before came back to him with a great rush, as if presented to him by some invisible hand.

As if it were a gift from heaven. When he was given a prayer book, he was at first afraid to open it because—what if he had, during his illness, forgotten to read? And when he had opened it and saw that he could read, he was frightened lest he misunderstand the meanings of the words. Then, when it was clear that he understood their meanings, he did not want to risk taking up a more difficult book in which, he was certain, meanings were concealed under seven seals. And when finally he did risk reading such a book and discovered that he understood everything, he was so superabundantly happy that it seemed to him that he was shedding gold from his sleeves, and that he was trying to fill his pockets with it, but there was more gold than there were pockets and the pockets were overflowing. And then like the miser whose eyes cannot get their fill of looking at his treasure and who forgets everything as he mirrors himself in its glow, so Alter in those first days was, like that miser, so delighted by his newly returned knowledge and intelligence that he could not bring himself to think of anything else and ignored the light of the sun by day and that of the moon and the stars by night.

A new world opened before him, as in a fairy tale someone comes after long wandering upon a great palace and walks round and round it, marveling at its beauty. Alter, who had been desperately poor, suddenly became abundantly rich. And as in a fairytale he seemed to be going from door to door, from room to room, unable to credit his eyes with the marvels he met on the way, but also with a lingering fear that the wonders might vanish at any moment.

Meanwhile, he was very happy. Since he had not yet established intimate contact with the members of the household, the world of books served as a sufficient substitute for intimacy. In that world he found a refuge where he could hide until his family got used to the change in him, until they could find a common language that would help them establish a new relationship. Until the time, that is, when they would no longer feel that he was a stranger in their midst.

There, too, he came upon places which, as he read about them by day, linked him with the nighttime yearnings that made him steal down into the kitchen where he stood beside Gnessye's bed so that he could feel emanating from it all the charms with which a woman's body can tempt a man, especially a man as deprived as Alter was. Coming upon such places in his books, he could feel day merging with night before his eyes, and he saw the whirling of fiery rings in the air, and other wonders such as an imagination like Alter's could call up from the strange depths in which they are hidden and which, had anyone else seen but one tenth their like, would have been regarded as spectacularly beautiful.

The world of books, then, opened him to an ecstatic world.

For instance, the ecstasy he experienced on Fridays when he recited the Song of Songs.

In the Mashber family there still survived an old custom that had been passed down for generations from father to son—that on Fridays the men of the family recited and sang the Song of Songs with great passion. Their father had done it in the synagogue where the congregation was so numerous that people crowded the doors and windows to hear him. Luzi had carried on the tradition and Moshe, too, though he was a merchant and a man of the world, did not depart from the custom.

Alter, too, recalled the practice. And on the Sabbath, after he had washed and put on clean garments, and was alone in his room that looked out on the garden, he began his recitation. He had no sooner pronounced the first verse when he felt a taste on his lips as of drops of honey which had not, after generations, lost their sweetness and which still had the power to nurture him—Alter.

And then his eyes glazed over and he found himself in a sunny land where on the far horizon there loomed mountains that seemed to tremble in the heat of the day, where sometimes stags in pairs and hinds in pairs yearned for light and water and height and love as they looked across the land and its valleys, at its shepherds tending their flocks beside wells, at the young women filling their pitchers, and at men and women who were keepers of the fenced or unfenced vineyards.

And Alter, at his recitation, joined those shepherds in dust and bright daylight as they drove their black and white sheep and kids and goats and cattle down from the mountains to water them at the wells.

"The Song of Songs."

He heard a voice singing in a garden, and the voice was like that of the one whom his soul loved. She whose body, "is black but comely, O ye daughters of Jerusalem," as the song goes. She who like himself was unable to sleep and sought her beloved, inquiring of the watchmen, the way he, Alter, when he could not sleep in his narrow bed rose feverishly from it and went out into the courtyard to stand beneath Moshe's window where he made his mute demand that his brother fulfill the promise he had made him.

I have put off my garment, how shall I then put it on?;
I have bathed my feet, how shall I then soil them?
My beloved put his hand to the latch of the door and my heart yearned within me at his coming . . .
Upon my bed at night, I sought him whom my heart loves; I sought him, but found him not . . .
Whither hath your beloved gone, O fairest among women? Whither hath your beloved turned, that we may seek him with you? . . .
My beloved has gone down to his garden, to his beds of roses . . .

And the voice seemed actually to fade away, leaving Alter standing there, openmouthed, as if he had heard it coming from the garden that faced his windows. He was exhausted, his hands trembled, his eyes wandered. And had anyone come into Alter's room just then it would have seemed to him that he was seeing Alter listening to an interior voice the way he sometimes did when he was ill, and that very soon he would reply to that voice with strange cries that came from his bowels. But no. Alter stood, dazed, drawn by that voice, overwhelmed by it. He felt feverish, weak, unable to breathe. He unbuttoned his shirt, then unable to keep to his chair, he leaned with his back against a wall, then lowered himself slowly to the ground.

That, then, was the distressing second consequence of Alter's recovery.

The third was that he became aware of the Mashber family problems.

He had very little to do with household matters and his routine of life even now was not much different than it had always been. Whatever he needed in the way of food, drink or clothing continued to be taken care of, so that as far as that was concerned he had no reason to notice any changes in the household. And yet from the looks on the faces of members of the famly whom he occasionally encountered, he sensed that something was not quite right in the household.

At first the explanation that occurred to him for the worried looks he encountered was that the family was concerned about Nekhamke's illness. But as he considered the matter more closely, the surer he was that there was something else going on as well. There was a nameless cloud hovering over the house whose vapors, penetrating the house through the windows and doors, through every gap and crack in the walls, everyone breathed. The very children in the house were made unusually silent by it, and the adults, as Alter observed, seemed possessed of such dark thoughts that they could not bring themselves to spare Alter a word of greeting when they happened to run into him.

And this, Alter understood, was the reason that Moshe had said nothing more to Alter about that vitally important matter they had talked about that night. Moshe had neither reassured him that he was still thinking about it nor promised to do anything about it. More than that, Moshe seemed to want to avoid him when, as occasionally happened, they chanced to meet face-to-face.

And this was why Alter, with no one to turn to, went about with his head filled with confusing ideas. He was afraid to ask anyone directly because, as he saw it, since they did not now confide in him, they would only give him evasive answers, the way people did when they talked with children or strangers to keep them from meddling. It was clear to Alter that the members of the family did not think it was possible or necessary to keep him informed because, as they saw it, he was not yet fully recovered and would not be able to deal with their problems. And so it was better not to involve him. The result was that he thrashed about like a fish trying to inform itself of what was going on on the other side of its fishbowl by beating its head against the glass. He had, finally, only one recourse. To keep to himself and wait for a chance to make things clear.

So he waited, and the chance he waited for was not slow to come.

One day, Mayerl, the oldest of the children in the house, came to see him. It happened that day that Mayerl's lessons had gone badly so that it was believed he wasn't feeling well. His teacher, Rabbi Borukh-Yakov, had come in the morning at the appointed time—Rabbi Borukh-Yakov, whose fee only the very wealthiest families could afford for the few hours of instruction he gave their children each day.

Borukh-Yakov was a staid man and, given the epoch in which he lived, well-dressed and very clean. The coat he wore in the middle of the week was tidier than those worn by others of his rank on the Sabbath. He always carried a clean handkerchief with which to wipe both his nose and his mustache, because he smoked and took snuff. And not as other people did because he was tense. On the contrary it was because he was so calm. He smoked when a lesson was going well, and he took snuff when it was going even better. No lesson he gave ever went badly. His capacity for explanation, his clarity of speech and his calm personal presence would be hard to match, not merely in the town of N. but anywhere else in the district.

It was a singular blessing for a child to have him for a teacher. There was no possibility that he would ever beat a child; it was even rare for him to raise his voice during a lesson.

Mayerl, Moshe's oldest grandson, was the only child Borukh-Yakov taught in Moshe's household. Mayerl was not only the oldest, but he was also the most gifted of the children. It had been obvious early that given Mayerl's talents, the extra cost of a teacher like Borukh-Yakov would be money well spent.

In summer, Borukh-Yakov and Mayerl used to study in a wooden hut in a remote and wooded section of the garden where they would not be disturbed. In winter, they had a room set aside for them in the house.

On the day of which we are speaking, Borukh-Yakov came, as he always did, promptly at his usual hour. Quietly, he had hung his coat with the velvet collar in the corridor closet where the members of the family hung their clothes. He had gone to the room set aside for lessons and there he had begun his usual work: to make the difficult understandable. Or if the child already understood the text, the rabbi knew how to interpolate a word—like a helping hand—that would keep him from becoming entangled in it.

Today, however, Mayerl was not his usual self and the lesson did not go well. It was obvious that his mind was elsewhere. Seeing that Mayerl was not proceeding with his usual skill, Borukh-Yakov, without raising his voice, without a show of anger of any sort, did what he could to make the text clear. But again, Mayerl was unable to grasp its meaning. Borukh-Yakov explained it once again, and when Mayerl was again confused, Borukh-Yakov asked him, "What's wrong with you today, Mayerl?"

It was then that Mayerl burst into tears.

And that was something to wonder at because Mayerl was neither a lazy nor a capricious pupil. It's true that Borukh-Yakov thought he was something of a daydreamer, but he had always been able to snap the boy out of his daydreams and to get him to follow him, Borukh-Yakov, down the road of clear and logical thinking. Never since he had first known Mayerl had the boy ever proved intractable in the very midst of a lesson, nor had he ever burst into tears.

He concluded, therefore, that the boy must be ill, and that it would be better to interrupt the lesson. "Go," he said. "Go lie down, Mayerl. You're not feeling well." And with that, Borukh-Yakov left the room and went to the closet in the corridor and took out his coat.

Mayerl's mother, seeing the rabbi, said, "Rabbi, why are you leaving so early?"

"I don't think Mayerl is feeling very well. He seems to have a headache."

"So suddenly?"

"I don't know. Just as we were getting started, he burst into tears. And I can see that he won't understand a thing today."

Yehudis went into the study room where she found Mayerl still sitting rigidly. She touched his forehead to see whether he had a fever. Nothing. No.

"Why couldn't you do the lesson today?"

Mayerl stammered something. And whatever it was that he was trying to say, it became immediately clear to Yehudis that he did not himself know what had gone wrong. And yet had one been able to look into his heart, one would have seen that Mayerl was experiencing in his incoherent fashion the very same family troubles which the adults were living through. But while the adults had clear and certain knowledge of what was going on, he had had to guess at it from exchanged glances and the looks on people's faces, from feelings hovering in the air.

Mayerl, who had the gift of seizing precisely those meanings that adults were trying to keep from him, who had indeed, as we have indicated, some gift of foreknowledge, experienced the present atmosphere in the house as an oppressive weight. He felt it not as an indication of what was to come, but of what was already there, and it was that knowledge that made him weep into his pillow at night. And that had caused him to burst into tears before the rabbi.

Mayerl, more or less comforted, continued to sit in the schoolroom for a while longer after his mother had left him. Then, simply to keep himself occupied and to keep from feeling superfluous, he went off to perform some essentially unnecessary and useless child's task. Then, hardly knowing how it happened, he found himself climbing the steps to Alter's attic room.

"Ah, Mayerl," Alter called the minute he saw the boy in his doorway. His tone was warm and welcoming, his smile delighted.

They were both pleased. Alter because he had a visitor, even though it was a child—still, it was a living soul—and he had such visits rarely. Mayerl was glad to be there because, being the kind of child who was drawn to attics and cellars, Alter's room had always been a kind of refuge for him, a place where he could be himself in an atmosphere considerably different from that of the rest of the house.

He used to come there even when Alter was still suffering from his illness. When there had been no possibility of any sort of discussion, but even then, Mayerl had found it interesting—even necessary—to visit Alter occasionally. And this was especially true now when it was possible to have real conversations with him.

"Ah, Mayerl," Alter said again. Then, seeing that the boy hesitated, he added, "Come on in. What's been happening to you?"

"Nothing," Mayerl said as he came in.

"Done your lessons today?" Alter said, simply to start a conversation.

"Yes," said Mayerl.

"You really know how to study?" asked Alter.

"Do you know how?" Mayerl shot back, allowing himself to ask Alter the kind of question he would never have put to any other adult. Mayerl felt that he could talk to Alter in this way because Alter's manner as he put his questions and his entire general demeanor were still those of a man who had recently recovered from a serious illness and whose mind and slurred speech, like those of a senile man or a retarded child, still showed its effects.

"Do you know how?" was Mayerl's question.

"Yes," Alter replied, smiling confidently.

"Let's see," Mayerl said going up to the table where he opened the first book that came to hand and offered it to Alter, inviting him to recite.

Alter, as if he were a student, took the book up obediently and began to read and comment with such clarity and perspicuity that Mayerl was convinced at once that Alter had told the truth.

It was a scene worth seeing: Little Mayerl examining his grown-up pupil, and Alter, with no hint of the sort of amusement or condescension with which adults sometimes treat a child, allowing himself to be examined. And it was then, because Alter had treated him as an equal, that Mayerl suddenly interrupted Alter's reading to confide in him: "Do you know what, Alter? My father doesn't have his gold watch anymore."

"What?" Alter turned his attention away from his book.

"His gold watch. He doesn't have it anymore."

"What watch?"

"The one he keeps in the chamois-skin sack. In his vest pocket."

"Do you mean it's been stolen? Or has he lost it?"

"No. Pawned."

"What does that mean, pawned?"

"He borrowed money on it. The watch and my mother's earrings and brooches. All the jewelry, and all the Sabbath candlesticks in the house."

What Mayerl said was true. Lately, he had observed that his father's watch pocket was empty. When he inquired about it, his father, Yankele Grodshteyn, had crimsoned and then said evasively that the watch had been sent to the watchmaker for repairs. "A spring snapped, one of the gears is broken." Unable to tell a lie, Yankele Grodshteyn had managed to tell two because he could not choose which of the two to tell.

At first Mayerl accepted his father's explanation but then when several days went by and the watch pocket remained empty, Mayerl, recalling that when his father's watch actually had needed repairs the work had been done within a very short time, because, as Mayerl now remembered, his father could not do without his watch and continually pressed the watchmaker to get the work done in a hurry.

And then there was a Friday evening, the beginning of a Sabbath. Mayerl had come into the dining room from some other room in the house and stopped in his tracks, openmouthed. The table which normally was covered with a whole row of large and small silver candlesticks whose blazing light reached all the way to the ceiling and to the walls of the room—the table was now in a sad state. In place of the silver candlesticks, there were now only a few shabby, worn brass candle holders shedding a light that not only did not reach the ceiling or the walls, but which hardly illuminated the table or the area around it.

Mayerl noticed, too, that each of the two women, his mother and his grandmother, had tears in their eyes after they had blessed the candles. Tears which each of the women tried to conceal from the children and from each other.

And he remembered, too, that after that candle blessing there had been a discussion in the kitchen between the two kitchen maids as they were finishing up their duties for the day. The older woman said, "Well, Gnessye, what do you think of the tale of the candlesticks? They're telling everyone that they've been sent to be replated. Well . . . that doesn't sound right. I'm not sure, but . . ."

"What? What do you mean?" the younger woman asked.

"Just get on with your work. It's not something you'd understand.

Just the same, if it comes to that, I'd be glad to have one tenth of the money that will still be theirs when it's all over."

"When what's all over?"

"Just get a move on. It's late. Well . . . Nice work if you can get it . . . move along now. Move along," the older one said as she hurried the younger woman on to finish her work.

The scene at the table had stunned Mayerl. He had been silent all that Friday night, making no replies either to the adults or children who spoke to him. And later on that same Friday night, it was a long while before he could get to sleep; and when finally he did he dreamed of watches with human faces standing before shabby candlesticks and moistening with their tears the hands with which they covered their eyes. He dreamed, too, that he saw his grandfather Moshe, along with his father and his uncle, poorly dressed and dirty, the three of them all in a row: his grandfather first, then his father and finally his uncle Nakhum. And he saw the three of them coming into the courtyard of their own house and humbly joining a line of beggars standing at the kitchen door where they waited for the scornful and indifferent servants to put some trivial coin into their hands.

Mayerl, after that night and those dreams, had gone about greatly distracted. He could not bring himself to participate in any childish games or pranks. Then after a while he began to see in broad daylight the same visions that had appeared to him by night. The well-dressed members of his household would suddenly appear to be wearing rags, like beggars. And since he could not confide what he was seeing to anyone—children would not have listened, and adults would only have scolded him—it had finally occurred to him that his best recourse was—Alter. The way to Alter was open. He could tell Alter everything. All that he had had to hide and to repress could be revealed to him.

And so when Alter had allowed Mayerl to examine him as if he were a pupil, Mayerl, reassured by the intimacy of that experience, had interrupted Alter, in the abrupt way that children can, to say, "Do you know what, Alter? My father doesn't have his gold watch anymore."

And then the confidences had followed: and Alter had learned of the dangers that threatened the household. Mayerl told him of a conversation that he, Mayerl, had overheard between his parents. About his grandfather, Moshe, who was frightened of something.

"Frightened? Of what?" Alter asked, pretending ignorance because he wanted to hear more of what Mayerl would tell him.

"What do you mean, 'of what'? Don't you know that bankruptcy is serious? You can lose everything."

After that, Alter asked no further questions. It may be that he simply wanted to keep the boy from conversations that might prove too complicated for him. Or he may have felt that Mayerl was in no position to tell him anything more. In any case, Alter asked no further questions and, much to the boy's amazement and for no reason that Mayerl could see, began to stroke Mayerl's head and shoulders in a gentle, fraternal fashion. Mayerl observed that Alter's eyes filmed over, as if he were no longer present, as if he had been transported to some distant place.

And indeed Alter's trance was so deep that he did not notice when Mayerl slipped away from him. And when Alter came to again, he seemed to sense that a message from the rest of the household hovered in his room. A message meant to reveal the family's secret to him. But Mayerl, after all, was still a child and could not be wholly counted on. Alter still needed word from some adult. And Alter set himself to wait for that.

He did not have long to wait. The situation in the household below was such as could not much longer be kept from anyone. Not even from the children. Not even from someone like Alter who was only brushed by the wing of the destiny that had seized the family.

Not long after Mayerl's visit, Gitl, his brother's wife, visited Alter.

This happened just about the time when her daughter Nekhamke's illness took a turn for the worse. It was not known whether it was that her original sickness had intensified or whether it was a second disease that caused Nekhamke's decline. But it was clear that her condition was mortal. The swelling in her feet expanded upward, and she had such difficulty breathing that not only could she no longer move about her room, but she was short of breath simply lying in bed. In addition to Yanovski, the family doctor, the Mashbers also called in a certain Pashkovski who, like Yanovski, was a Pole, and old and laconic, and who wore sideburns like him. These two were always consulted together because as the best and the wisest doctors in town they inspired hope in grave situations.

The two doctors spent long quiet hours at Nekhamke's bedside. First, one of them bent over her to examine her body, her face, her feet and to look deeply into her eyes, then the other did the same. And quietly they discussed her case, first in Polish, then in Latin. When as they were leaving and were followed from the room through the courtyard and to the street where they were asked for some reassuring words, they hemmed and hawed, replying finally that doctors could diagnose and prescribe. As for the rest, that was in God's hands.

That much was clear to anyone. Obviously, Nekhamke's situation was bad. That much Nakhum Lentsher, her husband, deduced from what the doctors said in Polish, which he understood. And the rest of the family got hints of the gravity of her situation from the incomprehensible Latin. When Nakhum, who had accompanied the doctors out, came back into the house, he turned to Gitl and said tearfully, "It's bad, Mother-in-law. It's bad. Something has to be done, but what?"

So it was that Gitl, accompanied by several of her poor relations, went one morning to the cemetery where, to deceive the Angel of Death, they would "measure" the graves. Then they would collect oil from the lamps burning in the tombs. Oil that was believed to be a remedy for the sick and with which they would later anoint Nekhamke.

Gitl went first to the tomb of Little Leah, the Pious, where women whose hearts were oppressed came to weep and to be consoled: barren women, who after years of marriage had not given their husbands children, prayed to become pregnant soon lest their husbands be compelled to divorce them. And desperate mothers of very sick children, young or grown, flung themselves down on Little Leah's tomb uttering prayers and lamentations.

And there, Gitl also wept. There and on other graves as well. And wept until she had practically lost her voice; and then because her weeping had made her hoarse, she avoided her daughter's room for the rest of the day lest Nekhamke guess from her voice where she had been.

And when the visits to the graves did not help Nekhamke, Gitl, one Saturday night, when the news from her daughter's room was worse than usual, put her coat on and, taking one of the older servants with her, made her way to a nearby synagogue.

It was already fairly late in the evening. The synagogue serving poverty-stricken workers was a solitary little building, perhaps the only synagogue in the street. I think that its members were candle-makers, rope weavers. Usually a synagogue this small would be empty on a late Saturday night, with no one in it but the synagogue caretaker and perhaps one or two beggars chatting under the light from a filthy lamp. But not this time. Tonight, the synagogue was brightly lighted and nearly full of people. There was something of a celebration going on. There was a considerable crowd of people standing or sitting around a table near the west wall where a cantor or some such person was sitting with pen and ink making entries into a book of records.

As we know, economically this had been a bad year. A year of scarcity, and, of course, it had been particularly bad for working people, and especially for people like these who even in times of prosperity are not in great demand; in *bad* times there was no demand for them at all. In such times, then, workers as little in demand as these did what they could to help each other out by forming "societies" in which they pooled such moneys as they had so that individual members when in need could borrow an occasional ruble to prepare for the Sabbath or a few groschen to buy bread for his family in the middle of the week. And where does one found a "society"? Usually in a synagogue. And usually on a Saturday night when the members are not busy and are still fresh from their Sabbath rest, and where one can always find a man who can create a book of records with its requisite finely engraved letters, first the title page, then the statutes: everything according to the custom of such books, with little painted birds on the first page, or a pair of hands clasped fraternally as a sign of mutual aid.

And there was just such a Jew putting the finishing touches on such a record book. Preoccupied and intent, he sat before a number of pens and vials of colored inks with which he was about to inscribe the names of the society's members. All around him the workingmen of the society craned their necks to see this folk artist at his work. And waited for the moment when their names would be called and they would step forward (those who could write) to sign the register.

The atmosphere was a bit noisy, but festive, as is generally the case when people are expecting some happy outcome from a venture they have conceived and accomplished together—even such poor people as these who had clubbed together their little bit of money here.

And it was just then that Gitl and her servant appeared. At first no one noticed their presence, but when Gitl, as was usual in such a situation, went up to the tabernacle and, with a swift movement of her hand, pulled back the curtain from the Ark of the Torah and uttered her first cry, then all those who were clustered at the west wall of the synagogue turned and took in the scene before the Torahs in the Ark at the east wall.

There, there were two women. One, it would seem, a servant who had simply accompanied the other woman, the one who had been compelled to come here, to utter her great grief before the Torahs.

The distressed woman was recognized at once by them all. It was Gitl who was well known to them as the wife of Moshe Mashber who owned a palatial house on a fine street in the town. A home the whole town visited on Sabbath afternoons, to have a drink of water from the cool well in the courtyard; and where as they drank they could look about at the enormous wealth that surrounded the house: at the paved courtyard, the array of rooms, the stables, the padlocked garden; and those who looked were filled with envy; and poor people, seeing it, sighed, not even able to wish for so much wealth. And now there she was, Gitl, well known as the wife of the wealthy Moshe Mashber, who it would appear had been driven here by some grief.

The work, and the conversation, around the book of records was interrupted and the place grew silent, as always happens when a grieving woman enters the men's section of the synagogue to call upon God, even when the men are in full recitation—and even in the most devout synagogues—the men interrupt their prayers and wait until the woman has finished uttering her lament.

So it was now. The congregation grew still, and then, from the depths of the tabernacle before which Gitl had fallen, Gitl's voice was heard, the pitiful cry of a mother who would not, who could not, accept the thought that she must part from a dearest and most beloved child, and oh, what a child. A woman fully grown and herself the mother of children.

Gitl, it may be, prayed even more intensely here than she had beside the graves in the cemetery. And the poor men watching her were undoubtedly sympathetic to her. On the other hand, the thought certainly occurred to them all that it would have been quite a different matter if one of their loved ones had been taken ill—a wife or a child. *Their* coming to lament in the synagogue (though it was open to everyone) would have had a different aspect altogether. It would not have been the way it was for Gitl who had come into the synagogue as if into her own home and who moved through it with a rich woman's ostentation and accompanied by a servant. Even her cries of woe seemed to them to be uttered in a tone that implied that God had greater obligations to her than to anyone else.

She made a contribution to the synagogue itself and gave some money to the caretaker with the understanding that the congregation would mention her sick daughter's name in their prayers. And before she left she gave the "society" some money for drinks so that when they celebrated founding the "society" with toasts, they would also drink to her daughter's early recovery.

Of course they readily accepted the donation and they promised to do what she asked. And then Gitl, having done all that she had come to do, called her servant and they left the synagogue together. And it was in the street, as they were walking along, that Gitl, feeling better and thinking more calmly, more clearly—as often happens after one has wept—it came into her mind that in addition to her daughter for whose welfare she had come to pray, there was someone else to whom she could pour out her heart. Alter! Who was in one sense so removed from everything, and yet was so close—almost like one's own child, or like someone saintly to whom one can tell everything down to the smallest detail . . . without even expecting a reply, since his mere presence is reassuring.

And so it was that not many days later, at a time when the entire house was permeated with medicinal odors and there was a constant coming and going of doctors, and a time, too, when the men coming home from the office had ever more gloomy faces—it was then that Gitl recalled the lucid thought that had come to her after her visit to the synagogue and, slowly, slowly, mounted the steps that led from the kitchen to Alter's attic room.

And as she mounted the stairs it was evident that she did not think she was on her way to visit someone who was her equal. Normally when one is on the way to discuss an important matter with someone, one thinks on the way there of what will be said. One tries to order one's thoughts and to choose which words to say. No. In this case, Gitl was solely preoccupied with her own needs. But she hardly knew where it was that her feet were leading her. And if she had an inkling that she was on her way to Alter's room, she had no idea what she would do or say there.

Alter was startled to see her because he was not used to having visits from grown-ups, and particularly not from Gitl, his brother Moshe's wife—so that it was clear to him that if she had taken the trouble to come there to see him, that the matter must be very grave indeed— either for him or for her. And so, inexperienced as he was, he turned to her a bit uncertainly and with more than a little fear.

Gitl who, as we have said, as long as a moment ago had not been sure just where she was going, now when she crossed the threshold and saw Alter, struggled to open the conversation in a way that would lead toward the confidences she had come to make. She glanced at him quickly and, though now he was better clad than he had been and looked generally better, her look was nevertheless like one that one might turn on a child or on a saintly simpleton—and yet that did not keep her from wanting to confide in him. On the contrary, it made her feel that she could open her heart to him, that she could tell him things which, if he had not been a sort of child, or a saintly simpleton, she could not have brought herself to reveal.

So she spoke with great directness to him as if when talking to someone like him, any preamble, any small talk, was unnecessary. She said, "You, Alter, who . . ."

But here she interrupted herself, uncertain what she meant by "who" as she saw Alter before her. True, he looked about anxiously, a bit confused, but he was clearly a grown man with a sound mind and a look in his eyes that seemed to require of her that she take some care in the choice of her words. She hesitated for a moment then resumed what she was saying—but with the same attitude and using the same words as when she had begun . . . as if she were talking to a child. "You, Alter, who are one of us. And who has required so much of our care before you could become what you are. You sit here in your room and you know nothing about anything. Everything is brought to you, as if you were a bird in a cage—you ought to intercede for the family now, pray for us, because we're in an inferno and we're going under. Do you hear, Alter?

"You know nothing and you understand nothing. Because you're a child and far removed from the world. But you should know that, first, our Nekhamke, God forbid, may leave this world, cut off before her time; and second, that the family business (you know what 'business' is, don't you?), the family business is in bad shape and it may be that we may have to give up everything we own, soon. The business itself as well. And the house. All of us. We down below, and you here. Do you understand, Alter?"

And here, Gitl shed some silent tears. But clearly it was not on Alter's account that she wept, but for herself. Because as far as Alter was concerned, she expected nothing from him beyond his innocence. No consolation and not even, as she might have expected from someone who was normal, not even a chance to ease her heart by talking to him at length. No. She wept because the tears would come, and with no awareness of who it was that sat or stood near her, wept as if she were alone in the room, as if she were weeping to the bare and silent walls.

Alter stood rigid and speechless. He did not know how to console her. He had neither the courage nor the social experience available to most people in such a situation to know what to do or say that might comfort her. In that regard he was indeed helpless and isolated. And so he said nothing, but stood awkwardly by, looking pale and as if he wanted to find a place to hide.

And when in the quiet interval Gitl had wept her fill, she rose from her chair and then, just as she was leaving his room, asked him a personal question or two: "How are you? Do you need anything. Just tell me what you need and I'll see about sending it up." Then she went down.

And now Alter was able to understand clearly what it was that Mayerl had brought to his attention by indirection: the real explanation for why the members of the household had been so depressed lately, and why it was that Moshe had seemed to be avoiding any discussion of the subject about which he and Alter had talked on the night we know of.

Beyond all that it was now clear to him that the fate that lowered over the family would certainly touch him with its wingtip soon. How it would touch him he did not know. But he had a premonition that Gitl's visit was not the only one he was destined to receive from the family. That there was a visit yet to come that would drag him into the caldron of the family's troubles, ending his isolation forever. When that would happen again, he could not be sure. But from that moment on he tried to prepare for that visit. And indeed it was not very long before he received a third visit. This time from his brother, Moshe Mashber.

It was all very abrupt and it happened at the very time that everyone in the household was so distressed. The older kitchen servant appeared suddenly in the dining room. It was obvious that she had not come on any kitchen or servant's business. For this occasion she had put her Sabbath headscarf on, something a servant will only do in the middle of the week when she is presenting herself to an employer for a possible new "place," or when she takes leave of her position. As she made the short trip between the kitchen and the dining room, she wiped her upper lip shyly, nervously, with a tip of her headscarf—as if the business she was on was a very serious one, or as if she did not believe she was capable of accomplishing it. And yet she was driven to it by her conscience, which would not let her keep silent over a matter which according to her pieties needed to be revealed.

She came to Gitl who just then was alone in the dining room. There, after some muttered incoherencies and a certain amount of hesitation, and considerable decent rubbing of her upper lip, she said, "Mistress, I hope you'll pardon me. But I have to tell you, it isn't right that our maidservant Gnessye, sleeps in the kitchen with me."

"What?" said Gitl, whose mind was on other, more important matters just then. "What do you want?"

"I have to say that it isn't right that our maidservant, Gnessye, sleeps in the kitchen with me."

"That she sleeps in the kitchen, you say? Why, where else should she sleep? In the living room?"

"No. That's not what I meant. I merely meant . . ." she stammered, unable to get to the heart of the matter.

"What's going on? What's happened?" Gitl asked pointedly, doing what she could to help her get past her stammering.

"Well, mistress, what's happened is that lately, Alter, your Alter, hangs about in the kitchen a little too much at night. And it's not on my account he does it. So it's because of her, the maiden, Gnessye."

"What," cried Gitl, getting to her feet as she threw the servant a look so fierce that the woman regretted having undertaken this task. Perhaps she might have done better to bury the dictates of her conscience deep in her bosom.

"Yes, mistress"—having begun she felt she might as well go on with it—"I had to tell you, because, after all, you're his relative . . . you need to know, because something . . . something scandalous may happen."

It was clear to Gitl that it had cost the woman considerable distress to bring her this news, and that what she had to say was no invention, no fantasy, but rather that she was reporting what was true—what, indeed, she may herself have witnessed. Difficult though it was for Gitl to have to hear such a tale from someone who was not a relative . . . who was moreover a servant; and though she kept her eyes on the ground for shame, unable to look the woman in the eyes as she talked, Gitl felt that it was her responsibility to hear the whole tale so that she might judge whether it was true.

The woman then lapsed into kitchen talk, and speaking confidentially as woman to woman, she gave Gitl various sordid details which made Gitl bow her head still lower, even more ashamed to look her servant in the eyes. But when she had heard all that it seemed to her she needed to hear, and when having heard it all she was convinced that the story was true, she got up from her chair, and speaking quickly to disguise how upset and humiliated she felt, she said, "Well, all right. Yes. Go, go. We'll see to it. We'll do what needs to be done. Yes," Gitl added, "and remember. Not a word to anyone else. Do you understand?"

"Of course I understand. I just had to tell you that Gnessye ought not to sleep . . ." Here she began to repeat her warning. "She can sleep in the dining room or anywhere else for that matter. But not there," the servant said, speaking with more self-assurance and with greater intimacy as she endeavored to reassure Gitl.

"Good, good," said Gitl, distracted. "Go on, go. We'll consider what's to be done."

Gitl did not delay. On that same day, just as soon as Moshe came home from the office, she called him into their bedroom where as soon as they were alone she told him the whole story, watching him anxiously to see how he would take it.

When he understood what she was saying, Moshe leaped to his feet as if scalded. And just as everything else he had lately undertaken to do had none of the marks of judgment and consideration one would have expected of a man like Moshe Mashber, so he behaved abruptly now when he heard the story of Alter.

"We'll have to call a marriage broker," he cried.

"A marriage broker? For whom?" an astonished Gitl asked.

"What do you mean, 'For whom?' For Alter. Who else, if not Alter?"

"And what sort of match will the marriage broker propose?"

"We'll see. We'll discuss the matter among ourselves, and with Alter, of course. And in the meanwhile," Moshe added as he remembered what the servant had suggested to Gitl, "in the meanwhile, we can set up a cot for Gnessye in the dining room." And with that he brought the discussion to an end.

As Moshe had listened to Gitl's account, several thoughts had entered his head all at once. First, that perhaps Alter and Gnessye might make a pair: Alter had seen her, she had pleased him, and perhaps they were destined for each other. And second, that it might indeed be a good idea. Because who if not someone like herself would be willing to be a wife to someone like Alter? Certainly there were no others who would want to share his life. Everyone knew the history of his illness, and who could guarantee what the future would bring? The third thought that raced through his mind was that under the circumstances it would be well to arrange the betrothal at once. Indeed, the sooner they were married the better. Moshe's own circumstances, as he well knew, were getting worse and worse. He was being assailed by troubles from all sides. And who could say whether arranging the marriage of an old bachelor—and especially an old bachelor like his brother Alter—might not earn him some merit from above that would avert the evil decree, stave off the flames or lighten the weight of the hand that seemed to be oppressing him. Fourth, he recalled that Luzi had also urged him to move quickly on this matter. Fifth, he remembered the conversation in which Alter himself, speaking lucidly and without shame, had asked Moshe to arrange a marriage for him soon. That, too, seemed a portent. Then what was the point of further consideration, of further delay? What needed to be done should be done at once.

Such thoughts, and others like them, rushed like a storm through his mind, and out of the welter and confusion of ideas, there was a single saving thread he was able to grasp, and it was the one that caused him to make his hasty remark to Gitl. A remark which not many days later he acted upon by inviting Meshulam the marriage broker to come to the house.

Meshulam was a small man with a reddish face and a white beard. He wore a shabby fur cap with a faded green velvet crown; and whenever he came into a home, the first thing he did was to remove his cap so that he was left with his skullcap on. That was not quite so easy to do since the cap and the skullcap were not lightly parted because they had grown so greasy after years of wear that they clung to each other. And yet with long practice he had acquired the skill needed to separate them. It was a trick he performed to make his work as a marriage broker easier, to show his prospective clients that he felt at home with them, and that therefore they could rely on a man like himself, Meshulam.

He arranged marriages, but for older people for the most part. For fifty- or sixty-year-olds, and for young male and female servants and poor workers. He was not the sort of marriage broker who would be called in by a family like Moshe Mashber's. Had it not been for Alter, Meshulam would never have had entrée into his home. For people in Moshe's class, there were other more respected and better known marriage brokers, like Nakhum Layb Pshotter, for example. A man who knew how to comport himself in such households. With gravity and tact. He knew how to propose feasible matches, and he commanded respect with his bearing. Meshulam was not like that at all. Meshulam understood only one thing: male and female. He was indifferent whether one was old and the other young, or whether they were both old. As long as they could be paired.

There was no need, then, to call in a matchmaker like Nakhum Layb Pshotter to arrange the strange match Moshe Mashber had in mind. A man like Meshulam was just what was wanted: a down-at-heels, silly fellow who knew enough to arrange marriages for servants. As for Alter's interests, Moshe would look after those himself.

It was altogether a difficult matter. And so Meshulam, in deference to the honor of the family and because he was unused to being in such wealthy homes, refrained from playing his usual matchmaker's trick of separating his cap from his skullcap. And indeed, Moshe and Gitl, who met him at the door, whisked him away to a private room where it was made very clear to him that only half of the match was to be his concern. He was to look after the bride's interests, but beyond those, he had no further function. *They* would look after the interests of the groom.

They regarded the situation as so delicate that they did not even introduce Meshulam to Alter, fearing the harm the crude matchmaker might do. They sent him off to the prospective bride.

It's easy enough to say "bride."

Though he was weighed down by his troubles and was assailed, as it were, by flames on every side, Moshe Mashber nevertheless retained a loyalty to his brother Alter which often made him heave a quiet sigh on his account. Though perhaps the sigh was not so much for Alter's sake as for his own, since the projected betrothal was closely related to Moshe's situation. Because had the situation in which Moshe found himself been different, then even Alter's betrothal would have been handled differently. There would not have been this need to link him literally to the nearest woman, the nearest servant, and one who worked in the Mashber household at that. At any other time, even a betrothal like this one would not have proceeded with such unseemly haste. It would all have been handled more respectably, with greater care, with an eye to the decencies, for Alter's sake as well as for the sake of the public at large. Now, it was all proceeding with such a great rush that Moshe could hardly catch his breath.

There is some reason to think that Moshe consulted his brother Luzi in the interval between his conceiving the idea of Alter's betrothal and acting upon it, and that Luzi had concurred in Moshe's decision to send for Meshulam the marriage broker.

Meshulam went immediately to work to persuade the prospective bride to agree to the match. We are not particularly concerned with how that was accomplished. Certainly there was a preceding conversation between Meshulam and the older kitchen servant. Meshulam had a certain affinity for older women who made up a large part of his clientele. At first, indeed, the woman apparently thought that Meshulam had a match for her, and managed to dart into a corner where she slipped her Sabbath headscarf on on her way to talk to him. But when after a long conversation with the marriage broker, a conversation filled with Meshulam's preambles and much marriage-brokerish backing and filling and much rubbing of the servant woman's upper lip—when she finally understood what he was up to and that she was not the one for whom a match was being proposed but that it was Gnessye; and when he had specified who the groom was meant to be, she was at first astonished, then she cried, "What, Reb Meshulam? Do you mean it? Really?"

She went on, still at the pitch of exclamation: "O dear me! What are you saying? It would never have entered my mind. A thing like that. Can you imagine? O my. Only a marriage broker could think up something like that."

"Tell me, Reb Meshulam," she continued, "does the family know what's going on?"

"Of course they do. Would I be here if I hadn't been sent for? Do you think I could have imagined such a thing? Of course they know."

The result was that Meshulam had an ally in the kitchen. It's uncertain whether he promised her a percentage of his marriage broker's fee or whether she helped him out freely and without payment of any kind because, like many older women, she loved the idea of pairing people off.

Gnessye, when the match was first broached to her, did not know which way to turn. All the while she was being spoken to, she kept unbuttoning her tight bodice, an action that drew Katerukhe's eyes (and the eyes of others as well) to her. She kept her head lowered and would look neither at the marriage broker nor at her comrade, the older kitchen maid, with whom she had served for so long doing the same work.

Then suddenly she burst into tears. Because she was surprised, because the whole idea was at once exalted and absurd—impossible . . . and demeaning. What did they mean? He . . . Alter, and herself . . . Gnessye . . . bride and groom? Man and wife? Alter, who not long ago had been shrieking so strangely, and herself . . . a strapping healthy full-bosomed woman whose dress concealed thighs whose mere touch could set Katerukhe or his ilk into ecstatic yearning. And then, even supposing that Alter had recovered his health, how could one imagine that she, Gnessye, the servant who had spent so many years working in the kitchen, could suddenly be lifted to a family relationship with her employers? To be their daughter-in-law—and an equal with other members of the family, to whom one could not give orders and who could expect to be waited on. Strange. Altogether strange.

She wept at first because she was startled. And because she believed that they were poking fun at her. And if they weren't teasing, how could the two of them—she and Alter—get on together? And if they did get together, how would she be expected to behave, and how would she be regarded by people like Katerukhe, for example, who had more than once when he had encountered her in one of the outbuildings, pressed her against a wall and played with her in the ways of a man with a maid.

And Gnessye was right. The whole idea of the match could only be thought of as strange. It could only have been conceived by a mind as confused as Moshe Mashber's. Judged by this scheme alone, one would have to conclude that there was a certain amount of Alter and of Alter's madness in Moshe's makeup which, in more normal times, was deeply hidden but which surfaced now under the pressure of events.

And in fact Moshe himself knew that, with the exception of Gitl and possibly of his brother Luzi, he could not expect approval from the family for his scheme so he neither sought advice nor discussed it with anyone.

As it turned out, an agreement on the part of the bride was arrived at quickly. A day or two went by during which Gnessye wept her fill after which she gave her consent. But that was not really Meshulam the matchmaker's work. For Gnessye, Meshulam was a stranger. Had he come to her on his own to propose a match like this it is very doubtful that she would have let herself be persuaded no matter how hard he worked. No. What made the difference was the help he received from the older kitchen maid. She, who was Gnessye's intimate friend, urged her on when they were alone together. "What," she cried, "still unwilling? What have you got to brag about? You have something that other girls don't? It doesn't please you? Just think what will happen to you. You'll be landing in a bed of roses. Did you ever, in your wildest dreams, think it could happen? Crying, are you? Well, would you rather have Katerukhe, the four guilden errand boy, who shoves his hand into your bosom to grab a free feel and who paws at you in the outbuildings and beside the well when it's dark? Well? Is Katerukhe a better match?"

And yet this same older servant, at any other time, if she had been asked what she thought of a match between a healthy and attractive Gnessye and a rich old man or some prosperous boor might very well have offered quite different advice. "Filth! Let them keep it for themselves," she might have cried. "Pure gold like you to be tossed onto that sort of garbage heap. May they choke . . ."

That might have been her reply at any other time. But now—and we do not know why—she rushed toward the making of the match. It may be that the match itself pleased her, that she saw it as a good thing for Gnessye, her friend, or it may be that she felt a certain vengeful pleasure of the kind that every servant dreams of, at seeing her exalted employers compelled to come into the kitchen to ask the servants for favors. Whichever it was, the net result was that after some more tears and much discussion, first with Gnessye alone and then together with Meshulam the matchmaker, she succeeded in getting Gnessye's consent.

From that point on whenever Alter descended from his attic room and made his way through the kitchen, Gnessye, standing to one side, blushed while her fingers worked the buttons on her bodice, or else she passed a hand through her hair. From that point on, Gnessye felt as if one of her feet had already crossed the threshold of the kitchen into the household. In one sense she was no longer a servant, and yet for the time being she was not quite something else. Though she no longer slept in the kitchen, and though one of the side rooms had been turned over to her, still, none of the members of the family (with the exception of Gitl) knew of the change in her situation; none of them had even noticed Meshulam the marriage broker's first visit to the house nor any of his subsequent recent visits. Gnessye, therefore, waited for the matter to be revealed and, in the days following her assent to the betrothal, continued to behave like a servant. For the time being the only change in her was that whenever Alter went by, she blushed, and lying in the new bed in the separate room, she tossed and turned because of the thoughts that came to her before she fell asleep.

As far as Gnessye was concerned, then, the matter was fully arranged. As for what regarded Alter, that could not be left to a marriage broker, and particularly not for a marriage broker like Meshulam. Moshe, as we have said, made those matters his own responsibility. That happened one evening not very long after what has been related.

It was an evening on which Alter, finding himself alone in his room, paced about, feeling restless. The blood in his veins seemed turbulent, mounting to his head in a way that made his temples feel too narrow to contain its pulsation; his head pounded as if it were constricted between hoops.

He tried the remedy that had helped him recently—leaning his back against the wall and lowering himself to a squatting position. But this time he could not assuage the pain; instead he started up, feeling even more restless than before. He was like a caged animal that exhausted from long pacing lies down, yearning for rest, only to start up again, driven to pacing even more quickly.

Something had happened to him today: whether it was a residue of the earlier illness that used to set him howling with pain, or whether it was because of his latest fall which, according to the doctors, had cured his earlier illness but whose effects might occasionally still assail him. Today, therefore, might be one of those times. It was possible.

One could see that he was oppressed as if by some heavy weight that made it hard for him to breathe, or as if someone were throttling him so that he had to unbutton his collar and his clothes in order to breathe. Anyone seeing him just then would have noticed that his eyes seemed to wander, and that because of his profound restlessness, he had been turned into a pillar of attention, that he seemed to be listening to his own innards, that he was waiting for something to happen— very soon.

Because he was so restless, and because he did not know what to do with himself, he turned once more to the letter writing that once used to occupy him. He hoped thereby to relieve some of the pressures that were tormenting him. He thought that he might describe his internal ferment, that he might speak of the repressed passions he carried about with him all day and which at night caused him to move between the maidservants' beds in the kitchen where he could hope for no more than the brief pleasure he could get from touching lightly the one he loved. And even that pleasure had been denied him lately, since her bed had been removed from the kitchen. That was one thing. Second, the events in the household around which he circled like a blind man feeling his way around walls. The details of those events reached him only in fragments or in Mayerl's childish gossip, or as he got them from Gitl who spoke with him as if he were some sort of golem, or a child—she said what she had to say and then left him without giving him a chance to respond.

"Sorrows, like ravens, circle over my head," he wrote in the letter he imagined himself writing. "They cluster before my eyes and over my body, pecking at me, tearing away bits of flesh."

"Woe unto me," he cried desperately in that imaginary letter. "The straw at which I grasped as I was drowning, and which I thought had brought me safely to shore, has deceived me. There is neither straw nor shore, no foundation on which to stand. I stare into my lamp but I see no light, and my heart is oppressed by my sense of alienation. I am like one who has sunk into quicksand—with only his hands still free to pray. I feel that something dreadful is about to happen—something from which I thought I had freed myself, but which is now gathering itself to seize me anew, to fling me into some dark and dreadful place.

"Woe unto me, and woe unto my soul," he seemed to write in that imaginary letter. "It seems to me lately that the entire house is under a cloud and the mist presses in through the windows and doors, through the keyholes—presses in and touches everyone's heart, my mind and heart as well; and the cloud is denser and denser, increasingly dark, and except for two guttering candles in the distance, there is no light to be seen. And those lights are my brothers who are all that I have in the way of support and all that I can cling to for consolation. Luzi and

Moshe. And yet one of them, Luzi, is not here, and the other, Moshe, is slipping farther and farther away.

Alter's thoughts, as he stood there in the middle of the room, were becoming increasingly tangled. It seemed indeed to be true that there was no solid ground beneath his feet. That he was hanging suspended upside down between heaven and earth, and everything in the room seemed to be topsy-turvy. He sensed that at any moment he would fall.

But just then his door opened and his brother Moshe stood at the threshold.

For a moment, Alter thought he was seeing a vision—like those that had been passing through his mind just then. He rubbed his eyes to make sure that what he saw was real. But when the initial moment of surprise was over, and he had heard his brother's "Good evening," he roused himself from his dream—from his confusion. He felt himself on firmer ground. His head cleared and he hurried forward to greet his brother.

Moshe Mashber saw that he had come upon Alter at a moment when he was very confused, and that any surprise might prove crushing to him. And so Moshe did not immediately broach his reason for coming. For a while after he was seated at the table, he talked of other more general matters, and then when he was assured that Alter had quieted down and was in a condition to hear more serious things, Moshe slowly, slowly, broached the reason that had brought him there.

"Alter, do you know why I've come? I've come to talk with you about the matter you asked me to think about not long ago. Do you remember? You asked me to keep it in mind. It's been very much on my mind, but lately I've been so tied up with business matters, as you know—and the anxieties about Nekhamke's illness . . . so I've had to put the matter off until now.

"And now, here's how it stands. I thought about it for a long time. Then I made some inquiries, and now I believe I've found you a prospective bride."

It was altogether difficult for Moshe to deal with this matter. The problem was how to get Alter to understand that a match which under any other circumstances could not possibly be suitable . . . a match that, had Alter been normal, no one could conceivably have proposed . . . was now, under the circumstances, the best that could be made. And Alter would have to confront that fact, as Moshe and those members of the family who knew about it had had to.

Moshe said, "She's a respectable Jewish young woman. We've investigated her carefully, though really it was not necessary since we know her well. She's a member of the household, almost a member of the family, who's worked here for the last several years. It's true her station is inferior. But Alter would remember that 'to marry beneath one is not degrading.' On the contrary, it is written that it is well to descend in taking a wife if one wants to assure happiness."

Moshe added, "Essence is essence. Human is human. And someone like herself, once she has become a member of the household, will certainly be transformed into a proper woman. . . . Though it has to be said, Alter—and I think you understand this—that someone like yourself is not considered a particularly brilliant marriage prospect. Because no matter how distinguished your background may be, or how excellent you are yourself, the fact is that your illness is well known. And there are not many people, except such poor folk as she comes from, who would be eager to link their destiny with yours. So that if it is not she . . . not the woman I'm presenting to you . . . then it would have to be someone like her, because I see no prospects for anyone better.

"Beyond that," Moshe added more quietly, as if he were whispering a secret, "you ought to know, Alter, that my own situation, my financial situation, is now at such a pass that even if there were a more fitting match available, if the bride's side, because of the difficulties I've spoken of, asked for a larger dowry or a cash payment, then I'm afraid I would be in no position to meet such demands. Because with the best will in the world, I haven't got the means. Though if with God's help I get past my present difficulties, I will certainly want to give you and your wife all the help I can. Beyond all that there's no reason to put it off. I hope you will give your consent so that we can arrange for the marriage to take place properly, as law and custom require, and as soon as possible. Because we already have the bride's consent. She has agreed and there are no obstacles on that side.

"And the family, too, has consented. I've talked with Luzi about it, and the idea pleases him too."

"Luzi!" Moshe's last words so perplexed and startled Alter that he cried out. "Luzi!" he said again, as if in the mists swirling in his brain he had caught a glimmer of light and was gratefully reaching to seize it.

From what Moshe had said, Alter clearly discerned first, that a match was being arranged for him; and that second, though her name had not been mentioned, it was a name he knew well because it was that of the woman over whom he had hovered at night; and third, that no other woman was likely to be proposed, whether it was because of himself or for other reasons; fourth, that the woman had already agreed and that he was now being asked to give his consent to the match. And finally that everyone knew about it and had agreed to it, including Luzi who, it would appear, was living somewhere in town. And yet he, Alter, had known none of this. And all of this now became confused in his mind so that he was not at first able to say whether he approved of what had just been explained to him or not. He was indeed unable to do anything but seize on the innocent first word that occurred to him and to put it to Moshe as a question: "Luzi? Ah."

Moshe understood his state of mind. It seemed to him that Alter's confusion, his inability to reply at this moment, was perfectly natural. Even for someone with normal capabilities, a conversation such as this one might have proved difficult, how much more so than for Alter from whom one ought not to expect an immediate decision. It would be much better to give him some time, to give him a chance to consider the pros and the cons of the match.

"Think about it, Alter. There's plenty of time. In a few days I'll come up again to get your answer." Had Moshe looked at Alter just then more searchingly and with greater understanding, he might not have risen from his place nor left the room quite so quickly because it would have been clear to him that for Alter, whose mind was already disturbed, the news he received was especially troubling. Its effect on him was like that of oil dripping on a red-hot iron.

Alter, however, said not a word just then because, as Moshe had understood, it was not the sort of thing to which one could instantly respond. And more especially because of something that Moshe did not know . . . that is, that Alter's mind had been buzzing with a number of thoughts even before Moshe had come up to his room and so he was in no way capable of forming any clear and thoughtful reply.

However, the truth is that Alter had already concurred in the match, and in truth there was nothing left for him to consider. And his answer was certain: he would say yes. He was perfectly aware that he was not a particularly desirable match and that no one was likely to offer him an opportunity for a more advantageous marriage. He knew, too, about the family's troubled situation as he had understood it from Mayerl, from Gitl and now from Moshe and which predisposed them to accept a match which in less difficult times someone like Moshe would not have considered.

His answer, then, would be yes. Because, in addition to all the other thoughts whirling in his head, there were those fantasies that had driven him to wander about in the kitchen at night in search of even the most minimal outlet for his passions, though in fact those wanderings inflamed them more.

Moshe left the room and Alter did not even hear his "Good night" because there were drums already beating in his blood. Alter yielded himself up to the sorts of fantasies about marriage that could only be imagined by someone as deprived and as famished as he was. Overwhelmed and surprised by his feelings, it would have taken very little encouragement (very little) for him to open his prayer book as he might on a Friday night and utter a sort of love song, a song of songs in praise of the surges in his blood that were driving him not toward a trundle bed in the kitchen around which he circled in search of hidden, forbidden delights, but to a real bed, like King Solomon's in his beloved Song of Songs ... a bed on which Alter's beloved waited all naked—to love him.

And now Alter's head began well and truly to spin. He was not sure whether his lamp was suddenly extinguished, or whether it was that it had strangely flared up and that the entire room had as a consequence burst into flame. He did not know whether he was still sitting where he had been when his brother left him, or whether he had not simply risen into the air and was flying about through the room. The room seemed to contract, the walls divided and suddenly he was in flight out-of-doors high among the cooling clouds. All he knew was that after what seemed an explosion of wild music in his head, like the sound of a thousand instruments, his mind was stunned by both light and dark and he found himself suddenly on the ground where he lay as if bound and paralyzed like one who has fallen with a crash from a great height.

The older kitchen servant is willing to swear that on that night, before she went to sleep, she heard Alter in his attic overhead moving about excessively. She could not confide the fact to anyone since the younger servant, Gnessye, as we know, no longer slept in the kitchen but had a room to herself somewhere else. She was alone, then, and heard a sound overhead ... a sound as if someone had thrown something heavy—a table or a chair, she was not sure which. Then, since she heard nothing further, she fell asleep.

That, then, was Alter's second fall, after the first one that had taken place before the whole family in the dining room. This time there were no witnesses. He was alone when he fell and he was alone when he came to and got to his feet. There were no apparent signs that the fall had done him any harm, but he felt himself deeply fatigued and as if every bone in his body had been broken.

BOOK TWO

BOOK
TWO

I

Then It Was That

1.

We do not know whether Mikhl Bukyer decided not to take his projected journey to Lithuania simply because he could not afford the trip, or whether, since he was able to find what he sought right in his own town, he felt that there was no need to go to so much trouble and expense. In either case, the fact is that Bukyer appeared one day at Yossele Brilliant's home—Brilliant, who would get to be called Yossele the Plague, was the leader of the local Jewish freethinkers.

Bukyer had trouble finding Yossele's house, distant as it was in a non-Jewish section of town—a district of dogs and gardens and high palings. A district in which invalids and asthmatics rented rooms during the summer where because of the fresh air they could find there, they went to heal their withered lungs. Bukyer's house, deep within a courtyard, was far from the hubbub of the town and the marketplace and safe from unwelcome or hostile observation and from the comment of slanderous tongues.

And here we must say a few words about Yossele.

Who is he?

The truth is he was a considerable problem to everyone, even before he was excluded from the Jewish community. He had a good head on his shoulders. He was a clever scholar who came, moreover, from a respectable family. He was the son of Mottl Brilliant, a quiet, extremely pious man, who led a peaceful life and did no harm to anyone. But he and his son, even while the boy was still quite small, were continually at loggerheads.

The clever boy, Yossele, was continually putting questions to his father which that quiet man could not always answer. While Yossele was still a child, his father managed one way or another to get along with him, but as Yossele grew older and his mind grew keener, he often reduced his father to staring, openmouthed impotence because of the questions his son put to him. When Yossele was older still, he swam about as freely as in a river among more complicated ideas: fate and free will, punishment and reward. But these were not matters his father could deal with. Mottl Brilliant lived quietly; he conducted his business quietly and he was just as quiet about matters of belief. Yossele's swarming words and thoughts seemed to his father to be like a storm that assailed—a storm that meant to uproot him from his quiet life.

As has been said, they quarreled frequently. At first, over matters that could still be accepted as within the framework of belief. About questions whose answers could be found in the works of great Jewish thinkers and about which discussion was permitted. But later, Yossele went far beyond those limits.

It is not known whether it was his own doing or whether he was pushed to it by someone else—a friend, perhaps. Or whether it was that he chanced upon a book written by some well-known figure of the Enlightenment and was captivated by it. In any case, it happened that in the midst of one of his quarrels with his father, the father suddenly perceived that his son was standing at the edge of an abyss. He had moved so far away that his father all but expected to see a crucifix hanging around his son's neck. Mottl Brilliant was horrified and interrupted the conversation so that he might have some time to think over quietly what was to be done.

For a while, then, he left Yossele to himself. But just then Mottl Brilliant was assailed by one more misfortune. His wife died. Because Yossele was an only child and felt the loss of his mother deeply, his father spared him from confrontation just then, thinking that perhaps the boy would see the tragedy of his mother's death as a punishment from above. But that did not happen and Mottl and his son moved ever farther apart. And if the mother had served to unite them to some degree, and to ease the tension between them, now that she was gone the last tie between father and son was sundered.

Mottl, moreover, as a deeply pious man, took seriously the injunction that a man must have a wife. He soon remarried and thereby enlarged the distance that separated him from his son.

All this coincided with a change in Mottl's business life. Until now he had been a money changer. He sat at a table in the marketplace and changed large bills into smaller ones, small bills into larger ones, coins into bills, bills into coins. But after his first wife's death (because her illness had proved very costly to him) and because of the somewhat lavish expenses of installing his second wife in her new home (naturally, he wanted to appear generous), he had taken steps to enlarge his business. In addition to changing money, he began to lend it, at interest.

To some degree this changed his quiet character. He became a bit harder-hearted, tougher-skinned—as moneylenders are apt to be. Yossele took note of this change and, already irritated as he was by his father's remarriage, it needed only the smallest occasion to ignite a full-scale battle between father and son. A battle that would fully and finally drive them apart so that they would no longer be able to live under the same roof.

That trivial occasion was not long in coming, and the battle erupted. Over what? As a matter of fact, it had to do with Mottl Brilliant's new business which had produced a surge of vitality in him. He rubbed his hands frequently with pleasure at the increase in his prosperity, and he sent up cheerful prayers of thanksgiving to God. Yossele, on the other hand, was profoundly displeased and cast bitter glances at his father.

It may be that Yossele could not abide seeing the defeated, humiliated and sickly faces of the poor artisans and small shopkeepers who were his father's clients, and who came shyly to borrow money as if they were asking for alms or as if they were committing a theft under compulsion. Or perhaps it was that he could not stand the sight of the new harshness in his father's face as he paid out the loans, or stood by estimating his profits as he fingered the goods presented to him as collateral. Whichever it was, Yossele could, finally, not tolerate the atmosphere in the house. An atmosphere that seemed to him to be pervaded with the smell of the perspiration of exhausted laborers. A smell that seemed to Yossele to be pleasing to his father's nostrils in the same way that the smell of wine is pleasant to a wine merchant.

All that, then, prompted Yossele to say to his father one day, "Father, what are you doing? It's all thievery and blood."

"What? What thievery? What blood? From whom am I stealing?"

"From those from whom you take the money. Money that's forbidden. It is written: 'You shall not take usury.'"

"Oh! And what about, 'It is permitted to collect interest.' It is permitted so that those in need, who cannot get on without borrowing, may be eased. It is a favor to them . . ."

"A favor? At those rates of interest? So that they can never crawl out of debt. You're flaying them alive. And you accept as pledges things they can't live without. The sorts of things that are specifically prohibited: 'Thou shalt return to them their pawned clothing at the setting of the sun so that they may cover their heads.' And you have whole chests and closets stuffed with cushions and quilts. Because of you, there are people sleeping on bare floors."

"Just listen to you. Are you wiser than the rabbis?"

"Rabbis! What are they to me? I wouldn't give you a groschen for them all."

Mottl Brilliant, at these words, stood dazed. Then as if he had heard the voice of a dybbuk in his son, he cried, in the manner of an actor in a Purim play, "Oh, my good Lord! Just hear what my depraved and rebellious son is saying." Then, "Satan, leave my son!"

Yossele, entirely understanding what his father meant, replied with a laugh, "Fool, leave my father." The word he used was not "fool" but another, so awful that it may not be printed and which, when Mottl Brilliant heard it, tore the last thread of any familial bond that still remained between him and his son. And not only the bond of kinship, but all ties that had existed between Yossele and the Jewish community as well.

From then on, it was as if Mottl had never had a son—or rather as if his son had died or become a convert to Christianity. Soon after the events described above, Mottl removed his shoes, placed a pillow on the floor and sat down, as one does during mourning. He asked for a stone to be set before him and he spent the day staring at it. It was meant as a symbol of bereavement. As a statement that he had lost what had once been his. And that the fruit of his marriage with his first wife had been taken from him, and that he must now wait for an heir, for a son to say Kaddish after him from his second wife. As for Yossele, he wiped him completely from his mind.

We do not know how Yossele supported himself without his father's help. It may be that he took a sum of money or various valuables from the house before he left. It may be that compassionate relatives interceded for him. Or that his father turned a blind eye on the gifts of money Yossele's stepmother gave him lest his son, left entirely without resources, might be compelled to even more dreadful courses.

How he supported himself at that time we do not know, but now, at the time of which we speak, Yossele was well provided for. He was an employee of a non-Jewish corporation in N. And he was already distinguished for his learning, both religious (which he had acquired before he left his father's house) and secular (acquired after he had established his independence). Beyond that, he wielded a ferocious pen and he had ready access to the journals of his time. All of which gave him considerable power because the press, as we know, has been feared and respected at all times and in all places—especially by those who have had reason to fear it.

And Yossele, when it seemed to him necessary, was quite capable of lashing out, sparing no one. Not even a banker as highly respected as Yakov-Yossi Eilbirten, who was well known not only in the N. district but in other places as well for his wealth and for the work he did with the government which had frequent occasion to consult him—a fact that enhanced Eilbirten's role as an intermediary.

But Yossele did not hesitate to speak his mind even about a man as powerful as the banker. It follows then that the banker did not take kindly to Yossele and kept a wary eye on him.

There is reason to think that Eilbirten hired a certain Jew to follow Yossele about, to observe what he did, whom he met, and who his companions were, hoping that sooner or later Yossele would say something against some highly placed government official—at which point Yossele's impieties and acts against the Jewish community might be pointed out to the authorities. The banker hoped that this would get Yossele expelled from N.

What actually happened is this: the hired Jew, paid by a special account Eilbirten set up for him, followed Yossele about. The spy used to come to the busy banker's office and whisper into his ear, "He's eating."

"Who? What?" Eilbirten, startled, jumped to his feet.

"Yossele," stammered the Jew. "Pork. Yossele Plague is eating pork. Lobster . . . and other forbidden foods."

Yes. The spy was certain. He had frequently taken the trouble to visit Yossele's house and done what he could to become an intimate there. But when Yossele understood the fellow's intentions and drove him away, the spy tried other methods. Sometimes he sent a child in to see what was happening, and to find out who Yossele's friends were.

Or he would report: "They're smoking."

"Who?"

"Yossele. As God is my witness. I've seen it with my own eyes. Smoke pouring out of his window. On the Sabbath."

Or, terrified, he might report, "They're doing—things."

"What kinds of things?"

"With women. With young women. They come together there. They chat. I've seen them with my own eyes."

But none of that was reason enough to turn him over to the authorities. Nor was it absolutely certain that all of those reports were true. What is true is that by then Yossele had a considerable reputation as a rule breaker, as one who had abjured his faith and who could not be brought back to belief by any means.

He had his own circle of disciples enlisted for the most part from among the Orthodox young people who regarded him as a leader. And since his influence over them continued to grow, more and more of them began to abandon the pious ways of their fathers. It is no wonder then that their parents began to regard Yossele as an enemy; or that they gave him the nickname "The Plague." From their point of view, he was contagious and everyone who came near him was in danger of death.

Mikhl Bukyer, like many pious folk of his sort, rose at night when house and street and town were silent to recite midnight prayers. He would wash his hands, touch his forehead with a bit of ash and then seat himself on the doorstep of his house where, together with God who, according to legend, wept two silent tears at that hour over the destruction of the Temple, Mikhl, too, wept and prayed:

"How long yet will there be tears in Zion; and sorrow in Jerusalem?"

Mikhl's wife, hearing his prayers in her sleep, felt both pleasure and pride because her husband here below had been chosen to share with God on high such an important matter as mourning over the grief of the world.

When Mikhl had said his prayers, he did not return to bed. He spent the rest of the night in study. Summer or winter, he was up at dawn, practically the first in town to recite the morning prayers.

Mikhl's wife never complained of those acts of piety, though of course they were exhausting to Mikhl. But because Mikhl was a healthy man, and because rising at night had become second nature to him, it seemed to her that he would not come to any harm. Lately, however, she had noticed that he was not quite himself in the morning. That there were blue shadows under his eyes, and that he often seemed to be in pain when he sat down. She called it to his attention, saying that if he was not well, he ought to see about getting help, but he always waved her away, as if to say, "It's nothing." And since in households as poor as theirs one generally ignored signs of illness, his wife managed to forget the matter almost at once.

But later she observed that it was not illness that was troubling him. That his getting up at night had now a different character. When she listened closely, she noticed that he no longer wept at his prayers. And when she followed him, she discovered that he no longer seated himself on the threshold of the house, but at a table where he sat writing, his head bent over his papers. And when he was not at the table, he paced about the room like a man lost within the confines of his own home.

She noticed these changes without understanding them. She observed that he had sundered his relationship with the other members of the Bratslaver sect. He did not attend their gatherings—not even on the Sabbath.

All of this made her wonder. It was clear to her that some sort of change was taking place in him. He was seething inside. And it was true that Mikhl was passing through a crisis.

We ought, perhaps, to pause here for a while in order to explain what it was that brought Mikhl to take his incredible next step. And yet we will not pause—first, because we have already spoken earlier in this book of his tendency to veer from one thing to another, from one contradiction to another, and second, we hope that the reader will understand from the event itself why it happened and why it took the violent form that it did.

Keeping in mind the period and its customs, what Mikhl did could have taken no other form. It follows then that for a man like Mikhl, undergoing so violent a spiritual upheaval was like a great leap from hot to cold; or, rather, it was the sort of act that however sickly and apathetic it might be, it would just the same be accompanied by a hysterical shriek.

And then . . .

One Friday evening, when it was already time to bless the Sabbath candles and when Mikhl was dressed to go to the synagogue, his wife noticed that he was standing rigidly, like a golem, or like someone who could not breathe because he had just experienced a sharp pain. His eyes were wide, the whites much larger than the pupils. He looked as if he had been transfixed and would stay that way until he was wakened (if he was simply in a brown study) or would have to be carried to his bed (in the event that he was actually ill).

The trance did not last long and Mikhl soon came out of it. But then instead of going to the door as he had started to do, he went toward the Sabbath candles on the table. He stood before them for a moment then he bent and, with a series of quick puffs, he blew them out, one after the other.

His wife, trembling, cried, "What are you doing? God help us!"

For a moment, he stood like one suddenly conscious that he had done something wrong of which he was now ashamed. In fact, he had his hand out as if he meant to relight the candles. But then he seemed to think better of it, and instead of relighting them, he went to the chest where his prayer shawl and phylacteries were kept and took them out. Then without a word he left the house, his prayer shawl and phylacteries under his arm.

"Mikhl, where are you going with the prayer shawl?" cried his wife, a new grief in her voice.

The whole thing was insane, because the prayer shawl is not used on Friday nights. So that his wife's astonishment was no less than when he had put out the Sabbath candles. Her outcry did not reach Mikhl, because he was already gone.

When he left the house, the brief autumn dusk had fallen and it was dark. Most of the people who lived in his street were already in the synagogue and there were only a few stragglers hurrying to get there themselves. Candles shone in the windows of the houses and shed a sweet, solemn glow that made one think of the emotions of those who had lighted them—people who after a week of hard labor had managed to arrive, as it were, on this peaceful shore after a tempestuous voyage.

As for Mikhl, once he left his house he was so disoriented that he had no idea where he was or where his feet were taking him. Until they brought him at last, after a long walk, to a non-Jewish neighborhood where there was no glow of candles in any of the windows facing the street. The houses, rather, faced onto inner courtyards and were surrounded by high walls.

And it was to the courtyard of one of those houses that Mikhl, bearing his prayer shawl under his arm, had come. He opened the gate and went in. Then he made his way to a non-Jewish house with a low roof, then down several stairs, through an entry door and then through the door to Yossele's home. Here, as in all such houses, there was the smell of earthen floors, of whitewashed walls and withered, already decaying, autumn flowers.

The place was clean. There was a simple lamp on an ordinary table that had been covered with a cloth. There was no sign anywhere in the room that it was a Sabbath evening. Yossele, blond haired, and blond bearded, his face amusingly freckled, sat at the head of the table with his friends, some of whom wore hats while others were bareheaded.

At the entry into the room of the strange Jew, conversation was interrupted and all eyes turned toward Mikhl as if everyone was asking the same silent question: how did a man who seemed to belong in a synagogue happen to be here, in this non-Jewish district and in Yossele's house?

There passed through their minds the suspicion that perhaps this was another spy sent by Yakov-Yossi, and they were quite prepared to throw him out. But a closer look made it clear that he could not possibly have been sent by the banker, because in Mikhl's face there was no hint of the flattery and deceit they had discerned in the other fellow. On the contrary, this man had a candid, open look and carried himself here as if he were an equal among equals.

Yossele, after looking at him first with suspicion then with more trust—indeed, with a certain sympathy for his appearance: the man was poor, but clean, his white shirt cuffs extended from his sleeves, his beard and earlocks were still moist from having bathed in honor of the Sabbath—Yossele said, "What do you want? Whom do you want to see?"

"You. You *are* Yossele Brilliant?"

"Yes. Well, then?"

"I've come to say that I want to join you. I think I belong among you."

"What do you mean?" Yossele asked, surprised as indeed his friends were, too. "What does that mean, 'Among you'?"

"Why should it surprise you?" Mikhl replied, a bit irritated, thinking that he was being rejected.

"I only wondered whether you know just where it is you are. And whether we're really the ones you're looking for," Yossele said, looking closely at Mikhl again as if to satisfy himself that the man before him, if not a spy, might not be some confused fellow with whom it would be a waste of time to have any further conversation.

"I know very well where I am," Mikhl said. "I'm here among you, who are outside the community, condemned for having broken all the rules."

"Well then?"

"I'm on your side."

"You?"

"Yes. No need to be surprised. And don't think I'm taking the matter lightly, God forbid. I think that you and your friends can see that

I'm not some careless fellow, and that what I've done I've done only after much soul-searching. It should be clear to you that I haven't just appeared from nowhere. I'm no wandering beggar. And it may even be that I've left a considerable fortune behind me on the other side of your threshold."

"A fortune?" Yossele and his friends were tempted to smile, but Mikhl went on.

"Yes, well," he said a bit angrily, "you understand that I'm talking about the spiritual wealth that a man accumulates who has served the Master of the Universe for many years. And you ought to know what it means to renounce all that . . . to be deprived of it entirely . . . And, too, you ought to keep in mind to whom this has happened and at what period in his life. It has happened to me, who was so deeply rooted in belief, to me in my old age when it is especially painful to lose what one has acquired, when it is hard to tear oneself away, and when, having once abandoned it, one finds oneself turning continually toward faith again the way a weeping child, afraid of being left behind, pleads to be carried because it is too weak to go on of its own accord."

"Well?" said Yossele as he and his friends waited for Mikhl to conclude.

"And yet," Mikhl proceeded, "I had the courage to turn my back on all that. Because, as you know, losing can sometimes make winning possible. And in order to reach a certain height, one has sometimes first to experience the depths. There is much more to be said on this matter. And things don't happen as quickly as they are described. I have had to endure hindrances and disruptions before what I had formerly deemed precious stones appeared finally to my sight to be shards, before tears for what I was about to lose no longer bleared my eyes.

"But after many difficulties, I was able to see clearly, helped to it by my ability to cling fiercely—until the blood flows from my fingertips—to what I regard as precious. As well as by my willingness to abandon whatever seems empty—the way one turns loose the empty air when opening one's fists.

"I was helped, too, by certain well-known books by various authors and (I am not ashamed to admit it) by my unhappy tendency to dream. This time my dreams served me."

"Dreams?"

"Dreams that used always to threaten my pious world because, whatever it was I accomplished by day, my dreams used to destroy it at night. . . . There are not days or nights enough for me to tell you about my dreams at length. But, if you and your friends like, I'll tell you about my last dream. The one that pushed me finally over the edge so that I became what I am now."

Yossele and his friends exchanged glances. "By all means," said Yossele.

Mikhl promptly recounted his dream: He had seen the Evil One one night. A tall, slim man with very narrow goat-hoofed feet. His face glowed as if there were a lantern shining under his skin. His eyes were narrow, long, sharply edged at the corners, and he looked through them as if through slits. He gave Mikhl a silent signal to follow him. At first Mikhl pretended not to see it, but the devil poked him with a finger that was at once cold as ice or steel at the same time as it seared and scalded worse than any fire. Mikhl, knowing that sooner or later he would be forced to follow, rose from where he was—he could not now remember where—and went with him.

The Evil One brought him to a large structure that looked like a temple . . . it was a place that had never been inhabited and it resonated with emptiness. The whole edifice was built on the edge of the Void. And there for the first time, the Evil One's true size was evident. Until then, only half of him had been seen. But now his head reached to the ceiling, and from that distant place his commanding voice descended. And suddenly spirits were visible, as well as spiders, flies, and bats, flying, alighting, crawling on the walls, on the floor, on the ceiling. Creatures compacted into huge masses, one on top of the other. And they all, when they beheld the Evil One's illuminated face, tried to crawl, climb or fly toward him as children might toward a father from whom they begged for love.

Then Mikhl, too, felt himself desiring that love, and he was assailed by an impulse to kneel before him, to crawl before him. And—sad to say—he actually knelt, along with the chittering sprites, and extended his hands toward the Evil One. Then, His voice was heard again, "Rise, poor but worthy one. It is well for you that you were prompted to kneel before me and well for you that you feared me. Now you will be rewarded." And the Evil One stamped his foot and the ceiling of that structure rose so high that it disappeared from sight. Mikhl threw his head back and, straining with all his might, was just able to see it. He saw the Evil One leaning his head against the ceiling and discerned a half circle of fire over the Evil One's head, like a crown in which fiery letters glowed, and Mikhl was able to read the letters which said: "I am the Lord thy God."

When Mikhl looked more closely still, he saw that there were other letters inserted in parentheses, another word which, joined to the others, made them read: "I (Samael) am the Lord thy God."

It was then that Mikhl, frightened, started up from his sleep, his face bathed in sweat. Nevertheless he fell back asleep at once. And then he saw The Other again, but not in the temple built over the Void. Now he was sitting on a high and jagged cliff overlooking the sea. His head rested on his knee and he looked like a man whose world has just come to a crashing end and who at any moment will fling himself into the sea, or like a man overwhelmed with wisdom . . . some sorrowing lawgiver whose intent has been to devise the best, the most appropriate, laws for all created worlds forever and who has etched the phrases expressing them into stone.

As Mikhl drew near, he heard him say, "I am the Lord thy God. I have been here a long, long while, thinking of the Law of Laws. Of the first and the greatest law that should be the basis of all beliefs. I have thought, 'Who is it who can say, "I am the Master of All, as well as sovereign over myself?" ' Surely it is He of whom it is said 'He alone is the creator of all things and He will permit no one to share power with Him.' Or perhaps it could just as well be said of him whom Mikhl had seen a short while ago, the Evil One, who regards himself as an equal sharer entitled to the same rights as He against whom he strives, demanding his share of the other's might. Or, it may be that everyone is entitled to power because no one has created anything, and everyone is self-created. They are here and have the power to say: I am I. No matter who I am, great or small, I am my own creator, my own God, my own Lord, my own opposite, my own destroyer, my own lawgiver.

"And," he said to Mikhl, "after great struggle it is to that last thought that I have finally come; it is the one that I want to share with the world. And, since I see that you have accepted it and are ready to go forth to preach its truth, I have nothing further to do here. My eyes are weary of sight, my limbs from sitting here so long. And so I leave this place . . . and now . . ."

At this, The Other flung himself from the cliff into the sea and, vast though he was, disappeared into it until there was only a final movement of his tail, like that of a fish—and he was gone.

"When I woke," Mikhl said, "I felt a constriction at my heart. I continued to lie still, like one paralyzed, and though I knew that a dream was a dream, still it gnawed at me. At first I trembled at the thought of being alone, without a master or lord, without a creator or destiny on earth. But when I considered what happiness was in store for the man who could say, "You are your own creator" . . . and that the idea was not the work of any one man, but rather that I had come upon it here and there in books by non-Jewish as well as Jewish writers who held that the creation and the creator were one and the same, that the glory and greatness ascribed to the creator could also be ascribed to his creation, and even to myself who was also, therefore, a wonder."

That, then, was the thought to which Mikhl had clung and he had felt not only that the idea filled him, but that he was capable of imparting its truth to others.

He had undertaken to explain all this in a book that was to be called *Anti-Rambam* in which he attacked Maimonides for the reproach he had made to Aristotle for having said that the world was immemorial—that is that it was not created by anyone, but that it had always existed in its present form. Always! That was the grand essence. And he, Mikhl, had undertaken to show that Aristotle was right. And Mikhl was certain that he would succeed in his task. And the book would bring down the entire straw structure of belief with its so-called prohibitions and commandments, its acts of grace and its sins, its rewards and punishments. There would be no need any longer to struggle against so many contradictions which were the natural consequence of the false notions accepted until now and which did not correspond to the Aristotelian ideas of knowledge and free will. There would be an end to all that!

And, said Mikhl, he had worked long and hard at that book and he hoped soon, for the sake of everyone's betterment, to be well on his way with it. Then with a modestly triumphant smile, because he had succeeded in putting his long-concealed thoughts before this group to which he had been drawn, he brought his discourse to its end.

Mikhl's sense of triumph was shared by Yossele and his friends who felt that they were in some way responsible for it as upholders of the Enlightenment. They formed a good-humored group around Mikhl, making him feel that he was one of them. And then they asked him what he did for a living, and what he had formerly done. To their questions, Mikhl replied with a shrug of his shoulders—as if none of that had any importance.

"What difference does it make? I'm a primary-school teacher and I don't make a living at it. I've lived in poverty for some time now . . . because I've long had a bad reputation and have been disliked, especially lately when I became more or less the head of the Bratslaver sect. But never mind. One way or another one gets on. What matters is that I'm here, now. Freed from a greater sort of need."

Here, Mikhl raised his eyes and examined the un-Jewish room. One could see that he was glad to be breathing the odor of the tamped-down earthen floor, of the whitewashed walls as well as the smell of the partly wilted peasant flowers. And he was pleased, too, by Yossele and his friends. Seeing them, and seeing how young they were, he seemed to become younger himself—as if he had shaken a certain number of years from his shoulders.

He was asked to sit down but he replied, "No. I still have someplace to go . . . something to do."

When he was asked why he carried his prayer shawl he said, "Ah, the prayer shawl. I need it for what I have to do."

"What is that?"

"That?" He smiled, and it was clear that he did not want to tell them. Or else that Yossele and his friends would learn what it was later on. Or, if they did not, that, too, would make no difference.

We will not describe here the rest of the time that Mikhl spent with Yossele and his friends nor what else they talked about. It is enough to say that when the conversation was over Yossele himself conducted Mikhl through the courtyard to ward off the dogs, and that Yossele invited Mikhl to return whenever he liked and promised that he would always be welcome.

Again, we will not recount here how Mikhl's wife waited for him on that Friday night. We will only say that when Mikhl left Yossele's house, the night was already very dark not only in the non-Jewish streets but also in the more populated Jewish sections of town.

In the synagogues, the congregations had long since finished the recitation of their prayers and had gone home. In the houses where the blinds in the windows were not drawn, one could see that the candles had burned down to half their length, and where the blinds were drawn, candlelight showed at the window edges.

The streets were silent and passersby were rare. Mikhl strode through the silence, his prayer shawl under his arm. He was heading toward the center of the town where the Open Synagogue and most of the study houses and other synagogues were.

There, too, opposite the synagogue and on the same square, there stood Reb Dudi's small two-story house. The lower story was a sort of demibasement reserved for Long Melekh, the shammes, the synagogue caretaker who functioned also as Reb Dudi's household servant. Reb Dudi lived on the second story which had more space and was better lighted.

One should say here that Reb Dudi was a sort of "state" unto himself. For one thing, he was the most renowned rabbi in the heavily populated town of N. He was, moreover, the representative of a Hasidic sect whose rebbe lived in distant Tchortkov; and, therefore it was something of a luxury to be one of his followers because only rich people, or those like Reb Dudi, could afford the cost of a visit to

Tchortkov. On top of everything else, one needed an exit visa to get there and *that* was a luxury beyond most people's means. So it was that Reb Dudi was frequently consulted as the fully accredited surrogate of the rebbe of Tchortkov. He gave advice, received petitions and was in charge of contributions to the sect.

Normally on the Sabbath, Reb Dudi presided not only over his own household but also over at least a full prayer-quorum of men (though usually there were more). The group was made up either of local Hasidim, but it could include various newly arrived rabbis from other towns and villages—young men or older—who brought with them various queries and problems that had been presented to them and which they were unwilling to deal with without first consulting the authority of someone older and more experienced than themselves—someone like Reb Dudi.

Generally, Reb Dudi wore a sable-trimmed hat as he presided over his Sabbath table. The others wore velvet-crowned hats that were also trimmed with fur. But theirs were trimmed with fox fur, not with sable.

To accommodate the Friday evening meal, the table had been opened out to its greatest length so that from wall to wall it occupied nearly the whole room. Reb Dudi sat at the head of the table. His wife and daughter-in-law at the foot. The meal was served by the rabbi's wife and the household maids with additional help from Long Melekh.

On this evening, too, there was more than a minyan of men seated at the rabbi's table. And as usual there were several visiting rabbis from other towns. The ambience was altogether respectable, animated and cheerful.

Because it was the Sabbath, Reb Dudi spoke very little, and the others at the table, out of respect for him, were also sparing in their speech. The table was lighted by tall silver candlesticks in which the Sabbath candles burned. There was also overhead light from a chandelier. All was as it should be in the home of a rabbi like Reb Dudi.

It was during one of the early courses of the dinner that a commotion was heard in the kitchen. Long Melekh's quarrelsome voice was heard, then the maids', followed by the voice of a stranger. The commotion was caused by Mikhl Bukyer's entry into the kitchen. Long Melekh, who happened to be there, asked Mikhl what he wanted to which Mikhl replied that he wanted to see Reb Dudi. Melekh then blocked Mikhl's way and pushed him back shouting, "It's the Sabbath. The rabbi is busy. Go on now and come back some other day."

Evidently Melekh's outcry did no good because the intruder in the kitchen, impudent or tenacious, or both, thrust the shammes aside and arrived at the threshold of the dining room.

"Good evening." It was the voice of the man at the threshold. Everyone at the table, including Reb Dudi, turned to gaze at the speaker.

"Good evening?" There was general astonishment at the sight of a Jew carrying a prayer shawl under his arm. "Certainly you mean 'Good Sabbath,'" everyone hastened to correct him, thinking that Mikhl had forgotten or had made a mistake.

"Good Sabbath," said several of the older rabbis using an archaic Hebrew form of the Sabbath greeting.

But Mikhl said again, "Good evening," and it was clear that he had neither forgotten nor made a mistake, that he had spoken with deliberate intent, with a cold provocation that no one could believe was possible for a Jew with a prayer shawl under his arm, a Jew in the home of a rabbi—and a rabbi of Reb Dudi's stature.

"He's drunk."

"He's insane."

"Touched in the head."

"A sinner." The cries came from all sides of the table.

"You," said the rabbi's wife, getting to her feet and moving toward Mikhl, "what is it you want?"

"I want to talk with the rabbi. With Reb Dudi."

"Now," said the rabbi's wife, "now, on the Sabbath? While he's at table?"

Mikhl replied, "There are those for whom it is the Sabbath, and then there are those for whom it is not."

"What? What day do *you* think it is, some holiday? Or an ordinary weekday?"

From the other end of the table, Reb Dudi's weak voice was heard, "Ask him what he wants? Why is he here?"

It was then that Mikhl left his place in the doorway and came into the room and moved closer and closer to Reb Dudi. When he reached him, he spoke directly to the rabbi, "I've come to tell you that I'm leaving the community."

"Which community?"

"Yours. And all the communities to which these people at your table belong. And see, I've brought my prayer shawl. I renounce it in life, and I renounce it in death. I do not want to be buried in it when I die."

Had a bolt of lightning erupted on a sunny day, the company would not have been more surprised than it was to hear these words uttered in the presence of a rabbi—and especially of a rabbi presiding over a ritual Friday evening meal in the company of devout fellow Jews in a room lighted by Sabbath candles. "Ha! What? What did he say?" Reb

Dudi inquired as if he had not heard—or had not understood——
Mikhl's words.

An angry old rabbi cried, "Evil one."

"Woe to the ears that hear this," cried another.

"Rend your garments," cried a third.

"Mad. Gone out of his mind," said a fourth.

"Jeroboam, son of Nebat . . . Troubler of Israel . . . Worthy of the
Great Ban . . ." The phrases came from all sides. Words such as are
rarely heard and particularly not on the Sabbath.

"What . . . what's happening here? Who let him in?" the rabbi's
daughter-in-law cried. "Melekh! Where is Melekh? Melekh, throw the
fellow out."

"Yes, out with him. Out. Don't let him spoil the Sabbath," added
the rabbi's wife.

And now Melekh, who had earlier been unable to withstand Mikhl
in the kitchen, emboldened now because he was needed in both of his
capacities as a shammes and as a domestic servant, started toward
Mikhl meaning to grab him by a sleeve or by his collar, but his hand
was arrested by the withering look Mikhl gave him. Then Mikhl, as if
it was a gesture he meant to make before leaving of his own accord,
took the prayer shawl from under his arm and put it down on an
empty space at the table. It was only when that was done that he
turned and made his way to the kitchen and, through it, back into the
street.

We will not describe how Mikhl Bukyer, on his way home, went
through the empty street on which the synagogue stood, nor will we
tell what happened when he arrived and found the door open and only
a small lamp (but no Sabbath candles) guttering out, nor how dreary
the place looked, nor that his arrival was unnoticed by anyone because
all the members of the family, their faces stained with tears, were
asleep in every corner of the house. We'll describe none of that because the reader can imagine it for himself. We will, however, talk
about what happened the next evening at Reb Dudi's house and how
the events of Friday were discussed and dealt with then.

That Saturday night there was, as usual, a sizable group gathered at
Reb Dudi's house. In addition to various foreign rabbis, there was an
assortment of local people: ritual slaughterers, meat inspectors and
other functionaries of the religious establishment. Also present was
Yakov-Yossi Eilbirten, whose custom it was on Saturday nights, when

he had completed reciting the prayers of the last religious service in his home, to order his high-seated light carriage to be harnessed so that he might be driven to Reb Dudi's house where he was sometimes involved in the affairs of the Jewish community but where, just as often, he simply sat listening to rabbinical discussions which seemed to him to be on a level with the Torah.

There was a hubbub in the household. The rabbi's wife, no longer in her Sabbath garb, was as usual busy in the kitchen preparing a beet soup, as well as other dishes for Saturday night. Reb Dudi, perhaps because of last night's excitement, did not feel very well and was lying down because his usual afternoon nap had not made him feel sufficiently rested.

But the fact that the rabbi was lying down made no change in the course of the evening during which visitors continued to gather. Along with Yakov-Yossi and the various religious functionaries, there were two people whose presence one might have remarked: the tavern keepers, Yone and Zakharye. No one was particularly pleased to see them there, but since a rabbi's house is to a certain extent a community institution and therefore open to everyone, there was properly no way to exclude them.

A few words about those two: Zakharye had his tavern in the butchers' district where he served butchers, meatcutters, porters and the like. He could broach a keg, pour a glass of brandy, hand snacks around, add up the bill in his head, collect what was coming to him and put it in his pocket—all with the greatest skill.

He was, too, a deft and skillful brawler. Before an opponent had time to look around, Zakharye was at him, and the man's face was a bloody pulp within moments. And if the fellow was handy with his fists and seemed willing to return as good as he got, Zakharye lowered his head and rushed his adversary, butting him in the chest with such force that his foe lost his balance and crumpled to the ground, helpless in defeat.

That, then, is Zakharye. Yone, the other tavern keeper, was a different sort of fellow. He was a man in his sixties, stolid and compactly built. He was a good ten years older than Zakharye, but his white bearded face still glowed with health, and it seemed certain that he had never been sick a day in his life.

His tavern was some distance away on the road that led to the cemetery. The place was frequented for the most part by young idlers and scoundrels, by pigeon fanciers, cardsharks, real or supposed thieves and pimps. They were at ease in the tavern and felt free to talk more or less openly about their shady professions: about perverted loves, or about young women who were going to give birth soon, about various "waters" or potions that could stimulate love or that could make the "other man" or "other woman" in a love triangle sicken and die.

It was rumored among honest folk that in Yone's place one could leave stolen objects in perfect secrecy because Yone was well connected where it mattered—with petty government officials who could be bribed with small sums of money or with a glass of brandy and a snack or two. He was skilled, too, at slipping larger sums of money into the hands of upper-echelon functionaries.

His tavern had been famous once because of his wife, whose antecedents were not particularly respectable. She was a full-hipped, desirable woman who, when she moved through the tavern, set pulses beating and made men catch their breath. Though she was no longer young, and acted always with the greatest propriety, it was not hard to imagine that she had once kindled many a man's desire. As was evident from the fact that she had gotten a man like Yone to marry her.

She had borne him only one child, a son who, at the epoch of which we now speak, was a tall youth in his twenties who took after his mother. But his parents derived very little pleasure from their son because (and this may have been his mother's fault) he came into the world afflicted with an illness which, because he had inherited some of his father's vigor, had masked itself until now. Or it may be that the youth had acquired the illness as an adult from his various dealings with depraved women. In any case it was clear that he was a syphilitic and the rumor among his neighbors in the compound where he lived was that he was not destined to keep his nose much longer.

Yone, then, was a man with a reputation. In addition to keeping his tavern, he was some sort of local government official to whom young men had occasion to come for various favors—favors for which he charged a fee.

It was something to see, the way a young couple—a man and a maidservant, for example, would come to Yone. "Reb Yone," the man might say, "I have to get married. I need a note to the rabbi." And Yone, his hands on his hips as he examined the young woman's every limb and feature, replying, "What the devil is your hurry? There's time enough to be married." Then he would add a remark or two of such crudeness that not only the bride, but the groom as well, flushed crimson, and he had to stare at the tips of his shoes. Yone's point was that money had to be paid before one could hurry on to the pleasures of marriage: fees to the rabbi, to the cantor, to the shammes.

Yone was, too, a collector of various taxes levied by the Jewish community for charities like the hospital and the religious school. And his word carried weight in those institutions because he had his toadies there who saw to it that he had his way.

Yone, then, was a man who was necessary to all sorts of people. And it was for this reason that he had entrée into homes to which otherwise he would never have been invited. In such houses he was a model of respectability, his Sabbath caftan was buttoned up even on weekdays. The moment that he heard the first measures of educated speech inside a proper household he was able to grasp why it was he had been sent for. He did not need to have things spelled out for him.

Yone was serviceable in all sorts of ways. He was competent to take on a quarrelsome tax collector, or a useless synagogue official, or indeed any other sort of person who had in some way offended the Jewish community and whom, therefore, the community would not tolerate. A fellow like Yossele Plague, for example, with whom as it happened Yone had once tangled. But things on that occasion ended badly for Yone. Because, as we have said, Yossele wielded a powerful pen—which he employed not only as a journalist, but also, at need, in writing letters to the government administration which for good reason the Jewish community feared. This is why Yone could not intimidate Yossele. But in dealing with someone less powerful than Yossele—someone like Mikhl, for example—that was an entirely different matter. There, Yone was under no apprehension. He could take on ten fellows like Mikhl and get rid of them one-two-three in any of a variety of ways: he could blacken their names, cripple their businesses, and, if it came to that, he could have the offender trapped in some dark alley where he would be beaten within an inch of his life.

Yone had been outraged when he heard what Mikhl had done: first, because of Reb Dudi, the town's chief and central figure—the very apple of its eye. A nobody like Mikhl who came from the devil only knows where, deserved a beating for daring to speak to the rabbi in that fashion. And then the thing itself was offensive to Judaism. And, though Yone himself was hardly a pious man—it was well known, for example, that stolen objects could not find a better hiding place than in his tavern—still, what Mikhl had done touched Yone to the bone. Because, just think of it! It wasn't right! It wasn't done. It disturbed the order of the universe. And Yone knew full well that such an event would not be without consequences. It would not be endured in silence. The town would find a means to punish Mikhl for his atrocious act, and when that time came, "hands" would be needed. That is, certain people would be needed to mete out punishment. And it is for that reason that Yone had thought it well to be on the spot where the event itself had taken place and where, without doubt, it would be discussed and considered.

On his way to the rabbi's house, Yone had picked up Zakharye and brought him along. And this is why these two were in that gathering of respectable folk at Reb Dudi's.

Reb Dudi was still resting in his nearby bedroom while the guests gathered quietly in the dining room. They stood about in clusters and, of course, they talked about the event of the previous day—an event which several of them had actually witnessed. And now, after the Havdalah service when the guests had had a smoke and something to drink and had made themselves comfortable, those who had been there the previous day told what they had seen to the others who listened avidly to the details.

Zakharye, unwilling to miss a word, stood with his head thrust forward. Though he was silent, it was clear from the gestures he made, that if he had Mikhl before him, he would certainly butt him in the chest and knock him flat with all the vigor he usually employed when he had an enemy before him who needed a more complicated lesson than mere blows could teach.

Yone, too, was part of the same cluster of men, but Yone was calmer. He stood there, his face crimson from the effects of the fatty foods he ate all year—and especially those he ate on the Sabbath. He was still flushed from the pleasant Sabbath nap he had taken after his meal. And flushed, too, from the several glasses of brandy which it was his wont to drink—especially on the Sabbath.

The man recounting what had happened yesterday was a small rabbi from out of town. A man who breathed piety. He was just offering his reasons for why such an event could happen. He talked of Reb Nakhman of Bratslav to whose sect, it was said, Mikhl belonged. A sect that was quite capable of any outrage because it had its roots in poison and bitter gall. The pious little rabbi was referring to Nakhman of Bratslav of whom it was said that when he came back from a voyage to the Holy Land and went to visit the rebbe of Berdichev, that rebbe called out to Nakhman, "Woe, woe. What has happened to the image of God in you?" And the wife of the rebbe of Berdichev, hearing those words, caught Reb Nakhman by the sleeve and said, "Go, Reb Nakhman. The rabbi of Berdichev doesn't want you here." "And this is because," the pious little rabbi went on, "the story was told of Nakhman that while he was in the Holy Land, he knelt at the grave of the Crucified One. Worse, it was even said that he 'threw stones at an idol.'"

"What? What does that mean?" asked Zakharye and Yone, the only ones in that group who did not understand.

"It's a form of religious belief in which people throw a stone at their idol."

"A stone?" The two tavern keepers stared and still did not understand.

"Yes."

"Well then, it's no great wonder," went on the pious little rabbi, "that that evil should give rise to this. One can expect any vileness from such people—even conversion—or the devil only knows what else."

"Rabbi," interrupted Zakharye, so excited that the veins in his throat swelled as if he had seen an enemy directly before him, "Rabbi, in that case why are we silent? Why don't we wipe them out, these miserable wretches, these idolators with their stones?" He thrust himself impetuously into the midst of the circle. "Why do we tolerate it? Let me at them. Me, and Yone."

"You, Yone!" He turned to Yone as toward a witness who would testify that they two, if they were so empowered, would take care of the matter.

But Yone kept still. And just as Zakharye waited for some assenting gesture from him, Yone nodded toward the doorway and said, "It's he. Reb Dudi."

And so it was. The rabbi, rested, and ready for the evening gathering, stood at the threshold. The room grew still.

The rabbi wore his dressing gown, as he always did on Saturday evening and he squinted—because of the brightness of the lamp, or because he was not fully awake, or because he was focusing on the people gathered in his dining room trying to determine the hierarchy of his guests—who were the least important and who could be ignored, and who were the prestigious ones, like Reb Yakov-Yossi, toward whom he directed his steps.

"A good week," he said quietly, offering his wish to them all.

"A good week. A prosperous week," everyone respectfully replied.

When Reb Dudi reached his place, all conversation in the room came to a stop and all eyes turned toward him as toward a chief speaker.

"What has been the subject under discussion?" inquired the rabbi, though he knew well what the answer would be.

"What is there to talk about? Last evening's event. Specifically, the man himself. Generally, the topic was: What are the roots of such behavior?"

"Good," said Reb Dudi. "That and that alone is the proper subject for discussion. The roots. Because the man himself is no guiltier than a conflagration that someone has kindled. The guilty one is he who ignites the flame."

"Who? What? Who does he mean?" There was a general shift of attention to what Reb Dudi was saying.

"Who? Certainly he who is their leader, who stands at the edge of the abyss and does not prevent others from approaching it. Indeed, he pushes them over."

"Of course. Of course," came a murmur of assent to what Reb Dudi was saying. "We should have seen it long ago. Though it's true that several attempts were made to talk with his brother, Moshe Mashber, but Moshe avoided the discussion—did not want to be involved . . . he waved the matter away, as if it did not concern him."

"Well, of course. A brother, after all," other voices spoke up. "He's not the one to talk with."

"Then who is?" others inquired.

"The man himself. He should be warned. It should be made clear to him that he is misled and that he is misleading others."

"No one but Reb Dudi can do that," said one of the more energetic people at the table as he turned to Reb Dudi with what amounted to a demand for action that could only be put to him as the most honored rabbi of the town, a rabbi whose word had to be obeyed and whose judgment was infallible.

"I?" said Reb Dudi, as if he was rejecting such a responsibility. "I?"

But just as he was about to say more, there was a shout heard from Long Melekh who was also in the dining room: "Look! Look. He's here again." It was as if Long Melekh had suddenly encountered a wild beast in a human dwelling. "Will you just look at that."

"Who? What?" The guests turned from Reb Dudi toward Long Melekh to see who it was he meant. There was not a person in the room who could have imagined that the man who had created yesterday's scandal would make a second appearance here, in the same room, in the same place and before the same people.

But it was he. Mikhl Bukyer.

A thunderclap . . . no. Ten thunderclaps at once, in broad daylight, would not have made such an astounding impression. Nor could there be any other explanation for his presence except that he was indeed insane, or that he was a man addicted to danger who enjoyed testing the edge of a knife against his throat, or putting his head into a noose. There was a final possibility: that because Mikhl's judgment was shaky, he had repented of yesterday's act and had returned to the scene of the outrage so that he might stand before the people who had heard his blasphemies. That he had returned now as a way of doing penance so that he might be forgiven by an all-forgiving God.

Undoubtedly, one of these possibilities was the right one, but whichever it was, Mikhl had the look of a dying man. And if in the first moment of his appearance in the doorway, Mikhl looked like a wild beast among men, when he stepped into the dining room, the scene took on an altogether different character. It was not he who was the wild beast. Quite the reverse. It was he, helpless and unarmed, who was the human who had stumbled into a cage of ferocious beasts that threatened his life. And all the recourse left to him was to murmur the deathbed confession with his pale lips.

"Ha! It's he." The cries were general as everyone turned to glare at him.

For a little while there was silence as the guests looked from Mikhl to Reb Dudi and back again, as if uncertain what to do or say about the intruder without permission from Reb Dudi himself. There was no question of attacking Mikhl just then, nor, though it occurred to some of them ... especially Yone and Zakharye, of tearing him to bits.

"Let him ..." Reb Dudi said. And it was clear that he meant first that Mikhl had permission to come in and second that it was forbidden for anyone to touch him, to interfere with him in any way until Reb Dudi had had an opportunity to clarify what it was that had brought him here. "Well, now what is it you want?" asked Reb Dudi when Mikhl stood near him.

"To repeat once more what I said yesterday," Mikhl replied. Everyone was amazed, especially Reb Dudi, who lately had been feeling a weakness in his limbs even when he was attending to calmer matters than this one. Now, seeing Mikhl, and hearing him repeat what he had said yesterday, Reb Dudi was so overwhelmed that he could hardly stand.

He felt his knees give and he grasped the table to steady himself. Then he turned to Mikhl again, but not in the manner of an interrogator who is indifferent to the fate of the accused who stands before him, but more as if he wanted him to emerge from the interrogation spotless and pure. Reb Dudi seemed rather to put words into Mikhl's mouth, words that would point him toward repentance.

"Why do you want to repeat what you said?" Reb Dudi asked.

"So that it may not be thought that what I said yesterday was spoken in a moment of madness or drunkenness."

"Perhaps it was. Think it over, Mikhl, son of ... ?" said Reb Dudi in his rabbinical style, as if he were presiding over a Levirate renunciation or over a divorce and was inquiring the names of the participants.

"Son of Sarah-Faygl," Mikhl responded.

"Well then, think, Mikhl, son of Sarah-Faygl, it may well be that you spoke in a moment of mental aberration, in anger, out of grief . . . in a state in which no one can be held responsible for his act."

"No. It was spoken with a clear and lucid mind."

"Then I take it that you are still of the same opinion."

"Yes," replied Mikhl.

"And you neither regret nor repent your words."

"No."

"And you fear neither the judgment of this world nor that of the World to Come?"

"No, because there is no law and there is no judge."

"In that case, in God's Name, and in the name of the community, I call you a betrayer of Israel, a sinner and one who conduces to sin."

"Rabbi!" A shout was heard. No. Not one shout, but many, but the loudest of all was the voice of Zakharye the tavern keeper who roared like a wild ox as he leaped up crying, "Rabbi! Just give the word and we'll make mud out of him."

"Mud," Yone echoed. Yone, who until now had had his hands behind his back, pushed his way through the crowd toward Mikhl.

"No," cried the rabbi, waving a trembling hand at the crowd, and interdicting especially the two tavern keepers who, as was clear from their furious faces, were determined to avenge the insult to the rabbi and who would indeed have fulfilled their threat to turn Mikhl into mud.

"No. Let no hand of ours touch him. Leave him to God." And so it was that no one touched him, and Mikhl left as he had come, unmolested by anyone. "Let God hold him to account."

"No, Rabbi. We'll hold him to account," cried Yone and Zakharye. "We will . . ."

The conversation remained an excitable one for the rest of the evening as the matter continued to be discussed. Arguments were often tumultuous and heated as Mikhl and the sect to which he belonged were excoriated. The bulk of the blame was directed at Luzi as its leader. The question foremost was, "What should be done about it?"

"Uproot the evil," one of the guests said.

"Destroy the nest," said another.

"They're not to be tolerated among Jews," cried a third.

"It's even worse than Yossele Plague . . . At least that fellow is not a member of the community . . . But these—they're like worms in one's own belly," came cries from all sides.

Naturally enough, a decision was arrived at that evening. The outcry took place in Reb Dudi's house, but it was heard by the whole of the Jewish community. And it follows, too, that because there was no way immediately to put one's hands on all those who might be guilty, Mikhl himself became the first target. As day followed day, fewer and fewer of his pupils showed up in the morning, until one day there was only one boy, and he was in any case so poor that Mikhl had never charged him a fee. On the following day, even that boy did not show up.

The whole thing smacked of an impromptu community excommunication. And its effects on Mikhl, on his wife and children, were soon evident. The household began to fast. In addition to that, chance (a bitter chance indeed) intruded an event into their lives in which pious bystanders were quick to see the hand of God who, as they would have it, pays sinners at once and in the appropriate coin for their deeds—though in fact it was the pious folk themselves who deserved such payment.

What happened was this. Winter arrived and there was no heat in Mikhl's house. In addition to that, the epidemic was going around that usually visits the homes of the poor where the ground is prepared for it at the end of the fall season. And the illness slipped into Mikhl's home. The first to be struck down was Berele, the oldest son, a puny lad with feet swollen from having worked from his earliest childhood for a knife grinder. The wind blew through the broken windows and reached the sick boy's bed so that it was not long before he was beyond the help of doctors or medicines and died.

There was no money for burial expenses and Mikhl had to bargain strenuously with the Burial Society, and later with its executive officer, who kept putting Mikhl off saying that the dead were plentiful enough and that there were others with higher priority and that Mikhl's dead would have to wait. It was not until the night of the second day after the boy's death that his body was taken from the house.

Mikhl's second son, Yankele, who worked for a bookbinder, was not to be outdone by his older brother and caught the illness from him. Berele's body was no sooner taken from the house than Yankele took his still warm place in bed. Nor did it take very long before Yankele died the way his brother had, and once again Mikhl ran about trying to persuade the Burial Society to do him a favor by removing the body of his second son.

And it was then, with the quick death of her second child, that Mikhl's wife, believing that the boy's death was not natural, grew distracted with grief. She felt that God was punishing the boys' father, Mikhl, for the accursed deeds he had recently committed. More, even, than she had raged over the bodies of her children, she ranted and raved against the living Mikhl: "Murderer. Assassin. You are the Angel of Death to your own children. Cry for help. Plead with the community, with the rabbi. Beg them to put out the fire. Plead for mercy."

And Mikhl made no reply. He stood, rigid as a stone, and looked down at the corpse lying on straw strewn over the miserable floor, lying with candles in two cheap candlesticks at its head. And all the while that his wife raged and cursed against him, Mikhl gave the impression that he was tempted to extinguish the candles that had been lighted for the dead. But in the end, he did not. He stood, rigid.

That, then, in the view of the Jewish community, was the first punishment from God. Later, and at the appropriate time, we will see what people did to get even with one who, as they saw it, deserved to be punished.

2.

As we will recall, there was a particular evening at Luzi's home when for certain particular reasons ownership of the deed to Moshe Mashber's house was transferred to Sruli Gol. The matter was expedited by Moshe's lawyer and financial counselor, Itsikl Zilburg, who had used every bit of his skill to see to it that there was not the tiniest loophole or ambiguity in the deed of transfer which any of Moshe's other creditors might take advantage of in order to file even the most minute claim to the property.

An agreement had been written which read: "On such and such a day, in the month such and such, in the year such and such, Moshe Mashber's house and the ground on which it stands, its courtyard, garden and every other structure including stables, storehouses and the like, are, in consideration of a sum specified that has been paid to the former owner, Moshe Mashber, now and in time to come the property of the new owner, Sruli Gol. Signed by Moshe Mashber, witnessed by a notary and stamped with his seal. No changes may be made in this agreement without the full consent of the party of the second part, the new owner, Sruli Gol."

And when Sruli Gol acquired this deed, prepared by Itsikl Zilburg's experienced hand . . . Itsikl had been unable to look Sruli Gol or (and especially) Moshe Mashber in the eye during the entire time that he, Itsikl, was busied with the document at the notary's. Sruli, at the moment when he acquired the document, though he felt a bit of moisture on the paper—a tear that Moshe had shed, perhaps. Or perhaps not.

But there was no doubt in Sruli's mind that he had seen a tear in Moshe's eye.

Though Sruli had foreseen this moment and prepared for it, now that he had the document in his hand he turned his eyes away from Moshe Mashber, and even averted them from Itsikl Zilburg and without so much as a "Good-bye" he left the notary's house and, turning his back on it, he went, for the second time since we have made his acquaintance, to a tavern.

But not, this time, to Sholem-Aron's tavern because he had no pleasant memories of Sholem-Aron from the last time he had visited his shop. He did not go to Zakharye's tavern either, because Zakharye kept a stand-up bar . . . a place for a quick drink only. His place was altogether too cramped for any sustained drinking, and so Sruli went to Yone's tavern which, because it was some distance away, would give him time to mull over how Moshe Mashber had looked at the notary's home while the transfer of the deed was being prepared. And to wonder what Moshe was doing now.

Sruli imagined that Moshe, among his other thoughts, was no doubt also thinking of Tsali Derbaremdiker. It was said of Tsali that whenever anyone in town who was on the verge of bankruptcy undertook to transfer the ownership of his shop or other property to someone else—a transaction that, naturally, took place at night when the goods in the shop were packed, weighed, measured or counted before they could be transferred to someone else's ownership, it was then, so it was said, that a knock was heard at the door. At first everyone was startled, but then someone would remember who it was who was likely to show up at such a moment—would remember that it must surely be Tsali who always managed to get his hooks into such a secret transaction by threatening to report it to the man's creditors. Tsali was quite capable of waking the whole town if need be, of creating an uproar. Everyone knew that. And so when he knocked at a door he did not come in when it was opened for him. He simply thrust his hand through the opening and everyone understood what it was that the hand wanted: money to prevent barking. And a certain amount was thrust into the outstretched hand with the hope that it would be enough. But generally Tsali, peering through the opening at what he had been given, would say, "Not enough." And more was added, because everyone knew that without it he would continue to stand there, and this could make people who were working at night by the light of a single lamp or candle extremely uncomfortable. Altogether a very undesirable event.

Yes. Moshe Mashber was undoubtedly thinking of Tsali Derbaremdiker's outstretched hand. And seeing Sholem Shmaryon, too. And, while Sholem did not stretch his hand out the way Tsali did but walked meekly, keeping close to fences to avoid being noticed, yet Sholem was Tsali's equal in every way. And in the given situation—Moshe Mashber's case—Sholem kept a lurking eye on Moshe's office so that he would know at once if anything was happening so that he, Sholem, might not lose a moment if action was required.

And, thought Sruli, Moshe must also be thinking of fellows like The Kitten who were no doubt keeping a sharp eye on his office and his home, keeping alert to take such advantages as might present themselves when Moshe's business came finally to its last gasp. They spied on him themselves or else they had their agents do it. People like Shmulikl Fist. And Sruli thought, too, that these days when Moshe Mashber went home from his office he must often find himself looking over his shoulder to see whether he was not being followed by someone who meant to shout something ugly or insulting behind his back—or perhaps to do even worse.

When Sruli reached Yone's tavern, he ordered drinks for two: for himself and for Moshe Mashber, as if Moshe were there with him as his drinking partner. Or as if, in addition to his own head, Sruli had borne Moshe's on his shoulders as well.

It must be understood that Yone was perfectly familiar with Sruli's position in the community. And he knew, too, just what his role was as regards Luzi. He was pleased to see Sruli in his tavern, though at first he could not precisely see how he could take advantage of the situation. Nevertheless, he looked upon Sruli in much the same way that a hunter might who saw his prey approaching his trap.

After a couple of drinks, Sruli, as he had in Sholem-Aron's tavern, began to talk confidentially to his glass. As he spoke, Yone made signs to the only other person who happened to be in the tavern just then, signs urging the fellow to eavesdrop on Sruli. At Yone's signal, the man, a ne'er-do-well and scoundrel, with slouching shoulders who looked out slyly from under the brim of his cap, returned Yone's signal as if to say that Yone might rest easy: he would not lose a word.

It was a long while since Sruli had last had anything to drink. And now, as we have said, Sruli was a man with two heads: his own and Moshe Mashber's. But it took only one drink for him to confuse the two. Then, since the two heads had only one tongue, he undertook to speak half drunkenly for them both.

"Maybe you know why I needed to get involved in this whole business. There are those who may think I'm a murderer, a highwayman who can only calm down by spilling blood, or that I'm still smarting from an insult that I can neither forget nor forgive. It's nothing like that at all. I swear by this brandy, that has nothing to do with it. The reason . . . it may be . . . is that I have been designated from on high to be your incarnate punishment, and that against my own will I am the whip wielded by your fate. And if that's the case, I swear by this brandy, I think you've been whipped enough.

"Eh. I saw Moshe at his brother's house in a certain situation. And I've also imagined the scene when Shmulikl Fist came to him on a particular occasion the details of which Shmulikl recounted to me later. Shmulikl had had to get himself good and drunk before he had been able to undertake The Kitten's business with Moshe. And however gently Shmulikl had borne himself in Moshe's house, he had nevertheless smashed his fist down on the table so hard that it had made the dishes rattle and the glassware in the cupboard and the panes of glass in the windows ring.

"As for that deed which I have in my pocket and which, or so it seems to me, has been dampened by a tear that you may—or may not—have shed . . . In any case, I saw it trembling in your eye . . . and if that's so, then perhaps, Sruli, you've had enough of being a whip. And it appears, doesn't it, that you've drunk your glass to the dregs and it must be time, therefore, to have it filled again as a consolation? Eh?" And here Sruli turned to Moshe Mashber as if seeking his assent.

"Yes," said Sruli. Then, assuming that Moshe had agreed, he turned to Yone's parasite and, mistaking him for a waiter, he asked him to be good enough to bring another glass because he wanted . . . he had in mind to . . . there was someone he wanted to treat.

"What? What is he saying?" Yone asked the fellow who passed Sruli's request on to him.

"I haven't the faintest idea. Except that he wants another drink," the fellow replied as he pointed his finger at his throat to indicate that Sruli was already drunk as a lord.

"Give him the drink. And pay attention to what he says."

"Why?"

"I have my reasons. Do what you're told."

When the waiter had brought Sruli what he ordered, Sruli stared at him for a while, perplexed, unable to remember what it was that he had just ordered. And when the waiter said, "A glass. You asked for a glass," Sruli remembered at last. "Yes, of course." And his eyes overflowing with tears, he filled his glass to overflowing intending it apparently for Moshe Mashber whom a moment before he had almost forgotten.

In the tavern, a midafternoon silence reigned. Except for the shirt-

sleeved Yone who stood behind the counter, and the underworld figure who did his bidding, and Sruli, who was already in a jolly mood,
the place was empty. From time to time, Sruli waved a finger of his
right hand before his eyes as if he was trying to warn himself about
something, though he seemed to forget immediately both the finger
and what it was he was warning himself about. When Yone's toady
gave him the glass of brandy, Sruli offered it to Moshe, his drinking
companion whom he imagined sitting opposite him and saying,
"Drink . . . and don't weep, Moshe Mashber, because it isn't you personally that the wielder of the whip has in mind. It's all of you . . . all
those like yourself. It's a form of allusion to the fact that those who are
on high can fall low while those below may be raised up high. As for
Sruli Gol, the rod, it may be that I do not regard fulfilling the wielder's
behest as a signal honor, and it's not something I get much pleasure
from. And you, who are sitting opposite me, Moshe Mashber, if you
want to know why I did it, it's all because I wanted to frustrate fate for
once—to pluck the rod from the wielder's hand—from fate's. That's
something I have wanted to do ever since I came to the age of reason.
Seeing how destiny exalts the unworthy and flings the others down, I
have tried this once to oppose it, to stand in its unpredictable way.
Though it may be that I did not do it for you, Moshe Mashber, but for
your brother Luzi who (can you keep a secret?) is very, very dear to
me. . . . Eh?"

"What's he going on about?" Yone asked the toady.

"I can't understand a word. He's talking with someone named
Moshe Mashber. About a secret . . . a hole . . . a whip . . . a rod . . .
blows . . . a stick and the devil only knows what else."

"You don't understand him? Well, let me do it," said Yone, taking
the fellow's place beside Sruli.

"Well," continued Sruli, who was utterly indifferent to what was
taking place behind him, "well, it's no great honor to be a rod, no matter whose hand is holding it. And, Moshe Mashber, I want you to
know, what I did was not a capricious act and not done to spite you. It
was something we all agreed on in Luzi's house. As for me it made no
difference. But for you it was shame and abasement. You care about
what the world will say . . . and now you haven't even got words to
express what you feel . . . only tears. And yet, the world has seen
worse. . . . Ah . . . ah . . . you're crying again. Clearly that's an indication of how drunk you are. Your head is all twisted around and you
ought to rest somewhere. You, Moshe . . . no . . . not Moshe . . . Sruli.
If you don't, the people here will take you for a drunkard and think ill
of you.

"Aha!" Sruli turned and saw Yone and his toady behind him. "Well, good people, what do you say? Can you find me a bed somewhere? Here, since I seem to be in no condition to get home."

"Of course," Yone said. "As long as you have the wherewithal to pay for it."

"Money. Of course I have money. How else does one pay." Sruli had his wallet out and started to pay first for his drinks and then for the bed which shortly they would be providing for him. Naturally, he paid, and overpaid, but even so, he was still left with a handful of money. Enough in any case to make the eyes of Yone's crony gleam like a cat's as he saw how little he would have to risk to get what he was perpetually in need of—money.

"Take him to Brokha's," Yone told him. And the fellow took Sruli's arm because Sruli, trying to get up from his chair, made it clear that he could hardly keep his balance. "Do what you like with him," Yone said. "Take whatever you want but let him have the full treatment." Putting Yone's words and gestures together, the fellow knew precisely what he had to do.

Brokha lived not far away in a back street in the Third Circle, where the houses seemed to have been built in the midst of huge empty spaces. No one standing outside their high walls would have believed that there were people in the world who would want to build a house or any other structure in a place like that.

One of those enclosures served as a safe house for people such as Perele and Iliovekhe of whom we have already spoken. These two did their business in the dark and, as far as possible, unobserved by anyone. It was in their house that pregnant young women lived until they gave birth to their babies. That enclosure was holy ground for Iliovekhe; it was there that she got rid of the "sucklings," the little "bastards" whom she cared for in a particular way—that is, by feeding them as little as possible until they turned yellow and green and without much delay gave up the ghost, leaving their beds free for others to take their place.

And it was there that Brokha lived. Brokha the Barrel Maker, as she was called. Not because her husband was a barrel maker. It was simply a dirty nickname and had to do with the way she earned her living. Here, for good and sufficient reasons, we will not clarify what the name really meant.

Brokha ran a house where, especially on Saturdays and holidays, young workingmen, alone or in groups, used to come and for whose pleasure Brokha provided a certain number of regular "women" with their room and board. And if her regulars were sometimes insufficient, Brokha could always turn to Perele's or Iliovekhe's newly delivered or soon-to-be delivered young women who for a small fee came to her aid.

The front room of the house smelled of rot, like an abandoned tavern. The walls were not whitewashed or else the whitewash had long since rubbed off. The ceiling was low, the floor was rough and splintered. There was no furniture in the room except for a rough-hewn table and chairs to match. There were a couple of pictures on the walls so that visitors might have something to look at in the event that they had to wait.

The first picture: a handsome Russian emperor with a sword in his hand and a lanyard across his chest, his face as pale as milk, like that of an angel in a chromo. He held his shako and one glove in one hand and one leg extended, cavalry fashion.

The second picture: a Turk wearing broad green trousers—gazing upon a naked woman rising out of a pool. This was a favorite viewing target for Brokha's visitors when they had to wait their turn.

Brokha, perhaps thirty years old, was a sprightly tall woman. When she saw a customer staring at the picture, she would slap him on the back in a comradely fashion and say, "What are you looking at? Looking only makes you drool. She'll be free soon," indicating the closed door of the room toward which the fellow was hankering.

Inside that unaired room that smelled of unlaundered bedding, there was a certain sort of bed on which certain kinds of women greeted the men. The women themselves gave off the sharp smells of various cheap foods.

Sometimes during the week when business was slow, a woman might spend some leisurely time with a customer. First in the front room, sitting with her bare warm arm around his shoulder. Then later in the other room she might stay a little longer with him than usual.

When in the full light of day Yone's toady led Sruli into Brokha's establishment, none of her regular women were in the house. But when the fellow had conveyed to Brokha just whom he had brought there and what would be required of her, she immediately went to one of the nearby houses—to Perele or to Iliovekhe—and brought back one of her women. The woman, breathing hard and still smelling of some acrid meal she had just eaten, approached Sruli and said, "Well, old fellow. What would you like?"

"From you? Nothing." Sruli, not understanding what she meant, looked curiously at her thin hoop earrings. "A bed. I want to sleep."

"Want to go bye-bye, eh? With . . . or without . . .?" the woman said impudently. She stepped close and looked into his eyes as she tried to put an arm around his shoulder. When Sruli turned abruptly away from her, she whispered something into his ear which, though Sruli was already drunk and had moreover not been involved in such things for a very long time, still what he heard made him feel suddenly sober at the same time he felt the effects of another kind of intoxication.

"Well?" Brokha's employee inquired.

Sruli's eyes cleared for a moment. He looked around the room and sensed that he had made some sort of mistake. That he was in the wrong place and that something unpleasant might happen to him here. But that moment of clear-mindedness did not last long and from then on whatever he remembered seemed all of it to be no more than a vague blur.

It seemed to him that he was lying in a bed with the woman who had whispered something immoral into his ear. And then it seemed to him that in addition to the woman there was a man in the room, standing beside the bed. It was the fellow who had brought him here from Yone's tavern. And that before the fellow came to stand beside the bed he had stood in the doorway of the room whispering to Brokha and making all sorts of gestures and signals to the woman in the bed meant to tell her what to do with him, Sruli.

And, furthermore, it seemed to him that Yone's toady came to the bed and moved him, Sruli, about as if he were a log. That the man went through his pockets and that—though it was shameful to admit this—when the fellow had taken whatever money Sruli still had after having paid his bill at Yone's, the fellow then rolled Sruli off the bed and took his place beside the woman. And what happened after that was altogether too shameful to report.

And furthermore it seemed to him that after he had lain on the floor for a while and had begun little by little to sober up, he saw that the room began to fill up with various crude folk who came in from the streets and neighboring houses of that remote district. And all of them were like the fellow who had brought him to Brokha's from Yone's tavern. And Brokha's women, too, were there, a crowd of women with loose skirts and low-cut, unbuttoned blouses and hoop earrings who cackled and laughed and pinched themselves when they saw him lying there on the floor, and they said obscene things to him. Then the men lifted him up off the floor and got him ready to go: they put his cap on backward and led him to the door. And it was then that Brokha's women, as if they had been offended, cried loudly enough so that the whole street, the whole neighborhood, could hear, "Pervert. Whore-monger. Going to women in broad daylight." And then, when others in the street came running, there were those who cried, "Hey, they caught him with a woman. Pull his pants down. Take the old sinner to the rabbi. Grab him. Take him, the old fool."

Oh, it was shameful. It was lucky for him that the fellow who had searched his pockets had not taken the Mashber deed which Sruli happened to have on him. The fellow had, no doubt, seen it, but not knowing what it was or what it was worth, had put it back. It was lucky, too, that there were no hotheads in the crowd to whom it might have occurred to drag him into the lower part of town and set him up there as a spectacle that would have drawn a larger crowd than a rich wedding or an important funeral. And lucky, too, we say, that they did not treat him even more shamefully—as often happens in such houses of ill repute where they pull a man's trousers down, or make him wear a sieve stuck through with feathers, or turn his coat inside out.

Yes, that, too, might have happened ... but no matter how little damaged Sruli was from his shameful exposure, still there was more than enough shame to have satisfied even Yone the tavern keeper had he seen it. Because though only a small crowd had seen Sruli, and nothing more had been done to him than that his cap was reversed, he made, nevertheless, such a sorry sight that Sruli shuddered remembering it later when he was sober.

He remembered that he kept moving as the crowd shouted at him, and that he had trouble keeping on his feet, that he wobbled and stumbled frequently over the stones and almost fell, and that he actually did fall, but the insults shouted at him brought him to his feet and he went on only to stumble and fall again.

He was ready to swear that when he came to his own street he fell and lay against a wall, certain that he could not make it to his house; and that there was someone there, some familiar person, who kept pushing through the circle of bullies and idlers to offer him his hand, to help him get back on his feet. But when whoever it was saw that Sruli was too weak to move on, he tried at least to drive the crowd of scamps away. "Why are you hounding him like this? Go on, beat it," he cried. And always it seemed to Sruli that he recognized the man's voice, and that he could almost say his name, but the drink had impaired his memory and he could not get it out. But even if had been able to speak the name, it seemed to him that pure shame would have kept him from pronouncing it.

It may be that it was someone from Luzi's sect who happened to be there just then. At other times it seemed to him (alas!) that it was Luzi himself who bent over him and touched him lightly. And that made him feel so ashamed that he turned his head away.

In a word, Sruli, though he recalled those hours of drunkenness, yet he remembered them only vaguely. He knew on the one hand what had actually happened, but he had, too, a sense of what else might have taken place. For example, that he had not lain innocently in the bed beside the woman who lived in Brokha's house.

Luzi heard the whole story a few days later. From whom? From Sruli himself who did not want Luzi to hear it from anyone else. Sruli neither hid nor denied any particle of all that had happened, and he made no effort to excuse himself—not even concerning those matters about which his guilt was doubtful. As, for instance, whether he had sinned with the whore in Brokha's house—which he very much doubted.

Luzi, hearing Sruli's account, was amazed. But he said nothing. Despite the fact that he knew that the whole town was in an uproar over the Mikhl Bukyer incident and that this matter of Sruli's would serve to splatter additional shame on Luzi and on all those who were close to him. Luzi knew all that and yet said nothing. It is true that Luzi could not bring himself to blame Sruli because it was clear from what Sruli told him that he, Sruli, had not gone to Brokha's house of his own free will. There one could discern someone else's hand: Yone, the tavern keeper's. Yone who for reasons of his own had seen to it that Sruli was led to the house of ill repute.

Yes, it is certainly true that had someone else been in Luzi's place, he would certainly have reproached him for drinking in general and particularly for drinking in a place like Yone's. Sruli himself had characterized Yone as the sort of man with whom no respectable person ought to have any dealings, or to cross the threshold of his tavern. Then why was it that he had crawled into the lion's den?

No. Luzi said nothing. And all the while Sruli talked, Luzi kept his head down to avoid shaming him. And not to prolong the interview, Luzi retired to his bedroom as soon as he had heard Sruli out.

That second room, small and badly lighted because the room's single window, which in any case gave very little light, had had a curtain drawn across it to keep strangers from peering in—as in that part of town people would if there was no curtain. There was a table in the room, a couple of chairs, a daybed. And a simple rug. There was one small corner of the room left bare where Luzi was accustomed to stand next to the wall when he recited the Eighteen Benedictions or practiced isolation.

Whenever he went in, he put the latch on the door as an indication that he did not want to be disturbed. It was a signal profoundly respected by Sruli who never disturbed Luzi at such times, and permitted no one else to.

Had anyone looked in on Luzi at such a time, he would have seen him standing in his corner with his head almost touching the wall as if he were expecting a door to open there. It was Luzi's hour for prayers, but he did not recite them in the traditional way by reading them out of a book. Instead, he turned to God with an overflowing heart and spoke directly to Him in Yiddish, as Nakhman of Bratslav had taught his disciples to do: "Father in heaven," Luzi said, taking up his position against the wall from which a living warmth seemed to flow into him, "You who carry on Your shoulders the weight of all three hundred and ten worlds with all of their suns and moons and stars, all of whom exist by grace of Your holy breath which gives them life and justification . . . Lord, forgive your creatures in this lower world who are no more than the dust of the earth, and from whom You can expect little enough.

"Forgive among others," Luzi prayed, "a creature like Mikhl Bukyer who dares, alas, in his absolute nothingness to oppose himself to You. But what value can the opposition of one who is as clay in the potter's hands have before You? In Your hands he either is or is not, as a wind may be here and then vanish. And Lord, forgive as well a creature like Sruli Gol from whom I have but just now heard—ah, Lord, what I have heard— And well for him if he did not experience all that may have happened to him, and yet even if he did, still there would not be the slightest shadow on Your honor nor any spot on Your garment.

"I pray for them as I would pray for myself, as if I had been in their place where, certainly, I would have done as they have done, and then perhaps they would be standing before the wall praying *for me* as I now pray for them. It has been said that the world was designed that way so that everyone is a pledge for his fellow creature, and every person must regard himself as a sharer with everyone else, whether of good or of evil. Otherwise, what would become of the human race which, dear Father in heaven, You have created for trouble and pain.

"Forgive and excuse," Luzi prayed and stood before his wall for a long time because the current of prayer had been roused in him and he felt a sweet essence surging from his mouth—the compassion of a man who is himself in dire straits but who at the same time has fellow feeling for the pain of others.

He stood beside his wall for a long, long time. As if he had become a part of it. When finally Luzi went back into the other room where Sruli had been waiting all that while, Luzi had the look of a man who had just bathed in holy waters. His face was damp—evidently from tears—but there was rejoicing in his eyes, and his demeanor was that of a man who comes from a place where after prolonged knocking at a high gate, he has received something—for himself or for someone else.

It was then that Sruli approached Luzi. A strange and abrupt approach, as was often the case with him. So that one could never know, from one moment to the next, what he might do. And now he handed Luzi a piece of paper.

"What is it?" asked Luzi.

"It's the deed to your brother's house. Signed over to me awhile ago."

"Well?"

"I don't want to have it in my possession."

"Why not?"

"Because I've already come near losing it, or having it fall into the wrong hands. On that day when I . . . happened into that house about which I told you. I'm afraid something like that might happen again."

"Again?" A shadow was visible crossing Luzi's forehead.

"Yes. There's no way I can guarantee my behavior."

"Then leave it at home."

"No. I'm afraid to leave it at home. I might be tempted to make use of it in some way."

"In what way," Luzi asked.

"I might want to borrow money on it. And that would be very bad for your brother, because his other creditors would get wind of it and there might be a premature run on his funds which would deprive him of the time he needs to work his way out of his troubles. Remember, too, that you're my guarantor. You assured your brother that the document was in safe hands. And that no ill use would be made of it."

It has to be said here that all of this was simply Sruli's way of testing how much confidence Luzi had in him. That is, of testing whether Luzi would believe that Sruli's word could not be counted on. And one has to say also that at first Luzi did not understand that, but that later he sensed that the weaknesses Sruli charged himself with were mostly imagined, and that in fact Sruli was quite capable of standing firm. Of keeping his word.

"No," said Luzi, with a wave of his hand as he gave the document back to Sruli, "I don't want it. I know I can count on you."

"Well, suppose the instinct for evil and the instinct for good should get mixed up and a situation develops in which I may want to help someone like Mikhl Bukyer, for example. You know of course that he has been abandoned by everyone, that he is losing his income and that in addition to the tragic loss of his two boys, he risks losing the rest of his family—his wife and other children. If I wanted to help him out, I would need money, but all I have in the way of assets is the deed. And since there's no way to eat the deed itself, who knows what I might do with it before your brother is finally able to buy it back? What do you say to that?"

"You'll have to do what you think best. You have good judgment in such matters. You'll know what to do." And he said again, "No. I don't want the deed."

Sruli, as if reluctantly, put the deed back in his pocket, but there was a gleam of satisfaction in his eyes and a smile on his face because Luzi had expressed absolute confidence in him. He felt his soul expand into a holiday mood and, having mentioned Mikhl to Luzi, Sruli was seized with a sense of urgency to help Mikhl Bukyer in some way. But just as in his impetuous fashion he started off to do something about it, the door of Luzi's house opened and there stood—Mikhl himself.

It was the period when Mikhl was still in mourning for his second son. He was wearing a shabby unlined cloak that gave him very little protection from the cold, so that he had to hunch his head and shoulders. It was freezing outside, though no snow had yet fallen. The autumnal mud—especially the deep muddy streets of the third ring, had frozen into great protruding clumps and clods.

Mikhl came in looking blue with the cold. His reddish beard had an untidy gray look to it now. The lines in his face were deeply carved and seemed to have loam in them.

He had just left his home where a lamp guttered in the window beside a rag and a glass of water—objects traditionally found in a home where someone has died. Mikhl's wife sat on the floor on a pillow without a pillowcase. Her remaining children, having nothing to do but think about the dead and about themselves, wandered about the house looking as if they were half dead.

Mikhl, during the period of mourning, had paced about his house, sometimes in one room, sometimes in another, sometimes through both. He went from one wall to another. Today he suddenly stopped pacing, caught up his cloak and, without knowing where he was off to, left the house.

Why he ended by going to Luzi's house instead of to someone like Yossele Plague's we do not know. Perhaps because Luzi's house was closer. Or it was because he was still unclear about the way to Yossele's house—or because he may have thought he would not be at ease there. Whichever it was, the minute he was out of the house and felt himself seized by the wind that had put a fine scrim of frost over the frozen ground, he turned his steps toward Luzi's house.

According to custom, Mikhl, because he was in mourning, was not greeted when he came in. Seeing Luzi at the head of the table and Sruli at one side, Mikhl, without waiting for an invitation, sat down opposite Sruli. Now there ensued a scene that was played out in uninterrupted silence. Luzi looked quietly at Mikhl who kept his eyes lowered. Sruli—for no clear reason—smiled. Perhaps touched again by a feeling of holiday joy he had experienced earlier.

Without further delay, and before Luzi or Mikhl had said a word, Sruli left the house.

And now there began for Sruli another of his strange wild days when, seized by an idea, he achieved in an hour what would have taken others ten days to do.

He went to the market and bought a wagonload of wood and hired a man to chop it up, then he and the woodchopper accompanied the wagon to Mikhl's house.

He entered the freezing house. Inside, the only light came from the lamp at the window. He invented a story to explain the wood delivery to Mikhl's wife—who had no idea why it should have come to her. When the woodchopper had cut the first bits of kindling, Sruli laid and lighted a fire, complaining that *he* was cold and that he wanted to see what a fire looked like in the stove.

Having explained to Mikhl's wife that Mikhl's friends had sent the wood, Sruli slipped her some money so that she could get her hands on some food for the children who had not seen a fire in the stove nor smelled the smell of cooking in a long while.

Having done that, Sruli said that she ought to know that when the time came to "close" the children's graves in the cemetery, all the arrangements had already been made with the watchman; and that all fees had been paid—again, said Sruli, by the same friends that had sent the wood and the money.

That done, Sruli left Mikhl's house. Out in the street he ran into

Shmulikl Fist. The pale film over Shmulikl's eye gave it a half-closed, sleepy look. His clear eye was bright—the result, evidently, of a drink Shmulikl had just taken.

"Hey, Shmulikl," cried Sruli, "you're just the man I want to see."

"What for?" a drunken Shmulikl grumbled.

"First, where have you been keeping yourself all this while? And, hey, the Luzi folk are having a dinner tonight. Why don't you come? You'll be more than welcome.

"And then . . ." Here Sruli dropped his voice and looked around to see that nobody was within earshot. "And then . . . I want you to remember something. If sometime soon The Kitten should want to send you on a certain errand to Moshe Mashber—in a case that might involve bankruptcy—just remember, whatever The Kitten offers to pay you, I'll double it if you don't go. And that's not all: I want you to keep any other enforcers from going. Do you understand?"

"Understand? Of course I understand. Do you think I'm dumb? Of course I won't go. No matter how much Kitten offers."

"Good," said Sruli. "Remember, come to the dinner tonight." With that he turned to go because he had something important to do before it was time for the dinner. He was on his way to Brokha's house.

To Brokha's house?

Yes. And though he had some trouble finding it—because when he was there last he had been quite drunk—still, with careful searching, he came to it.

When he came into the house, Brokha, as she had been when he came there the first time, was alone. Sruli studied her for a while, as if he did not at once recognize her, then in the familiar tone of an old acquaintance, he said, "Ah, it's Mother Bawdyhouse."

"Bawdyhouse? What are you talking about?" said Brokha, surprised and a bit frightened.

She recognized Sruli, and remembering that in addition to the various insults heaped on him when he was last there, his pockets had been emptied, she worried lest he had come to demand his money back. She knew, furthermore, that anyone else who had wandered into a house such as hers and who had been treated—and plundered—in the same fashion would have taken great care not to come back again. He would have avoided coming near the street or so much as turning his head in its direction. So that if *he* was here again, it was an indication that he felt himself powerful enough to retake by force what had been taken from him, using teeth and claws if need be. Or, she concluded, it might be that he had an accomplice nearby on whose help he counted.

"Bawdyhouse?" she said again. "What do you mean?"

"Just look at her, the poor little kid who doesn't know what we're talking about," Sruli said in his most familiar manner—as if he were accustomed to slapping people on the back. "Don't play the fool," he said. "Bring what's ordered."

"What? Whom?"

"A woman."

"What are you talking about?" Brokha cried, raising her voice as if she expected her neighbors to hear and to come to her aid.

"I'll pay for two," he said. Brokha could see that she was not dealing here with some yokel. When she saw the wallet he produced, she softened her manner considerably.

"Hey, do you really mean it?"

"Actually, I don't want just any woman. I want you."

"What? What are you saying?" Brokha stammered, embarrassed.

"Not for . . . that. I need you to be a witness."

"A witness? To what?"

"If it happens that today . . . or tomorrow . . . you are asked what happened when I came to your house, I want you to tell what you know. The whole truth: that I was drunk, and that I neither came here nor left of my own free will."

"Of course that's what I'll say," said Brokha, clucking her tongue as Sruli counted money out for her.

His business done, Sruli turned and left without a word of farewell. Outside, he peered about, trying to identify landmarks in the event that he had to come back here at night. After that he went into town to shop for the dinner planned for that evening.

While Sruli was taking care of his errands, Luzi and Mikhl were having a quiet encounter which earlier we did not describe but about which we want to say a few words now.

Mikhl, finding himself face-to-face with Luzi, allowed himself to say all that he had repressed during his mourning. He told how he had been avoided by everyone, how he and his wife and children were getting poorer daily. "Well, perhaps I have it coming. But why must they suffer?"

He went on to say that he knew whom it was that he had offended: people who ascribe to God all the lesser characteristics with which, alas, they themselves as creatures of flesh and blood are endowed: envy, hatred and so on. The very greatest and most devout Jewish scholars have inveighed against ascribing lesser human characteristics to God. And not only the lesser . . . even the most exalted human attributes must not be ascribed to Him. Because how can one measure the Superhuman with merely human perceptions?

"Those people," continued Mikhl, "say that the death of my two children is my punishment sent by the Holy Name because I have rejected His service. It is written, they say, that 'The sins of the fathers shall be visited upon the children.' And they forget what was said in later times: that one must endeavor to explain the Torah so that even unlettered men will understand it. And that if those lines about 'the sins of the fathers' were literally true, they would be among the most bloodthirsty ever written."

It was unheard of because someone else would not have permitted the slightest hint of such words to reach his ears because they were forbidden to the pious.

It would be a mistake to suppose that Luzi regarded Mikhl as being out of his mind and that he excused him on that account. It is more likely, given the era and its customs, that Luzi saw Mikhl's break with the community as an exceptional event. And clearly, Luzi, too, was an exceptional person. If Luzi listened to Mikhl patiently it was not, heaven forbid, that Luzi was a less pious man than he was reputed to be. It was, rather *because* he was a member of an especially pious sect and because, as has been said, he was himself something of an exceptional figure, even within that sect.

It would require an entirely separate treatise to explain how someone like Luzi had been brought to open his home to people like, for example, Shmulikl Fist. Shmulikl, whose scandalous reputation and violent deeds are already known to us. It is utterly contradictory—utterly ununderstandable—how someone whose hands were stained with the blood of the innocent as well as the guilty . . . and blood-stained for the sake of money . . . how such a person could be permitted to enter one's doors. Strange. Others would have turned their eyes away from the very sight of him. And yet there he was, with free entrée into Luzi's home.

Because, yes. This needs to be clarified.

It was because on more than one occasion a fellow like Shmulikl at whom the entire town might look askance, and who was regarded with revulsion and fear . . . it happened that when such a person was received by the sect, and was made to feel therefore that the doors of repentance were not closed even to him . . . it had happened that such a person had turned his back abruptly on his past. That he had burst into tears one day in the presence of the members of the sect who until then had regarded him merely as an indifferent guest who kept himself apart and uncommitted . . . that he had burst into tears and pleaded for them to accept him as one of them. That had happened, we say, and when it did, it was not only because of the nature of the sect itself, but more particularly because of the way that its leader stood before it, for the sake of purity and spiritual betterment, as a man half or entirely condemned, as one who was nearly or entirely lost.

And that was how he had treated Shmulikl and that's how, now, he was with Mikhl. And that may be why Luzi listened so patiently to Mikhl's bitter words of rejection, neither interrupting nor turning away to avoid hearing words that anyone else in a similar situation would have regarded as being a revolting assault on his ears.

Luzi listened attentively to all of this. And, wonderful to relate, he seemed actually to agree with what Mikhl was saying. And indeed there was the trace of a smile on his face as he listened—and that was truly astonishing.

But in fact Luzi was smiling not because he was in accord with Mikhl's words, but rather because he chanced to remember that Sruli, earlier in the day, had, a moment before Mikhl appeared at the door, spoken Mikhl's name and linked it to the use he might make of the deed to his brother's house which he asked Luzi to take from him lest he, Sruli, might need to make use of it. In the event that he might need money, for instance, to support someone like Mikhl. Luzi knew well that if Sruli had made up his mind to something he would not rest until he had accomplished it. Certainly, thought Luzi, the fact that Sruli had absented himself from the house just as Mikhl came into it—that was done so that Mikhl's family might get the help it needed (behind his back as it were) at the same time as he was spared embarrassment.

And indeed, as we know, that is what happened. And that is why when Mikhl poured out his bitter grief and then added that he had not come for consolation—because he knew that mankind was dust, and dust was his consolation—he had come because he could not bear to be at home with the sorrows of his wife and children before his eyes. When Mikhl added this observation, to which Luzi said not a word, it was immediately evident what a great weight had been taken from Mikhl's shoulders, if only because he had been able to speak openly and directly.

Mikhl felt better, too, because Luzi's house was well heated and the pleasant warmth served to drive the cold from his limbs and to relax him. And then when Sruli, having done his errands in town, came home bearing a full basket, his hands and his pockets full of delicacies—and liquor—intended for the evening's festivities . . . and when Sruli invited Mikhl to wash up and to taste of the things he had brought, Mikhl did not decline. He washed his hands, then took his place at the table where he was offered some of everything that was there. And it was evident that Mikhl was delighted, not only by the food itself, but also by the manner in which it was offered and the generosity with which it was served to him.

Neither Luzi nor Sruli watched Mikhl as he ate. While he was appeasing his hunger, they averted their glances and acted as if they were involved with something else altogether. When Mikhl was done, he left Luzi quietly, with no trace of contention about him. On the contrary, he left feeling that Luzi's door would always be open to him, just as it had been in the past, and as if nothing had changed between them.

And it was then that the spirit of celebration descended upon Sruli. He was overtly cheerful and relaxed, a consequence on the one hand of the various labors he had accomplished that day and on the other because of the way Luzi had just treated Mikhl. He turned energetically to the preparations for the evening's festivities as if he were undertaking the first work of the day.

He pushed all the tables in the house together, forming from wall to wall a single long table in the room where the gathering was to take place. Then he set benches in place and put such tablecloths as Luzi owned upon the tables. At each place where a guest was expected to sit, he set out plates, knives, spoons and forks. And everything he did was done with a broad hand. Generously. Not as was done in poverty-stricken homes on the occasion of a sparse meal when there were not plates or silverware enough to serve the guests and one knife had to accommodate all the guests at a single table. Nor was his preparation for the meal all hugger-mugger, catch-as-catch-can.

This time, Sruli's provision of food and liquor for the evening had been carefully thought out. He gathered all the lamps in the house and set them on the tables so that the house might be brighter than usual. And when everything was ready, he passed the practiced eye of a skillful waiter over his work and if he noticed that something was missing that was not to be found in Luzi's home, then he went at once to a neighbor's and asked to borrow what was needed. And there is reason to think that that evening, when he was concerned that there might not be enough liquor, he went into town to buy some more.

That night after the second evening prayers were over, Luzi's guests began to gather. Luzi's poverty-stricken people squinted against the unaccustomed light of three lamps instead of the usual one at the table, and they were dazzled by the unaccustomed table setting. It was then that Sruli Gol, exhausted from his long day of hustling and bustling, sat down in a corner of the room, as if it was not he who had made all the preparations for the evening, as if he had nothing to do with the unusual brightness of the room, with the expanded table laid with a white cloth, with the variety of courses and the supply of brandy. He sat in a corner as if none of that had anything to do with him, and waited for the guests to be seated. Later when more food needed to be brought to the table, it was he who brought it, like a host who does not partake of his own dinner because he prefers to please his guests by serving them. And he particularly saw to the comfort of those of the guests who, coming late, could find no place at the table and had to stand.

That included various of the inhabitants of The Curse who, having seen the unusually bright light shining in Luzi's window and deducing from it the promise of a festivity, had come in uninvited. Sruli made it his business to please these folk as well and welcomed the cripples and the deranged ... people like Wednesday and Ten Groschen Pushke who had been drawn to the house by the bright light, and who, having edged their way through the kitchen quietly and on tiptoe, contented themselves with looking on at the festivities some portion of which might fall to their share.

At the table itself there were a number of the Luzi people whom we have already met: Avreml, the Three Yard Tailor, with the scrawny neck and enlarged Adam's apple; Menakhem, the harelipped dyer; Yankele Eclipse. The Couple and still others whom we will not list because we are well acquainted with them. There was also a small number of newcomers to the sect who felt themselves not quite at ease. Finally, there was Shmulikl Fist, the enforcer who had eagerly accepted the invitation he had received earlier in the day.

Some of the courses of the meal had already been eaten, and considerable brandy had been drunk. The cheeks of the famished members of the sect acquired a rosy tinge as they relaxed. In a little while they would begin to sing, and after that, in the very midst of the festivities, they would dance until they were drenched to the skin.

But just as all eyes were turned to the one among them who usually led them in song, another sound was heard. A quite unexpected sound from one side of the room—a musical instrument of some sort. Everyone's eyes turned toward the side of the room where the inhabitants of The Curse had stood in a cluster. And there they saw Sruli with a flute between his lips. The same flute with which he used to entertain newlyweds. The guests turned toward Luzi inquiring silently whether it was fitting for Sruli to appear before them playing on a flute. And whether it was permitted for them to listen.

They read good-humored assent in the smile on Luzi's face, though it was clear that he, too, found Sruli's appearance strange and that he, like them, was curious to hear what music Sruli would make.

They were entranced. Those who were sitting at the table and those who were standing. As well as people like the Wednesdays and the Ten Groschen Pushkes who had crowded into the kitchen and who, hearing his instrument, moved to the door of the foyer and stretched their necks toward Sruli.

Then Sruli played. And now he surpassed himself. His tone was so pure, the notes he struck so remarkable, that his hearers immediately forgot the poverty of their lives and who they were. Sruli seemed to have led them to a lofty palace, a spacious structure built on an appropriately elevated site amid splendid surroundings. A palace with a gate closed against intruders and against those who were unworthy to enter.

And it seemed that Sruli stood before that gate—Sruli and his listeners whom he had brought with him. And as he played he seemed to be persuading the gates to open for them because they were worthy of that honor.

"It is what they deserve," his flute seemed to say. "Now, they are the poor and the disappointed. But who can say what tomorrow will bring or who will inherit the earth on the day after tomorrow?"

With that the gate opened. Sruli and those who were with him went in. At first those who followed him felt constrained and embarrassed, because they were not sure that they had been admitted because of their own merits. But Sruli walked before them, encouraging them with the sort of music one plays to welcome guests into a palace.

And then they entered halls that were richly decorated and where there were tables with beautiful place settings. And there were people sitting there, like those whom Sruli had just brought in. They, too, were poorly clad, they, too, were sorry-looking, but they were relaxed and happy and hospitably made place for the newcomers and encouraged them to feel at ease.

Then the owners of the palace came in. They were beautifully dressed and gave the impression that they had never before had anything to do with the sorts of people Sruli had brought there, and yet they were proud of their guests. They sat with them and shared food and drink with them. Later, when they had eaten and drunk, and the newcomers started to dance, the owners of the palace danced feverishly with them all until, for sheer joy, the palace roof began to rise and all who were there cried, "Let the world be free. Let all who will come share our celebration. Everyone, from the highest to the lowest, the wise as well as those who have but a penny's worth of wit. All. All. And not only people, but the creatures of the forest and the cattle in the fields are welcome too."

And then as the ceiling rose one saw that it was a bright starry night. And then a group of old men dressed in a variety of garments came in out of the cold. They carried candles in their hands as if they were going to a wedding. And they were followed by a crowd of wanderers, people who carried staffs of walnut wood and who had sacks over their shoulders. They were the kinds of people who never have a roof over their heads. And following them—just imagine!—herds of field cattle . . . no, not field cattle. These animals came from poorly built stables that sheltered them so poorly from the cold that they still had rime on their hides. And they seemed to be looking for someplace warm where they could give birth to their young.

And that's what they did. There was a soft lowing of cows, then the bleating of nanny goats, and the baaing of ewes—as calves, kids and lambs were born by the joyful light of the candles the old men carried. And when all the creatures had finally emerged from their mothers' wombs, the old men turned to those in the palace and cried, "Congratulations. Congratulations to the world." While outside in the cold night a green and gold star shone over the heads of those who had witnessed those many births.

"Baa, baa."

"Congratulations."

And here, Sruli broke off abruptly, as he always did when he played. And again he managed to give his audience the feeling that they were still in the grip of their vision, and that the flute was still in his mouth, though in fact it had been in his pocket for some minutes past.

It was a shepherd's song of some sort that had so entranced the guests that those who were at the table sat with their mouths open. Those who were standing had no sense that they were on their feet. The cripples and the half-demented people of The Curse, the Wednesdays and Ten Groschen Pushkes, stood with outstretched necks and gaped toward the vestibule. Sruli's playing elicited an occasional laugh from them, sometimes even an enthusiastic shriek.

They felt themselves under the spell of his music even after it was over. They could still see the images his playing had set before their eyes: the grief because of which Sruli had played the march for those he brought with him; the mutual rejoicing with the owners of the palace; the old men holding candles in their hands and the cattle giving birth—baa, baa ... congratulations. In all of which the listeners had felt, masterfully expressed, some touch of their own fate.

All eyes were on Sruli, as if they were all hoping to hear more. And still more. But all at once someone whispered, "Hush. Hush. Luzi's going to talk." This was a rare enough event, because Luzi was sparing with speech and usually delegated someone else to make the discourse the members of the sect expected on such occasions. And now without anyone having requested it, he was about to speak—a clear indication that he, too, had been moved by Sruli's music.

Yes. Luzi, too, had had a full day. First, hearing from Sruli an account of all that had happened. Then sequestering himself to pray beside the wall of his room as he begged forgiveness for Sruli on the other side of the wall—and for Mikhl, who showed up a little later and who, as we will recall, stayed for a considerable while. And now this celebration which he had watched Sruli prepare as if it were on his own account, working hard to make everything come out just right. Then the pleased Sruli playing his flute.

Evidently it was all these events that made Luzi modify his usual routine. Especially when he saw how the ears of his guests pricked up because of Sruli's playing. It was then that Luzi felt an impulse not to let the attention Sruli's playing had quickened in them subside and to scatter some seed of his own over the field that Sruli had just plowed.

"Beloved fellow Jews," he began quietly, speaking in short, terse phrases, "Blessed is Israel whom neither exile nor the fact that he has been driven from his father's table has kept him from feeling that he is a child of God, and chosen to live in the Kingdom to Come.

"Let not the nations of the world rejoice," he went on, "with their generous portion and let them not regard Israel with contempt though his shame is as black as the tents of Kedar. Yes, it is true that Israel now has the poorer portion and lives under the threat of the swords dangling over his head, that he is compelled to beg his sustenance at the hands of all sorts of murderers and assassins. Yet let them not rejoice at his woes, nor let them despise Israel.

"The light of redemption is coming. That which was prophesied will come. But even now there are holy men, as there always have been in every generation when Israel was beset with trials and tribulation ... holy men who undertake to interpret Israel's destiny and to guide him with love and compassion along his thorny way, holy men who are willing to intercept with their own bodies the spears and arrows intended for Israel. And this wish is shared, too, by those intimates of the holy men whose happy grace it is to have experienced the exalted sorrow of Israel, who is himself the suffering and grieving heart of the world.

"Israel is loved because of his sorrows, because he gives to the world an example of constancy, because he holds fast to his vision even with the knife against his throat. Israel is loved, because in his darkened eyes there rests a tiny opening through which he continues to look toward the coming redemption. Redemption not only for himself, but for all those on whose account he is the blessed sufferer and for whom he is a reminder of the promise that there will come a time when the tears of all the world will be dried.

"A time is coming," Luzi continued, warming to his theme, "that will be filled with hope. When a wedding canopy will be erected on the holy mountain. Wise men and saints from all the world, wearing crowns on their heads and carrying candles in their hands, will surround the Anointed One in their midst, and the people of the world will follow after them: man and wife and child. And not only mankind. Beasts, cattle and fowl will rise up to be filled with the knowledge and the joy of that day. Every wise man and his disciples and admirers; every prophet and those who have been nourished by their pure speech and hallowed deeds. All those who have tended to the holy fire, defending it against storm and wind, and who have kept it from going out in the dark.

"I urge you, therefore, my brothers in Israel, to guard the light that is your inheritance until the time of the Messiah when every knee will bend before the Saviour. And all heads will bow to receive His blessing. All men, as well as all other creatures that have the breath of life . . . a living soul.

"Guard the flame," said Luzi, becoming even more animated. His audience stared eager to hear more, and still more of his consoling words, more about the exalted mission of the holy man in which all who stood near him would have a part.

"Ah, ah," his listeners groaned with pleasure at the vision of an end to general as well as particular human sorrow. "Ah, ah," they groaned, pleased to think that they carried beneath their tunics the light whose glow they must guard until the coming of the Messiah—as the Rebbe Nakhman of Bratslav had promised. "Ah, ah."

The guests were still entranced by what they had heard when suddenly there was a crash and a stone came flying through a front-room window. In addition to shattering the glass, the stone just missed cracking somebody's head (and came close to Luzi, too, for whom it may have been intended).

The startled guests looked about wildly. The cluster of cripples gathered at the kitchen door began slowly, slowly, to disperse and made their way out the back door. The guests who had been standing beside the table in the front room began to stir restlessly; so, too, did those who were seated. Sruli alone, of all those in the room, grasped what had happened and what needed to be done.

With a quick nod he alerted Shmulikl Fist, who was sitting at the table, to follow him out of the house where if they were lucky they might catch the stone thrower and give him what was coming to him.

Sruli understood at once that the flung stone was but a sequel to what had been done to him at Brokha's house where he had been led when he was drunk, and, if certain people had their way, it was also a presage of things to come.

He squeezed his way through the crowd, and when he and Shmulikl were outdoors, they set themselves like hunting dogs on the trail of the rock thrower, but though they searched everywhere they found no one and had no choice but to abandon their plans for vengeance. Near the house they ran into a tall individual whose face in the dark they did not recognize. The tall man, seeing Sruli and Shmulikl, asked, "Does Luzi Mashber live here?"

"Yes. What do you want?"

"I want . . . I've been sent by Rabbi Dudi to give him a message."

The three of them went into the house through the kitchen and from there to the front room where they found those who were assembled there still shaken by what had happened. The tall newcomer looked toward the head of the table where he immediately recognized Luzi, the man whom he sought. But wanting to make sure he turned and asked, "Is that Luzi Mashber?"

"Yes. Yes."

"I've been sent by the town rabbi to say that he, Reb Dudi, would like to have Reb Luzi come to his house as soon as possible. Today. The matter is important."

The tall man was Long Melekh, Reb Dudi's servant. When he had delivered his message, he stood there, disconcerted by the atmosphere in the room, disconcerted, too, by the inexplicable look of distress on the faces of those who were there. With nothing further to say for himself, he just stood by and waited for Luzi's answer.

"Very well," said Luzi. "I'll come. But . . . Melekh . . . you under-stand . . . we're having a celebration. When we're done . . . when we've finished our last prayers, I'll come without delay."

Later, when the meal and the prayers in however abbreviated a fash-ion had come to an end, the guests, still disturbed by the stone throw-ing, and concerned, too, because of the message from Reb Dudi, gathered around Luzi to wish him well, to urge him to be wary of the danger he might meet where he was going.

One by one, and then in small groups, the guests left Luzi's house leaving only Sruli, Luzi and Shmulikl Fist, who at a sign from Sruli, had stayed behind. When Luzi, readying himself to go to Reb Dudi's house, put on his coat, Sruli put his on as well. "I'm going too," he said. "And Shmulikl's going with me."

"Why? You haven't been sent for."

"It doesn't matter. I'm going anyhow."

The three of them, with Luzi walking in the middle, left the house. They walked warily through the dark and unfrequented streets, careful lest they meet another attack against Luzi, like the stone thrown at the house.

Then all at once Sruli stopped. Giving Shmulikl to understand that he must stay with Luzi all the way to Reb Dudi's house, and that he was to stay with him until he, Sruli, showed up. Then he muttered that he had something he needed to do, and abruptly left them.

He went off to find Brokha's house. And though by day he had done his best to remember the landmarks that would lead him to her house, still he stumbled about considerably in the dark before he found it.

When he came into the house there were, as was typical on a week night, only a few clients and they tried their best to avoid being seen. Sruli turned to Brokha at once and whispered, "I need you now. I want you to come with me, as we agreed you would."

"Where?" Brokha inquired.

"To the rabbi's house."

"Ah. Ah. To the rabbi."

"Yes. Does it scare you?"

"Yes. Of course, I'm scared."

"Then put your hand to the place you hold when you're scared."

The answer made Brokha smile and she understood that this stranger, Sruli, was no babe in the woods, that he knew very well how to deal with women like herself. And for the second time that day it was clear to her that he was a man who would know how to compel the fulfillment of a promise. It seemed to her that if she tried to wriggle out of doing what earlier she had promised, that this Sruli, whom she did not know, was capable of making a scandal, a dreadful scene that could do considerable damage to her by no means proper establishment. An establishment that was better off for not being seen and that did better to avoid all hullabaloo.

And so she yielded. Though she did not know precisely how she would serve this stranger by going to the rabbi's house; and though she had reason to believe that her testifying there might prove not to be in Yone's interests—Yone, with whom evidently she was quite familiar and who, as she knew, had been the one who for some purpose of his own had engineered the entire episode that had brought this stranger to her house. And she considered, too, that quarreling with Sruli was not wise since Yone was not on the premises to help her. And she considered, too, that earlier in the day Sruli had paid her well for the help he now required, and that he was not the sort of person who would allow himself to be cheated twice in her house. . . . All this considered, she replied, "I'll be ready in a minute." And indeed a moment later she was ready, with a shawl over her head and a winter cloak thrown over her shoulders. "A deal," she said, "is a deal. You told me to tell them the truth. Whatever they ask me, I'll tell them what I know."

There were not many people in Reb Dudi's house when Luzi came in. It was much different than it would have been on a Saturday night. But the few who were there had not come by chance, as was clear to Luzi who could tell from the look on their faces that they had been talking about him just moments before his arrival. Reb Dudi, seeing Luzi, rose from his chair and greeted him respectfully. There were a couple of rabbis in the room as well as various town notables and—surprisingly enough—Yone the tavern keeper. Since Yone did not dare to sit among the higher folk at the rabbi's table, he had found a place to stand behind the chair of a respected personage. He stood there with his hands folded in his usual fashion behind his back.

When Luzi came in, Yone had taken note of Shmulikl Fist's presence. Shmulikl had followed Sruli's orders and had accompanied Luzi all the way into the rabbi's house. Yone had noted, too, that when Shmulikl came in, he had looked around the room with his filmed-over eye as if uncertain whether to stand or sit. Finally, Shmulikl, who was in the same social class as Yone, decided, like Yone, to stand, but Shmulikl took up his position some distance away, as if he had no right or entitlement to be in that company.

Seeing him and knowing that he had not been invited, various people asked, "Who is he?"

Others, who knew something about him and his profession, murmured, "Ah, Shmulikl." They were not particularly pleased to see him.

"Ah, Shmulikl," Yone exclaimed, as if to an old acquaintance, and it was clear that *he* knew Shmulikl and that Shmulikl knew *him*. The result was that those who were irritated by Shmulikl's presence had no way to protest, since Yone had been admitted as a witness for one side, the other side had a right to its witness: Shmulikl.

And that is how it was settled. Yone stood behind the respected person's chair and Shmulikl in his place some distance away.

Then, when Luzi and Reb Dudi had completed their exchange of polite greetings, they both turned their attention at once to the matter at hand.

A few words about the meeting between these two.

At first glance one might think that the two of them had been shaped out of the same clay. They both shared the same God and the same religion, and even their modes of belief were similar. And yet they were profoundly different as regards their goals, their personal characteristics and the places each of them occupied in the community.

Reb Dudi, a brilliant Talmud scholar whose learning had been the means by which he had achieved the rabbinate in a city like N. where he was profoundly respected, where his every word was treated as if it had been spoken on Mount Sinai by God Himself. He was a proud man who had an entire town at his beck and call, as if he were its lord, and ruler. It was Reb Dudi's custom—as the reader may recall—to go out on his porch early every morning and there, shading his eyes, to scan the whole town like a man looking at an inheritance which required his care.

So much, then, for Reb Dudi. Luzi was a quite different sort of person. He was a man given to isolation and had spent most of his life in a small town somewhere on the frontier. Though he was deeply learned he was not drawn to power. Rather, he was a man of feeling. Not only was he not a proud man—he seemed to have some sort of inward flaw. We have already described how in his abstracted pacing he would come to a stop and pass a finger over his right eyebrow, like a man who means to calm some feverish thought. . . . He was a man of interior disturbances, like a receptacle that keeps wobbling until the turbulence of the wine it contains has subsided. He had been like that in his youth, and he remained that way until after a long spiritual pilgrimage, he joined those to whose school of thought he now adhered, though (here we make a revelation) it was uncertain whether he would remain with it to the end. That, then, was Luzi.

Now to the matter at hand.

When Reb Dudi saw Luzi standing before him, he exchanged a few polite words of greeting then he said, "Are you aware that the community is very upset by you, and that it is my duty as its spiritual leader to give you a warning?"

"Yes. I understand," Luzi quietly replied, his tone at once melancholy and ironic. He smiled. "I've already had one warning today."

"From whom?" asked Reb Dudi.

"From a rock that was thrown through my window this evening."

"A rock?" Reb Dudi said, surprised even as he shrugged his shoulders as a way of dismissing Luzi's not particularly covert accusation—as if denying that anyone like Reb Dudi could possibly have anything to do with rock throwing. "I have no idea what you're talking about, nor is there anyone here at my table who does. Well, do you?" he said, turning to his guests as toward witnesses who could establish both his and their innocence.

"No. We don't." They all rejected the idea since in fact none of them knew anything about it. None of them but Yone, that is. And had anyone been looking closely at him, they would have seen how, at Luzi's mention of the thrown rock, Yone turned his head away, and how the hands he kept clasped behind his back trembled.

"Very well, then. They know nothing," said Luzi, altering slightly his half-melancholy, half-ironic manner. "What is the warning you want to give me?"

"I want to call to your attention the fact that there are those under your wing who, if Israel were still a power, would deserve to be excommunicated ... or worse." And here, Reb Dudi recounted the whole of Mikhl's story as it had transpired here, in his house, before the very table at which Luzi now sat.

"It is impossible even to discuss extenuating his behavior, since he continues to stand by his blasphemies. And no one has the right to protect or excuse a heretic who ought to be treated with the full severity of the law. But more than that, it is necessary to deal with the roots from which such wild growths spring and by which they are nourished. I mean that school of thought to which the man of whom we speak belonged, and which sustained him until he made his disastrous plunge. I mean the sect to which you, too, Luzi Mashber, belong and which has its origins in the teachings of that outcast Reb Nakhman of Bratslav who was attacked in his day by all the great men of his generation and who was spared excommunication because no one wanted to dishonor the memory of his sainted ancestor, the Bal Shem.

"It is clear, then, that he who opens a path for a sinner is as guilty as the sinner himself. And there's no way of knowing whether he may not himself become a transgressor since the members of that sect are as those who inhabit a ruin in which demons and spirits dance and where they entice people away from the straight and narrow path.

"And that is the matter about which I want to warn you. You will either separate yourself from this doomed sect and help to destroy its nest or others will do it in the Name of God and the community to which it is already a reproach that under the guise of patience it has delayed extirpating such a great evil.

"Now, I want you to think carefully about what I've said," Reb Dudi went on, "and if you wish to make a reply, I am prepared to listen."

It must be said in all truth that Luzi had nothing he could say against Reb Dudi's central charge. Luzi's shoulders were simply not broad enough to hold the full weight of an act as dreadful as Mikhl's—an act which all pious minds, including Luzi's, were bound to condemn. Then why had Luzi prayed for Mikhl earlier that day? Though it exceeded the strict letter of the law, that had been done on an impulse of his own because Luzi had recalled the phrase that says that God's pity is available to all his creatures no matter who they are or what they may be guilty of. Luzi had, then, prayed out of compassion. But that was a good deal more than he had a right to expect Reb Dudi to do, Reb Dudi, who was the official guardian of the law and its standard-bearer. Reb Dudi would have been right to reply that to treat every sinner as an exceptional case was to open God's garden of commandments and laws to trampling feet. It would shake the established order of the world.

As a result, Luzi Mashber, sitting in Reb Dudi's presence and hearing what the rabbi had to say against Mikhl, felt himself unable to make a direct reply that would openly defend him. And so he undertook to do it by indirection and disguise.

What Luzi did say was, "Mikhl, for as long as I've known him, has been a man of vacillating character. A fearful man but astute as well. Drawn, therefore, on the one hand to the proper path and distracted from it on the other. I know that from his youth upward, he has been frequently tormented by doubt.

"But would it not have been better to wait such a man out rather than to condemn him so quickly, a man whose error, strange though it may seem to us, is the consequence of a good intent . . . as can sometimes happen when one is entangled in high thoughts; but who knows whether such a man may not find his own way out of his confusion and back to the proper path. And how could one be certain that his present confusion was not a manifestation of the light from on high, one that would send Mikhl back to what he *ought* to believe just as darkness had driven him toward what was wrong.

"In any case," Luzi went on, "perhaps he ought to have been handled differently. Instead of irritating him, it might have been better to calm him, as true healers often do when their intent is to drive an illness away—they calm the patient, not because calm is a specific for the illness, but because it eases the patient. In this case, it is not the sin that matters, but the sinner whom we want to separate from his sin. But what was done to Mikhl was quite the reverse: it was as if the intent were to heal the patient by pouring hot lead over his head. I mean by that the severe measures the community took against Mikhl who was condemned without being given an opportunity to bethink himself— as if one could beat an illness out of the body with sticks. Mikhl's livelihood was taken from him, the last bit of income with which he supported his family. The resultant poverty and illness (the first perhaps more than the second) lost him his sons. A disaster that some regarded as sent by the Hand of God, a punishment from the Holy Name . . ."

"It was . . . it was by the Hand of God," cried several of those sitting at Reb Dudi's table.

"No," said Luzi speaking a bit more sharply. "While I am not authorized to say what is God's Will, still, to the degree that any man can understand it, I feel confident that the Lord would not have behaved toward Mikhl the way the community has. It is said of Him that 'He is slow to anger.' I think the Lord would have shown more patience."

"So that's what you think," Reb Dudi snapped angrily. "How is it that you are able to be so generous with someone else's purse? With God's patience or His impatience. Especially in a matter concerning a man whom no reasonable person could believe worth pardoning. It is written that 'He that blasphemes against the Lord must die.' And it is becoming increasingly clear that you are within a hairbreadth of washing this Mikhl clean of guilt. The question that rises, then, is who has given you the right . . . where do you get your authority? From what great man or Talmudic commentary?"

"I claim no right and I have no authority," Luzi replied. "But since we are dealing here with a man whose soul has gone astray, one needs to find some gate of repentance . . . some means to rescue him. That being the case, I do not need to be one of the great to undertake such a rescue.

"So much, then, for what concerns Mikhl. As for the charges Reb Dudi has made that the sect to which Mikhl belongs is responsible for his sin and that other schools of thought are free from and guard themselves against such error . . . Forgive me for saying that Reb Dudi is mistaken. Because as we have seen in the case of the rebbe of Lvov in recent times . . . and surely the rebbe of Lvov was not just anybody . . . he was a personage, one of the distinguished men of Israel . . . the son and brother of distinguished men. And yet he, too, did something similar; he ran off and sought refuge with the free thinkers of Chernowitz who were delighted to have him and offered him their protection as a way of outraging their pious enemies.

"Everyone knows the story, despite the efforts of his friends, his parents and his brothers to hide what happened, and despite the squalid means they employed to get him back. Not that they succeeded. The point is that there is no way for any community to guard against error because, as it is written, 'All is in the hands of heaven—except the fear of heaven.' Everyone is capable of choice, but none of us is responsible for the acts of another: neither a father for those of his child, nor a child for those of his father . . . nor any sect for the acts of one of its members, however dear he may be to it."

"Yes," interrupted Reb Dudi, and it was clear that he had been made uncomfortable by Luzi's last example: the story of the rebbe of Lvov who had caused his followers and his family considerable heartbreak because of his defection to the ranks of the heretics who hailed it as proof that they had right on their side since such a God-fearing man had joined them.

"Yes," he said again as he groped for something to say that would weaken the effect that Luzi's last example had had on him and on those who sat at his table. "It appears then that you have an excuse for your protégé, as well as one for the sect to which he belongs. But what have you got to say about the fact that one of your intimates is reported to have strayed into a place which I would prefer not to name lest it defile my lips? And yet unhappily for me, name it I must. It was a whorehouse from which he was shamefully driven. After that he was seen staggering drunkenly about in the street. What do say to that?

"There is a witness here," Reb Dudi said, indicating Yone who stood behind a notable's chair waiting to be remembered, to be called on, to be the sworn witness of the shameful behavior of one of Luzi's followers. It was clearly a scenario that had been prepared for in advance. "There is a witness here who saw or who heard the details from those who were there—it makes little difference. Well, then, what will you say to that?"

Those at the table stared warily at Luzi as if readying themselves to draw away from him as they might from a dangerous man, or from one who gave off a terrible stink.

"To that?" Luzi seemed ready to undertake a defense of the newly accused Sruli.

"To that?" suddenly echoed Shmulikl Fist who had been standing there and who naturally enough had not participated in the conversation since he did not understand any of the high matters discussed by Luzi and Reb Dudi. Now, however, hearing Reb Dudi say "whorehouse," a word which he did understand, and hearing him making an accusation against one of Luzi's intimates (which one he did not know) for whom, evidently, Luzi was in some way being held responsible, Shmulikl was determined to justify Luzi. And this is why Shmulikl, hardly aware that he was doing it, began to echo Luzi, as if his sympathetic repetition would make Luzi win this part of the argument just as, evidently, he had won the argument that preceded it.

"To that," Luzi said, meaning to proceed, but just then two people appeared in the doorway: one was a woman who wore a winter cloak and had a scarf over her head, the other was a man directly behind her who seemed to be urging her on, giving her no time to regret having come.

These two were Brokha and Sruli who arrived just as Sruli's name was about to be mentioned—exactly the way a hero shows up in a story when he is most needed.

"Go on in. To the table," Sruli whispered as he pushed her forward.

Brokha was confused first by the rabbinical air of Reb Dudi's house—an atmosphere that was foreign to her—and then because she suddenly saw Yone among those who were in the room. She sensed that whether she liked it or not there would be an altogether undesirable clash between them that evening.

"Ah, Brokha," Yone exclaimed without thinking, as if calling out to an old friend. And speaking her name, he felt that he had sufficiently warned her about where she was and that she was to behave in a way that would protect their common interests.

"Ah, Yone," cried Brokha, pleased the way one is at seeing an old acquaintance among a crowd of strangers among whom one is not very comfortable. She all but started toward him but changed her mind when Reb Dudi spoke to her—not to *her* but rather to the space just above her head: "You, woman. What is it you want?"

"Yes. What does she want?" said the inquiring glances of those at the table.

Brokha stood, speechless. Then, "I'm a respectable woman," she started to say, but after the word "respectable" the words froze in her throat.

"Well, what do you want? And why have you been brought here?" Reb Dudi said, with a glance at Sruli who stood behind Brokha. It was clear that those two had come on the same business.

Here Yone interposed on behalf of the stupefied Brokha: "Rabbi, this is the woman into whose house he went—the fellow we were just talking about. She runs the house and there he is, that's the fellow," he said, pointing at Sruli.

"That's who I am," said Sruli, and to everyone's astonishment, the words were spoken without the least embarrassment. "And I'm the one who brought her so she can tell what actually happened and to make clear what part that fellow"—here he pointed at Yone—"played in the whole affair."

"He?" asked Reb Dudi in confusion as he turned toward Yone.

"Yes. That Yone, and that whore," said Sruli, employing the word most calculated to be offensive to those in Reb Dudi's house.

"What's going on here?" Reb Dudi cried as loudly as his aged voice permitted. "Who is that man?" In his perplexity he turned to Luzi.

"He's the man you were just talking about. He's brought a witness to testify to his innocence."

"Brokha!" It was Shmulikl Fist. He had been standing quietly listening to the accusation Reb Dudi made. Then, seeing Brokha and Sruli, he understood who was being accused: Sruli. And it was clear to him, too, that Sruli had brought Brokha with him because he felt confident that he could prove his innocence. Worried then that Yone might intimidate Brokha, Shmulikl shouted, "Brokha, tell the truth. Don't let anyone scare you. Do you hear? It's me. Shmulikl Fist."

"I'm a respectable woman," Brokha began again, weeping because she felt herself in the midst of several fires: there was Yone whom she knew well and with whom she had business dealings she would have preferred to protect; and then there was the stranger Sruli; finally there was Shmulikl Fist with whose physical strength in the service of those who paid him she was familiar. "Rabbi, I'm a respectable woman. It's just the way I earn my living. I'm telling you the truth. That man . . ." she pointed toward Sruli, "was drunk when he was brought to my house from Yone's tavern," and here she looked toward Yone as she named him.

"Mmmm," Yone grumbled, irritated because Brokha had identified him. Clearly she had not understood his silent signals, or had chosen not to understand them. For a moment he looked as if he meant to fall upon her. Thoroughly frightened, she drew her head down between her shoulders.

Yes, she was, as we have said, caught in many cross fires: on the one hand, simply being present before the rabbi and in the presence of people who were on intimate terms with God whom Brokha feared, despite the not quite sanctified profession she practiced. On the other hand, there was her fear of Yone who evidently had on more than one occasion sent a bit of business her way and whom, therefore, she would have preferred to please instead of thwarting him in his affairs. And then there was Shmulikl who also from time to time could do one a favor, or considerable harm—he was capable of both. And then finally there was this Sruli who had visited her twice today and who, the first time, had given her money. And who, both times, had asked one thing only of her, that she tell the truth. Which, if she chose not to, why he, too, was a man who could find the means to repay her. Considering all these things so addled her mind that as she looked about and discerned danger on every side, it seemed that there was finally only one thing to do and that was the easiest of all—to tell the truth, which she could speak without strain or tongue twisting and which required neither covert speech nor any disguise.

"Rabbi," she cried, and here she indicated Sruli, "Rabbi, he didn't do anything with the woman. Because he was too drunk. He didn't touch her."

"Melekh," Reb Dudi cried, utterly beside himself at having to hear such language. He shook himself with revulsion, as if reptiles were crawling over him. "How shameful," he said helplessly. "What's going on here?"

"Yes. What's going on here?" his guests chimed in, as stupefied as he by the proceedings.

"My home has become a den of thieves," Reb Dudi shouted, beside himself. "Go," he said with disgust and waved a hand toward Brokha, Shmulikl and Sruli. And at Yone who, though he was well known to the rabbi, had by his participation in these shameful events lost Reb Dudi's confidence.

"Do you see," the rabbi said, turning to Luzi who all this while had sat feeling humiliated by the repulsive affair into which he had been drawn. "Do you see where it has led you: to shame, to whores, to dealings with men who cannot be blamed for what they do. The guilt is on those who lead them. On you. You, Luzi Mashber. And we . . . I and all those who are gathered here warn you now that the community will not bear this in silence. The matter will be looked into, irrespective of the perpetrator's rank or the high connections he may have. A flame has been lighted, and it must be extinguished by the community with whatever means are available to it. He may need to be driven from the town, or turned over to the Gentile government. If necessary, blood may have to be spilled," Reb Dudi cried, his voice at its highest pitch.

"Yes. Blood may have to be spilled," came the echo from those seated at the table. Yone, who was especially pleased by Reb Dudi's last words, spoke most loudly of all.

"Yone," called Shmulikl Fist who, like Yone, had turned alert at the mention of blood and understood at once that the threat was directed against Luzi's people. His filmed-over eye glistened and he looked primed for battle against the man whose name he had called. "Yone, I'm not dead yet. It's me. Shmulikl. You'll have me to deal with."

"Be still," Yone said, and waved his hand as if discounting Shmulikl's words as well as his prowess in battle.

"Go, go," cried Reb Dudi as much to Yone, who seemed to be on his side, as to his enemy, Shmulikl. And to Brokha and Sruli. All of them polluted his house and he wanted them to leave it—the sooner the better.

"As for you, Luzi Mashber . . ." Reb Dudi, exhausted first by his earlier quiet discussion with Luzi and by the shouts of the last few minutes, now turned his attention to Luzi. "In the community's name, I warn you once again. Bear in mind that it will not be silent. It will carry out the excommunication."

"What excommunication?" said Luzi, meaning to say something in Sruli's defense. Pointing to Sruli, he said, "But the man has brought a witness."

"A witness! That kind"—Reb Dudi indicated Brokha—"are unfit witnesses. They are a shame unto Israel, and only the members of your sect, and perhaps you, yourself, can justify having dealings with their sort. . . ."

"What?" stammered Luzi.

"What did Reb Dudi say?" Sruli inquired, starting forward as if he were breaking a chain. It was clear that if he were not restrained he meant to say such things as would make not only Reb Dudi cringe with shame, but all those who were in the room, and the very walls as well.

Yes, that was the pass at which things at that moment stood. But just then two newcomers appeared in the doorway. Two women in winter coats, wearing scarves over their heads. A single glance at their clothing and one knew they were women of rank. Wealthy, very wealthy.

The two were Gitl Mashber and her older daughter Yehudis with both of whom we have long been acquainted. They had come by coach to the rabbi's house, though not from the Mashber residence. Instead, they came from The Curse, the neighborhood in which Luzi lived. Not finding him at home, and learning that he had gone to the rabbi's house, they had instructed their driver to bring them here.

The last few days had been very difficult ones for Moshe Mashber. He had made the secret contract with Sruli as well as similar contracts with other people—about which we will say nothing here. About the same time, it became clear from the frequent visits of the doctors to his house, and the number of long consultations they had, that there was little hope left for his ailing daughter. Her days . . . perhaps even her hours, were numbered.

It was then, when Gitl, Moshe Mashber's wife, had out of sheer anguish taken frequently to avoiding her sick daughter's bedroom and when Moshe Mashber, who for the same reason wanted to leave the room with the same haste with which he entered it, but could not bring himself to do so because his daughter detained him and would not let go of his hand, saying invariably, "Who are you leaving me for? Stay near me. Be with me. Don't leave me alone" . . . it was then that Moshe's face was bathed in tears and he felt sobs choking him each time she pleaded with him.

It was then, on that evening which we have just spoken of, that Gitl took her older daughter, Yehudis aside and whispered a few words in her ear. . . . A little later, dressed to go out, they entered the carriage they had ordered to wait for them at their gate and asked to be driven to a certain address in The Curse district.

Gitl had known from hasty conversations with Moshe over his meals that he and Luzi had been reconciled and that he, Moshe, had made several visits to Luzi. To the degree that she was able to rejoice at all in those difficult days, Gitl had been delighted by the news. But now, when the Angel of Death was poised in the doorway of her daughter's room, now that all the efforts she had made to save her had proved fruitless: money dispensed to synagogues for candles and brandy so that congregations might pray for her daughter's recovery, and tombs in the cemetery had been measured, and finally (as a way of deceiving the Angel of Death) her daughter's name had been changed. None of it had helped.

It was then that it had occurred to Gitl to find Luzi whom she thought of as her last consolation. Not that she believed he could perform a miracle, or that his prayers would be more acceptable to God than her own or the prayers of others. It was simply that she wanted to confide in him, to open her despairing heart, to put her face against his breast the way a child does to its father.

When she and her daughter appeared in the doorway, all those in Reb Dudi's house grew silent: Reb Dudi with anger still on his lips, Luzi with the question he meant to pose still in his mouth, and Sruli frozen into an attitude of attack. Everyone else in the room, no matter which side of the quarrel he or she was on, was frozen into the pose they had before Gitl's arrival. When Gitl looked around and saw Luzi, she moved quickly toward him but she stopped before she reached him and turned toward the head of the table, toward Reb Dudi and to the other respected rabbis who sat with him. "People! Rabbis," she cried, then interrupted herself as she turned to Luzi, who was her reason for being there. "Luzi!"

Because it was clear that she was too exhausted to stand before Reb Dudi as custom required, someone offered her a chair. But Gitl waved it away. "Dear, dear Luzi. God's anger is turned against us. Our young tree, Nekhamke, is about to be cut down. Ah, Rabbis, people, pray for Moshe Mashber's daughter who is dangerously ill."

The faces in the room turned somber. Some of those at the table lowered their eyes and murmured sympathetically, "Ah . . . Moshe Mashber's daughter. May the Lord help her."

"Luzi!" Gitl cried, turning once more to him as if there were no one else in the room, "Come with me. There's a coach outside . . . Forget the wrong Moshe did you . . ." Then, as if sensing that Luzi, just before she came into the house, had been on the verge of being insulted again, she added, "There's no insult that can touch you, Luzi."

"I'll come with you, Gitl. Of course I'll come," said Luzi. All those in the room looked on awed by the reverence with which she treated him. Though he was a near relative, she stood before him with her head bowed. The shameful reproach Reb Dudi had made to Luzi—of the sort that one would make only to a sworn enemy—seemed to dissolve under the influence of Gitl's reverence. Insult, as Gitl had said, could not touch him.

Reb Dudi was not the only one who felt uneasy and more than a little guilty in Luzi's presence. All of Reb Dudi's sympathizers felt the same way. Even Yone stood with his hands at his sides, as if unwilling, even if authorized, to do Luzi any harm.

After Gitl's appeal to Luzi, the minor characters in the brief drama left Reb Dudi's house. First, Brokha disappeared, unnoticed and without a word of farewell. Then Shmulikl went, at a signal from Sruli. Shmulikl could see for himself that his work in this place was done. Yone, after what had happened, was not likely to perform any Yone tricks for a while, and Shmulikl's ardor for combat had also cooled.

It was then that Luzi rose from his place and took leave as best he could of Reb Dudi and those who were at the table. Then he followed Gitl and her daughter from the house. Sruli followed after, and when they were all outside and had taken their places in the coach, Luzi gestured for Sruli to join them.

That was how Luzi, after so long an absence, appeared again in his brother's house. And if anything could make the Mashber family happy just then, it was Luzi's presence among them once again. He was led immediately into the sickroom where the family gathered around him as if they regarded him as a source of comfort and healing.

When he saw how hopelessly ill his niece was—her altered features, her sharply outlined cheekbones, her clay-colored nostrils; when he heard her labored breathing—harsh gasps such as a fish makes out of water—he did what people usually do in such cases: he maintained an equable calm and treated her the way he did the rest of the family, as if there was nothing unusual about her condition at all.

And for a while Luzi's behavior had a salutary effect on the patient. Because however greatly she had declined in recent days, when she saw Luzi in her father's house again, Luzi, whose coming had always created a festive air in her home, she experienced a wash of pleasure and managed to forget her illness for a while. And in those days pleasure was as rare for her as a normal breath of air.

The visit, then, was conducted around her bedside for as long as possible. For the sake of appearances there was some talk of her health, but in order to distract her and to keep her from being fully aware of her grave condition, the talk was mostly about other things.

While Luzi was in the sickroom, Sruli waited for him in the dining room. In the same dining room to which, formerly, he had been a frequent visitor when he had wanted to be, and an infrequent one when he had not cared to go. And the last time he was there, as we will recall, it had been on his return from his summer's wanderings that he had set his knapsack down in a corner of that room; and it was from there, in the course of the quarrel between the brothers, that he had been driven from the Mashber house, taking his knapsack with him as he went.

He sat now looking at that corner. Then he glanced around the rest of the dining room as well as at such of the other rooms as he could see through the doors that opened into it.

If Sruli had not been Sruli, strange thoughts would undoubtedly have passed through his mind. One thought in particular: that he, who had been driven from this house, was now the owner not only of this dining room, but of all the rooms in the house, and of the courtyard, of the garden, of the entire property that had belonged to Moshe Mashber. Yes. Had Sruli not been Sruli, all he would have needed to do to confirm the truth of that thought was to touch the billfold in his breast pocket in which reposed the deed of transfer he had received not long ago from Moshe Mashber. A touch, to confirm that he was the owner.

But whether such a thought occurred to him, or whether he touched his billfold, we do not know. Though we rather think he did not. Because now when he encountered Moshe Mashber walking with his brother, Moshe merely glanced at him indifferently, as at someone on whom one's eyes did not need to linger. And this is something he would not have done had Sruli, on the occasion of their meeting, served to remind him that he, Sruli, was a man of substance, a man of worth, and that indeed a large portion of his, Moshe Mashber's, worth was now in Sruli's hands. All of which simply indicates that Sruli was not one of those people who are willing to take advantage of another's misfortunes—or of his own good fortune—to aggrandize himself at the other's cost. Especially not now, when he knew what was happening in Moshe's home.

He sat alone in the dining room. And it may be that he listened to the sounds of the freezing night in which, as he and Luzi, Yehudis and Gitl were returning from the rabbi's house, he had noticed as they passed under a streetlight, the first flakes of a light snow falling from the darkened vault of the sky—the sort of snow that just barely covers the surface of the hardened earth at the beginning of winter—while at another time, the same light snowfall could intensify and turn plentiful and so dense that by morning one could not open the gate before a low-built hut. Nor the gates before low-built huts only.

It may be that sitting alone in the dining room he thought of Moshe Mashber's senile porter, Mikhalko, whose small wooden hut stood facing the entrance to the Mashber kitchen. Sruli, coming through the courtyard, had noticed the weak light of a candle stub glowing behind a dusty windowpane of that hut.

Sruli recalled the last time he had waited in the courtyard for Luzi with whom he had become acquainted earlier on that very morning. And how on the evening of that day, he had had his first conversation with him. He remembered, too, that he had spent part of that morning in Mikhalko's hut, and that he had had a refreshing nap on Mikhalko's wooden bed. And we may conjecture that Sruli, exhausted from his long, wearying day, wished that he could have a similar nap now.

But just then the members of the family came out of the sickroom. Luzi, Gitl and Moshe as well. Everyone took leave of Luzi and urged him to come frequently again. Then Luzi, accompanied by Moshe, went out into the courtyard where Sruli followed them.

It was Sruli who noticed that the ancient Mikhalko, who was performing some evening task in the courtyard, that Mikhalko was taken aback when he caught sight of the tall, dignified, somewhat stern Luzi standing there with his brother Moshe. Mikhalko grumbled unhappily and stepped aside to let his employer and Luzi pass on toward the gate leading to the street, but it was clear that the old porter regarded Luzi with suspicion and fear.

The truth is that the sight of Luzi made Mikhalko shudder, just as it had last summer when Luzi had come on a visit. Back in those days Mikhalko used to come upon him often at night, moving about in the moonlight (when there was a moon in the sky) or in starlight (when the stars were out). "The man is a sorcerer," Mikhalko had even then said to himself. "He bodes nobody any good."

Mikhalko believed that some part of what he had prophesied last summer had already been fulfilled. Despite the fact that Luzi had disappeared from Mikhalko's ken—and though Mikhalko had not known about the quarrel between Luzi and Moshe and therefore had no idea where Luzi had disappeared—still, there were traces of Luzi's sorcery to be seen. Though Mikhalko was old and weak and his sight was dim, he had only to look at his employer and the members of his family to see that things were not going well with them. He knew it from the size of the portions of food on his plate which recently had become much smaller. It was evident that for them Fortune's Wheel had stopped turning. He knew, too, that his employer's youngest daughter was gravely ill, and that it was feared that she would not recover. There was no way to avoid noticing the constant coming and going of doctors who continually prescribed new medicines. And he noticed, too, how preoccupied everyone in the family was, how no one had time to exchange so much as a word with him, with Mikhalko.

And what was worse, he felt the effects of his prophecy on his own person. Because lately he dreamed frequently that a swarm of bees clustered over his bosom seeking to enter into his chest the way bees enter a flower to extract its nectar.

No, it bodes ill, thought the aged Mikhalko when he saw Luzi standing beside Moshe. He turned away to avoid the sight of Luzi, and as he did so he decided that when he went back to his hut that night he would make the sign of the cross many, many times before his dusty and cobweb-covered icon. Only then would he go to bed.

"Yes, I'll cross myself a lot," he said, and having made that decision he cast a fearful, if concealed, glance at Luzi.

II

Two Deaths, One Marriage

Mikhalko's prophecies were fulfilled—above all, those concerning him.

On the night that Luzi and Sruli visited Moshe Mashber's house, the snow, as Sruli had foreseen, fell so hard that when the family woke in the morning they found that everything outside was veiled in snow so bright it made one's eyes water. The trees in the garden were knee-deep in it. And the same was true of the courtyard and the drive and the stone steps that led to the kitchen. The roof of the house as well as those of its outbuildings were blanketed, as indeed were all the streets and houses of the district.

When Mikhalko rose that morning he had much to do. First, he had to struggle to open the snow-jammed door to his hut which would not yield at first to the pressure of his trembling hands. Then he had to create a path between two of the outbuildings as well as one between his hut and the kitchen, and still another path from there to the gate leading into the street. In addition to that, he had to pump water from the well and carry it to the kitchen. Today, pumping the water seemed especially difficult, first because he was already exhausted from making the paths, and then because the change in the weather had turned the air moist so that he had trouble breathing. Finally, he had trouble carrying wood to the house where the stoves, because of the change in the weather, required more than usual.

Watch Chain, the voiceless dog with the dragging belly, followed his master Mikhalko about all morning. He stood and watched him when he paused and followed after him slowly when he moved. On this occasion, Watch Chain had an unusually concerned look in his eye, as if he was looking at something that needed to be well observed because he was likely to lose it at any moment. Watch Chain watched how Mikhalko continually interrupted his work to stand as if thinking whether he had not forgotten something when in fact he paused because he was having trouble breathing. He stood, looking as if at any moment the load he was carrying would drop from his hands and he would be left standing there like a golem.

Watch Chain also noticed that when Mikhalko received his food in the kitchen that morning he did not devote himself eagerly to it as he usually did. No, this time he hardly touched his food and gave most of it to the dog.

Watch Chain noticed, too, that when Mikhalko, having finished doing chores in the courtyard, in the kitchen and in his master's house, returned to his hut and there began to stoke his stove—that Mikhalko, instead of kneeling before the fire and looking into it as he usually did, he knelt absently before it, as if he were dozing. Then when he started awake he had trouble getting up and had to sit down. And then he had to lean on his hands, like a crawling infant or a paralytic, before he could manage to get up off the floor.

That day, a severe frost, rare after a snowfall, set in. In the evening, when candles were being lighted, Mikhalko, who was in the courtyard on some need of his own, felt the cold and concerned lest his stove cool down during the night, he decided to carry in more wood for his fire. Evidently he carried in more than he needed because the hut soon became so hot that he began to gasp and had to unbutton his collar.

He felt a weakness in his hands and feet, as if fumes had overcome him. He made his way to his cot where he sat down, first at the edge of the bed, then, as more fumes assailed him, he eased himself farther into the bed so that he could rest his back against the wall. The hut seemed to be whirling and he saw spots and bright lights before his eyes which little by little took on shape, forming a larger picture.

He dozed off and saw:

It was summer, not winter. Evening. He was in the courtyard, the only member of the household still awake. Suddenly, he saw a tall man who looked like Luzi standing on the roof beside the chimney. The man was performing sorceries and speaking to the heavens.

Mikhalko was startled and drew back so that the man on the roof would not see him in the courtyard, but he did not succeed. The man saw him and called to him, and Mikhalko, without knowing quite why, felt himself compelled to join him beside the chimney. And it seemed to him that there was a sort of smoke rising from the chimney, invisible smoke which Luzi, by means of such tricks as sorcerers perform on summer nights, made him feel. Mikhalko tried to turn his head away so as not to breathe the smoke. But the tall man forbade him to do that and Mikhalko continued to breathe the smoke until he grew dizzy and almost, almost fell from the roof into the courtyard where he would certainly have shattered his bones.

It was then that he woke up, trembling, and found himself sitting on the bunk bed in his overheated hut. He had a feeling that there was something he needed to do, there was some work he must undertake . . . get up . . . open the door . . . let in fresh air. Or go into the court-yard with Watch Chain. But he could not bring himself to move.

Then he dozed off again and it seemed to him that Watch Chain was standing on his hind legs and that the dog was pushing at him with his forelegs, trying to wake him because Mikhalko's old head was hanging sideways strangely and his trembling hands hung limply at his sides.

And it seemed to Mikhalko that Watch Chain, when he was unable to wake him with his forelegs, tried to make some kind of sound with his mute throat, and that the distressed Watch Chain, had he been able, would now have uttered the bark he had suppressed so long.

Mikhalko slept again, and again he saw the tall Luzi on the roof. Luzi was calling him, asking him to join him, and once again Mikhalko felt compelled to go. And again he joined him, but this time it was not only he who was there. Moshe Mashber's entire household was there on the roof, their faces grave as they watched Luzi perform his spells and sor-ceries. They stood silently by unable to move or to say a word, and they, too, had to breathe in the smoke until they grew dizzy and nau-seous. But the two who suffered most from the smoke were himself, Mikhalko, and Moshe Mashber's younger daughter, the one who had been ill for some time and for whom there was no hope of recovery. Then all who were there uttered a fearful cry when they saw the two of them—Mikhalko and Moshe's younger daughter—overcome by ver-tigo, fall to their deaths. And Mikhalko saw two funerals forming at once in the courtyard: One was a Christian funeral—his own . . . he lay in a coffin with his face uncovered; the second, a Jewish funeral—his employer's daughter . . . she lay on a stretcher with her face covered.

And then Mikhalko heard a cry whose origin he did not know: perhaps it was made by Watch Chain's mute throat as the dog strove to wake Mikhalko; or maybe it came from his employer's house across the way. It was the sort of cry one hears coming from homes in which someone is mortally ill, homes in which people wail to keep the soul from taking flight.

It was then that Mikhalko lost consciousness for the final time. He turned rigid and his head dangled to one side, like a weight he was no longer able to carry.

For a while Watch Chain stood guard beside him. The dog stood on his hind legs with his forelegs pressed against Mikhalko's chest. He, too, was rigid.

The candle stub cast its glow over them both. Watch Chain did not take his eyes from Mikhalko's face until late, late into the night, until nearly dawn. And at last he saw that Mikhalko's immobility was not the result either of sleep or of drunkenness, and that his master had experienced the last event of his life. He sniffed at Mikhalko's hands and sensed that there was nothing more to be expected from them: they had grown cold and hard. Then had anyone been near Mikhalko's hut at that moment, he would have heard the beginning of a canine cry that ended on a gentle and bitter note of grief.

For a while, Watch Chain's voice was returned to him.

The report of Mikhalko's death was one more bit of dreadful news in Moshe Mashber's already chaotic household. It was already a home filled with misfortune, a home verging on the catastrophe which . . . today or tomorrow . . . was sure to come. Even Nakhum and Nekhamke Lentsher's little children felt it in their own way: they understood that their mother would be with them for a limited time only, and that their lives were threatened by some nameless peril.

They understood it, too, from the way that their mother was not available to them recently: she did not dress them or undress them; she did not feed them or put them to bed. Other people took care of that for her: sometimes their grandmother Gitl, uttering angry cries; sometimes their aunt Yehudis who did not distinguish between her children and them; and sometimes it was their father, Nakhum who, not being used to woman's work, did it clumsily, the way men do.

But all of that was not yet the worst of it. They knew that mothers sometimes took sick. But one could still go into her bedroom to tell her of their joys and sorrows, and get a loving glance or hear a kind word from her. Now that was no longer possible. The children had been forbidden to go into the bedroom, except now and again when they were allowed to stand in the doorway and look toward their mother who looked different, unfamiliar. And if she chanced to see them, she turned away at once, especially when she saw them together with their father, Nakhum Lentsher.

That, then, was how it had been until now. In the last couple of days, however, even the brief doorway visits were forbidden and their little coats were held in readiness in case it was necessary to send them away to relatives or friends.

That almost happened to them last night but at the last moment it was decided to let them stay. And they would swear that during the night they were wakened out of their sleep by the wild cries uttered by the family, or friends who, for their mother's sake, were spending the night in the house. The outcry was brief, and when the children started up they found several members of the household there who had come to comfort them. Among them there was one who was not of the household. That was Grandmother Shayntse who, traveling on a late train, had arrived that evening while the children were asleep.

Yes, it was Grandmother Shayntse, Nakhum Lentsher's mother, who, having been alerted about the misfortune that was closing in on her son, had come in her winter coat all the way from far away Podolia, almost in the vicinity of Kamenets.

She had gone at once into Nekhamke's sickroom. Nekhamke hardly recognized her—or if she did it no longer mattered though she did notice how her mother-in-law stood at one side of the room, her eyes brimming with cold, mute tears.

Nekhamke noticed, too, that shortly after her mother-in-law had wept secretly for a while, she took her son Nakhum to one side where evidently she gave him advice and consolation. Perhaps of the usual sort: "It's all in God's hands." Or, "Don't let yourself be overwhelmed. Such things happen . . . there's nothing you can do."

Yes. Of course. Seeing that the end was approaching, Grandmother Shayntse did what she could to keep her son Nakhum away from the sick woman's bedside to make things easier for him. She encouraged him to take thought for himself. To prepare himself for any eventuality.

"You're a father, a young father. You have children to think of. You mustn't waste your life."

"What are you talking about?" even the cold and inconstant, but now despairing Nakhum said. "Nekhamke," he sobbed. "What's to become of us? The children and me."

"God," said Grandmother Shayntse, "is a father to all—and to orphans as well."

Yes. Even in these moments of extremity, the narrowness and egotism of Nakhum's family showed through. If it was not apparent in Nakhum, who was situated at the exact center of the misfortune, it showed up in his mother Shayntse who, as a guest in the house who had arrived at last moment but who conducted herself in a way that made the other family members draw away from her, and kept them from regarding her as one of them because of the way she only half participated in their sorrow. It was as if she had come to their misfortune the way she might have gone to a wedding, representing only the groom's family.

In the moments of the greatest distress she actually (shameful to say) went about examining closets and bureaus, checking their contents and sorting with her eyes her son's clothes from those of his wife, the way a married couple might do before a divorce when they have to take stock of what they own so that they will know how to divide it when the time comes for them to part.

Of course, none of this was intended to be noticed, and yet, grief-stricken as the members of the family were, it did not escape them that Grandmother Shayntse was the sort of person who at a time like this had such matters on her mind.

It was the morning after Nekhamke had had her very difficult night in the course of which the cries of the family (including, this time, too, that of Grandmother Shayntse) had called Nekhamke back from the dead.

No one in the household (with the exception of the smaller children) had slept a wink all night. They all looked sallow, exhausted and were certain that the appalling night through which they had just passed did not mark the end, but rather the beginning of a greater sorrow. The true crisis was yet to come—perhaps today or tonight . . . but come it would.

They awaited the coming of the doctors who had been sent for early on the morning after that difficult night, though everyone knew that their visits would produce no improvement beyond those final remedies that they would prescribe, like camphor and cathartics.

The weather, sharp and frosty, looked in through the bleared windows in which as the night ended it had already begun to etch its angry pictures which diminished the light in the house where now there reigned a gloom that seemed to have turned everyone silent.

It was then that Mikhalko's death was suddenly discovered. The older servant who had been calling him for some while without getting a reply finally went to his hut to get him. There, when she opened the door, she found him—as she found him. She went back at once to the house where as if that was all that was needed after what had already happened, she announced her bit of news. "Someone had better look to Mikhalko. I think he's dead. Mikhalko."

"Dead? Where? What? When did it happen?"

"I don't know but I think that . . ."

Various members of the household went to Mikhalko's hut to see for themselves and they confirmed her news.

One of the members of the family said, "We'll have to do something, inform someone. See that he's taken away."

"It seems to me that he has a daughter," said someone else.

Then one of the store assistants, Elyokum or Katerukhe who had spent the night so that they might prove useful to the family, went to look after Mikhalko.

Grandmother Shayntse, who had made a long, tiring journey—a distance nearly all the way to Kamenets—and who had been up all night at her daughter-in-law's bedside, now retired into a nearby room and there, still in her traveling clothes and wearing her veil, she settled herself on a couch and had herself a good sleep. No one had seen her go, and no one missed her.

The doctors who had been called that morning, and who waked out of their sleep and made to rise before their usual time, came reluctantly to the house and as if only for the sake of appearances, and for the sake of a family to which they were frequent visitors and from which recently they had earned considerable sums. There was nothing further that they could do beyond, as we have said, prescribing cathartics; and indeed they contented themselves with that, and wrote no further prescriptions. This time they were not pleased when members of the family accompanied them to the gate. When they were asked about the patient they made generalized replies like, "It's in God's hands," a phrase which rang false coming from them. It was, too, a sign of hopelessness and an indication that there was no point in asking them anything else.

Naturally enough, none of the men in the household went into town to conduct business. On the contrary, every employee, every clerk or bookkeeper, who could be spared from the business was asked to the house, or came of his own accord to be helpful.

As for Moshe Mashber, feeling aimless because he had nothing to do, he stood in the middle of the dining room and, moving with greater haste than usual, he put on his prayer shawl and tefillin and then recited his prayers rapidly, as if he feared an interruption from his daughter's room. He read without enthusiasm, and without being particularly aware of what the words meant, because all the while he was reciting, he kept turning toward his daughter's room to see how she was doing. Once, he actually crossed over into her room. His daughter, just then, was surrounded by various family members. She had just closed her eyes. Then she opened them and looked suddenly toward the door where she saw her father carrying his prayer shawl and phylacteries. She was startled and took him for a stranger or, what was worse, for a phantom or the Angel of Death wearing a prayer shawl.

But it was not long before she recognized him. "Ah, Father," she said, motioning him to come closer. She took his hand and clung to it and pleaded with him to stand beside her because she felt safer with her hand in his.

But when she closed her eyes and dozed off, Moshe took advantage of the moment to take his hand away and leave the room.

It was after that that Elyokum or Katerukhe—whoever it was who was sent to give Mikhalko's daughter the news of her father's death—returned to say that he had brought the daughter back with him.

She was, in fact, in Mikhalko's hut just then. When she saw him sitting all rigid in his bed, with his head against the wall, she burst into a loud lament that reached to his employer's dining room.

Moshe Mashber was standing at the window in his prayer shawl and tefillin when he heard her outcry and it made him tremble.

But she quieted down at once and evidently got busy doing what needed to be done for her father. She laid him out and changed his clothes and got him ready for his burial.

Awhile later, several people, members of his family or people hired for the occasion, came with a coffin and a wagon. They took Mikhalko and drove slowly away with him. For some reason it occurred to nobody to close the gate after they left. And it was through that same open gate that Moshe Mashber's daughter, Nekhamke, was driven away at the same time the next morning.

On that final night, Nekhamke's children, after very little discussion, were sent away from the house. They were bundled, weeping, into their coats; warm scarves were wrapped round their necks, and they were buttoned up and sent to spend the night where it was judged it would be quieter and therefore better for them.

That night, nobody, absolutely no one, not even Grandmother Shayntse, slept a wink. The sick woman was several times "called" by wailing and each time that those voices waked her she looked around wildly as if astonished, like someone who has returned from another world. Those gathered in Nekhamke's bedroom were no longer concerned that the presence of so many anxious faces might unsettle her. The store and office employees who had come to make themselves useful—though there was nothing left to be done—stayed on until dawn. Then when the first light of day appeared and the marks of a severe frost showed in the windowpanes, Nekhamke spoke: "Dark. It's so dark? Father, where are you?"

Moshe came near. Bending over her he wiped the cold sweat from her forehead. "Ah, child," he said.

"Light! Turn on the light!" she cried with what was left of her strength.

Moshe, unable to restrain his tears, said desperately, "My child. It's not dark here for anyone but you. Your world is passing."

And now her mortal agony began. There were spasms and groans, all the gestures of finality the body makes.

Then someone handed Moshe Mashber a prayer book, long kept in readiness and open at the proper place. An anguished Moshe, taking it, bent closer to his daughter and said, "My child, repeat after me . . ." And he read the prayer of confession to her in proper form: "I thank Thee, O God, and the God of my fathers that my healing is in Thy hand and that my death, too, is in Thy hand."

Those who were there and saw it, the members of the household, the relatives and even the employees who were now gathered in the sickroom were without exception silent. Even the most hardened of them had tears in their eyes and were choked by grief. Nevertheless, they all maintained a reverential silence and not one of them wept aloud.

It was not long before Nekhamke's breathing grew calmer, quieter. So quiet at last that one might have been deceived into thinking that she had just fallen into a healthful sleep while in fact it was not sleep at all. It was the final end.

Those with some experience in these matters saw it at once in Nekhamke's face and moved quickly to lead the members of the family away from the bed. Gitl, like a wounded animal, made a move toward her daughter, crying wildly, "Oh . . . my darling." Yehudis, the sister, clutched at her head and echoed her mother's cry. Moshe Mashber, too, stood for a while as if paralyzed until someone woke him from his trance with a gentle word and pointed once again to a place in the prayer book. And now Moshe read the prayer that exalts God's righteousness:

You who live in clay houses,
What makes you proud?

God has given and He has taken away.
Blessed be the Name of the Lord.

Then Moshe also left the room.

At times like this a somewhat distant relative who knows what needs to be done with a corpse is given the task of tending to it. In this case, that was Esther-Rokhl who was also known as The Leather Saint. She was a distant relative of Moshe Mashber's and she had spent her life in piety and poverty, a result of her marriage to her husband whose two professions—he was a bookbinder during the week and the caretaker of a workingmen's synagogue on the weekend—whose two professions combined produced hardly enough to feed them. And yet she never complained and, except for a bit of beet soup at Passover time, she never asked for help from any of her relatives, including Moshe. And when she was asked, "Esther-Rokhl, how are you doing?" she always replied, "Not bad, thank you. My husband Moshe, the bookbinder, and the good Lord look out for me. Somehow we get on." It was as if she meant to shake off such sympathetic inquiries, despite the fact that her face was evidence enough of the dire poverty that had turned her features hard as leather and rendered them incapable of expressing joy.

Prosperous relatives employed her at weddings where she looked after the cooking and the baking and supervised the servants. She was employed by women in labor or to sit at the bedside of a sick member of the family. Or, as now in Moshe's house, to perform the final duties for the dead.

It was Esther-Rokhl, as we have said, who now made her appearance. She approached the bed and bowed. Then, as if she were speaking to a living person, she said, "Holy spirit of Nekhamke, daughter of Moshe, return to the place from which you have come, and may your body serve you." With that, she closed Nekhamke's eyes, drew out her hands and feet, removed the pillow from under her head and covered her face.

When she had done all that, she covered the mirror on the wall. Then she turned to the bystanders and said, "Let them pour out water."

Later, the necessary things were done to the body. It was lowered to the floor and lighted candles were placed behind the head. But all of this was done by men, not by Esther-Rokhl who at the same time went up to Moshe, to Gitl, to Yehudis and to Nakhum Lentsher and cut the seams of their garments: Moshe and Nakhum had the seams in their lapels opened with a knife, then the men tore the rent wider with their hands so that some cloth would dangle; Gitl and Yehudis had similar rents made in their bodices.

We will not describe what happened then: how the members of the household, other relatives and family intimates seated themselves around the body and wept over it. Nor will we describe how Gitl, who did not sit, wandered about through the other rooms, sometimes in one, sometimes in another, moving silently from wall to wall as if she was waiting for someone to come at any moment from the room in which the body lay with the news that the impossible had happened. That her daughter was alive again.

She moved about this way until dawn when the members of the burial society showed up. Later, a couple of poorly dressed women appeared carrying strange-looking pots and cannisters that had not seen scouring in a very long time—implements with which to wash the corpse. Later still came the stretcher bearers. One of them carried three long rods under his arm; another, a black cloth which, for the moment, was folded; and the third carried a sheaf of straw which he would later spread over the stretcher.

When the various samovars in the kitchen and the anteroom were boiling, the women carried them skillfully to a room in which the corpse had been laid across a couple of tables that had been pushed together. It was the room in which the corpse was "given its due" and no one was admitted into it who did not have strong self-control. But Gitl thrust her way in like a mother tiger.

Esther-Rokhl noted the wild look in her eyes and went up to her at once. Gitl uttered a brief cry and was silent. Then, like one who was half out of her mind and also strangely yielding, she said to Esther-Rokhl, "Just tell me one thing, Esther-Rokhl, dear. I beg you. Is what I see really true?"

"Yes," Esther-Rokhl said without ambiguity. "It's real. Now, let us give her her due, as becomes a good Jewish daughter. Go on, get out of here Gitl." Esther-Rokhl spoke harshly thus to Gitl to bring her back to her senses, which she was very close to losing.

From then on, all that needed to be done to the corpse was done: it was washed in hot water; it was dressed in grave-clothes; the bonnet prescribed by piety was placed on her head, and the appropriate verses, such as, "I shall sprinkle pure water upon thee . . ." were recited.

Outside the house, the stretcher to carry the dead was being prepared by a stretcher maker who leaned two long rods against a kitchen chair and then bound them together with diagonal lengths of rope. He took a handful from the sheaf of straw and deftly created a sort of pillow at one end of the stretcher and a foot rest at the other. Then he scattered straw over the length of the stretcher. A bit later, two other stretcher bearers appeared who wrapped the body in a white sheet. Each of the bearers held a bunched end of the sheet in his hands as the two of them staggered with the heavy weight of the body into the courtyard.

It was then that the women of the immediate family, relatives and neighbors and such other females who were in any way close to the Mashbers, approached the stretcher and surrounded it. And then out of the small, densely packed circle, out of the tremulous confusion that was seething around the stretcher bearers who were hastily doing their work around the body—measuring it, covering it—various voices and wild cries could be heard.

"May good angels come to greet you."

"May the gates of Heaven be opened to you."

"Ah, woe. Such a young tree . . ."

"Intercede for us."

And Gitl paused at the threshold over which the body had just been borne. She did not go down toward the stretcher but cast a disordered look toward it, and all the while that the others were wailing, she continued to repeat to herself the question she had been putting to Esther-Rokhl: "Is what I see really true?"

Then the funeral procession began to move. Then one heard the rattling sound of the alms box that an officer of the Burial Society was holding, and everyone moved through the gate through which, yesterday, Mikhalko had been carried, and which no one had thought to close—nor was it closed now.

Awhile later when the funeral procession, made up of members of the family, relatives and friends as well as all those who had come to pay their respects to Moshe Mashber—people from the market, from the synagogue and all sorts of others—when the funeral was gone, one person out of all that crowd stood alone in the street outside the gate.

It was Alter, to whom in the last few days no one had paid any attention, whether he came down into the house or not. No one noticed that he, like every one else, had stayed awake during the last terrible night. No one had seen him wandering about like a shadow, and no one in the hubbub of preparations had taken note of him today. Or had seen him standing before a wall in the dining room, weeping quietly to himself. Alter, since he was not used to people, had not thought to take his place in the funeral procession. And so it was that he was in the street now, staring after it.

He stood there, as perplexed as an animal that has lost its way . . . and it was then that the dog, Watch Chain, came out to him, as if meaning to comfort him. Watch Chain who since yesterday no longer had an owner, and who, like Alter, had been ignored or forgotten by everyone in the house. And the two of them, Watch Chain and Alter, looked in the same direction. The direction toward which the body had been carried.

Alter might have stood there for a long time—well into the evening—turning rigid with the intensifying cold if Gnessye, the young servant woman to whom he was secretly betrothed, had not chanced to see him when she came out into the courtyard and led him back into the house.

The house had the look of a house from which a body has been carried. The doors of every room were opened wide. The damp residue left by the washing of the corpse was on the floor as well as the footprints of those who had moved back and forth through the opened doors.

At the cemetery, which the funeral procession reached somewhat late in the evening because of the great distance it had to go, the usual rituals were performed: the mourners circled the corpse seven times, then they recited the prayer Tsiduk Hadin, then they approached the open grave which because of the frost had been difficult to dig and was not quite ready. There was, then, a delay before the body could be lowered by lamplight into the earth.

This time, because Nekhamke belonged to an important family in town, Hirshl Liever himself stood beside the grave and held the lantern over it as he issued commands to the shammes's wife: "Uncover her face . . . the shards . . . where are the shards? And the forks . . ." he cried when it was necessary to cover the eyes of the corpse and to put a fork-shaped twig into its hand as the ritual required.

Then, because Nekhamke had not left grown children who could say the Kaddish, the mourner's prayer after her, Moshe Mashber undertook to recite it. But, at the first word, *Yisgadal*, he uttered a strange sob, and the rest of the prayer seemed to dissolve between his trembling lips.

Every customary condolence was offered to the family, but when everything was done and the cortege began to move away, then Moshe

Mashber, with the words of the mourner's prayer still half-congealed in his mouth, continued to stand there, like a broken man whose destroyed world lay beside the hillock formed by the newly filled grave.

Moshe's brother, Luzi, naturally enough, was there as one of the mourners. He came up to Moshe and did what he could to ease his grief. Moshe turned and looked at him in amazement—as if he were looking at a stranger—then in an unearthly, flat and toneless voice, he said, "Ah, Luzi. There lies half my world. And it won't be long before the other half lies there, too."

"What are you saying?"

"Yes," Moshe replied. "I'm talking about myself. That's what I mean."

And Moshe began preparations for his own burial.

Just after the seven-day mourning period was over, but while they were still in the thirty-day mourning period, Moshe took Gitl aside and said, "Our world, Gitl, is almost over. It's time to think of the *other* world."

"What?" said Gitl who, having endured so much already, sensed the onset of some new misfortune and she turned to him for an explanation.

"I mean that there's nothing to hope for *here* and we must get ready for what's to come."

"Yes, but what is it you want?"

"Before all, I want to see Alter married."

"Alter? At a time like this?"

"Yes. Especially now. Time is passing. Our own situation is perilous and Alter's will be determined by what happens to us. If we don't look after him, who will? And if not now, when?"

"But where's the hurry?" Gitl asked, fresh tears starting in her eyes.

"It's a good deed not to delay a marriage. Especially one like Alter's."

Yes, it was strange. It sometimes happens that someone who has been dealt such a blow, or several, by destiny that he no longer has the strength to rebuild what has been destroyed. Abandoning everything he has ever had, he makes a small packet of the remnant of his strength and lets it serve him on his poor, defeated final way when the time comes to give over his former grandeur.

It is strange, we say, the way Moshe Mashber became indifferent to his business affairs—as if they were beyond despair. At a time when anyone else might have taken measures to do something, to make some kind of move, even a reflex thrashing like that of a fish out of water, or a half-slaughtered fowl—when he might have formed a partnership with someone or found some other sort of help.

The matter of Alter's marriage so occupied Moshe's mind that he put all other business aside. Because during the period of mourning, Moshe one day had observed an encounter between Alter and Gnessye in the doorway to the dining room. He had noticed how Alter looked at *her* and how she had looked at *him*. And the way that Alter and Gnessye, as if oblivious of the misfortune in the household, then looked at him, Moshe, as if they were reminding him of his promise to look after them.

Moshe Mashber moved with dispatch, and there is reason to think that he discussed the matter with Luzi even during the period of mourning when Luzi paid his condolence visits. Hushed discussions away from anyone else's ears, in the course of which one of them had murmured the phrase, "Funerals precede marriages," the meaning of which is that the death, even of a close family member, must not be permitted to interfere with a planned wedding. And that, therefore, according to the law and with due regard to the actual situation, the matter must be taken care of as soon as possible.

Moshe, therefore, undertook to hurry the matter on. Especially when he had taken a good look at Gnessye and had seen from the way her body pressed against her clothing that she was fully mature, and that if he had not betrothed her to his brother, there would have been men enough . . . men of her own rank . . . a fellow like Katerukhe, perhaps, who would be glad to have her.

He was certainly right about Gnessye. Whenever she appeared in the marketplace she elicited many a sly wink from the cheerful crowds of younger butchers, meat cutters and the like. Seeing her, they poked each other in the ribs and made vulgar sounds with their tongues. Sounds which, in their butcher language, meant, "Hey, just look at that, will you!"

There is reason to think that even Mazheve, the butcher's apprentice who worked for Meyer Blass, a youth whom we have already met . . . there is reason to think that even he, that well-known breaker of women's hearts, had often looked after her and rubbed his hands in lustful anticipation.

In all likelihood her name was on his list of conquests to come. She was often on his mind, and he fully intended to accost her one day so that he might get to know her better.

Yes, there is reason to suppose that Mazheve was deeply offended when he heard the news (from someone like Katerukhe) that Gnessye, forgetful of her rank, had been betrothed to some sickly upper-class fellow. First, because he, Mazheve, had missed an opportunity, and then even supposing him out of the picture, she would, in the normal course of events, have married someone like himself: an artisan or a butcher. Now that he knew what she had done, he watched for his opportunity, and catching sight of her, he slunk after her, following her closely as she left the marketplace on her way home. And thus it was that he suddenly appeared before her, standing before a recessed gate.

Of course she knew who he was, because who among the maidservants and chambermaids had not cast an eye on Mazheve as she passed her tongue over her parched lips. But, seeing him now, directly before her, gave her a start, particularly since Mazheve asked her to come in behind the gate, a request she found herself unable to deny. She felt like a bird paralyzed by a serpent's gaze. She tried unsuccessfully to lower her eyes. To cover her face with her hands—and could not. And was afraid. His dreadful proximity induced a warm glow in her that rose from her knees to her thighs. Standing heavyhearted before him, waiting for him to say the first word, she felt herself entirely in his power. It was impossible to run, equally impossible to scream. But what mattered most was that the heat rising past her knees was terrifying—and pleasurable.

"You're a maidservant, aren't you?" Mazheve asked.

"Yes," Gnessye replied. And she was suddenly petrified as she recalled where she was a servant and with whom she was now speaking. And given the family she served and the tie that bound her to it, what it would look like to be seen in a blind alley talking with a man . . . a man like Mazheve. "What do you want?" she asked, frightened.

"Nothing. It's just that I've heard you're going to marry some rich simpleton and you imagine he's going to make you happy. I just wanted to say . . . better think it over because those people don't have the knack."

"What knack?" Gnessye asked for the sake of saying something and embarrassed because she did not understand.

"This one," he said, giving her an unspoken but gross explanation by pressing his stiff masculinity against her.

"Leave me alone." Gnessye turned away half unwillingly, trying to tear herself away from his proximity which suffocated her and made her catch her breath. "Leave me alone or I'll scream."

"Where we come from, screaming will get you a punch in the mouth—and someplace else as well," Mazheve said. But then, seeing that given the frequency with which people passed by, there was not much in the way of dalliance he could accomplish in the gateway, he acted as if he were turning her loose. "Go on. But think it over. And don't do anything you'll be sorry about."

When Gnessye got home, she was still pale and frightened. In the kitchen she was so weak in the knees that she had to sit down. The older servant, who knew her every expression intimately, cried out, when she saw her, "What is it? What's happened? Why are you so pale, girl? Why are you sitting down?"

"It's nothing," Gnessye said, thinking that she could not possibly tell even her closest friend about her encounter with Mazheve.

"But something's happened. Go on. Tell me. You met somebody. A man. Right? Go on, tell me."

Gnessye lowered her eyes, unable either to deny or to confess what had happened. The older servant caressed her, soothed her, reassured her: "There, there. Just you wait a little while. Just now the master and mistress have their misfortune on their minds. But a promise is a promise. You've been betrothed and I'm sure the wedding will be soon.

"I know," she said, speaking with a mother's devotion above Gnessye's head. "Your need is great. I know. You're filled with it. The hoops cannot contain the cask nor your clothes your virgin body. Just wait a little. Your time will come, and soon."

The encounter between Mazheve and Gnessye took place at the same time that Moshe Mashber observed the exchange between Alter and Gnessye about which we have already spoken, and which prompted him to talk to Gitl about getting Alter married.

Gitl, grieving over the death of her daughter, did not at first want to hear anything about it. But she yielded when Moshe, with whom it was her habit to agree, put the marriage in a context of exalted ways, eternity and good works that one must not put off.

It was after that first conversation with Gitl that he said, "We'll have to see about getting her ready to be a member of the family." A short while later she and Moshe asked Gnessye into their bedroom for a talk.

There after much backing and filling and an awkward search for words that would be appropriate to use to someone who was several levels lower on the social scale but who now for certain reasons had to be reckoned as a member of the family, Gitl said, "As you know, we've not been able to think about the betrothal until now. But it's time for you to get ready. Just do what is right, and you'll be treated like our own child. Very well, go now, Gnessye. We'll be celebrating the wedding soon."

After that conversation, Gitl left the room, her face flushed and her heart in a turmoil. She pressed her hands against her bodice as if fearful that something might fall from it. And when she got to the kitchen, she flung herself into the older servant's arms, sobbing, "Oh, my dear!"

"What is it? What's happened? Who's been picking on you?"

Then Gnessye told her what Moshe Mashber and Gitl had discussed with her in their room. She wept and sobbed as she spoke, as if she was reliving the conversation about the match.

She had wept that first time because she had been required to make up her mind; now, the second time, she wept because the wedding (as they had discussed it in the bedroom) loomed before her and she still had no idea what sort of a man Alter was, or how she would live out the rest of her days with him.

It had been hard for her at first, when the older servant had urged the match on her. She had allowed herself to be persuaded because the idea of being a daughter-in-law in such a family—like landing in a bed of roses—had dazzled her. But knowing what Alter had been like earlier, she had had misgivings then, as she had them now when to all appearances he was entirely well.

"I'm scared" she sobbed. "I don't know where I am . . . or where I'm going . . . or what I'm going to do."

But the thing was done. And the older servant had more than one pang of conscience when she considered that she had perhaps been foolish to encourage Gnessye to this betrothal. But betrothed was betrothed. And it was too late to unsay it. Then, because she was after all the older woman (and because she felt more than a trace of guilt), she plucked up her courage and, as if she were scolding Gnessye, said, "Don't be a fool. Why are you crying? You're not going to the slaughter. You're going to be married. Well? Don't you want that?"

"No . . . yes," Gnessye replied tearfully. "But I'm scared."

"Then say your prayers. What are you afraid of? That a prince will carry you off? Or that the butchers' dogs will tear your silk dress?"

She spoke thus harshly to Gnessye first, to interrupt the flow of her thoughts, and second, to drown out the cries of her own conscience that were driving her to think of reconsidering the matter.

Little by little, Gnessye calmed down. Later, after her conversation with Moshe and Gitl in their bedroom, Yehudis, their older daughter, called Gnessye into her room and speaking to her as to one of the family she advised her how to prepare for the tailor who was coming to measure her for her wedding clothes. Gnessye crimsoned and listened, her hands pressed against her bodice because she did not feel at ease with Yehudis, who, though she did her very best to talk to Gnessye as to an equal, delivered her advice as though she were standing on a ladder.

Yes. Yehudis went to considerable trouble and did what she could for her parents' sake. And to do what she thought was necessary, too. She understood that, for Alter's sake . . . for someone like himself, one needed to step down from one's own social level, even if that meant being on an equal footing with Gnessye, to treat her like a relation, and to give her access to the family. So she did what she could, as did the other members of the family, even the sons-in-law who, in recent days when they learned of the betrothal and the approaching marriage, had begun to alter their treatment of her, to minimize the distance that had formerly separated them, naturally, from their maidservant. Now they treated her more kindly, more like a relative.

During this time, understandably enough, the family disregarded their straitened financial circumstances and to the limits of their ability, freely incurred whatever expenses the marriage preparations entailed. Within days of the first conversations between Moshe, Gitl and Gnessye, a woman's tailor and a man's tailor were sent for. When they had been shown the materials that had already been purchased and it had been made clear to them that the clothes were to be ready just as soon as possible, the tailors began to take measurements of the prospective bride and groom.

The measurements were taken in separate rooms: the bride was measured in one and the groom in the other.

The tailor hired to make Gnessye's clothes was Yoshua, a very pious man with a neat, well-tended beard who always wore his Sabbath hat and caftan. Yoshua never took any measurements lest he should chance to touch a woman; indeed, he did not want to risk looking at one, especially in those moments of undress that his profession sometimes required. And this is why he never came alone to take measurements but always brought with him one of his skilled older assistants who did the measuring while Yoshua carried on a respectable conversation with his clients while he wrote the measurements for the garments into his notebook.

This time, too, Yoshua brought an assistant who, knowing what was happening in the household and what Gnessye's rank was, behaved with more freedom than usual when he took the measurements of daughters in respectable households where the slightest unnecessary touch of their bodies was forbidden; but in Gnessye's case his hands lingered when he had her raise her arms so that he could measure from her armpits to her sides; or places like her high bosom or her back and thighs which he sometimes caressed under the guise of an adjustment to his tape measure, though all the while he was thinking of what he would brag about to his fellow assistants when he got home.

Gnessye, whose measurements were being taken in the presence of both Gitl and the older kitchen maid, felt tense, unhappy and confused. She stood there with tears in her eyes, and each time that Yoshua's assistant permitted himself a liberty, her hands went to her bodice and she trembled, imagining that it was Mazheve doing something indecent. Her eyes were so narrowed that she saw no one. Not Gitl, not the older servant who was her most intimate friend. But what she saw, as through a thin veil, was Mazheve calling her to join him in a recess behind a gate.

And all the while that the tailor's assistant worked around Gnessye, Gitl kept her eyes averted from her, because even for a woman the sight of the too-ripe female body straining at the seams was forbidden. She kept her eyes from Gnessye and kept up a conversation about clothing styles and about various things she had ordered from the tailor. Yoshua, who looked at none of the women, promised her whatever she asked for and went on recording numbers in his notebook.

In another room, Alter, too, was being measured for his wedding clothes. His tailor was Gershon the Lithuanian or Gershon Shtoglitz, as he was also known. He was a man of advanced years. A little nothing of a tailor. A man partly naive, partly stupid, with weak red-rimmed eyes, a thin high-pitched voice and a way of pronouncing "sh" sounds as if they were "s."

He was not usually given work to do in well-to-do homes but the fact never distressed him. He was convinced that he was as fine a tailor as those who worked for wealthy clients because his work, like all fine tailoring, was in the "stoglitz" manner. But what the word "stoglitz" meant, no one, including Gershon, could say. But clearly he thought it signified first-class work, the last word in fashion in N.

His work was indeed "stoglitz," though that could mean that a collar stuck out too far or had a way of creeping up the neck. Sometimes the front of a coat or caftan was longer than the back, or the other way around. But it made no difference. He was suitable enough for Alter. Everything had to be done quickly and cheaply. There was no point in getting involved with well-known tailors who charged the moon and then did not keep their promises.

The only bystander in the room where Alter was being measured was Moshe Mashber himself who looked on with erratic attention as

Gershon turned Alter about every which way while he, Gershon, kneeled and rose, his exertions sending his aging blood to his face and to his weak eyes. Moshe watched him write the measurements in his book in an angular tailor's hand, notations he finally did without because he forgot them just as soon as he reached home. Moshe, standing by, urged Gershon to two things: to do the best work he could and to do it as quickly as possible.

"Certainly," said Gershon. "I sall work quickly. Shtoglitz quality. And quickly, too."

And the work moved on apace. Both of the tailors worked expeditiously, and it was not many days before the clothes were brought to the groom and the bride for a first fitting. They, in separate rooms, were, each of them, as if enclosed in fumes of haste. Speed was essential and Gitl urged Yoshua on while Moshe Mashber hurried the Lithuanian Gershon to finish as quickly as he could.

As the wedding day approached and all the clothes and linen and everything else that was needed was ready, Gnessye, who could hardly read Hebrew well enough to move even haltingly through her prayer book, was given a tutor: Esther-Rokhl, the pious relation whom we have already met. Her task was to teach Gnessye the various laws dealing with women which every Jewish female is expected to know as she approaches her marriage.

Esther-Rokhl taught Gnessye how to bless the Sabbath candles and the prayer to make over the bread dough. Later, she took Gnessye into a room where, opening the collection of prayers called *Korban Minkhe*, she found "The Pure Fountain" from which she read the laws and commandments a woman is expected to obey and perform when she unites herself to a man, as well as those that pertain when she is separated from him. As always, Esther-Rokhl spoke with clarity and directness, naming by their real names such things as made Gnessye blush and squirm and look about to see whether anyone was listening.

A few days before the wedding, in the presence of a very small number of people (mostly members of the family), the wedding contract was written and signed.

And now we are at the wedding.

The day before, the bride was turned over to the care of Esther-Rokhl and the older servant who prepared her according to various Jewish rites. They led her to the ritual bath where, as was customary, they turned her over to the *tukerns*, women who administered the ablutions. The *tukerns* trimmed Gnessye's finger- and toenails, then they immersed her in the water crying, "Kosher, kosher, kosher." This was done for a predetermined fee, but the fee to one side, the *tukerns* admired Gnessye's plump white body, and each time she rose from or descended into the water, they exchanged knowing female glances that signified, "Ah, may every man be lucky enough to enjoy so fine a treasure."

Gnessye submitted herself to everything without exception. But when she caught a glimpse of her freshly bathed, clean body, its loveliness turned her dizzy.

And all that the women had done for Gnessye, Moshe, who regarded it as a brother's duty, did the next day, the day of the wedding, for Alter. He led him to the ritual bath and saw to it that he performed the appropriate ceremonies there.

On the wedding day, the bride and groom, as is the custom, fasted. Gnessye was dressed and bedecked by Esther-Rokhl and the older servant while Alter was brought by his brother into another room. There, when Alter had recited a prayer of confession and wept for a while over the various misfortunes of his life, and when, as is traditional, he had by means of certain prayers invited his departed parents to his wedding—after all that, Moshe sequestered himself with Alter so that he could convey to him by means of euphemism and innuendo the information from the *Korban Minkhe* that Esther-Rokhl had passed on to Gnessye.

While Moshe talked, Alter, who seemed not to understand what was being said, turned pale, partly because of his illness and partly, too, because he was fasting. He was helped to put on his wedding garment, a white tunic, like a shirt with broad sleeves. The tunic made him look even paler, almost like a corpse.

He flung himself into Moshe's arms and then into Luzi's, who was also there helping to dress him. Overcome, he was able to say only, "Moshe . . . Luzi . . . my brothers." To a bystander taking in that scene, it would have been clear that the groom did not have high hopes of the joy to come, and that those who were with him, and who wanted to see a bit of happiness in his life, had no great expectations either.

The marriage was celebrated quietly in a room in the house, the way such marriages are celebrated by families that, for one reason or another, do not want to make much of a stir.

Not many people were invited, and those that were were not really intimates of the family. There were no marketplace merchants, no members of the synagogue to which Moshe belonged and yet there was a full prayer quorum of Luzi's people.

Gitl and the rest of the family were at once hosts to the wedding celebration at the same time as they were people in mourning. This was especially true of Gitl and Yehudis who before dressing for the wedding had had to remove their black aprons. Aprons which they would don again after the wedding.

They were still in the midst of the prescribed thirty-day mourning period so it was perfectly understandable that there was not much joy in the faces of Moshe and his family. Moshe moved hurriedly, as if he were in a dream. He was hasty now as he had been when he made the wedding preparations. He cut short the wedding jester's performance both at the "seating" of the bride and at the "seating" of the groom. He cut short the performance of the shabby little band of musicians that had been invited, allowing it to play only the most necessary numbers. He urged the shammes to set up the wedding canopy quickly. And he made the cantor hurry the wedding ceremony itself.

And that's what was done. Then there was the dinner at which Meshulam the matchmaker was also present. Meshulam who, as the man who had arranged the match, could not be omitted.

He felt himself now to be on intimate terms with the family. Because the bride had no parents and no relations beyond her close friend, the older servant, Meshulam took it upon himself to be in loco parentis. Taking advantage of his new intimacy with the family, Meshulam allowed himself to drink a bit too much. The result was that his naturally roseate face turned scarlet and his white beard turned even whiter by contrast. His felt cap was drenched with sweat so that when as was his habit he tried to take it off so that he could wear only his skullcap, he had, this time, to work even harder to separate the two. But he succeeded at last and started to dance clumsily, drunkenly. Had he been seen dancing this way on any other occasion when people's hearts were less heavy, he would have been the butt of laughter and would have been led to one side and invited to sit down.

But now, no one interfered with him. And yet his was a strange dance indeed: he moved with his eyes closed, apparently half asleep, as he gestured and made grimaces like a goat. Strange as his dance was, it was no stranger than the entire ambience surrounding the marriage of this couple who, when the ceremony was over, were seated side by side and who, after their prenuptial fast, now ate what was put before them without exchanging so much as a word as they stuffed themselves while their eyes looked in every direction but at each other.

It was strange, too, that Gitl had permitted the older servant, as the person most nearly related to the bride, to sit beside her. Strange, too, the sparse company that included some fifteen of Luzi's followers whom Moshe Mashber had asked Luzi to invite. Because people who were closer to the family, and intimate friends who usually participated in the Mashber family's celebrations, were this time not invited. So that no one close might have to witness this strange wedding.

Strange, too, the sight of the Luzi people who, endeavoring to amuse the bride and groom, started a dance such as Moshe Mashber's walls had never seen. They made a crush of bodies, throwing their heads back, then bending close to the ground as if they meant to unite heaven and earth within the compass of their gaze.

Strange, too, the sight of Moshe Mashber and Luzi dancing together. Moshe, though he was in mourning, wanted to please Alter; and Luzi went along so that Moshe would not dance alone. They made a strange sight, circling around each other—Moshe followed by Luzi, then Luzi followed by Moshe so closely that each time they turned they found themselves almost face-to-face.

It was strange, too, to see Gitl dancing with the older servant as if they were equals, the one representing the groom's and the other the bride's families. Gitl gave no indication at all of her superior walk in life. The older servant, flushed with pleasure, kept wiping her upper lip with the holiday kerchief she wore.

Then Esther-Rokhl danced with Yehudit. Esther-Rokhl, whose face was leather hard as a result of poverty and unsated hunger . . . Esther-Rokhl who, as we have said, was usually employed to watch over a corpse, or to supervise the waiters at a wedding or who, sometimes, on occasions like this one involving Alter and Gnessye, was given a more important part to play: to teach the bride the religious laws relating to women, to take her to the ritual bath and later to place her, as now, at the bridal feast. And then she, Esther-Rokhl, might dance with some important member of the family, as she now danced with Yehudit.

Esther-Rokhl danced silently. Not an artery or vein in her face moved—as if no ray of festive light could penetrate to her interior. Nevertheless, she was celebrating in her own way. A way that expressed itself by an authentic stillness which is, perhaps, more exalted, more meaningful, than other, louder forms of celebration.

Then her husband, Moshe Einbinder, danced. He, who was never invited to a wedding—or if he was invited, he generally chose not to come. Because he firmly believed that no one needed him to grace a festivity. This time, however, he not only had been invited, but he had accepted the invitation because on this occasion he felt that his kinship to the Mashbers made it appropriate for him to participate in the festivities without feeling embarrassed and having to sidle off into corners because of his small size and his poor-man's smile, and his dirty hands that he could never wash clean of his bookbinder's paste and glue.

He danced with Meshulam. Meshulam in his skullcap, and without the felt outer cap that he had permitted himself to remove out of sheer marriage-broker's exuberance and as an indication that he was a family intimate. And because he had already drunk a great deal. Much too much. And dancing with him was Moshe Einbinder, wearing a hat that anyone else would long ago have consigned to weekday wear and which he wore on Sabbaths, on holidays and at weddings—to which he was never invited.

After that, Luzi, as the oldest of the brothers, danced Polish style with the bride. Gnessye held one end of a red kerchief while Luzi held the other. He led her in the dance while all the guests formed a circle around them. Luzi, on any other occasion would have taken the opportunity to show the audience his dancing skill but, evidently on a signal from Moshe, he brought the dance to a quick end.

And thus the festivities, too, came to an end. The guests, Luzi's people and others, said their farewells and left early. Only the family remained and they too were urged to retire to their various rooms for the night.

Meanwhile, Esther-Rokhl and the older servant made up a bed in one of the bedrooms. Over it, they recited various prayers and proverbs that are customarily recited at the bedding of a newly married pair.

Then the house grew still. And here it would be appropriate for us to lower the curtain, as it were, and say no more.

But since the situation is an exceptional one, and since it involves Alter, we are compelled to call attention to a matter which we would otherwise pass over in silence. That is, that something quite abnormal transpired that night between the young couple in their room. We will say no more than that Alter's share in the proceedings might have been predicted.

One more word.

In the morning at dawn, while the house was still silent, Gnessye got up and dressed. She wandered about the room for a while as she gathered her things together and bound them in a bundle. And if the older servant, who slept as usual in the kitchen, had not been so exhausted from the festivities of the night before, she would certainly have heard when someone came into the kitchen, roamed about it for a while then opened the kitchen door and left.

It was Gnessye. We have no idea where she went that morning when fully dressed she left Moshe Mashber's home. We don't know whether it was to some acquaintance, or to an agency for servants, or whether she simply wandered off somewhere without goal or purpose.

But we do know the effect her leaving had on Moshe Mashber's household and we will say a few words about it.

Later in the morning, the family, naturally enough, looked about for the young couple to make its appearance. When they did not come out of their bedroom, Esther-Rokhl, who had been asked to spend the night so that she could be serviceable on various marriage matters . . . Esther-Rokhl received a delicate signal to knock at the door of their bedroom and inform them that it was time to get up. And when Esther-Rokhl knocked and received no reply, she tried the door and, finding it open, went in and found Alter, fully dressed, standing in the middle of the room. It took but a single look at him for her to see that something very strange had happened.

It may be that Alter had been asleep and had not seen Gnessye getting ready to leave, or it may be that he had seen her and pretended to be asleep. Whichever it was, it was clear that Alter, pale and dismayed, had been standing alone in the middle of the room for a very long while—as if he had just had one of his seizures or as if he was about to have one.

Esther-Rokhl asked him about Gnessye, but her experienced woman's eye had already told her that there was no need to ask. Not only was there no sign of her, but even the memory of her seemed to have drained away.

Alter hardly heard her questions. She left the room hurriedly and whispered something to Moshe. Shortly afterward, those in the room exchanged looks of disquiet as they asked, "What is it? What's happened? Where can she be?" They put worried questions to the older servant and waited anxiously for her replies. "Do you know anything? Did you think something like this might happen?" And the older servant, too, did not know what to say.

Gnessye was gone. That was the message written in all of the anxious faces. And for a while it did not even occur to them to send someone to search for Gnessye because it seemed to them that there was no point in it because it would only double the shame and embarrassment that must follow the questions that would necessarily be asked.

There is reason to think, however, that some kind of search was undertaken. One suspects that Esther-Rokhl and the older servant were sent discreetly into town on the chance that they might find her and bring her home.

And there is even reason to think that they employed certain wise-women, seers and "prophets" to whom people turned when they had been robbed but none of the seers had any idea where Gnessye might be, though they promised to do what they could to find out. Meanwhile, they demanded a rich fee now for what they promised to do later.

But nothing came of any of those gestures. Gnessye disappeared from the house forever and left not the slightest trace behind. All that she left behind was her wedding dress ("Decent of her," said some members of the family). She took with her only those clothes which she had bought with her earnings as a kitchen maid—and not even all of those. But she also left Alter behind . . . a man without a wife, and yet, a man who now wore a prayer shawl when he prayed, as a sign that he was married. And for Moshe Mashber, she left behind one more disaster, another downward movement of his steadily worsening fortunes which would not allow him to rejoice in the marriage he had arranged for his sick brother.

Yes. Had anyone taken a good look at Moshe Mashber during those days, he would have seen how the blond hair of his head and beard darkened and turned gray. And that there was now an aged slope to his shoulders, and that this all but imperceptible slope made him look shorter—the way a house looks when it has grown old and is about to collapse.

III

Bankrupt

Properly speaking, the Moshe Mashber tree had been nearly sawn through. It would have required only the very smallest push for it to fall with a crash. And yet he was spared.

By whom?

People like Tsali Derbaremdiker and Sholem Shmaryon, whose profession it was to profit from the bankruptcy of others and who might have profited from his, refrained nevertheless from falling upon him like the carrion dogs they were. Yes. Though they were used to following along behind a stronger creature so that they might snatch a bone from his prey, and when he turned weak and became the prey of someone stronger than himself, turning upon him to tear tasty strips mercilessly from his flesh; still, though that was their profession, this time the Tsalis and the Shmaryons refrained from exercising it.

Why?

For one thing they had invested large sums in his business and they knew the sorts of dangers any bankruptcy could entail; and they had reason to be concerned that they risked losing considerable sums of their own money in his fall. Second, scavengers though they were, they had been shaken by the visitations from God which, as they saw them, had overtaken Moshe Mashber: first the death of his younger daughter and then the disastrous marriage of his brother Alter. And finally, of course, there were his business reverses which had brought him to the edge of the abyss. All of these taken together had, we say, roused a little pity even in the hearts of a pair like Tsali and Sholem.

And . . . let us acknowledge . . . let us acknowledge that when Tsali Derbaremdiker, along with everyone else, accompanied Moshe Mashber to the cemetery, and later when the earth had closed over the grave and people came up to Moshe to condole with him as is the custom, that he, too, Tsali, had said, "May God keep you from sorrow, Moshe Mashber." Let us acknowledge that Tsali was touched to see that Moshe had buried a part of himself under the heaped-up earth of the grave.

And let us acknowledge this about Tsali and about a good many others. Because in those days people still maintained the archaic manners of their ancestors—even in business matters. Not as later on when it became a dictum that "Livelihood is not brotherhood." And when pity in business was regarded as irrelevant. No. At that time and in that place, in cases such as the present one of Moshe Mashber's, people behaved better. It was still possible for them to manifest compassion.

And so for a while they were patient with Moshe. Both the prosperous merchants who were in good financial condition and could wait, and even those who were not, those whom we have described elsewhere who had taken their small savings to him in perfect security and who now desperately needed the money.

The times just then were hard for everyone. It was a year of bad harvest. The peasants throughout the district were unable either to buy or to sell; as for merchants, even the major ones went about with their heads bowed. As for the lesser traders, they jingled sadly the last few groschen in their pockets.

It stands to reason that if it chanced that one of these petty merchants had at some time managed to put aside a bit of money for a rainy day, it was now that he wanted to lay his hands on it. He either dug it out from its hiding place, or he asked for it back from the rich merchant with whom he had invested it.

The misfortune that waited upon these petty traders had two aspects: aside from the fact that there was no profit to be made anywhere there was also an increasing scarcity of goods.

On Sundays or on Friday evenings, one could see worried housewives standing before shops that sold flour dismayed because the coins knotted in their handkerchiefs would not be enough to pay for what they needed. And similar scenes were repeated in the meat markets where the women turned away from that morning's fresh cuts of meat to buy the dried tough leftovers from the day before. And the same distress was visible in the groats' shops where the women blanched when they found themselves unable to buy what they needed. And in the wood depot established by the community to supply firewood to the city's poor. It was something to see: the amounts of wood and the kinds of wood those poor women, alone or helped by a child, took away with them. An armful or a faggot or two, but never enough to keep anyone warm.

And it was something to hear the talk of the shoemakers in taverns like Sholem-Aron's where they continued to gather on Friday afternoons after their work, just as they had done in better times. What they said, what they shouted as they were drinking (but particularly when they were drunk), when their eyes grew inflamed and they gave free rein to their tongues as they poured their hearts out to each other, even as they worried about their wives at home and the anguish that waited for them there when they got home and the women learned that there was not going to be enough money with which to prepare for the Sabbath.

"Damn it all to hell," a voice was heard above the hubbub. "You're shoemakers? You sew shoes and slippers? Scholars, that's what you should have been. . . . May they go barefoot. May the whole town go barefoot. Eh? Reb Dudi, that great man, can't open his mouth to say a good word about the poor? And Reb Yakov-Yossi Eilbirten is too weak to untie his purse strings?"

"Right," several of the drinkers echoed, but it was clear to them all that nothing further would come of it, and that the helpless "Right" was all that would remain of this show of anger, because weakened as they were by their poverty there was nothing else that they could do.

It is clear, then, let us repeat, that any of these folk who had managed to invest their money at low interest with some rich man felt compelled now to ask for their money back.

It should also be clear that such petty lenders had in recent days begun to appear at Moshe Mashber's office with greater frequency and in larger numbers. If their notes had matured, then well and good, they were well within their rights to demand payment. If not, they begged and pleaded to be paid before the due date. If not the whole amount, then at least a portion of the principal.

During the period of Nekhamke's illness, these creditors had found neither Moshe nor Nakhum Lentsher, his son-in-law, at the office, and the creditors had been put off with the excuse, "Well, you see how it is. This is a very bad time just now. They have other things on their minds." Then when Nekhamke died, and they came to the office and found it locked, they turned away, saying, "Well, yes. A misfortune." Then, when the month of mourning was over and Moshe and his son-in-law still put in only rare appearances, there was still the excuse that this was not a time to be too demanding. But then, when the month of mourning was over, these poor creditors, hounded by their poverty, would hear no more excuses and crowds of them began to arrive at the office. And if Moshe was not there, they waited long hours for him. When he was there, they besieged him closely and would not leave. Those whose notes had matured made demands, those whose notes still had time to run begged.

It was then that Nakhum Lentsher took his father-in-law aside and, pointing out that they were at the end of their rope, and that they had no other recourse, suggested that they ask Yakov-Yossi Eilbirten for help.

It's easy enough to say, "Ask Yakov-Yossi."

A brief sketch of Yakov-Yossi:

What does he look like?

A well-fleshed, broad-shouldered man well into his sixties with a well-kept white beard cut moderately short. During the work week, he wore a black caftan of fine English cloth. On the Sabbath his caftan was of satin. He was very rich. The richest man in town where he had the largest loan office as well as a variety of other businesses.

To all outward appearances, he was a quiet, modest man and yet he was not without a rich man's caprices.

He had a taste for fine books in rich bindings lettered in gold. He was, too, a collector of religious and cultural objects. His box for holding the citron used on the Feast of Tabernacles was made of gold on which Jewish artisans commissioned by him had etched scenes of Mount Zion and Jerusalem.

He had a Hanukkah candelabrum that occupied more than half a wall. Its heavy silver branches were designed to look like a stag's horns.

He had, too, a true delight in melody. On any Sabbath or holiday, after he had recited his prayers in his own tiny synagogue in the company of a selected group, he made his way to the Old Synagogue where the famous cantor Yerukhim the Great sang. There he took up his usual place along the west wall where he continued to stand despite the entreaties of the shammes and the synagogue officers who offered him a place at the east wall. There, leaning against the wall or against a bookstand, he stood, his eyes closed, listening attentively to the cantor's song or to the choir assisting him. At such times he had his arm through only one sleeve of his caftan, while the other hung empty—a rich man's affectation, no doubt.

He was also something of a scholar who could hold his own not merely with rabbis of minor fame but with those even of Reb Dudi's quality. He was skilled at interpreting knotty questions of religious law, and he knew whole sections of the juridical texts, *Khoshen Mishpot* and the *Yore Dea*. He was also well schooled in subjects about which rabbis have no knowledge: astronomy and geometry; he had several poor scholars in these fields whom he paid for the pleasure of contending with them.

He came, too, of fine stock and was descended from no ordinary line. In his family, marriages were concluded only with families of the highest rank whose ancestry included famous wonder rebbes of the region—from Ramistrivke and Karlin—as well as from abroad: from Sadigure and Shtifinesht.

Naturally, he was envied. And when he was seen on the Sabbath and on holidays standing at the west wall in the Old Synagogue, wearing his satin caftan, with only one of his arms inside a sleeve, and when it was seen how he refused to go to the prestigious east wall, many an eye was impressed by his broad shoulders and his pale scholarly forehead that was so expressive of the sweetness of his comprehension and his delight in the prayer melodies.

But what he was most envied for was his wealth which was estimated to be immense and which consisted of cash and of businesses which he wholly or partly owned. Then, too, there were the estates of various of the nobility that had been mortgaged to him. He was the legal owner of stone houses, farmland and the apartments of various local residents; he owned also a palatial apartment building of several stories which he had had built for himself and for his family: a separate story for each of his sons- and daughters-in-law, so that they could continue to live in the style to which they had become accustomed in the homes of their wealthy wonder-rebbe fathers. He even indulged himself by owning two carriages. One, a smaller one with a high seat—a sort of cabriolet—was devoted to his personal use. And a second, larger one upholstered in expensive white material which he used rarely, except when a young niece felt a sudden urge to go for an evening ride; or when a wonder rebbe was due to arrive and his followers wanted to honor him with a fine reception; or sometimes the local administration borrowed it to use in welcoming a provincial governor, or a bishop, or a metropolitan when one of those officials came to visit the Christian community of the town.

In a word there was much for which to envy him. As they said of him in town: He has Torah scholarship and wealth in one hand. And there were many who wished for themselves one tenth . . . no, one hundredth of his fortune.

But in addition to his wealth and his learning and his famous lineage, he had a quality that was neither exalted nor noble. Those who envied him whispered among themselves that he was a "silent killer."

"And how did that square with everything else?" asked the secret whisperers. He served as something of a bugbear: a sort of sharp-toothed pike that terrorized the mud-dwelling darter fish. Of course that's how he appeared to those whose misfortune it was to find themselves clamped between his teeth.

As long as all was well, they had nothing to worry about. Then he was gracious, never a word spoken in anger. But the moment a man was in financial trouble, Yakov-Yossi knew it because he had hired informants who told him. *Then* one could see his shoulders stiffen under his caftan; and though his features altered but little, yet one could see behind his black eyes, under his pale high forehead, the shadowy movement in his mind of financial speculation. "Yes," those shadow movements implied, "the matter's worth looking into."

Yes, it's easy enough to say, "To Yakov-Yossi." But anyone who knew the role he played in the town, and in the entire region, knew also what a heavy hand he had; and that anyone caught in his grip could escape more easily from a pair of steel tongs.

He lent money readily. And was forthcoming whenever anyone was in need. No. Especially when one was in need. When the noose was already around one's neck and he was beginning to choke. It was then that he showed up with his offer of help. And it is easy to imagine just how gratified the half-throttled man in the noose was, and just how much of his hide he was required to sign over to Yakov-Yossi as the mark of his gratitude.

He treated landed noblemen that way when he learned that one of them was at the end of his resources. He knew when a government official with a passion for gaming had squandered public funds at cards; he knew when a local businessman was in the sort of straits from which he could not extricate himself—and it was then that he came to their rescue, requiring only that he be given a share of their business or that it be signed over wholly to him. After which he gave the owner some trivial sum and dispensed with him altogether. He did the same thing with the owners of financial companies, with near-bankrupt noblemen who pledged their estates to him for half of their value. With high government officials; though he did not take over their properties his goal was to get them into his power so that he could make use of them either for personal gain or for the good of the Jewish community.

There were many who had fallen into his trap. Many well-known men had been reduced to poverty because of him. The fact was well known and people tried to avoid his "help." If they turned to him at all, it was when they were at their last gasp. And if it happened that his victim, feeling himself driven to the wall without hope of rescue, pleaded with stifled voice with Yakov-Yossi not to take advantage of his situation, not to crush him utterly, saying, "How can you do such a thing? A man like yourself. What about Judaism? Humanity? You're cutting my throat without a knife." At such times, Yakov-Yossi rose from the chair in which he had been sitting while he conducted the business with his client—his victim. Then, his voice cold, as if the matter was of no concern to him, he replied, "It's not convenient for you? Then let's forget it. You don't want to do it? Then don't. As for Judaism, you'd do better to search for it in the *Yad Hakhzoka*. And if it's humanity you want, come to my home for that. But in this counting-house where business is transacted, I am indeed a robber if the favor of credit extended to someone who is no longer creditworthy is considered robbery, and a murderer, if helping a man out of the mire is the same as cutting his throat with or without a knife."

There was nothing for it but to yield. To accept his terms. And woe indeed to the man who had to have recourse to Yakov-Yossi. He might arrive at Yakov-Yossi's office with his head held high, still the proprietor of his own business; but when he left, he was utterly transformed into hardly half a man whose downcast eyes stared at the tips of his shoes.

It was, then, to this Yakov-Yossi that Nakhum Lentsher advised his father-in-law, Moshe Mashber, to go for help.

It was easy enough to say. Moshe was already indebted to Yakov-Yossi because, like most of the smaller moneylenders, even in good times he had had occasion to borrow from the wealthier ones. But if he were to appear before him now to apply for a new loan . . . when it was well known that he was in no condition to pay out even the small sums that had been confided to him, it could not fail to be interpreted as meaning that he, Moshe, was at that stage of his business when he was ready to liquidate it entirely, one way or another—by walking away from it or by taking on a partner who had large sums of money, then stepping aside and assuming the role of a sort of employee with a small share of the business and little influence.

Nevertheless, Moshe agreed to go to Yakov-Yossi. But it was not done as a consequence of an active decision on his part. It was not the act of a man who, struggling to save himself at all costs, does not concern himself with whether the means within his grasp are good or evil so long as they serve to save him. No. Moshe acted out of a failure of will, with a sort of negligence. Like a man who is equally indifferent to a rescuer or to an executioner.

"Ah," he said, "Yakov-Yossi? Very well, then, to Yakov-Yossi."

It needs to be said that by then Moshe Mashber generally looked like a man in whose brain something had snapped and who was no longer touched by the events around him. It was evident from his behavior at home where, as if he had used up his supply of words, he hardly spoke, even to Gitl. It was evident, too, from his behavior in the parlor in which guests were usually received and where there was a full-length mirror on a wall. Whenever Moshe passed the mirror and saw himself in it, he would stop short as if he had seen a stranger who had suddenly emerged from *Olam Hatohu*, the World of Chaos. Then he would look vaguely, helplessly at himself, until slowly, slowly his interest faded and he walked away, still musing, until in his pacing he came upon himself once more and was again astonished.

The degree to which he was in a state of shock might be gauged, too, in the way that he spoke to the children in the household. Above all, in the remarks he made to the oldest boy, Mayerl, of whom he was especially fond. When they met, Moshe would stop the boy as if he had something particular to say to him. Mayerl would stand expectantly, waiting to be told something, but each encounter always ended with Moshe saying, "No. Never mind. Ah!"

Alter, like Mayerl, was treated the same way. Alter, in the days after the wedding, had withdrawn once more to his attic room and rarely came down. Moshe visited him frequently in those days, but he usually did not stay very long. And coming or going, he had a distracted look, and seemed not to know why he was visiting him.

That then was his behavior at home, and it was the same at the office where, now, he did not show up as he used to do with an employer's regularity. Now he came at sporadic intervals. He would put a question to one employee or another and then turn away before he had heard the reply, leaving the employee with his half-uttered answer in his mouth.

Distracted. Very distracted. So confused that lately he had been unable to find a place to sit down at his office. Instead, he walked back and forth without need or purpose from his own room to his employees' room and then back again. So confused was he that he was perpetually unable to find the exit door of the office and ended by standing before the locked rear door. And if someone called that to his attention, saying, "No. Not that way, sir," he would say with a start, "Of course not. Not that way." Nevertheless he continued to hold the bolt in his hand. And when having pulled the bolt open he found that the chain was on, he unchained it and went out by a door that nobody ever used.

Yes. He was indeed very confused, and it was in this state of mind that he started off to see Yakov-Yossi. The consequences of the interview, given the circumstances, are only too easy to imagine.

Just think how even a calmer, more deliberate man—a man gifted with the wisdom of two heads—might feel if he had to appear before Yakov-Yossi. Yakov-Yossi would instantly have guessed precisely where his shoe pinched. Then think what it was like now with Moshe Mashber whose desperate situation Yakov-Yossi understood after the merest glance.

As soon as Moshe entered Yakov-Yossi's office, he explained that he had some pressing business to conduct that required a confidential interview, and he asked that Yakov-Yossi lock the door so that their discussion would not be interrupted. Yakov-Yossi readily agreed and locked the door himself.

The minute Moshe Mashber was seated opposite Yakov-Yossi, he began to search for something in his pockets. Whether it was his handkerchief he wanted before turning to the matter in hand, or whether he was searching for a piece of paper which he meant to show Yakov-Yossi—a copy of a balance sheet that would demonstrate to Yakov-Yossi that everything was well with Moshe, God be praised, and that it was only because the times were difficult that he had come—whatever it was he was searching for, he kept turning in all directions, looking first in his breast pockets, then in his trousers pockets in which he never carried anything. He even stood up and looked at the seat of the chair to see whether whatever it was he was looking for might not be *there*.

He became thoroughly confused, seeing that Yakov-Yossi was regarding him with a demeaning look of pity, as if he was looking at a man who was desperately trying to maintain his dignity but who, unable to master himself, was becoming more and more demoralized and dismayed.

Moshe's confusion was immediately manifest when he began a hesitant explanation of why he had come. He had come, he said, to ask for the loan of a certain sum for a short period of time . . . until business conditions improved. Then he would be in a position to pay the loan that was now outstanding as well as the new one. He would certainly be in such a position. There was no doubt about it. And there was something else he wanted to say. The rate of interest . . . there was no need to talk about that now. It was not a stumbling block. He was prepared to pay whatever Yakov-Yossi asked. If that was agreeable to Yakov-Yossi.

Certainly, it was very foolish to say that he would pay whatever interest rate was demanded. It was anything but businesslike. It did not take a shrewd businessman like Yakov-Yossi to know that only a man whose shoe hurt was willing to accept whatever interest rates were offered. Anyone else would push for the best deal that he could get, knowing that he could take his business elsewhere.

"No," Yakov-Yossi said in an offhand manner, "the interest rate is not important. It's the principal."

"The principal. Of course, the principal. Surely, after doing business with me for so many years, you have no doubts about that. The Lord be thanked, everyone I ever dealt with has been treated well and . . ."

"No," Yakov-Yossi reassured him, "there's no suspicion of any sort. I simply remarked that interest, in this case, is not the issue. But nowadays even a man's good name is no security. Even a man who could get loans on every side because his notes were as good as cash can find it hard to get credit now. There's a terrible scarcity of money. No one will let go of it. No one will trust anyone, and for good reason."

"What do you mean?" said Moshe anxiously as he stood up.

"God help me, I certainly didn't mean you. The fact is, things are hard just now for me. I'm not doing any business. And when, as rarely happens, I do, I have to take great precautions."

"What kinds of precautions?"

"I have to know where the money is going and to what use it will be put."

"What does that mean?"

"If the money goes to a borrower without causing difficulties for a lender, that's one thing. If not, then the lender is surely insane not to take precautions. You know very well that huge sums can disappear as if they have sunk into a deep hole."

"What sort of security do you have in mind?"

"First of all, I'd like to become familiar with the business itself. To see how it's doing. To calculate how much the owner needs to put into it and to determine by just how much he is in the red. And then, if the matter seems worth pursuing, I would want to become a partner in the business."

"No. I can't do that," Moshe said resolutely as if to make sure that both he and Yakov-Yossi heard him.

"What can't you do?"

"Be partners. A man may be partners with his wife, with his children, and finally he may be a partner with God. But with no one else. No. There's nothing more to be said."

"Very well. No is no." And with that, they both got up from their chairs because the interview was over almost before it had begun.

Because Tsali Derbaremdiker was a gross fellow with a reputation for being extortionate with the poor folk who borrowed petty sums from him, and because he was also a supremely uncultivated man who, except for things to do with money, could hardly tell the difference between *a* and *b*, he did not normally have access to the home of a man like Yakov-Yossi, though in connection with various financial transactions, he was received in his office.

If, then, a few days after Moshe Mashber's visit to Yakov-Yossi, Tsali Derbaremdiker chose to visit Yakov-Yossi, one was right to think that Tsali had weighty matters on his mind.

Yakov-Yossi was, as always in the morning, wearing his blue flannel, lightly tied robe whose front was slightly open. He sat in a dining room that was as vast as a field. It was a room he had had built at the start of the construction of this house. He had first supervised the design on paper, and then as it was being built, he had supervised its construction specifying to the workmen the length and the breadth he required. The room was one of his rich man's caprices. The other rooms of the house were like rooms anywhere, but he had wanted his dining room to be unique in the town; for his own use; for guests and for celebrations; and to match this room, he had ordered an oak table that would accommodate ten or twelve people at its width and some thirty at its length and which, for a banquet, could be extended to nearly double its size.

Yakov-Yossi was seated now at that table which was so vast that one had to shout across it to be heard. Beside him there was a boiling samovar, one of three that were used on various occasions. Except for the servant who handed him his snuffbox or poured his tea or adjusted his footstool, he was alone.

Tsali Derbaremdiker, getting ready to pay his visit, did not feel entirely at his ease. He approached Yakov-Yossi's outer door where he paused to look himself over, to see to his clothes and to check whether his shoes were dirty. Before he crossed the threshold, he coughed to clear his throat.

And still he delayed just as he had delayed for a long while his coming here. But finally a decision had to be made.

What had brought him here?

A rumor had reached Tsali that some while ago Moshe Mashber had quietly signed all of his assets over to his children and to various relatives. It was not yet known whether it was true, but the mere rumor of it was enough to send someone like Tsali Derbaremdiker into a tizzy.

Just think of it. He, Tsali, who always skimmed something off every bankruptcy whether he was involved in it or not, had been so outmaneuvered that not only had he not been able to rescue the money of the small investors whom he had counseled to invest with Moshe, but he was himself caught in the trap and was in danger of losing money of his own.

"Ugh," he said, keeping up a stream of self-accusations. "This is a situation for others. Not for me. Not for Tsali Derbaremdiker. Never since I came to manhood has anything like this ever happened to me. Or could have happened."

His anger kept him sleepless, and in the course of his wakeful nights, he would sometimes groan aloud as if something had suddenly bitten him.

"Eh, what is it?" said his wife in the next bed, each time she was startled awake by his outcry. "Is someone ringing? Is there a fire?"

"What fire? There's no fire."

"Then why are you yelling."

"*I'm* burning."

"What? What?"

"Go to sleep. It's nothing to do with you," Tsali said, trying to calm his wife at the same time as he wanted to keep her from interfering with his business. After that, he continued to stay awake, sitting up or lying down. At intervals, he would cry out again as if he had been bitten.

That's how it was at night. By day, he went about depressed, his mouth clamped shut, unwilling even to talk with his fellow money brokers like Sholem Shmaryon and afraid to confide anything to them.

Finally, after much thought, he decided to take counsel with Yakov-Yossi.

What he wanted to know was, first: had Yakov-Yossi heard the rumors; second, if, having heard them, he believed them to be true; third, if he had heard them, which did he think was the better course: to let Moshe Mashber declare bankruptcy alone and at a time of his own choosing; or by concerted action to force him to declare it at a time favorable to his creditors? The last was easy enough to manage. There were plenty of means at hand with which to give Moshe a final thrust when he was not looking.

"Good morning," Tsali said as he entered the famous dining room and found Yakov-Yossi taking his tea. It is more than likely that he said, "Good morning" twice. The first time with great deference as he crossed the threshold. But because the room was too large and the table at whose farther end Yakov-Yossi sat was so far away, he was not heard. His second "Good morning" was spoken as he came quite near and presented himself.

"Good morning and a good year," replied Yakov-Yossi who was busy with his tea. There was a book beside him into which he occasionally looked. "What have you come to say so early in the morning?" Then, turning to his servant, a decrepit-looking, extremely nearsighted man who held the right side of his body twisted to the left like a warped wagon yoke, "Shepsl, pour tea."

"No, thank you, I've had mine," said Tsali, out of politeness and because he did not feel at ease in a home like this. "I'm here on business," he said as he cast a wary eye on Shepsl. "I was hoping we might talk in private," he went on as if he was inquiring whether they might safely talk in the presence of the servant.

"No," said Yakov-Yossi, who understood what Tsali meant. He looked scornfully past his servant as though he were a mute creature of some sort before whom one could say anything.

Reassured, Tsali said, "I was wondering whether you would consider selling the promissory notes of one of your debtors who is feeling pressed just now. And who, so goes the rumor, is on the verge of bankruptcy. Obviously," he added offhandedly, "given the risks, the notes would have to be discounted."

"And who is the debtor and who wants to buy?"

"Moshe Mashber . . . and I'm the one buying."

"And why are you doing this?"

"Why? It's a business matter. There are very disturbing rumors about Moshe Mashber."

"All the more reason to wonder why."

"I'm willing to risk it."

"What does that mean?"

"It means that if the rumors should turn out not to be true, I would make a profit on the notes that have been discounted because of them. If, on the other hand, the rumors are true—well, that's the risk I take—as with any business matter, as with any card game."

"Of course. But what makes you think I'm less interested in risk taking than you are?"

"Of course you are, of course you can. I only thought that this was a matter that would not be interesting to you. That you might not want to be involved with someone who, so the rumors say, has secretly signed his business over to other people, to protect himself so that when the crash comes his creditors will be unable to recoup so much as a hair."

"So that's what's rumored, is it?" he said uneasily and got up from his chair. "Shepsl"—he turned to the servant who had been standing absently by paying no attention to the conversation—"pour tea."

One suspects that Yakov-Yossi already knew at least half of what Tsali had told him and that he had deduced it from his own conversation with Moshe. But the other half that concerned the secret transfer of assets as a means of defending himself against his creditors was news to him. And that so upset him, so destroyed his calm, that he rose from his chair and began to pace along the width of the table as he ordered his servant Shepsl to pour him more hot tea—though in fact he was not thinking of tea at all but rather of the electrifying news that made him now say what follows, though the words were addressed more to himself than to Tsali.

"Ah," he said, "Moshe is much mistaken if he thinks he can do a thing like that and still keep his good name. No. If a debtor is in trouble and he comes in good faith to plead for some relief, then why not? One performs a good deed. But this sort of thing. These deceptions, these devious means. This swindling. There's a law for that. There's a rabbinical court. And finally, there are the government courts. I've seen such things before and I know well how to guard myself against them."

"But how can one prove that the transfer of ownership was not made before the debts were incurred, as he will, of course, claim? How can one prove that it's a scheme to outwit his creditors?"

"How? The means are well known. And because of them, more than one man has been carted off to live at the cost of the czar."

"Well then, let me ask you another question. What do you think? In a case like this, which would be the better plan: to wait, to be patient for a while? Because all we have are rumors, and perhaps the debtor has not yet taken the actions that are rumored. Perhaps, if one waited, he might think better of his scheme and might abandon it. Or, instead of waiting, would it be better to take immediate action. Is the rumor alone a sufficient justification for his creditors to take action to prevent the scheme we have been talking about? I mean, is it legal or ethical from a business point of view to push the debtor into bankruptcy even before he declares it, and in that way keep him from doing what a man in his situation has been known to do—with harm to his creditors as well as to himself? Would it not be a favor to him? What do you think?"

"Of course it would be legal. Of course it would be ethical. Because nowhere is it written that if a man wants to hurt you that you have to go meet him halfway. Quite the reverse. It is said: 'If a man threatens to kill you, kill him first.' And in this case, there is no reason to pity him. On the contrary, the greatest pity would be to be pitiless. It makes no difference. . . ." And here, Yakov-Yossi explained what he meant: "It makes no difference that it is only a rumor, because in the first place, when you hear bells ringing, it follows that it's a holiday. And it may be that he himself started this rumor in order to ease his crooked conscience. So that he can say that since there are such rumors, and since he is believed capable of swindling, then why not swindle in good earnest? Because in any case his reputation is damaged, soiled. So that if his creditors take timely steps to keep him from accomplishing his swindle, then they rescue not only themselves, but, and this is the heart of the matter, they rescue the man as well who risks a truly bad ending. So that it is above all for his own good."

"Ah," Tsali said, appreciating Yakov-Yossi's witty way of showing that it was a good deed to thrust Moshe into a pit in order to keep him from falling into it by himself. "Ah . . ."

"Yes. According to the laws of Israel and the laws of the state, one may do it," said Yakov-Yossi in a firm voice, pleased to have found a justification for something which at first glance might have appeared to be a wicked act—almost a crime. "One ought to do it, and it is also just."

By now, the two men, Tsali and Yakov-Yossi, had quite forgotten the promissory notes which the former never had any intention of buying or the latter any intention of selling. They were both content. Yakov-Yossi because he had acquired important information without having to stir a finger, and Tsali, first, because he now knew what to do

in a situation whose like in all his years as a usurer he had not encountered, and then because having Yakov-Yossi's permission and approval, he felt himself in a comradely relationship with a man of
stature who, whatever happened, would give him his support.

Yakov-Yossi resumed his place at the table, expecting to pick up
what he had been doing when Tsali made his appearance: to drink his
tea and to turn the pages of the book beside him. It was his signal to
Tsali that the interview was over. Tsali rose to go. Just then the door
opened and a silent, early morning visitor came in. It was Sruli Gol.

In the long time since he had allied himself to Luzi, Sruli had not
been a visitor in any rich man's home. And if he was here now, it was
because he had a compelling reason.

Knowing the sort of power Yakov-Yossi wielded in the town, and
knowing, too, how oppressive his hand could be in business affairs—
he could make them or break them—and knowing that Moshe
Mashber was heavily indebted to Yakov-Yossi, Sruli was anxious to
discover just how far Yakov-Yossi would, as an interested party, allow
himself to proceed in this case. Whether he intended to crush Moshe
Mashber at once, or whether he meant to wait and would advise others
to do the same.

When Sruli opened Yakov-Yossi's dining room door, he paused for
a little while on the threshold, as if he was considering whether to go
in or not. Then he made his decision and strode into the room as he
always did when he entered a place where he was not especially
welcome. And his long stride was meant to indicate that it made
not the slightest difference to him whether he was welcome or not,
and that he was indifferent to anything except the exercise of his own
will.

He approached the table without so much as a "Good morning," and
without waiting to be taken notice of by the master of the house,
Yakov-Yossi, or by his guest, Tsali, Sruli went up to the samovar and,
entirely unbidden, poured himself a cup.

His reasons for coming here were quite the reverse of Tsali's. Tsali
had come to contrive the push that would send Moshe over the edge,
and Sruli, to prevent him from being pushed over.

Silently, and with the air of a man who was not observing them, he
nevertheless looked shrewdly out at them from under the low visor of
his cap. His guess was that these two had just concluded a piece of
business which had left them both feeling pleased.

"Ah, a guest," Yakov-Yossi said ironically as if he was speaking to someone who did not much interest him and for whom he had very little respect.

"I haven't seen you in a long while."

When Sruli made no reply—indeed, he acted as if he had not heard him, Yakov-Yossi, making a third attempt at conversation, said, "What are you angry about?"

"What difference does it make if I'm angry? It won't spoil a rich man's digestion."

"I just wondered," Yakov-Yossi said, pleased to have irritated Sruli. It put him in a good mood and so he asked, "At whom are you angry?"

"Not at anyone . . . at myself," Sruli muttered as if reluctantly.

"But why?"

"I came close to becoming a rich man, but somebody saw it and interfered."

"Who?"

"Him," Sruli said, pointing to the heavens. "God, who keeps peering down: if someone like you has money, then all's well and good. You get to keep it—and may it be fruitful and multiply. But if someone like me has it . . . ugh . . . let it go the way it came—from one rich man to the next."

"What do you mean?" Yakov-Yossi asked.

"There's my witness," Sruli said, pointing at Tsali.

"What are you saying? That you've had money?"

"Yes, he did," Tsali agreed.

"Invested with Moshe Mashber?"

"That's right," said Tsali.

"And now that Moshe Mashber is going up like a puff of smoke, all those who invested with him are going to go puff too, isn't that so?"

"That's right," Tsali said, but he caught himself and turned to Yakov-Yossi to check whether he had done right to reveal to Sruli even such a little bit of what he and Yakov-Yossi had talked about.

"If that's your situation, you have every right to be angry," Yakov-Yossi said, "because you've been cheated."

"Cheated?" Sruli said.

"Yes."

"And what do you advise me to do?"

"There's nothing you can do—unless . . ." Yakov-Yossi began, meaning to console Sruli with a joke.

"Unless what?" Sruli asked.

"Unless Moshe Mashber had been kind enough to sign over to you the ownership of his oil and kerosene business, his countinghouse or his expensive home. If had he done that, you would have some recourse."

"Is that right?"

"Yes."

"Well, that's precisely what he did. Here, look." Sruli reached suddenly into his breast pocket and pulled out a stamped document that had been folded over into fours. He unfolded it and showed it to Yakov-Yossi and to Tsali. They looked it over and it was plain to them that what had earlier been a mere speculation between them had actually happened.

What prompted Sruli to display the deed which until now he had kept hidden is not clear. Perhaps it was meant to pay Yakov-Yossi back for his scornful treatment of him and to provoke his anger. Or he may have thought that if Yakov-Yossi and Tsali learned that Moshe Mashber had anticipated them and had taken steps to thwart his creditors, after his bankruptcy, that then they would no longer be interested in pushing Moshe toward insolvency and would instead want to prevent his collapse, that they would, indeed, want to help him as a way of safeguarding their own interests because they, too, would lose every penny they had invested with him.

We do not know why he showed them the document. The moment Yakov-Yossi and Tsali saw it, Yakov-Yossi abandoned his bantering tone and Tsali turned suddenly speechless. They stared at each other, and then they stared at Sruli.

"Why are you staring at me?" Sruli asked with bitter humor. "What's the matter? I don't seem to be one of your rich men? Or is it that you don't think the document is authentic or that the signature is real? All right, then. Very well. I'll show it to you again. Or is it that you think someone else ought to have grabbed it and made sure of it before me? Or is it that you wouldn't have touched this deal if it had been put to you? That you would have washed your kosher hands of the matter, that you wouldn't have sullied the kosher hems of your garments by going near it. Eh?"

"That's right," said Yakov-Yossi, looking past Sruli at Tsali, as if Sruli were not standing right beside him at the table. "Just remember this," he went on, addressing Tsali and completely ignoring Sruli, "just remember that Moshe Mashber is not the only one who will have to suffer. . . . This one, too . . ." And here, Yakov-Yossi turned and pointed toward Sruli. "The collusion is so clear, a child could see it." He pointed at Sruli once more. "How does *he* come to have any money? Does he have an inheritance? It'll be the easiest thing in the world to prove that right from the beginning there was collusion here.

The whole thing is a cheat in which, no doubt, that disciple of Shabbatai Zevi, Moshe Mashber's brother, and those followers of his are involved. Along with this fellow," and here he pointed again at Sruli, "whom one ought to shake to see if he has any money, and if he has, to find out where he got it. You may be sure it isn't his—and if it is, that he got it dishonestly."

Show some respect, please," interrupted Sruli. "You," he pointed at Tsali and then at Yakov-Yossi, "you talk about honesty and dishonesty? You?"

"Out of here. What are you doing here? Get out," cried Yakov-Yossi, and turned as if he were calling on the walls to witness Sruli's presumption. But they made no reply.

"What are you doing here?" he asked again. Then, suddenly remembering his servant Shepsl, he shouted at him, "Why are you standing there like a dummy? Go on, go get him . . ." He was so frantic, he could not think who it was he wanted Shepsl to get. Then it came to him, "The coachman, the policeman . . ." he cried, and it almost seemed that he would shortly add, "The chief of police, the governor."

"Put him in chains, take him to jail," he went on furiously. He pointed at Sruli as if with his finger he meant to turn him to ash or to transform him into a pile of bones.

"Not so loud," said Sruli. "What's gotten into you to make you shout at the top of your lungs? Has someone stepped on your favorite corn?"

"Out. To jail with you. Arrest him," shouted Yakov-Yossi.

"Not so loud. I'll go of my own accord," said Sruli again, and indeed he fully intended to get up from his chair, to turn to the door and go. But though this is what he intended, he suddenly saw someone who, in the course of the uproar following on Yakov-Yossi's outburst of anger, had not been seen by anyone coming quietly through the dining room door.

It was a woman. Moshe Mashber's wife, Gitl. Sruli, who was about to say again, "Not so loud," said instead, "Not so loud. It's Moshe Mashber's wife."

They turned to look. It was indeed she. She was dressed in her best holiday garb, including her fur coat whose wide collar, sleeves and skirts were trimmed with sable. She had come in so silently they had hardly heard her.

"What is it you want?" Yakov-Yossi inquired.

"I've come on business."

"You?"

"Yes, it's strange, but it's true. I who have never meddled in my husband's business have come of my own accord—nobody sent me, and indeed it would upset my husband if he knew I was here. I've come to talk with you about a certain matter."

It should be said that Gitl's decision to make this visit to Yakov-Yossi was not an act of courage such as one might make during a fire when one has a sudden access of strength and is able to snatch more from the fire than one might normally do. No, it was rather the act of one who no longer cares whether it is fire or water that is raining down upon him. In this respect she was just like her husband, Moshe Mashber, who, though he was externally still himself, might, if the truth be told, just as easily have been called by another name.

She, too, was troubled, confused. And often there were tears in her eyes. Cold tears that seemed not to belong to her. That came of themselves, uncalled for.

Gitl was a pious enough woman, the way women of her background were. But the calamity of her daughter's death had made her more pious still. No, not more pious. Rather, she had become otherworldly—as if things of this world no longer touched her.

She was, lately, rarely seen in the dining room, and she was less and less involved in the ongoing running of the household, depending for that on the older maidservant, the only one who was left, to do the shopping and tend to the other essential household details.

For the most part, she sat in her bedroom, withdrawn, continually reading, even in the middle of the week, from her women's translation of the Bible. She would read a couple of lines, then she would think over what she had read.

"When, because of Nebuchadnezzar, the children of Israel are on the road to exile, Rachel will rise from her tomb and will pray to the Lord and God will hear her prayer." She imagined the Jews being driven, young and old, in chains; and as they pass Mother Rachel's tomb, they stop, refusing to go on, waiting for her to rise and pray for them.

In her mind's eye, she saw Mother Rachel as, sometimes she walked before the band of exiles, sometimes behind them. And always her arms were raised. Then not only her arms, but Rachel herself grew, rising higher and higher, almost touching the heavens and her voice was heard as she bewailed her children.

Gitl read by day, and at night she dreamed of what she read. As for example: that her dead daughter appeared to her and Gitl asked her how things were with her. And her daughter had nothing to complain of. She did not weep. But being a devoted woman who was attached to her family, she continually reminded Gitl, "Mother, do look after

Father. I think he's being harassed." And each time Gitl woke up frightened and became aware that in the next bed her husband was not sleeping. Often she heard him talking to himself or groaning, "Ah, Mother." And then one night he left his bed and, sitting beside her in the dark, told her of the visit he had made to Yakov-Yossi and what its purpose was and how he had been received. And what had come of the interview. Nothing.

After hearing that account, Gitl was sleepless for the rest of the night. She could hardly wait for dawn. Then after the family had had breakfast and everyone had gone about their various business and the house was quiet, she went into her room and put her finest clothing on. After that she went off to Yakov-Yossi's house.

She came at a bad moment, arriving just as the scene described above was taking place when Yakov-Yossi, outraged by Sruli's impudence and by his refusal to keep still, was furiously shouting at him.

It would have been entirely natural for Yakov-Yossi, seeing before him the wife of the man he had just been discussing . . . it would have been natural for him to want her out of the room, or to be unwilling even to look at her, or to greet her rudely, or even to drive her from the room as he had been driving Sruli.

But that isn't what happened. Instead, amazingly enough, when Yakov-Yossi heard Sruli cry, "Not so loud. Not so loud. It's Moshe Mashber's wife," not only did he not do any of the things mentioned above, any of which would have been likely for a man in his situation; instead, he suddenly quieted down as if the name he had heard was that of a highly respected person whom it behooved him to accord all honors. And so, incredible as it may seem, instead of turning angrily on her, he turned to greet her politely.

So much, then, as regards Yakov-Yossi. As for Gitl, what happened to her was also remarkable. Instead of being distressed, as she had been when she left her house, she felt alert, as if she had just risen from a fall from which she had lightly brushed away the dust that had barely touched her.

She had to walk across a considerable distance from the doorway to the head of the table where Yakov-Yossi sat, and yet she continued to feel good, unconstrained in any way by the looks the men gave her. Indeed, she hardly noticed them. And when she reached Yakov-Yossi who was about to offer her a seat, she forestalled him, dismissing the invitation with a wave of her hand, and started in at once to say what she had come to say.

"Do not wonder that I, a woman, who has never had any understanding of business, have come here in the interests of my husband who, I should say, has not sent me. On the contrary, if he knew what I was doing, he would not approve of it at all. It would seriously distress him.

"I hope, too, that you will not be surprised if having made my decision to take this step, I first ask you, Yakov-Yossi, to let me speak to you in private and not in the presence of others about matters that are properly kept confidential.

"Because, and I say it openly, this is the final hour. The day of judgment when my husband's entire worth—and world—are on the scales. Punishment or salvation, this way or that, destruction or mercy. At a time like this, a time for action, one dispenses with all sorts of hesitations; at such times, it is said, even a kitchen knife is a weapon. And the dumb speak, as now you hear me, who until this moment has never spoken a word on such matters.

"I've come," she said, "to rescue my husband who is on the brink of absolute ruin . . . he may be left without a penny to his name. I say it without shame. Such things happen to people. Sometimes the ruin is deserved. Sometimes it is not. And my husband Moshe Mashber belongs to the second category.

"It may be that you—and others—will think that Moshe's downfall is the result of poor business management or because he lived beyond his means. That's not true. I am Moshe Mashber's wife in this world and in the world to come. And I will testify in this world before everyone; in the world to come I, an honorable Jewish daughter, will tell the Creator that my husband Moshe was never a gambler or a spendthrift and that he always lived within his means. The misfortune that overwhelmed him was not of his doing and he has nothing to be ashamed of.

"On the contrary, I believe that my husband deserves to be helped instead of having a knife put to his throat. It seems to me, then, that those who over the years profited by doing business with him—as he also profited—should be in the forefront of those helping him. People like you, Yakov-Yossi, to whom I have come with my request.

"If you help him," she went on, "you will see that you, Yakov-Yossi, will lose nothing. On the contrary, when things get better, you will not only have done a good deed, but you will be gratefully paid and paid with interest. And Moshe's lesser creditors will also escape unharmed. But what matters most is that a reputable businessman will be able to restore his fortunes. A man who, everyone knows (I take God as my witness), never took anything from anyone and who never enriched himself by underhanded means.

"I say this in good conscience, as if I were standing before God

Himself, and at the same time I want to remind you who my husband's forebears were, and to point out that he has not inherited deception from them, and that neither in his nature nor in his character is there the least hint of evil intent or the desire to harm anyone, so help me God."

Amazingly enough, as Yakov-Yossi listened to Gitl (keeping his eyes averted from a woman, as a pious man should), he was nevertheless aware of the wide sable collar of her coat, its trimmed sleeves and skirts. Amazingly enough, the sight softened him and he experienced for a moment the sort of woman-induced pleasure that makes a man weak and yielding. But he mastered himself at once. Then, just as Gitl was coming to a close . . . and while she was reassuring Yakov-Yossi that as God was her witness, her husband had never intended to deceive anyone . . . it was then that Yakov-Yossi, fresh from his earlier conversation with Tsali with whom he had concerted to take action against Moshe—Yakov-Yossi, having before him Tsali and Sruli, against whom he had not yet been able to vent his spleen—and seeing Gitl, who, gentle and feminine though she was, had come, no doubt, with the connivance of her husband, to soften him, to wake his compassion. With all this to consider, Yakov-Yossi got to his feet and, seizing on Gitl's last words, he mimicked them back at her.

"What? You say your husband is innocent as a lamb? Is he? So there's no intent to swindle or cheat? You're prepared to swear, are you? And you want me to help him for no better reason than his honorable behavior? Well, why didn't he consider the needs of others instead of only himself?"

Gitl, disturbed and unable to understand Yakov-Yossi's bitter words, stammered, "Who?"

"Who? Your husband, that's who."

"My husband? Looked out only for himself? I don't know what you're talking about?"

"Of course you don't, but your husband does. Ugh. It's repulsive. One doesn't do such things."

"What things?" she stammered again.

"Such as . . ." He pointed toward Sruli who, all the while that Gitl was addressing herself to Yakov-Yossi had stood a little to one side, and who now looked out at Yakov-Yossi from under the visor of his cap. "Such as . . . that." And he drew his finger back with revulsion. "That's the fellow through whom your husband thought to outwit everyone by signing the house and other properties over to him so that no one would be able to get at his assets in case his position weakened and he came close to bankruptcy. Ugh. It's not done. No merchant . . .

no Jew, especially not a man like Moshe, who, as you've pointed out, comes from a distinguished family."

Then, getting even more excited, he said, "And we'll see where it ends. He won't wiggle easily out of this."

Then because he was unwilling to hear any further defense of her husband, and because he wanted to bring the matter to an end, Yakov-Yossi undertook to move Gitl politely toward the door. "Good-bye. And if you care for your husband and want to do him a favor, tell him not to treat the matter lightly. Let him take care how and to whom he gives offense lest what he does ends badly . . . very badly."

"Dogs. Pickpockets," Sruli grumbled, but loudly enough so that it was impossible for him not to be heard by anyone at the table.

And it was then that Yakov-Yossi uttered a final cry, "Shepsl." And this time there could be no doubt that there would be no peaceful ending to the scene as there had been the last time he had called his servant.

Sruli, without further delay, started toward the door followed by Tsali who had long ago finished the business that had brought him to Yakov-Yossi's house. After that, it was Gitl's turn. She turned from Yakov-Yossi's table without saying good-bye. Anyone watching her as she went to the door would have noticed that she made no effort to keep the tears that rolled down her cheeks from falling into the broad collar of her sable coat.

Finally, the inevitable happened—a day such as one would not wish on anybody descended on Moshe Mashber. He sensed that the end was near and by then it would certainly have been better if he had not gone to his office. But he could not keep away. For one thing, what would he have done at home where the fear of what was coming was manifest on every face? And then his presence in the office was in fact necessary to fend off the creditors who besieged the place . . . to make them believe that at some time—now, later, soon—they would be paid.

It was necessary for him to show himself. But oh, how sad it was. Had anyone seen him walking to his office, hunched over, his head drawn into the collar of his winter coat, he would have taken him for his own shadow, or for a memory of his former self. This was espe-cially true when he came into his office where he was unable to escape the crowd of his creditors who surrounded him, begging for a reassur-ing word. Frightened and evasive, he managed finally to stammer something out.

There was no longer anything enviable in Moshe's situation. As soon as he had put off a group of creditors by deceiving them a little (and indeed they allowed themselves to be deceived), he left the office, his head, hunched by shame, between his shoulders and the untrue words he had spoken rising in his gorge.

One day Moshe came into his office a bit late. His eyes were still dimmed from the freezing weather outdoors and for the first moment or two he saw only what was immediately before him. It was not only because his eyes were not fully functioning but also because of the tension he had been feeling on his way there. And so it was that as he looked around, the scene he observed seemed unfamiliar to him, and strange.

The place was noisy and jammed with men and women, all of them dressed in winter clothing that made it seem that they were occupying more space than usual. Seeing them, Moshe shuddered. Frightened, he wanted to turn and leave the office at once but before he was able to do that, the crowd became aware of him. Quietly, and as if it was a concerted action, they made a space for him even as they surrounded him.

For a while they were silent, then one of them, as if he had been empowered by the others, said with quiet restraint, "Reb Moshe, it's time. We can't wait much longer. We've been waiting for months. Think who you're dealing with. We're not the sort of creditors who get rich by lending. No. We're poor folk who gave you our money as if we were putting it into a safe."

"Our money," was heard from others in the crowd who, emboldened to speak, named the thing itself as they advanced upon him.

Then a small bent fellow who wore a rope for a belt stepped forward. This was The Kitten who, in addition to everything else that he wore, had, also, a scarf tied as a bandage over one cheek—whether against the pain of a toothache or because of the cold no one knew. "Of course, it's time," he said in his squeaky voice, as if he was speaking for them all. "The due dates on our notes have come and gone for us all. Where's justice? Even God wouldn't wait any longer."

"Yes, the due dates," echoed the others.

Because he was confused and had nothing to say to those who surrounded him, Moshe began to edge toward the door through which he had just come. It was then that he saw his son-in-law, Nakhum Lentsher, in the other room, looking as if he meant to come to his aid, to free him from his besiegers.

"Why are you crowding the office like this?" It was the voice of Nakhum Lentsher. He pretended not to know why they were hemming his father-in-law in so closely. His sudden appearance drew the crowd's attention to himself and distracted them from Moshe.

Moshe, harassed though he was and unfocused though his mind had recently been, had wit enough to realize that this was an ideal moment for him to take advantage of the crowd's shift in attention to slip away. And to let the mob's anger fall upon his son-in-law.

And that, precisely, is what he did. He acted quickly, without hesitation. And to avoid pursuit he made his exit not by the usual door but by a little side door where, or so he hoped, his departure would not be noticed.

Moshe, in his flight, understood very well that the confrontation between Nakhum Lentsher and the crowd could not but end badly. Even at its beginning, they were not likely to treat him kindly and who could say what might happen later? But what would be much worse still would be what might happen when the crowd, realizing that Nakhum, after all, was not the real culprit, turned from him and trailed Moshe to his home into which they would intrude, shouting insults, banging on his table and smashing windows—as such crowds had been known to do in similar instances.

But for Moshe there was no other recourse. And so, his head bent, his collar turned up, he hurried on. Anyone seeing him just then might have supposed he was looking at a hunted beast.

At Moshe's office, one of the persons jammed together there said to Nakhum Lentsher, "Why are we crowding the office like this? We'd like to see how you would behave if you had been treated the way Moshe Mashber, your father-in-law, has been treating all of these people. Would you wait any longer, and would you be more patient to those who owe you money if you were in the same situation *they* are in?" Here he pointed to the crowd, and as he did so both he and various others noticed that the man to whom they had earlier been making their complaints was no longer there. Disappeared.

Someone shouted, "Why are we talking with him? We didn't lend *him* our money. He didn't sign our notes. Mashber? Where is Moshe Mashber?"

"Not here," someone shouted.

"Sneaked away."

"Ran off."

Other voices cried, "Where's he gone?"

"Hiding somewhere."

"We know where he lives."

"We'll find him there."

"Let's go."

"He can't be far. He's only just left."

"Bankruptcy? Is that what he thinks?"

"To rob . . ."

"Whom . . .?"

"Us . . ."

"Of money earned by our sweat and blood," came the outcry. Then not having before them the man on whom they wanted to vent their spleen, they tumultuously vilified Moshe Mashber and Nakhum Lentsher as well as each of their employees and even those who, having heard the noise in the office, had come in from the street and the nearby shops to see what was going on and who now stood perplexed and helpless, as if they had been stricken by a blast of hail.

The mob moved toward the door as with a single will. Various old people, threatened by the crush, cried, "Heaven help us." Others repeated, "Our money. Our hard-earned money."

Then all at once the office was empty and the mob was on its way, running . . . at first all together, but very soon the younger folk outdistanced the rest, while the older and weaker followed, panting, as if afraid they would be late and that something would be snatched away from them by those who preceded them.

And Moshe now was at home, having arrived there only moments before the crowd set off in pursuit of him. When he came into the dining room there was nobody there. Gitl, as was her custom, was in her room reading her "women's" Bible commentary. Moshe stood for a moment, running through his mind the various rooms in the house in which he might hide, but just then, seeing his grandson Mayerl coming toward him, he said, almost without thought, "Mayerl, into your room, quick. And lock the door."

"What is it, Grandfather?" said Mayerl, seeing his grandfather so frightened—looking like someone who has just escaped from a band of robbers and who is still so agitated that he is willing to turn to a child for help.

It was then that Moshe Mashber took Mayerl's hand, and it was clear that it was not to lead Mayerl, but rather so that Mayerl could lead him. That is, he expected the boy to lead him into the children's room where Mayerl usually studied or passed the time.

"Lock the door," Moshe said again hastily. "Ah, Mayerl." He spoke almost as if he were speaking to himself. Mayerl saw how his grandfather's lips trembled. "Ah," Moshe said.

And it was then that Mayerl heard the sound of many voices in the dining room. At first they were hushed, as if the speakers were intimidated by the luxurious surroundings, but after a while they spoke

more loudly, as if they had gathered courage to utter, in however suppressed a fashion, their just complaints.

"Oh, how dreadful."

"Who could have foreseen it?"

"A man whom God and man might envy."

A little while later, as more and more people pressed into the house,
and as they became more habituated to it and were no longer impressed by their surroundings, the crowd became bolder and abandoned their restraint.

"We won't leave till he's paid up. To the last penny."

"We'll stay here day and night. As long as it takes."

"We'll tear the place apart."

The mob, not seeing any of the members of the family before it,
shouted their demands to the walls, to the ceiling, to the doors leading
to the other rooms in which there was now apparently no one.

In Mayerl's room, the frightened boy was beginning to understand
what was going on and why his grandfather was hiding. "Hush," said
Moshe wiping the tears from the boy's cheek. "Don't cry."

All at once the house grew silent. Gitl, when she heard the first
sounds of the crowd's entry into the house, had been reading her
women's Bible commentary. Now when the volume of sound increased, she made her way slowly to the dining room to see whether
there actually was the noise she heard, or whether she had perhaps imagined it. Gitl moved slowly, pervaded as she was by the profound
sense of indifference that had come over her since the misfortunes that
had overtaken her husband—and particularly after her disastrous visit
to Yakov-Yossi's home (it seemed to her that there could be nothing in
the world more dreadful than that visit had been).

On the threshold she listened more or less calmly to the cries of the
crowd and simply observed the disorder. She noticed the strange
smells that were now in the room: smells of misery. She observed that
mud and snow had been tracked in by the worn-out shoes and boots
the people wore. It was not long before the crowd became aware of her
and the result was that for a moment they grew suddenly silent, as if
struck by her calm demeanor as she stood there on the threshold. As if
respectful of her dignity, and yet pleased, too, that at last someone
close to Moshe Mashber had appeared. Someone to whom, whether
for good or ill, they could speak as they might have spoken to Moshe
himself.

It was then that The Kitten, wearing his light topcoat, slipped out
from amid the crowd. Seating himself at the head of the table he
pounded on it with his fist and cried, "My money."

"Money," echoed various women whose look of ferocity was intensified by their disheveled hair.

"People," said Gitl quietly as the mob surged toward her, "take whatever you like. Take whatever you see. None of it belongs to me. It is all God's and yours."

At that the crowd swarmed from the dining room all over the house, one by one or in clusters of two or three or in larger groups. Made fierce by their own impetuosity, they grabbed up whatever came to hand: bedclothes from the beds, clothing from closets and bureau drawers. As well as pots, dishes, linens and towels.

In their excitement many of them flung what they found into sheets, the way people do in great haste when their house is burning. They felt ashamed of their pilferage and justified it to themselves by the magnitude of the misfortune that had driven them to it. "God forgive me," some cried, even as they snatched what they could, "to think it has come to this."

Various strange scenes were played out: two people grabbing at the object they had both caught sight of at the same time, each one trying to take possession of it for himself, quarreling over it to the point of blows.

Gitl went from one cluster of looters to another, soothing them, encouraging them and, as it were, giving them good counsel. "Don't quarrel. There'll be enough for everyone. Take it. Take it. And may it do you some good."

It should be clear that Gitl herself was not the one saying these words. It was, rather, as if someone else were speaking through her. Someone who was at once victim and tormentor, the person condemned and the one condemning.

It was an anguishing sight, Gitl standing in the middle of the room, her hands over her eyes. But more anguishing still was the sight of Moshe Mashber cowering in his grandson's room, pressing himself against the boy, clutching him as if expecting his help to come from the child.

It was worse still later, after the poorer creditors arrived and began to do what we have described above: making up bundles and hurriedly grabbing whatever they could, as if in a riot. Later, when the more substantial creditors came, they made less noise and were more patient, but their complaints were of a graver sort. "How," they cried, "can a man like Moshe Mashber, a man like your husband, steal what belongs to us?"

Gitl, wringing her hands, replied, "Please, do as these others are doing. Take what you will." But these more solid citizens replied,

"What good will that do us? And do you really think that our debts can be settled with a handful of household goods? No. No. We won't hear of it.

"Understand something. We've not lent you any money, and we ask nothing from you. All we want is a chance to discuss the situation with your husband. He understands these matters. Where is he? Why is he hiding? We want to see him."

Above the tumult was heard Tsali Derbaremdiker's voice—tall Tsali jostling his way through the crowd to stand before her so he could shout into her face, "You think it's going to be easy to be rid of Tsali? Oh, no. I'm not going to leave the house. I'll stay here day and night. I'll lie in Moshe's bed, in your bed. No one gets away without paying his debts to Tsali."

Just then there was the sound of shattering glass—something snatched from a shelf by some petty creditor who, not knowing what use it was intended for, had flung it to the ground, or who, handling it incompetently, had let it fall. The crowd immediately thought that windows were being smashed.

There were cries of "That's right. They've got it coming. Smash the windows. Wreck the place."

It was then that Gitl shuddered. The sort of shudder that is usually followed by a mind-piercing scream . . . or by the kind of silence that precedes a fall from which there is no recovery.

And it was then that the names he was being called reached Moshe Mashber in his hiding place. And it was then, though it is hard to know why, that he decided to leave Mayerl, to unlock the door of the room and to go down to show himself to the mob.

But again there was a moment of silence—as if someone had appeared unexpectedly before the crowd. Someone whose presence had abashed even the most vociferous of them.

It was a municipal official. Dressed in full uniform he stood on the threshold. Behind him stood a policeman who was flanked by Sruli Gol and Shmulikl Fist.

The municipal officer who had come in at the height of the looting cried, "Halt." Going to the head of the table, he unrolled a paper from which he read. The reading did not take long, and those who had even a minimum knowledge of government proceedings understood its purport almost at once: what the crowd was doing—taking up Moshe Mashber's property in payment for outstanding debts—was illegal because none of the household effects belonged to him any longer. They were now the property of the person to whom Moshe had signed over the house, the courtyard and everything contained in them.

"What?" came the astonished voices of those who had understood the announcement and who now heard the name of the person to whom Moshe Mashber's fortune belonged. Sruli Gol.

"Yes," said the municipal official. Then he added that from that moment on, anyone who touched the slightest thing in the house would be answerable to the law which had now taken the whole matter under its control.

"What law? What's he babbling about?" asked those who had not understood him (that is, the majority). They felt baffled and upset because the heavy weight of authority had interfered and was keeping them from getting their own back.

"We're forbidden to take anything? Because it's in somebody else's name?"

"In whose name?"

"In his," said someone, pointing at Sruli who was standing beside the official. Sruli, suffering from his inability to say anything at that moment, stood, his face immobile.

"Who's he? And what did he invest? And what's it got to do with him?" asked several people who still did not know what was happening.

"*Panyi, Hospodar*," several people began in Polish and Ukrainian, endeavoring to address the official, but since "Sir" was the only word in either language they had mastered, they could not go on.

"Good Lord, what a mess," cried several of those who had already appropriated individual household items or whole bundles which they already considered as their own and who, now, obedient to the official order, had to bid their new possessions good-bye.

"Lies and deception," cried those who had spurned taking any of the small stuff because its value did not match the sums they were owed. And The Kitten, dejected and helpless, moved silently, sadly, toward Shmulikl Fist for whom, over the last several days, he had been unsuccessfully searching, meaning to hire him to look after his interests. He had expected to find Shmulikl here because he was usually present at bankruptcies, but now The Kitten felt that Shmulikl was trying to avoid him because he was unwilling to be hired for one of his usual tasks.

"God help me," mourned The Kitten in his whining chant. He turned to Shmulikl Fist and demanded, "Where have you been hiding? Haven't I paid you enough? Or has someone paid you more than I have, you thief? And why haven't you said something to me? The devil take you."

On a signal from the official, the policeman said, "All right, everyone. Disperse." He advanced on the people as he pointed to the door toward which he was driving them.

Little by little the house began to empty. Those who did not understand Russian but who nevertheless trembled at the mere sight of a uniform, went first; later, they were followed by those who like Tsali were less fearful but who felt compelled to obey an official order. At the door, Tsali Derbaremdiker turned to call back threateningly, "We'll see. Just wait. He can't get away with it. I'm not the only one involved here. I'll expose the whole swindle."

"Enough, enough," said the policeman, pointing to the door, and Tsali, like everyone else, had to go through it empty-handed, with nothing to show for their pains but the loud curses and threats that they uttered.

Only one person was left. The Kitten had managed to stay longer than the others because he was so small and insignificant looking. He continued to stare up into Shmulikl's face as if he meant to climb toward it on a ladder, and he kept repeating softly, "Damn you and your father's father to hell. Why wouldn't you do my work for me? And where have you been hiding all the while I was looking for you, when I really needed you?"

And now to bring this matter to its end we need just a few more minor details. First, one must imagine what Sruli's feelings were at this scene in which his role was to defend the interests of someone with whom his relationship (as we will recall) was hardly of the best. And especially when that defense was likely to harm those who were dear to him—the poor to whose miseries he would not willingly have added.

There is, indeed, a contradiction here and it is one that would repay lingering over, but there is no time for that now.

The contradiction is one thing. The second is a tableau which now we mean briefly to sketch: Finally, the crowd was gone and only Gitl was left in the dining room. She was touched and in some way comforted by the fact that the creditors had not been permitted to take anything away from the house. A moment later Moshe and Mayerl came in quietly from the room in which Moshe had been hiding. The two held each other's hands, but it was not Moshe who held Mayerl's hand. Rather, it was the other way around: Mayerl led Moshe by the hand as one might lead a blind man.

When he and Moshe came into the dining room and found Gitl there, they went toward her without speaking a word. It was the first time that Moshe, in anyone else's presence, had stood so near his wife, and Gitl allowed the closeness as she would have allowed it for a child or for someone who was ill. It was then that Mayerl, finding himself between them, took his grandfather's hand and joined it to Gitl's, uniting them both in their mute sorrow.

IV

Fraudulent Bankruptcy

No sooner did Moshe Mashber's bankruptcy become public knowledge, and when the scenes that had taken place in his home were bruited about—how his impoverished creditors had grabbed up whatever they could, and how at the last moment they were prevented from taking anything by the appearance of a government official accompanied by Sruli Gol who, the official indicated, was the true owner of the property which until then had belonged to Moshe Mashber—when all of that was known, then meetings were held in Yakov-Yossi's house. First, Yakov-Yossi met with his attorney, then with various of Moshe's creditors. In the course of these long discussions, a decision was finally reached, one part of which was promptly put into action. A few words were spoken in the right government quarters and Sruli Gol was detained by the police and subjected to interrogation. The interrogator wanted to know who Sruli was and how it was that he had come to be in his district. And then he wanted to know how someone like Sruli came to have money.

Sruli, as custom required, stood hatless before the official. At first his manner was whimsical, as if he were talking with an old friend: "Money? How do I come to have money? Who knows? Maybe I stole it from a church in Kiev or in Potchaiev." But then seeing that he was in the wrong place for whimsy, he abandoned it and gave serious, intelligent and detailed replies to the questions put to him by the shrewd interrogator who was studying him with a practiced eye. It did not take long for the official to realize that those who had denounced Sruli had done it without the slightest shred of evidence and, from the very first interview, the interrogator's impulse was to let Sruli go. And yet, thinking that he was perhaps dealing with an especially sly fellow, he delayed releasing him. He interviewed him a second and a third time. But he did more than that: he put the secret police to work and from their reports he was able to establish that everything Sruli had claimed was in fact true down to the smallest detail. That established, there was no legal basis for detaining him any longer.

The result was that Sruli was turned loose. Nothing came then of the plan set in motion by Moshe's creditors to show that Moshe had dealings with a notoriously shady character. But they had no trouble proving that Moshe had behaved dishonestly by making it appear that he had creditors to whom he had lent money well before anyone else, creditors whom he was obligated to repay before any of the others.

Moshe's bad faith was easy to prove because it soon appeared that in addition to the properties he had signed over to Sruli Gol, he had also assigned ownership of his various other businesses to his sons-in-law. The kerosene and oil depot now nominally belonged to Yankele Grodshteyn; the brokerage house had been turned over to Nakhum Lentsher.

Ugh! It was unheard of. To deprive anyone except those who were not members of the family of any possibility of recovering their losses, however small.

Such proceedings angered everyone, and in particular, people like Yakov-Yossi who could not bear to leave such behavior unpunished because they believed it would serve as a precedent to others. It was then someone from among the most respected, the most highly regarded, of Moshe's creditors passed the word in the right official quarters that resulted in Moshe's being taken up for questioning. The interrogator who was empowered to detain Moshe for as long might be necessary was the same one who had questioned Sruli Gol.

But now, when Moshe's arrest was imminent, a recourse to keep him from it was found. A money bond assuring that he would show up at his trial could be posted, or else some reputable person in the town could sign as a guarantor to the same effect. Such a person was found.

No sooner was Moshe's liberty assured than Itsikl Zilburg, his confidential adviser, was sent to talk with the angriest of the creditors. His task was to persuade them that Moshe had not acted out of evil intent. Moshe had merely meant to avoid the dispersal of his holdings, as would certainly have happened had all of his creditors made a run on his funds all at the same time in the spirit of people who save only what belongs to them in a fire. Such a run would have harmed everyone, and Moshe had thought that it was better for the time being to put his holdings into trusted hands until such time as things got better and he was in a position to liquidate his debts to everyone.

Itsikl Zilburg tried this argument on various of Moshe's creditors with very poor success. They replied that there was no way that anyone could believe Moshe Mashber anymore because his behavior had been despicable. And even supposing that what he said was true, he ought to have confided in his creditors openly, telling them the true state of his affairs. Had he done that, they would certainly have given him what support they could. Perhaps they would even have extended the due dates on their notes.

"No," came the reply from each of the creditors to whom Itsikl now proposed a delay in payment. "It's too late now. He'll have to pay now or stand trial for what he's done. And the verdict is easy enough to predict."

In brief, Itsikl accomplished nothing. Then, since Moshe Mashber was in no condition to compound with his creditors—not even to the degree of offering them a percentage of what he owed them—there was nothing he could do but wait for the inevitable.

And now that trial was approaching.

Since his bankruptcy Moshe did not leave his house. He cowered at home, strangely silent, pacing from wall to wall as if he was drawn to them.

He rarely talked with anyone, and when he did he would forget what he was saying in midsentence. He also forgot to eat unless someone reminded him, and when he did eat he would pause vaguely, with the food in his mouth unchewed and unswallowed.

Sometimes, too, he would shudder, as if he was chilled, or as if someone was tugging at his sleeve; or he would turn his head sharply to the right or left as if someone behind him had suddenly called him.

He was indifferent to everyone. And yet, a little while before the trial was scheduled to take place, when every possibility that he might come to some agreement with his creditors—either on his own account or with the help of members of his family, or through the intercession of his business adviser, Itsikl Zilburg who in this matter labored as if his own interests were at stake to persuade the creditors to withdraw their charges at the last minute . . . then, when that hope, too, had faded and Moshe Mashber felt the shadow of the sword above his head, and there was no help, no help from any source; when even Gitl, his wife, had no word of comfort for her husband, or for anyone, because she herself no longer knew where to turn for consolation, then, in that time of despair, Moshe sent word to his brother Luzi that he was not well. That he had an important matter to discuss with him, and that he would be grateful if Luzi would come to him.

Luzi came. He was no sooner in the house when Moshe took him into one of the sitting rooms. "Do you know why I've sent for you? No? I want to say good-bye. You know what lies ahead for me: a trial and a verdict that will please my enemies and bring sorrow to my family. As regards myself—I'm prepared for what is to come. Undoubtedly I deserve it. As you've pointed out to me, our father, of blessed memory, cautioned us against the pursuit of wealth. Now you see where that pursuit has brought me, though if the truth be told, I was never one of those who tears up the world in my haste to become rich the way some others have done. But that's the nature of man: whatever he does, he wants to climb higher, to achieve more—whether doing good deeds or doing business. And since business is generally something of a swamp, the more you go into it, the deeper you sink—even as you imagine you are mounting. Certainly it's too bad, and it grieves me deeply that you see me now with soiled hands and my head bowed in shame because of unsecured debts—and, oh, what debts they are! Though I had thought that the pain and anguish I've already been through would stand me in good stead with the Lord in the world to come, I see that it has not been enough.

"My family, I know, will complain that I have thrown up my hands and given in to despair. That I'm not taking counsel with anyone for means to get out of my situation, as people usually do. But I don't feel that way. For me, it's not just a matter of finding my way out of a temporary difficulty. What's at issue and what I cannot bring myself to tell them is that it's not only my good name that is about to be lost. It's me . . . myself. I no longer feel that I'm an inhabitant of this world. It's as if I have one foot already on the other side. One step more and I will have passed over altogether.

"No doubt you remember what is written in one of the Hasidic books: 'When the hour of death destined for a man approaches, his luck immediately turns bad. His mouth and his eyes are sealed.' And lately when I am among people, fully awake, I find that I neither see nor understand much anymore. And at night in my dreams I hear the tread of silent feet approaching. Sometimes one person, sometimes several. When I look closely, I see it is our father and mother and various other now-dead relatives. They come before me and arrange themselves in a line. And there is always an empty place in that line and it seems to me that it is there for me. I haven't told any of this to anyone because—what would be the point? But I've told you. And it's the reason that I've sent for you.

"I can't say when I will pass over. Perhaps when I am in prison, or later. But whenever it is, since you've decided to stay in N., I'm asking you to look out for my family. You know how much they all love you and what confidence they have in what you say. Be generous with them when I am gone. They will need your generosity."

All the while that Moshe sat facing his brother, spoke with his brother, he spoke calmly, as if he was making preparations for someone else. And though what he said was in the nature of a farewell speech, Moshe's demeanor was serene; his eyes were clear, not veiled or troubled as they had recently been.

Luzi, of course, tried to reject what his brother was saying and did what he could to make him ashamed of the tendency of his thoughts. "How can you possibly talk like this? What makes you think you have the right to borrow trouble? And what makes you think you can know what is concealed from everyone else—the end of Man? And how can you bring yourself to believe foolish dreams and signs? Furthermore, it is said that 'Dreams speak falsehood.'"

But as Luzi spoke, one could see Moshe's eyes turning hooded once more; it was as if he was no longer listening, as if he was concentrating on something else altogether, and that Luzi's lecture did not reach him.

Whether Luzi noticed this or not, we do not know. But when their conversation ended and as the two brothers were leaving the sitting room, Moshe, who was walking beside Luzi, suddenly put his head on his brother's shoulder—and there is reason to believe that a sob escaped him. "What will become of Alter when I'm gone?" Luzi, as moved as his brother, had no better consolation to offer him than to murmur, "God is pitiful." And we may suppose that a lump rose in his throat that kept him from saying anymore. He turned his head away. And when the two brothers entered the dining room where the family was gathered—each of them was anxious to talk to Luzi, to get some sort of comfort from him—whatever it might be. But Moshe said that Luzi was too busy, that he had come only in response to his, Moshe's, request and now that their discussion was over, there was no point in detaining him and that he must be permitted to go.

· · ·

The trial began, and from its very first day it was evident that the judge's sympathy and judgment were on the side of Moshe's opponents. And everything suggested that it was an open-and-shut case. It was even clear that when Moshe's lawyer undertook to make a defense of what Moshe had done that there was uncertainty in his voice. The court and the spectators heard the defense lawyer irritably and quickly rejected anything he had to say.

The trial lasted several days. And each morning when Moshe had to pass through the crowd that was gathered in the courtyard and in the street before the Hall of Justice, he kept his head down to avoid encountering the various looks that were directed at him. And when the time came for Moshe to testify in his own defense, he could hardly move his lips. He spoke haltingly and without any hope that anything he said would make any change in the outcome. Not only was he himself in despair, but even his attorneys, Itsikl Zilburg and the lawyer whom Moshe had hired to plead for him at the trial, could not offer him any hope that the verdict would be anything but the one that Moshe himself had foreseen.

Toward the end of the trial, the opposing attorney, in his final speech, called the court's attention to the dangerous precedent that Moshe Mashber's behavior would set if he was found not guilty—or even if his sentence was merely eased. Others, he threatened, would follow Moshe's lead, and the result would be a weakening of the very foundations on which the business world was built and therefore would weaken the state itself.

It was only too evident that Moshe was being squeezed in a vice from which there was no possibility that he would be freed by words.

And he was found guilty. It was the verdict that Moshe had expected all along. On the morning before it was handed down, he was certain that he would not be returning from the courtroom that afternoon—that he would be sent to prison instead. And so he had spent part of the morning bidding farewell to the members of his family.

Before he left the house, he had asked to be given the sack containing his prayer shawl and phylacteries and had filled it beyond its capacity with a prayer book, a Bible, a Code of Jewish Law and a copy of *Crossing the Yabbuk* which he had quietly taken down from some bookshelf. He could not get that book into the sack because his hands trembled so. Finally he put it aside saying, to the astonishment of the bystanders, "Who knows, maybe Luzi is right and it isn't time yet." Curiously enough, no family member of those who were standing there offered to help him, nor did they hinder him in any way. It was as if they were watching someone digging his own grave.

The older kitchen servant—the only servant left to the family—had, without asking anyone's permission, left her work in the kitchen and had come out to say good-bye. She stood with the family and, using a corner of her headscarf, wiped the tears from her eyes and nose, weeping.

Gitl, on the other hand, shed no tears. Nor did Yehudis, Moshe's older daughter. She kept her eyes fixed on her mother, anticipating the possibility that Gitl might faint, or scream, but nothing like that happened. Gitl controlled herself, unwilling to add more grief to his already overflowing cup.

As we have said, neither Gitl nor Yehudis wept. Moshe's sons-in-law looked quietly on, too distressed to say a word.

The office employees were also present, as well as those who worked in the kerosene and oil businesses. Moshe had sent for them, perhaps as an act of humility, to let them see what their employer, the source of their livelihood, looked like as he was leaving his home. Like everyone else, they stood silently, stiffly, as if they were at a deathbed.

When finally Moshe had finished his packing, he made his farewells. He went up to each of his employees and his servant and the look in his eyes more than his words begged their pardon for any wrongs he might have done them.

The children standing there, though they did not understand why Moshe was packing, knew at least that everyone was very sad and that it was an occasion for keeping still.

Then he went to Yehudis and in a low voice pronounced a blessing over her. Then to Gitl to whom he murmured something indistinct. Finally, he turned to Mayerl, his oldest grandson. Mayerl did understand what was going on, and that was why he turned his head away and why he withdrew his hand from his grandfather's grasp.

It was now that Alter showed up. Alter who had come down from his attic room without being noticed. And it was then that Alter and Moshe, overwhelmed, simultaneously sobbed.

Moshe Mashber did what he could to bring this scene quickly to an end. He took a final look around—at the walls, at the people around him. Then he moved to the door through which he must pass, but before he went through it, he raised his eyes to the mezuzah on the doorjamb. He touched it briefly with his fingers which he then kissed.

Some of the family members as well as some of the employees accompanied him, while others stayed home, including Gitl, whom everyone had urged to stay behind—nor did she have the heart to go.

On that very afternoon after the verdict was pronounced, Moshe Mashber was turned over to the authorities who were now charged with looking after him. He was surrounded by guards and taken to the prison where he was to be incarcerated for a fixed time.

There was a considerable crowd before the Hall of Justice standing around in clusters waiting patiently for the trial to end and to see Moshe being led out by guards with their swords drawn.

And finally it happened. Some of Moshe's relatives fainted. Others wept, and even his enemies who had had a great deal to do with pressing the edge of the sword to his throat found themselves unable to rejoice at their victory and turning their heads away sidled off, hoping not to be noticed.

A large portion of the crowd followed Moshe and his guards for a considerable while. Some followed behind, as if at a funeral; others, the more curious idlers, were eager to watch Moshe's face and so they ran before him. Finally, the crowd trailed away until only the prisoner and his guards were left: he in their midst, a guard with his sword drawn walking before him while another walked behind.

Throughout the course of that long march, Moshe, carrying his prayer-shawl sack, kept his eyes on the ground. It was only as they approached the gates of the prison and the small entry door was opened for him that he looked up. Then realizing where he was, he glanced about at the doorjambs as if checking to see whether there was a mezuzah on one of them. But when one of the guards shouted at him, Moshe pulled himself together and crossed the threshold.

And here we will leave Moshe for a while in order to tell what transpired after those members of his family who had accompanied him to his trial returned home.

When Gitl saw them—first the sons-in-law who looked pale as after a fast, and then her daughter Yehudis whose face was tear-stained, Gitl knew at once that what they had most feared, and expected, had happened. She took a step toward her daughter as if she meant to hear what she had to say, but almost at once, as if she regretted that impulse, she stopped where she was and said quietly, "Yehudis. Hold me. I'm falling."

And when Yehudis ran up to her and put her arms around her, Gitl's whole body sagged and she became so heavy that Yehudis, who was not strong enough to support her, had to call for help. The sons-in-law ran up, as well as others who had come back with them from the trial; and with their combined help, Gitl was carried to her room and put to bed.

Yes, after having repressed so much pain and suffering without being able to express it either by outcries or tears, she was now stricken by that illness that paralyzes people, turning them so inert that they cannot blink an eye or move a limb. And what is worse, unable to say a word.

The doctors, who were immediately sent for after she had been put to bed, studied her carefully for a while, and all came to the same conclusion: it was indeed the illness of which we have just spoken. And from what they said later, it was clear that her situation was not good, that there was practically no hope for her beyond the possibility that she would stay just as she was perhaps for days, for weeks or years. They did not know.

She lay quietly, uttering no sound and staring straight ahead, like a wax figure.

It was indeed fortunate, we say, that she was able to be put to bed in her own house, with her own roof over her head—all of which could have been taken from her by any one of Moshe's creditors. That this did not happen was the result of a ruling of the court which held that the transaction in which the ownership of Moshe's property was transferred to Sruli Gol was legally binding and that Sruli was now its legal owner.

And it is well, too, we say, that the family was given the undisturbed use of the house and that Gitl, its former mistress, could continue to live in it as if she were its mistress still. Because all that Yehudis could think to do to make her sick mother's situation easier was to treat her as if she were still in charge of the household. This, in spite of the fact that Gitl was utterly incompetent to do anything at all. Yehudis often wept silently when, as if she had come for advice, she stood before her impassive mother and put various questions of household management to her, though her mother was not able to make the slightest reply to any question she was asked. But Yehudis felt that the very asking was a debt she had to pay her mother. It continued to nourish the illusion that Gitl was still her mother and that the household was still being run as it always had been.

It was fortunate, too, yes, it was fortunate, that Luzi, Moshe Mashber's brother, did what Moshe had asked him to do before the trial, when, as we will recall, he had a discussion with Luzi before taking his leave. And now that Moshe was gone and that Gitl's misfortune had come upon her, Luzi kept his promise to Moshe and made frequent visits to comfort the family.

That, too, was fortunate, but beyond all that good fortune, Moshe Mashber's family was hardly fortunate at all.

Consider: Moshe Mashber was in prison. Gitl was bedridden, half-dead; the business was at a standstill, though some while later various creditors working together made some effort to get it moving again and put its management in the hands of knowledgeable people who had a financial interest in the matter. But nothing came of that. Why not? Because when Moshe's business was left without the guidance of those who had run it— his sons-in-law and himself—their usual clients and customers, who had done much of their business with the Mashbers on credit, were heavily indebted to the firm. They now took advantage of Moshe's bankruptcy and, as a way of avoiding payment of their debts, declared themselves bankrupt as well. The least ethical among them said simply, "If he doesn't pay, we don't pay." Well, there was nothing to be done. Other, more reputable merchants, had more reputable excuses, but they, too, withheld payment. As a consequence, even if anyone had devoted himself to the task of collecting all that was owed to the firm, it would have required a great deal of time and trouble, lots of tugging and hauling, with finally nothing to show for one's pains.

In the event, those who had pushed Moshe Mashber to the wall profited very little from it. All that happened was that several of his creditors who had businesses similar to his drew his customers to them, hoping that over time the profits from those transactions might make up for the losses they had incurred with Moshe Mashber; another result was that the minor creditors were left without any hope at all of recouping their losses. The net result was that those of the creditors who had no businesses of their own, and who therefore could not recover their money by taking on Moshe's customers—those creditors were left with nothing in hand but their promissory notes. And perhaps the consolation that Moshe Mashber was in prison . . . much joy may it give them.

And now to return to Moshe Mashber.

When he passed through the gate of the prison courtyard, he was turned over to the director of the prison, who then inscribed his name into a book that listed the convicts under his care. Moshe's civilian clothes were taken from him and he was given a uniform. Finally, clothed in prison garb, he was led to one of the prison's communal cells. There the door was unlocked for him and he went in.

He entered the place like any other prisoner: with nothing except for the sack containing his prayer shawl and tefillin, which, as religious articles, he was allowed by law to keep. He stood, clutching his sack, and looked around, very much like a man entering a new synagogue for the first time; and in his confusion he raised his eyes to the door-jamb to look for a mezuzah to kiss.

Instead of the mezuzah, however, what he saw was a man who had just left a cluster of prisoners and who was coming toward him. He was the sort of man, the sight of whom made one forget not only mezuzahs but even one's own name.

He was a short, stocky convict half of whose head had been shaved; he had a yellow complexion, like that of all the prisoners who lived for long periods in cramped and airless rooms. He had a short rippling beard and a repulsive-looking upper lip that was shaved so closely that it looked quite blue.

He was a long-term convict who was being sent by stages to some other prison, but he had meanwhile been assigned to this one at N., where he waited for the administration to recall him to mind, after which he would be sent on.

He wore a convict's gray, visorless cloth cap, a short jacket stamped with a government number at the shoulder, and trousers made of the same sort of cloth as the jacket. He came close to Moshe, very close, and without saying a word he took the sack containing the prayer shawl and tefillin from him.

"What is this?" he asked.

"Things I use to pray with," said Moshe, finding a few non-Yiddish words with which to answer the convict so that the fellow would know what the objects were and would treat them with respect.

"And what is this?" the convict asked, taking the books out of the sack into which Moshe had put them before leaving home.

"Also things to pray with," Moshe said.

"And you? Who are you?"

"A merchant," stammered Moshe.

"Do you have money?"

"No. That's why I'm here," Moshe said, making a feeble joke (if you can call it that) as he saw the group of convicts who now surrounded them and were staring at him.

The stocky fellow, who appeared to be the leader of the group, took up the prayer shawl Moshe had brought and clumsily, heavy-handedly, he tried to put it on and to enfold himself in it. With equal awkwardness, he tried to do something with the tefillin. And yet, however clumsily, he handled the objects with respect. As if they were things that he had once known something about but to which he had been long unaccustomed.

Moshe, seeing what the fellow was doing, turned pale. He was afraid that the other convicts, who kept up a continual laughter as they

watched their comrade manipulating the religious articles . . . that they
might be tempted to profane them.

"Stop laughing," said the *starost*, the leader, the fellow with the wavy
beard and the closely shaven repulsive upper lip. "These are things
that belong to *my* God and to *his*," he said, pointing to Moshe who
stood there, depressed by his environment and by having to deal with
this *starost* who was handling the religious articles, evidently to make
fun of them.

But that turned out not to be the case. The *starost* was a Jew. What
sort of a Jew may well be imagined! With a tin earring in one ear, with
the low forehead of a bull, with hands like logs—hands that he was
prepared to use on all occasions. And it was evident that he would find
strangling an opponent no more trouble than it would take to kill a
kitten.

He was called "the fellow from Novorossisk." He came from the recently settled prosperous Novorossisk region where they eat white
bread even in the middle of the week, and where Jews become coars-
ened and rattle their r's.

His was not a very elevating story. He made a living stealing horses
which he sold at distant fairs. If the horse stealing went without incident, then well and good. But if there was resistance, he did not hesitate to use violence; and it had often happened that he had had to flee
to the steppes where he hid. There, when he was hungry, he would
steal a "head" from a flock, kill it and eat it raw. It was said that even
here, in the prison, when he was sent to the kitchen to bring his fellow
convicts their food, or when he helped the cook in some way—it was
said that he managed to steal some raw meat and eat it.

In a word, he was something of a legend. An orphan who had grown
up in a distant peasant settlement in Novorossisk, he had worked as an
errand boy for a long while; then as a stable hand, for which he was
paid a miserable pittance and was considerably mistreated as well. The
result of it all was that when he joined a band of thieves, he was able to
link his knowledge of horses and of the steppe with their thieving
skills.

He could not remember when any of this had happened, having long
ago forgotten the details of his youth. And all that remained to him . . .
all that bound him to his forebears, was that he could not bear to see
anyone being shamed. When he saw it happening, he often took the
victim under his protection.

Yes, Moshe was lucky indeed to have encountered this fellow, because otherwise there is no doubt that he would have been treated the
way other newcomers to the lockup are treated when they are initiated

to prison life by their fellow convicts—that is, with blows—wet and dry—from which they . . . especially someone like Moshe . . . would not have escaped with their limbs intact. So Moshe was lucky that his religious articles had stirred the *starost* to respect and that he had taken Moshe under his wing the moment after he walked through the door into the cell.

But, oh, what woeful luck. As Moshe felt, looking more closely at this fellow with the tin earring in his ear, his low forehead, the stubby hands that made him look more murderous than his fellow convicts. It was because of his hands, no doubt, that he had been chosen by them to be their leader, maintaining discipline among them and looking after their interests, often risking his life on their account even as he put theirs in peril of his knife which despite the watchfulness of the authorities, he had managed to keep hidden from them and which he had always in his possession.

What pathetic luck, as Moshe would be well aware, later when he got to know this *starost* with the repulsive closely shaven upper lip with its blue cast on which there occasionally gleamed a ferocious drop of sweat whenever he grew angry and was about to give someone his comeuppance.

Ah, Lord in heaven, thought Moshe when he was able to leave the circle of convicts that surrounded him when he first came into the cell. Where hast Thou brought me? And where am I placed?

He was afraid to say more lest he draw the attention of the others to himself. He clamped his mouth shut, deciding that this was no time to say anything; but later, at night, when the others were asleep and he was alone, he would finish what he had begun to say.

And so it was. When he left the cluster of convicts, he was shown a bunk where he could dispose of his few possessions by day and on which he would lie at night. Somehow or other, he settled in. Naturally enough, he kept severely to himself and was careful not to interfere with anyone. And in the evening, he, too, received his portion of the usual food which he excused himself from eating, saying that he did not care for it as he offered it to anyone else who might want it.

Then he examined his bunk more carefully. It was shiny from long rubbing against bodies. He glanced, too, at the slop bucket which his eyes had long been avoiding and to which he was by now accustomed. To it, and to those who used it without embarrassment.

Finally, the time came when the prisoners got themselves ready for bed, when a small lamp was set in a niche in the wall to shed its weak light over the room. The gray-clad prisoners with their dim yellow features were now indistinguishable from each other.

And so they all lay. Moshe Mashber, too, in his prison bed for the first time. Then when the convicts, after a certain amount of stirring and movement, began to fall asleep, he finally found the time to think through his situation.

Had anyone seen him there by the weak light of the lamp, lying in his bunk among the other convicts, he would have seen that Moshe's face was wet with tears which seemed to flow not from his eyes but from some deep inward source without a name.

Moshe, lying on his smooth, well-polished bunk without a hint of bedclothes, was not aware that he was weeping; nor did he notice when his tears stopped and he fell into a doze or at what moment it was that he saw his father standing before his half-opened—or perhaps even closed—eyes.

His father was wearing his white linen robe and there were several rams' horns tucked into his waistband the way a man who is going to sound the shofar, foreseeing that one of them might prove defective, provides himself with several just in case.

"What is it, Father? Is today Rosh Hashanah?" Moshe asked, astonished.

"No, my son. An anathema."

"Against whom?"

"Look," replied his father.

And here, somehow, Moshe saw himself inside a synagogue, one of those in which all the popular solemn days are celebrated, whether for joy or, God forbid, for the reverse. He saw himself standing to one side, like a condemned man for whom the congregation has cleared a space so that whatever may happen to him will not touch or harm them in any way.

His father was standing on the podium together with several other respected men. The podium, as if it were the eve before Yom Kippur, was alight with candles and lamps. A large, silent and awed congregation was assembled, and was evidently waiting for some event to occur. The synagogue and the heads and faces of the congregants were illuminated by the light that shone down from the hanging candelabra and from the candles on the podium. The curtains over the Ark were drawn and its doors were open. And the Torah scrolls, too, like everyone else, seemed to be waiting for something to happen.

All at once, a shofar was heard that made everyone tremble, Moshe more than the others. He stood to one side and saw that it was his father who had blown the shofar and who now announced that it was his son who was to be separated from the community.

A voice was heard to say, "Cursed be he, the supreme curse from the chapters of malediction; and the curse of Joshua, the son of Nun, and the curse of all the others on the head of him who stands before us, sundered from the congregation; on him who trod the ways of the apostate, and the paths of shame and falsehood."

"Cursed be he," repeated the congregation, careful to repeat each word of the uttered curse.

And here Moshe Mashber lifted his eyes and recognized many of his poor creditors from whom he had borrowed money and who not long ago had besieged his office with their entreaties, and from whom, when they had pressed him too closely, he had escaped by going out a back door, making his way home where the crowd followed him and where they behaved riotously until they were driven away by a Gentile official.

Yes, Moshe, ashamed, condemned by the entire congregation and by his father, who stood on the podium with others like himself and who had to his shame to repeat with his own lips the general anathema against his son . . . Moshe bowed his head as under a storm of hail and accepted it all as no more than he deserved and prayed for death.

Then all at once, the scene vanished: the synagogue, the assembled congregation and only he and his father were left standing together. And his father (a father, after all) came to greet him as if he was greeting one who was prepared for everything. His father came toward him wearing the same white linen robe as before, and he showed Moshe how roomy it was, indicating that he, Moshe, should also wrap himself in it, so that he might accompany him to the place from which his father had come, a revenant from the other world. And Moshe was ready to follow where he was bidden, but here he woke up and saw by the light of the weak lamp where he was.

It was night. He was lying in his bunk among gray-clad convicts who had drawn their greatcoats over their heads. And since, not long ago, he had been prepared to pass from one world into the next, he did not feel humbled by the harsh reality which the weak light of the lamp revealed to him now.

He lay awake for a long time, his eyes open. It was still early, not past midnight, and Moshe, in his half doze, felt himself transported to the town where it seemed to him he stood, hearing himself talked about by various groups in the marketplace. Some people sympathized with him while others on the other hand said that Moshe had gotten what he deserved. That justice had been done.

Then he imagined that he made his way home, where it seemed to him that he first stumbled about like a stranger in his night-darkened courtyard; and then it seemed that he approached the doors, but he did not have the courage to cross his own threshold. And when finally he made his mind up and went into the house, it seemed to him that he moved stealthily, silently, from room to room. First he peered into his grandchildren's room to see how they were sleeping. Then he came to his daughter Yehudis's room and saw that she was not asleep; that her pillow was wet with the tears that continually flowed from her eyes; and finally he entered his own room where he saw that his bed was made, that no one was sleeping in it, and that Gitl, his wife, lay in the next bed. But see—how strange. She was neither awake nor asleep. She frightened him by the way she stared with glazed eyes at some point straight before her. A horrified cry started in his throat as if he actually were seeing Gitl in trouble of some sort. She seemed so close, so real, that though he had no inkling of what had really happened in his home when he did not return after the trial, yet he felt now that something like what he was seeing had taken place; and so a cry rose in his throat as when one cries for help at the time of a disaster.

But here, he woke once more and remembered where he was. Not at home. Far from the town. In prison, at night, among convicts. He knew that he was lying on the smoothly rubbed bunk. And that an outcry here was futile.

All that night he lay on his bunk unable to close his eyes. When the first signs of dawn showed through the high barred windows, Moshe was to be seen wearing his prayer shawl and tefillin, facing the window. The prayer shawl drawn over his head sharply outlined the edges of the phylactery he wore on his forehead, making it look like a strange protuberance. He stood silently, not moving a muscle through all of his prayers, as if he was reciting a long Shimon Essre. And when one of the convicts, coming awake just then, looked up to see what time it was, the sight of Moshe Mashber in his Jewish morning garb frightened him. He could not tell what it was he was seeing: whether it was someone human and alive, or a ghost which had somehow survived into wakefulness from his dreams.

And now for a while—until the time when we will bring him home again, a man utterly broken and transformed from what he once was—we will leave Moshe Mashber in prison where he remained despite the intervention of various members of his family; and even of certain of his creditors who finally understood just what it was they had accomplished and *whom* they had consigned to *what* hands. And though—let us say it again—thanks to such intervention with the right people, Moshe was accorded privileges that made his lot a bit easier than that of the other prisoners—for instance, he was not assigned, like them, to hard labor in the town—so that he might be spared the shame of being seen in his convict's clothes; and he was permitted to keep the religious articles he needed for his prayers on the Sabbaths and on the other holidays; and he was allowed, according to the law, to have kosher food; and when it was learned that he was ill—whether it was because of stress, or because of prison life—he was immediately transferred to the prison hospital where he received better food and was looked after by a doctor who was, of course, well paid for his good care . . . though all of that had been accomplished, still it was not enough to heal the great wound he had received, nor to make him change his view that he would do better not to stay in this world after all that had happened to him in it and that it would be better for him to take leave of it and go to the one to which his father had led him.

V

Luzi Off Balance

1.

For the sake of our narrative, we will now look back for a while.

When Luzi returned home on the night when he was called away from Reb Dudi so that he could be at the sickbed of his perilously sick niece, and when he had a little recovered from his grief for her and her family, his mind turned again to Reb Dudi and all that had happened in the rabbi's house.

In his mind's eye, he saw Reb Dudi with his cleanly white beard, his intelligent, half-closed eyes whose look penetrated into one and bent one to his will. In the man capable of such a glance, Luzi recognized one who was profoundly steeped in the Torah as well as one who was surrounded and sustained by people like the tavern keeper whose presence Luzi had taken note of on that night. Luzi especially remembered Yone's hands and the way he held them behind his back.

He recognized in Reb Dudi one of those men whom Luzi had avoided for so long—those comfortable and cosseted people who took the choice front seats in the coach to which the poor masses were harnessed. He could hear the pleased clucking of their tongues as they drove the coach. Perfectly satisfied with themselves, they never took the trouble to see whether those who drew the coach were strong enough for the task.

He sensed in Reb Dudi a man who had forgotten that the weight of the load must be in proportion to the strength of the one who pulls it, otherwise he may collapse and fall. He was one of those who believed in the sanctity of the law *because* it was the law and not because it served some purpose. People like him did not judge their fellowmen according to the circumstances that prompted them to action.

For instance, in the case of Mikhl Bukyer for whom, even according to the law, he might have had compassion, he had reached instead for the rod to chastise a man whose circumstances he did not know, nor did he ask himself how he would have behaved in the same situation. A man like Reb Dudi should have remembered that "Sinful Israel is Israel still." That even a sinner is human. And that before imposing punishment on a man it is necessary to know the reasons for the crime before thrusting him away and denying him his rights both in this world and the next.

And each time that such thoughts occurred to him that night, he thought, too, of Mikhl Bukyer, and his image was accompanied each time by that of the diminutive gray Reb Dudi who stared fixedly at Luzi as if to say that the quarrel about Mikhl Bukyer which he, Luzi, had begun was not over.

It was not much later that an event profoundly unsettling to Luzi occurred. And again it concerned Mikhl who had been suddenly taken ill. And Sruli one day brought the sick man to visit Luzi.

What happened.

It was the middle of the day. Luzi's door was opened and two people came in. Sruli, leading an apparently reluctant Mikhl by the hand. As Mikhl walked, the right side of his body seemed to lurch forward while his left side, as if it were in no way related to him, was dragged along. He shuddered as he came in; at the same time the smile of a pleased simpleton appeared on the right side of his face while the left side maintained its half-dead, wooden look.

Sruli led him up to Luzi's table and as if introducing him, said, "See what they've done to him."

"Who? What?" asked Luzi, startled.

"The respectable folk of the town, those skillful designers of his misery."

"Ah, Luzi. Shalom," said Mikhl, smiling with half of his face as he thrust out his functioning right hand. But that was all he was able to say.

Luzi, regarding Mikhl, was both frightened and tense. He stood and for appearance sake returned the greeting. "Shalom." Then seeing that there was nothing more to be gotten from him, he turned his eyes away and spoke to Sruli as if Mikhl were not there. "What is it?" he asked. "What's happened?"

Sruli, who could give no clear account of what had happened, did not know what to reply except to say that Mikhl was, as Luzi could see, no longer himself. That he was broken in body and crippled in soul. And that he, Sruli, had just met him being led by his weeping wife who was taking him to beg at the houses of his former employers to show them what he looked like so that they might take pity on him.

"This is the direct consequence of his quarrel with the community," Sruli added. "It's they who have brought him to this pass, and there will be more to come. I mean, of course, that he isn't long for this world."

And as regards Mikhl's illness Sruli was right. Here is what happened.

After the deaths of his children, after the loss of his primary school which left him not only with no income but with a tarnished reputation as well, so that he could not even get a job (for which he applied) as an assistant shammes in a tiny synagogue—after all that, Mikhl, to feed his family, had no recourse but to borrow wherever he could, and then when there was no one left from whom to borrow, and when the kitchen stove as well as the house itself grew cold, all that he could manage to do was to get a bit of kerosene from a shopkeeper or from a neighbor so that when his hungry family went to sleep at night, he would be able to sit at his table by the light of his cheap lantern and there with industrious devotion continue writing the book on which he had been so long engaged: the book in which he quarreled bitterly with the Rambam, refuting his arguments, the book which Mikhl hoped would with its newly developed arguments remove the blinders from the eyes of the world.

One night while Mikhl, by the light of his lamp, sat deeply engrossed in one of the Rambam's convoluted arguments about *maskil* (He who thinks), *muscal* (What one thinks about) and *sekhel* (Thought itself)—arguments which, given the compression and the difficulty of the language in which they were expressed, would have been difficult enough for a man with a clear brain—how much more difficult, then, for a man like Mikhl, who was lately both ill fed and exhausted with worry. It was then, engrossed as he was, that suddenly there was a crash and the matter he was mulling over seemed to shatter, as if a glass had shattered in his brain. At one and the same moment he expe-

rienced both an intensely bright light and a profound darkness. And at
the same time he lost sensation in half of his body. Saliva dripped from
the paralyzed side of his mouth, and had his wife—or anyone else who
might chance to be there—waked up and found him there, she would
have seen that when the flow of spittle stopped, he was left sitting
there, a completely emptied man. On half his features the sweet smile
of a simpleton, on the other half, nothing. Death. A riddle, cold and
rigid. And if Mikhl had been able to stand by himself or with the help
of someone else, it would have been clear that he was finished. That he
was already possessed of all the symptoms we described earlier in our
account of Sruli's encounter with him and of the subsequent visit to
Luzi.

"Ah, woe," said Luzi, casting a compassionate look at Mikhl.

"Woe to whom?" asked Sruli, at once content with what Luzi had
said and at the same time with a trace of mockery in his voice, as if to
say that it had taken Luzi long enough to arrive at the thought that was
now in his mind.

"Woe to those whom you have just named," replied Luzi.

"So be it," said Sruli coldly, curtly, as if unwilling to talk more about
the matter. Instead, he went on to give details about Mikhl: when it
was that it had happened and how he had run into Mikhl and his wife
today, and how she had led Mikhl by the hand as she wept, and how
he, Sruli, had taken her place holding Mikhl's hand and how they were
left alone, and how Sruli had led him from house to house, to collect
such money as he could.

Sruli, reconstructing all this, did not so much as look at Mikhl, who
stood nearby, but acted as if Mikhl was incapable of hearing or of understanding what was said. And indeed, all the while that Mikhl had
been in the house after he had uttered the single word "Shalom," and
all the while that Sruli was describing what had happened to him,
Mikhl stood nearby, like a stranger, as if it were not he who was being
talked about. He stood there shifting from foot to foot while on the
paralyzed right side of his face there beamed an idiotic smile.

After the first visit to Luzi's house, Sruli led Mikhl into a number of
other homes as well. One might have thought, seeing the way Sruli led
Mikhl about by the hand or adjusted the clothing that Mikhl, given his
illness, was not always aware needed to be adjusted . . . one might have
thought that Sruli was a close relative—a brother, perhaps—or else a
paid companion. But of course he was neither the one nor the other.
There is reason to think that he saw in Mikhl an opportunity to pursue
a matter he had long wanted to discuss with Luzi.

That opportunity was not long in coming.

A little while later, when he returned home from having led Mikhl about the town, he reported to Luzi that as they were passing Reb Dudi's house, Mikhl had come to a stop and had refused to go any farther. The message seemed to be that he wanted Sruli, without explanation or excuse of any sort, to take him into Reb Dudi's house. Mikhl, until then, had never shown any special interest in any of the houses in which people he knew lived. But he refused stubbornly to pass by Reb Dudi's house and made it clear, by various signs, that he wanted to be taken in.

And Sruli indulged him. They went into the house where they found Reb Dudi sitting at the head of his table dealing with a rabbinical matter: resolving a question of law or simply having a discussion with his followers.

They had no sooner crossed the threshold when Mikhl pulled himself away from Sruli and started toward Reb Dudi's chair of honor where he stopped in the attitude of a man who means to say something decisive, or indeed who means to deliver an extensive speech. But the sounds he uttered were mute and incomprehensible; his face was suffused with blood. And then, because of some impediment in his thought but more because of the frustration of being unable to express himself, he came to a dead stop and a stream of saliva issued from his mouth. And now, just as before he had grasped Sruli's hand to make him lead him into Reb Dudi's house, so now he grasped it again to make Sruli lead him out of it.

"Yes," added Sruli, as he recounted all this, "it was clear that Mikhl remembered his encounter with Reb Dudi and the business of the prayer shawl. And this visit was his silent form of protest."

"Reb Dudi," continued Sruli, "seeing Mikhl, said not a word. It may be that he might have said something, but seeing what state Mikhl was in when he came in, and when he left, seems to have reduced the rabbi to silence. And furthermore Mikhl hurried us out so quickly that even had the rabbi had something to say, he would not have had time enough to say it.

"But at the door, I turned and pointing to Mikhl, I said, 'You may be proud of yourself, Reb Dudi. See what you have accomplished. This is your work.' "

"Yes," Luzi said in spontaneous agreement.

"No," said Sruli, as if rejecting Luzi's support, "it isn't only Reb Dudi's fault. It's the fault also of all those who aided and abetted him."

"What do you mean?" Luzi asked.

"I mean that if you are out to kill and you use a double edged knife it doesn't matter which edge you use."

"I don't understand you."

"No? Well then, if you think you haven't had a part in all this, then you are very much mistaken."

"What part have I had? What are you talking about?"

"Yes. Well, if you think that just because you are not in the dead center of the marketplace where God is sold, because you stand to one side and do not cry your wares . . . if you think that makes them either purer or more precious, then you are wrong again."

Luzi stared in astonishment at Sruli who in all the time they had known each other had never spoken to him like this.

"You ask what part you have in this? I reply: What is the difference between you and those who oppose you? What is the difference between your forms of belief and theirs? Since the root of all belief systems is that those who share in the belief in one system are permitted to regard those who believe in something else as dust that may be trampled on.

"Isn't that so?" asked Sruli without waiting for a reply—as if replying himself. "You may sneer at what I've said. You may ask, 'How can you compare those who have the majority on their side, who are allied with the powers that be and who use all sorts of brutal oppressions and persecutions against those who do not share their beliefs; how can you compare them with this group, small in number though steadfast in conviction, who have no intention of forcing others to their belief?

"Inoffensive lambs to look at them. Oh, I know them well. To look at them it would never occur to one that they, too, could be capable of persecutions because they have experienced persecutions themselves. But the truth is, the differences between Reb Dudi's crowd and these is a difference in numbers, not in kind, a difference in degrees of power, not in essence.

"Who knows," said Sruli with a harsh and bitter glance at Luzi, "what you and your followers, for the time being small in number, will become if your numbers were to increase."

"Me? Us?" Luzi said, returning Sruli's look.

"Yes, you. Why does that surprise you? What makes you immune from the touch of evil when in fact it is to be found under your own roof and, in a manner of speaking, in your own bed."

"What?"

"Yes," said Sruli unable to restrain himself. "But I don't want to talk about that now. But as regards the Mikhl affair, which is what we are talking about now and about which there may be more to say later . . .

if you think that your share of guilt in it is smaller than Reb Dudi's then you are very much mistaken.

"In general I've minded my own business, but now since we are talking about it, I want to say that the way you deal with your followers who cling to your skirts, who look up to you, who drink in your words—you are no less guilty regarding them than a man who leads the blind into a ditch.

"I'm referring now to the second blade of the two-bladed knife. Look at Mikhl. Doesn't he have the look of a man who has escaped the slaughterer's knife? But not only Reb Dudi's knife, but yours as well, and even from his own toward which he stretched his throat and from which he received a mortal wound.

"Because, after all you know the sort of lives your devotees lead: the kinds of homes they inhabit—their wives and children dragging about like autumn flies before they die. They spend days, months, years, without getting their hands on a coin from their men, a coin that might buy them a bit of nourishment.

"Yes. You know how they freeze in those homes in winter. Ramshackle homes with nailed boards or pillows instead of glass in the windows. Have you any idea what the children in such houses look like even when they're healthy, much less what they look like when they are sick? And they are not sick one at a time, but in their numbers because they get sick in groups and lie together in the same bed with no bedclothes to speak of. And that's how they have always lived. From the time that the marriage was sanctified always and hopelessly in debt to usurers.

"Yes," continued Sruli even more heatedly, "and all because the men in those households, instead of providing for their families, squander their last bit of strength in the service of their God, who, if he ever chanced to look down from on high, would be moved to laugh (or to weep) at the sight of such sacrifices and such praise being uttered (if you'll pardon me) by such ill-smelling mouths.

"And you, to whom they look up, whom they honor, is it not your responsibility to keep them from their own destruction? Why don't you, as one should expect that you would, why don't you say something to keep them from acts forbidden, as I think, by God and His laws?"

And here, Sruli came to a stop and waited for Luzi to reply.

But his waiting produced nothing. There was no reply. Luzi was silent. No matter how agreeable it might be to maintain a silence in the face of such questions, no matter *who* it was who asked them, and no matter what might be the relationship between them, still, once the questions were uttered—once they were in the air, as it were—it behooved one to respond one way or another, whether with anger or by dismissing them with contempt. And yet Luzi made no reply? Why not? Was it because he thought it would cut off further discussion? Or was it because he did not regard Sruli as an equal with whom such matters could be debated? Sruli, for his part, was not really expecting an answer so that now, when it became apparent that Luzi was not going to make one, he was neither distressed nor insulted.

On the contrary. In order to keep Luzi from embarrassment because of his silence, Sruli now pretended that he had suddenly remembered something he had been meaning to do and left the room abruptly. He passed through the adjoining room and hurried out into the street feeling rather pleased that Luzi had not engaged him in a lengthy conversation, and pleased, too, that he, Sruli, had managed to put various ideas before Luzi . . . ideas which for a considerable while Sruli had had on his mind. His hope was that sooner or later his words would not be without their effect on Luzi.

We will see later just how right he was as regards Luzi. He was not, generally speaking, a man who was indifferent or insensible to influences. Had anyone else but Sruli spoken to him as Sruli had, it is certain that Luzi would not have heard him in silence. There is no question that Luzi would have been touched and would have blamed himself because he had been assailed by doubts before now, and it was not likely that he would be able to avoid others yet to come.

As we will see in what is to follow.

Early one very cold morning in which the weak light of a late rising sun struggled to touch not only the twisted streets of the town but also the outlying districts where the streets and highways were so shrouded by a heavy snowfall that one could not see what was happening on them . . . on that morning a man who had been walking on the highway could be seen passing through a field barrier on his way to the boundary of the town.

He was a tall, well-built man. Still young—not yet in his thirties— and dressed the way most Jews were in those days, in pious garb: a long winter coat below which there showed an even longer caftan that occasionally interfered with his steps.

He carried a small sack under one arm so that at first glance he looked like a local resident going through the streets and carrying his prayer shawl and tefillin on his way to the synagogue. In fact, he came from very far away. From a village, a town or from some godforsaken settlement many, many versts away from N., and he had been traveling for a long time, as one could tell from his clothes. His coat, his hat and his shoes were covered with frost as were the branches of the dimly seen trees. There was frost on his face, too, so that his intense dark eyes were as hard to see as his short beard.

He walked quickly, more quickly than one might expect of a man who has already traversed a long distance. This suggested either that he was a hot-blooded individual whom the cold and the crackling snow had stirred to action or else that he had something on his mind that compelled him to move at such an abnormal pace.

And indeed he did seem to be distracted, as was indicated by the way that despite his vigorous build he kept his head lowered and thrust forward, as if he was sending it hurriedly before him to be the guide to the rest of his body.

When he passed the field gate and sensed the presence of the town—the smoke of early morning fires in stoves and ovens—he looked around to see where he was and to decide which way he now had to go. He made inquiries of the people he met and with their help he moved from street to street until he arrived in The Curse district and found the home of one of its inhabitants whose address he had. There he asked at once to be taken to Luzi who he knew was living in N. but whose address he did not know.

The man's name was Avremele Lubliner. And he traveled on foot not because he was poor or because he could not rent a wagon but because he *always* traveled on foot. It may have been because he had taken a vow of some sort or for some other reason which in those days among people like him would not have seemed strange.

His pace was always quick and he never seemed to tire because, as has already been said, he was sustained by his thoughts, and then, given his youth and his vigorous build, no amount of effort could tire him.

When he was shown into Luzi's house, though he was still in his overcoat, he thrust his hand out to greet Luzi. But it was only when he had taken his coat off that one could get a sense of his size first in relationship to Luzi who was himself a man of more than average height, and then in relationship to the rooms themselves whose low ceilings he all but touched with his head.

He was dressed all in black. His caftan as well as the rest of his clothing was made of fine cloth, and despite his extensive travels and the fact that he had occasionally to stay with people who were not exceptionally clean, he always managed to keep his clothing in good shape and was in every way much cleaner than others like himself.

This was the result of his background. He was both a son of rich parents and a son-in-law of equally rich people in the distant city of Lublin in Poland. He had been born and married there. And yet despite all his wealth, he had, either because he had met someone who persuaded him to it or because of some process in his own mind—whichever it was he had abandoned his parents, his in-laws and his wife and children to join the Bratslaver sect. Among them he was widely known.

It was said of him that he had visited Palestine many times. The story was told that when he arrived in Palestine, still a very young man, he flung himself down on the shore where he was disembarked. He kissed the ground and wept so passionately that he astonished the people who were traveling with him—members of his own sect to whom Palestine was equally dear.

On another journey, provided with a great deal of money by his rich parents, he undertook to see and to walk over the length and breadth of the land. With that in mind he hired a non-Jewish native guide to show him everything, beginning on the coast where he, Avremele, had landed and ending on the other side of the Jordan. So much then for the breadth. After that, he made the journey through the length of the Land as well, from one end to the other.

He had a terrifying experience one day as he and his guide approached the Jordan River. Suddenly a fierce outlaw, hooded and brandishing a spear, appeared before them. The bandit placed the point of his spear against Avremele's chest and he was within an inch of losing his life when his native guide interceded for him.

You may well imagine that the rescue cost him dear. Every penny that he had brought with him. And more. The bandit demanded Avremele's clothes as well, and he was left standing there in his underwear.

His parents, of course, replaced what was lost. New money was sent, much of which he distributed to the poor, especially when he visited the graves of such holy men as Shimon ben Yokhai and Reb Maier Bal-ness, where beggars and the poor swarmed all over him like flies while he distributed alms with a generous hand so that, having dispensed huge sums—almost a fortune—he had again and again to write to his parents to ask for more.

It was said, too, that when he approached the Wailing Wall with its ancient moss-grown stones and saw what a ruin it was, the same thing happened as when he debarked from the ship and came ashore. He went nearly mad with excitement and flung himself upon one of the stones, pressing first his forehead then his entire body against it and could not be made to leave . . . like one who clings to the grave of a loved one meaning to warm the body back to life.

He stayed for a long time in the Holy Land and visited all of the sanctified places mentioned in the holy books as well as certain pious societies which, as he believed, had been graced with the responsibility of guarding, in this land, the gates of heaven.

It is not known what caused such a rich young man to join such a rigidly pious sect as the Bratslavers. Perhaps it was that he had committed some sin for which he wanted to repent or it may have been something else. But one sensed that his devotion to the sect was so intense that he would cheerfully have smashed his head against a stone wall for its sake.

It was said of him also that he had once joined a secret society known as The Ten Brothers. This was a society whose members took a powerful oath to come to each other's aid. So constraining was this oath that it was said that if one of them after death was condemned to hell, the others were required to share his punishment there, share and share alike. And this clause, like the others in the agreement, was signed by The Ten, not in ink, but by blood drawn from their hands and fingers.

There were more and yet more tales told about him. For instance that he had visited Rome.

Rome?

Yes, like all the Bratslavers, he shared with the Radziner sect the practice of weaving a single blue thread into the fringes of his ritual undergarment. It was a practice which in those days was not permitted because it was believed that the Khalzon, the worm that provided the blue dye that colored the wool used in making the curtains of the Ark—that that worm had disappeared with the destruction of the Temple. The Radziners, however, believed that the worm still existed and that they had found it. And this was a source of great contention between them and other sects.

And it was in order to make an accurate comparison of the ancient color with that of the contemporary blue that the Radziner had sent a delegation to Rome where, it was said, the original curtain of the Ark is kept to this day in the Vatican archives.

We do not know whether the delegation accomplished anything in Rome. It would seem not. But travel expenses alone cost a mint of money and Avremele undertook to pay most of the charges himself. And those sums, and others like them, were provided by his parents and his in-laws. And throughout everything, his parents, though impoverishing themselves in the process, continued to help him. As now, for example, even though he had left behind wife and children and business and was wandering from place to place, now, that he was a member of the Bratslaver sect and was a sort of supervisor who went from one small group of members to another—even now, his parents, who were by now reduced nearly to poverty, managed to muster love, devotion and loyalty enough so that they sent him money from the little that remained to them.

Nor were the sums they sent trivial. As one could tell from his clothing which was made of expensive cloth, as well as from his general health and vigor—characteristics he did not share with other members of his sect.

It was only after Avremele had removed his coat and stood in his black caftan in Luzi's hallway that Luzi recognized him with delight. It was as if he were seeing a youthful version of himself: a vigorous, lively man with the extravagant gestures that come from an excess of good humor.

Indeed, Avremele coming into Luzi's house brought not only the frosty freshness of the outdoors with him but his own personal vibrant freshness which now filled the room as with pleasing odors.

Avremele's bearing toward Luzi was at once candid and respectful and it was clear that Luzi treated him in the same way. He behaved toward him like an older, more experienced man, but unceremoniously, too, the way a father might treat his own child.

They plunged almost at once into a lively, frequently interrupted, conversation in which Avremele, the younger man, did most of the talking as he described in general what he had seen on his extensive pilgrimages, and in particular his visits to various small Bratslaver communities.

Luzi listened closely to him, and as always happened when he heard something cheering, he turned cheerful himself and his features, as if forgetting how grave they had lately been, allowed themselves to relax. And all the while that Avremele spoke, Luzi, looking up at the taller young man, kept his eye on Avremele's lips as if unwilling to lose a particle of the pleasure Avremele was giving him both with the manner and the matter of his speech.

Then it was time for prayers, and it was here that he showed himself a true member of the sect to which he and Luzi belonged and just how much of their wealth he possessed.

From the first blessing he uttered, his prayers were all leaping flames. As he prayed, he paced Luzi's room with such fervor, such animated gesticulation, that even Luzi, who was used to such or similar manifestations, seeing his wild frenzy could not keep his eyes from him.

Actually, Avremele's enthusiasm disturbed Luzi's prayers as he became engrossed in seeing the way Avremele found the room too small to accommodate his gestures, the way he seemed to want to press the walls apart so that in the grip of his passion he could get more air so that like a small fire touched by a breeze, he could burst into flame.

Awhile later, they sat down to eat. Luzi, the host, sat at the head of the table with Avremele, his guest, beside him. Sruli Gol sat at his usual place, facing Luzi, and noted the way Luzi looked at Avremele—with great affection but also with a certain degree of envy that had, in fact, begun to express itself in the very first moment that Avremele made his appearance in Luzi's house.

And yes. There was something to be envious of. After the passionate recitation of his prayers, he turned equally passionately to the meal so that it almost seemed that his mouth could not accommodate to the speed with which he swallowed his food—and not because he was a glutton or greedy, but because it was his nature to be impetuous and everything he did was done in haste: walking, talking, praying, eating. And all of this reminded Luzi of his own younger days and he watched Avremele as if he, Luzi, older and calmer now, were looking at a portrait of his younger self. He gazed at him as one might at someone deeply loved, of whom, though he was destined to be his inheritor, he was, as Sruli noticed, more than a little envious.

A few days later on an evening when only Luzi and Sruli were at home (Sruli was busied with something off in a corner), Luzi and Avremele had the kind of intimate conversation such as we have described earlier when Mikhl Bukyer unburdened himself to Luzi in the Living Synagogue.

Though it was not the appropriate time for it since it was not the month of Elul which was the month when the members of the sect generally revealed to each other their hidden needs and exchanged confessions, nevertheless something like one of those confessions took place then. And this time, the one who was meant to be the spiritual guide, the one hearing and judging, was not Luzi, the older man to whom Avremele his junior should have confided, but the other way around. Avremele was in charge and Luzi was the one who had the need to be heard.

Neither of them, before the event, had any idea that it would take place. Sruli, on the other hand, had guessed that it would from the very first moment when Avremele crossed the threshold of Luzi's house. And why was that? Because it had been clear to him that Luzi, lately, was not quite himself, and he had had some inkling that it woud happen from the way that Luzi had kept still on the occasion of the conversation we have described above. "A sign," Sruli said to himself, "not of firmness or self-assurance of the sort that allows one to dismiss objections with the wave of a hand." Nor was it that Luzi's regard for Sruli was so small that what he had to say did not deserve attention and could be calmly, even coldly, ignored. No. It was that Luzi was inwardly divided and was unwilling to reveal that to anyone. It might be that he would always be that way, or else that he was simply waiting for someone to come along to whom he could reveal himself as he could not to him—to Sruli. And, lately, seeing how warmly Luzi always received Avremele, and noting, too, the trace of jealousy Luzi felt for the younger man, Sruli was certain that Avremele was the one to whom Luzi would unburden himself in the way that certain pious folk take it as their duty to prostrate themselves before those whom they envy, arguing that if they mean to maintain themselves at a high spiritual plane, they must have the strength and the courage to endure such a confrontation.

And now the confrontation that Sruli expected was about to take place.

It was night. No one was at home. It is not important whether it was a coincidence that no one was there or that Sruli, as he was capable of doing, had arranged matters so that Luzi should be at home alone and undisturbed. What is important is that the two of them, Luzi and Avremele, were in Luzi's room seated at a small table illuminated by the friendly light of a lamp. The door leading to the vestibule was latched. Avremele was seated, Luzi was standing, and there was a look of surprise in Avremele's face even before Luzi had said a word.

The reason for it is clear. The very fact that Luzi on coming in had latched the door and hooked the chain was sufficient indication that something of a very serious nature was about to take place in their tête-à-tête. That this was true was even clearer when he heard Luzi's first words which implied that he, Luzi, meant to confide something to him, which is why Avremele, though he was usually restless and had difficulty sitting still, now sat quietly looking straight ahead as if he was about to hear something that would require the attentiveness of more than his ears—of his whole body.

To make the scene between Avremele and Luzi more striking, let us summarize a few details: it is a quiet winter evening in a godforsaken part of town where even in daylight the noises of the city hardly reached. At night it was even quieter. And quieter still on a winter's night such as this one. Outdoors the snapping cold had driven everyone inside the snow-covered houses in whose windows small (very small) lamps glowed.

The exhausted inhabitants of that part of town neither had nor were capable of having any other goal than to warm their limbs, which had been chilled all day, at the scanty fires that burned in their stoves. Anything more spiritual than that was far from their minds. And it was there, among those silent, badly lighted, snow-covered houses, that an exception was to be seen. One house with a brighter lamp glowing in it. A house that was so warmly and pleasantly heated that two people, isolated, removed from the concerns of daily life, could concern themselves not with their surroundings but with spiritual matters.

Luzi approached his subject tangentially, citing the passage, "Man sees what is before his eyes; God sees into the heart." Luzi went on: "Sometimes one sees a man who seems to have good luck as a permanent guest, and misfortune avoids his door. But his reality is far otherwise. The truth is that the merest touch of a finger will reveal that the vase of his happiness has a crack in it.

"Take me, for example," Luzi continued. "Many people who see me only superficially find much in me to envy; they suppose that my accounts with God are like those springs that flow not rapidly but with deep clarity, that I am one of those for whom heaven stretches out an arm to point me toward what I care for and for which I am destined. But the truth is far otherwise. Not only have I not had such advantages, but indeed it is as if I had a malevolent eye looking down at me which, seeing that my tree was more fruitful than others, continually sent thieves and vandals over my fences to steal and damage my crop."

Then Luzi, moving from the general to the particular, described in detail those matters which we have already touched on briefly: how he had freed himself while still a youth from the constraints of a religious asceticism that had almost destroyed him, and how his rebbe had saved him by showing him how he could serve God with joy.

It was in that period that he had married, he said. He was then young and vigorous, so broad-shouldered that he sometimes split the seams of his caftan. "And then all at once—I don't know why—whether it was because we had no children or for some other reason . . . I cooled toward my wife. And then since I was a popular man in my circles, that very popularity went to my head so that without at first being aware of it I found myself looking for an outlet for my natural vitality, not only in ways that were permitted, but in forbidden ways as well."

And here, Luzi, employing innuendo more than direct speech, spoke softly of sexual matters. He was then, he said, in the full vigor of his manhood when he began to notice that, at the very least contact with a woman, the soles of his feet turned hot, as if they were being licked by flames. Usually it happened at festivities, when everyone was relaxed and had been drinking. Then a slight touch or a passing glance was enough to excite his concealed and dangerous sensuality.

Once at a wedding in the home of a wealthy family there was a guest, one of those women who stands out on such occasions because of her clothes, but more particularly because of her liveliness.

He noticed her hovering near him; sometimes she approached him; sometimes she touched him inadvertently or served him something; but always, and when he least expected it, she was in his vicinity, making him sense her presence and her excitement.

Later that night, Luzi, who had been drinking, went to one of the more distant rooms in the house to cool off. It was a room in which a number of beds had been set aside to accommodate sleeping children. And suddenly there she was. Inflamed, exhaling the excitement of the wedding. He did not know how she came to be there, but there she was, talking familiarly with him.

She started to talk about her husband, and it was clear from what she said that she was not particularly fond of him, and that she was very, very attracted to Luzi.

"And here," he said, "though I don't know how it happened, her head was against my chest, and the reason she had absented herself from the wedding festivities was suddenly clear."

He was young and she was very near his own age. She kept her eyes on a level with his chest, and he sensed her closeness. In a word, the two of them in that room far from the festivities were within a hair-breadth of committing (God save us) the most terrible of terrible sins.

It is not clear whether someone walked into the room just then, or whether one of the children sleeping there stirred. In any case, though they had entered the room without being remarked by anyone, they left it feeling ashamed and unable to look each other in the eye.

He went to confide in his rebbe, Luzi said. He asked him whether he was being punished because he had not fulfilled the commandment, "Be fruitful and multiply." That he, Luzi, was a sterile tree without leaves or blossoms in whose branches no birds nested. And that was the reason, he thought, that he was assailed by impure thoughts. His rebbe listened compassionately and comforted him as he could, giving him advice such as to arrange the beds in his room so that they pointed from north to south, and to fumigate his bedding every Friday by burning the feathers of a black cock. Or to drink an infusion made with an herb called rue and so on.

But nothing helped. During the Days of Awe, Luzi went to visit his rebbe with whom he used to stay until Succoth and sometimes on into the winter until Hanukkah. And it was on the day before Rosh Ha-shanah when according to custom he was preparing for the New Year and was weeping over the year that had passed, his rebbe, studying him, made a suggestion in whose efficacy he may not have believed. In the spirit of a man offering a desperate remedy, he said, "Stay until Yom Kippur."

"But what does that mean?" Luzi wondered. "I always stay much later than that."

"No," the rebbe said musing sadly. "This time there are weightier matters to consider than usual."

Then it was the night of Kol Nidre, when as usual the congregation was overwhelmed by passionate prayer. And now it was time to offer the recitation of the Adon Olam prayer to the oldest or the most re-spected member of the congregation, to men without a blemish in their characters and who had lived admirable lives. And then, to everyone's surprise, the rebbe commanded that Luzi was to be honored with the recitation.

The congregation was stunned. He was so young, so inexperienced. A man in whose veins the blood still ran turbulently. But never mind. If the rebbe commanded . . . perhaps he had something special in mind.

Luzi came to the reading stand and, his voice trembling, recited the exalted prayer: "Lord of the Universe, You who ruled before any crea-ture was born . . ." He did not feel himself worthy to say these words but the freshly shaven rebbe in his prayer shawl and white ceremonial garment, and wearing his embroidered Spanish skullcap, gave him an encouraging look as if to say, "It's all right. Just do it . . ."

Later, the younger people in the congregation went home and only a few selected people stayed gathered around their rebbe. They would stay up late studying and reciting psalms, engrossed in this pious labor on the day before the Great Judgment.

Luzi, too, was there. The synagogue, according to custom, was as fully ablaze with candles and lamps as it had been during the service. It was late. The pious bustling of the pre-Yom Kippur day—the frequent visits to the ritual bath, the passionate Kol Nidre prayers, the meal eaten in preparation for the fast and the long hours spent in study—had exhausted everyone and they lay asleep, some on benches, others with their heads leaning against lecterns, still others lying on the floor which tonight was covered with fresh straw. Even the shammes, who did not usually sleep, was asleep now. Only the rebbe, in his sacramental white garb, but no longer wearing his prayer shawl, moved quietly among the benches. To what end? So that he might look into the faces of the sleepers and watch for signs of night pollution, which, God keep us, could happen. He could recognize the signs at once and when he saw them he woke the sleeper with a touch of his rigid finger.

Luzi, too, was there. And suddenly he was started awake by the touch of a hand. "Who is it?"

"Woe." Luzi saw the rebbe bending over him.

Luzi came awake, overwhelmed with chagrin that he whom the rebbe had so honored, so distinguished that day, had so soon—on that very same night—shown that he was unworthy; and that because he was still under the dominance of his seething blood, that something like this could happen to him. And in a holy place, on Yom Kippur . . . and under the very eyes of his rebbe.

For a long while afterward he could not look the rebbe in the eye. After most of the holidays were over, and he was almost the last of the disciples still left in the rebbe's court, he went to bid him farewell. He stood before him, his head bowed, too downcast to say anything. The rebbe looked regretfully at him as if he were saying, "Well, see for yourself . . ."

Finally he said to a weeping Luzi, "Seek to find your flaw."

"Of course, he was right," Luzi said to Avremele after a pause. "As you know, one sin brings on another. And when I searched within myself I soon found that in addition to that shameful event that had so lowered me in my own eyes as well as in those of my rebbe that I was unable to bring myself to ask him for what I most wanted . . . when I looked deeply I found that there was even worse within me. An inclination—may God forbid—an inclination to idolatry. My grandfather, the follower of Shabbatai Zevi, began to come frequently to me in my dreams and his visits did not, as they should have done, arouse revulsion in me.

"For instance: I seemed to see my grandfather as a beggar at a fair. And when I wanted to pass him by, he tried to catch the skirt of my garment and pull it, stammering something in his beggar's language: 'Do you see what's become of me. I sit on a heap of threshed straw, forced to beg, a stranger at a foreign fair.' And when I looked closely at him I saw that indeed he was a stranger. Dressed in Turkish clothing, with green breeches and a green jacket and a cylindrical red hat. And his speech, too, was strange: not quite Yiddish. And his tears were strange . . . not the tears of a Jew. And all this served to alienate me still more from him. I looked about warily to see whether we were being observed, which I very much did not want to happen.

" 'Yahoudi,' the old man said, his accent strange as he spoke the ancient words, 'I am a Jew, of the seed of Israel. I beg you, in my name and in your father's name, pray for me.' As he spoke, cold senile tears rolled down his beggar's face and I felt myself pitying him.

"That, then, was one of his appearances: as an old, decrepit beggar at a fair. At other times he appeared as a young man in the full flush of his errors, when he was still newly a member of his sect.

"It was in a large maritime and commercial center, very like Istanbul. I seemed to be in a large square before a palace where a huge crowd had gathered. And there in the midst of the crowd I saw my grandfather. The crowd, men and women, were dressed in their holiday best, their heads turned toward the palace from which their venerated leader whom they meant to honor was expected to come.

"And all at once there he was surrounded by his seven closest disciples, 'the seven branches of his menorah' as they called themselves. At that, the crowd gathered before the palace cried out in unison, 'Our Lord . . . our Light. Messiah, son of David. God-sent redeemer.' They prostrated themselves to the ground; they kissed the dust which, as it seemed to them, their leader had trodden or would tread one day.

"And all at once the crowd disappeared as well as he who had appeared before them from the palace, and I saw my grandfather, all alone, still lying on the ground. He knelt, kissed the earth, crawled the circumference of the palace, kissing its stones. As he crept from place to place he came at last to the place where the leader had stood, and there my grandfather knelt, compelled to lick what was for him the holy dust. When finally he rose from licking the dust he had the look of a man who has crawled out of a swamp.

"And every time I saw him in one of those foul and shameful situations, and without having heard him speak a word, I found myself holding a ewer in my hand which I showed my grandfather; he, seeing it, came closer to me and I poured water over his hands the way a Levite does for a kohen before he gives his blessing. The point being that before saying a word to him, before reproaching him in any way, I wanted to clean him up. And this suggests a certain compassion on my part, a certain willingness to excuse him whom to excuse is forbidden; and with whom all ties are to be cut without pity. Ah, woe."

Later, Luzi recounted all this to his rebbe who looked mournfully at him and said no more than, "You would do well to look behind you to see who it is with whom you've gone into partnership."

Luzi, shuddering, had looked around and wept, knowing full well what the rebbe meant.

"What have I done?" he pleaded. "I was lost and aimless as a youth, and now that thanks to you I've found the right path, I'm in danger of losing it again. Why do I deserve this?"

"Perhaps," replied the rebbe, "because he is most punished who is most loved."

"What must I do *not* to be so loved?" Luzi said without thinking. "I want neither the suffering nor its rewards."

"Ah," said the rebbe, outraged, "in that case you must do what Job's wife counseled Job to do. Curse God and die. Then you will avoid the suffering."

Luzi went away crushed, like a man with a miserable fate for whom no remedy can be found.

After a short pause, Luzi recounted another event that evidently still affected him. "At that time, in the little town where I lived, I met a man named Shmerl Bass. He was a Lithuanian. A great scholar who was moreover well schooled in secular matters. There was no one to equal him in all the town unless it was the nobleman to whom the town and a number of villages belonged. He was not only wealthy, but he had an avid thirst and a talent for learning which is why he sometimes invited a priest or some other cultivated man to his home where they could discuss scholarly matters. He became friendly with Shmerl Bass with the result that the Jewish community occasionally received favors from him. Whenever the community wanted something from the nobleman, Shmerl Bass, whom he respected, was the intermediary.

"Well and good. And yet Shmerl was not well liked in the town, though either in his home or out of it he behaved no differently from anyone else, whether in secular or religious matters. As for the poor, toward them he always showed a generous hand. But because he did not perform certain minor religious rites which in any case are not believed in by all Jews, he was regarded with suspicion and various hardened fanatics began to spread rumors of things he had done, though not of things anyone had seen. They were, rather, what the rumor mongers wanted people to believe. One such rumor, for example, was that he went bareheaded when he visited the nobleman. Nor was that all. He was said to have participated as an equal with non-Jews at the nobleman's meals at which nonkosher foods were served. And so on.

"Things had come to such a pass that on those holidays when people get drunk, various people had thrown stones through his window.

"He was, moreover, independent of his fellow townsmen because he had a profitable business relationship with the nobleman and yet the people in the community were dependent on Shmerl. No one who came to him for help was ever denied it. His generosity was such that sometimes he helped even one of those who kept a stone in readiness to throw through his window. And though Shmerl was well aware of this, he pretended to know nothing lest he shame the man in his time of need. Shmerl's behavior should have been instructive to the community, and yet it was not. It was one thing when in need to present oneself to him for personal or communal help, but it was quite another to pardon the violation of certain religious rules which they regarded as important.

"Things had reached such a pass that when Shmerl wanted to make a match for his son whom he dearly loved and who loved him in return . . . things had come to such a pass that no family in the town or in the district would be allied with his. Shmerl's ill fame had spread so widely that he had finally to go abroad to find a bride for his son."

It was after that that Shmerl came one day to discuss his situation with Luzi, to pour his heart out to him and to make clear that the things he had been charged with were only trivial departures from tradition and that whatever he had done had no bearing on religious law; or to the degree that it did touch upon it, it was no more significant, as he saw it, than brushing against cobwebs in the darkest corner of a room. As evidence, he cited the fact that various notable authorities shared his point of view. That these small matters could be interpreted in either of two ways. But in any event one did not deserve to be turned into an outcast because of something like, for example, the custom of sacrificing a fowl at Yom Kippur time, a custom which Rabbi Shlomo Kruger also opposed.

If the truth be told, he, Luzi, had taken a position in support of Shmerl and had thereby provoked considerable hostility from various people who attacked him as if he were a participant in Shmerl's apostasy. They cried, "What do you mean? Dear Lord in heaven, how could you have allowed someone like him, whose very breath is tainted by the plague, to cross your threshold?"

Then, seeing that Shmerl's daughter-in-law, whom he had brought from abroad, was not the sort of woman who could set herself against her father-in-law's practices and put him on the right path . . . seeing that, the anger of those fanatics blazed even higher and they cried that the community was in danger of being caught up in the conflagration Shmerl had kindled.

But then disaster struck. Soon after his marriage, Shmerl's son was taken ill and died. The Burial Society demanded a high fee to bury him, though they were less interested in the money than in a chance to humiliate Shmerl. They assumed that if he sensed he was being humiliated that he would resist paying their fee, augmenting thereby his humiliation. Because the money was not important for Shmerl. What mattered was his son, his dearly beloved son, the apple of his eye, his whole support in this world—and the unabashed cruelty the Burial Society was willing to show to the dead. They haggled for a day or more. It was summer, and Shmerl finally agreed. But it was the great anguish of that experience that hardened his heart so that when they reached the cemetery and the body was lowered into the grave and they turned to him, as the father, to recite the prayer for the dead, he refused. No doubt it was grief that made him do it. Seeing himself deprived of his only son, he was rendered mute, and as sometimes happens, he could not open his mouth to perform the rites required by religious law. Eventually, a member of the Burial Society had to recite the prayer.

Shmerl's despair reached such a pitch that when his daughter-in-law returned to her parents and his house was empty, he would pace from room to room. Later, he settled into one room in which he paced diagonally from one corner to another silently. He refused to do business of any kind. The end, when it came, was dreadful, may God keep us from the like. He was found hanging in his attic.

As for the fanatics, they were as unforgiving as before and said, "So, he killed himself. It was no more than he deserved: a hook in a timber. We're well rid of him." And as far as Luzi remembered, he was the only one who attended Shmerl's funeral.

When he was denounced for this to his rebbe (Luzi reported it to the rebbe himself, being unwilling to hide anything from him), the rebbe was very severe with him, saying, "I see. I see. There is the good Lord, and then there's Shmerl. You've made some choice."

To tell the truth, the rebbe's irritation did not, this time, touch Luzi, because it was the first time since Luzi had become his disciple that he had found himself disagreeing with his judgment.

And from that time on, this Shmerl, as if it were a form of punishment, had accompanied Luzi everywhere, as if he were actually growing out of his side.

Here Luzi cited a couple of examples. One Thursday evening, Luzi was at his books in the synagogue making his customary preparations for Friday. It was late at night. The other scholars were asleep and only Luzi sat before his reading stand, the candle in his hand illuminating his book. He, too, was dozing off, but he resisted falling asleep. There was darkness on every side. Suddenly he saw two people standing in the doorway. It was not possible to know who they were, but what was notable is that they moved from west to east and that, when they reached the Ark of the Torah, one of them kissed the curtain over it while the other did nothing.

Then both of them approached Luzi, and the one who had not kissed the curtain came up to him and like a guest who has come from abroad, he put his hand out in greeting, saying "Shalom."

"*Aleikhem,*" replied Luzi, then, after a moment when he was unable to see the man's face, he said, "Well, if it isn't Shmerl."

"Yes," replied the man behind whom the second of the visitors was still concealed.

"How are you? Where have you been?" Luzi asked.

"What does that mean, where? Why, *there*, of course." And Luzi understood it was the other world that was meant. Surprisingly enough, he was not frightened. It was as if he had been told no more than that Shmerl had come from some other town or from some other street in the same town.

"And who is that with you?" Luzi asked, gesturing toward the other man who continued to stand half concealed behind Shmerl.

"Shalom," said the other man and put out his hand.

"*Aleikhem,*" replied Luzi. Holding the stranger's hand and seeing him more closely, Luzi was frightened. Why? Because what he saw before him was himself, his own form, dressed just as he was, wearing the same coat and hat and everything else down to the last detail.

Turning to Shmerl for an explanation, Luzi asked—again, more by signs than by words, "What does this mean?"

"What you're seeing?" said Shmerl with a smile as if what was happening was perfectly ordinary. "Why are you surprised? In this world, you and I always lived in perfect amity. We never quarreled. Is there any reason why we shouldn't continue our friendship in the other world?"

"No," said Luzi, half unwillingly.

"In that case, until you show up *here*, I'll continue my friendship with your double with whom I'm on perfectly good terms, except for an occasional minor difference of opinion. As for instance, you'll have noticed that 'he' kisses the curtain of the Ark and I don't. There's no harm in it, eh? Or do you have strong feelings about it?"

"No," Luzi said even as he looked at his double with a mixture of fear and curiosity. The double who a moment ago had stood before him quite clearly was now beginning to fade away like a fog. "Well, how are things *there*," said Luzi, turning his attention away from the double.

"The way things are here," said Shmerl, smiling.

"Really." And here Luzi affected by Shmerl's light tone began to talk almost mockingly about matters that one did not ever take lightly. "And what about the hell with which your parents threatened you because of your impious ways and prideful acts for which, where you are, one is not handed a bed of roses."

"The flames of hell," Shmerl quipped, "have been put out. The place is empty. No one is burning, boiling or roasting."

"No one?" Luzi asked, and suddenly felt his hand being scalded by the wax from the candle he was holding to light the book on the lectern. And it was here that he started out of the sleep into which, like his fellow scholars, he had fallen. And he saw that his candle had tilted, that wax was dripping from it, and that its flame was so perilously close to the book that at any moment it might have started a fire.

He rubbed his eyes and of course the other two forms, Shmerl and Luzi's double, disappeared. And then—how astonishing—not only was he not oppressed by this visit from *that* place at such a time in the synagogue, a visit that could have been taken as a presage of evil—instead, it was as if there was not the slightest hint of depression or gloom in his mind. Instead, he resumed the study of his text with greater assiduity, as if he had had a most desirable encounter.

"And here is a second instance, the last of several, about which I'll say little because it would take us away from our subject."

This happened when his rebbe, his spiritual adviser was dying. He was sick, swollen, and then the swelling spread from his stomach to his heart and his face puffed up. It was the holiday season when Luzi and many other of the rebbe's adherents and intimates were gathered together from all over not, as they usually did, because it was the holiday season but because it was well known that his end was near.

The Days of Awe passed, then Succoth. And now it was Simhat Torah. In the jam-packed synagogue a voice cried out, "Make way," and the rebbe was brought in. He was in his bed and could no longer sit up or even move his legs.

It was on a day, too, when the congregation had had a good deal to drink because the rebbe himself had encouraged it: "Never mind anything but Simhat Torah. Let Jews rejoice."

He was breathing heavily when he was brought in. His beard was stiff, wiry. His eyes were half closed. Then, keeping in mind the rebbe's condition and that he ought not to be detained today, the congregation quickly recited the evening service and got ready to make the procession around the synagogue with the Torah scrolls.

And then, the Ark of the Torah was opened and the shammes, as he usually did, began to call out the names of those who were to be honored with Torahs to carry on the first circuit. Naturally, the first name that he called was the rebbe's. "Our great and learned master." And the first of the Torah scrolls taken from the Ark was offered to the rebbe, though no one supposed he would actually take it and carry it around the synagogue. In his condition, that was unthinkable. All they meant to do was for him to hold the scroll there, in bed, while members of the congregation came up to wish him well and to receive similar wishes from him in return.

But that isn't what happened. The minute the Torah was offered to him, he sat up and swung his feet out of the bed and reached his arms out for it. Several of the respected older people, fearful lest something go wrong, hurried over to urge him against taking it. To tell him that it was not right. That there was danger both to himself and to the Torah he would be holding in his trembling hands.

But he paid no attention to their warnings. "What am I, and who am I," he asked, "that on a day like this when Jews rejoice that I should spare my swollen old feet?"

There was no help for it. Nothing anyone said would dissuade him. And so the cantor stood at his right side and a synagogue officer at his left, each of the three carrying a Torah scroll. The cantor sang out, "O Lord, be Thou our help; O Lord let us be fortunate." And they started forward, carrying the scrolls round and round as is the custom.

The synagogue was packed to the rafters, with people jammed into doorways and standing on windowsills. They were packed so closely that the men had to hold on to each other's waistbands not to lose their footing. Everyone stood, openmouthed, at the man who walked between the cantor and the official. A man so sick that it seemed unlikely that he would be able to put one foot before the other.

And yet he walked. More than that, as the congregation watched with bated breath, it saw him suddenly begin to dance. The old and cherished habit of delight in the meaning of this day, Simhat Torah, the Festival of the Torah, had awakened in him as he made the circuit of the synagogue so that he forgot his condition and acquired the strength not only to move his limbs with ease but to inspire others to do the same. They watched as his lips formed the words, "Rejoice in the celebration of the Torah," and packed though the congregation was from wall to wall, from ceiling to floor, so densely that the men clung to each other's waistbands, still they found the bit of space they needed to imitate his movements. They moved, and danced.

The rebbe, seeing this, smiled and encouraged them. And weakened by illness though he was, he summoned up the strength to bless them, giving them the assurance thereby that they were not to worry about him. There would be no accident. The Torah was safe in his hands.

It was a striking scene. The congregation was at once silent and jubilant as it rejoiced and mourned, and both kinds of tears were shed by many.

But of course the rebbe paid almost at once, and dearly, and on the spot, for his dancing. When he had finished the circuit of the synagogue and was approaching his bed, the Torah was snatched from him just in time to keep it from falling and it was only with difficulty that he was gotten back into bed—utterly exhausted and more dead than alive.

Once again the cry was heard, "Way, make way." And he was carried home from the synagogue, hardly breathing.

And it was at that celebration in which Luzi had taken part, when there was hardly room to move, and he, too, obeying the rebbe's injunction, had had a great deal to drink, it was then that he suddenly noticed two people who stood out from the crowd. The same two he had seen on that night when he had been up late in the synagogue.

"If it isn't Shmerl," he said, recognizing the man who now stood quite near him. "How come you're here?"

"What do you mean, how come? Jews are rejoicing. I'm a Jew. I have a right to be here."

"Well, did you see how the rebbe's feet moved for the last time today? He wanted to dance with everyone because he'll not be doing that again. He's on his way. He's being taken from those who depended on him as their leader. You saw that?"

"Yes, I saw."

"Well?"

"Nothing?"

"What does that mean?"

"It means that I, Shmerl, am not one of those who is dependent on anyone. I stand on my own two feet, not like all of these people whose minds for the most part are weak and whose ideas are vague and childish. Particularly today when they are as drunk as he is." And here Shmerl smiled as he indicated the man he was with, the man whom Luzi, when he looked, recognized at once. Once again, it was his double. Wearing again his holiday clothes. His silk coat and velvet hat and holiday waistband.

As Luzi watched, he saw that the second man—himself—was crying and that he had trouble holding up his head, and that his eyes were clouded because he had been drinking and it was clear that if he had not been hemmed in by the crowd that he would have fallen to the floor.

"See," said Shmerl again, "see his tears. They are tears of weakness, as his reverence for and dependence on his rebbe are weaknesses. Because if this fellow were sober and could reason clearly, he would know that there is no reason to weep and that the best source of strength is within oneself." And here, Shmerl's words seemed to take on a special meaning.

It was then that other people, too, noticed that the double was so weak that he was in danger of falling. People took him by the arms and he was led through the crowd into the outer lobby and from there into the street so that he could have some air. Then he was taken home to the room he rented and he was put to bed so he could sleep himself sober until morning. And that, in fact, is what happened and what Luzi discovered when he woke in that bed the next day.

"I'll finish this very soon," said Luzi, his voice weakened by his long narrative. "Because all I've said to this point ought to make clear to you that I have not been slandering myself nor have I suspected things in myself that are not there. The truth is that there are worms of some sort gnawing at my vitals, worms invisible to others but perfectly clear to me—and to those who know about worms."

And here, Luzi turned to describe the various forms of the fear of God as they are described in pious books. "There is," he said, "the fear of punishment, the fear of a dreadful life in this world and the fires of hell in the next. And then there is the higher fear of the Lord of the Universe whom no mind can fathom and to whom no thought can attain. The first fear serves children and ordinary people. The second is a fear one must earn and on occasion I have had the happiness to think that I had earned it only to discover that I had actually plunged from its heights. And though I know that even by falling one can attain to a degree of enlightenment, because he who has not experienced the vertigo of falling can not savor what it is like to ascend and cannot perceive the great, expansive rounds of earth and sky which, too, can make one dizzy with extraordinary delight . . . though I know all this, still I find these ascents and descents painful, these wobblings from one end to another, from the good Lord to Shmerl as my rebbe put it. It is always painful to stand at the edge of the abyss where, as one knows, there are two dangers: first of falling and second, may God keep us from it, the temptation to jump in."

And here Luzi resumed his former manner of narration with a view of justifying what he had been saying. "This happened after I had lost my rebbe and when for a time I traveled from one court to another in search of a rebbe to whom to attach myself. I came, at that time, to N. to visit my brother Moshe Mashber who lives here. I was feeling renewed and alert. And it was then I got to know, and formed a relationship with, Sruli Gol whom, since you have been a guest here, you must have noticed. He's not an official nor a servant nor a poor man whom I support. In fact, and here I am confiding a secret to you, he's rich, though he shows no signs of having wealth because he does not want it to be known. He's a strange man; what his antecedents are is not quite clear and there's a touch of the licentious in his nature. But he pleases me because I see virtues in him that no one else sees or is willing to acknowledge. He has bound himself to me and I, for my part, have done the same to him and to the extent that I cannot even imagine how I could get on without him. It's almost as if we were related by family ties. He seems to be taking Shmerl's place whose task it was to open the way for my thoughts even before I was fully aware I was having them.

"For instance, this year when the Days of Awe arrived and I went to Uman to visit the rebbe's tomb, Sruli went with me, though it was utterly unexpected of him since he generally doesn't believe in pilgrimages of any sort.

"On the day before the New Year, when I came to the cavern where the rebbe is buried, the crowd was so great that a line had to be formed so that people could be admitted a few at a time.

"And when I finally got in and wanted to recite the necessary prayer, and to put several questions that were in my mind to the rebbe whose replies, I felt certain, would be the same as if he had made them when he was alive; it was then, I say, as I began that I heard someone beside me weeping loudly and bitterly and it was apparent if he had been standing next to a wall he would have dashed his head against it the way, as happens, someone will do who is determined to achieve some impossible goal, like bringing the dead back to life.

"His behavior distracted me. Others, who had finished, were starting to the door, while those who were outside, seeing them leave, started to stream in to take their places. And there I stood, unable to say a word. Unable to think a clear thought because the man weeping continued to disturb me.

"I was there long past the time allowed me. I ought to have ceded my place to the others who were waiting outside and who kept putting their heads in to see whether there was room for them. I began to hurry my prayers when—ah, me. I have no idea where the ideas came from but two questions occurred to me, each more wicked than the other.

"First, I asked, is it right to go to the dead for counsel as if they were alive? And second, if it is right, will I continue to have faith in Reb Nakhman of Bratslav whom I have chosen after much troublesome wandering?

"I was frightened and looked around the cave to see whether anyone had divined the wicked thoughts that had occurred to me. Or worse, whether anyone had actually heard me utter them? And just then I saw Sruli who had, evidently, come into the crowded cave with me and who now stood looking at me with—I swear it—the sort of smile on his face that a man has who has guessed what you are thinking.

"As we left the cave . . . I first, with Sruli following, Sruli came up to me and said, 'Right from the start, I knew that for all the good it would do me, the money spent on this trip was a waste. But if I am any judge, I would guess that you, too, felt that you were a stranger in there. Because otherwise that man's weeping would not have disturbed you. And you would not have looked as depressed and confused as you looked not only in there, but here, now, in the open air.'

"And it was true. Even outdoors my head was bowed with shame, and I could not bear the pleased look on Sruli's face, the look of a man, who having found a weak spot in your character, insists upon talking about it with you."

"So you see," Luzi said to Avremele as he, Luzi, came to the end of his narrative, "that my life has not always been an easy one. I have had my share of struggle, and continue to struggle to this day . . . so that I have to hide my tears. . . .

"It's good that you have come," Luzi said, exhausted from so much speech. "I want to hand over my responsibilities as head of the community. Sensing my own imperfections, I find it hard to preach perfection to others. I only agreed to take on the leadership of the sect after being entreated to it by Mikhl Bukyer, its former head of whom you've surely heard . . . and of what's become of him. I am myself too old—and, as the rebbe, Reb Nakhman said, 'Old is not good.' One has constantly to renew oneself.

"I have decided to do either of two things: to return to my town on the border and there live out my life, or else to take the whole world as my 'border,' that is, with the help of God, to undertake a perpetual spiritual pilgrimage and wander through the Diaspora."

With that, Luzi was done.

And now we must say a few words about how Avremele responded to what Luzi had said.

He listened as he usually did to the confession of a member of the sect who generally told not only what had happened to him but also what his thoughts were as it happened. Avremele was familiar with the way the members of the sect besmirched and denigrated themselves in order to make of one's humiliation a footstool on which to ascend once more. That's what they usually do, he thought and he was, therefore, not surprised at all.

But when Luzi concluded what he had been saying by announcing his decision to leave the leadership of the group because he no longer had a call, and that he meant to retire to some corner of the world where he might mourn his lack of courage . . . when Avremele heard that, he got to his feet abruptly and taking a step toward Luzi said, "Oh, but you've no right to do that," said Avremele, moving toward Luzi. "Not that I'm in any position to make you change your mind. But because you've chosen to confide in me, and because I'm the first person to hear what you have in mind . . . for those reasons alone I'm going to risk telling you as energetically as I can that what you want to do is wrong.

"You will pardon me. It may be that I am young, inexperienced and unimportant. But it is said that it is well for the great sometimes to listen to those who are smaller than themselves if it leads to good and to the welfare of the community.

"What I see here is that you are allowing your personal modesty, your self-denigration to approach a slander against God's work. You are mistaking the shadow of the thing for the thing itself—that is, you are treating what might have happened as if it had happened in deed.

"So much, then, for you, yourself. But now let us talk about the harm your decision to abandon it will bring to the community. You know very well that I can't take your place. The result will be that the community will be left a flock without a shepherd, a group of blind men with no one sighted to guide them."

Luzi, however, would not be persuaded. Dear as Avremele was to him because of the way he reminded him of himself in his youth, his reply was "No," accompanied by a wave of his hand that dismissed whatever further reasons Avremele was prepared to muster. "No. My mind is made up."

Had there been a bystander there then, he would have seen a rare sight. Avremele unbuttoned his vest, then his shirt and pulled out a little sack filled with something. It was a sack filled with earth from the

Land of Israel, earth that he had brought back with him from one of his voyages there. In addition to the earth, which he carried always with him, he had a document in which it was written that no matter what the community was to which his body might chance to be brought in case he died, he wanted this sack of earth to be buried with him and not the usual earth provided by burial societies.

Seeing that Luzi did not understand the import of what he had in his hand, Avremele came closer and said, "This is the most precious thing I have, and I will take it with me into the Next World. I beg you, in the name of all that's holy . . . and in the name of this soil which will serve me at the time of my death . . . I beg you to reconsider your decision."

"Ah, no," said Luzi turning away, unwilling to look at what Avremele insisted on showing him, and it was clear that he was exasperated that Avremele should have brought such a thing into play as a means of persuasion. "No," he said. "I won't."

Had there been a bystander also in the adjacent room, he would have seen that Sruli Gol was standing with his ear to the door. Nor had this just happened. He had been standing there throughout the long secluded conversation between Luzi and Avremele. All that while he had stood pressed close against the door as if unwilling to miss a syllable of what passed between them.

And that bystander would have observed that Sruli's face showed increasing signs of pleasure as the conversation on which he was eavesdropping progressed. And when Sruli heard Luzi's conclusion and the way Avremele sought to dissuade him from it and how Luzi held firm against his urging, then, had there been a bystander there, he would have seen the smile of contentment in his face. A contentment which he experienced at first silently but which, it was clear, he was almost ready to utter aloud in a burst of speech. It is not inconceivable either that if there were such a bystander he would have seen that Sruli did not merely content himself with that smile but that softly, so he could not be heard on the other side of the door, he began to dance. And what was even more likely was that at any moment soon he would knock at Luzi's door and being admitted he would, with no explanation offered, begin to dance before Luzi and Avremele. And that Sruli was particularly happy when he heard what Luzi's plans were. Plans that were dear to his, Sruli's heart, and which he had been urging on Luzi since the time that he had first joined him.

He had been urging it especially lately after what had happened to Mikhl when Luzi had been terribly disturbed by what the community had done to him, driving him to illness and taking his livelihood away. It was then that Sruli had added kindling to the flames by urging Luzi not to take the contentions of the community lightly because he, Luzi, was no match for them if it came to a quarrel. It was then, too, that Sruli noticed that in addition to Luzi's general temptation to withdraw from society, there was now the added fact that Luzi saw himself, in the matter of Mikhl, being drawn into a conflict that could have ugly consequences not only for himself, Luzi, but also for the sect that he represented, and that it would be better if he left the role of leader to someone else. Seeing this, Sruli had, at every opportunity, encouraged Luzi to loosen his ties in N., and to that end he had recently, as we have recounted, brought the sick Mikhl Bukyer to him to show him what his antagonists were capable of and to make the point that others, too, might share the same fate when one contended with people who would stop at nothing to rid themselves of their opponents. Just as Avremele secretly carried his little bag of Holy Land earth with him, so Sruli had been secretly cherishing the notion that he would be able to persuade Luzi to withdraw from his work with the sect and, accompanied by Sruli, that he would leave the city. If it meant settling in some other community, then well and good. But what would be better (and this idea was very dear to Sruli) would be for the two of them to undertake a perpetual pilgrimage, wandering from place to place, stopping occasionally to spend a day here, a day there.

And he came within an ace of walking in on them, but just then the door leading to the kitchen opened and Mikhl Bukyer's wife appeared. A tall thin woman whose shawl made her look even taller, thinner. She came in silently, but one sensed an inner tension in her as in someone who is repressing speech, who is waiting to be in a particular place and before particular people. She had made a long journey all the way from her home, compressing in her heart a great anguish about which she said nothing, having no one to whom she could speak her grief. But now the instant she found herself inside Luzi's house and in this lighted room and saw Sruli before her, she could contain herself no longer and uttered a despairing cry, "Help," she cried. "People, help. My Mikhl is dying."

And indeed it was true. On that very night Mikhl had had a second and final attack. A great smile spread over his face and now streams of saliva flowed from both corners of his mouth and he turned blue as a spleen. He began to tremble, and by the time his wife got him into his bed it was almost too late. He was no longer himself: the paralysis which until then had affected one side of his body was now total. He lay like a log.

His wife snatched up her shawl and started out to call the neighbors, but then she remembered that Mikhl's recent behavior had alienated them. Then she remembered Luzi as a member of the sect to which Mikhl had belonged. And that Luzi had come to N. the previous summer and had been a guest in their house for an entire Sabbath; and she remembered, too, that Sruli had come to the house when her children died and how on those occasions he had provided the family with firewood and money for burial expenses. And she knew, too, that Sruli had a close connection with Luzi and that if she came to the one she was likely also to find the other. Knowing all this, she started off. Turning first to her older daughter, Esther, she said, "Stay at your father's bedside. He mustn't be left alone. He's dying, God help us all. Oh, Lord, Lord, we will be left without our provider. Cast adrift . . ." Then she left.

The smaller children, afraid because their mother was gone, huddled around their older sister as if she were their mother, but Esther, too, was terrified. She stood, trembling, at the other end of the bed and watched Mikhl whose gasps for breath were becoming shorter and shorter. "Don't die, Father," she cried. "Who will look after us?"

Meanwhile, her mother, Mikhl's wife, hurried through the cold night with her shawl over her head. She did not weep, though from time to time she exhaled a muted sob. It was only when she was in Luzi's house and she saw Sruli with his back to her that she burst into tears and cried, "Help."

When Luzi, Avremele and Sruli entered Mikhl's house they found him at his last gasp. He was beyond answering any questions. They stood quietly at his bedside and waited for the inevitable, for his breathing, which had become very shallow, to stop. And then it did.

Sruli bent down and did what was needful: he put a feather to Mikhl's lips and observed that it did not move. Then he closed his eyes, undressed him and covered his face. After that he led Mikhl's wife and children, who were shrieking and tearing their hair at the sight of their husband and father lying rigid before them with his face covered . . . he led them out of the house.

Later, Sruli and Avremele (such work was beyond Luzi's strength) lifted Mikhl's body from the bed and set it on the floor. Then Sruli searched for a sheet with which to cover the body, but there was no such thing to be found in the house. Finally, they covered the body as best they could with a ragged bit of quilt that was not long enough for the task: whatever they did with it, either the head or the feet remained uncovered.

Then Sruli asked Mikhl's wife for all of her Sabbath candlesticks— in this case a few dried-out bits of clay. But there were no candles in the house, so that they had to make do with the cheap lamp under whose faint light Mikhl had been working on the book we have described earlier. The lamp was put at his head. Its effect was to make the room seem even darker.

And that is how the room remained for the rest of the night. Sruli would not permit Mikhl's family back into it. At first only he, Luzi and Avremele stayed with the body. But later he made a sign to Avremele to take Luzi home while he, Sruli, would stay to watch the corpse as custom required.

And that is what happened. Avremele and Luzi went from the bedroom into the next chamber and from there to the kitchen, from the kitchen to the vestibule and from there out into the street where they made their way home. Luzi was silent all the way and Avremele read in that silence a continuation of the discussion he had had with Luzi earlier that evening, a reiteration of the conclusion to which Luzi had come and which had been such a surprise to Avremele.

Seeing Mikhl's death, his squalid surroundings, his wife and orphans who were still in the house and who without guidance or support woud later be at the mercy of a cold world, having to beg for help from strangers—seeing all this and knowing that Mikhl's case from its beginnings to its end was probably the occasion that had pushed Luzi to his confrontation with not only the community but himself as well . . . seeing all this, even Avremele was rendered mute. Avremele, in whom there had never appeared the smallest crack through which the breeze of unbelief might blow.

He walked beside Luzi with his head bowed all the way from Mikhl's house to Luzi's. Even there they did not exchange a word. And when Avremele went to bed and thought over all that had happened—all that he had heard and seen—then, amazingly enough, he no longer blamed Luzi for his decision.

Meanwhile, Sruli who had stayed at Mikhl's house in the room where what little light there was not only did not reach the ceiling, it hardly even touched the corpse in whose presence Sruli, who was not pious, did not, as others would have done, read psalms or devote his time to study. For a while he sat stiffly in his chair, then when he got bored, he began to pace the very narrow limits of the little room, thinking thereby to make the long winter's night pass more quickly. Then when that, too, bored him, he sat back in the chair and, wearied by his long and depressing wait beside the body, drifted off to sleep.

He dreamed:

That Luzi was somehow the owner of a large garden fenced in on all sides and kept closed and locked. And Mikhl was the watchman there. But then he noticed that the garden fence was not a normal one. Rather it was like a prison wall. It was too tall to climb over and there was no crack or opening in it anywhere that would have permitted anyone to look in. Then Sruli saw that Luzi no longer had the look of an owner, but rather of a prisoner of this garden. Sruli was very distressed by this but there was no way to get in to help him. Then suddenly he saw that the wall was warping, groaning, and the deeply rooted pillars holding it up heaved and toppled, bringing the entire wall crashing down with them. And then when the wall had fallen, Mikhl, with a pleased smile on his face, appeared in the garden as if he alone, all by himself, had demolished the wall . . . or in any event as if he had been made very happy by its fall. And then the look of joy on his face was changed to the look of deep woe on the face of one who has labored with might and main to destroy something only to feel himself destroyed in the process. Sruli, grateful to him for his work of liberation, hurried over to thank him and to express his sympathy. But it was too late. There was a grimace now on Mikhl's face which, though it was not accompanied by groans or cries, was an indication nevertheless of an anguish so deeply repressed that it would shortly undo him.

And indeed that's what happened. Mikhl was undone. And there he lay silent on the gound. And then Sruli saw himself and Luzi standing over the body in reverential silence as one does when paying one's last respects to the dead. But they did not stay long. Hand in hand they strode past the body. For a while they looked back and then they found themselves all alone in a distant field on a lonely road at whose end the rounds of heaven and earth were revealed and opened to them.

"Ah!" said Sruli, startled out of his sleep and seeing what there was to see in Mikhl's chamber. Yes. Mikhl laid out upon the ground, the cheap little lamp beside his head shedding a weak light that was now almost invisible because the pale dawn was already peering into the room.

2.

The next morning Sruli had a great deal to do. First, he had to inform the Burial Society of Mikhl's death and to order a grave and grave clothes. Nor did he ask for them free, as for a pauper. Sruli paid for everything without bargaining, as if the deceased were well-to-do and had left him a fair-sized estate.

And then, having made all the preparations for the funeral, he went off to that non-Jewish part of town in which Yossele Plague lived. How did he know where he lived? What a question to ask about Sruli. Perhaps he had inquired earlier where he lived, meaning to visit him . . . who knows what for? Or out of sheer curiosity. Or because he had a serious interest in him. With Sruli, anything was possible. In any case, Sruli found Yossele that morning and informed him of Mikhl's death. "You know who I mean?"

"So. He died. How did it happen?"

"As it does with everyone. And the funeral, to which you are invited, will be . . ." And here he gave Yossele the details.

That done, Sruli hurriedly got in touch with various members of Luzi's sect and asked them in Luzi's name to reach as many people as they could and invite them to the funeral.

Finally, and as a result of Sruli's pell-mell activity, all that was needful was properly prepared. There were candles burning beside the body until it was purified, and after the purification, there were samovars boiling. In the courtyard before Mikhl's house a considerable crowd of people was gathered—a considerable surprise to Mikhl's neighbors who supposed, after what he had done (vis-à-vis Reb Dudi), that no one would come to his funeral.

There were two sorts of people who followed the body to the cemetery: those who had been Mikhl's friends earlier—people like Avreml the Three Yard Tailor, Menakhem the dyer, Sholem the porter, and other members of the Bratslaver sect, who walked together, shabbily dressed, their shoulders bowed, their faces haggard and blue with cold. The other group were Yossele's followers who looked altogether better nourished and better dressed.

Yes, it was a strange enough sight. Here and there, one of Luzi's people found himself paired with one of Yossele's men, holding the handles of the bier on which the body was being carried.

There was also another sight to see: Sruli tenderly leading a boy of five or six by the hand as if the child were his own. The child, in addition to being raggedly dressed, also limped. This was the last of Mikhl's boys, his only male survivor.

Arrived at the cemetery, the body was set down and as custom required, people walked around it seven times. But when they raised the body, meaning to carry it through the second gate of the cemetery to the grave sites where Mikhl's grave, ordered and paid for, should have been ready by now, there was suddenly a third remarkable event— impossible to believe at a funeral like Mikhl's. First Sruli saw it, then others who were familiar with the affairs of the town.

Suddenly, Hirshl Liever, the caretaker of the cemetery, appeared. A rare event because Hirshl showed up only at the funerals of the very rich. Beside Hirshl stood Yone the tavern keeper who had a finger in everything that went on in town. Yone, whom the community sent for when a task no respectable person would perform needed to be done.

"What are they doing here?" Sruli asked the minute he saw them. He understood at once that something was amiss.

And indeed what that was was soon clear. Because as the pallbearers raised the body, meaning to carry it through the gate and along the path that led to the grave site, Hirshl the caretaker cried out, "No, not there. Over there." He pointed to a place along the wall, opposite the path where there were dirty footsteps still to be seen in the snow. The place to which he pointed was rarely used for a burial—except for an occasional nameless abandoned child, or a woman of ill repute or a thief well known to the town.

"What?" said Sruli, dropping the boy's hand and going up to the caretaker. "Why there?"

"It's so ordered by the community," said Yone the tavern keeper, coldly, calmly as he stepped forward, his hands crossed over his belly, and made his way to the pallbearers intending to bar their way so they would have to take the direction indicated by Hirshl Liever.

"Oh, no," said Sruli, turning to the pallbearers and barring their way in the other direction. "You won't take him there."

"It's so ordered," said Yone coldly to the pallbearers who, as employees of the municipality and therefore frequently dependent on Yone, were inclined to obey him. They knew only too well that when he set his mind on something, he achieved what he wanted.

"No, it is not," said Sruli sharply, barring their way.

It was then that Yossele Plague, who had not at first understood what was happening but who now saw that an insult was intended to Mikhl's body, stepped forward.

He was better dressed than anyone there because he was a well-paid and very important employee of a major highly regarded foreign business concern in the town. No doubt that emboldened him to face Hirshl and Yone. But, as we will soon see, he was anything but a pushover. Well then, he emerged from the crowd and approached Yone the tavern keeper and looked him up and down contemptuously. Yone, his assurance shaken, especially when Yossele moved toward him, took a step back.

"So! It's you, is it? Reb Yone, the tavern keeper, if I'm not mistaken. Yes. Well then, pay attention. Do yourself a favor and take my advice. Don't start anything . . . not with me, not with any of the people here who've come to a funeral. Just go your way and let us bury the dead in the manner to which he is entitled. If you don't, let me warn you, things will go badly for you." Here, Yossele bent down and spoke more softly as if confiding a secret to him: "You're well known, you know. You sell bootleg liquor, you hide stolen goods. And," Yossele added, "on top of all that, you can't speak the language of the Gentiles, so you're scared of the officials. Do you understand me, Reb Yone? If you like, tomorrow, the official who would be most interested in your case will be informed of your various activities in this world (they will be held against you no doubt in the next world as well). Have you understood me, Reb Yone?"

Yossele's words so overwhelmed Yone that he stood speechless. Then he slunk away like a whipped dog with his tail between his legs.

Sruli and Yossele undertook to direct the pallbearers, who now set the body down before the mortuary (custom forbade them to carry it back the way they had come) while Sruli and Yossele arranged with Hirshl the caretaker to have a grave dug at a site that would not dishonor the body.

And that is what was done, but it took a long while before the grave was ready. Because it always takes a long while to dig a grave, especially in winter when the ground is hard. In the interval, Yone the tavern keeper, after his fiasco, slipped into Hirshl the caretaker's hut, and from there made his way back to town.

The mourners meanwhile huddled together against the cold in the mausoleum where they gathered into separate clusters: Luzi's followers and Yossele's followers. When a while later Yossele caught a glimpse of Luzi among his disciples, he found himself being drawn to him. He saw Luzi dressed in the rabbinical style, wearing his gleaming black furred hat and holding his unbuttoned winter coat closed in his hands, his face pale and refined . . . saw him in the midst of a group of people who pressed around him, eager to swallow his least word. And seeing him thus, Yossele went toward him.

Luzi's followers, seeing him, made room for him, and indeed moved away from Luzi assuming, with some pride, that Yossele was coming to talk to Luzi because Luzi had impressed him. They edged away from the well-dressed Yossele as from someone not in their circle. Some of them, indeed, were afraid to stand near a man with such a bad reputation. Others, the most deeply pious, felt a certain revulsion at being inside the same four walls with him.

Luzi, then, was left almost entirely alone with him and Yossele opened the conversation at once by asking Luzi about Mikhl on whose account they had all come. "Perhaps you know the details about his sudden death. It was not so long ago that he seemed to be perfectly all right." Having said so much, Yossele was emboldened to say, "You must pardon me if I ask a second, more personal question. How is it, given the sharp break between Mikhl and your sect, that you and your people haven't cast him off, as other pious groups have done?" And here, Yossele gave Luzi a shrewd look of inquiry, seeking verification of his suspicion that it was Luzi himself who was responsible for such strange behavior which certainly other pious groups would have condemned.

Luzi's answer to Yossele's first question was that he, Luzi, knew no more about what had happened to Mikhl than Yossele did. That as far as he, Luzi, could tell, the chief cause of Mikhl's death was the treatment he had received from the community which had cast him off and deprived him of his livelihood. It had destroyed him physically and spiritually. As for Yossele's second question, Luzi made almost no effort to answer it. He waved the matter aside, as if leaving it to Yossele to think about. Given the place in which this conversation was taking place it is remarkable that Luzi nevertheless managed to put a slight smile on his face as he talked, which only made Yossele conclude that the suspicions he had had about Luzi were well founded.

He was confirmed in that feeling, too, by the way that Luzi talked about Mikhl. Without resentment. Rather, the way one would talk of someone with whom he had been on an equal footing for years and with whom he had an affectionate relationship despite occasional small differences of opinion which others, but certainly not he, were inclined to make a fuss over.

Yossele was delighted by Luzi's modest demeanor. He listened to him closely as he talked, he scrutinized his clothes and his features and forbore to interrupt him with either word or gesture.

Finally, the gravediggers announced that the grave was ready. By then it was evening. As the body was carried toward the grave, Sruli once again led Mikhl's son by the hand. The boy was cold because of the long wait, and oppressed by the many strangers among whom he had been so long as well as the strangeness of his father who since yesterday had lain covered up, and to whom people with mournful faces did all sorts of strange things which he permitted. When the boy neared the grave and saw the mounds of earth heaped up on both sides, he burst into tears and turned toward Sruli as toward a parent. And Sruli promptly played the part and took the boy up into his arms.

The crowd quieted down. The gravediggers busied themselves for a few moments longer in the grave, then they were done. Then people seized the two edges of the sheet in which the corpse was wrapped and the body was lowered into the grave. Then all at once the sob and cry of an adult was heard. It was none other than Avremele Lubliner who, of course, was among Luzi's followers at the funeral and who now burst into tears. This sometimes happens to particularly vigorous men who are suddenly overwhelmed by a death. Or it may be that Avremele was still reacting to his long conversation with Luzi yesterday when he had sensed the coming of a calamity over which he, Avremele, had not yet had time to weep because the events involving Mikhl had interrupted his conversation with Luzi.

And now, again, Mikhl's son burst into such violent tears that when it came time for him to recite the mourner's prayer and one of Luzi's adherents urged the boy, saying, "Go on, now. Begin the prayer, *Yisgadal*" Sruli turned angrily on the man and said, "What's the matter with you? Don't you see that he can't? You recite the prayer."

It was time then to fill the grave. Luzi threw the first clod in and was followed in turn by other members of his sect. Nor did Yossele and his adherents abstain from the task.

It was already well into the evening when the mourners made their way back to town. Again, Sruli held Mikhl's son by the hand, and when Sruli noticed that the boy was showing signs of fatigue he took him up in his arms. Luzi and Avremele went home to Luzi's house and the other mourners scattered to their various homes.

And so it ended. And so Mikhl Bukyer's name was stricken from the roll of the living.

Late, late that night after Mikhl Bukyer's funeral, the light of a lamp was to be seen shining through a crack in the blinds of Yossele Plague's house in a non-Jewish quarter in a distant part of the city. Yossele was at his desk writing an article for the journal to which he was a contributor, *Hakol*, in those days a well-known Hebrew journal published abroad, in Königsberg, one supposes.

He wrote in the highly florid style then current among Enlightenment writers, with citations from the Bible in which, as in an arsenal, such writers found powerful weapons: moving rebukes and outcries against the community leaders of the previous generation with whom the Enlightenment contended the way the Prophet Elijah and the other prophets of their day contended with the false prophets and bad kings who oppressed the people.

"Ah, woe unto the obscurantists, the stubborn quenchers of light who having gone astray now lead others to do the same. Woe unto them. God's flock is scattered on the mountains and there is none to gather them in. Forgetful shepherds lie sleeping while famished desert wolves, biding their time, stalk the flock . . ." and so on and so on, wrote Yossele, still outraged by what he had seen today at Mikhl's funeral and by what he remembered of the poverty-stricken household from which the body had been carried. And how Mikhl's wife and children had looked, and how, on the other hand, the hired agents of the community such as the inspector Hirshl and Yone the tavern keeper had, on orders from above, endeavored to bury Mikhl shamefully under a fence, in a sort of donkey's grave, because he had had the courage to look beyond the limits that God, from time immemorial, had set up to keep people from crossing over toward what was desirable and good for them.

"Woe, woe . . ." Yossele remembered Mikhl's son, the boy with the splinter in his foot, who had limped along after the funeral and whom later Sruli took by the hand. He remembered how at the graveside the child had wept bidding farewell to his father who had left him without prospects and abandoned him and his mother and the other children. "Why? Why?

"And woe to those who keep the people poor and ignorant and who impede the amelioration of their pain and who drive to despair not only those who need help but those who endeavor to give it to them, those in whom God's spirit breathes and in whose hearts there is grief when they see that their labor is in vain, and that their goodwill is wasted because like voices crying in the wilderness, they are unheard."

Sitting in his distant room in a non-Jewish quarter of the town, by the light of his lamp, Yossele felt himself to be like the other decriers of his generation scattered about the country, who were endeavoring to find a common language with those whose cause they had shouldered like a heavy load, and who had for various reasons been received not as they deserved, with celebration, but as outcasts, as evil enemies to be greeted with hatred and flung stones.

As always when Yossele began to write, he felt awkward, unnecessary to the task, superfluous, but as he warmed to his work he began to see himself as a warrior in combat on a battlefield. He, along with a few comrades, was fighting against many and was *therefore* filled with the hope that always surges in those whom the people have chosen as the front-runners of a new generation sent to confront the old and worn-out one that has preceded them and which has been in power too long and which sooner or later must cede its place to those whose coming triumph is predestined.

Yossele took comfort when he remembered the small group of resolute and faithful who had crossed over entirely to his side, as well as those who for the time being still kept their distance, though occasionally they made an effort to come nearer to him or put a tentative foot into his domain and who, it was certain, would one day cross over entirely, bringing with them all the secret weapons of the other side.

Someone like Mikhl, for example, who had died today and who must have found it difficult, given his time of life, to sunder his ties with his sect. At his age it was hard to tear up one's roots and yet the fact that he had done so might well serve as a sign that all was not well with the other side if even a man like Mikhl, in his search for new spiritual possibilities, could find the strength to come to someone like himself, to Yossele.

Encouraged by these thoughts, Yossele, like many of his like-minded contemporaries, finished his article with the prideful prediction that however long the night might be, its reign was over because the light of a distant dawn was already beginning to show through the cracks as it sought for a way to rise.

"There," said Yossele, pleased with himself as he finished, happy now to have been entrusted with his mission which, despite all the obstacles put in its way, was moving forward like a column of light which at its beginning had seemed to shed no more of a glow than the smallest of lamps in the hands of an unhappy porter but which now, because there had been so many who had cherished it and shielded it with their own bodies, and sacrificed everything for its sake, was able to blaze up to serve as a guide to all who deserved to ascend to the heights so long desired.

Yossele rubbed his hands together for pleasure. He was especially pleased when he remembered Luzi whom he saw in his mind's eye. Luzi, with whom he had spoken yesterday near the grave as they waited for Mikhl to be buried. He remembered Luzi's black fur hat and his coat of rabbinical cut, the two edges of which he held together with one hand and how Luzi had stood there seeming to be at once a bit distant and yet at the same time giving the impression that he would be easy to talk to and that the two of them could find things on which to agree.

For a while longer he paced his room and then he went to bed, but even there the image of Luzi lingered in his mind and made him smile.

Yes, we say as we move on, Yossele retained the memory of Luzi for the next several days. And then he inquired where Luzi lived, and when he learned the address, can you believe what he did? He started off all by himself to Luzi's house.

Strange! Because what business could someone like Yossele have with someone like Luzi? Especially strange if one considers the period and the circumstances in which Yossele's activities were taking place and which would make it seem that no rapprochement of any sort was possible between two such differing sides.

Yes, it was strange, but it can be explained.

How? Because Yossele did not see it as his mission just to preach to the young people and students who from time to time came to him for help in escaping from the "four *ells* of the Talmud" as they are called. His goal was to reach the masses as well. However, long and bitter experience had taught him that only those who had time to look upward could search the clouds for "Heaven's daughter" as the Enlightenment was called. And that was not possible for the masses exhausted as they were by their toil. They needed to be approached with something substantial, bread before dancing, before they could appreciate its nuances. They had neither the time, the patience nor the understanding necessary for such sensitivity.

It was clear to Yossele that he with his small group of followers constituted no more than a small island in a great sea of need and ignorance, and that it would be mean-spirited and narrow to boast of one's own greatness or to be content with purely personal achievements.

And this is why he sought some ample gate to the masses through which he could pass, believing that if he could get them to approve and accept what was immediately clear and accessible to them, they would then become alert to the reasons for their oppression.

And so he endeavored to reach them with something more than empty, well-intentioned promises which are hard to believe. He wanted rather to propose practical, well-thought-out plans and ideas that would ease their intolerable burdens.

Here is plan one: to found a savings and loan bank for mutual assistance. That is, as he explained, a bank in which people would deposit what they had saved in prosperous times so that long- or short-term loans, with or without interest, could be made available to those who were in need.

Plan two: to found cooperatives, as we would nowadays call them, that would buy up the goods produced by a group of artisans, bypassing thereby the middlemen who always took a considerable cut of the price of an article simply for being the mediators between producers and consumers. What he told the workers was, "You be the middlemen; organize yourselves so that all the profit comes to you and does not end in the hands of the wholesalers who neither sow nor reap but who live off the labor of others."

And there were other plans as well.

In a word, Yossele had often tried to bring together a crowd of various sorts of workers to explain, with many examples, how right *he* was and how backward *they* were if they did not understand that his proposals were intended only for their advantage and profit.

The audience at first had listened attentively to him and nodded their heads in agreement. "Of course, what a good idea that is, and how profitable it would be for us." But later when Yossele tried to move beyond words to deeds, to bring some of his plans to immediate fruition, they turned cold and shied away. Why? Because each of them thought he was about to be tricked and they became suspicious first of each other then of Yossele, and a Babel-like confusion of tongues arose in which no one listened to anyone else as each of them imagined that the other had plans to earn more than himself. Then there were quarrels and they parted with nothing—the way they had come.

"Don't you see," said one of them who passed for Yossele's friend and well-wisher and who hated to see him losing his labors and who therefore drew him aside and spoke confidentially and like a faithful counselor to him, "don't you see that there's nothing to be done with our comrades? That they're blockheads. And no matter how you hack away at them they'll stay blockheads to the end."

Yes, Yossele's schemes often came to naught. He thought it was his fault because he couldn't sway his hearers with the right words, and so he labored long and hard to compose a pamphlet in which he would explain in plain speech what he meant.

He wrote the pamphlet and took it to the local printer, Reb Sheftl Katz, who always wore a silk skullcap in his printshop, partly as a sign of self-respect, and partly as an indication of the character of his business which provided his genteel customers with such important works as the Talmud, the Mishnah, the Eyn-Yakov and the Bible with thirty-two commentaries finely printed on the best "royal paper," with letters that still smelled of printshop ink and which had festive title pages with pictures of Moses and Aaron on both sides, with rays of light like horns coming from Moses' head and Aaron wearing a breastplate that looked like a Catholic priest's pectoral cross complete with the chains from which a censer hung.

In addition to his skullcap, Sheftl Katz also wore a pair of spectacles at the tip of his nose as he moved among his employees, supervising a printer here, correcting a proofreader there, hurrying a workman on or passing out advice or warnings: "See to it that the column is straight . . . Go over that proof and get it right. . . ." He wore those glasses, too, when he dealt with his customers, squinting through their lenses at them like a rooster, sometimes good-humoredly, sometimes grumpily, depending on his mood or on what he felt the customer deserved.

Sheftl knew all about Yossele and his reputation in the community even before he came to him and asked him to print his pamphlet. He gave Yossele a sidelong glance the way one might look at a man with whom it might be better not to be involved. And when, for form's sake, he did take up the manuscript, he turned it in his hands indifferently from one side to the other as if he wanted to avoid soiling his fingers with it. Then he returned it saying, "No. It's not for me."

"Why not, Reb Sheftl? This is your line of work. You do have a printshop, don't you?"

"Yes. But not for that sort of writing."

"What sort do you mean?"

"Gibberish and poppycock and such other trifles. Who knows what you've written there?"

"You can read it and see that, God forbid, there's nothing improper in it."

"No. I don't want it. I want nothing to do with it. I don't want it." And Yossele's work was not only refused, but Sheftl favored him with one of his squinting looks of rejection.

So that, too, did not work out. Then Yossele thought to have announcements and proclamations put up on synagogue walls and other public places, but he knew that just as the printer had turned down his pamphlet out of fear that among his printshop customers he would lose his reputation for respectability, so, too, the long arm of the community would reach the synagogue officers with whom Yossele would have to deal with a signal to tear down any of Yossele's announcements the moment they appeared on the walls.

Yossele finally addressed himself to the less-bigoted religious groups, believing that they might be willing to hear what he had to say once he had persuaded them that, God forbid, he intended no harm to religion but that he meant only to relieve the distress of the many poor who were now a charge on the community which, with the best will in the world, could not help them. But that, too, did not work. There were those who right from the beginning would not let him cross their thresholds, as if he was someone it was better to avoid. And others who received him and heard him out, and who even seemed to agree with him, saying, "Yes. You have a point. It's worth discussing." They, too, after being frightened by their more fanatic colleagues ("Who knows what horrible thievish business he has in mind?"), later regretted talking with him.

Now at last it seemed to Yossele that he had come upon someone who would sympathize with the schemes he had been nurturing for so long, and so as he walked toward Luzi's house he saw him as his last chance of salvation before all his fine schemes and his social mission were shipwrecked once and for all.

Luzi was at home alone when Yossele came in. At first, seeing Yossele, he looked a bit confused, thinking that he had mistaken his way and had come in by accident. When, however, it was clear that, no, Yossele intended to see him, he invited him in courteously and offered him a seat at the table.

Yossele accepted the invitation with pleasure, and once the initial exchange of greetings was over he began at once to explain why he had come.

He said, "I'm here on a matter of the general welfare for which I would very much like to have your help."

"And that is?"

"For a long while now, I've had the idea of providing a firmer basis of support for those of the poor who are now a charge upon the community, not because they have no trade or are lazy, like the beggars of the town for whom alms are their livelihood. No, I have in mind those who because of accident or illness or for other reasons over which they have no control have lost their jobs and have been, as it were, unhorsed and, having fallen, have been unable to recover their former prosperity."

"And what is your plan?" asked Luzi.

'It's like this," Yossele replied, and he developed in detail the various plans which were, literally, so near to his heart. That is to say, that at this point in the conversation he took a notebook out of his breast pocket from which he read the notations and statistics meant to make clear to any reasonable person that he, Yossele, was not some vague vaporizer building castles in the air, but that all of his notions were well-founded and consistent with reality and common sense.

At this point Yossele permitted himself a witticism, saying that the phrase in the Bible, "The poor shall not vanish from the earth," was neither a commandment nor imposed any obligation, nor was it the expression of a wish that the poor should be with us always. No, the Torah was simply indicating a misfortune and it would have been better for the Torah if that passage had been missing if it meant that poverty, too, would be gone from the earth."

"Yes," agreed Luzi, smiling.

"And so I've come to you as a man who has influence and followers, who is listened to and whose word is respected. I've tried several times to do something on my own, but for one reason or another I don't get listened to, whether because of fear or that I inspire a lack of confidence, I don't know. Whatever the reason, people turn away from me and I'm left with nothing."

"No," said Luzi, rejecting Yossele's proposal that he join him in his projects. "I can't do that. The idea of it pleases me. I'm by no means opposed to you. As far as I can see there is nothing wicked in it (God forbid). But as regards the help you want, I'm afraid I have to say no. It's not something I'm able to do. I don't have the call. And even if I wanted to do it, I've no idea how to go about it. No."

Yossele made no effort to persuade him. Seeing Luzi sitting before him, seeing his refinement of manner and deducing the spiritual nature of the thoughts which filled his mind, Yossele was as considerate of him as if he were an object one used only on holidays. He did not, then, insist, and made no effort to make Luzi do what he had described as being unnatural to him.

Having received a refusal, Yossele regarded the visit as over. If he did not immediately take his leave of Luzi, it was not because he had any hopes of achieving anything further, but simply because he wanted to extend his visit a bit longer. To chat with Luzi, who made him feel as if he was in the presence of a . . . yes . . . yes . . . of a beloved father who elicited a great deal of respect as well as love.

Yes, he wanted to attenuate his visit by any means whatever. He turned the conversation to another subject which had no bearing at all on the reason for which he had come, but just then Sruli Gol appeared in the doorway.

When Sruli saw Yossele and Luzi seated side by side and so engrossed in their conversation that they did not notice him, he smiled just as he had smiled, as we will recall, when he had overheard the discussion between Avremele Lubliner and Luzi in Luzi's room when Luzi had reached the point at which he said that he meant to change his way of life, to give up the leadership of the sect and that it was very likely that he would leave town.

Yes, now, too, something made Sruli happy seeing something that evidently he had long wished to see. He stood quietly for a moment or two—perhaps longer—and then feeling that he could not continue to stand there without seeming to be eavesdropping once he was noticed, he started into the room toward Luzi and Yossele, and in a loud voice, as if he were speaking to an entire congregation, he said, "Mazel tov."

"Eh? What?" Both of the men at the table turned and one of them, Yossele, looked his surprise while the other, Luzi, expressed his: "What's happened? Why a mazel tov all of a sudden?"

"Nothing. Never mind," said Sruli, as if withdrawing the word, as if it was a mistake or as if it was some foolish whimsy he had spoken aloud. "There's pie in the sky. The cat has had kittens."

"Are you crazy?"

"No. It's just something that slipped out."

"Ah," said Luzi irritably, looking at Sruli as if he might have to apologize for him before a stranger to keep him from being offended. As if Sruli were a jester or a wag whose words were not to be taken seriously.

Yossele did not understand the scene. He did not in general understand why these two had such a close relationship, though he had some notions of his own about it. What surprised him was that a man like Sruli could feel himself entitled to make jokes and foolish remarks before Luzi as if he was a member of his family. Naturally enough, Yossele, not being an intimate of Luzi's, did not interfere in the scene. In any case, Sruli's arrival had effectively interrupted his conversation with Luzi and Yossele abandoned any hope that it might be renewed.

He waited for a decent interval, however, unwilling to let Sruli see that he was disturbed. But as soon as he could, he rose and announced that he had to take his leave. And as he left, he asked Luzi's permission to come again sometime, giving as his reason that Luzi might be interested in hearing more about the matter in which Yossele had hoped to involve him.

Yossele left and Sruli came even closer to Luzi. His face, which a moment ago had glowed with giddy delight, was now grave as he looked silently at him. Then he said, "Do you know who that was who paid you a visit? Do you know what his reputation is in the community?"

"I do," replied Luzi.

"Well, are you aware that the fact that the two of you were in a single room without witnesses can be interpreted by certain sniffers and peerers as an indication that you and he share the same ideas? And are you aware that these same sniffers and peerers will put the sorts of words into your mouth that will delight your enemies, and that you'll never be able to wash the stain of this meeting away because they will say that they saw and heard everything, that they were there behind the door and peering through your window?"

"Well, what of it? There's no way to escape from tale bearers and slanderers so why think about them? Let them say what they like," said Luzi, turning away, evidently unwilling to hear any more and leaving Sruli with unspoken words still in his mouth.

This, too, pleased Sruli as much as he had been pleased earlier when standing on the threshold, he had come upon Luzi and Yossele chatting comfortably away. It was clear to Sruli that Luzi no longer cared what might be said about him in the community because for a variety of reasons his ties to it were loosening . . . loosening, so Sruli believed, because of his, Sruli's efforts.

Then Sruli came even closer, and to intensify his pleasure and to persuade himself again that what he wished to be true was true, he undertook to startle Luzi out of his wide-ranging musings by giving him a final warning. "Just the same, I have to tell you. Don't take the matter lightly. There's a heavy debit side in your account with the community. Things can get much worse."

"All right, then. Let them," said Luzi, startled out of his reverie. He waved Sruli's warning away with a hand. The gesture seemed to say, "I've heard that before. I know. Leave it alone."

VI

Letters

At about that time, Luzi received a letter from his imprisoned brother Moshe who among other things wrote as follows:

"Luzi, if you want to know how I am, then remember 'Thou hast enclosed me in shadows.' If it were not that I am always watched, I would no doubt bash my head against a wall, as people in the last stages of despair sometimes do. Things are so bad that occasionally I find myself unable to believe in the existence of justice or universal order. There are times, too, when I lose the capacity for the most ordinary common sense which links thoughts to deeds and cause to effect. For me, the links in that chain have snapped. I don't want to go on in this way because if I do I will end by distancing myself, God forbid, from the Creator of all our destinies.

"Can you imagine? I've reached such a pass that my situation has elicited pity even from my worst enemies—the very people who have cast me into this pit. I mean, of course, my stubborn creditors, whose present concern for me has reached me inside these prison walls. I feel its effects from the various privileges that have been accorded me. For example, I have been exempted from doing prison labor in town along with other prisoners, and I am not required to do any work here inside the prison. Work such as other prisoners are required to do but which would be beyond my strength, like carrying wood, water or slops. And they permit me to eat the kosher foods that are sent to me from home. Otherwise, I'd have to fast, permanently, because the prison food is not only not kosher, it is inedible.

"Of course it is all God's doing who has softened the hearts of those who have interceded for me. And I have to thank Him, too, for having miraculously sent me the help of a Jewish prisoner who is the leader of the other prisoners and who, from the first moment that I entered this place, took me into his care and who has seen to it that I haven't been harmed by any of the people he commands.

"And I thank God, too, that I am able to fulfill my religious duties as a Jew—at least as much as is possible in a prison."

And here, Moshe described in detail how he spent his week and how he celebrated the Sabbath. He described how every Friday night he set out the Sabbath loaves his family sent him—set them out on the hard wood of his bunk—how he lighted a candle and how he blessed the Sabbath wine, and how the other prisoners gathered around him in a solemn silent circle and watched him as he performed his ritual duties. And he told how, every Friday evening, the prisoners came by to remind him to "Pray to God, Moshe. It's the Sabbath today." And all this was thanks to the prisoner mentioned earlier. He, too, stood by and watched Moshe's proceedings, openmouthed and awed as, little by little, memories of long-forgotten acts and ceremonies came back to him.

"Yes, for all of that, I thank God. But when the Sabbath day is over, and evening falls, I get so depressed that my heart constricts, and the only way I have of getting any relief is to write letters home. Letters such as this one.

"By the way, my letter to you has the notation *bh' dr' g,* which signifies that only the addressee is permitted to read it, because I don't want anyone, except you, to have even an inkling of what will shortly follow.

"Because the truth is that, as I suspected before I left home, I do not have long to live."

And here, Moshe implied rather than said that he was sick with an illness he had lately acquired in prison. A cough of some kind that night and day kept him from his rest. So that not only were his nights sleepless, he had, too, to worry about keeping his fellow prisoners awake.

Evidently the intervention of various reputable people in town had made it possible for him to be taken to the prison hospital where the doctor, who had, of course, been well paid, had given him a long and careful examination after which he had prescribed various remedies as well as better food—just as one's own doctor might have done. But Moshe noted that the doctor looked at him with ill-disguised pity, as if it was clear that he was thinking that no prescriptions or better food would be of much use to him, Moshe.

And, indeed, when, one day, Moshe caught a glimpse of himself in a pane of window glass as he passed he hardly recognized himself and was frightened by how thin and sallow he looked.

"Yes. Luzi, for God's sake, don't breathe a word of this to anyone in the family, but my greatest fear lately has been that I will soon have to return the pledge I've had from God . . . that is, my soul. That I will do it here, in prison, and not at home in my own bed.

"Of course, God is compassionate," Moshe wrote, "but to the degree that anything that is to come is in our hands, I want you to undertake to comfort the family, and especially Gitl about whom, ever since I left home, I have had disturbing premonitions. I know that something has happened to her. I deduce this from the fact that I haven't had a single word from her since my arrival here. And though the children keep telling me I have no cause for anxiety, and that she doesn't write because her hand trembles, I know that it's not true, and that they are simply trying to reassure me."

And here, Moshe ended his letter, tearfully, as one could tell from the dark spots on the paper, as well as from the disordered signature.

We feel it needful to say, for our part, that Moshe was quite justified in shedding tears—both for himself and for his wife Gitl, as well as for his entire household which had had such a precipitous decline that he would not have recognized it had he been able to see it just then any more than he had been able to recognize himself in the window glass.

A decline so abrupt that it surprised even someone like Malke-Rive, Moshe's impoverished distant relative whom we have already met. She was the mother of Moshe's employee, Zisye, who had been taken ill while working for him, and who, after long weeks of illness, had died, like all of Malke-Rive's sons, of consumption.

Malke-Rive continued to come to the Mashber home to collect her son's wages: the ruble and a quarter that was paid to her, not because anyone thought she was entitled to it, or that the family had an obligation to pay it, but rather, in the tradition of those times, it was given her as a sort of alms because Zisye's wife, his children and his mother had, after Zisye's death, been cast adrift, as it were, and would have had to go begging as their only other option.

Malke-Rive came now without her veil and without her dangling brass earrings as she used to do. Because, first of all, she was in mourning and second, as regards her earrings, cheap though they were, still when things were at their worst during the time of her son's illness the earrings too had to be sold for whatever little sum they could bring.

Though she herself could hardly be said to have come from luxurious surroundings, Malke-Rive, when she entered Moshe's house after the death of his daughter, after his bankruptcy, after he had been sent to prison, and after Gitl's illness—Malke-Rive felt the foreboding that emanated from the walls, from the faces of the adults and even from the children who seemed to have abandoned their games . . . Malke-Rive was so struck by all this that for a while she forgot her own sorrows which, if the truth be told, could hardly be compared with those that had overwhelmed the Mashbers.

Arrived in the house, Malke-Rive went immediately into Gitl's bedroom. "God be with you, Gitl. Do you recognize me?" Her visit with Gitl was as short as she could make it, after which she took her leave and retraced her steps through the dining room through which she had to pass in order to get the bit of money she had come for, then she was out the door of the house and in the street, moving as quickly as she could in order to free herself of the prevailing gloom, some of which, it seemed to her, still clung to her shoulders and which she had trouble shaking off.

Naturally enough, Luzi, too, had his budget of sorrows to deal with when, partly because he wanted to and partly because his brother had made it a request, he visited the Mashber household. Even as he approached the house, and well before he entered it, he sensed its decline. Images of its former repose passed through his mind—its gracious locale, far removed from the town, the approach to the house by means of the bridge that led across the river whose banks were overgrown with reeds that in the summer showed a restful green and which even in winter seemed to murmur summer sounds. And the courtyard of the house, and the garden, in which sometimes as a guest he strolled with his brother, sometimes by day, sometimes in the evening; sometimes alone or sometimes seated pleasantly on a bench or in an arbor with some member of his brother's family.

He recalled how at ease he had been in his brother's house with its high-ceilinged, airy rooms, with their enameled walls and waxed floors, and especially how he had felt in the best guest room that had been assigned to him, and how he used to look out of the window of that room on a Sabbath afternoon and watch the townspeople who came there to stroll through the garden which was open to the public and to drink water from the well, and how those strollers looked about them, assessing his brother's wealth shrewdly but without envy: the buildings that belonged to him, the flower garden before the entryway that had been created by the skillful hand of a gardener, and the carefully tended garden behind the house which, too, with its sanded walks, its shaded benches and latticed arbors was designed for the delight of young and old.

In his mind's eye, Luzi saw his brother who despite his wealth was not one of those who bragged about what he owned or who forgot who they were and what were their origins, or that there were other goals in this life beyond narrow self interest. No, his brother was not one of those.

It's true that Luzi also thought about how the quarrel between himself and his brother had come about and how at that time it had seemed to Luzi that he had caught a whiff of a rich man's self assurance in Moshe; on the other hand, Luzi was convinced that that had been circumstantial, in the way that sometimes someone manifests behavior that is by no means characteristic of him, because essentially Moshe was not the sort of person whose self-esteem was so great that it kept him from knowing the difference between right and wrong and who therefore was beyond defending even though he had, in the course of a momentary aberration, lost track of that difference.

He had seen that in his brother's behavior both before the bankruptcy and during it when he had made use of every possible recourse to avoid harming others; and now, now after the bankruptcy, it was even clearer from the desperate guilt that so overwhelmed him because of it that there was reason to fear that something truly dreadful was lowering over him, as one could tell from the prison letter that Luzi had received from him and in which there sounded a true cry from the depths.

This is why Luzi chose not to describe the grief in the household to his brother. When Luzi wrote to Moshe, he felt that his primary duty was to console him, to strengthen him, to encourage him. To keep him from falling into a despair that would undermine both his body and soul. "Peace and blessings, and may the Lord send you His help," he wrote. "Undoubtedly, the punishing hand of God rests heavily on you just now. But do not give up hope, and continue to trust in God's compassionate spirit. Above all, do not despair.

"What is essential is this: keep in mind that just as the best part of a human destiny is vain, hollow and brief, so, too, is its opposite, the worst. It is all, all a spark that flies upward and is of brief duration in our briefly enduring world.

"And therefore, dear brother, do not let yourself be tempted by the Tempter whose goal is to deter you from faith, to darken your reason, and to encourage you to rebel against Him, against whom one may not rebel, for His ways, though they are veiled, yet they lead unto good, though to mortal eyes they may appear tangled and delusive.

"Nor ought you to be astonished if I urge you to feel pleased that you have been chosen as being one of those from whom payment is demanded in this world so that they may be spared making payment in the next.

"And I take it that you are learned enough to understand that it is better to be punished for things you have not done, than for those that you have. You know how much better that is than to have merited your punishment.

"Finally, I want to say (if you have ears to hear) what you certainly know: that you are the son of our father, may he rest in peace, who used often to say—sometimes with envy, sometimes with regret—that in times past a man who did not have sufficient sorrows of his own used to go in search of them, wandering an exile through the world.

"Our father, may he rest in peace," added Luzi, his meaning half-hidden, "was on the verge of such a pilgrimage, but he died before he could achieve it. And I, too, am prepared for such a journey, but I don't know whether I will manage to do it either. You ought to consider yourself worthy to have received the precious gift of suffering in your own home.

"And thus I end my letter, setting down my signature. I remain your brother Luzi who now utters a prayer to the Lord of the Universe and the Master of Help that He may redeem you from the straits that you are in and that He will soon bring you home to peace and happiness and make you whole in spirit and in flesh. Amen."

And now we turn once again to what it was that Luzi observed in Moshe's house.

As soon as he came into the house, he went, naturally, to Gitl's room to find out how she was. He always found Esther-Rokhel there, "The Leather Saint," whom we met earlier when she was employed in Moshe's house at the time that his daughter was dying; we saw her again at the time of Alter's wedding, and now we see her as a faithful nurse tending to Gitl.

Esther-Rokhl was so poor that her own housework required hardly any time at all, so that she could devote entire days and nights to caring for Gitl. Not for money, naturally, but because, in her view, caring for the sick was a most important act of piety.

She tended to Gitl even more devotedly than Gitl's own daughter Yehudis. She understood every one of Gitl's mute gestures and desires and brought her whatever it was that she required. She was able, too, to assess Gitl's condition with the precision of a doctor or a nurse. Always, when Luzi asked Esther-Rokhl, "How is she doing?" she always replied, so long as they were in Gitl's presence, "Good. Things are going well." She said this lest Gitl was able to understand what was going on. But Luzi had no sooner left the room than Esther-Rokhl always followed him into the next room where, feeling less constrained, she told him what she believed to be the truth, "God help us, she is getting worse and worse."

When Luzi visited Moshe's family to inquire generally about them, and about what was happening to Moshe's business—and whether there was a plan afoot to reestablish it—he was always given a gloomy report.

Little as Luzi understood about business, especially the complications attendant on a bankruptcy, he nevertheless understood from what Moshe's family told him that the situation was and would continue to be bad. It made no difference whether everything stayed closed, or whether the creditors were taken in as partners and business was resumed. In the latter case, the creditors' primary concern would be for themselves and not for the welfare of Moshe's family.

It should be said here that the business *was* about to be reopened, but chiefly it was to be run for the profit of Moshe's creditors and with hardly any gains for him. Because, as we have seen, Moshe's former clients had soon after his bankruptcy seen fit to take their business elsewhere. In that way, they had avoided paying the debts they had accumulated over the years of doing business with him.

Certainly it's not right when people allow themselves to ignore payment of debts that they owe on the grounds that their creditor is not paying his debts . . . of course it's not right to ignore the reasons for his bankruptcy and to take advantage of his situation to pull off a piece of chicanery of one's own. But never mind, that's how it was and that's what was done and what they said with a clear conscience was that "It's right to steal from a stealer."

These, then, are the things Luzi heard from Moshe's family. They described what was happening in great detail, much of which he did not understand. But the heart of the matter was clear even to a man with as little business sense as he, Luzi, had: his brother's business was in a decline, and as a consequence, various family ties, too, were being loosened. Moshe's sons-in-law, who, when all was going well, had been united, were now backing away from each other and looking about for other things to do.

Nakhum Lentsher, Moshe's younger son-in-law, for instance, who after his wife died and after Moshe went bankrupt and was sent to prison . . . Nakhum Lentsher wrote to his mother, Shayntse, whom we have already met when she came to visit at the time when Nakhum's wife was dying. We saw how Shayntse behaved then, and her behavior now was no improvement.

She continually pointed out to Nakhum that there was no point in his suffering for his father-in-law's sake. And that, furthermore, it was time for him, Nakhum, to stop grieving for his wife and to think about remarrying. Of course, a woman with money which would for one thing free him from having to care for the children; then it would give him, who had such a talent for it, a chance to begin a new business.

"You have a head on your shoulders and you're young. And may I have as many good years as you will have matches offered you: maidens or young widows or well born divorcées with large dowries."

Nakhum, reported other family members, had begun to keep to himself; and he had no sooner taken care of the needs of his children—to the limits of his masculine abilities—then he would take to pacing back and forth in his room, smoking his cigarettes only halfway down, after which he spat on their tips and threw them into the spittoon in the corner of the room.

Luzi, too, observed how Nakhum was keeping his distance, particularly, as we have said, after his mother Shayntse came to visit. Despite the fact that Shayntse was an in-law, she rarely crossed the threshold of Gitl's room. Luzi took note of the way she manipulated Nakhum, how Nakhum continually mulled over her suggestions, readying himself to act on her self-serving and coldhearted suggestions.

He saw, too, how Moshe's older daughter, Yehudis's eyes were continually red with weeping. And she had what to cry about, because over and above all the misfortunes that had overtaken her father's house, she had to put up with her husband, Yankele Grodshteyn who even in the best of times had never distinguished himself by his intelligence or skill in business. He had been in constant need of Moshe's supervision, so that Moshe could correct the mistakes his somewhat slow-witted son-in-law committed.

He was very quiet, extremely naive and moreover, deeply religious. He was, like the Patriarch Jacob, drawn more to the tents of the Hebrews than to the tumultuous marketplace with its raucous buying and selling, and he seized avidly the slightest opportunity to avoid close contact with people in the business world. He had a distaste for the marketplace where he felt like a stranger, and he found a better world in books and in the company of those whose tastes were like his, young sons-in-law, well-to-do young men who could permit themselves the sorts of indulgences for which Yankele Grosdshteyn would have given the shirt off his back.

In a word, he was a "silent lamb," as the clerks and small businessmen who could not understand his behavior called him. The sort of person who, if his father-in-law, Moshe Mashber, had not poured some oats into his feeding trough from time to time, that is, if he had not made up for the sums squandered by Grodshteyn with his lamb-like ways, would have ended naked long ago, truly without a shirt on his back because of his unfortunate and inept business dealings and his poor understanding of money.

In those better days, Yehudis's mistakes made no great difference. Business was good and there was plenty of money to go around. Then, Moshe quietly corrected his errors and overlooked his ill-conceived expenditures that bordered on the profligate. But now, when everything was turned topsy-turvy—Moshe not there, the business at a standstill, the household in dismay, and the money supply so low that they had to worry about each day's expenses—at such a time, Yankele Grodshteyn was not only useless in acquiring any money that might be used for the general welfare, but he had not the faintest understanding of how to economize. Instead, he maintained his old habits of open-handed generosity.

Yehudis, his wife, had no one in whom to confide her sorrows. How does one account for that? Because former friends of the Mashber household now tended to stay away. And the only one to whom she might have been able to say a word or two was Esther-Rokhl, the poverty-stricken relative who, night and day and without payment of any sort, looked after Gitl, and was more attentive to her than even she, Yehudis. Yehudis could not bring herself to confide in Esther-Rokhl because she, Esther-Rokhl, had spent a long lifetime being poor. The decline in the Mashber fortunes could not appear dreadful to her, and so she could hardly expect much sympathy from Esther-Rokhl.

That left only her uncle Luzi.

"Ah, Uncle," she wept as she all but threw herself on his breast, after he had heard and seen all that was transpiring in his brother's house. Her shoulders trembled as she stood before Luzi and she held a handkerchief to her eyes as she talked.

When Luzi concluded his visit, he always asked about Alter who more than all the others had been affected by the recent events. He kept more to himself in his bachelor quarters in the room in the attic, and when Luzi visited him there he was astonished to find that Alter, instead of sitting empty-handed in his room or musing outstretched on his bed, was busy writing away.

"Ah," Alter said, startled when he sensed the presence of another person. When he saw that it was Luzi, he blushed, embarrassed to have Luzi find him at his work, and as he stood up, he tried with his hand to hide what he was writing.

"How are you doing," asked Luzi, making no endeavor to sit down or to stay for very long. Later, he said, "I'll see you again when next I come." Alter, surprised by Luzi's visit, was so rattled that he forgot to accompany him to the door as politeness requires. Or it may be that he did not forget, that he simply stood rooted to the spot in sheer surprise at the visit.

When he had recovered, as it were, from the great pleasure of his brother's brief visit to him, he would stand immobile where Luzi had left him, immersed in thought. At other times he would go to the window seeking to calm himself by looking out at the winterbound garden until with a start, as if remembering something, he would return to his work—writing.

These days when members of the family spoke of Alter, they often said to each other, "Yes, the letter-writing sickness is about to begin again."

And here is the "fruit" of that activity—a disordered mixture of a trance state with the unclear feelings of a mentally disturbed person. In order to give the reader some sense of their essence, it has been necessary to arrange and to order them and to discard what is unessential.

But here it needs to be said that Alter's letters this time were not, as they once used to be, addressed to the ancient names of the Bible, such as Nebuchadnezzar, the king of Babylon, and so on. Now they were addressed to more familiar people. To members of his own family, and especially to his brothers Luzi and Moshe who, it would appear, stood before him lately like two burning candles from whose sight he could not turn his eyes.

Here is one such letter:

To my brother Moshe, my help and my protector:

I do not really know what a prison is though these days there is a lot of whispering about it in the house. But if it means being separated from people and being locked away, I understand that, because from my childhood upward I have been separated and closed off in the mute walls of my fate which acts as if it did not hear my frequent and horrible laments which leave me as exhausted as a woman after her first childbearing.

Alas, I do not know why you are being punished any more than I know why I have been made to suffer. Because if one were to judge merely by actions, then you ought to be rewarded by being raised to the heavens, to the stars and higher and still higher for the more than brotherly way that you have always acted toward me.

Ah, brother. Ah [wrote Alter]. You were always ready to keep in mind even those who had no need of it. And if I, condemned as I am for no reason, make no complaint about being sent imperfect as I am into this world, it is only because I was fortunate enough to have you for a brother who have done everything you could to keep my lips from uttering a complaint; nor is it the least of what you have done that you have not turned me over to the cold care and supervision of strangers, but you have kept me under your own fraternal roof so that I might live out my destiny, part ruin though it is, instead of being driven into the streets as others in my situation are.

I often look out of my window into the garden where I see you in dazzling white snow beneath trees whose branches are like purified silver: That garden, morning, noon and night, is enclosed, at its edges, by a blue mist which quietly distinguishes it from all the nearby gardens.

And each time I look down into the garden I seem to see you, Moshe, standing straight, pale, tranquil and so light that the earth seems not to notice when you have taken leave of it, nor the air when you ascend into it. And I, too, become aerial though I cannot tell just how I floated through the attic window before which I stand. And then I am near you. You above me, I below you. You are carrying nothing, but I carry a bundle the way a servant carries one for his employer. We rise, and keep rising, higher and higher. So high that we can no longer see the earth. And then we come to a place in the sky where there is an opening for us.

We enter into a wide empty vast round space in which the Lord of Hosts sits quietly, and at the border of that round space, there are rank upon rank of heads, each rank higher than the others. They are all looking at a scale at the feet of the Almighty toward which we approach. I am instructed to put the bundle I've carried for you onto the scale. And I no sooner put it there when thousands upon thousands of voices are heard in your praise crying, "The scale has tipped . . . the scale has tipped on the side of compassion. He is pure, pure. There is no need to descend to earth. He is asked to stay here."

And all of the heads that are gathered in that space turn to each other and pass among themselves the wished-for news that someone like themselves has arrived to join their circle.

And it is at this point, dear brother Moshe, that I wake up and am no longer with you as you are invited into the circle. And then I am in my own room. And lo, whenever it chances to be, whether morning, noon or night, I always find a lighted lamp waiting for me. A memorial light, but who has lighted it for me, I cannot say. Perhaps myself, or someone else. And always I stand before an opened Mishnah text where I find myself searching for three commentaries that begin with the letters *Mem, Shin, Heh,* the letters that spell your name. And I study passionately, heatedly, for the sake of the ascension of your soul.

Ah, me. [Here Alter gave a start and interrupted himself.] What am I saying? May there be no such hour! Moshe is here among us for many a year. And all that I've been saying is nothing more than a manifestation of my addled brain.

Because . . . yes. As regards me, Alter. It seems to me that I am ill once more. Sometimes my thoughts fly about inside my head like clouds being driven by a strong wind; at other times I am as perfectly calm and empty as a stopped mill . . . without work to do, empty as on a Sabbath. Sometimes, feeling myself cursed, I have an impulse to tear my shirt. At other times I feel as silent as a worm beneath a rock, a worm that has indeed earned no more for itself than the bit of soil that it inhabits beneath the rock.

As now, for instance, when I have an impulse to lie on the floor in some corner of the room, and to stay there, like some furry animal which has no other ambition except to lie still all curled up, ignored, and possessed of only the least bit of awareness that there is, in addition to the bit of earth which it is its destiny to inhabit . . . that there is a spacious other world in which more fortunate people move about.

And again, as now, when I with my minuscule, minimum mind see myself as a poor little bird soaring high in the heavens near the circle of the sun, looking for a gate whereby I can enter into its dazzling center so that in a rapture of flight I may immolate myself, feathers, wings and all.

And here we interrupt our reading of Alter's letter because it is evident that he is being so carried away that in a little while it will be impossible either to read or to edit him. Enough, then.

Now, here is another letter:

"*L'akhi Luzi e'uzi u m'uzi,* To my brother Luzi, my strength and stronghold," he began, establishing an exalted tone, as if he were standing at the foot of a mountain and was calling up to someone directly above him.

Whenever you come to mind, I feel proud to have you for my brother; and whenever I look past my darkened being, as through a window, all I see is you who are a consolation to many, but especially to me, Alter, who has received no other gifts but the capacity to dream of the unattainable. You should know that were I like others and not, as I am, condemned to muteness, then I would never quit your presence. I would cling to you as a child clings to its mother, or walks in her footsteps and is perpetually near her. But I am one who is deprived of all worldly joys—well, let that pass. But the worst of it for me is that having a brother like you, I nevertheless seem to have only the title page, as it were, and not you, yourself, your substance, your essence.

When you visit me, I am as overwhelmed as a child who has just experienced more delight than his heart is capable of and who feels, therefore, that it is about to burst. And my excitement is so great that instead of wishing that you would stay with me, I wish for you to leave me so that I can be alone to savor how joyful I would be if we could be together and to grieve over how much I would lose if Heaven should deny my wish.

When you leave, I go to my window where suffused with happiness because of your visit, I look out into the garden which is all white, all snow . . . entirely winter. And I seem to see you there in the form of a lighted pyre hidden under the trees in an isolated corner of the garden, a pyre without smoke, that doesn't darken the soil or give off a red glow; rather, it gleams with small white flames, like silk hovering in a breeze. And above it, high in the heavens, a small window opens through which the pyre is observed, and its soft, hushed white glow is found to be acceptable and it is blessed.

And when I gaze for a while at the pyre, it seems to me that I, too, rise in the form of a piece of burning paper. Light and aerial, I fly wheeling and turning like a swallow, and as I fly, I read what has been written on me, and that is, that I, the lesser brother of him by whose grace I am ascending higher and higher, am a petition to whom it will concern requesting that when my brother's pyre is received into heaven, that mine, too, as an additional act of compassion, will be permitted to enter.

Again, we interrupt our reading because we see that Alter is plunging into a wilderness into which we do not need to follow.

VII

Darkness

Let us reiterate what has been said several times already: it was a year when the harvest was bad. The peasants in the surrounding settlements had nothing to sell, and were even less able to buy anything. The small towns were the first to experience hardship because they were unable to sell off the goods they received from the larger center. And then, the center itself began to suffer, a town like N. which served as a distribution center for the small towns in the region.

That winter even the more prosperous merchants heaved sighs over the lack of customers as they moved about their shops and of course the less successful shopkeepers frequently groaned at the sight of their empty shelves . . . empty, not as in good times because their goods had been sold, but because such money as came in was spent on household expenses and there was not the slightest hope of replenishing their shelves with new goods because they could no longer get credit from their richer colleagues.

So much, then, for the shopkeepers. Then think what it was like for those who hover around the shops: porters, packers, middlemen and so on. And what of the simple craftsmen whose livelihood depended on orders from the upper stratum which, when things were going well, could think of buying shoes and clothes and other such things?

Poverty spread at a dreadful rate. Anyone who had put aside a few pennies for a rainy day now had to dig them up and spend them. But who among the workers had ever been able to put any money aside, even in good times? In their homes, one began to notice the absence of bedclothes on the beds of both adults and children. And the absence, too, of holiday clothing that had been carefully tended from the beginning of a marriage and which no one had ever dreamed of replacing. Missing, too, were copper and brass implements: samovars, frying pans, pots, dippers as well as candlesticks which had secretly and with great embarrassment wandered into the hands of the avaricious usurers in exchange for coins of low denomination.

The greater part of this impoverished group had to turn to the benevolent societies whose treasuries were, thanks to their willingness to help the poor, constantly empty. Especially now when so many of those in need reached their hands out for what little help they could get.

All too often on a Sabbath morning in the synagogues, before the reading of the Torah, one heard tearful appeals from various benevolent societies being read by the shammes. "To so-and-so and such and such benevolent congregation, help us ease the plight of your needy brethren whose children are dying of hunger, cold and disease. And, thereby," the appeals went on, "you will aid in the coming of the Messiah. Amen." The appeals were heard with indifference.

Meanwhile, the winter did what it would. In the household of the poor there was no money to buy firewood, so that in addition to being hungry, people froze. The result was an increase in sickness and death, and those who took to their beds had very little hope that they would ever leave them.

Truly, it was a good time for doctors: they earned a lot from their visits to the homes of the poor who did whatever they could to keep their sick alive and who believed that for that a doctor was essential and that simply with his visit part of the illness would go away. There were some of the town's doctors whose eyes glowed and whose cheeks shone with the money they earned from their visits and from something else: from the rake-offs they got from the pharmacists who filled out the prescriptions the doctors signed. And the pharmacists, too, did not do badly as they stood behind their pharmacy counters grinding away at the remedies in their white porcelain pestles, grinding slowly, as was proper, while they appreciated the prosperity that was descending upon them.

But for the sick, neither doctors nor remedies helped, because in addition to remedies, the poor needed something else that in their homes was very scarce: heating, nourishment, trained bedside care and so on. As a result, anyone who took to his bare plank bed at home rose from it only with the greatest difficulty, and those whose misfortune it was to find themselves in the hospital did well to bid farewell to their own homes forever, because for the most part most of those who went to the hospital soon had their poverty-stricken bundle of bones huddled off, quick-march, to the cemetery, where one indigent was laid out beside another and where their graves were marked by a bare bit of paling which did not last very long but which, together with the memory of the poor, soon sagged to the ground.

The Sabbath appeals to the rich intended to wake their compassion were no help. Even as they listened, they turned their heads away, as if the appeals were intended for someone else. And if they were approached directly, they waved off the appeal, crying, "What do you want of us? We're the ones who have contributed and contributed, well beyond our means. Why are you hounding us? When times are this bad, do you think we can support the poor of the entire town?"

And that's where the matter rested. And the result of these outcries was that the purses of the rich remained tightly closed and what then happened was that on the day after the Sabbath various benevolent folk, men and women, in twos and threes, went from house to house carrying red kerchiefs to collect what money they could. When at some rich home they were given a donation larger than they had received at a neighbor's, their faces glowed with enthusiastic perspiration because of the generosity their labors had provoked.

Still, the net result was poor. Gifts of this sort did not diminish the sea of need by so much as a drop and the poverty intensified. And poverty brought illness, and illness in the homes of the poor at times like these meant simply that the door to the other world was already more than three quarters open.

Then as always in a time of misery, various false healers flocked to the town, like ravens to a cadaver, to extract the last bit of coin from the pockets of the poor. First, and frequently to be seen, there were certain withered and sorry-looking "grandchildren" who came of good Jewish stock that was now much declined. They had no reputation to speak of and had never achieved any rank or distinction in the towns in which they lived. These "grandchildren" attained a livelihood of sorts because of the merit they derived from the possession of a mangy sable hat or a fur-lined cloak they had inherited from some famous and pious grandfather. They received donations from their followers, various workingmen who came to them in order to hear them speak a few words of religion. On holidays, the Sabbath or even on ordinary days of the week, they received such offerings as the workers were able to make: sometimes food or drink, sometimes even a small coin.

These "grandchildren" prospered more than ever before because, living in the very midst of the populace, they were familiar faces, always nearby and always accessible at need. Consolation from them was easy to get: one came to them bearing a bit of a coin and was given an immediate response—"Don't worry, the Creator will come to your aid. Because of our grandfather's merit, those for whom we pray will be helped soon."

These "grandchildren" to whom access was easy, who were not surrounded by rabbinical assistants, to whom one did not need to write petitions, and for whom one did not need to wait behind closed doors as was the case when one visited famous wonder rebbes, these "grandchildren" also had simple wives who helped their husbands by developing congenial relationships with the women who came for help and who listened attentively to their complaints and who then helped them to explain their griefs when they brought them in to their husbands.

In addition to these hole-in-the-wall miracle workers, all sorts of fortune-tellers, Jewish and non-Jewish, coming from the devil only knows where appeared suddenly, like mushrooms: grizzled hundred-year-old doddering and toothless Ukrainians who kept up a continual whispering, silent Tartars who healed by rolling an egg about, or by means of smoke, or the use of various herbs, or melted wax, or by giving the patient water to drink in which a talisman inscribed with Tartar script had been soaked for several days.

There was, too, a great demand for those who could read fortunes from cards. These did quite good business using an old pack and a pair of candles stuck into candleholders that were set on a table in a tiny room in which the blinds were drawn. Everything was set so that when a client came in, the candles were immediately lighted and he saw a *Korban Minkhe* on the table and beside it a worn copy of a book entitled *The Wisdom of the Hand*. There was a picture of a hand on the title page, with all of its lines and wrinkles identified as to their meanings: long life, good or bad fate, a long journey, illnesss, death and so on.

And as if that wasn't enough, there were also other seekers after easy money: magicians, mezuzah examiners, squint-eyed cabalists who wore sheepskins and woolen socks in summer and in winter and who pulled their magic remedies and philters out of their filthy breast pockets. In addition to all these, there was an influx of famous *real* miracle rabbis from abroad who were well known because of their forebears, or because they were famous in their own right. Men to whom their followers made continual pilgrimages to the towns where they lived, bringing with them gifts to which the rebbes were entitled. But now when the suffering of the people was so great, these wonder rebbes journeyed to them, calculating that though there was but small coin to be gotten from each poor man, yet there were so many of them that in the end, putting coin upon coin, the journey would prove profitable.

And, as if that wasn't enough, there appeared exotic pilgrims from strange and distant lands—from Jerusalem and Safed, from Turkey and Yemen, from Persia and other unknown places like Morocco and Algiers. Some wore rolled white turbans instead of hats; others wore tall lambskin caps. They all wore caftans down to the ground and had tightly wound long ear curls that descended to their waists. Others had shaven heads and mustaches. And they all spoke a mutilated Hebrew—more Aramaic than Hebrew—which, even as it made them seem alien, nevertheless inspired both fear and respect.

They did not come alone. They had their wives with them—though one could not be certain that they were actually their wives or whether they were simply partners in the begging venture. And these plump, tanned, full-bosomed women in Turkish shawls, wearing many skirts and vests one on top of the other, kept washing their hands as they helped their mendicant partners tell tales of wonder that they said had happened in the lands from which they claimed to come.

These women spoke a familiar Yiddish interspersed with words from the women's prayer book. And the stories they told always had the same form: lately in the City of Jerusalem a cave had been discovered. When it was entered, a light was seen at a great distance away beneath which an old man was discovered sitting at a table on which there was a book. Beside him, there was a ram's horn. The man was the prophet Elijah, and the ram's horn was the one with which he would announce to the world the coming of the Messiah on the day when he would manifest himself. At that moment all the Jews everywhere would gather in Jerusalem. When the old man was asked, "When will that be?" he replied, "When the Sabbath prevails over all the earth, in the seventh millennium of our era. And," the women said, "we are now almost in the seventh millennium. And," the pious women added piously, "if we are deemed worthy (for the sake of the alms we give), weekdays may be counted as days of the Sabbath. And that will bring us sooner to the seventh millennium. And so, because of your generosity, it may be our happy destiny to hear the old man sounding his shofar to announce the coming of the Messiah. Amen."

These men and women gave off an aura of foreign perspiration; they cast sharp, penetrating looks from their bright, reptilian eyes. Sometimes their eyes had the amber look that follows on a fever, or that is the result of endless staring at the desert distances in the places from which they had come. Sometimes, too, one sensed a sea-salt aura coming from them, as if one were smelling the seas through which they had sailed. All of this gave them the upper hand in their competition with those soothsayers who came from regions closer by and who, like them, had been drawn to the city by their hopes for gain.

All these folks, the "uncles and aunts from Medea and Persia" as the local freethinking wits called them, brought various holy things with them to sell: candles, oil in long-necked Oriental jars and bottles, thread with which to measure graves (this had a wide sale among the superstitious). These objects, coming from distant, holy lands, were the outer and visible signs that their bearers, too, came from holy places.

Of course, it was in the interest of such people to keep the unhappy populace in a state of anxious turmoil, and so they encouraged the spread of tales of dreadful events in the town itself; such terror tales, exploited by their tellers, were listened to attentively and with beating hearts.

Tales, for example, about demons that had recently appeared in various ruined houses in distant streets. Passersby, it was said, would hear the clicking of tongues and would catch glimpses of eyes blazing as brightly as lanterns; sometimes someone would be hurt when the demons threw shards, bits of plaster and sometimes whole pots at them from the roof.

There were tales told, too, about a newborn child who would not nurse at his mother's breast if she washed it, and who recited the morning prayer and uttered prophecies regarding a two-headed calf, and about some other beast that had four legs sticking out of its back.

And there was the tale, too, of a certain local cabalist named Yokton and his nephew who practiced black magic together. They meant that short, black-bearded Yokton who wore a fur coat both summer and winter and who always kept a hand at his left eye which continually flowed with tears because, as everyone knew, he had looked at something that was forbidden; Yokton who along with many of the homeless lived in the Open Synagogue with his seventeen-year-old nephew who was also short, stunted like his uncle, and who also always wore a cloak that served him all the year round and who was, more-over, something of a cripple, carrying his head bent toward his shoulder. The two of them, Yokton and his nephew, had been beaten several times by local fanatics for their behavior and for undertaking to heal the sick by means of amulets they themselves had written and which they carried stuffed into their breast pockets and sold at affordable prices. And those who assaulted these two repeatedly swore that while they were striking Yokton and his nephew they felt sharp pains in their hands as if they had been striking their fists against stone or iron. Proof that they were dealing with no natural creatures but with the sorts of beings that were not to be permitted to cross a Jewish threshold because they were close kin to "those folk" with whom they were in league and that that was why these two looked like "those folk": short, skinny, squint-eyed, and that was why, too, no one had even seen either of them washing or eating, as if they were angels who had no stomachs.

It was said that Yokton had lately been observed staying up late at night in the Open Synagogue. And sometimes when one of the people who slept in the synagogue with them woke up, he saw Yokton and his nephew near a bookcase from which they pulled various dusty old papers over which they busied themselves for a long time, looking at them intently and anxiously; but then, overjoyed, they seized each other as if something very wonderful had just happened, and as if they had found something in the papers that filled them with rapture. They exchanged a long, lingering gaze, after which they fell into each other's arms and kissed each other the way men and women kiss—God keep us from the like.

Another rumor that was current then was that there was a young woman who walked the streets at night who choked to death everyone she met: tall and short, young and old, weak and strong. Children stopped going to primary schools in the evening. Shopkeepers closed their shops while it was still daylight so that they could get home before dark. The streets stood empty; midwives gave up visiting women who went into labor at night. Neighbors in the same courtyard were afraid to risk going from one building to the next, and no one dreamed of crossing over into the next street at all.

The town undertook remedies against the maiden. First, they turned to the police, the so-called guardians of the peace, and offered to reward them well if they captured her and took her where she belonged. The police agreed and, to celebrate their anticipated certain success, tossed off many a congratulatory drink. But except for the emptied glasses and the glowing promises, nothing came of the police venture.

Night after night heartrending screams were heard coming from distant streets. Cries made, no doubt, by some deaf person who had not heard about the predatory maiden, or by someone who knew about her but who was forced by necessity to go out into the night. Screams that chilled the blood.

The town hired local butchers and knackers armed with cleavers and knives to capture the maiden. They accepted the task, but they were no more successful at it than the police had been. No, they fared worse. They actually encountered the maiden and one of them, felled by her hand, died, while the others just barely escaped with their lives. And these were the sorts of men—butchers and knackers—who could wrestle a bull to the ground.

In a word, things were bad. And the haunting lasted a long while—almost the entire winter. And it ended appropriately enough: there was no demon maiden. It was merely a thief in disguise who was instigated by the town's thieves to frighten people and thereby give the brotherhood of thieves opportunities to do what thieves generally do. To break and enter, to smash window glass with impunity.

It was indeed such a good season for thieves that the brotherhood commissioned the writing of a new Torah scroll and gave it to the synagogue, and since no one knew what sort of money had paid for the scroll, the synagogue dedicated it with a festive parade, with music and dancing.

That, then, is the way ordinary thieves took advantage of the occasion. But so, too, did extortioners like Yone the tavern keeper and his cronies who invented a libelous tale about the Bratslaver sect and against the man who headed it: Luzi Mashber. They let it be known that the sect had a little bone from a corpse in their keeping. (Among the Bratslaver, this was not such a farfetched possibility, since they were frequently involved with the dead, spending whole days and nights lying on graves.) And by means of that little bone they performed various scandalous acts unheard of among Jews: putting the bone under an armpit, they asked it questions about the future. With the bone under a thigh, they summoned the dead. And more and more of the kinds of tales that used to be told in times of idolatry, the times of our forebears, as the Bible tells us.

"Woe, woe," cried those who heard all this and put their hands to their heads while the younger ones spat and their elders turned fearfully away as they whispered something hateful, unable otherwise to express their anger at such vileness.

"Woe, woe," cried others who were readier to undertake action against evil with slaps, shouts and curses. "Woe, woe. Why is it that children and older folk as well are taken from this world by illness and misfortune before their time?"

Yes, it was a time when the Bratslavers were much spoken of, and they were in very great danger of attack, of having their homes destroyed while they, their wives and children were stoned or driven from the town.

And indeed that was about to happen. And the hostility of that was about to be vented against the head of the sect, against Luzi Mashber of whom it was told that he was the possessor of the little bone which he kept locked away in a bureau drawer. Surely it was he for whom the curses of the *Tokhekha*, the Mosaic curses of Leviticus, were insufficient. A town worthy of the name would not permit a man like him to spend so much as a single night in it.

Indeed it was clear that sometime soon a crowd of Jews, whether members of one synagogue or simply a mob formed in the street, would set out toward Luzi's house where, seizing him, they would throw him into a dung cart after which to the accompaniment of the shouts and whistles of youthful hooligans, they would run him out of town.

Yes, such a moment was imminent because the town's nerves were on edge—partly because of the decline in its prosperity, and partly because of the recent deaths that had emptied many beds and caused many a mirror to be turned to the wall as a sign of mourning. And so the town sought someone on whom to fix the blame as a way of explaining the visitations that the God of Compassion had lately sent upon the heads of the innocent.

And so, various sources of the trouble were identified. First there was Yokton, the cabalist sorcerer who had, not for the first time, been beaten for his activities; now those who had beaten him reported that they hurt their hands as they were delivering their blows because his body was not like that of a human's at all but more like that of a stone. The town also blamed the Bratslavers and their dead man's bone. Not only had they profaned a grave by digging up the limb of a corpse, but they also made use of it to learn secrets that should properly be shrouded. Their behavior was altogether unheard of—it was enough to make a Jew want to cut the seams of his garments; and surely anyone guilty of such acts deserved to be severely punished.

And punishment would have been imminent except that the men of the town were so busy that they could not find the time to get together long enough to decide what to do. And so they delayed and delayed. Finally, it was not the men who triggered the action. Its chief instigators (though at the beginning to a very minor degree) were the women who once their blood was up were quick to come to an agreement, and when they moved, it was with the force of a dam that has burst in a storm.

It began with Pesye, the wife of Sholem the porter. He, too, as we have recounted earlier, was a member of the Bratslaver sect. He was a giant of a man, capable of downing three pots of cabbage stew and three loaves of bread all at once. He was the sort of fellow who before he joined the sect was quite capable of betting his fellow porters that he, Sholem, could eat up all the food prepared by Zakharye the tavern keeper for his customers. Everything down to the last morsel, until the table was empty: goose giblets and livers, goose crackling, knishes—everything. "All you have to do is bet, and pay for what I eat. I'll show you what I can do." And it was done. The bet was made and Sholem kept his word. While the other porters stood about, he gobbled every-thing that was on Zakharye's display table, leaving it as bare as a kitchen that has been cleared of traces of leavened bread before the Passover.

That's the sort of fellow Sholem had been. A powerful eater who, when he was asked what he wanted in the World to Come, replied that he wanted the green hill on the outskirts of town to turn into a loaf of bread, and the river that flowed nearby to turn into a stew so that he might dunk the bread into the stew.

In those days Sholem did what a market porter was expected to do. He worked hard hauling heavy loads. And he lived peaceably with his wife, according to God's command and according to the law. And liv-ing with her, he begot a fine little crowd of children, God keep the Evil Eye from them: boys like bear cubs, girls like tubs, all of them broader than they were long, and all of them with appetites as hearty as Sho-lem's.

And Pesye was happy and contented with her husband's great size, his porter's apron that hung down in front and in back and was tied by a rope in the middle, and happy, too, with his earnings, every penny of which, like a good and decent husband, he always brought home to her. She, for her part, carried out the duties of a market-porter's wife. She seemed to have acquired some of her husband's health. Her shoul-ders and hips were broad, and she had the vigor to "carry" and to "have" frequently; when she was done "having" she had the energy to care for her children, to provide them with food, to see to it that they had the proper clothing. She washed, fed and tended, as was proper.

That's how things had once been. But lately after Sholem abandoned his porter's trade and immersed himself in the Bratslaver sect, and devoted himself to piety, the household peace was shattered. At first Pesye did not understand what he was doing and treated his behavior as if it might be a form of illness, or else something that would pass with time—as can happen; but when it became clear that he was steeping himself more and more deeply in piety, and that as a consequence he was earning less and less, and that there was progressively less money available for her household needs, then Pesye began to grumble. She complained gently at first. She tried to reason with Sholem, to persuade him that what he was doing was wrong, that his fellow porters were laughing at him, and that his actions were beginning to harm her and the children. She pointed out, for example, that that very day she had not had enough money with which to do the marketing and that the children were hungry and that the boys had been sent home from their primary school because so much time had passed since last she had been able to pay their fees. And so on. And so on.

Sholem heard it all in silence. And since he was a simple man and not yet well versed in his new creed, he deduced from it that what he ought to do was to deprive himself of food and drink and even to put some distance between himself and his wife and children. Nor did his new creed provide him with sufficient skill to persuade her that what he was doing was right. And so he kept silent. And Pesye, too, after her initial attempts to persuade him, kept silent and waited to see what would happen next, believing that when he thought the matter over, and when he saw how his household was suffering, he would repent and come to his senses on his own.

But that's not what happened. And when Pesye saw that he became more and more engrossed in his new piety, and that his income continued to diminish to such a degree that there was now insufficient money for even the most minimal expenses, and when in addition to all this Sholem began to avoid performing his conjugal duties, then Pesye decided that he *must* be ill. But then she realized that it was not illness but the tenets of his new belief that kept him from her bed. And so one Friday evening she said, "Look here, Sholem. Are you an angel or a priest? Is that why you don't need . . ."

"No," he said. "It isn't that I have no need . . . I'm not allowed to need . . ."

"What do you mean?" she burst out. "What kind of talk is that? You're joking." Then she added, "Just remember this. I'm not going to keep this to myself. I won't let them take away your manhood, or your work or keep you from being my husband and the father of your children. I won't let it happen. I'll yell and scream. Do you hear, Sholem?

Those people who are pushing you to this . . . I'll scratch their eyes out."

Again Sholem listened in silence. If she did what she threatened, she would shame him, and as we may recall, Pesye had already shamed him once before when she went to complain about Sholem to Mikhl Bukyer when Mikhl was still the leader of the Bratslaver sect. But then she had done it quietly, all alone, calmly and respectfully, the way one comes to put a question to a rabbi. But as time went on and her husband continued with his new ways and as a consequence his earnings continued to decline, and when the other porters openly poked fun at him, and when as a consequence of too little food and too much prayer his health suffered so that he was no longer able to lift the heavy chests, sacks and bundles which formerly had been child's play to him . . . when it became clearer and clearer to Pesye that disaster crouched at her doorstep and poverty had become a steady boarder in her house, and when such a severe winter set in that even people who were in good health and who were energetic about making a living were having a hard time making ends meet because there was little work available and no one needed porters . . . especially not Sholem who had become physically weak and who in any case was not diligent about looking for work, and when he did try to find something someone else snatched the job out from under him and Sholem made no complaint but naively yielded his rights and allowed the other man to get ahead of him . . . and when Pesye saw how weak and pale Sholem had become and noted, too, that her own dress was becoming roomier and that more and more of the most necessary household items were finding their way to the pawnbrokers: Sabbath candlesticks, cushions from her own and her children's beds; when she saw that all the pawning netted only money enough to get by for another day and sometimes a little more, and that there was nothing left in the house that could be pawned, and that there was no place she could borrow any money or buy anything on credit because the little shop where, as the wife of a healthy and prosperous porter, she had cheerfully been given credit, now when it was learned that her husband was no longer a wage earner, treated her rudely and withdrew that credit . . . when Pesye, after she had seen all that and after she had time after time tried angrily or gently to reason with her husband and pointed out their disastrous state to him, and demanded to know where it would all lead; and when Sholem, hearing her, continued to maintain his silence while his eyes misted over like those of a man who has inhaled fumes; and when after all those conversations she saw how things in the household were going from bad to worse, and when her children took to their beds because the house was unheated and there was not enough to eat, then Pesye seethed with anger like a lioness whose cubs are threatened. She experienced first a wrenching at her vitals and then she charged as if she meant to knock over or trample on anything that stood in her way.

She charged those who were responsible for her huband's misfortune.

It happened on a day when Luzi was at home sitting at his table with Avremele Lubliner who was still in N. and who paced back and forth as he listened to Luzi's utterances: a word here, a phrase there, and Avremele, in the manner of a good disciple, stored them up in his heart as if they had been Torah.

Sruli Gol was not in the house. Lately, he had taken to disappearing for long hours at a time. As he left the house, he would sniff the air outside like an animal scenting danger on all sides. Then he would wander about the streets, sometimes standing at the edge of one crowd, sometimes at another, listening to what was said. At other times he slipped into a synagogue or a house of study where again he took note of what was being said as if he was trying to discover something. When he got home and saw that everything was in order—that the thing he was apprehensive about had not happened, then he felt very cheerful and regaled everyone with the news he had brought back from town.

As for instance that the town was in an uproar and was looking for someone on whom to blame its misfortunes. And it had settled on Yokton who that day had been severely beaten. And here Sruli imitated Yokton burying his head in his hood and, from that hiding place, crying as he was beaten, "Help, Jews. They're choking me." He recounted, too, how Yokton's nephew, meaning to use a cabalistic spell to help his uncle, kept crying, "I am my beloved's and my beloved is mine." After which, he, too, was beaten.

He recounted, too, how the town was searching for remedies against its misfortune. For instance they had arranged the marriage of a mute ragpicker to a blind old maid; Sruli told how delighted everyone had been to see the bride being led to the wedding canopy, and how the mute groom recited "Thou art in holy bonds . . ." After that Sruli performed so many other imitations that he made even Luzi laugh.

Another time he told a longer and more detailed story about Avram the convert and his wife Anastasia who, when she was converted had, as was the usual custom, been renamed Sarah, a name that she did not earn because, down to the present moment, it would have been better had she kept her original name, Anastasia.

The story had to do with a convert whom everyone in town, adult or child, knew well. A short, stocky, powerful Ukrainian—a Katzap, as they used to say, who in the days of Nicholas the First served in the army where he achieved the rank of colonel after which, for some reason, he left his own people and became a Jew.

He still retained his "Gentile" strength: he had a vigorous, erect spine and his broad chest still looked as if it were bedecked with the crosses and decorations he had worn while he was in the army. On the other hand, there was a smiling look on his roseate, healthy face that looked both old and young at once, a gentle, yielding in his clear twinkling eyes, as if he had acquired wisdom, or had traded something very good for something even better, and it was because of that smiling look that everyone, but especially children, loved him. Despite his wretched Yiddish and his non-Jewish manners and his bearlike gait rocking back and forth when he walked, despite his broad white flowing beard, meant to look Jewish though it did not, despite all of that he was regarded as a member of the community. Though he was a convert, yet he had been one for so long that no one could imagine the community doing without him anymore than it could do without one of its religious officials.

He performed various good deeds of his own. Every Friday evening he went from house to house carrying a sack into which he put the loaves of bread he begged for the travelers' hostel. His voice could be heard several streets away as he sang a song of his own making in a high voice cracked by age: "Little Jewish children, the dear Sabbath is coming . . ." And so on. And the children, hearing him, gathered around him as they might have gathered around a Gypsy with his monkey, and they followed him, singing along with him. Nor did he drive them away. Quite the reverse. He caressed their heads and was kind to them, because he had no children of his own.

And so he was much loved. His wife on the other hand, Anastasia who, when she was converted had been named Sarah, was not very well liked because it had been clear that she had not been especially happy at all that she had had to do when she left her own people to become a Jew. She had been particularly repelled when she was led into the ill-smelling ritual bath after which she spent a long while spitting to get its taste out of her mouth. And there is reason to think that if it were not for the love she bore her husband, the former soldier in the army of Nicholas the First, she would never have agreed to put up with anything like that.

And her views had not changed despite the years and years she had spent living among Jews. She continued to keep herself aloof, and, with the exception of blessing the Friday-night candles and the offering of white bread (when a bit of the dough is thrown into the fire) and various other ritual deeds that she performed like the other women, she remained in every other respect who she had been so that she was hardly ever counted as a Jewish woman. Her neighbors avoided her and came very rarely to borrow something or to discuss some problem with her the way housewives often do.

She had no children, and that, too, served to keep her apart. For this reason, her husband, who deeply loved his new religion and who desperately wanted to leave a "Kaddish" (a son who would recite the mourner's prayer) when he died, seeing that it was unlikely that they would have a child of their own, urged his wife, Sarah-Anastasia to adopt a boy.

It was easy enough to find one, and they did. A boy, Moshele, a fatherless and motherless orphan. The boy was sent to school and was raised like every other little Moshele with this difference, that Avram the proselyte's wife, Sarah-Anastasia, kept the boy considerably cleaner than his schoolfellows.

And now (Sruli said) Moshele's bar mitzvah was celebrated. It was an event in which the whole community participated. The rabbi who lived in that quarter of the town was there, and the ritual butcher, as well as all the other pious householders of the street where Avram the proselyte lived, as well as the members of the synagogue where he prayed.

Moshele made a speech which, naturally, Avram the proselyte did not understand. Sarah, his wife understood even less. There was a great banquet, with all sorts of food to eat and a variety of spirits to drink. And everybody drank. Avram the proselyte, sitting among the pious folk who were drinking, felt at first a bit constrained, but when finally the liquor relaxed him, he began to utter drunken oaths: "As I am a Jew . . . may I live to see the Messiah, the real, the Jewish Messiah come . . ." And Sarah-Anastasia, his wife, as she was serving people, Anastasia who had evidently also had something to drink, went then, compelled by old habit, into a corner where quietly she crossed herself.

No doubt all those strange Jews, the rabbi, the ritual slaughterer and the others, had frightened her by their behavior, by the way they dressed, so that tipsy as she was she had gone into a corner, back to her old god to whom she prayed that he would protect her from her new coreligionists.

Sruli had other funny details to recount as if he had been there, a guest at the feast.

But these were all humoresques performed by Sruli when he was in a good mood. But lately when he came home from his wanderings in the streets, he had been more and more somber and worried-looking. Why? Because in addition to the various rumors and bits of news which he brought back and treated comically, there was one to which he paid intense and anxious attention: the rumor that the town regarded Luzi's sect as in some way responsible for the troubles that had overtaken it, and that there were plans afoot to get even with them. It was no joke.

And lately whenever Sruli came home from his sorties into town, he would stand quietly contemplating Luzi, as if he hadn't seen him for a long while, or as if he had seen someone with malevolent intent standing behind Luzi. Luzi asked him one day, "What is it you're peering at?" Sruli replied with questions of his own: "Who? Me? No, it's nothing. I was just musing." But if the truth be told, he did have a worried look on his face, as if he had seen the embodiment of a danger which at any moment now he would call by its right name.

For the time being he refrained from naming it. But each time he was about to leave the house, he would move about restlessly, organizing, arranging things so that Luzi was always left in the company of a trusted friend. Recently, he had empowered Avremele to undertake that task. And when Avremele asked him, "What's the point of guarding him like this?" Sruli replied abruptly and without much thought, "It's necessary. If I say it's necessary, you may be sure I have my reasons. But," he added, "it's important that Luzi not be aware that we're doing it." Avremele, studying Sruli, was struck by the seriousness of his demeanor and, without any certain knowledge of what it was all about, he obeyed Sruli and accepted his role as Luzi's guardian.

The same thing was true on the day of which we are about to speak: Sruli was not in the house and Avremele was alone with Luzi who was developing his ideas on the various kinds of suffering that afflict people.

"There is" said Luzi, "the suffering that comes from love of God and the enlargement of the spirit when a person, like a bird struggling in its cage, tries to tear loose from his poor corporeal garb in order to unite himself with the Supreme Essence. It sometimes happens that the bird, driven by its desire to sing, bird fashion, its praise for the Creator, and to be again a bird in nature, from which it was wrested by force . . . it happens then that the bird bruises its head against the bars, and it turns away with revulsion from the small heap of birdseed that is meant to be the price of its caged and compelled song.

"So, too, is it with mankind who aspires to become the purest image of his Creator of which he is a reflection, who aspires to be engulfed in the Whole from which as a particle with neither knowledge or will, he was created. He wants to correct that imbalance by renouncing all that is material in his creation: the two hundred and forty-eight bones and the three hundred and sixty-five sinews which he can feel and touch . . . he renounces them so that he may be worthy to ascend into the heights and wheel above God's spiritual waters from which the first created things emerged, the way the least breath that issues from the nostrils of a newborn infant rises upward.

"There are griefs of a different sort when a person absolutely refuses to turn away from the narrow limits of his mortality. It is so dear to him that he would prefer to be permanently invested in it, to serve forever the shameful instrument of flesh and blood, unwilling to free himself of it even at the coming of the Jubilee—like that slave we know of whose ear was pierced as a sign that he refused his freedom. That is a great decline, when a man has fallen so low that, alas, even his master looks scornfully at him, saying, 'See what you have earned by selling yourself.' And the slave replies, 'I love my Lord. I don't want my freedom. My essence is to serve, slavery is my delight.' And the slave trembles lest he be forced to provide for himself, lest he be deprived of a stick to lean on, of a master whom he can adore and whose shoes he can lick like a dog.

"There are also the sorrows of love, the love of false gods.

"There are," Luzi went on, "Jobian griefs, when a person is tested without his being able to fathom why. And yet the testing has been decreed by a Higher Wisdom and one hopes the reasons for it will one day be revealed to him who is being tested.

"But there are also meaningless sorrows, foolish ones." And here Luzi, who had been going through the various categories of grief, began to explain what he meant by the last one.

All the while Luzi talked, Avremele stood still, gazing at him. Sometimes when he was overwhelmed by the importance of what Luzi was saying, he started from his place and took a couple of vague steps simply to relieve his feelings.

It was after tea, just before the morning prayers. A time when people like these two, rested from their night's sleep and purified by their morning's ablutions, were most relaxed and inclined for such discussions.

Very soon they would begin their prayers, but they lingered in conversation. Luzi was caught up in organizing and intelligently presenting what he had learned in the course of his life, and Avremele, who was much younger than he, listened intently, respectfully, eager to hear and to remember, as among the most cherished memories of his life, every bit of the spiritual and moral wisdom that his teacher uttered.

The house was quiet; that distant quarter of the town where Luzi lived was quiet as it usually was on a winter's morning when the poverty-stricken women of that district were busy behind closed doors with their domestic duties, and the men were at work behind the same closed doors.

Then as Luzi and Avremele were in the midst of their discussion, they heard the sounds of a small crowd of people—as when one distantly hears the outbreak of a quarrel, a fight or some other unusual event.

Luzi, sitting at the table, simply turned his head in the direction of the noise, but Avremele went directly to the window to see what was happening. It was soon evident to them both that the crowd was at no great distance, and that it was in motion and was getting closer and closer—to Luzi's house.

It was a crowd of men and women who had been joined by an assortment of young workers and ne'er-do-wells who grew like weeds in that part of town.

"What is it?" Luzi asked Avremele, surprised at the interruption.

And Avremele at first did not know what to say. But when he perceived that the crowd was getting closer and closer and that everyone's eyes were on Luzi's house and that their goal was in fact that house, he had a dark intuition that whatever was going on, it had not yet happened but rather it was about to begin. Then, remembering, too, what Sruli reiterated each time that he left the house—that he, Avremele was never to leave Luzi alone (words which until that moment he had not understood), he cast a glance at Luzi which Luzi instantly understood to mean that something very unpleasant was in store for him or for his household.

Meanwhile, the approaching mob continued to grow and the voices they heard were beginning to take on a threatening tone. Then all at once there was silence. Luzi's door opened and two people were pushed through the doorway, which they managed to get through though it was too narrow for them both.

They were, first, Yone the tavern keeper whose flushed face, closely cut white beard and goose's waddle identified him at once, and second, a woman so stocky that a woman and a half could have been carved from her. Her girth was an indication, too, that she was married to a man who by making her frequently pregnant had given her plenty of opportunities to expand.

That was Pesye, Sholem the porter's wife. She and Yone were the first to enter. They were followed one by one by men and women, by young laborers and street hooligans whose quilted jackets were draped over their shoulders. Once inside and confronting Luzi, who, astonished and anxious, stood up as if to greet them, they seemed to lose the energy that had impelled them while they were outside.

"Is that him?" said Pesye, egged on evidently by Yone who stuck close beside her.

"Is that him?" replied Yone with a question. "Of course it is. Who else could it be?"

"So, then, you're the one who keeps people from making a living, and who keeps husbands from their wives."

We interrupt our narrative here in order to say what follows: It is hard to know how it happened that these two, Yone and Pesye, had found a way to work together. What sorts of sympathies were at work that made it possible for them to concert an attack against Luzi? It may have been simply a matter of chance. Or perhaps not. Perhaps Yone and his accomplices—of whom he had many in the town, and especially in *this* part of town—sniffed about until they found someone whom they could inveigle into such a venture. And they had found Pesye. Whatever the truth was, these two, Pesye and Yone, had found a common language that enabled them to plan and execute the assault we are now describing.

Pesye was the first to speak; and it was Luzi at first who did not understand what she was talking about or why all the others had crowded into his house and what it was they wanted to accuse him of. He did hear something but he could not understand it. Looking about him at the densely packed mass that had shoved its way into the house, he saw some angry faces while the others looked simply curious while still others showed real fury, and it seemed to him that if he so much as opened his mouth to reply to Pesye that all those mouths before him would speak not only with the reproach she, Pesye, had made first, but with much worse in the way of insults and imprecations as can happen when a mob gets excited.

And so he simply looked on, waiting in confused silence. Avremele, too, who stood at one side and who, like Luzi, had never been in a situation like this, surrounded by a mob without knowing what to say or how to calm it, he, too, stood speechless, unable to help Luzi in any way. Ought he to go into the street to call for help, or should he stay because it would be wrong to leave him alone, for who could say what might happen if Luzi was left face-to-face with such an excited crowd that was capable of God alone knew what?

He waited for someone in the crowd, or all of them together, to indicate more clearly what they had in mind and what it was they wanted of Luzi.

Looking at the people massed before him, Luzi observed that they were of various kinds. Most of them were the merely curious, people who loved a good scandal, the sort who will dance at any wedding whatsoever. Then there were the others, who like Yone were there with other intentions. But there were still others, a smaller number who like Pesye had truly suffered and who came here driven by the pain that was only too visible in their faces.

"What is it you want?" Luzi asked abruptly, turning to Pesye but addressing all those who had crowded into the house and the others who were in the kitchen and in the vestibule as well as those who were still outside. "What is it you want?" a frightened Luzi said to the mob, to the uninvited strangers, to the women who had left their kitchens, and to the men who had come from their workshops bringing with them the smells of paper, of paste, of shoe leather and sawdust.

"What do we want?" someone said, laughing.

"Water to cook gruel
Thread to string pearls."

Apparently it was one of the hooligans, and a sizable portion of the crowd was ready to encourage him with its laughter.

"What do we want?" said Pesye who had been the first to utter her complaint and who now stepped forward with Yone.

Her stance before Luzi was respectful, since she was in the presence of someone like Luzi whose very appearance seemed not to permit disrespect; at the same time, she was conscious that it was he who had been indicated to her as the one chiefly responsible for her sorrows, because he had interfered with her life as a woman by taking from her her breadwinner and had moreover so changed him and separated him from her that she and her husband had lost the intimate and loving language they had used in peace and harmony over many years. "We want you to stop taking away what God has given us."

"What do you mean?"

"Our bread during the week and our white bread on the Sabbath, our children's fathers without whom the children are no better than orphans. Ah woe . . . woe," an excited Pesye cried, turning for sympathy to the crowd. "What is it we've done? And what do they want from men like my Sholem who was not born or bred to this rabbi business: to fast and to wear himself and his family out for the sake of sins he knows nothing about. What is it they want of him? Why can't they let him serve God the way he and his kind do? The way he can. Making a proper living for his family. Where are they taking him? Where are you dragging him?"

"Who's dragging him?"

"You are," Pesye said. "You and your kind who have turned his poor simple head around and hauled him into your pious chicken coop. You who, as far as I can see, have an income, can afford to pray and study as much as you like. But we can't—not people like my Sholem who if he doesn't feed his belly hasn't got the strength to work; and if he doesn't work, he earns nothing; and if he earns nothing, the grocer stops giving credit, and the schoolteacher won't teach the children, and so they turn into scamps who can do nothing. Is that what God wants? Is that the way for Jews to behave?"

"Jews? What Jews?" interrupted Yone the tavern keeper from the sidelines, addressing the crowd like a preacher. He spoke loudly, gesticulating heatedly. "What kinds of Jews are we talking about? Let me tell you what's being said about them in town?" Pointing at Luzi and Avremele, he cried, "Sorcerers and idolaters. That's what they are."

"Sorcerers?" came the voice of a frightened woman in the crowd.

"Yes," Yone continued, with the same momentum. "See him," he said, pointing to Luzi, "him with his holier-than-thou look. But the fact is that he's a prime hypocrite and the one responsible for all of our troubles. And he's supported by his brother, Moshe Mashber, the bankrupt who's robbed old folk and widows and orphans who entrusted to him their last pennies without receipts, without notes of any kind, because they counted on his integrity. And he betrayed them all, and set them adrift.

"Of course it's true. Since he's neither a rabbi nor a rebbe what does he live on if not his brother's ill-gotten gains? Or else, as is whispered in the town, he does forbidden things with the little bone he's taken from a corpse.

"We have to put a stop to all the wicked things they do in the dark," the flushed and drink-excited Yone cried. "If the town is embarrassed to do it, if they don't want to get their hands dirty, well then we're here, and here he is before us, looking scared and guilty. Well then, let's make him confess the evil he's been doing or else we'll tear him apart and destroy his filthy nest. Let him do it now, at once. Let him speak. We can't wait another minute because who knows, if we let him go now, he may disappear and continue to do his evil from his hiding place."

"That's right." The mob, hearing Yone, grew sullen. Not only those who like Pesye had come here oppressed by real grief, but those, too, who had merely come as spectators of what might prove to be an interesting scene, began to edge away as if they feared not only some uncanny power near them but Luzi, too, who controlled it, and who at any moment might direct it at them.

Yone noticed that, and still flushed from the success of his earlier speech, he plunged on to make a second one, though one would be hard put to say where he found the words that came to him.

"There's no need to put it off. We have to do what needs to be done, *now*, at once. Because, as you see and as you have just heard from her own mouth"—here he indicated Pesye—"this fellow and all those of his persuasion have reached such a pass that they and those whom they corrupt have no need (*ptui, ptui*) for women in the normal way of the world, but they do what they need to do—men with men (*ptui, ptui*) . . . it's not to be spoken of."

There was a gasp, and again the frightened crowd retreated a pace to avoid being near Luzi and Avremele who stood still and turned paler and paler which the mob read as a sign that the charges Yone was making about them were true.

"Asses. Donkeys," someone cried, and it was soon clear that shortly other cries would follow uttering worse insults than the first one.

"Bankrupts! Corrupters!" came from the midst of the excited crowd.

"Rams and goats."

"Trousers with trousers," cried several of the young street hooligans who were delighted with Yone's charges and who took the occasion to give each other significant winks and to whisper and poke each other in the ribs. "Behhh, mehhhh." Evidently this hateful joke affected Luzi and Avremele more than the preceding serious and threatening outcries, because it was suddenly clear who it was that was judging them, and that words would not suffice to exonerate them in any way. Because whatever the mob with its mixture of serious or ill-intentioned people in it decided, there were certain to be eager volunteers to carry out its decree.

The situation was bad. There were outcries from all sides, "Shabbatarians! . . . Bankrupts . . . The money of widows and orphans . . . men with men . . . bread with bread."

"Why are you silent? How can you tolerate such a thing?" cried several others, inciting each other as they pointed to Luzi and Avremele, who stood paralyzed beside him as was Luzi himself who saw that the crowd was at once surging toward them even as, for the moment, it was still restrained, since, being still unsure of themselves, no one wanted to be the first to attack.

"Goddamned plagues coming from God alone knows where to descend on our heads to our destruction. Because of them, our children have the scurvy. We're all of us endangered by them."

"Rams and billy goats! *Meh, meh. Fee, fi, fo.*" This was followed by a piercing whistle by one of the more excited street toughs who carried his vest over one shoulder.

The situation was so bad that any moment now one could expect what often happens at moments like this: that someone from the mob would step forward who meant to settle the score against Luzi and Avremele with his fists. And indeed that seemed about to happen, because one of Yone's accomplices, evidently hired by him to do precisely that, approached Luzi and was on the verge of grasping him by the collar meaning to shake him—or worse, grabbing him by the beard or slapping him resoundingly in the face.

It was about to happen, but just then a new voice was heard coming from Luzi's doorway. The voice of someone who, it appeared, had come in inadvertently and who, seeing what was happening, let out a yell which was heard over the racket of the jostling mob.

"What's going on here?" cried Sruli in the voice of a master of the house who coming home without warning finds an unexpected and noisy crowd in his home. "Who are you?" he demanded. "Who's brought you here?

"Out! Every last one of you. I don't want to see so much as a hair of your heads," he cried more loudly still as he pushed his way through the crowd toward Luzi and Avremele who, as he could see, were in imminent danger.

"Who is he?" came the countercry from the mob, uttered, it would seem, by another of Yone's accomplices or perhaps by Yone himself who, if Sruli had not appeared just then, had intended to direct whatever action was to follow.

Sruli made no reply. Silently, he approached Luzi, and with an authoritative gesture as from an older man to a younger one who needs to be looked after, he pointed toward Luzi's room. Its door was closed and Sruli opened it for him so Luzi could enter. That done, Sruli directed Avremele to stand with his full height and his arms outstretched before the door in order to prevent anyone's getting through.

When that was done, and when a pale, stunned Luzi, followed by jeers and threats, was more or less safe behind the door and in his own room, and when Avremele, following Sruli's orders, had taken his place before the door and stood there, like one crucified . . . it was only when all that was accomplished that Sruli turned to peer into the mob to find, if he could, who in it was responsible for its being there.

It did not take him long. He identified his head among the many thronged together in the room. Yone, who always stood out by his extortioner's massive build, his broad shoulders that took up considerable space even in tight quarters. Sruli took one look at him and . . . it may be that he had overheard Yone's inciting words as he, Sruli, came into the room or he may not have heard them but he intuited their import and understood at once that Yone was the ringleader, the one who had egged on to the attack those who were otherwise innocent, as well as those who were of his cohort with whom he had arranged to be at a particular place at a particular time.

It was all clear to Sruli then, and he cried out, "Ah, Yone. The fellow who always takes the town's side and whose face and neck therefore get redder and redder. There he is, the do-gooder who always looks out for your interests. Wherever there's thievery afoot, he has his share in it; wherever there's some dirty business to be done, he is the first to be consulted. When you're young he gets a rake-off from your weddings. And from your poverty when you get old. And from your illness when you have to go to the hospital. As a member of the Burial Society he profits even from your deaths when you have to be sent to the cemetery. He gets his cut, from the living and the dead."

"That's right," came a voice from the densely packed crowd. And it was clear then that Sruli had succeeded in turning the mob's anger from Luzi toward someone else.

And here, let no one wonder that Sruli was not frightened when he came into the house and saw all the commotion, as if he had walked into a lion's den, and that he acted instead with great courage and with such firm vigor not only to hide Luzi, but more than that, to attack his attacker as he had just attacked Yone . . . let no one be surprised, because what else could Sruli have done who had been so stunned by the unexpected scene he had come upon that it had seemed to him that there was only one thing, surprising even to himself, that would work on the howling mob the way one dashes a glass of cold water into the face of an overexcited man.

And the distraction almost worked, but the mob soon understood that it had been deceived. And that what had brought them excitedly together from all sides was suddenly gone. Those who like Pesye had come meaning to utter their real griefs were now deprived of the person to whom they had meant to pour out their hearts—Luzi. The others who had come along for the sake of curiosity or for the simple fun of it were now deprived of the hoped-for spectacle. Again, Luzi.

They stood, feeling cheated, like children who have had a toy snatched from them and who find themselves suddenly empty-handed and who neither know what has happened to the toy nor what to do with their hands.

So now they turned upon Sruli who, it was clear, had frustrated their desires. "Who is he? Who is this fellow?" came the cries of those who did not know Sruli, while those who knew him shouted, "What's he doing here, the bum? That beggar who hasn't got a home of his own. What the devil brings him here? Who needs him?"

"What's going on," cried Yone who had now recovered from the splash of cold water he had received from Sruli. "Who is this fellow who has no father, no roof of his own, and who comes from the devil only knows where? From chains and bars where he was sent for making counterfeit money. Or for something else as vile. Look at him. There stands a man whom nobody has ever seen pray or study or do a day's work. Lately, he hasn't even made his begging rounds. So the question is, how does he get his living unless it's from the dark doings that go on here?

"And as for that one," Yone pointed to Avremele who stood like a crucifix, with outspread arms before Luzi's door. "Just see how the two of them have connived to protect and hide the man we had before us, how they have kept us from giving him his just desserts."

"You!" It was a cry meant to come to Yone's assistance and to spare him from going on with his speech; it came from a fellow who now appeared before Sruli, his fist clenched before his face. It was clear that that fist would very soon meet that face and that Sruli's would be awash in blood, or that he and several of his front teeth would part company. But just then Sruli turned abruptly, and running to the double window that had been sealed with padding to keep the winter cold out, he tore the inner window open and an instant later the outer one as well. Hardly another instant passed and Sruli was half out of that window—not at all intending to run away, but simply to make it possible for him to get his head outdoors so he could cry out, as now he did, "Police, police. Here . . ."

Sruli knew very well that there was no point in shouting "Police," because in that part of town there was never so much as the shadow of a policeman to be seen . . . except on those rare occasions when the police stumbled into the neighborhood to have their palms greased, or when they were sent by the town's higher authorities on some special assignment. Though Sruli knew all that, yet he cried "Police," first because he had no other option, and second because he instinctively knew that the word itself would have a cooling effect on the mob.

And as it turned out he was right. The crowd, though there was not the slightest trace of a policeman to be seen, turned fearful. First of the word itself, and then of the remote possibility that Sruli might by pure coincidence have seen a policeman nearby. That was all they needed—especially that half-innocent part of the crowd that did not belong to Yone's cohort—to believe that a brass-buttoned uniform representing power and law and order might appear at any moment either in the window or at the door.

Well, there were no volunteers for a meeting with officials. The result was that the dense crowd began a hasty exit from the house. And shortly there were only Yone's cronies left, but even with Yone at their head, they had lost their earlier momentum. And with the room half-empty their combativeness, too, faded away.

And so those fellows who wore their jackets hung over their shoulders began to edge toward the walls and closer to the door. Finally, they, too, left the house, though it's true that they continued to mutter threats between their teeth, "Never mind . . . we'll see . . . when we meet them"—meaning Luzi's followers—". . . they'll get theirs . . . break every bone . . . Never mind. If not today, a day will come . . ."

Finally, Sruli, who all this while had been straddling the window, seeing that they were all gone, climbed back into the room. First he closed the outer window then the inner one. Then approaching Avremele who stood like a statue before Luzi's door, his arms still outstretched, he released him from his task. Then he went into Luzi's room. Luzi was, as was only to be expected, considerably depressed. Sruli then, without preamble, because he, too, had just been through a great strain . . . Sruli said, "As you see, Luzi, I was right to say that the town was planning some ugly thing. I think you ought to know that what just happened is merely the prelude of the play that is yet to come. A test. A beginning whose consequences, fortunately for us, we have been able to escape. But those who are out to get us have not put up their weapons. And after this first, unsuccessful attempt, there'll be another that may prove successful. It could all end very shamefully . . . with you paraded out of town in a dung cart, which is what they do to people they hate. Well, what do you think, Luzi? Haven't I been right in telling you to get out of town?"

"Yes," Luzi replied, staring at Sruli, "you have," he said, still stunned by all that had happened. "You have been right," he echoed, his lips pale.

VIII

Sruli Gol Prepares to Travel

In the evenings that followed the events described above, Sruli could often be seen fussing with the knapsack that he carried with him when he went on his annual after-summer wanderings. He had found it in some out-of-the-way corner where it had lain, long unused. When he found it he studied it for a while and concluded that it was not large enough for all that he planned to put into it later, and so to enlarge it he cut its seams and sewed in additional canvas to enlarge it. He also sewed on an additional strap so that he could carry it over both shoulders instead of, as he had always previously done, over one shoulder only. And late one evening after he had modified the knapsack to accommodate to his new plans, he even tried fitting into it all the things he would need personally as well as the things Luzi would require, such as prayer shawls, phylacteries, linens and Sabbath garments. When the knapsack was well packed, he put his arms through both armholes and tried it on to see whether it was light or heavy, comfortable or not, and whether now that he had enlarged it, everything was in order. And when everything checked out, a smile of quiet satisfaction appeared on his face.

Once he had finished remaking his knapsack, Sruli took to disappearing during the morning hours ... particularly on Sundays and Wednesdays, which were light market days. Sruli could then be seen wandering about in the various marketplaces, looking into people's faces as if he were hoping to recognize someone in the general chaos. He seemed to be especially interested in those who were shabbily dressed, unemployed and even those who were not especially bright.

And one morning that was precisely what he found. A twenty-year-old Gentile lad with a clerical overgarment that reached down to the ground and was tied at the waist. He wore, too, a shabby velvet hood which indicated that he had once been in a monastery which he had for various reasons chosen to leave or from which he had been sent away because of his clumsiness.

The moment Sruli saw him, he went up to him and struck up a conversation. Clearly the fellow pleased him, because it was not very long before they were both seen moving through the crowd evidently on some errand upon which they had agreed. Sruli walked in front, empty-handed, and the Gentile youth followed, carrying a bundle which, it seemed, held in it all that he owned and which he had taken with him when he left the monastery.

Sruli meant to make a watchman of this youth whom he led out of the market, then through the streets of the town until they came to Moshe Mashber's house. But he did not, as would have been normal, take him into the house so that he could discuss the terms of his employment with his prospective employers. Instead, Sruli had him wait outside Mikhalko's hut while he, Sruli, went into the house where, meeting with Moshe Mashber's daughter, Yehudis, he said abruptly, "I've brought you a watchman for your courtyard. He can help around the house as well."

Yehudis heard what he had to say and made no reply. But in effect she assented with her silence as she would have consented to any proposal whatever that Sruli might have made, knowing that he could have made himself the master of the house and that he had not done so out of simple goodwill.

Yehudis had seen him lately, sometimes in the morning, sometimes later in the day, wandering about in the courtyard, doing nothing at all. He never came into the house to report what he was up to. No one inquired whether he needed anything, and Sruli offered no explanations of why he was there. Until now, when as the culmination of several recent visits, he had come into the house to say that he had hired a watchman.

Now why was it that Sruli installed him here? It may be that Sruli hired the watchman because, seeing how the house and grounds had been neglected and realizing, too, that, come summer, the garden, too, would suffer, a sense of pride of ownership was awakened. Or none of that may be true. It may only have been a caprice.

Whatever his reasons, Sruli hired the Gentile to be a watchman, and after showing him Mikhalko's hut where he would have his quarters, Sruli gave him terse instructions about his duties in the yard and in the house.

And we say that it was well done. Because the slightly dim-witted youth adapted himself quite well to the Mashber household and to his house and yard duties. Simpleminded, silent, smiling frequently to himself, he had no complaints against the world which had let fall into his hands some tiny portion of its riches.

Because, indeed, he did not need much: he had no need of superfluous clothing since he had no one before whom to display himself or whose friendship he sought, with the possible exception of a cat sometimes, or a lost dog or, later, in summer, with the birds in the garden whom he knew well, their names and their characteristic song in the morning when they waked as well as in the evening before they slept. Moreover, he ate very little, contenting himself with a bowl of hot water into which he crumbled the loaf of bread which every morning and evening he was given in the kitchen.

Yes. We say that he fitted nicely into the impoverished Mashber household generally, and he got on particularly well with several members of the family, like Alter, with whom, at their very first meeting, he established a friendship without having so much as uttered a word.

Only an artist could properly depict the way Vassily (the ex-novice's name) stood one morning in the garden into which he had wandered with no particular purpose, raised his eyes and encountered Alter, who was looking out of his attic window; and how these two, with a mixture of astonishment, distance and familiarity, regarded each other; and how despite the differences in their origins (Alter, a Jew, Vassily, a Christian), they felt a fraternal bond between them, possibly because each of them was a man with a diminished destiny; and how they let their mingling glances and their smiles take the place of speech between them as they looked at each other. A true tableau.

Sometimes they encountered each other more nearly and carried on brief, half-incoherent conversations in which gestures more than speech were involved. Vassily's eyes, Russian and cornflower blue, looked warmly into Alter's equally warm dark Jewish gaze.

At summer's end, a similiar sort of comradeship was established between Vassily and Mayerl, Moshe Mashber's grandson. These two sometimes spent hours silently together—first because Mayerl could not speak Russian, and then because there was nothing to talk about with Vassily. But Mayerl would sit or lie beside him under a tree and listen to Vassily singing a monastery melody, or listen to him as he carried on a conversation with some bird of his acquaintance, imitating birdsong so exactly that one could not tell which was the man and which the bird.

And so we say that Sruli did well in hiring Vassily. Later, Sruli did something else. A few days after he had installed the watchman, he showed up again at Moshe Mashber's house, and encountering Yehudis once more in the dining room, he broached a new subject to her.

"You do know, don't you, that your father owes me money?"

"I know," a perplexed Yehudis replied.

"And you know that the house has been signed over to me and that I have the right to treat it as my own—and I haven't exercised that right?"

"Yes, of course I know," Yehudis replied, stammering a little with confusion and the fear that now on top of all their other problems a new one was about to surface. She studied Sruli's every feature as if hoping to discover why he was putting his questions to her. "Of course I know," she said again. "I know very well that you haven't treated us the way other people in the same situation would have. On the contrary . . ."

"Well now," said Sruli, interrupting her, "let me ask you to consider. What if I were a married man . . . and what if I wanted . . . not the whole house, but merely a single room in which to install my family? What would you say? Would you be against it?"

"Good Lord, no. You have the right. You can do anything you like. But . . ." and here Yehudis was a trifle embarrassed, "I had no idea that you had a family."

"No. Not actually a family, but people very close to me for whom I am anxious to provide."

"By all means," Yehudis said, relieved because it was evidently not a question of the whole house but only of a single room. "By all means, let them use it in good health. Come, we'll pick out a room right this minute. They can move right in—today . . . tomorrow."

There were tears in her eyes which she did her best to hide from Sruli, but he did notice them and was therefore very, very careful about selecting the room. He made his choice quickly, choosing the smallest one, one that was fairly removed from the center of the house so that its inhabitants would disturb the family as little as possible.

Later when he had done his business with Moshe Mashber's daughter, he could be seen in that poverty-stricken part of town where Mikhl Bukyer's house was. He was seen going into the courtyard, then bending so he could enter the low doorway into the house.

He stayed in the house for some little time, and it would appear he carried on a serious and lengthy conversation with Mikhl Bukyer's widow as he persuaded and cajoled her to agree to some project of his own.

"Why?" she demanded, perplexed by what he had proposed. "Why to *them*? Into such a wealthy household. Isn't it better to stay here, where I am, where I'm used to things . . . (if only the rent money can be found)?"

"But you haven't got the rent money," Sruli said irritably. "And there you can stay free."

Hearing Sruli's last words, Mikhl Bukyer's wife allowed herself to be persuaded. What options did she have?

The next morning at the same hour of the day, Sruli could be seen driving a wagon into her courtyard. And a little while later such poverty-stricken remnants of furniture as she still possessed were put into the wagon: an aged, worn-out chest of drawers, worm-eaten wooden beds that had been handed down through generations, a folding bed whose mattress was stuffed with straw, and other household objects of the same sort on which the youngest members of the household, a boy and a girl, were seated astride. Mikhl Bukyer's widow and her grown daughter walked behind the wagon. The driver, leading his horse, walked in front accompanying that wagonload of household goods through the town on their way to a street and to a courtyard in which such a rickety wagon carrying such a dismal and bulging load had never been seen before.

Evidently the arrival of people and furniture had been arranged in advance, because as soon as the wagon turned into the courtyard, Yehudis, Moshe Mashber's daughter, came out of the house to the courtyard gate to greet them, the way one customarily greets guests to whom one ought (or wishes) to be friendly.

It should be clear that this time Yehudis was not especially enthusiastic. There is no doubt that she would have preferred to seem more spontaneous. But when she saw Mikhl Bukyer's widow and the children to whom all those household goods belonged, she could not help turning to Sruli and in the tone of a rich man's daughter, inquiring as she indicated the loaded wagon, "Why did they bring all that? There's plenty of furniture in the house for all their needs." Her subvert message was, "Up till now, I've yielded to you. Now, it's your turn." The shabby sticks of furniture made her quail.

Sruli, for his part, put up no resistance. No harm would come to Mikhl Bukyer's widow and so he undertook to persuade her that neither she nor her bits of furniture would be injured if they were stored in some empty room in the house for a while.

At first the widow was unwilling to be parted from the things to which over so many years she had become accustomed. But when Sruli said, and frequently repeated, that it was all being done for her own good, and that she would not lose a single stick of her furniture, and that anything she might need would be provided for her, she finally acquiesced.

Though it must be said that after she yielded, her eyes looked longingly after her furniture as it was being carried away to some distant part of the house, as if she felt the depth of the insult to which they were being subjected.

Finally, with Sruli at her side she entered the house empty-handed. Sruli introduced her to Yehudis, to whom he hinted delicately that she should not condescend to Mikhl's wife, and to Mikhl's wife that she was not to regard herself as in any way an inferior. As he was leaving, Sruli turned back to tell Mikhl's wife not to be backward about offering to help around the house if she saw ways that she could be useful, and that she should think of herself as a servant who, instead of being paid money, was being housed rent free.

And so that was accomplished: Mikhl Bukyer's widow and her children were installed in the Mashber residence. It was an idea that could have occurred only to Sruli.

And now there was a third thing that Sruli did.

One day when Luzi had gone to visit Moshe's family and Sruli and Avremele Lubliner, who had not yet left N., were together in Luzi's house, Sruli took a bottle of brandy from his pocket and, approaching Avremele, said, "I hope you won't say no to a little drink."

"Why now? It's neither a holiday nor the first of the month." Avremele shrugged, meaning to decline Sruli's offer. First because there was no public occasion for drinking, and then because he could not understand what was prompting Sruli to invite him to drink now since Sruli, from the very first moment that Avremele appeared in Luzi's house, had kept his distance and had treated him as if he were not even there.

"It's the anniversary of the death of one of my parents."

"An anniversary," Avremele said, astonished. "Then why didn't you observe it during morning prayers and in the presence of a minyan?"

"I don't believe in the minyan. I prefer to observe it personally."

"What do you mean?" Avremele inquired, even as Sruli, clearing the table, found a couple of glasses somewhere and was already pouring brandy into them as if Avremele had already agreed to drink.

"L'khaim," said Sruli, raising his filled glass and holding it out toward Avremele so that he, to keep from shaming Sruli, was constrained to raise his glass as well and for the sake of appearances to put it to his lips as he replied, "L'khaim."

"L'khaim," Sruli repeated, and Avremele was struck again by Sruli's elevated mood, as if he had already downed more than one glass of the brandy.

And then Sruli, in a great gush of speech, began to talk in a way that Avremele, in all the while he had lived in Luzi's house, had never seen before. Usually, Sruli, silent and aloof, had kept to himself. As if no one interested him, as if he did not want to be involved with any of those who hovered around Luzi ... like Avremele, for instance, to whom he had never spoken directly and whom he seemed always to have regarded as an interloper.

But now, to the amazement of Avremele, Sruli talked. He moved rapidly from subject to subject and then, as if involuntarily, Luzi's name was in his mouth and Sruli found himself talking compulsively about him.

"L'khaim," he said. "I drink to Luzi, too, to whom I am very attached and who deserves to have a health drunk to him. You don't think so?" He turned his half-drunken irritation on Avremele as if he suspected him of disagreeing with him.

"Oh, no. Quite the contrary," said Avremele who as a fervent admirer of Luzi's who had always been too shy to express that admiration in public now felt himself compelled to do so before Sruli. "Of course he does. He ..."

"Well, in that case," Sruli said, catching at his words, "if you really are capable of appreciating his worth, then you may be in a position to understand how ridiculous the prophet Elisha, the prophet Elijah's disciple, must have seemed when seeing Elijah ascending into Heaven, Elisha burst into tears like a child abandoned by his father and cried, 'My father, my father, the chariot of Israel ...' because he had not intelligence enough to encompass what was beyond him."

"What is your point?" asked Avremele, looking at Sruli as if what he said made no sense, like the words of a man half mad.

"My point is that there was a time when I saw you in the role of an Elisha."

"When, how?" Avremele said, still unable to understand.

"You don't remember? Well, try to remember the night awhile ago when Luzi took his leave of you, when he made his confession to you. When he told you that he was thinking of leaving town, of leaving the work he was doing here in God's service for another somewhere else. And you did not understand. And you wept like a child at his ascension . . . that is to say at the prospect of his taking his own road instead of following the beaten path."

Yes, Avremele remembered. And now hearing what Sruli had just said, he was struck by what was suddenly revealed to him: that he and Sruli shared the same goal though their methods for achieving it were different.

"Go on. You can tell me that you think I'm wrong," Sruli said as if demanding something from Avremele.

"No, you're right," he said as he studied Sruli—that strange person who had revealed that he could be as spiritually moved by Luzi as he, Avremele. "How is it that he is suddenly endowed with a quality that no one has ever suspected before?"

Sruli understood what Avremele was thinking and was delighted by it. It prompted him to sing Luzi's praises again in the accents of a King Solomon praising his Shulamite. And Avremele, who would not have believed just a little while ago when he had been invited to join Sruli at the table that such a withdrawn and surly fellow . . . who seemed entirely indifferent to all that happened in Luzi's house, and even to Luzi himself . . . Avremele would not have believed Sruli to be capable of talking with a fervor so intense that it seemed he would be compelled at any moment to move from speech to dance.

And indeed Sruli got to his feet, and whether it was the effect of the brandy or whether it was because his hitherto concealed feelings of admiration for Luzi suddenly surfaced—or whether it was both together, we do not know—but all at once he began a paean of praise for Luzi such as a father might have uttered for a beloved child or, better, such as might have come from a child in whom the floodgates of affection for its father had burst.

"I swear," said Sruli, among other things that he imparted to Avremele as if he were confiding secrets, "that I have seen him in a vision walking around a row of lighted candles lighted in memoriam to previous generations. He tended them well, he trimmed their wicks. Nevertheless, the candles seemed about to go out because their wax was dwindling away. The only hope left against the oncoming darkness was that Luzi had secreted an additional candle in his lap which for the time being he showed no one, saving it for when the world should grow dark.

"You know," continued Sruli, as if he was imparting another secret, "it is said that Luzi in his youth was a great dancer at Hasidic celebrations and at the courts of the rebbes. In those days he used to dance around the illumination of others, but now that he is older, wiser, he dances around his own secret candle set in a silver candelabrum on the ground. He hardly lifts the skirts of his coat when he dances and there is not the slightest breeze to make the candle flame tremble as he moves carefully, delicately, around it, as in a magic circle.

"I could swear—" Sruli was about to go on but then as if he was suddenly aware that he had drunk too much, he interrupted himself and said, "I'm babbling away, isn't that so?"

"No, on the contrary," said Avremele, encouraging him to continue because he, Avremele, would be pleased to hear more.

Sruli obliged him, and in the same spirit with which he had begun, he went on to elaborate his praise of Luzi which, once again, so enraptured Avremele that had there been a third person there he would have believed that at any moment the two of them, both Sruli and Avremele, would get up from the table and, taking each other's hands, would, in unison, utter praises to him whom Sruli had been exalting, only to be joined in the course of the conversation by Avremele who employed the same tone.

It would not have taken very much for that actually to happen, first, because of the drink that Sruli, willingly, and Avremele, unwillingly, had swallowed, and also—and this is the heart of the matter—both Sruli and Avremele felt such high regard for the man under whose roof they now happened to be that despite the fact that he, the object of their reverence, was not in the house so that his near presence could not be felt coming through the wall from his bedroom, still, the movement of his ever-present breath in the air sufficed to transform their workaday thoughts and to give them a Sabbath quality when they talked about him who was capable of inebriating them even when they were sober, and much more so now, when they had been drinking. But suddenly Sruli's mood unaccountably darkened and he lapsed into silence. "What's the matter?" Avremele asked. "What's bothering you?"

"I'm angry."

"At whom?"

"At you."

"What have I done?"

"I'm not angry at what you *have* done but at what you might do."

"What is that?"

"You wanted to make Luzi change his mind about his decision to go on a pilgrimage—and that, in my best judgment, would have been very bad for him in every way."

"Why?"

"*Al te'iru v'al te'uru*. That is, Do not awake or provoke Luzi to alter his decision. For one thing it'll do you no good since he is not one of those hasty thinkers who do not consider their actions, and then keep in mind the attack he has just been through. You may be sure that matter will not end there, and if Luzi decided to leave after the first attack, he will hardly change his mind after a second or a third. No. I don't think you understand what is at stake here, what his enemies are prepared to do to shame him. It's not a matter to be taken lightly."

"No, of course not. I understand," Avremele said, agreeing with Sruli partly because he was persuaded, partly, too, because the brandy had softened him and made him agreeable. "I haven't said anything to him. I haven't even thought about saying anything. As you see I'm getting ready to leave town. And since the night you spoke of, neither he nor I have said anything further about the matter."

"In that case, good," said Sruli. And it was clear that the drunkenness of his drinking bout with Avremele was gone. And that the invitation to him had been nothing more than a ruse that had given Sruli a chance to unburden himself to him.

That, then, was the third thing Sruli had to accomplish before he could be on his way.

There was one more thing he had to do:

This time he waited for an occasion when he was alone in the house with Luzi. He came into Luzi's room quietly, as if on tiptoe. As soon as he was inside he turned and hooked the door chain.

Luzi gave him an inquiring look and asked him why he had latched the door, and whether he had some secret to impart.

"No," said Sruli. "I have no secrets. But I do want to clear up an important matter. I want to ask whether when you leave N. your intention is to go to some other town, or do you mean simply to begin your pilgrimage and choose a place to settle in later on?"

"The second," Luzi replied.

"In that case," said Sruli, "I have something else I want to ask you. Would you mind if I went with you? I could be useful since I'm an experienced traveler."

"That would be just fine," Luzi said, casting a warm look at Sruli. "You've just anticipated my own wish. I've been planning to put that very question to you."

"Really." Sruli's face was radiant with relief, because when he had entered Luzi's room, he had been in an agony of doubt lest Luzi should deny him his secret wish. Now that he had heard what he had so desperately wanted to hear, he felt so exalted that he did not think he could contain himself.

Then like a child who has received an utterly unexpected gift, he found himself uttering warm expressions of reassurance and loyalty as well as (Who can say why?) a stream of jokes and buffooneries, of which he always had a plentiful supply.

"You can be sure that I'll prove useful before the trip as well as on it. For instance," he said, going right on without a pause, "I've been getting my knapsack ready. It'll do for two; and there's a needle and thread with which to sew our clothes, as well as a shofar for the Messiah in the event we meet him riding upon an ass." Though Sruli spoke soberly, there was a musing smile on his face as if he was already seeing Luzi and himself on some morning or evening, hand in hand, sharing their pilgrimage, making their way across some distant field.

Seeing the look of delight on Sruli's face because his hidden desires were going to be fulfilled, Luzi also smiled, pleased by Sruli's joy. And it seemed that when Luzi's smile reached Sruli, Sruli, had such a thing been permitted, would have thrown himself at Luzi's feet to kiss the hem of his garment.

Luzi, meaning to cool a little Sruli's extreme ardor, put a practical question to him: "So you really have made everything ready?"

"Yes," said Sruli, grateful to Luzi because he had prevented him from expressing his joy in a humiliating fashion, "everything is ready. Including a blade for a ritual slaughterer, and a knife for a circumciser, just in case there's a chicken to be killed in a village or some farmer's son to circumcise.

"And I have, too, a bundle of talismans to give to country wives who have not had children either from their husbands or from the wagon drivers with whom they sometimes have to spend the night in some wood or field on their way to market towns."

Sruli went on and on in this vein, uttering vulgarities and obscenities which he would not have permitted himself to speak at any other time. But when Sruli after the third and the fourth such tale seemed inclined to continue, Luzi, who had listened good-humoredly until then, turned his head away as an indication that the discussion was over. That it was time for Sruli to unlatch the door and go.

And just as Sruli had come in quietly and as it were on tiptoe, so he now left the room in the same way except for the look of happiness on his face.

Leaving Luzi's room, Sruli's joy was so great that at first he did not know what to do with himself. For a while he simply stood in a daze, rubbing his hands for pleasure. Then he wandered into the kitchen where was the folding bed on which he usually slept, but now he could not think *why* he was there. Was he meant to undress or not? He started to take his caftan off and ended in a brown study sitting on the edge of the bed, his arm through one sleeve of the caftan.

Little by little he got himself ready for bed. The minute his head touched the pillow, he whispered, "Enough for today, Sruli. Good night and sweet dreams."

And there is reason to believe that his wish was fulfilled.

He dreamed he saw a plain on which there were no trees to be seen and no birds in the air. But far on the bright horizon, there were two men about whom one could not yet be sure whether they were coming from the horizon or going somewhere else, and one had the sense that one of them was being led and that the other was leading him.

"That's us. That's Luzi and me," Sruli said.

For a while he waited, then the horizons of the earth and sky suddenly contracted and the two men who had been hardly visible were now so close to him that he could have reached out his hand to touch them.

"That's us . . . ?"

"Yes," said the man who seemed to serve the other one.

"Well, where are we going?"

"Into the wide world, carrying this pack," said the man, indicating it with a backward movement of his head.

"And what's in it?"

"Almonds and raisins / For snacks and for trading," said the servitor in the same comic vein Sruli had employed earlier, and he would have gone on that way but the man whom he served gave him such a stern look that his witticisms died in his throat.

Then, more soberly, the servant took the knapsack and unbound it and Sruli, looking into it, saw tiny souls with no bodies, only faces. They looked like beads on a string. They were grimacing in pain. But in addition to their sorrow, there radiated from them also a sense of hope not only for themselves but for everyone, for every suffering soul in the world that waited for redemption.

"Well, if that's how things are," Sruli said, "then *my* place is in the knapsack, too." And he was prepared to be strung on the same string, but just then he woke up. He sat up in bed and his hand touched his own knapsack . . . the one he had worked over, getting it ready for his journey. He wondered now how it came to be in the bed with him. Had he put it there deliberately, or had he, in his bedazzled state, done it unawares?

IX
Winter's End

It was already the Purim season. The Jewish calendar showed that it was time for the Judgments-Offerings section of the Bible to be read in the synagogue. It was a time when primary-school children no longer came home from school in the dark, trooping out of lanes and alleys following tin or paper lanterns, singing as they walked,

Teacher, teacher is a liar,
His nose is as long as a telegraph wire.

Often during the day patches of the sky showed pure blue amid rifts in the clouds, and at night the entire vault of the heavens seemed as if purified and studded with glistening stars, one more indication that soon someone with sharp ears would hear by day, but especially by night, the distant wild cry of flocks of birds returning from their last year's homes in the south and now northward bound.

In a word, signs upon signs that winter was declining.

Sometimes on a Saturday morning and sometimes even on a week-day morning, bright drops of water began to flow down roofs and into gutters. Again, a sign that the worst of the cold was over, and that the birds would soon be more likely to find food than while it had been winter.

And it was on such a morning that Moshe Mashber was called to the office of the prison director. There, the director, who seemed to be regarding Moshe with a more friendly sympathy than usual, told him that he was free and could go home. "On foot if you like, or if you want to avoid the long walk through town, in a carriage if you are willing to pay for it."

All this was the result of the intervention of important people in the town who had petitioned the proper authorities for Moshe's release on the grounds that the law allowed for some diminution of penalties for reasons of health and so on. And they requested, therefore, that Moshe Mashber be freed before the full term of his sentence.

The petition was granted. And no doubt it was a great boon for Moshe, but evidently the boon came a bit too late—as we will soon learn.

Moshe left the director's office and returned to his cell block where he reported that he had been freed. As he was gathering his things together for his return home, his fellow convicts, wearing stamped jackets and round visorless caps on their partly shaved heads, gathered around, their eyes fixed on his hands. Moshe understood what they meant and he immediately distributed among them the things he had brought from home—everything but the objects his religion required; his prayer shawl and phylacteries. His clothes, pillowcases, quilt and pillow he turned over to one of the prisoners who would sell them for money that would buy the drink with which they would all toast his freedom.

The things were received gratefully. And just as Moshe's relationship to the other prisoners had been good, thanks to the intervention of the *starost*, the man from Novorossisk, so now their farewells were warm and without any trace of envy, particularly when they saw the items in the *starost*'s hands and calculated their worth and imagined the drinks they would be able to buy with the money.

They wished him Godspeed. Several of them looked closely at him, and others, seeing how emaciated he had become, shook their heads, saying, "Well, if it comes to that, it's better to die at home in one's own bed among loved ones."

They were right to wish him that. They recalled that several times since his arrival in the prison, he had been sent to the hospital, and that he had stayed there several weeks at a time and had come back to the cell block showing no improvement. In fact each time there had been a decline in his health—and his cheekbones, like those of a corpse, showed more prominently under his beard.

All of the inmates bade him farewell. Only the *starost*, the block leader, who wore a tin earring, the fellow with the untrimmed beard whose upper lip was shaved so closely it showed blue—only he stood aside as if he was waiting for something. Then when Moshe, accompanied by them all, went to the door, the *starost* followed Moshe into the corridor where he helped him carry his few bundles. He went with him as far as the exit door where they had to part. There he stopped and looked strangely at Moshe. Seeing him there, a worn-out, weak man who could hardly stand on his feet, and sensing that Moshe was just then closer to Heaven than to earth, and, it would seem, remembering an old picture he had seen somewhere in which a Jewish father or a grandfather, on the occasion of some holiday or celebration, blessed his children, the *starost* then, with that image before his eyes as he was saying good-bye to Moshe, whom he regarded as one of God's favorites, turned and said, "Bless me, Moshe." With that he put Moshe's bundles down and bowing his head waited to be blessed.

They made a strange tableau: Moshe, who had never been in a position to bless anyone before, especially not someone like the *starost*, stood confused for a moment. But then seeing how piously the fellow inclined his head, and considering that it was dangerous to anger such a man by denying him anything, he put his hands on his head and whispered the requisite benediction, "God bless thee and keep thee . . ." The *starost*, much brutalized as he had been and uprooted long ago from his traditions, received the blessing with excessive (and un-Jewish) reverence and gratitude, and when Moshe had taken his hands from his head, the *starost* (again, the gesture was not Jewish), seized one of Moshe's hands, meaning to kiss it; when Moshe, partly embarrassed, partly irritated, drew his hand away saying, "No, you mustn't. It's not done," the *starost*, confused and even more grateful, seized not one but both of Moshe's hands and kissed them. . . .

When Moshe drew up to his home in a carriage ordered at his request by one of the prison guards, the first person who saw him was the older servant who, after the disappearance of Gnessye the kitchen maid, was the only one of the servants left in the house. She happened just then to be out in the courtyard on some errand—emptying ashes in the trash can or for some other need—when she saw him drive up, and saw that he was so weak that he could not get down from the carriage by himself. At first she stood bewildered, then she put her hands to her headscarf and set it to rights, just as she had done when she had to appear before her employers (not in the course of her service in the kitchen but in happier times). But she understood at once that straightening her headscarf was not enough, that she was not the appropriate one to greet Moshe at the moment of his return. She thought instantly of Yehudis for whom, as Moshe's daughter, it was more fitting. And so without a moment's delay, she went to fetch her. And when she came upon Yehudis, who was utterly oblivious of what was happening, the maid cried out confusedly, "Look at you, sitting quietly here and you haven't the faintest notion that the master is here, and that he's outside in his carriage."

"What? Who?" a startled Yehudis cried. Because though Yehudis knew that her father was to be freed, there had been no mention of the particular date on which that would be. Hearing the news then, from the servant, that the event had already taken place and that her father was, at that very moment, outside, Yehudis felt her knees quaking and she, too, like the servant, cried out, "What did you say, woman? When? Who?"

She went outside and was in time to see her father still seated in the carriage. She went toward him and he, seeing her, made an effort to get up, but he could not get down from the carriage, first because he was too weak and then because meeting with his daughter at the gate of the house he had not seen for so long made him dizzy.

Yehudis helped him down and in the course of helping him into the house looked into his face and found that he was almost unrecognizable—as if someone else had been substituted for him. Seeing that, she pressed against his shoulder as she tearfully repeated the single word, "Father, Father," unable to say more, unwilling to grieve him by letting him see just how greatly changed she found him. And so she restrained her tears when she could or wiped her eyes against his shoulder.

Moshe, too, when she embraced him, caressed her hair with a tender, paternal hand and consoled her, doing what he could to keep her from noticing his condition. But he lacked the energy to maintain the illusion before his daughter that he was stonger than he was. The small bundle he had brought with him from the prison, the bundle that contained his prayer shawl and phylacteries, and a book or two, was beginning to be too heavy for him to hold, and Yehudis had to take it from him. The bundle in one hand and her other arm around her father, Yehudis held him close as she led him as if he were an old or much weakened man who could walk only with difficulty . . . from the gate through the courtyard and from there into the house.

Once in the house his first movement, Yehudis observed, was toward his bedroom as if he meant to discover what had happened to

Gitl from whom throughout his absence he had not received a letter. From which fact he had concluded that there was something wrong with her, that perhaps she had been taken mortally ill when he had gone away, or, worse, that she was dead.

Yehudis tried to detain him long enough to give him some particulars of her mother's illness and to prepare him so that he would not be startled by his meeting with her, but Moshe refused to delay. "I know. I know," he muttered confusedly, inattentively as leaning on Yehudis he passed from one room to another.

"I know. I know," he said under his breath as silently, stubbornly, and in spite of his physical weakness, he tried to hurry.

When he entered his bedroom, he went to Gitl's bed at once. And here something happened that would have proved instructive to the most experienced and most skillful of physicians: Moshe, when he came close to Gitl's bed and saw her lying helpless there, inert, with no light of understanding in her eyes—seeing that, we say that Moshe, who recently had readily endured the various calamities that had hailed down upon him, now endured this one, too, as something unavoidable, fated, and against which there was no defense. His lips closed, and he leaned against the nearest wall to keep himself from trembling, then he looked silently at Gitl.

So much, then, as regards Moshe. As for Gitl, the moment she saw Moshe who had been absent for so long in a place from which in the weakened condition of her mind she had had very little hope that he would return . . . at that moment, if an experienced doctor had been there, he might have expected one of two things to happen: she might have given a surprised shudder and cried out "Moshe," which would have been an indication that she had had, as sometimes happens, a healing crisis in her illness which would lead to the restoration of her speech and mobility to her body; or on the contrary that the surprise of seeing him might have induced a shock that, tearing at her already weakened roots, would kill her.

The first possibility was the more likely because the moment Gitl saw Moshe, she uttered a choked cry that verged on the comprehensible speech she was trying to achieve. And then in spite of the paralysis of her body, she made a spasmodic movement which seemed to imply that in another moment she would get up from her bed and go to Moshe and put her head against his shoulder in mute grief the way her daughter Yehudis had done—though it should be said in passing that for a pious woman to express such tenderness toward her newly returned husband might not have been deemed proper. And yet for such an exceptional encounter whose consequence might be her own miraculous recovery, she might consciously or unconsciously have permitted herself behavior which was frowned on by the pious and which was even forbidden by the strictest of strict laws.

Yes, all of that might have happened. But it did not. Gitl's single outcry was not repeated. The spasm of her body was as brief as a lightning stroke and turned out to be no more than an inconsequential twitch. She lay in her bed as she had lain in it before: inert, staring, silent. With one exception: her stare was now directed at Moshe, who stood at the foot of her bed, and it seemed to be saying, "Ah, Moshe, do you see? Here I lie in bed, sick, and you stand near me, apparently well, but I think, and I'll take my oath on it, that you, too, belong in a sickbed."

Yehudis, who had witnessed the meeting between her sick father and her paralyzed mother and who wanted to cut the scene short, turned to her mother and said as if Gitl could understand her, "Mother, Father is tired and needs to rest." Then turning to her father she took him by the hand and said, "Come, Father. You're tired. You can come again later."

Moshe obeyed her. He turned away from Gitl, because he could see that there was no point in staying there any longer, that nothing would be eased, and, too, because as Gitl had noticed, his body, exhausted from long lying in his prison bunk, longed desperately for a bed.

With Yehudis helping him along, Moshe left Gitl's room and was led into the living room where, well before the scene we have just described, Yehudis had instructed the older servant to set up a bed and to get everything ready that might be needed.

Moshe's face lighted up when first he saw the bed with its clean white sheets. At last he was home. He looked around the airy room which with its rugs, its potted plants, its tall mirror and its many windows had always been exceptionally comfortable. And for the first few moments he let his eyes linger over the bed as he remembered the prison from which he had come and the sort of sleeping arrangements he and the other prisoners had had there.

That was in the first few moments. But as soon as he began, at Yehudis's suggestion, to take his shoes and his clothes off so that he could get into that clean bed, he was suddenly deeply depressed with a depression that reduced him to silence as he was taking his clothes off. The depression did more than that. It confused him so that he was unable properly to undress himself, to remember which of his garments should be removed first—his caftan or his vest or his shoes or his socks.

One would have sworn that he was frightened of the bed. And he continued to be fearful during Yehudis's attempts to rouse him from his reverie as he was undressing. He showed most fear when finally undressed it was time for him to get into bed.

At last he got into it. And that was how Moshe, freed from prison, came home to lie in a bed in the best and airiest room in his house. And a look of pleasure played at intervals in his face and it was evident that he was thinking that at last, here, he would shake off his illness, that he would recover from his shortness of breath, and that here, in this spacious room with its high ceiling, its tall, wide windows through which the sunlight shone, here his health would be restored.

But that was only at intervals. For the most part, after he got into the bed, he lay there so dazed that he hardly knew where he was and hardly noticed the anxious devotion with which his daughter Yehudis moved around him, concealing from him any sign that might make him think that he needed special care.

He was so dazed that when on the evening of the day that he returned home and his daughter, his sons-in-law and his grandchildren gathered at his bedside, some standing, some sitting, and asked him how he was and told him the news of the household from which he had been gone so long . . . he was so dazed that he registered nothing that was being said. He made no reply to the questions put to him about his health, and as for the news they reported hoping to distract him and to help him forget his recent dreadful experiences, it was evident that he had no interest in it whatever.

He heard nothing, understood nothing and nodded only rarely to indicate yes or no. And then in the midst of the family hubbub going on around him, he suddenly said, speaking to nobody in particular, "Children, I can't quite remember. Have we enclosed Nekhamke's grave?"

"What are you saying, Father? Of course we have," replied Yehudis quickly to this bizarre question, hoping to distract him from further memories of his departed daughter, memories which evidently were oppressing him.

"So you say yes?" And then he withdrew again into the thoughts that were uppermost in his mind and took no further part in the conversation going on around him.

Then, all but discourteously, he interrupted his visitors and said, "Children, I'm tired. Go on to bed." And the family dispersed, and Moshe was left alone, still as dazed as when they had gathered around him.

He continued to be so disoriented in the first few days of his return that he did not even notice the visits of the oldest of his grandchildren, Mayerl, who sometimes approached his bedside, though more usually he paused on the threshold of the room as if he feared that Moshe would notice him and ask him what he meant by his visits.

Yes, for his part, even Mayerl, we say, felt himself so out of touch with his grandfather that he actually thought Moshe did not recognize him, or if he did, that he no longer regarded him as in any way different or closer to him than any of his other grandchildren.

And, again: Moshe was so withdrawn from his surroundings that on the morning after his return and after the evening spent with all the members of the family around his bedside except Alter, who because his own illness made him keep to himself in his attic room and who therefore was overlooked and had not even been notified that Moshe had returned home—when Alter learned of it in the morning . . . on his own or because the maid servant had imparted the news to him, when Alter, then, came to Moshe's room, Moshe was so withdrawn that all he could bring himself to say was, "Ah, Alter. How are you?"

Alter, when he came into his brother's room, had an impulse to rush toward him as toward his only protector from whom he had long been separated, and to pour out to him his long-gathering grief, if not in words at least by throwing himself into his brother's arms. But when he heard Moshe's half-chilling, absent "How are you?" Alter was taken aback and entirely lost the spontaneous impulse with which he had started toward his brother, and all he could bring himself to say was a flat "Moshe." But it was evident that even Alter, ill as he was, had been able to gauge his brother's condition and did not feel offended by his cold greeting. Because a glance at his brother's face had told him that Moshe was too sick to be concerned with other people's feelings—not even those of his own brother. The tears came to Alter's eyes.

On the second day after Moshe's return home, Yanovski, the family doctor who was generally sent for on serious occasions, arrived in the house. He studied Moshe for a long while; he listened to his chest and tapped it carefully. Then he became very, very grave and said nothing. The result was that the members of the family who were there, and especially Yehudis, who had been standing beside the doctor watching his every move, concluded that Yanovski was not willing to make a diagnosis alone, that he did not want to announce a grim assessment of the case and that he was very anxious to consult a second doctor, particularly Dr. Pashkovski, another Pole who was Yanovski's age and who like himself wore white side whiskers that looked like tufts of wool that had been pasted on his cheeks.

The consultation was arranged. And the two doctors were to be seen at Moshe's bedside on that very same day. Yanovski reported to his colleague the impressions he had had of his patient earlier that day. And then the two doctors were seen gravely studying Moshe and discussing him in their secret medical language. They peered into Moshe's face at great length, which Moshe found very disturbing because he deduced that they were reaching an unhappy conclusion from what they saw.

Naturally they said nothing to him about what they thought. But when they left the room, led by Yehudis who accompanied them out of the house into the courtyard and then to the gate—there at the gate they let her know in their terse and yet sympathetic fashion, the way doctors impart their judgments in such cases, that her father was very ill and that she must be prepared for him to get worse.

"Who needed them?" Moshe said to Yehudis as he emerged briefly from his lassitude. Looking into her face, he read the news that she had been given by the doctors standing at the gate, news which in silent agony she was trying to keep from him.

"We needed them. To give us something. To prescribe something."

"Bah," said Moshe turning angrily away with a movement that rejected all those who presume to heal by "giving" and "prescribing" and angrier still with himself for having had even the most minimum hope of being helped by such "givers" and "prescribers."

"Bah," he said, and one could see him sinking back into the apathy from which it would be difficult indeed to bring him back to a more cheerful way of thinking.

Then more or less in the same dazed condition, he asked one further question and that more of himself than of anyone else: "Do you see? Luzi hasn't come yet."

"No, not yet," Yehudis replied. "But he'll be here, soon. We sent for him some while ago."

These last words of Moshe regarding Luzi will become clearer to us if we explain that on the day after Moshe's return home, there was no appropriate moment that Luzi could be sent for, first because it did not occur to anyone until quite late, and then since Luzi's home was in such a distant section of town, it was too far to send for him that day. Which is why on the second day at Moshe's insistence a special messenger was sent whose instructions were first to impart to Luzi the news that Moshe had returned, and then to say that Luzi was invited to come at once, to return with the messenger if possible.

But Luzi did not come at once, nor did he come after an hour or two—or even later, after the doctors had made the two visits that so depressed Moshe. And so Moshe was beginning to feel considerably irritated.

But we ought to say a word or two in Luzi's defense. He did not show up not because of any lack of interest in his brother but because today was the day he had arranged to bid farewell to Avremele Lubliner whose time in N. had come to an end and who was about to start off on foot to go from city to city, from town to town and from village to village, wherever there might be a community of the Bratslaver sect and where he could accomplish the mission he had set for himself. That mission was to strengthen the trembling hands of those who endured persecution from various other Hasidic sects, or to encourage those who had weakened and drifted away from the living root of the faith.

Avremele's time in N. was over but not his desire to remain near Luzi from whom he had received spiritual gifts in bountiful measure, and whose guest he had been for a long while, and whom he regarded as a flag beneath which gathered all those who believed as Avremele did, and whom he loved as a father who brings honor both to himself and to his house.

One may well imagine, then, that for Avremele this parting from a revered master was a most difficult experience. So difficult that in these final days before he was due to go he could hardly bring himself to meet Luzi's eyes lest Luzi divine his weakness of spirit, or lest he, Avremele, break down and cry like a child, or, worse, lest his intense yearning tear something inward in him. Yes, it was something to consider, because given Avremele's love for Luzi there was no way to ensure that some such thing might not happen.

As an instance of how he felt, he had only to remember his emotions on the Friday preceding the last Sabbath he was to spend in N. He remembered how Luzi looked in his white linen and his caftan with its cincture after his visit to the ritual bath; and how Luzi, as was his custom, recited the Song of Songs, even though he knew the words by heart, holding the prayer book in his hand, his eyes fixed on the page as if not only the Song of Songs had the power to open the gates of Heaven but the very letters of the song printed on the page had such power as well.

Luzi's words so warmed Avremele that he began, almost without noticing it, to read along with him. At first quietly, then louder, and with such excitement that when he came to the passage, "I open to my beloved . . ." he almost . . . almost felt life leaving him as it yearned for what his body loved: the Lord God, one of whose manifestations in the form of a Son of Man stood before him, freshly bathed—Luzi, who was walking about before him wearing white garments, his collar turned down over his caftan, his prayer book in his hand, and to whom Avremele, in a rapture of love wanted to cry out: "Who will give you to me as a brother, nursed by one mother at the same breast?"

Such was Avremele's love for Luzi, and it was the same with Luzi as regards Avremele, who reminded him of his youth when he was in the full flush of his powers and passionate to serve the Lord, blessed be His Name.

And now these two were about to part. And it was then that Moshe Mashber sent his messenger to Luzi asking him to come and see him. And Luzi had had to put the visit off.

Both Avremele and Luzi finished their morning prayers early. Avremele began to pack the bundle that he usually carried with him on his travels, and Luzi sometimes stood by and watched him and sometimes drew aside because he could not bear watching him, and sometimes he returned again to Avremele, and like a father advising a son, he urged him to pack more and still more food and whatever else he might need on his journey, though Avremele was not thinking of such matters and hardly heard what Luzi said.

At last Avremele was ready. He reached for his coat, meaning to take his leave in the house beside the mezuzah in the doorway which he assumed was as far as Luzi would accompany him. But that is not what happened. Luzi, too, put his coat on and they both left the house. Nor did Luzi say farewell when they were outside. Instead he went with Avremele in the direction he would have to take on his way out of town.

They walked on silently together, each of them thinking his own thoughts. Avremele cast sidelong glances at Luzi in order to engrave his image on his mind, while Luzi did the same thing, the way a man does when he parts from a well-loved disciple in whom he sees his spiritual heir.

And then moving from street to street, they came at last to a field gate at the edge of town beyond which, evidently, Luzi did not mean to go. Here, Avremele put out his hand even as he kept his head lowered so that Luzi would not see the grief in his eyes nor hear that he was whispering, almost against his will, the same words that Elisha whispered when his master Elijah was taken from him.

Then Luzi, too, gave Avremele his hand, and clasping it a bit longer than is usual, he whispered *Lekh l'shalom*, Go in peace. Then turning their backs on each other, they parted. And that was that.

When Luzi arrived in Moshe's house, he found his brother lying in the bed that had been set up for him in the parlor. One may imagine what their meeting was like, following on the separation we have described above.

No, there was not much joy waiting for Luzi in his brother's house. When he came into the parlor, accompanied by various members of the family who had welcomed him as someone for whom they had been longing, Moshe Mashber made a sign to them that indicated very clearly that he wanted them all out of the room, that he had sent for his brother because he particularly wanted to be alone with him. They obeyed and left.

Luzi, when he was face-to-face with his brother, noted that Moshe, even before he had a chance to reply to Luzi's first polite question regarding his health, did not speak even the familiar words with which one usually answers such questions—perhaps because he could not find them or it may be because he regarded them as wasted or superfluous.

At the same time, Luzi noted, there was a certain gravity in Moshe's face which seemed to imply that the conversation to come was not to be like that of an ordinary bedside visit. He was not interested in hearing the usual reassurances about his health and about the likelihood of his recovery.

"No," he said as if to himself and then continued, addressing Luzi, "I'm being called."

"Where?" Luzi asked, pretending not to understand.

"There," Moshe said, raising his eyes toward the ceiling, and then to keep Luzi from the need to pretend that he did not understand, he spoke directly and with the tone of one "who is preparing to take the way of all mankind," he said, "Say nothing of this to any of the others in the family. I don't want to distress them. But I know it is so, and I think you ought to know it too."

He went on to describe portents of the event: he was frequently frightened even during the day by his sense of the presence of someone who always stood behind him at the head of the bed. Some tall stranger dressed in black from whose interior gleams of light seemed to show, as through cracks in a ruined building. He heard him, too, walking barefoot beside the walls of the room at night. Whenever Moshe closed his eyes for a while, the stranger looked closely at him, but when Moshe opened his eyes, the man pretended not to be looking and resumed his barefoot walking.

"It's known," said Moshe, speaking ambiguously but assuming, nevertheless, that Luzi understood who the figure was that frightened him, that stood at the head of his bed and that stalked him barefooted in his room at night.

Yes, Luzi heard portents enough from his brother. But the gravest, the most fearful portent of all was the sight of his brother lying in his bed, his brother sitting up for Luzi's sake when Luzi came in. But after that he grew weak and insensibly sought his pillow until finally he was fully leaning on it. And there he lay, weary, exhausted, speaking softly, almost incomprehensibly, so that Luzi had to move his chair closer to the bed in order to hear his words as they issued from his mouth.

That, then, was the first portent. The second was the sickly cast of his features which showed yellowish islets under the skin of his face and under his beard.

Luzi sat beside his brother's bed for a considerable while and to the degree that he could he did his best to drive away Moshe's dark thoughts, reassuring him that things were not quite the way Moshe saw them, that summer was on its way, the season when those who are ill feel better, as Moshe certainly would because as the weather improved with the end of winter and he was out in the fresh air of the courtyard and the garden, he would lose his cough. It was, after all, almost Purim time, nearly Passover.

No doubt Moshe was readier to be comforted by his brother than by any other members of his family, not excluding his daughter Yehudis who, from the moment he came home and took to his bed, talked to him in a tone of voice in which one could detect not the slightest doubt that he would recover. She pretended not to have any anxieties about his illness which, she seemed to say, was a temporary and passing thing that posed (God forbid) no danger.

And this was why Moshe relied more on what Luzi said because he deemed him incapable of lying even to console his own brother.

And so Moshe felt heartened a little by Luzi's visit and as long as he was at his bedside. But when Luzi rose to take his leave of him, Moshe's depression returned at once so that before he said farewell to Luzi, he pleaded with him to repeat his visits often. "Because, as you know," Moshe said quietly, hesitantly, "at a time like this, standing on the threshold between 'yes' and 'no' . . . between 'today' and 'tomorrow' . . . at a time like this, the presence of a man like yourself is absolutely essential."

Luzi, seeing that he was indeed the one who could keep Moshe's spirits up, promised.

Luzi made his farewells and took his leave, after which Moshe was except for a very few moments again subject to a depressing apathy. In addition to that, he became aware of a presence in his house for which he could not find a name, but each time he caught a glimpse of him, he felt his blood congeal and his eyes grow wide with terror. This was a tall stranger dressed in black whom he saw standing sometimes at the head and sometimes at the foot of his bed.

Lately, Moshe was generally fearful. Especially at sounds that seemed frequently to come at him from no clear direction. It happened then in the days following his return home that the new caretaker, Vassily, whom Sruli Gol had hired, carrying a log that was meant to be used in heating a nearby room, passed by the open door of the parlor. Moshe, in bed, frightened at the sight of a hooded stranger wearing a monk's robe and cincture, cried out, "Who's that? Why is there a priest in the house?" And it took a long, long while before Yehudis could calm him down, could persuade him that there was nothing to worry about and that he had misunderstood what he had seen. That it was not a priest, but a caretaker who had taken Mikhalko's place. But Moshe remained distrustful of her explanations, believing that Vassily was another of the manifestations he had lately been seeing.

And Mikhl Bukyer's widow frightened him in the same way. Sruli Gol, we will recall, had installed her in the house in the same way. She sometimes did the work of a servant or any other specific tasks that might be needful. Moshe, catching sight of an unusually tall woman, lean and dark and one who was, moreover, a stranger moving about as if she belonged in the house was as terrified as if he had seen a ghost.

Nor was he reassured by anything Yehudis said. In all such instances, she did what she could to distract him, to soothe his fears away, and to turn the conversation to more cheerful subjects. Nor did he feel any better because of the visits he was paid by officers of his synagogue who came to express their sympathies, as well as various merchants of the town who came because they felt guilty at having had something to do with precipitating his various troubles and who wanted to express their regrets and to smooth things over if they could. He received them all more or less indifferently; he listened to them with only half an ear because he was in fact listening to an inner voice whose presence he could not ignore and which reminded him continually that nothing that was being said around him had very much to do with him anymore, because he was as one who had one foot ready to step over the certain threshold into the other world.

He was even indifferent to the fact that Sholem Shmaryon and Tsali Derbaremdiker came one day, sent openly on a mission of reconciliation by Yakov-Yossi Eilbirten, the richest man and the most important creditor in town, who could not quite bring himself to visit the sick man's house, first because it was unfitting for a man of his stature, and, too, because he felt guilty as regarded Moshe Mashber and was therefore uncertain how Moshe would take such a visit—whether he would forgive him or angrily turn his back on him; therefore Yakov-Yossi sent those two, Sholem Shmaryon and Tsali Derbaremdiker, whom he had taught to say that what had happened had happened and there was nothing to be done about that; however, as regarded the future, when Moshe, as was to be hoped, recovered from his illness, then he, Yakov-Yossi engaged himself to do all that he could to help Moshe reestablish his good name and his former situation. But Moshe received even that news with chilly indifference and his face showed not the slightest trace of satisfaction.

And so the days went by and now it was almost Purim, the holiday that marked the coming of spring. It was the holiday that filled the town with childish delight as well as grown-up pleasures that were deeply rooted in an ancient legend that was read aloud from a yellowed old parchment scroll in which was told the story of the defeat of an ancient enemy of the people who had determined to destroy them; and in addition to the recounting, the legend itself urged that the tale be accompanied from generation to generation with celebration—with eating and drinking and jollity and with the giving and sending of gifts.

But not even the coming of this holiday lightened Moshe's spirits. It made no difference to him that now a bright sun shone frequently through the parlor windows, or that the new watchman, as the season grew warmer, stood among the still-bare and snow-laden trees, staring up at them as he listened to the chirp of a bird for whose song he had waited all winter and whose first notes he believed he had just heard. No, Moshe sank deeper and deeper into his despondent mood so that he hardly even noticed the care his daughter Yehudis lavished in order to bring some of the holiday spirit into the house so that the sick Moshe might be cheered and distracted from thinking of the danger he was in.

No. Moshe either could not or would not exert himself even for the sake of his beloved daughter and remained indifferent to almost everything. There was one thing he did still care about and that was Gitl into whose room from time to time he asked to be taken. And he would be helped down from his bed and moving with difficulty would be led into her room where he did not stay very long—but stood at the foot of her bed for a short while, looking at her, after which he would ask to be taken back to the parlor and to his own bed.

But in recent days he lingered longer at her bedside, clasping the bedpost with his hands until he felt the strength leaving them, and only then did he ask whoever had led him there to take him back.

Usually when he paid his visits he said nothing to Gitl, knowing that it would be useless, that it was impossible that there would be an answering groan such as he had had from her on the occasion of his first visit to her. But on this day, Purim, when Yehudis had succeeded in creating for her father's sake a little of the cheerful atmosphere of the holiday, he went in to see Gitl, himself in something of a holiday mood—and this time he did venture to speak to her even though there was no likelihood that she would hear him and almost no possibility that she would reply.

He asked to be led closer to her and then bending over her he said, "May you and those who are dear to you be granted another year of life." But even as he spoke, it struck him that as regarded one of her loved ones, namely himself, he had uttered a blessing that rang untrue. He straightened up quickly, as if he had caught himself uttering a lie, and asked whoever it was who had brought him there to lead him back to his room at once.

Moshe left Gitl's room utterly devastated. He lay in his bed, wondering about his visit to her. And then when he had caught his breath from the laborious exertions involved in going to her and back, various vague images of Purim, in which he could not now take part, passed before his eyes.

In his mind's eye he saw how the poor young people of the town, youths and maidens, went from place to place carrying gifts of food on plates (if they were from poor people) and on platters (if they were from the rich), and how the gift bearers bustled about and how their eyes sparkled as they calculated the sums they would earn this year and compared them to what they earned last year and looked forward eagerly to the year to come.

From these thoughts, Moshe drifted to images of the marketplace and to the open stalls of the honey-cake bakers who all year long sold sweets, and who now were besieged by customers buying up sweet goods for Purim: candies, aniseed cakes, poppy-seed cakes, sweet biscuits, as well as various toys made of snow-white sugared starch: some in the form of violins, ducks, birds and so on. Things which the children used first as toys and which turned later into snacks.

Moshe imagined, too, how the streets were full of strange-looking poor folk and beggars going about in great numbers, singly or in groups, as well as men and women dispensers of alms who, dressed in their holiday clothing, had volunteered to go about from house to house searching out poverty-stricken dwellings whose inhabitants were too proud to ask for charity.

And lying in bed Moshe imagined, too, how the door to his own kitchen, which was at some distance from the parlor in which he lay, was being opened at intervals, sometimes by the usual beggars who were paid off on the doorstep with their usual groschen, or sometimes a respected man or woman alms collector dressed in holiday garb in honor of the charitable task they had undertaken, and so that they might make a better impression on those from whom they sought alms. These alms collectors were invited into the house where they bargained with their hosts for larger donations to which they were entitled first because they were better dressed, then because of the charitable work they had undertaken to do, and finally because they let drop hints of the circumstances surrounding the "fallen" clients on whose behalf they were soliciting.

Lying in his bed Moshe thought he could hear the arrival at intervals of one or another gift bearer sent by a relative or a friend, and it seemed to him that he heard Yehudis receiving the gift from each new arrival, giving each of them some money "to make their journey easier" and sending her regards to those who had honored her father's house by sending the gifts.

Yes. It needs to be said that Yehudis had her hands full just then. She had first of all to do the work that was expected of women during the holiday, but also because she undertook to celebrate it by fulfilling every custom and form the holiday required in order to create for her father the impression that everything was normal, that their Purim was no different from anyone else's.

She had even prepared and arranged the usual Purim banquet at which people generally lingered far into the night. But this time because of her father's illness, the meal was served in the parlor where his bed had been set up instead of in the dining room to which it would be difficult for him to come and where it would be hard, too, for him to sit for any length of time. And she had so arranged matters that Moshe's bed was at the head of the table.

And then, to cheer Moshe, she also invited her uncle Luzi to be with them from the beginning of the meal, or in the event that he was presiding over a meal of his own, then she urged him to come later, whenever he could.

Moshe, for his part, exerted himself to act as if all was well on this occasion, partly as an exercise in self-deception, but partly, too, because he did not want to spoil the evening for his children. But there was no member of the family at that table, beginning with Yehudis and ending with the least small child, who expected their grandfather to turn toward them instead of upward toward the ceiling at which he had been staring in self-engrossed silence over the last several days.

No, it was hard for Moshe to maintain the illusion that everything was normal. And hardly conscious of it himself, he began slowly, slowly to sink into his bed on one side of which Yehudis had placed a pillow against which he could lean. Yehudis, naturally enough, was the first to notice what he was doing, and to relieve him from the strain and irritation of pretending that all was well, she said, "Father, if it's hard for you, lie down."

He put up no resistance and obeyed her at once. And despite his every intention not to betray how weak he was, he could not help wincing with the pain that was the price of his brief effort to take a normal part in the banquet. From that moment on he lay in his bed, withdrawn from all further activity. He touched none of the food or drink that had been prepared and that was being served all around him.

Luzi showed up late in the evening accompanied by a cluster of his fellow Bratslavers with whom he had been celebrating at his home. To continue those festivities, Luzi had invited them to come with him to his brother's house.

And now Moshe had another access of energy. As a gesture honoring his brother, he tried to sit up. More than that . . . he even made a movement to get off the bed but that was a maneuver that did not succeed. As soon as he sat up he had an attack of coughing so severe that all who were there, family or visitors, gathered around his bed and stared openmouthed as he fought for breath, choking, gasping, and wheezing. Some of them thought that Dr. Yanovski should be sent for, and others suggested a traditional "wailing" against the spirits that had brought on the attack.

A little while later Moshe felt better. Various members of the family stayed beside him for the rest of the night, maintaining an anxious watch, afraid that he might suffer another attack. But the visitors, Luzi's disciples, that is, overwhelmed by a gush of the sort of piety that was unique with them, and which when they felt themselves compelled to fulfill one of God's behests—to pray, for example—rendered them deaf and blind to whatever was going on around them, seemed now to have all but forgotten the sick man. It was not because they were ill-intentioned. On the contrary. It was more likely that they wanted to cheer him by including him among the number of those who could forget even their own illness in the fervor of celebrating the holiday. These people, then, began to sing from the moment that they sat down at the table where place was made for them. They sang the songs that are usual on Purim, such as the melody, "Rejoice, thou Rose of Jacob." And then ignoring the sick man, they began to dance, because there is no delight without dance. They sang and danced with such exalted tenacity that we are certain that had Moshe Mashber not been dangerously ill, and had he been able to cast even a fleeting glance at them, and had he been able to hear a fragment of their song, we are certain, we say, that he would have been tempted, however briefly, to join them, and we are certain, too, that a tiny smile of delight would have shown on his face and in his eyes.

Because it was clear that those dancers did not dance, as others did, because of any superfluity of food and drink. Rather, they danced for joy in the great miracle that had been granted to them and to their ancestors many generations ago, a miracle by whose grace those ancestors in their time, and now they in their generation, were permitted to celebrate and praise and serve Him who lives forever.

Yes, if only Moshe had been able . . . But he was not. All the while that Luzi's people were singing and dancing, Moshe, as if unable to see or hear them, lay in his bed with his eyes fixed on Luzi as if he was waiting for an appropriate moment to say something which he did not think it was fitting to say during the celebration. It was as if he had hidden something away that he would only divulge to his brother when the festivities were over and he was taking leave of him.

And that is what happened. When it was all over and the final blessings had been recited, and when Luzi's adherents said their good-byes first to Moshe and then to the members of his family, and when as is customary they had wished everyone a good year, and when Luzi neared the head of Moshe's bed, meaning to make similar wishes for him, it was then that Moshe gestured to him to bend closer—as if to say that he could not hear or perhaps that he did not have the strength to speak up. When Luzi did what he was bidden, Moshe said, so softly that no one else could hear, "It's over, Luzi. I'm not going to be here much longer. I beg you, come frequently, because in a little while there'll be no one to come to."

Purim always comes on the fourteenth day of the month of Adar. Passover comes on the fourteenth day of Nisan, and in the interval the town is busy with the preparations that usher in that happy festival that always comes arm in arm with spring when nights sparkle as if the stars in the dark vault of the sky had been washed and refurbished during the winter, and when the cloudless sky in daylight looks scoured. It is the time when migratory birds have made their long journey back from their distant southlands, and when the nonmigratory birds greet the arriving guests with loud twitters and flapping of wings, and when hens in the Passover season utter clucking promises of new generations to come as they settle down to lay expansively and at their ease, and when turkeys proudly display their blue-coral wattles as they walk stiffly, as if on stilts.

As happens annually in the days immediately following Purim, various ruined huts which have stood empty and idle in obscure streets all year long are now rented for this month only by commercial bakers who turn those huts into matzo factories.

Planed plank tables are set up in the small rooms. These tables are for the use of women and girls who hire themselves out for a month as matzo dough rollers. An oven is built, and near it, is a tin-covered table on which the dough is scored. And there is always a small dark room in those houses set aside for the kneading of the dough which is then cut into smaller pieces and carried out to the long tables and turned over to the "rollers."

The scene in these bakeries is busy, cheerful. There is the sound of chattering and joking women and girls who, as they knead and roll the dough, talk constantly, carrying on loud conversations with those at the same table as well as with others even some distance away.

The cries of the *shieber*, the man who slides the matzos into the oven, are frequently heard urging the women on because without matzos, the oven's heat is squandered. Cries, too, of the *rigler*, the man who scores the matzos, also urging the women on. And the cries of the employers when they catch sight of the women and girls slacking off at their work or not fully observing the religious rituals prescribed for it, or when the kneading is delayed, or when one of the "rollers" has fingernails that are not trimmed to the quick as they are supposed to be. Or when one of the women pops something not kosher for Passover into her mouth and then does not shake off the crumbs or wash her hands as she is required to do.

There are the cries, too, of mothers scolding when their children pull at their apron strings demanding some of the matzo that has just been pulled out of the oven.

In the street, porters are already to be seen carrying flat wicker baskets loaded with matzos to the homes of householders who can afford to buy their matzos well before the holiday, unlike poorer people who have to put off buying them because they haven't yet got the wherewithal.

And in the evenings one can see whole tribes of men gathering at the cold river in which ice is still floating. They have gathered to sell all sorts of utensils for the holiday: pitchers and buckets with which to gather "our water" before the sun sets. And one can see the water being taken quietly, ceremoniously, and later one can see how the water drips from those pitchers and buckets as they are carried carefully homeward.

And just after Purim, as is customary in prosperous households, the borsht for Passover is prepared and given a place of honor in a corner of the parlor or in some other handsome room. And that corner of the room is carefully watched, almost as if the borsht were in hiding. The crocks are covered with clean white cloth and the children are severely cautioned against going anywhere near them ... indeed, not even so much as to look at them. And the householders come in from time to time and uncover the crocks and skim off the foam that has gathered, then they cover the crocks again until their next visit.

In more prosperous households, preparations for the Passover generally begin early. One room is cleaned at a time. Barrels and dishes are bought, and orders are given to a variety of tradesmen—shoemakers, tailors—so that whatever is ordered will be ready in plenty of time for Passover.

There is a bustling about in poor houses as well, among those who must exert themselves to find the means with which to provide for the festival, as well as among those who are too poor to provide for themselves but who know that there is help available for them in the town's various charitable societies.

The mood is high in the marketplace, too. The petty retailers display a great choice of remnants and bric-a-brac on their stands, leftovers from last year's stock that the wholesalers have sold off cheap and which are now being hawked as if they were the latest fashion, newly manufactured.

Cheap buttons, tape, socks, neckties, lace and clothing of all sorts are to be found there, as well as remnants of more expensive goods: draperies, wool, calico and so on.

Dealers, their voices hoarse, shout their wares. They weigh and measure and count the money that comes in and give change hurriedly, feverishly—as if someone behind them were driving them on to take care of their customers with the greatest speed. But all of that haste is merely put on and is meant to inspire those who are merely looking on with the desire to buy.

The chief marketplaces are bustling. There, shopkeepers and their assistants look into the eyes of the more prosperous buyers, knowing that they have the wherewithal and are serious shoppers, and if necessary they lower their prices for these buyers rather than lose an opportunity to take in cash ... which is so vital for them. Especially now when they have to be ready to pay their creditors in the larger towns for last year's goods so that they can get long-term credit to make purchases in time for this year's summer season.

The press is tremendous. There is a constant coming and going, a constant bargaining and measuring in those shops where local customers and those from out of town gather. A constant buying and selling of bolts of cloth, leather goods, shoes and so on.

And the weather helps out. It has passed the season of caprice when it is partly winter, partly not, when it is unstable, unpredictable, changing from cold to warm, from clear and bright to fogs that often bring rain or snow, and sometimes even a mixture of sunlight and icy rain—almost hail. No. It is different now. "Mild and gentle breezes," as the almanac, to everyone's great satisfaction, always predicts about the weather preceding the holiday. And it is always right . . . and when it isn't, it's no great matter.

As is customary, the boys in their primary schools study the easier Bible chapters, Mishpatim, in which is described the Ark of the Covenant that Moses caused to be built in the desert after the exodus of the Jews from Egypt—the Ark with its altar and its branched candelabrum decorated with knobs and flowers. These are the easier chapters that come after the head-cracking Terumah-Tetzave chapters, those dealing with the tithes.

The schoolboys are occupied with sketching and painting the Ark of the Covenant: its curtains, its entrance and its roof made of goats' wool; with making a model out of ordinary cloth of the breastplate with its twelve precious stones representing the twelve tribes of Israel; with its shoulder straps and waistband which the high priest wore on his breast, back and thighs. And their teacher always allows one of the boys to wear this homely model of the breastplate so that the other boys may form some notion of what the real one looked like when, long ago, Moses caused it to be made in the desert.

In a word, the whole town is caught up in a fever of preparation that intensifies day by day and week by week as the holiday approaches. The men are busied with what concerns men; and the women are driven distracted by all they have to do: shopping and cleaning the houses that, throughout a long winter, were cleaned only for the Sabbath and even then not very thoroughly.

It is, then, understandable that people in that season have very little time to concern themselves with much of anything but what is immediately necessary; they do not even have time for bad-mouthing their neighbors as during the long winter nights they have been quite willing to do. No. Not now. Everyone is so caught up being busy that he or she hardly has time to discuss even weighty events that might have happened in the town, events which at any other time they would chew the fat over for days on end, for weeks and for months. Events such as a wealthy marriage, or the death of some well-known person. Now there is no time even to talk about even the most important ones—except for a quick mention—because any longer consideration is interrupted by "What am I doing going on like this? I still haven't finished with . . ."

And yet Moshe Mashber's death and especially the events that followed it disturbed the town to such a degree that it forgot its preoccupation with the coming festival and for a while it could talk of nothing else.

Moshe Mashber began to decline shortly after the Purim festival described above, and his condition soon went from bad to worse. Not only was he forced to give up his brief visits to his wife Gitl, which had taxed all his strength, but he became so weak that he was unable to take care of his elementary needs without making use of somebody's arm or shoulder.

His doctors not only despaired of curing him, they also gave up trying to ease his pain with the narcotics that are usually given to a patient in such cases to numb his consciousness and to keep him from understanding his true condition.

Moshe no longer slept either by day or night. And those who were at his bedside observed how he lowered his eyelids, like a dozing hen, while trembling and half-wakeful thoughts flitted across his face like dark shadows that have just come near a cloud from whose vicinity they show no inclination to leave.

Yes, there was someone at his bedside then both night and day . . . though most of the time it was his daughter Yehudis who did everything she could to make things easier for him by seeing to it that he found her, the person most devoted to him, always there. But not even she, Yehudis, could help very much. Because whatever care she exerted was countered by his progressive deterioration, and finally all that Yehudis could do was to adjust her father's pillows. There was one thing more she could do: she could remind him to take the medicines the doctors had prescribed on the occasion of their last visit, medicines which her father stubbornly resisted taking. And when sometimes he yielded and obediently swallowed them, it was clear that he did it not so much for himself as for her sake.

And yet there was one more thing that Yehudis could do. She could sometimes leave her father's bedside and go into another room, or into a corner of the parlor itself . . . and there she could weep silently, wiping the tears away in secret so that no one—and especially not her father—could see them.

It needs to be said that Moshe by then spoke very little. So little that it was as if his tongue had atrophied because he no longer had any words either to address to others or for himself. So one can well understand Yehudis's astonishment when one night as she kept her vigil at Moshe's bedside he suddenly made a sign for her to bend down because he wanted to tell her something. But what he had to say gave her little joy. She did as he asked, of course, and bent over him attentively, but the moment she heard his first word, expressed with great difficulty, she understood what he had in mind: that he was uttering a last wish. He said, "See to it that the family is kept together. Whatever God sends don't let the family fall apart. Your mother," Moshe went on (and the words that followed were even more startling), "won't linger much longer. You must be ready for two memorial services at once. One for me, one for her," he said, indicating Gitl's room with a movement of his head.

"Father!" cried Yehudis, shuddering. "What are you saying? Wherever did you get such a notion?"

Moshe said no more but waved his hand to indicate that he was too weak to go on and that the conversation was over.

Yes. After that Moshe hardly spoke another word. And only Luzi, who lately had taken to spelling Yehudis at Moshe's bedside because Yehudis was near collapse after weeks of attending on both her father and mother—only Luzi from time to time was the recipient of such of those confidences that Moshe's weakened condition permitted him to make.

And so it happened one night when Luzi was alone with him that Moshe signaled to his brother to stand beside him at the head of the bed. Then Moshe, breathing with great difficulty, said quietly that he had been seeing that which no one else could see: their father in his skullcap sitting opposite him looking as he had once looked when he rose in the morning to study and his wife in her bonnet handed him his lime tea. Moshe was not frightened of the apparition. His parents seemed so lifelike that he had not the slightest doubt that he was actually seeing them, though he knew that that could not be true. But then suddenly something else had happened. A cock appeared above his father's head. It seemed to be both hovering in the air and perched on a bar or a rail. And that amazed and frightened Moshe terribly.

Then the cock spread its wings as if it was about to crow, and then their father's head disappeared and was replaced by that of the cock. What could that mean? asked a fearful Moshe, breathing heavily.

"Dear Moshe, it's nothing. It's just the play of your fancy . . . because you sleep badly and not enough," said Luzi to calm him, though the look on Moshe's face as he turned it in the direction in which he had seen the vision of the cock caused Luzi considerable distress.

"You really think that?" Moshe asked, half disbelieving his brother, and it was clear that if it had not been Luzi, Moshe would have dismissed his words with a wave of his hand.

On evenings after such gloomy conversations with his brother, Luzi would sometimes sit at his bedside in order to reassure him. Occasionally he would get up and go over to a side table in the parlor where there was a book into which he looked far into the night. At other times, with the lamp turned low, Luzi walked quietly, quietly along the walls of the spacious room so as not to disturb his brother and tried to think how he could be helpful to someone whose days, perhaps whose hours, were numbered.

Luzi was at his book or pacing in the room so late that Moshe, starting from his slumber and catching sight of him, would take fright, or he would call him again to his bedside and tell him of the latest apparition he had seen.

During the last several nights he had seen the house full of flies. Flies on the walls, on the ceiling, in the air, and even on the floor. A tremendous mass, flying and humming. "How can that be?" he asked, amazed. "I don't think it's summer yet. No. It's not summer. Then where did so many flies come from?"

Luzi, of course, did what he could to calm his brother's fears. But there came a final night when it was so clear to everyone that the end was near that no one went to bed. On that night, with all of them standing around his bed, just as someone was handing Moshe some medicine in hopes of keeping life in him a little longer, Moshe, with a sudden wave of his hand, as if directing them all to go off to one side—all but Luzi, who, as Moshe requested, bent over him . . . Moshe spoke calmly, tersely, in the tone of a man who is about to go on a journey and who cannot brook delay: "What time is it, Luzi?" And then he immediately said, "Grave clothes and a cemetery plot. It seems to me I got those ready a year ago."

That said, he turned silent and seemed to be waiting for an answer to a question that had really been a statement. Then as if finished with that matter, he said to Luzi, "Confession."

Luzi did what was needed. He read the prayer of confession and

Moshe, without a trace of self-pity and with such strength as still re-mained to him, repeated the words.

It was quiet in the parlor. So quiet that if those flies that Moshe had imagined had been real, they would have now stopped in midflight and turned silent at the sight of what was happening.

Muffled sobs were heard from various parts of the room. Yehudis's especially. She stood behind a curtain of the door and there, hidden from everyone's sight, she stood, her shoulders shaking.

Esther-Rokhl wept along with her, as well as the other relatives who in the last several days had been invited to the house to give the exhausted members of the family some help. Everyone was silent, as if in those final moments they had been stricken dumb. Only Luzi, as befitted the role required of him, stood at the head of the bed and led his brother through the rites of farewell as he watched his soul depart.

Moshe himself, hardly able to breathe, was now entirely calm as he lay dying. Then he was still, and those who were with him could see that there was nothing more to be done—except those things that are done to one who has been so stilled.

It was then that a loud cry burst from Yehudis's throat. Her hus-band, Yankele Grodshteyn, and her brother-in-law, Nakhum Lentsher, as well as the other relatives and synagogue officers who had been called to watch beside the bed that night, formed a circle around her and kept her from going to her father, though she strove against them with exceptional force.

As for Moshe they did for him what custom and the rites of the dead required. His body was lifted from the bed and set on the ground. The Sabbath candlesticks that belonged to Gitl his wife and to her daughter Yehudis were placed at his head. The burning candles cast a glow over the body that was now wrapped in a sheet.

And that was that. The end of Moshe Mashber.

The following morning, when the news of his death began to spread, first to his own place of business and into the marketplace where it was heard in the shops and stores, everyone was moved. And particularly the merchants who had done business with him, as well as those who knew him personally, or who had heard of him and who respected his position in the mercantile world. All of them now, at the news of his death, expressed their surprise.

"Ah, blessed is the True Judge," they said. And almost all of them added, "A pity. A pity."

"Left the world before his time," said others with some anger as they recalled those who had had a small hand in his death.

"Just think of it, to turn a man over to his enemies. And such a man, too. To send him to prison!"

"It's unheard of. A father of children. A notable. Not just anyone. To knock him down that way. To lay him so low. Damn them, whoever they are."

"Who?" inquired several people who had not been part of the circle at the beginning of the conversation and who, happening by, now thrust their way in.

"Who?" said the one who had expressed anger first. This time he did not refrain from going on, though it may be that when he first started to speak he may have had reasons for being specific; while among those who heard him there may have been those who had reasons for not inquiring too closely who was meant—because they knew perfectly well whom he had in mind. "Who," continued the angry speaker, "those who do not have God in their hearts. The Yakov-Yossis of the world who are quite capable of sweeping anyone out of their way who, by seeming to prosper, threaten their mouths and pocketbooks. They think nothing of putting someone like Moshe Mashber in prison; they think it's perfectly fine to shove such a man into a hole in the ground."

Everyone had something to say. Some spoke bitterly, others were more measured, and some spoke because they liked to be part of a conversation about the death of others because it gave them an occasion to meditate on their own lives.

And then after all the talk among the various people clustered in the marketplace, a considerable number of those who were there started off at noon toward Moshe Mashber's house to follow him to the cemetery and to pay their last respects.

The funeral took its usual course. First, a quiet crowd gathered at Moshe's house. There, people went in to look at the body that was laid out in the parlor whose many windows looked out on the courtyard, and since they were already there, several of the visitors who had never been in Moshe's home before and who ranked several ranks below him as regards fortune, now that they were inside, inspected the furniture that was still left from the days of his prosperity: the soft couches and the chairs with white covers, the tall mirror in its gilded frame which now stood draped in a sheet, the potted plants now set in a corner where they formed a sort of garden. And these folk, many who were many levels lower in rank than Moshe Mashber, not only mourned for him whose corpse lay on the ground with lighted canlesticks at its head, but they also experienced a bit of envy as they thought of him once upon a time entertaining guests in this airy and comfortable parlor and who, as they supposed, had been many times happier than they had been in their own homes.

Then these same people looked also into other rooms in the house, rooms which had been left open because it had not occurred to anyone to shut them, as one usually did on the occasion of a festivity or a bereavement.

As we have said, people at first crowded into the house where they gathered in quiet, respectful clusters. They walked about in silence, raising their voices only in the courtyard where they waited while the body was purified. There they spoke of the departed, praising him. Each of them told of having known him at a distance over the years, or claimed to have had a close relationship with him.

Then in the house when the ceremony of the purification of the body was over, and the body was being carried from the house, a bottleneck developed in the doorway leading to the courtyard. It was Yehudis who stood there and prevented the body from being carried through. She stood against the doorpost of the house, her head pressed against it, oblivious to the cries of "Let us pass. Let us pass." Oblivious, or pretending to be oblivious, so that she might keep her beloved father in the house a bit longer.

Then when the body had been carried to the bier that stood leaning against a chair in the courtyard, it was Alter, looking dreadfully pale, who prevented the body from being placed on it.

Throughout the time when Moshe's end was drawing near, Alter had not come near his bedside, though sometimes he would stand in the doorway and look in. Then he would go quickly off. Now, however, when it was all over and he had to bid farewell to his brother—and because he knew that, given his illness, he would not be permitted to go to the cemetery—he had tried, first in the parlor where the body lay, to fling himself on Moshe's body, meaning to kiss his face, perhaps, or to say something dictated to him by his own malady, or perhaps he wanted merely to weep over him. He had, however, been prevented from doing anything, because as he bent over the body it had been clear that he intended to do something. It was then that he had uttered one of his piercing, now truncated, but still piercing screams. It was so powerful that it seemed that he was about to be overwhelmed by a seizure that would produce a series of his ferocious leopard cries, one after the other without letup. All of which would have added a strange subplot to the present tragedy. But to everyone's astonishment, and who knows where he got the strength for it, Alter managed to control himself and repressed the cries, evidently feeling that respect for the dead required him to do so. And so he did—at great cost. And this is why as the body was being placed upon its bier, that one saw Alter, who had been standing beside his brother Luzi who in his turn had chosen to be near the body so that he might watch all that was being done to it . . . it was then that one saw Alter flinging himself into Luzi's arms, and like a child pleading mutely for something from his parents, he pressed his head against his brother's bosom.

This made such a deep impression on all who were there that for a little while the body was actually forgotten. Even the pallbearers, who because of their profession had seen many a sorrowful sight, paused before the bier and delayed placing the body on it.

"Let us pass, let us pass," cried one of the pallbearers at last, and Alter, dazed and pale as a corpse, tore himself away from Luzi and moved off to one side.

The pallbearers did whatever needed to be done to the bier. Mayerl, Moshe's grandson, pressed against his mother's skirts just as Alter had pressed himself against Luzi's bosom. He hid his head so that one could not tell whether he was weeping, or sobbing, or whether his entire young body trembled.

The assembly followed the bier from the courtyard and again there was a delay at the gate. This time it was because Yehudis, who, unable to bear watching the preparations around the body, had placed herself at the head of the cortege, and just as she had earlier done, so now she leaned her head against a gatepost, hoping, evidently, to rouse sufficient compassion so that her father would not be borne so abruptly away from his courtyard.

She was moved to one side and from that moment the procession went on as usual. The body was brought to the cemetery and lowered into its grave. And because Moshe Mashber had left no male children, his brother Luzi recited the first Kaddish, the mourner's prayer, over the body before it was covered.

So it was finished. The town as usual expected to forget Moshe as God commanded, and as the dead are usually forgotten. But a couple of days later, in the same week that Moshe died, Gitl, his wife, died, too, and followed him to the grave.

No one knows whether Gitl, who was herself so sick, had been in any condition to understand that her Moshe was dying, or whether she had guessed at it from his appearance during the visits he had made to her bedside, whether she had observed that he was turning progressively more sallow, more withered, his cheeks more wrinkled, that he looked more and more like a ruin about to collapse; or whether she guessed at it when his visits suddenly stopped; or when Yehudis, who usually preceded her father, came in looking even more distracted than usual and spent increasingly less time with her—an indication that Yehudis now had a patient more gravely ill to look after than herself, Gitl. Or perhaps none of that happened. Perhaps Gitl was in no condition to notice anything though it may have been that on the day Moshe died and was laid out on the parlor floor ... that on that day, when there was a sudden influx of many people into the house, she may have seen some strange things through her open door. It may be that then she guessed what had taken place. There is further evidence that this may have happened from the fact that on that day Yehudis had failed to visit her altogether—except once when no matter how much she tried to conceal the marks of her tears, it was clear that she had been crying. And so it was that Gitl might have been able to guess that something unusual had befallen the family.

And Gitl may have received an additional hint when one of the people who had come to purify Moshe's body, a fellow wearing a very greasy caftan and carrying a copper basin inadvertently walked into her room, thinking that the body was there. Gitl, catching sight of him, must certainly have understood to what uses the copper basin was meant to be put.

Yes, there are grounds for thinking that if a member of the family had been in Gitl's room on the day that the fellow with the basin came in he would have seen a transformation in Gitl's face—a sudden rush of blood which, given the nature of her illness, ought to have been impossible for her unless she had received some quite unusual stimulus which might have led to an improvement in her condition—or to a decline. "Red or dead," as the saying goes.

But there was no one in the room to see that at the sight of the intruder, she began to tremble as if she was feverish. And from then on and throughout the considerable while the body was being purified and it was time for it to be borne from the house, no member of the family came into her room because they wanted to keep her from being aware of what was happening.

So that there was no one to see her reactions. But later when Esther-Rokhl who was usually at her bedside had taken leave of Moshe's body after uttering the requisite cries of lamentation and had come back to Gitl's room, having first revived Yehudis from the fainting fit into which Yehudis had fallen ... it was then that Esther-Rokhl noticed the change in Gitl. She saw that Gitl was trembling and was aware that something in addition to her own illness had happened to her, and so far as she was able, Esther-Rokhl did what she could to help her. She pulled Gitl's quilt up and and covered her with woolen shawls and blankets as well. But Gitl, for the first time since the beginning of her illness, now made a meaningful gesture and uttered a meaningful word. "No," she said as she indicated that the quilts and blankets were not necessary. She was not cold. In fact she was suffocating with heat.

It was then that blood rushed into Gitl's face, so frightening Esther-Rokhl that she hurried to Yehudis who, not fully recovered from her fainting spell, was lying in her bed, overwhelmed by having seen her father's body borne from the courtyard. Unwilling as Esther-Rokhl was to add to Yehudis's sorrow, she had nevertheless to say, "Dearest Yehudis, the Lord keep you from further sorrow. Bethink yourself: you are a mother of children. Have pity on them, and on yourself, and on your mother who does not seem to be feeling well. She may have gotten wind of something . . ."

Yehudis went to her mother at once. A message was sent to Dr. Yanovski urging him to come as soon as possible. Yanovski came. The moment he set eyes on Gitl, he turned his head away because he could see that there was nothing more to be done for her and so he said very little, but like all doctors, he prescribed something. He felt himself very close to this family from whose midst one of his patients had been taken away that very day, and for the family's sake he had left his own house in much greater haste than comported either with his age or with his girth.

He left and was followed by Esther-Rokhl who asked haltingly, "What do you think? What's going to happen to her?" He hardly replied but made a mute gesture whose meaning was clear.

Yanovski was right because a few days later Gitl was no more. She did not suffer very much. She died quietly, the way the flame of a lantern goes out. Her face turned alternately red and then white. Sometimes it seemed that she was seeing something that delighted her and a pleased smile appeared on her face. Sometimes she seemed to be seeing dreadful sights and then she stared gravely straight before her.

Her struggles lasted a day and a half. At the end, one had the impression that whatever it was at which she had been staring and which had seemed to be at some distance from her was now very close— touching her forehead or at the very tip of her nose. So close that she seemed to be trying to touch it either with her hands or with her mouth.

She seemed to be murmuring continually, "Moshe . . ." In her final moments, one of her hands seemed to have overcome her paralysis and moved as if she meant to wave farewell, but the movement failed and her hand fell across her breast, immobile once again. It was then clear that Gitl was gone and that she had fallen asleep with her eyes wide open.

"God save us," cried the frightened women who heard about Gitl's death. They were amazed, as if they had seen something incomprehensible. "Two in one week. Dreadful."

"To barren fields, to desolate woods," said others uttering the exorcism as they spat and turned away, unwilling to hear any further details that the news bearers were willing to add.

And this is what the men said concerning her death: "It's not natural. It's a sign from Heaven. A punishment from the beloved Name."

"Yes," said others who wanted to be clearer about the matter, "but a punishment for what? Moshe Mashber, as everyone knows, was hardly the sort who deserved such punishment. Neither was his wife. Nor are his children. Then why have they been punished?"

"You'll have to ask the good Lord Himself. He knows what He's doing. 'Mysterious are the ways of the Lord.' "

"They're not so mysterious. The matter is clear," said others who were determined to point an accusing finger at someone. "Not mysterious at all. It's well known that sometimes one is punished not for one's own guilt but for the sins of a near one: a member of the family, one's parents. It is said, 'The sins of the fathers shall be visited upon the sons . . .' And if you look closely, what do you find? A grandfather who was a follower of Shabbatai Zevi. And now a brother of the same sort of whom it is said that the Mashber family luck began to decline with his coming to town. Not to mention the trouble that that brother has been to the community. There's no need to look very far, the truth is much closer to hand. The wonder is why the guilty one hasn't been made to pay. But wait awhile: 'Nothing is forgotten before the throne of the Lord.' Just wait and see, his turn will come. Never mind. The reward of the wicked is as it were in a good bank. Payment for what they deserve." And in saying this of course they meant Luzi over whom the hand of punishment was raised and on whom at any moment it would fall.

"Yes. Never mind."

X

The Beginning of Summer
or
Two Pilgrims with One Knapsack

The Angel of Death slipped in among the personages of this story with deadly earnest. In the same month of Nisan, in the interval days of Passover, Reb Dudi, the great rabbi of the town, died.

The day on which he was buried was beautifully sunny. No matter where one looked, the sky had a clean-washed appearance. There was not a trace of a cloud to be seen anywhere in its vast expanse. It was one of those days that made one want to open doors and gates to release the last traces of winter, to watch them disappear like thin wisps of smoke into the farthest reaches of the sky.

It is true that older people still wore their winter coats, but they no longer wore them buttoned up. As for the children, they seemed to have grown wings at their shoulders and wouldn't think of wearing coats any longer. They swarmed into the streets on that day with such lively, untrammeled spirits that one might have thought they were a flock of swallows readying themselves for flight—straight or zigzag, high or low, in avian madness.

It was, in a word, a day unfit for sorrow.

. . .

From very early in the morning, people from the most distant houses in the farthest corners of the town began to gather. Merchants did not open their shops—or if they did, it was only for appearance sake, to turn the keys in the locks out of habit, after which they closed the shops again and together with their assistants made their way to the street on which Reb Dudi had his house and where the funeral was to begin.

And what was true for the merchants was true, also, for the artisans and their apprentices who, as always in the interval days of Passover, were free early. They, too, gathered from all parts of town and drifted in chattering groups toward Reb Dudi's house. But when they entered the square where a crowd was already gathered, and when they saw the two-story house with its door leading to the upper story where there was the balcony on which every morning Reb Dudi used to make his appearance—the earliest riser in the town—and when they saw the window of the room in which his body had been set on the ground . . . (It was something they could not see but they seemed to sense the light of the many candles that had been placed at Reb Dudi's side and at his head and feet); when they saw all that, the new arrivals grew suddenly silent as a respectful shiver ran up and down their spines and they interrupted their talk as a murmur rose from the crowd like the busy humming of bees in a hive.

A little while later the community clerical functionaries began to appear: rabbinical judges, rabbis, ritual slaughterers, before whom the less exalted people in the crowd gave way.

The assembly in the square before Reb Dudi's house continued to grow, swollen by the arrival of the town's schoolmasters accompanied by their older students, all of whom flowed into the square like tributary streams into a spring river so that there was hardly room to drop a pin into that crowd. And the press was even greater inside Reb Dudi's house which was so besieged that even the pallbearers who arrived later could not make their way in.

And as if there wasn't a sufficient throng of men in Reb Dudi's street, women, too, poked their heads out-of-doors and through gates to see what was going on. But almost at once one heard the men's voices warning, "In. Women, get back in." And the women, like frightened hens, drew back inside the gates, after which they only occasionally risked peering through a gap in a paling or fence.

Children at first thought that they might be able to push their way through the crowd, but when they saw how futile their efforts would prove because of the way the adults continually drove them away, they took to climbing up on fences, on gas lamp standards and even onto rooftops, which they reached by going through the attics of houses so that all along the streets through which the funeral would pass, one could see such masses of children glued to high places that one would not have thought the town had so many.

In Reb Dudi's house, the purification of the corpse was proceeding. Rabbis, rabbinical judges, slaughterers and other such clerical folk wearing their holiday caftans were busied with those tasks around the body which, had it been anyone else but Reb Dudi's, would have been performed by members of the Burial Society. Passages from the Mishnah were read and psalms. Then the body was tended to: it was dressed in its grave clothes after which, in a ceremony deemed fitting for a man of Reb Dudi's importance, those who were there circled the body several times carrying Torah scrolls.

None but the community's most important personages were permitted to be present at these ceremonies, and indeed others, because of the press of people, were not even allowed into the house.

Out in the street the pallbearers put up a barrier of laths and poles so that everyone would know where the bier was to be placed so that the crowd would leave room for the body and its bearers. Then all at once there it was. There was a gasp from the crowd as the body was brought down. It was quickly placed on the bier, and then the poles and palings were raised as a signal that the funeral procession was about to begin. But it had no sooner started when it came to a stop.

A man appeared in the doorway of Reb Dudi's house. A man carrying a shirt in one hand and a shears in the other. It was the shirt Reb Dudi had worn at the moment of his death. The man mounted a bench he had brought out with him and showed himself to the crowd. In the voice of one who calls men up to recite Torah passages in the synagogue or to read the You Have Shown prayer at Simhat Torah, he called out, "The learned and pious so and so and the Important Personage such and such have the honor of the first portion." With that he began to cut the shirt into segments as many hands reached toward him to receive them. Large sums of money were paid, ostensibly to build a synagogue or study house in Reb Dudi's honor. Very rich or very distinguished people received larger swatches of cloth; lesser folk got smaller portions, but everyone wanted to participate in this act of piety. And in addition they wanted to own a piece of what the entire crowd had designated as a talisman. Just think! the shirt that Reb Dudi had worn at the moment of his death. Thousands of hands reached for it. Those who were close by succeeded in getting a scrap; those some distance away begged those who were closer to get them a piece. Those with money paid for their bit of cloth on the spot. Those who had no money pleaded to be given their piece on credit. And some, in the tumult, removed clothes—caftans, coats or jackets—and offered them as pledges for the money they promised to pay.

But by then the last bit of the shirt was gone. The pallbearers' poles and laths waved over the heads of the crowd as a signal that the body was about to be moved. And then over the hubbub a voice was heard crying, "A great man in Israel has fallen." A shudder went through the crowd. Even the children perched on walls, on roofs and lampposts, hearing the cry felt fear mingled with curiosity and forgot for the moment the marvelous weather, made for children, and watched the surge of black-clad men, like the movement of a flock of sheep, toward the spot where the body was being carried, watched how frequently and reverently people took over the task of carrying the bier. Women—and girls—looked out through shutters and gaps in fences, frightened by the body as well as by the increasingly threatening tones of the men as they cried, "In, women. In."

The body was carried slowly, carefully, with frequent pauses at wayside synagogues so that the memorial prayer, O Compassionate God, could be read. Then finally the procession arrived at the cemetery. Here there was a long pause as the entire community gathered around the cortege.

The body was carried to its grave where it was again treated differently from anyone else's. Instead of members of the Burial Society, whose task it normally would have been, synagogue officers dressed in satin caftans gathered around the corpse to do it the honors to which Reb Dudi was entitled.

The body was lowered into the grave. Then those who were present asked pardon of Reb Dudi's remains: "Our teacher and rabbi, all the members of the community that you have served for so many years, making no distinction between great and small, now ask your pardon." And the tone of those who prayed was so intimate and seemed to have so little to do with separation that it sounded more as if one were merely taking leave of someone who was about to go on a short journey and whom one would shortly meet again. Before the earth was thrown into the grave someone called down to the body, "And your son, Leyser, will stand in your place, and the community promises to revere him as he deserves and in a manner pleasing to the departed Reb Dudi."

The rabbi's son recited the Kaddish. The man in the grave who was making final preparations around the body was pulled up by various bystanders. Then clods of earth were thrown in. The first clods were thrown by the dignitaries who had prepared the body for burial, the rest by anyone else who could push his way near enough. The final lumps of earth were thrown in by a professional grave maker who then smoothed out the mound.

And then the assembly should have dispersed. And yet it lingered. The funeral had begun well before noon on this lovely day, and it was ending late, when the day was even lovelier, as a golden spring sun shed its light on expanses of meadow from which rose the mingled scent of a departing winter with that of the spring that was on its way. The trees, too, though still black and bare, were instinct with green. And it was this magnificent weather that affected even the most pious of those who were there so that they could not bring themselves to leave, so that they continued to cluster in groups in the cemetery where they could continue to talk a bit longer about the man whom they had just left under a mound of freshly turned earth.

"He was one in a generation," said one of a cluster of rabbis as he half-closed his eyes and drew his rabbinical mantle closely about him—either to ward off the fresh air to which he was little accustomed or out of respect for the memory of Reb Dudi who, as he put it, had no peer in his generation.

"An irreplaceable loss," said someone else, averting his head because he was unable to look into the eyes of those who were there.

"You'd have to search the wide world over to find his like," said a third rabbi in the same tone, and he was followed by a fourth and a fifth who were equally ready to sing the praises of Reb Dudi.

Those, then, were the comments of the calm, reflective folk, but there were others who under the guise of piety had attached themselves to this cluster of rabbis and who meant to give vent to their vindictiveness. These fiery folk said something like this: "If the cedars fall and the willows stand, must we not draw conclusions?"

"Such as?" they were asked.

"That there is something wrong in our midst to which we are not sufficiently attentive," said those who were choked with envy. Then to make clear why they were so agitated they spoke first of Yossele Plague, the well-known apostate who, as his nickname implied, was dangerous. And then there was the case of Mikhl Bukyer, cursed be his name. The fellow who one Sabbath day this winter came to Reb Dudi's house and handing him his prayer shawl announced that he, Mikhl Bukyer, wanted to be considered as one who had left the community of Israel. And then there's Luzi Mashber who is another source of trouble. And all of these things taken together, said the angry speakers, certainly had not gladdened Reb Dudi's heart and they must certainly have helped to shorten his days.

"May *their* days be shortened." The words came from an unexpected quarter, since the speaker was one of those who, having succeeded in joining the group, nevertheless, out of respect for its original members, had been standing slightly apart from it. "It would be better if *their* days were shortened," he said, now more boldly.

Which "their"? came the question from the more respectable members of the group who, puzzled by the curse, now turned to look at the speaker.

"There they are," he said, indicating Yossele Plague and his adherents on one side of the cemetery and Luzi Mashber and his followers on the other.

The man uttering the curses and who was doing the pointing was Yone the tavern keeper who was accompanied as usual by Zakharye. These two, like everyone else in the community, and particularly those who would not miss the opportunity of being present at the funeral of a man like Reb Dudi, had naturally enough been present at the funeral and at the cemetery where, indeed, they had shed tears. First, Yone, who at Reb Dudi's grave had watched what was being done to the remains of a man whom the entire town regarded as the apple of its eye . . . Yone, then, and perhaps for the first time in his life, had drawn a moral from what he saw: that this was the end of mortal men, even of a man as distinguished as Reb Dudi, and that if this could happen to Reb Dudi, why, then, what was likely to happen to someone like himself, Yone? And so he had wept, spurting tears like a leaking barrel. It may be that he wept because of the moral he drew from Reb Dudi's death, but perhaps, too, because of something else—because of the frequent "four cups" he had drunk beginning in his own home on the eve of Passover and later in the homes of others. And Zakharye wept along with him. Zakharye, his partner in all of Yone's shady or extortionary ventures in town, wept less, contenting himself with wiping away an occasional dry tear from his eye.

These two, then, finding themselves at the edge of a circle of respected rabbis, had at first restrained themselves, but when they heard some of those rabbis excitedly ascribing Reb Dudi's death not to natural causes but to the acts of specific persons whom they had actually named without knowing that they were there at the cemetery . . . it was then that Yone and Zakharye, who knew Yossele and Luzi on whom they had been keeping a wary eye for some time, pushed themselves forward to revile them openly and to point them out. "There they are, Yossele and his band on one side and Luzi with his followers on the other."

And it was true that those two, Yossele and Luzi, were there at the funeral. Yossele because he had little work to do in the interval days between Passover and Purim and because the weather was fine, and since everyone else in town would be there, he, Yossele, might as well be, if only to experience the secret satisfaction of the atheist whose most intransigent enemy has been rendered powerless. So much then for Yossele's reasons. Luzi had others. While it is true that a quarrel is a quarrel and an enemy is an enemy, still, Reb Dudi had been the rabbi of the community whom one ought to honor because one honors the Torah thereby. Then how could Luzi not be there?

"There they are, Yossele who looks as if he were at a wedding, and the other fellow, Luzi. They don't seem to be sharing the community's grief. On the contrary. They seem to be enjoying the fact that he who had them closely watched and who sooner or later would have made them feel the weight of his punishing arm is gone." It was thus that Yone the tavern keeper spoke to the cluster of rabbis regarding Yossele and Luzi who were standing nearby. As he spoke, the blood rushed to his face and it was clear that had he been given permission he would very soon have found an action to suit his words, and in spite of the holiness of the place, and no matter that he whose wrongs he meant to avenge was lying in his newly made grave and that the acts Yone was prepared to undertake would not at all behave redounded to the rabbi's honor.

"There they stand." This time the words came from Zakharye coming to the aid of his comrade whose lead he always followed and whose every command he obeyed. Indeed, Zakharye already had his head lowered like a buffalo ready to charge when Yone should give the word.

"Oh, no. God forbid," came from the circle of rabbis as they rejected any share in such an undertaking. Even if they who proposed it had right on their side, this was neither the time nor the place for actions that would bring dishonor to the Lord's Holy Name and to a holy place.

With that the assembly dispersed after its brief interlude in the "field." And when everyone returned to town where it was still broad daylight, they all sensed how the place had been diminished by the passing of Reb Dudi. Even the children whom one met on the way back, despite the short attention span of the young, nevertheless retained on their faces signs that they still felt the mixture of fear and curiosity that had been theirs when they had watched the crowd thronging like a flock of sheep around the laths and poles erected to prevent their jostling.

So that was that. And now Reb Dudi was gone. And since the interval days were after all an interval—and since the interval was followed by a holiday, there was no time to make eulogies, and so that particular debt owed to Reb Dudi was put off until after the holiday.

But then many memorial services were convoked. First, by means of announcements put up on the doors of synagogues and study houses. And then shammeses were sent out who went from street to street crying at the tops of their voices that in such and such a place a memorial service for Reb Dudi was to be held, and all those who had grief in their hearts were invited to hear such and such a rabbi or the great preacher so-and-so.

In the synagogues and study houses, local preachers as well as those from distant places stood in their prayer shawls before podiums or tabernacles—sometimes they were not even preachers but merely pious men who had been moved by Reb Dudi's death. And these always began their discourses with ragged cries that moved the entire congregation. As for the professional preachers, following the usual tradition they began by citing a text that was difficult to understand except as it served to point some moral. And should one moral prove insufficient, they had a second one ready to hand until step by step they arrived at the heart of the matter toward which from the beginning they had been tending. At that point they cried out, "Woe, oh, woe teachers and congregants, the holy man dies and no one has considered that it was not because his time had come to pass from this world to the World of Truth, but because of the sins of the present generation." And then they came to the very essence of the matter: "And when one sees such a pillar of the Torah, such a luminous column as Reb Dudi who was one of those for whose sake the world is spared—when one sees the fall of such a pillar it is incumbent upon us to seek and to find the source of the decay. Each one of us must search first within ourselves to find our sin and to expiate it, and then we must examine those close to us—family and neighbors—and from there we must look through the town itself. And wherever the sinners are we must not recoil from action. Not even from the shedding of blood, as the Levites, obeying Moses' instructions, were prepared to draw their swords against the children of Israel lest the Lord God (may His Name be Blessed) take vengeance on all for the sins of a few."

"Woe, oh, woe," cried tenderhearted women as they reiterated piously and with approbation the words of the preachers. And the men, too, gave their assent and shed tears of contrition and regret as the preachers urged them to do.

"Woe indeed," interjected several who were by no means kindhearted and who, having an ax of their own to grind, made good use of the opportunity given them by these preachers to egg the populace on against those against whom for a long while they had been nursing vengeful thoughts.

And these troublemakers now had the chance for which they had been waiting. Mingling with the crowds with intent to incite them to action, they let drop the names of those who might be deemed guilty of Reb Dudi's death—as well as the deaths of others. And they found attentive ears and willing hands.

Yes. As very shortly we will see, those malign efforts that had failed several times before succeeded now that they were linked to the events connected with Reb Dudi's death.

One evening shortly after the events described above, Shmulikl Fist, with whom we are already well acquainted, came to Luzi's house. His filmed-over eye had a baleful look, while his other, normal eye, bleared by drink, looked out at the world cheerfully. Evidently he had just come from a tavern.

In the vestibule Shmulikl found Sruli doing some not very masculine work: he was stitching away at the knapsack which in recent days he had frequently taken up to repair. Shmulikl passed him by as if to say that it was not Sruli with whom he had come to do business and went directly to Luzi's chamber. First poking his head in he looked about with his normal eye, then he went in.

Usually when Shmulikl came, Luzi greeted him silently and without asking him what he wanted, he allowed him to sit in a nearby chair for as long as he liked. And Shmulikl was always grateful for Luzi's hospitality because it gave him a chance to breathe a little the air of respectability for which from time to time Shmulikl yearned when he wanted to purify himself of the moral effects on him of his enforcer's profession—a profession which often weighed heavily on him because he knew that his sort of work was little honored in this world and that even in the next world it would bring neither mercy nor reward.

Luzi, now, seeing him poke his head into the room, invited him silently in and with a gesture indicated that he was willing to listen if Shmulikl had anything to say. And if he did not, then that was all right too. Shmulikl obeyed and sat in the chair to which Luzi had pointed. Luzi then resumed what he had been doing before Shmulikl arrived— pacing from wall to wall.

Shmulikl watched Luzi's pacing closely as he walked from one wall to another. The effort of watching, as well as the many drinks he had taken, fatigued him so that as he often did when he sat in Luzi's room with nothing to do, he lowered his head on his breast, closed his eyes and dozed, sometimes snoring, sometimes silently.

But this time he fought against sleep. He started up, and turning to Luzi who kept up his continual pacing, he said, "Ha! If you were to ask me, I'd tell you to get out of town as quickly as you can. You're in for some bad stuff," he said. "No, worse—" He caught himself up short, unwilling to utter a word which no matter how much it concerned Luzi, he would not normally have spoken in his presence. "They've hired bruisers. You can guess what that means." Shmulikl's tongue knotted up as he tried to convey to Luzi what might happen when such hired toughs attacked him. "People like me, Shmulikl, with hands like these. For instance . . ." And here Shmulikl displayed one of the hardened hands with which he did his enforcer's work. And as he looked down at it, he could not help feeling a professional pride in it: its massive size, its power when he delivered a proper blow. "Of course," he confided disingenuously, "they offered me the job. They tried to persuade me. Promised to pay me well if I did what they wanted.

"Just think, damn them to hell"—the improper words slipped out— words such as he never allowed himself to use in Luzi's presence— "just think . . . Well, they came to the wrong man. They wasted their time talking to me. I'd rather let my hands rot. But I can't guarantee that they won't find others who won't be willing to do it. Oh, they'll find them. And then, dear as you are to me and with the best will in the world, I won't be able to help you. They'll be too many and too strong for me. And that's why I warn you, for the love of God and to save your life, try to avoid what's coming.

"Because the danger is real," he added, and as he spoke, his normal eye had the rational, sober glow that one sees in the eyes of a person who means to keep someone from harm.

Luzi listened quietly and regarded Shmulikl with an air of disbelief, wondering whether it was not the drink manifesting itself in him or whether the matter was indeed serious. He concluded finally that Shmulikl was in earnest and he was about to thank him and to press him for details.

But just then, even as Luzi was going to speak and Shmulikl was setting himself to listen, Sruli appeared in the doorway, and from the look on his face it was clear that the news Shmulikl had just imparted to Luzi had reached Sruli who evidently had been listening on the other side of the wall and had heard everything.

Luzi had no need to reply because Sruli took that upon himself, though instead of addressing himself to Shmulikl, Sruli spoke past him, as if he were not there, and addressed himself to Luzi. He said, "I want to know whether you've understood what he told you? And do you intend then to wait, as you have been, for the sword over your head to continue to hang there miraculously? And how much longer do you mean to tempt Providence, which forbids such temptation and which enjoins one to use one's intelligence to take timely precautions against danger which in this case means to do without delay what has already been agreed upon?"

"Yes," said Luzi thoughtfully and in a tone that expressed the regret he felt for having carelessly and indifferently dismissed Sruli's earlier counsels.

"Good," growled Sruli, satisfied at the effect of Shmulikl's warning which, it may be, Shmulikl had undertaken on his own account, or it may be that Sruli had a hand in the matter and had contrived this warning and perhaps others like it.

As for Shmulikl, Sruli paid no more attention to him now than he had when he first came into the room. As if he were not even there. As if the chair on which he sat did not exist, and as if the very words Shmulikl had spoken had not come from him but had emanated from the walls.

Sruli knew that Shmulikl was drunk, and that now having given Luzi his warning, there was nothing further left to keep him awake, and that very soon, following his usual custom, Shmulikl would be dead to the world.

And that is precisely what happened. Shmulikl's head was now entirely empty of any thought, and he was utterly indifferent to anything that might pass between Luzi and Sruli. His head dropped and he fell asleep at once, though he started up from time to time with a drunken cry or some curse on his lips on the order of, "Damn them all. Damn them for trying to get me on their side."

Sruli, seeing that Shmulikl slept, took advantage of Luzi's changed feelings to ask him quietly, "Well, when?"

"Whenever you like. I see no reason to delay," Luzi said, placating him as he turned over to Sruli the right to make all decisions regarding their undertaking.

And we say that it was high time that he did so.

And here let us add a few words, not so much for the sake of our narrative itself, but as a sort of lyric variation.

The evening described above, when Shmulikl came to Luzi's house, was one of those true spring evenings that follows the first rumbling of a summer thunderstorm when the earth seems to open. In town, storm windows had long been taken down and the shutters were wide open. Luzi's window, too, was wide open. Shmulikl, his head bowed, slept for a long while until, starting up, he looked and saw that it was time for him to go home. Then with hardly a word of farewell, he left Luzi's house as quietly as he had come to it.

Luzi, left alone, went to the open window and looked out at the sleeping town and up at the heavens whose entire expanse was sprinkled with gleaming stars. And standing there in that solitary hour in the presence of that silent vault of sky, Luzi looked as if he had absolutely forgotten that according to the warning he had just received from Shmulikl, the town had ugly—very ugly—plans for him.

Seeing him standing there under his own roof, looking out of his window at the mild, expansive spring night, one would have understood that the reason he had just made the decision to leave town had nothing to do in fact with his quarrel with the community nor with any fear of the consequences for himself of that quarrel. No, his reason was a quite different one: it was an inborn yearning for far horizons that is characteristic of former wanderers who are drawn from their own haunts by distant places and who feel themselves cramped within their own four walls and the life they must lead in them year in and year out.

Yes. One might swear that Luzi, seeing such wanderers in his mind's eye, saw among them his ill-fated grandfather of whom it was said that one night, before he became an apostate, he left the house wearing slippers, not shoes . . . and when he was missed, the whole town ran about searching for him; they even went down to the river thinking that perhaps he had had an accident bathing. Then finally it became clear that there was no further point in searching for him because later reports were received from reliable persons who had seen him, first in Podolia, then in Moldavia and in Walachia, and finally in Istanbul dressed in the half-Jewish, half Turkish garb of those who belonged to Shabbatai Zevi's sect.

Though Luzi was not permitted to think well of his apostate grandfather, it seems to us nevertheless that he did, if only because his grandfather was among the number of those who had shown himself capable of severing his ties with his family, with his wife and children, with his community, to walk out into the world wearing his slippers.

Standing there before his window and looking out at the spring night and thinking about such wanderers, he saw among them also his grandfather who before he had come to his decision to leave must have stood before *his* window and yearned for far horizons the way he, Luzi, was doing before he, too, undertook to be one of those wanderers.

Yes, Luzi standing there before the window of his bedroom looking out at the summer night had his mind made up, and Sruli, in the next room, knowing that Luzi was silently casting up his accounts in the light of the stars, left him alone as he waited for him to finish. And indeed when Luzi was done, he stood for a considerable while looking out at the night, then he turned and walked into the other room where he found Sruli busy at his beloved task—repairing his knapsack. Then Luzi, with half-closed eyes and a pleased smile on his face, gave Sruli and his knapsack a look that implied that they were intimate sharers with him of the starlight into which he had been looking.

It was then that Luzi undertook to put his affairs in town in order and to make his farewells.

With whom?

First of all with the members of his sect. He found time to be with each one of them separately and for as long as was necessary. He allowed them to warn him of the difficulties he would encounter on the "road to completion," that is, on his way toward the Creator of the World, the road all Jews, and particularly the members of the Bratslaver sect, are commanded to take. And then beyond that, each of them had other things to warn him about: the lack of income and the way that that would interfere with the free movement of his spirit or with the necessary broadness of vision that is required for one who means to attain the ways and to do the work of the Lord. Luzi stayed closeted with each of them for so long that at the end of the discussions in which his followers unlocked their secret worries, each of them when they left had tears in his eyes, as did Luzi who had been listening to them.

When Luzi had made his farewells to the members of his sect, he undertook to make frequent, almost daily, leave-taking visits to his brother Moshe's children. First, because he was mindful of the request his brother had made that he would continue to look after his family, and because he knew that when he left town he would no longer be able to honor that request.

He visited first Yehudis, whom he wanted to comfort and encourage as much as he could, because as mistress of the house she had had to contend with the diminished financial resources of the family, and with the illness and deaths of her parents.

"Ah, Uncle," Yehudis said, wincing when she heard that the uncle to whom she was so close was going to leave, "Ah, Uncle, who will look after us when you're gone?"

Luzi did what he could to comfort her; he urged her not to give up hope, to remember that one is enjoined against despair even when the edge of the sword is at one's throat. And Yehudis especially, as a daughter in Israel and as Moshe Mashber's daughter, must not lose hope, because the destiny of the family depended on her—whether it would be as it had always been or whether it would collapse.

Then Luzi undertook to talk with Yehudis's husband, to Yankele Grodshteyn, to that model of piety and commercial incompetence. He upbraided him saying, "Which is it to be? One thing or another? Either one is what one is—a merchant—or you give up the mercantile world altogether.

"Because," Luzi went on, "if it was once possible for you to stand aloof from business matters, it was because there was someone who could step in to take your place, and whenever you made a mistake, Moshe, your father-in-law, could correct it. Now, however, Moshe is gone, which means that if you go on as you used to, you are very likely to bring yourself and your wife and children to the verge of starvation."

And then Luzi went on to say that though he himself was far from a hand at business, it was his understanding that Moshe's creditors, before Moshe's death, had indicated that they were prepared to make all sorts of concessions regarding the original debt and were willing to accept payment of a smaller sum just as long as they saw some signs that Moshe's brother and his children were prepared to get the business back on its feet. Because the creditors who had precipitated Moshe's bankruptcy now saw that it was not only his business that suffered, but that they, too, the creditors, had lost whatever opportunities they might have had to recoup any of their losses.

"And so," Luzi said, "the time is ripe to begin building once again."

It was thus that Luzi advised Yankele Grodshteyn, the older of Moshe Mashber's sons-in-law, and he did the same with Nakhum Lentsher, the younger son-in-law, to whom he pointed out that it was not wise for Nakhum to withdraw from the family business—an idea Nakhum had been cherishing for some while . . . and especially lately. Luzi pointed out that though the idea might have made sense earlier when there had been some possibility that if he withdrew from the business he could take a certain share of the money with him, money with which he might have made a fresh start elsewhere, but now, when there was nothing but unpaid debts, all he would take with him from the business was a reputation as a bad credit risk, a bankrupt. Then what sense did it make to leave, what good would it do him? "Not only that," continued Luzi, "why, since you'll have no cash of your own to invest, should you end by using your talents as an employee (because you will certainly not be a partner) in someone else's service? You'd do better staying where you are, in your own well-founded business whose clients, even if they scattered for a while, will come back when they see that it is once again on its feet. After that you can do as you like. You can pull out or not.

"By the way," Luzi said, "you ought to consider that if you leave the business, you will also be leaving the family with whom you would no longer have any relationship and that, as I see it, is not in your interest. Now you are a man without a wife, a widower with small children whom you have to look after by yourself. Here you have Yehudis, who looks after your children as if they were her own, leaving you free of that yoke."

On his visits to his brother's house, Luzi also went to see Alter. One day he said to him, "Alter, you know that soon I'll be going away and that we won't be seeing each other for a while." Alter, who was standing in front of him the way one does in a conversation, threw himself into Luzi's arms in precisely the same way that as we will recall he had when Moshe's bier was in the courtyard a few moments before it was to be carried away. In Luzi's arms, Alter was at first silent, and stood with his head bowed, but then he looked up, and speaking like a perfectly sensible person, he said after a painful pause, "And what will happen to me, Luzi, now that Moshe is gone . . . and now you?" Unsettled, Luzi did not quite know what to reply except to let Alter bury his head once again in his breast. "God will not abandon you," Luzi said, and it was all he could bring himself to say by way of consolation because the tears choked him.

Before he left town, Luzi bade farewell not only to his brother's family but also, if one may put it that way, to his brother's house and grounds as well. Amazing as it was, and nobody was quite sure why, Luzi used often to wander about the grounds by himself. He even made a final visit to the garden where he recalled the rare silences that had pleased him when he moved about alone or accompanied in the days when he used to visit his brother. And he particularly remembered what happened a year ago at this time when he and his brother were strolling in the garden at the end of the day, discussing various matters as we will recall, and how his brother's ears had turned red with vexation while he, Luzi, delighted by the mild evening air of the garden, had looked on good-humoredly while his brother stood, disconcerted and baffled and at a loss for words.

Now it was spring in the garden. There were sticky blue buds on the dry stems of the lilac bushes beside the palings, a promise of blossoms soon to come. And the same was true of the carefully trimmed fruit trees. For the time being, these were hardly perceptible but they were the presage of an efflorescence, white and rose.

The garden paths had been cleared of last year's fallen foliage and swept, though here and there there were still little mounds of heaped up leaves waiting to be burned or to be carried off to the mulch pile.

The garden was still naked and transparent, not yet clothed in its summer garb, and one had an unobstructed view of everything that was happening in the courtyard and in every nook and cranny of the garden itself.

And so one was able to see the recently hired caretaker at his work in a distant corner of the garden. Sometimes that work required him to dig up a tree or to sweep the paths. Sometimes he could be seen taking his ease, staring after a bird whose passing flight had roused his simple wonder.

When Luzi paid his final visit to the garden, he saw Vassily in a distant corner of it. But he was not alone. There was a child with him. Mayerl, Moshe Mashber's oldest grandson.

Luzi moved quietly through the garden, feeling the approach of summer. Without his being aware of it, he approached the corner of the garden where Vassily was. Mayerl, without anything better to do, was standing beside Vassily. Seeing that Luzi was approaching, the boy turned shy and with downcast eyes moved away from Vassily and toward his uncle Luzi.

Luzi then, again without his being aware of it, took one of Mayerl's hands and led him away without a word. Then, moved evidently by the special kinship that had always existed between him and Mayerl, in whom he sensed an inheritor of all the good qualities of the family. Then he bent over the boy, and without transition from anything that preceded that moment, he said, "Well, Mayerl, do you think you'll remember your uncle Luzi when you grow up?"

Then Mayerl, rendered even more shy by the surprising question from the uncle he so much admired, looked down at the ground and mastering his intense shyness replied, "Of course I'll remember."

And we, for our part, want to add that of course Mayerl did remember his uncle Luzi, particularly as he saw him on that last day in the cool, transparent springtime garden: tall, with a short white beard, striding alone and unaccompanied, like a stranger and not as Mayerl had been wont to see him, in his grandfather's company.

Certainly he would remember his uncle Luzi who just then looked as if he had stumbled into the garden by chance, or, rather, like someone who was hiding from scrutiny and who comes to bid farewell to one who has given him pleasure and whom he expects he will not see again, someone like Mayerl, for instance, whose hand he had taken and to whom, as they walked, he had put that surprising question that could only have come from someone whose thoughts are confused and who meaning to say one thing says something else so that the one spoken to—even if it should chance to be a child—looks at the questioner strangely as if *he* were a child.

Yes, we repeat that Mayerl would certainly remember him. And we want to add as well that this Mayerl to whom until now we have not devoted much time because of the small role that as a child he has had in the narrative . . . this Mayerl in what is to come will play a much more important part because, to anticipate a little, we want now to make the timely observation that a considerable portion of the continuing story of the house of Moshe Mashber will devolve upon Mayerl as chronicler and believable witness of what is to come. And we want to say further that we have decided to present here and now a particular extract from that chronicle which has bearing on what we will shortly be describing, that is, Luzi's and Sruli Gol's departure from the town; because we remember that the form Mayerl's chronicle takes is more appropriate to the coming matter than the one which up to now we have used. Yes, that is our decision. But before we do that, we need to delay for a little while longer in order to answer a question which interested readers will no doubt ask at this point in the narrative. And that is:

What would have happened if Luzi had not taken Sruli Gol's advice or had not heeded Shmulikl's warning to leave town as soon as possible? That is, what would have happened had Luzi stayed in the town awhile longer?

To that question we answer as follows: On the very day that Luzi and Sruli left town before dawn—a departure that we will describe later—on that very day a very rare sight was to be seen on one of the town's main streets which swarmed with busy merchants, secondhand dealers, buyers and sellers and people of all sorts hurriedly coming and going.

Two fellows in short, threadbare trousers, their bare feet stuck into their low topped boots, stood harnessed to the shaft of a long dung cart with removable side panels that permitted the loading and unloading of dung. One of the men, a starveling named Sharfnogl, had passed his youth in synagogues and study houses among scholars whom he served as an errand boy who in summer bought them kvass and in winter the frozen apples that study house habitués are so fond of. As payment he sometimes got a mouthful of whatever he had bought—at other times he had to content himself with looking on at the contentment of others. Now he was something of a market porter who made deliveries to the homes of local customers or to the inns of merchants from out of town. He earned very little because he was too weak to carry sizable bundles. He was anemic, and because of the pallor of his face, one could not tell whether he was intelligent or a fool, whether he was capable of joy or whether his character was essentially tragic. He was generally silent, but once he was moved to speech he spoke in a rhyming rush, never stopping, never at a loss for words, like a real master of ceremonies at a wedding.

That, then, was one of them. The other was of the same mold: a failed student, too dense to have profited by his studies. He had, however, developed a considerable appetite. In satisfying it, he had grown into a burly fellow with sturdy hands, feet and shoulders. He had a grown man's thick brown beard. In order to feed his appetite he had taken service as an assistant to a primary-school teacher. He looked after the smaller children, carrying them from home to school on muddy autumn days. He could carry five or six at a time: two or three on his back and one in each arm. He was quite skillful at stealing from the small fry when be brought them their lunches, removing as much as half or more of the food in their pots (depending on how much the food might please him). His job had an additional advantage: it gave him access to the maidservants who attracted him in the various households that he served. Several of these servants had had sufficient commerce with him so that their employers had had much ado to get them married off and to drive him away from their homes. After that he, too, took to working in the marketplace, but he was a stout fellow for the task and was crowned with the nickname, Sher-Ber Girl Maker, no one knew why—or perhaps they did.

In short, these two whom we have just described were now seen harnessed in traces, like horses, to the dung cart with the movable side panels. Sharfnogl carried a tall pole to which a broom had been attached. One of those brooms that are carried every Thursday when people are called to the baths that are heated on that day. There was, too, a sort of chair on the cart . . . on which someone of his own free will would sit—or perhaps against his will.

All at once Sharfnogl broke his silence and addressed an invitation to the considerable crowd that had already gathered around him. He spoke in rhyme:

"Men and women, boys and girls
In skirts, in pants, straight-haired, in curls"

And so on, always in rhyme, promising all that if they followed him and his comrade they would see wonders and marvels—and telling them of a prince and a princess who ate with their spoons reversed, of spotted cats in great number and more and more which for the moment he was not permitted to reveal but for whose truth he begged them to take his word.

And as he made his announcement, Sharfnogl signaled to his partner in harness, "Pull, Sher-Ber," and Sher-Ber gave a hearty yank and the dung cart began to clatter over the poorly cobbled street and a crowd of idlers, responding to Sharfnogl's invitation, took off after it, their eyes on the pole with the broom attached to it and on the as yet unoccupied chair which, it was understood, had been prepared in somebody's honor.

The crowd ran: porters, errand boys, and as the procession moved on it attracted more and more children, though later in the outlying streets older people joined it, too: artisans and tradesmen: shoemakers in their aprons, tailors in their waistcoats and others who were not artisans, but who appeared at their doors and windows and egged on by the instinct for evil, also joined the hurrying mob.

The crowd in the street was by then so densely packed around the two who drew the cart—around Sharfnogl and Sher-Ber Girl Maker— that Sher-Ber had great difficulty pulling it because his partner, Sharfnogl, was too weak to help him with anything more than words. We say, then, that the crowd in the street had grown so packed that there was hardly room in it for the newcomers who having heard the racket in their homes had come streaming out onto the sidewalks and were having difficulty squeezing their way into the mob.

The mob, continuing to grow, moved from the center of town to the outlying streets, and whenever one of the new arrivals sought to inquire, "Where are we going, and what are we going to do?" the only reply he got was a dismissive shrug of the shoulders which implied that there was no time for talk, and that the thing to do was to keep moving without question and that when they got where they were going and the thing was done everything would be clear.

But it was already clear that the broom-tipped pole which everyone could see, and the dung cart which could no longer be seen because, like something sweet, it was covered by flies—it was clear that the pole and the cart were leading the mob to some purpose, that the intent was to "honor" someone with the treatment often reserved for an informer or the like, by riding him out of town in a particular fashion: at the head of a whistling, ululating procession of half the town's employed or unemployed ne'er-do-wells.

The fact is that there were directing hands raised above the heads of the mob that showed it the way it should take. Themselves lost in the press of the crowd, these ringleaders shouted and waved their hands, their faces flushed by zeal as they pointed the way.

And now they approached the street on which Luzi Mashber's little house stood in all innocence, awaiting its fate. No, not only the house but he who lived in it and on whose account this vast crowd had been put into motion and given its proper direction by those who were its leaders.

"Bring him out," came the commanding voice of one of those leaders when the dung cart and the pole to which the broom was attached reached the house.

"Bring out the wolf in sheep's clothing, bring out the Shabbatarian, that so-and-so . . . that such and such," came other cries as whole sheaves of fists were raised ready to greet him as he deserved when, frightened or helpless, he should show himself either at a door or a window.

"Where is the fellow? Him and his filthy followers?" Some of Luzi's neighbors who knew of Luzi's cordial behavior not only to his followers but also to anyone who chose to walk into the house for whatever reason, if only to hear some pious words spoken, when these people saw the mob that certain people with malign intent had directed here, they made a risky attempt to get through the crowd and into the house, meaning to give Luzi warning—but these neighbors had no sooner made the attempt when they were spotted and greeted by such violence from the many clenched fists that they retired with bloody heads while others who had had the same intention, seeing what had happened to those who had made the attempt, hastily withdrew without a word, happy to escape without broken bones.

Well, when the crowd saw that the man they wanted was not about to present himself willingly for the trial that awaited him, and that he was hiding, evidently with the hope that the mob, when it had tired of shouting, would go away—seeing that, the mob burst into Luzi's house, first into the foyer which could not accommodate all those who tried to push in, then into the first of Luzi's rooms which, too, proved insufficient for the crowd. Then, not finding the man against whom they meant to vent their rage in either of these two rooms, they avenged themselves furiously on such mute and innocent household objects as fell into their hands: they smashed, broke and banged tables, chairs, dishes and the like, and flung the debris out the windows to incite and inflame those who were still outside to do what they, who were already inflamed, were doing.

Yes. Now even those who were at the sidelines and who had been calm at first, once they were caught up by the general frenzy also imitated those who had initiated the destruction. There was a sound of glass smashing, dishes crashing, the crack of furniture being flung through doors or windows, and the crowd waiting outside received those objects with the same vengeful eagerness with which those inside had flung them out.

Awhile later, when the ringleaders realized that broken crockery was not what they had led the crowd here for, and that there was no sign of those for whom they *had* come either in the vestibule or in the front room, they turned their attention to the second room—to Luzi's chamber which, as they now noticed, had its doors closed. There they hoped to find those whom they sought cowering in some corner or under a table, or under a bed, fearful of the punishment that awaited them.

Yes. With a rush they burst into Luzi's chamber, but there—imagine the astonishment and the disappointment of the ringleaders as well as of those who followed them when instead of finding Luzi Mashber with one or more of his people, they came upon two persons sitting perkily there—Ten Groschen Pushke and Wednesday, both of whom we have already met on another occasion.

They sat opposite each other in two chairs, these two half-mad characters who lived in The Curse district. Pushke, with his many tin rings on his filthy fingers, was wrapped in a mountain of rags and looked like a turtle. He sat on one side of a table and Wednesday sat opposite him, looking out at the world with his glass eye that was as large as an apple and at which one could hardly bear to look . . . while from his other, his natural eye, good humor seemed to flow like water from a mountain stream into a valley.

They sat before a pot of stewed carrot preserves which someone had placed between them, and though they had no spoons, they were doing a fine job of licking their way through its contents.

How did they come to be there? And who set them there on either side of the pot?

None other than Sruli Gol who despite the seriousness of his mien as he and Luzi left the house that morning (and we will speak of that departure shortly) had been unable to resist the clown in him—the impulse to make a practical joke. Knowing from reliable sources that an assault was being prepared against Luzi, and knowing, too, about the dung cart and about all the other things of which we have already spoken, he had not been able to resist turning the tables on the ringleaders so that when they broke into Luzi's house they would find, much to their shame and chagrin, these two: Pushke and Wednesday instead of Luzi.

He did this in the same spirit as when he used to leave the town even for a few months when having traveled some distance he would stop, turn around and make a fig against the city. So, now, he did the same thing when he was leaving it for a long time—who could say for how long?

He staged the scene with Pushke and Wednesday so well that when the mob burst into Luzi's room and found the couple comfortably ensconced, cheerfully licking away, they were unable at first to believe their eyes and thought for a moment that they were seeing the people they sought who were disguised as Pushke and Wednesday. Later, however, when they looked more closely and saw that the pair, who were already a bit stupefied from their gorging at a food whose like they had never eaten before in their lives, could not tear themselves away from their gorging, even though they were no longer alone but surrounded by those who had flung open the doors—seeing all of that, the ringleaders stood helpless and beaten. Those in the crowd who had merely followed them in, laughed loudly as Pushke reached out grubby fingers toward the pot to take another sticky gob, while Wednesday, smiling sweetly, did the same.

The crowd in the next room, hearing laughter instead of shouts and yells directed against those whom they sought, came to the door and seeing what their predecessors had seen, also burst out laughing.

The news of the couple was carried quickly to the vestibule as well as to those who were outside the house. Finally, it reached the two who were harnessed to the dung cart: Sharfnogl and his comrade, who stood waiting for those whom, pale and beaten bloody, they expected to see led out of the house in bonds so that they could be seated in the chair of honor after which, accompanied by the cursing, swearing and jubilant mob, they—Sharfnogl and Sher-Ber—would haul them away with even greater fanfare than when they had hauled the cart here empty.

Then Sharfnogl in despair recited a desperate rhyme:

Jews with hemorrhoids
Jews without
Back to your homes
Of wood or of clay
Because, without doubt,
Here's the end of the play.

He ended the recitation sadly, since now he and his partner, Sher-Ber Girl Maker, would not be paid what they had been promised to carry out their work, and for which they had thus far received only a small sum. He and Sher-Ber started off pulling the cart through the now much quieter crowd which began to disperse.

Then all at once a plaintive voice was heard. It was Luzi's landlady crying, "Criminals, murderers. What has my house ever done to you?" She wept, standing amidst the smashed crockery which had been cruelly thrown from the house into the street. It appeared that she had not been at home when the attack began, but now having just arrived, she stood wringing her hands in the midst of the havoc that had been wrought on her poor possessions and complained bitterly, "Help, good people. What have I done to be ruined like this?"

"She's right," said several people who were standing around looking on at the destruction that not so long ago they themselves had helped to create—if not as actual participants, at least by not resisting what the others had done.

But others—the ringleaders who were still there—frustrated because they had not been able to vent their anger at the culprits who were their target, turned harshly on her saying, "You got what you deserved. Woe unto the wicked, and woe unto his neighbor. That will teach you to rent to a nest of serpents."

Those who were sympathetic to her as well as those who were not left her in tears after listening to her grief for a while. Turning their backs on her, they dispersed.

The ringleaders, shamed by the ill success of the venture they had undertaken so eagerly and chagrined because their prey had slipped out of their hands, lowered their heads and edged their way out of the crowd.

Those who were merely bystanders, or who were only there because they had meant to take part in a rare performance in which an accused person was placed in a dung cart while a huge crowd followed it . . . these people, now that the performance had not taken place, were not particularly regretful and they dispersed more calmly than they would if it had. They had just heard the grief of an innocent woman who had been wronged and it may be that they were pleased that a second wrong had not been done to someone else about whom it was not even known who he was or whether he deserved what had been planned for him. And so these people who had no ax to grind may well have been pleased that they had not participated in an act which, later, they would have regretted.

And they were spared that regret because on the morning for which the outrage was planned, Luzi Mashber and Sruli Gol, who would certainly have been the victims of it, left the house, which later would be besieged, early in the morning, quietly closing its door behind them while the town was still asleep.

And now, as we promised above, we turn the narrative over to its future chronicler, Mayerl, who coming in at this point in the narrative begins slowly and solemnly and with an epic, biblical tone: "And then Jacob left Beersheba and went to Haran." And what Mayerl says is, "And Luzi and Sruli left at dawn of such and such a day in the month of Iyar when no one was yet to be seen in the streets.

"Luzi kissed the mezuzah before he crossed the threshold and Sruli turned to look back into the house before he did the same. On three sides of the horizon the sky was still dark, but in the east there showed the first pale signs of the birth of the sun which later would emerge mirror-red and radiating heat.

"The city still slept behind closed doors and shutters. The street dust lay inert. The dawn sky overhead was blue and mild. As they went they met no one whom they might have greeted or whose greeting they might have returned.

"As Luzi and Sruli went down the street that took them to the thoroughfare that led to the railway station at the end of the town, they had on their right the cemetery with its tall linden trees and low hazel bushes; on their left there were open fields and plains which drew the eye toward far distances. Again, there was no one to be seen except for these two: Luzi in a summer coat such as traveling merchants wear, Sruli in an unbuttoned coat and carrying a heavy knapsack on his back which contained, in addition to his own things, various things that belonged to Luzi who appeared to be empty-handed.

"When they had left the town a good way behind them, the morning defined itself as the sun rose out of a distant horizon: a wild monster, a round, red idol rising from a secret, subterranean region.

"Just awakened fledglings greeted the rising of the sun with an outburst of idolatrous song, thankful for its radiant and encouraging warmth, and to honor the sun with deeds, they began to fly wildly about in search of the food they needed to celebrate the beginning of the day.

"Later, when the sun had climbed the steep slopes of the sky, our two walkers felt the first sweat of the day. Sruli, because of the weight of his knapsack, and Luzi because he was not accustomed to walking.

"But later, when it was almost noon, they came upon a rivulet—the last remnant of melted snows that collect in low-lying places and do not finally dry out until summer. There they stopped to rest. Sruli removed the pack from his shoulders and put it on the ground, then he and Luzi washed their hands in the clear stream, put on their prayer shawls and tefillin and said their prayers, after which they washed once more and Sruli took out some of the food he had packed for the road.

"When they had eaten, they resumed the route that Sruli had mapped out for them along the path that led across the fields. Late in the afternoon they turned into an oak forest which gave off the strong fresh smell of bark and last year's leaves. And of the oncoming summer.

"A marvelous calm of oak ruled over the place, and when they had taken several steps through the rustling fallen leaves—still with no sign of a road—they came suddenly upon one made by the passage of peasant carts and wagons which in both summer and winter leave deeply carved signs in the earth.

"When they had traveled some distance through this wood, they sensed a village, or a farmhouse, or an isolated inn nearby. They heard the faint resonance of a human voice through the trees and the familiar bellowing of a cow and the dismal groaning of a pole lowering an empty bucket into a well and bringing it up full.

"And indeed they came upon an inn in a clearing there in the very midst of the wood. A low hut with tiny windows and a thatched roof and a badly fenced courtyard with a stable in it for peasant carts and wagon drivers who had sometimes to spend a day or a night there.

"The inn belonged to a certain Jew named Yekhyel Tryeryer, a short, plump man with poor eyesight which was, nevertheless, good enough for him to be able to see when one of his calves was about to lose itself in the woods or get into trouble of some kind. He was a man who even in summer wore wadded trousers tucked into his boots, and whose food and mead were so highly reputed in the district that no one went by without stopping.

"The inn smelled of sourdough and stagnant well water, of chickens raised in the house who laid their eggs and hatched them under the stove.

"It was into this inn that Luzi and Sruli went at the end of their day, both of them pale and tired and dusty from much walking. When the proprietor, Yekhyel Tryeryer, saw them, he knew at once that they were not the sort of guests from whom one could 'get' much. He took them for the sort of poor wanderers who sometimes stop to spend the night or to rest for a day. When they came in, Yekhyel was busy in another room looking over various articles that peasants had pawned with him: coarse coats, furs and so on. These things lay heaped in piles in the dark room so that he paid no attention at first to Luzi and Sruli, thinking that they were not the sort of people for whom one needed to hurry or to interrupt one's work.

"But later when he took a better look at the people who had crossed his threshold and took in the tall Luzi in his traveling coat and the other one, Sruli, carrying the knapsack on his back who seemed to be some sort of synagogue employee or a servant to the first man, he regarded them with more respect and did not wait for them to put to him a pauper's request for lodging for the night. On the contrary, wiping his hands on his wadded trousers first, he went forward to return Luzi's greeting as was customary. Then he also replied to Sruli's greeting. He sensed that with these people he would not have to wear himself out and end by giving them free lodging for the night, as often happened with people of their ilk, but that indeed there was a possibility that he might make a profit on them, the way one can with rich people.

"Sruli set his knapsack on a bench and Yekhyel, having greeted them both, asked 'And where might you be coming from? And where are you going?' To which Sruli in turn replied with another question, 'What sort of food and drink do you have to offer? And do you have rooms in which the two of us can stay for as long as we may want?'

" 'I have,' said Yekhyel.

"It was evening. Through the inn's tiny peasant-windows there came from far beyond the forest the weak glow of the setting sun. A servant, a crippled old peasant woman, came in bearing two swaying pails of water on a curved yoke over her shoulder.

"Both Luzi and Sruli washed their hands, then they recited their early and late evening prayers. Then a lantern was lighted because the fading light of the sun no longer served to illuminate any part of the inn.

"The table was set for the guests: a coarse linen cloth, a glass salt shaker, tin forks and spoons. Then the food Sruli had ordered was served: black homemade rye bread and various dairy products made in the village.

"Yekhyel studied Luzi from a distance, watching him as he prayed, then as he ate. And his respect for him grew. It grew even more later when he went outside and found Luzi standing in the ill-fenced courtyard, his head thrown back, looking at the sky. He could not understand what it was that this strange guest was looking for in an ordinary village sky at night.

"His respect continued to grow the next morning when very early Luzi, after praying with Sruli, got ready to resume his journey. In fact,

Yekhyel was so awed that when Sruli tried to pay for their food, drink and lodging, Yekhyel refused to accept payment . . . as he would not have accepted payment from the occasional famous 'wonder rebbe' who stopped at his inn.

"More than that, when Luzi and Sruli were taking their leave, he turned to Luzi and asked him for his blessing in the manner of such backward village Jews, asking him to pray that his cow would calve safely, that his horse would not fall and that his inn would continue to prosper. Luzi did what he was asked, at first with a certain ill grace, but then with the smile of a scholar when he has before him a yokel of a village Jew who in his ignorance believes in things that are forbidden.

"He bade farewell and together with Sruli resumed his journey, passing through the same oak forest which yesterday they had entered.

"When they had walked for several hours they came to the edge of that wood and saw a tiny village before them. A village with one street and two rows of houses, each house opposite another. The silence that reigned over this village was no less than that which ruled the forest from which they had emerged.

"Luzi expressed a desire to stay here for a while. They rented rooms, and Luzi spent several days in the village's single synagogue, reciting his prayers in the morning, and still wearing his prayer shawl, studying when his prayers were done.

"From there, several days later, he journeyed through that region of towns still famous from the time of Chmielnicki: Zvil, Koretz, Anapol, Zaslav and the like.

"And as he went he was followed by various vague rumors that emanated from the city of N., rumors which were interpreted for good by some while others took a contrary view. There were those—very pious people—in the various towns through which Luzi had to pass who kept themselves aloof from him . . . and indeed they wished he would leave their towns as soon as possible because who could say whether the rumors about him and why he had had to leave N. were true? Others, however—and this included most people—seeing Luzi did not believe the rumormongers and were confident that he was in the right. They said that while it was true that Luzi had been assailed by doubts he now meant to put them to rest by making this penitential pilgrimage which in any case had nothing to do with those false rumors.

"Whatever anyone thought, the fact is that in that summer the entire region felt that there was a hidden presence moving through it. And when Luzi came even to those places where his evil reputation had preceded him, he nevertheless found willing ears to hear him. And when people caught sight of him—him and Sruli who carried the knapsack like a servant—the respect he elicited was so great that even the most pious folk were not hardy enough to reproach him to his face nor indeed to mutter an insulting word under their breath.

"Luzi acquired such stature in his wanderings that not only those of his own race, Jews, but the non-Jews who met him stood out of his way, and when he went by they looked after him with respectful glances.

"And the same thing happened, for instance, when Luzi and Sruli, coming to a village at harvesttime in the heat of the day when the peasants were in the fields and only a very few old men and women were left at home—when Luzi and Sruli came to a courtyard and asked for a drink, the drink was instantly and respectfully given them, and when they had drunk they were led to the garden behind the house where they were offered apples, and pears taken from the trees, or blue sweet plums misted over with gray ... blue plums in a bowl with a rooster painted on the bottom.

"They were wished 'Good health' in unbegrudging peasant fashion as the peasants stole glances at the weary-looking Luzi who elicited from them the same feelings of piety that were roused in them by their own wandering pilgrims who went from church to church and from one renowned monastery to another.

"It would happen, too, that sometimes in that summer when Luzi and Sruli came to a town where they understood that a wedding was to be celebrated that evening and they presented themselves, as was customary for new arrivals, to the wedding household to offer their congratulations to the bride and groom and to their families—no matter when they came, whether before or after the ceremony or when the wedding celebration was in full swing, they would be noticed immediately and people would come toward them to invite them to the table where they would be offered food. Everyone—the exhilarated in-laws and their not so exhilarated guests—would for a little while quiet down as they cast glances at Luzi and asked each other in whispers, 'Who is he? Is he a beggar?'

" 'God forbid!' came the immediate answer from someone who knew more and who had some inkling about the matter. 'Why it's he, Luzi Mashber, who has been wandering through the district.'

" 'Really?'

"Thus it was, then, of an evening in a town. But it happened, too, when before dawn they were ready to take to the road, that hearing wedding music they would go toward the house to greet the young married couple and their families, as custom required; there, too, when

Luzi in his traveling coat appeared on the threshold with Sruli behind him carrying the knapsack like a servant, a path to the young couple was respectfully opened for them. Then when all the guests including the musicians had stopped their playing and dancing, these two, Luzi and Sruli, were invited to take their places at the table and to taste something. When they refused because they had to be on their way, one of the women in-laws would ask Sruli to open his knapsack into which she would put in a selection of the delicacies that are prepared for weddings: sponge cakes, honey cakes, fruitcakes as well as roasted meats enough to last our travelers for a day or longer.

" 'Who is he?' people asked each other.

" 'You don't know! Why, it's Luzi Mashber who is wandering through the district.' And as they spoke, they kept their eyes on the tall, stately Luzi who by coming into that house had given it an importance everyone felt the family would always retain."

Well, that's it. And now we take the narrative back from Mayerl and we undertake to report what is to come in our own fashion and in the style that is unique to ourselves.

Again, that's it. And with this, we believe that our first book is finished.